The Iliad
and
The Odyssey

The Iliad
and
The Odyssey
by Homer

Wilder Publications, LLC.
PO Box 3005
Radford VA 24143-3005

ISBN 10: 1-934451-43-6
ISBN 13: 978-1-934451-43-4

First Edition

10 9 8 7 6 5 4 3 2 1

THE ILIAD

Book I.

How Agamemnon and Achilles fell out at the siege of Troy; and Achilles withdrew himself from battle, and won from Zeus a pledge that his wrong should be avenged on Agamemnon and the Achaians.

Sing, goddess, the wrath of Achilles Peleus' son, the ruinous wrath that brought on the Achaians woes innumerable, and hurled down into Hades many strong souls of heroes, and gave their bodies to be a prey to dogs and all winged fowls; and so the counsel of Zeus wrought out its accomplishment from the day when first strife parted Atreides king of men and noble Achilles.

Who among the gods set the twain at strife and variance? Apollo, the son of Leto and of Zeus; for he in anger at the king sent a sore plague upon the host, so that the folk began to perish, because Atreides had done dishonour to Chryses the priest. For the priest had come to the Achaians' fleet ships to win his daughter's freedom, and brought a ransom beyond telling; and bare in his hands the fillet of Apollo the Far-darter upon a golden staff; and made his prayer unto all the Achaians, and most of all to the two sons of Atreus, orderers of the host; "Ye sons of Atreus and all ye well-greaved Achaians, now may the gods that dwell in the mansions of Olympus grant you to lay waste the city of Priam, and to fare happily homeward; only set ye my dear child free, and accept the ransom in reverence to the son of Zeus, far-darting Apollo."

Then all the other Achaians cried assent, to reverence the priest and accept his goodly ransom; yet the thing pleased not the heart of Agamemnon son of Atreus, but he roughly sent him away, and laid stern charge upon him, saying: "Let me not find thee, old man, amid the hollow ships, whether tarrying now or returning again hereafter, lest the staff and fillet of the god avail thee naught. And her will I not set free; nay, ere that shall old age come on her in our house, in Argos, far from her native land, where she shall ply the loom and serve my couch. But depart, provoke me not, that thou mayest the rather go in peace."

So said he, and the old man was afraid and obeyed his word, and fared silently along the shore of the loud-sounding sea. Then went that aged man apart and prayed aloud to king Apollo, whom Leto of the fair locks bare: "Hear me, god of the silver bow, that standest over Chryse and holy Killa, and rulest Tenedos with might, O Smintheus! If ever I built a temple gracious in thine eyes, or if ever I burnt to thee fat flesh of thighs of bulls or goats, fulfil thou this my desire; let the Danaans pay by thine arrows for my tears."

So spake he in prayer, and Phoebus Apollo heard him, and came down from the peaks of Olympus wroth at heart, bearing on his shoulders his bow and covered quiver. And the arrows clanged upon his shoulders in wrath, as the god moved; and he descended like to night. Then he sate him aloof from the ships, and let an arrow fly; and there was heard a dread clanging of the silver bow. First did the assail the mules and fleet dogs, but afterward, aiming at the men his piercing dart, he smote; and the pyres of the dead burnt continually in multitude.

Now for nine days ranged the god's shafts through the host; but on the tenth Achilles summoned the folk to assembly, for in his mind did goddess Hera of white arms put the thought, because she had pity on the Danaans when she beheld them perishing. Now when they had gathered and were met in assembly, then Achilles fleet of foot stood up and spake among them: "Son of Atreus, now deem I that we shall return wandering home again—if verily we might escape death—if war at once and pestilence must indeed ravage the Achaians. But come, let us now inquire of some soothsayer or priest, yea, or an interpreter of dreams—seeing that a dream too is of Zeus—who shall say wherefore Phoebus Apollo is so wroth, whether he blame us by reason of vow or hecatomb; if perchance he would accept the savour of lambs or unblemished goats, and so would take away the pestilence from us."

So spake he and sate him down; and there stood up before them Kalchas son of Thestor, most excellent far of augurs, who knew both things that were and that should be and that had been before, and guided the ships of the Achaians to Ilios by his soothsaying that Phoebus Apollo bestowed on him. He of good intent made harangue and spake amid them: "Achilles, dear to Zeus, thou biddest me tell the wrath of Apollo, the king that smiteth afar. Therefore will I speak; but do thou make covenant with me, and swear that verily with all thy heart thou wilt aid me both by word and deed. For of a truth I deem that I shall provoke one that ruleth all the Argives with might, and whom the Achaians obey. For a king is more of might when he is wroth with a meaner man; even though for the one day he swallow his anger, yet doth he still keep his displeasure thereafter in his breast till he accomplish it. Consider thou, then, if thou wilt hold me safe."

And Achilles fleet of foot made answer and spake to him: "Yea, be of good courage, speak whatever soothsaying thou knowest; for by Apollo dear to Zeus, him by whose worship thou, O Kalchas, declarest thy soothsaying to the Danaans, not even if thou mean Agamemnon, that now avoweth him to be greatest far of the Achaians."

Then was the noble seer of good courage, and spake: "Neither by reason of a vow is he displeased, nor for any hecatomb, but for his priest's sake to whom Agamemnon did despite, and set not his daughter free and accepted not the ransom; therefore hath the Far-darter brought woes upon us, yea, and will bring. Nor will he ever remove the loathly pestilence from the Danaans till we have given the bright-eyed damsel to her father, unbought, unransomed, and carried a holy hecatomb to Chryse; then might we propitiate him to our prayer."

So said he and sate him down, and there stood up before them the hero son of Atreus, wide-ruling Agamemnon, sore displeased; and his dark heart within him was greatly filled with anger, and his eyes were like flashing fire. To Kalchas first spake he with look of ill: "Thou seer of evil, never yet hast thou told me the thing that is pleasant. Evil is ever the joy of thy heart to prophesy, but never yet didst thou tell any good matter nor bring to pass. And now with soothsaying thou makest harangue among the Danaans, how that the Far-darter bringeth woes upon them because, forsooth, I would not take the goodly ransom of the damsel Chryseis, seeing I am the rather fain to keep her own self within mine house. Yea, I prefer her before Klytaimnestra my wedded wife; in no wise is she lacking beside her, neither in favour nor stature, nor wit nor skill. Yet for all this will I give her back, if that is better; rather would I see my folk whole than perishing. Only make ye me ready a prize of honour forthwith, lest I alone of all the Argives be disprized, which thing beseemeth not; for ye all behold how my prize is departing from me."

To him then made answer fleet-footed goodly Achilles: "Most noble son of Atreus, of all men most covetous, how shall the great-hearted Achaians give thee a meed of honour? We know naught of any wealth of common store, but what spoil soe'er we took from captured cities hath been apportioned, and it beseemeth not to beg all this back from the folk. Nay, yield thou the damsel to the god, and we Achaians will pay thee back threefold and fourfold, if ever Zeus grant us to sack some well-walled town of Troy-land."

To him lord Agamemnon made answer and said: "Not in this wise, strong as thou art, O godlike Achilles, beguile thou me by craft; thou shalt not outwit me nor persuade me. Dost thou wish, that thou mayest keep thy meed of honour, for me to sit idle in bereavement, and biddest me give her back? Nay, if the great-hearted Achaians will give me a meed suited to my mind, that the recompense be equal—but if they give it not, then I myself will go and take a meed of honour, thine be it or Aias', or Odysseus' that I will take unto me; wroth shall he be to whomsoever I come. But for this we will take counsel hereafter; now let us launch a black ship on the great sea, and gather picked oarsmen, and set therein a hecatomb, and embark Chryseis of the fair cheeks herself, and let one of our counsellors be captain, Aias or Idomeneus or goodly Odysseus, or thou, Peleides, most redoubtable of men, to do sacrifice for us and propitiate the Far-darter."

Then Achilles fleet of foot looked at him scowling and said: "Ah me, thou clothed in shamelessness, thou of crafty mind, how shall any Achaian hearken to thy bidding with all his heart, be it to go a journey or to fight the foe amain? Not by reason of the Trojan spearmen came I hither to fight, for they have not wronged me; never did they harry mine oxen nor my horses, nor ever waste my harvest in deep-soiled Phthia, the nurse of men; seeing there lieth between us long space of shadowy mountains and sounding sea; but thee, thou shameless one, followed we hither to make thee glad, by earning recompense at the Trojans' hands for Menelaos and for thee, thou dog-face! All this thou threatenest thyself to take my meed of honour, wherefor I travailed much, and the sons of the Achaians gave it me. Never win I meed like unto thine, when the Achaians sack any populous citadel of Trojan men; my hands bear the brunt of furious war, but when the apportioning cometh then is thy meed far ampler, and I betake me to the ships with some small thing, yet my own, when I have fought to weariness. Now will I depart to Phthia, seeing it is far better to return home on my beaked ships; nor am I minded here in dishonour to draw thee thy fill of riches and wealth."

Then Agamemnon king of men made answer to him "yea, flee, if thy soul be set thereon. It is not I that beseech thee to tarry for my sake; I have others by my side that shall do me honour, and above all Zeus, lord of counsel. Most hateful art thou to me of all kings, fosterlings of Zeus; thou ever lovest strife and wars and fightings. Though thou be very strong, yet that I ween is a gift to thee of God. Go home with thy ships and company and lord it among thy Myrmidons; I reck not aught of thee nor care I for thine indignation; and all this shall be my threat to thee: seeing Phoebus Apollo bereaveth me of Chryseis, her with my ship and my company will I send back; and mine own self will I go to thy hut and take Briseis of the fair cheeks, even that thy meed of honour, that thou mayest well know how far greater I am than thou, and so shall another hereafter abhor to match his words with mine and rival me to my face."

So said he, and grief came upon Peleus' son, and his heart within his shaggy breast was divided in counsel, whether to draw his keen blade from his thigh and set the company aside and so slay Atreides, or to assuage his anger and curb his soul. While yet he doubted thereof in heart and soul, and was drawing his great sword from his sheath, Athene came to him from heaven, sent forth of the white-armed goddess Hera, whose heart loved both alike and had care for them. She stood behind Peleus' son and caught him by his golden hair, to him only visible, and of the rest no man beheld her. Then Achilles marvelled, and turned him about, and straightway knew Pallas Athene; and terribly shone her eyes. He spake to her winged words, and said: "Why now art thou come hither, thou daughter of aegis-bearing Zeus? Is it to behold the insolence of Agamemnon, son of Atreus. Yea, I will tell thee that I deem shall even be brought to pass: by his own haughtinesses shall he soon lose his life."

Then the bright-eyed goddess Athene spake to him again: "I came from heaven to stay thine anger, if perchance thou wilt hearken to me, being sent forth if the white-armed goddess Hera, that loveth you twain alike and careth for you. Go to now, cease from strife, and let not thine hand draw the sword; yet with words indeed revile him, even as it shall come to pass. For thus will I say to thee, and so it shall be fulfilled; hereafter shall goodly gifts come to thee, yea in threefold measure, by reason of this despite; hold thou thine hand, and hearken to us."

And Achilles fleet of foot made answer and said to her: "Goddess, needs must a man observe the saying of you twain, even though he be very wroth at heart; for so is the better way. Whosoever obeyeth the gods, to him they gladly hearken."

He said, and stayed his heavy hand on the silver hilt, and thrust the great Sword back into the sheath, and was not disobedient to the saying of Athene; and she forthwith was departed to Olympus, to the other gods in the palace of aegis-bearing Zeus.

Then Peleus' son spake again with bitter words to Atreus' son, and in no wise ceased from anger: "Thou heavy with wine, thou with face of dog and heart of deer, never didst thou take courage to arm for battle among thy folk or to lay ambush with the princes of the Achaians; that to thee were even as death. Far better booteth it, forsooth, to seize for thyself the meed of honour of every man through the wide host of the Achaians that speaketh contrary to thee. Folk-devouring king! seeing thou rulest men of naught; else were this despite, thou son of Atreus, thy last. But I will speak my word to thee, and swear a mighty oath therewith: verily by this staff that shall no more put forth leaf or twig, seeing it hath for ever left its trunk among the hills, neither shall it grow green again, because the axe hath stripped it of leaves and bark; and now the sons of the Achaians that exercise judgment bear it in their hands, even they that by Zeus' command watch over the traditions—so shall this be a mighty oath in thine eyes—verily shall longing for Achilles come hereafter upon the sons of the Achaians one and all; and then wilt thou in no wise avail to save them, for all thy grief, when multitudes fall dying before manslaying Hector. Then shalt thou tear thy heart within thee for anger that thou didst in no wise honour the best of the Achaians."

So said Peleides and dashed to earth the staff studded with golden nails, and himself sat down; and over against him Atreides waxed furious. Then in their midst rose up Nestor, pleasant of speech, the clear-voiced orator of the Pylians, he from whose tongue flowed discourse sweeter than honey. Two generations of mortal men already had he seen perish, that had been of old time born and nurtured with him in goodly Pylos, and he was king among the third. He of good intent made harangue to them and

said: "Alas, of a truth sore lamentation cometh upon the land of Achaia.
Verily Priam would be glad and Priam's sons, and all the Trojans would
have great joy of heart, were they to hear all this tale of strife between
you twain that are chiefest of the Danaans in counsel and chiefest in
battle. Nay, hearken to me; ye are younger both than I. Of old days held
I converse with better men even than you, and never did they make light
of me. Yea, I never beheld such warriors, nor shall behold, as were
Peirithoos and Dryas shepherd of the host and Kaineus and Exadios and
godlike Polyphemos [and Theseus son of Aigeus, like to the Immortals].
Mightiest of growth were they of all men upon the earth; mightiest they
were and with the mightiest fought they, even the wild tribes of the
Mountain caves, and destroyed them utterly. And with these held I
converse, being come from Pylos, from a distant land afar; for of
themselves they summoned me. So I played my part in fight; and with
them could none of men that are now on earth do battle. And they laid to
heart my counsels and hearkened to my voice. Even so hearken ye also,
for better is it to hearken. Neither do thou, though thou art very great,
seize from him his damsel, but leave her as she was given at the first by
the sons of the Achaians to be a meed of honour; nor do thou, son of
Peleus, think to strive with a king, might against might; seeing that no
common honour pertaineth to a sceptred king to whom Zeus apportioneth
glory. Though thou be strong, and a goddess mother bare thee, yet his is
the greater place, for he is king over more. And thou, Atreides, abate thy
fury; nay, it is even I that beseech thee to let go thine anger with Achilles,
who is made unto all the Achaians a mighty bulwark of evil war."

Then lord Agamemnon answered and said: "Yea verily, old man, all this
thou sayest is according unto right. But this fellow would be above all
others, he would be lord of all and king among all and captain to all;
wherein I deem none will hearken to him. Though the immortal gods
made him a spearman, do they therefore put revilings in his mouth for
him to utter?"

Then goodly Achilles brake in on him and answered: "Yea, for I should
be called coward and man of naught, if I yield to thee in every matter,
howsoe'er thou bid. To others give now thine orders, not to me [play
master; for thee I deem that I shall no more obey]. This, moreover, will I
say to thee, and do thou lay it to thy heart. Know that not by violence will
I strive for the damsel's sake, neither with thee nor any other; ye gave and
ye have taken away. But of all else that is mine beside my fleet black ship,
thereof shalt thou not take anything or bear it away against my will. Yea,
go to now, make trial, that all these may see; forthwith thy dark blood
shall gush about my spear."

Now when the twain had thus finished the battle of violent words, they
stood up and dissolved the assembly beside the Achaian ships. Peleides
went his way to his huts and trim ships with Menoitios' son [Patroklos]
and his company; and Atreides launched a fleet ship on the sea, and

picked twenty oarsmen therefor, and embarked the hecatomb for the god, and brought Chryseis of the fair cheeks and set her therein; and Odysseus of many devices went to be their captain.

So these embarked and sailed over the wet ways; and Atreides bade the folk purify themselves. So they purified themselves, and cast the defilements into the sea and did sacrifice to Apollo, even unblemished hecatombs of bulls and goats, along the shore of the unvintaged sea; and the sweet savour arose to heaven eddying amid the smoke.

Thus were they busied throughout the host; but Agamemnon ceased not from the strife wherewith he threatened Achilles at the first; he spake to Talthybios and Eurybates that were his heralds and nimble squires: "Go ye to the tent of Achilles Peleus' son, and take Briseis of the fair cheeks by the hand and lead her hither; and if he give her not, then will I myself go, and more with me, and seize her; and that will be yet more grievous for him."

So saying he sent them forth, and laid stern charge upon them. Unwillingly went they along the beach of the unvintaged sea, and came to the huts and ships of the Myrmidons. Him found they sitting beside his hut and black ship; nor when he saw them was Achilles glad. So they in dread and reverence of the king stood, and spake to him no word, nor questioned him. But he knew in his heart, and spake to them: "All hail, ye heralds, messengers of Zeus and men, come near; ye are not guilty in my sight, but Agamemnon that sent you for the sake of the damsel Briseis. Go now, heaven-sprung Patroklos, bring forth the damsel, and give them her to lead away. Moreover, let the twain themselves be my witnesses before the face of the blessed gods and mortal men, yea and of him, that king untoward, against the day when there cometh need of me hereafter to save them all from shameful wreck. Of a truth he raveth with baleful mind, and hath not knowledge to look before and after, that so his Achaians might battle in safety beside their ships."

So said he, and Patroklos hearkened to his dear comrade, and led forth from the hut Briseis of the fair cheeks, and gave them her to lead away. So these twain took their way back along the Achaians' ships, and with them went the woman all unwilling. Then Achilles wept anon, and sat him down apart, aloof from his comrades on the beach of the grey sea, gazing across the boundless main; he stretched forth his hands and prayed instantly to his dear mother: "Mother, seeing thou didst of a truth bear me to so brief span of life, honour at the least ought the Olympian to have granted me, even Zeus that thundereth on high; but now doth he not honour me, no, not one whit. Verily Atreus' son, wide-ruling Agamemnon, hath done me dishonour; for he hath taken away my meed of honour and keepeth her of his own violent deed."

So spake he weeping, and his lady mother heard him as she sate in the sea-depths beside her aged sire. With speed arose she from the grey sea, like a mist, and sate her before the face of her weeping son, and stroked him with her hand, and spake and called on his name: "My child, why weepest thou? What sorrow hath entered into they heart? Speak it forth, hide it not in thy mind, that both may know it."

Then with heavy moan Achilles fleet of foot spake to her: "Thou knowest it; why should I tell this to thee that knowest all! We had fared to Thebe, the holy city of Eetion, and laid it waste and carried hither all the spoils. So the sons of the Achaians divided among them all aright; and for Atreides they set apart Chryseis of the fair cheeks. But Chryses, priest of Apollo the Far-darter, came unto the fleet ships of the mail-clad Achaians to win his daughter's freedom, and brought a ransom beyond telling, and bare in his hands the fillet of Apollo the Far-darter upon a golden staff, and made his prayer unto all the Achaians, and most of all to the two sons of Atreus, orderers of the host. Then all the other Achaians cried assent, to reverence the priest and accept his goodly ransom; yet the thing pleased not the heart of Agamemnon son of Atreus, but he roughly sent him away and laid stern charge upon him. So the old man went back in anger; and Apollo heard his prayers, seeing he loved him greatly, and he aimed against the Argives his deadly darts. So the people began to perish in multitudes, and the god's shafts ranged everywhither throughout the wide host of the Achaians. Then of full knowledge the seer declared to us the oracle of the Far-darter. Forthwith I first bade propitiate the god; but wrath gat hold upon Atreus' son thereat, and anon he stood up and spake a threatening word, that hath now been accomplished. Her the glancing-eyed Achaians are bringing on their fleet ship to Chryse, and bear with them offerings to the king; and the other but now the heralds went and took from my hut, even the daughter of Briseus, whom the sons of the Achaians gave me. Thou therefore, if indeed thou canst, guard thine own son; betake thee to Olympus and beseech Zeus by any word whereby thou ever didst make glad his heart. For oft have I heard thee proclaiming in my father's halls and telling that thou alone amid the immortals didst save the son of Kronos, lord of the storm-cloud, from shameful wreck, when all the other Olympians would have bound him, even Hera and Poseidon and Pallas Athene. Then didst thou, O goddess, enter in and loose him from his bonds, having with speed summoned to high Olympus him of the hundred arms whom gods call Briareus, but all men call Aigaion; for he is mightier even than his father—so he sate him by Kronion's side rejoicing in his triumph, and the blessed gods feared him withal and bound not Zeus. This bring thou to his remembrance and sit by him and clasp his knees, if perchance he will give succour to the Trojans; and for the Achaians, hem them among their ships' sterns about the bay, given over to slaughter; that they may make trial of their king, and that even Atreides, wide-ruling Agamemnon, may perceive his blindness, in that he honoured not at all the best of the Achaians."

Then Thetis weeping made answer to him: "Ah me, my child, why reared I thee, cursed in my motherhood? Would thou hadst been left tearless and griefless amid the ships, seeing thy lot is very brief and endureth no long while; but now art thou made short-lived alike and lamentable beyond all men; in an evil hour I bare thee in our halls. But I will go myself to snow-clad Olympus to tell this thy saying to Zeus, whose joy is in the thunder, [perhaps rather, "hurler of the thunderbolt."] if perchance he may hearken to me. But tarry thou now amid thy fleet-faring ships, and continue wroth with the Achaians, and refrain utterly from battle: for Zeus went yesterday to Okeanos, unto the noble Ethiopians for a feast, and all the gods followed with him; but on the twelfth day will he return to Olympus, and then will I fare to Zeus' palace of the bronze threshold, and will kneel to him and think to win him."

So saying she went her way and left him there, vexed in spirit for the fair-girdled woman's sake, whom they had taken perforce despite his will: and meanwhile Odysseus came to Chryse with the holy hecatomb. When they were now entered within the deep haven, they furled their sails and laid them in the black ship, and lowered the mast by the forestays and brought it to the crutch with speed, and rowed her with oars to the anchorage. Then they cast out the mooring stones and made fast the hawsers, and so themselves went forth on to the sea-beach, and forth they brought the hecatomb for the Far-darter Apollo, and forth came Chryseis withal from the seafaring ship. Then Odysseus of many counsels brought her to the altar and gave her into her father's arms, and spake unto him: "Chryses, Agamemnon king of men sent me hither to bring thee thy daughter, and to offer to Phoebus a holy hecatomb on the Danaans' behalf, wherewith to propitiate the king that hath now brought sorrow and lamentation on the Argives."

So saying he gave her to his arms, and he gladly took his dear child; and anon they set in order for the god the holy hecatomb about his well-builded altar; next washed they their hands and took up the barley meal. Then Chryses lifted up his hands and prayed aloud for them: "Hearken to me, god of the silver bow that standest over Chryse and holy Killa, and rulest Tenedos with might; even as erst thou heardest my prayer, and didst me honour, and mightily afflictest the people of the Achaians, even so now fulfil me this my desire: remove thou from the Danaans forthwith the loathly pestilence."

So spake he in prayer, and Phoebus Apollo heard him. Now when they had prayed and sprinkled the barley meal, first they drew back the victims' heads and slaughtered them and flayed them, and cut slices from the thighs and wrapped them in fat, making a double fold, and laid raw collops thereon, and the old man burnt them on cleft wood and made libation over them of gleaming wine; and at his side the young men in their hands held five-pronged forks. Now when the thighs were burnt and they had tasted the vitals, then sliced they all the rest and pierced it through with spits, and roasted it carefully, and drew all off again. So when they had rest from the task and had made ready the banquet, they feasted, nor was their heart aught stinted of the fair banquet. But when they had put away from them the desire of meat and drink, the young men crowned the bowls with wine, and gave each man his portion after the drink-offering had been poured into the cups. So all day long worshipped they the god with music, singing the beautiful paean, the sons of the Achaians making music to the Far-darter [or, "the Averter" (of pestilence)]; and his heart was glad to hear. And when the sun went down and darkness came on them, they laid them to sleep beside the ship's hawsers; and when rosy-fingered Dawn appeared, the child of morning, then set they sail for the wide camp of the Achaians; and Apollo the Far-darter sent them a favouring gale. They set up their mast and spread the white sails forth, and the wind filled the sail's belly and the dark wave sang loud about the stem as the ship made way, and she sped across the wave, accomplishing her journey. So when they were now come to the wide camp of the Achaians, they drew up their black ship to land high upon the sands, and set in line the long props beneath her; and themselves were scattered amid their huts and ships.

But he sat by his swift-faring ships, still wroth, even the heaven-sprung son of Peleus, Achilles fleet of foot; he betook him neither to the assembly that is the hero's glory, neither to war, but consumed his heart in tarrying in his place, and yearned for the war-cry and for battle.

Now when the twelfth morn thereafter was come, then the gods that are for ever fared to Olympus all in company, led of Zeus. And Thetis forgat not her son's charge, but rose up from the sea-wave, and at early morn mounted up to great heaven and Olympus. There found she Kronos' son of the far-sounding voice sitting apart from all on the topmost peak of many-ridged Olympus. So she sat before his face and with her left hand clasped his knees, and with her right touched him beneath his chin, and spake in prayer to king Zeus son of Kronos: "Father Zeus, if ever I gave thee aid amid the immortal gods, whether by word or deed, fulfil thou this my desire: do honour to my son, that is doomed to earliest death of all men: now hath Agamemnon king of men done him dishonour, for he hath taken away his meed of honour and keepeth her of his own violent deed. But honour thou him, Zeus of Olympus, lord of counsel; grant thou victory to the Trojans the while until the Achaians do my son honour and exalt him with recompense."

So spake she; but Zeus the cloud-gatherer said no word to her, and sat long time in silence. But even as Thetis had clasped his knees, so held she by him clinging, and questioned him yet a second time: "Promise me now this thing verily, and bow thy head thereto; or else deny me, seeing there is naught for thee to fear; that I may know full well how I among all gods am least in honour."

Then Zeus the cloud-gatherer, sore troubled, spake to her: "Verily it is a sorry matter, if thou wilt set me at variance with Hera, whene'er she provoketh me with taunting words. Even now she upbraideth me ever amid the immortal gods, and saith that I aid the Trojans in battle. But do thou now depart again, lest Hera mark aught; and I will take thought for these things to fulfil them. Come now, I will bow my head to thee, that thou mayest be of good courage; for that, of my part, is the surest token amid the immortals; no word of mine is revocable nor false nor unfulfilled when the bowing of my head hath pledged it."

Kronion spake, and bowed his dark brow, and the ambrosial locks waved from the king's immortal head; and he made great Olympus quake.

Thus the twain took counsel and parted; she leapt therewith into the deep sea from glittering Olympus, and Zeus fared to his own palace. All the gods in company arose from their seats before their father's face; neither ventured any to await his coming, but stood up all before him. So he sate him there upon his throne; but Hera saw, and was not ignorant how that the daughter of the Ancient of the sea, Thetis the silver-footed, had devised counsel with him. Anon with taunting words spake she to Zeus the son of Kronos: "Now who among the gods, thou crafty of mind, hath devised counsel with thee? It is ever thy good pleasure to hold aloof from me and in secret meditation to give thy judgments, nor of thine own good will hast thou ever brought thyself to declare unto me the thing thou purposest."

Then the father of gods and men made answer her: "Hera, think not thou to know all my sayings; hard they are for thee, even though thou art my wife. But whichsoever it is seemly for thee to hear, none sooner than thou shall know, be he god or man. Only when I will to take thought aloof from the gods, then do not thou ask of every matter nor make question."

Then Hera the ox-eyed queen made answer to him. "Most dread son of Kronos, what word is this thou hast spoken? Yea, surely of old I have not asked thee nor made question, but in my heart sore afraid lest thou have been won over by silver-footed Thetis, daughter of the Ancient of the sea, for she at early morn sat by thee and clasped thy knees. To her I deem thou gavest a sure pledge that thou wilt do honour to Achilles, and lay many low beside the Achaians' ships."

To her made answer Zeus the cloud-gatherer: "Lady, Good lack! ever art thou imagining, nor can I escape thee; yet shalt thou in no wise have power to fulfil, but wilt be the further from my heart; that shall be even the worse for thee. And if it be so, then such must my good pleasure be. Abide thou in silence and hearken to my bidding, lest all the gods that are in Olympus keep not off from thee my visitation, when I put forth my hands unapproachable against thee."

He said, and Hera the ox-eyed queen was afraid, and sat in silence, curbing her heart; but throughout Zeus' palace the gods of heaven were troubled. Then Hephaistos the famed craftsman began to make harangue among them, to do kindness to his mother, white-armed Hera: "Verily this will be a sorry matter, neither any more endurable, if ye twain thus fight for mortals' sakes, and bring wrangling among the gods; neither will there any more be joy of the goodly feast, seeing that evil triumpheth. So I give counsel to my mother, though herself is wise, to do kindness to our dear father Zeus, that our father upbraid us not again and cast the banquet in confusion. What if the Olympian, the lord of the lightning, will to dash us from our seats! for he is strongest far. Nay, approach thou him with gentle words, then will the Olympian forthwith be gracious unto us."

So speaking he rose up and sat in his dear mother's hand the twy-handled cup, and spake to her: "Be of good courage, mother mine, and endure, though thou art vexed, lest I behold thee, thou art so dear, chastised before mine eyes, and then shall I not be able for all my sorrow to save thee; for the Olympian is a hard foe to face. Yea, once ere this, when I was fain to save thee, he caught me by my foot and hurled me from the heavenly threshold; all day I flew, and at the set of sun I fell in Lemnos, and little life was in me. There did the Sintian folk forthwith tend me for my fall."

He spake, and the white-armed goddess Hera smiled, and smiling took the cup at her son's hand. Then he poured wine to all the other gods from right to left, ladling the sweet nectar from the bowl. And laughter unquenchable arose amid the blessed gods to see Hephaistos bustling through the palace.

So feasted they al day till the setting of the sun; nor was their soul aught stinted of the fair banquet, nor of the beauteous lyre that Apollo held, and the Muses singing alternately with sweet voice.

Now when the bright light of the sun was set, these went each to his own house to sleep, where each one had his palace made with cunning device by famed Hephaistos the lame god; and Zeus the Olympian, the lord of lightning, departed to his couch where he was wont of old to take his rest, whenever sweet sleep visited him. There went he up and slept, and beside him was Hera of the golden throne.

BOOK II.

How Zeus beguiled Agamemnon by a dream; and of the assembly of the Achaians and their marching forth to battle. And of the names and numbers of the hosts of the Achaians and the Trojans.

Now all other gods and chariot-driving men slept all night long, only Zeus was not holden of sweet sleep; rather was he pondering in his heart how he should do honour to Achilles and destroy many beside the Achaians' ships. And this design seemed to his mind the best, to wit, to send a baneful dream upon Agamemnon son of Atreus. So he spake, and uttered to him winged words: "Come now, thou baneful Dream, go to the

Achaians' fleet ships, enter into the hut of Agamemnon son of Atreus, and tell him every word plainly as I charge thee. Bid him call to arms the flowing-haired Achaians with all speed, for that now he may take the wide-wayed city of the Trojans. For the immortals that dwell in the halls of Olympus are no longer divided in counsel, since Hera hath turned the minds of all by her beseeching, and over the Trojans sorrows hang."

So spake he, and the Dream went his way when he had heard the charge. With speed he came to the Achaians' fleet ships, and went to Agamemnon son of Atreus, and found him sleeping in his hut, and ambrosial slumber poured over him. So he stood over his head in seeming like unto the son of Neleus, even Nestor, whom most of all the elders Agamemnon honoured; in his likeness spake to him the heavenly Dream:

"Sleepest thou, son of wise Atreus tamer of horses? To sleep all night through beseemeth not one that is a counsellor, to whom peoples are entrusted and so many cares belong. But now hearken straightway to me, for I am a messenger to thee from Zeus, who though he be afar yet hath great care for thee and pity. He biddeth thee call to arms the flowing-haired Achaians with all speed, for that now thou mayest take the wide-wayed city of the Trojans. For the immortals that dwell in the halls of Olympus are no longer divided in counsel, since Hera hath turned the minds of all by her beseeching, and over the Trojans sorrows hang by the will of Zeus. But do thou keep this in thy heart, not let forgetfulness come upon thee when honeyed sleep shall leave thee."

So spake the Dream, and departed and left him there, deeming in his mind things that were not to be fulfilled. For indeed he thought to take Priam's city that very day; fond man, in that he knew not the plans that Zeus had in mind, who was willed to bring yet more grief and wailing on Trojans alike and Danaans throughout the course of stubborn fights. Then woke he from sleep, and the heavenly voice was in his ears. So he rose up sitting, and donned his soft tunic, fair and bright, and cast around him his great cloak, and beneath his glistering feet he bound his fair sandals, and over his shoulders cast his silver-studded sword, and grasped his sires' sceptre, imperishable for ever, wherewith he took his way amid the mail-clad Achaians' ships.

Now went the goddess Dawn to high Olympus, foretelling daylight to Zeus and all the immortals; and the king bade the clear-voiced heralds summon to the assembly the flowing-haired Achaians. So did those summon, and these gathered with speed.

But first the council of the great-hearted elders met beside the ship of king Nestor the Pylos-born. And he that had assembled them framed his cunning counsel: "Hearken, my friends. A dream from heaven came to me in my sleep through the ambrosial night, and chiefly to goodly Nestor was very like in shape and bulk and stature. And it stood over my head and charged me saying: 'Sleepest thou, son of wise Atreus tamer of horses? To sleep all night through beseemeth not one that is a counsellor, to whom peoples are entrusted and so many cares belong. But now hearken straightway to me, for I am a messenger to thee from Zeus, who though he be afar yet hath great care for thee and pity. He biddeth thee call to arms the flowing-haired Achaians with all speed, for that now thou mayest take the wide-wayed city of the Trojans. For the immortals that dwell in the palaces of Olympus are no longer divided in counsel, since Hera hath turned the minds of all by her beseeching, and over the Trojans sorrows hang by the will of Zeus. But do thou keep this in thy heart.' So spake the dream and was flown away, and sweet sleep left me. So come, let us now call to arms as we may the sons of the Achaians. But first I will speak to make trial of them as is fitting, and bid them flee with their benched ships; only do ye from this side and from that speak to hold them back."

So spake he and sate him down; and there stood up among them Nestor, who was king of sandy Pylos. He of good intent made harangue to them and said: "My friends, captains and rulers of the Argives, had any other of the Achaians told us this dream we might deem it a false thing, and rather turn away therefrom; but now he hath seen it who of all Achaians avoweth himself far greatest. So come, let us call to arms as we may the sons of the Achaians."

So spake he, and led the way forth from the council, and all the other sceptred chiefs rose with him and obeyed the shepherd of the host; and the people hastened to them. Even as when the tribes of thronging bees issue from the hollow rock, ever in fresh procession, and fly clustering among the flowers of spring, and some on this hand and some on that fly thick; even so from ships and huts before the low beach marched forth their many tribes by companies to the place of assembly. And in their midst blazed forth Rumour, messenger of Zeus, urging them to go; and so they gathered. And the place of assemblage was in an uproar, and the earth echoed again as the hosts sate them down, and there was turmoil. Nine heralds restrained them with shouting, if perchance they might refrain from clamour, and hearken to their kings, the fosterlings of Zeus. And hardly at the last would the people sit, and keep them to their benches and cease from noise. Then stood up lord Agamemnon bearing his sceptre, that Hephaistos had wrought curiously. Hephaistos gave it to king Zeus son of Kronos, and then Zeus gave it to the messenger-god the slayer of Argus [Or, possibly, "the swift-appearing"]; and king Hermes gave it to Pelops the charioteer, and Pelops again gave it to Atreus shepherd of the host. And Atreus dying left it to Thyestes rich in flocks, and Thyestes in his turn left it to Agamemnon to bear, that over many islands and all Argos he should be lord. Thereon he leaned and spake his saying to the Argives:

"My friends, Danaan warriors, men of Ares' company, Zeus Kronos' son hath bound me with might in grievous blindness of soul; hard of heart is he, for that erewhile he promised me and pledged his nod that not till I had wasted well-walled Ilios should I return; but now see I that he planned a cruel wile and biddeth me return to Argos dishonoured, with the loss of many of my folk. So meseems it pleaseth most mighty Zeus, who hath laid low the head of many a city, yea, and shall lay low; for his is highest power. Shame is this even for them that come after to hear; how so goodly and great a folk of the Achaians thus vainly warred a bootless war, and fought scantier enemies, and no end thereof is yet seen. For if perchance we were minded, both Achaians and Trojans, to swear a solemn truce, and to number ourselves, and if the Trojans should gather together all that have their dwellings in the city, and we Achaians should marshal ourselves by tens, and every company choose a Trojan to pour their wine, then would many tens lack a cup-bearer: so much, I say, do the sons of the Achaians outnumber the Trojans that dwell within the city. But allies from many cities, even warriors that wield the spear, are therein, and they hinder me perforce, and for all my will suffer me not to waste the populous citadel of Ilios. Already have nine years of great Zeus passed away, and our ships' timbers have rotted and the tackling is loosed; while there our wives and little children sit in our halls awaiting us; yet is our task utterly unaccomplished wherefor we came hither. So come, even as I bid let us all obey. Let us flee with our ships to our dear native land; for now shall we never take wide-wayed Troy."

So spake he, and stirred the spirit in the breasts of all throughout the multitude, as many as had not heard the council. And the assembly swayed like high sea-waves of the Icarian Main that east wind and south wind raise, rushing upon them from the clouds of father Zeus; and even as when the west wind cometh to stir a deep cornfield with violent blast, and the ears bow down, so was all the assembly stirred, and they with shouting hasted toward the ships; and the dust from beneath their feet rose and stood on high. And they bade each man his neighbor to seize the ships and drag them into the bright salt sea, and cleared out the launching-ways, and the noise went up to heaven of their hurrying homewards; and they began to take the props from beneath the ships.

Then would the Argives have accomplished their return against the will of fate, but that Hera spake a word to Athene: "Out on it, daughter of aegis-bearing Zeus, unwearied maiden! Shall the Argives thus indeed flee homeward to their dear native land over the sea's broad back? But they would leave to Priam and the Trojans their boast, even Helen of Argos, for whose sake many an Achaian hath perished in Troy, far away from his dear native land. But go thou now amid the host of the mail-clad Achaians; with thy gentle words refrain thou every man, neither suffer them to draw their curved ships down to the salt sea."

So spake she, and the bright-eyed goddess Athene disregarded not; but went darting down from the peaks of Olympus, and came with speed to the fleet ships of the Achaians. There found she Odysseus standing, peer of Zeus in counsel, neither laid he any hand upon his decked black ship, because grief had entered into his heart and soul. And bright-eyed Athene stood by him and said: "Heaven-sprung son of Laertes, Odysseus of many devices, will ye indeed fling yourselves upon your benched ships to flee homeward to your dear native land? But ye would leave to Priam and the Trojans their boast, even Helen of Argos, for whose sake many an Achaian hath perished in Troy, far from his dear native land. But go thou now amid the host of the Achaians, and tarry not; and with gentle words refrain every man, neither suffer them to draw their curved ships down to the salt sea."

So said she, and he knew the voice of the goddess speaking to him, and set him to run, and cast away his mantle, the which his herald gathered up, even Eurybated of Ithaca, that waited on him. And himself he went to meet Agamemnon son of Atreus, and at his hand received the sceptre of his sires, imperishable for ever, wherewith he took his way amid the ships of the mail-clad Achaians.

Whenever he found one that was a captain and a man of mark, he stood by his side, and refrained him with gentle words: "Good sir, it is not seemly to affright thee like a coward, but do thou sit thyself and make all thy folk sit down. For thou knowest not yet clearly what is the purpose of Atreus' son; now is he but making trial, and soon he will afflict the sons of the Achaians. And heard we not all of us what he spake in the council? Beware lest in his anger he evilly entreat the sons of the Achaians. For proud is the soul of heaven-fostered kings; because their honour is of Zeus, and the god of counsel loveth them."

But whatever man of the people he saw and found him shouting, him he drave with his sceptre and chode him with loud words: "Good sir, sit still and hearken to the words of others that are thy betters; but thou art no warrior, and a weakling, never reckoned whether in battle or in council. In no wise can we Achaians all be kings here. A multitude of masters is no good thing; let there be one master, one king, to whom the son of crooked-counselling Kronos hath granted it, [even the sceptre and judgments, that he may rule among you"].

So masterfully ranged he the host; and they hasted back to the assembly from ships and huts, with noise as when a wave of loud-sounding sea roareth on the long beach and the main resoundeth.

Now all the rest sat down and kept their place upon the benches, only Thersites still chattered on, the uncontrolled speech, whose mind was full of words many and disorderly, wherewith to strive against the chiefs idly and in no good order, but even as he deemed that he should make the Argives laugh. And he was ill-favored beyond all men that came to Ilios. Bandy-legged was he, and lame of one foot, and his two shoulders rounded, arched down upon his chest; and over them his head was warped, and a scanty stubble sprouted on it. Hateful was he to Achilles above all and to Odysseus, for them he was wont to revile. But now with shrill shout he poured forth his upbraidings upon goodly Agamemnon.

With him the Achaians were sore vexed and had indignation in their souls. But he with loud shout spake and reviled Agamemnon: "Atreides, for what art thou now ill content and lacking? Surely thy huts are full of bronze and many women are in they huts, the chosen spoils that we Achaians give thee first of all, whene'er we take a town. Can it be that thou yet wantest gold as well, such as some one of the horse-taming Trojans may bring from Ilios to ransom his son, whom I perchance or some other Achaian have led captive; or else some young girl, to know in love, whom thou mayest keep apart to thyself? But it is not seemly for one that is their captain to bring the sons of the Achaians to ill. Soft fools, base things of shame, ye women of Achaia and men no more, let us depart home with our ships, and leave this fellow here in Troy-land to gorge him with meeds of honour, that he may see whether our aid avail him aught or no; even he that hath now done dishonour to Achilles, a far better man than he; for he hath taken away his meed of honour and keepeth it by his own violent deed. Of a very surety is there no wrath at all in Achilles' mind, but he is slack; else this despite, thou son of Atreus, were thy last."

So spake Thersites, reviling Agamemnon shepherd of the host. But goodly Odysseus came straight to his side, and looking sternly at him with hard words rebuked him: "Thersites, reckless in words, shrill orator though thou art, refrain thyself, nor aim to strive singly against kings. For I deem that no mortal is baser than thou of all that with the sons of Atreus came before Ilios. Therefore were it well that thou shouldest not have kings in thy mouth as thou talkest, and utter revilings against them and be on the watch for departure. We know not yet clearly how these things shall be, whether we sons of the Achaians shall return for good or ill. Therefore now dost thou revile continually Agamemnon son of Atreus, shepherd of the host, because the Danaan warriors give him many gifts, and so thou talkest tauntingly. But I will tell thee plain, and that I say shall even be brought to pass: if I find thee again raving as now thou art, then may Odysseus' head no longer abide upon his shoulders, nor may I any more be called father of Telemachos, if I take thee not and strip from thee thy garments, thy mantle and tunic that cover thy nakedness, and for thyself send thee weeping to the fleet ships, and beat thee out of the assembly with shameful blows."

So spake he, and with his staff smote his back and shoulders: and he bowed down and a big tear fell from him, and a bloody weal stood up from his back beneath the golden sceptre. Then he sat down and was amazed, and in pain with helpless look wiped away the tear. But the rest, though they were sorty, laughed lightly at him, and thus would one speak looking at another standing by: "Go to, of a truth Odysseus hath wrought good deeds without number ere now, standing foremost in wise counsels and setting battle in array, but now is this thing the best by fat that he hath wrought among the Argives, to wit, that he hath stayed this prating railer from his harangues. Never again, forsooth, will his proud soul henceforth bid him revile the kings with slanderous words."

So said the common sort; but up rose Odysseus waster of cities, with sceptre in his hand. And by his side bright-eyed Athene in the likeness of a herald bade the multitude keep silence, that the sons of the Achaians, both the nearest and the farthest, might hear his words together and give heed to his counsel. He of good intent made harangue to them and said: "Atreides, now surely are the Achaians for making thee, O king, most despised among all mortal men, nor will they fulfil the promise that they pledged thee when they still were marching hither from horse-pasturing Argos; that thou shouldest not return till thou hadst laid well-walled Ilios waste. For like young children or widow women do they wail each to the other of returning home. Yea, here is toil to make a man depart disheartened. For he that stayeth away but one single month far from his wife in his benched ship fretteth himself when winter storms and the furious sea imprison him; but for us, the ninth year of our stay here is upon us in its course. Therefore do I not marvel that the Achaians should fret beside their beaked ships; yet nevertheless is it shameful to wait long and to depart empty. Be of good heart, my friends, and wait a while, until we learn whether Kalchas be a true prophet or no. For this thing verily we know well in our hearts, and ye all are witnesses thereof, even as many as the fates of death have not borne away. It was as it were but yesterday or the day before that the Achaians' ships were gathering in Aulis, freighted with trouble for Priam and the Trojans; and we round about a spring were offering on the holy altars unblemished hecatombs to the immortals, beneath a fair plane-tree whence flowed bright water, when there was seen a great portent: a snake blood-red on the back, terrible, whom the god of Olympus himself had sent forth to the light of day, sprang from beneath the altar and darted to the plane-tree. Now there were there the brood of a sparrow, tender little ones, upon the topmost branch, nestling beneath the leaves; eight were they and the mother of the little ones was the ninth, and the snake swallowed these cheeping pitifully. And the mother fluttered around wailing for her dear little ones; but he coiled himself and caught her by the wing as she screamed about him. Now when he had swallowed the sparrow's little ones and the mother with them, the god who revealed him made of him a sign; for the son of crooked-counselling Kronos turned him to stone, and we stood by and marvelled to see what was done. So when the dread portent brake in upon the hecatombs of the gods, then did Kalchas forthwith prophesy, and said: 'Why hold ye your peace, ye flowing-haired Achaians? To us hath Zeus the counsellor shown this great sign, late come, of late fulfilment, the fame whereof shall never perish. Even as he swallowed the sparrow's little ones and herself, the eight wherewith the mother that bare the little ones was the ninth, so shall we war there so many years, but in the tenth year shall we take the wide-wayed city.' So spake the seer; and now are all these things being fulfilled. So come, abide ye all, ye well-greaved Achaians, even where ye are, until we have taken the great city of Priam."

So spake he, and the Argives shouted aloud, and all round the ships echoed terribly to the voice of the Achaians as they praised the saying of god-like Odysseus. And then spake among them knightly Nestor of Gerenia: "Out on it; in very truth ye hold assembly like silly boys that have no care for deeds of war. What shall come of our covenants and our oaths? Let all counsels be cast into the fire and all devices of warriors and the pure drink-offerings and the right hands of fellowship wherein we trusted. For we are vainly striving with words nor can we find any device at all, for all our long tarrying here. Son of Atreus, do thou still, as erst, keep steadfast purpose and lead the Argives amid the violent fray; and for these, let them perish, the one or two Achaians that take secret counsel—to depart to Argos first, before they know whether the promise of aegis-bearing Zeus be a lie or no. Yea, for I say that most mighty Kronion pledged us his word that day when the Argives embarked upon their fleet ships, bearing unto the Trojans death and fate; for by his lightning upon our right he manifested signs of good. Therefore let Trojan's wife and paid back his strivings and groans for Helen's sake. But if any man is overmuch desirous to depart homewards, let him lay his hand upon his decked black ship, that before all men he may encounter death and fate. But do thou, my king, take good counsel thyself, and whate'er it be, shall not be cast away. Separate thy warriors by tribes and by clans, Agamemnon, that clan may give aid to clan and tribe to tribe. If thou do thus and the Achaians hearken to thee, then wilt thou know who among thy captains and who of the common sort is a coward, and who too is brave; for they will fight each after their sort. So wilt thou know whether it is even by divine command that thou shalt not take the city, or by the baseness of thy warriors and their ill skill in battle."

And lord Agamemnon answered and said to him: "Verily hast thou again outdone the sons of the Achaians in speech, old man. Ah, father Zeus and Athene and Apollo, would that among the Achaians I had ten such councillors; then would the city of king Priam soon bow beneath our hands, captive and wasted. But aegis-bearing Zeus, the son of Kronos, hath brought sorrows upon me, in that he casteth my lot amid fruitless wranglings and strifes. For in truth I and Achilles fought about a damsel with violent words, and I was first to be angry; but if we can only be at one in council, then will there no more be any putting off the day of evil for the Trojans, no not for an instant. But now go ye to your meal that we may join battle. Let each man sharpen well his spear and bestow well his shield, and let him well give his fleet-footed steeds their meal, and look well to his chariot on every side and take thought for battle, that all day long we may contend in hateful war. For of respite shall there intervene no, not a whit, only that the coming of night shall part the fury of warriors. On each man's breast shall the baldrick of his covering shield be wet with sweat, and his hand shall grow faint about the spear, and each man's horse shall sweat as he draweth the polished chariot. And whomsoever I perceive minded to tarry far from the fight beside the beaked ships, for him shall there be no hope hereafter to escape the dogs and birds of prey."

So spake he, and the Argives shouted aloud, like to a wave on a steep shore, when the south wind cometh and stirreth it; even on a jutting rock, that is never left at peace by the waves of all winds that rise from this side and from that. And they did sacrifice each man to one of the everlasting gods, praying for escape from death and the tumult of battle. But Agamemnon king of men slew a fat bull of five years to most mighty Kronion, and called the elders, the princes of the Achaian host, Nestor first and king Idomeneus, and then the two Aiantes and Tydeus' son, and sixthly Odysseus peer of Zeus in counsel. And Menelaos of the loud war-cry came to him unbidden, for he knew in his heart how his brother toiled. Then stood they around the bull and took the barley-meal. And Agamemnon made his prayer in their midst and said: "Zeus, most glorious, most great, god of the storm-cloud, that dwellest in the heaven, vouchsafe that the sun set not upon us nor the darkness come near, till I have laid low upon the earth Priam's palace smirched with smoke, and burnt the doorways thereof with consuming fire, and rent on Hector's breast his doublet cleft with the blade; and about him may full many of his comrades prone in the dust bite the earth."

So spake he, but not as yet would Kronion grant him fulfilment; he accepted the sacrifice, but made toil to wax increasingly.

Now when they had prayed and sprinkled the barley-meal they first drew back the bull's head and cut his throat and flayed him, and cut slices from the thigh's and wrapped them in fat, making a double fold, and laid raw collops thereon. And these they burnt on cleft wood stript of leaves, and spitted the vitals and held them over Hephaistos' flame. Now when the thighs were burnt and they had tasted the vitals, then sliced they all the rest and pierced it through with spits, and roasted it carefully and drew all off again. So when they had rest from the task and had made ready the banquet, they feasted, nor was their heart aught stinted of the fair banquet. But when they had put away from them the desire of meat and drink, then did knightly Nestor of Gerenia open his saying to them: "Most noble son of Atreus, Agamemnon king of men, let us not any more hold long converse here, nor for long delay the work that god putteth in our hands; but come, let the heralds of the mail-clad Achaians make proclamation to the folk and gather them throughout the ships; and let us go thus in concert through the wide host of the Achaians, that the speedier we may arouse keen war."

So spake he and Agamemnon king of men disregarded not. Straightway he bade the clear-voiced heralds summon to battle the flowing-haired Achaians. So those summoned and these gathered with all speed. And the kings, the fosterlings of Zeus that were about Atreus' son, eagerly marshalled them, and bright-eyed Athene in the midst, bearing the holy aegis that knoweth neither age nor death, whereon wave an hundred tassels of pure gold, all deftly woven and each one an hundred oxen worth. Therewith she passed dazzling through the Achaian folk, urging them forth; and in every man's heart she roused strength to battle without ceasing and to fight. So was war made sweeter to them than to depart in their hollow ships to their dear native land. Even as ravaging fire kindleth a boundless forest on a mountain's peaks, and the blaze is seen from afar, even so as they marched went the dazzling gleam from the innumerable bronze through the sky even unto the heavens.

And as the many tribes of feathered birds, wild geese or cranes or long-necked swans, on the Asian mead by Kaystrios' stream, fly hither and thither joying in their plumage, and with loud cries settle ever onwards, and the mead resounds; even so poured forth the many tribes of warriors from ships and huts into the Skamandrian plain. And the earth echoed terribly beneath the tread of men and horses. So stood they in the flowery Skamandrian plain, unnumbered as are leaves and flowers in their season. Even as the many tribes of thick flies that hover about a herdsman's steading in the spring season, when milk drencheth the pails, even in like number stood the flowing-haired Achaians upon the plain in face of the Trojans, eager to rend them asunder. And even as the goatherds easily divide the ranging flocks of goats when they mingle in the pasture, so did their captains marshal them on this side and that, to enter into the fray, and in their midst lord Agamemnon, his head and eyes like unto Zeus whose joy is in the thunder, and his waist like unto Ares and his breast unto Poseidon. Even as a bull standeth out far foremost amid the herd, for his is pre-eminent amid the pasturing kine, even such did Zeus make Atreides on that day, pre-eminent among many and chief amid heroes.

Tell me now, ye Muses that dwell in the mansions of Olympus—seeing that ye are goddesses and are at hand and know all things, but we hear only a rumour and know not anything—who were the captains of the Danaans and their lords. But the common sort could I not number nor name, nay, not if ten tongues were mine and ten mouths, and a voice unwearied, and my heart of bronze within me, did not the Muses of Olympus, daughters of aegis-bearing Zeus, put into my mind all that came to Ilios. So will I tell the captains of the ships and all the ships in order.

Of the Boiotians Peneleos and Leitos were captains, and Arkesilaos and Prothoenor and Klonios; these were they that dwelt in Hyria and rocky Aulis and Schoinos and Skolos and Eteonos full of ridges, Thespeia and Graia and Mykalessos with wide lawns; and that dwelt about Harma and Eilesion and Erythrai, and they that possessed Eleon and Peteon and Hyle, Okalea and the stablished fortress of Medeon, Kopai and Eutresis and Thisbe haunt of doves; and they of Koroneia and grassy Haliartos, and that possessed Plataia and that dwelt in Glisas, and that possessed the stablished fortress of lesser Thebes and holy Onchestos, Poseidon's bright grove; and that possessed Arne rich in vineyards, and Mideia and sacred Nisa and Anthedon on the furthest borders. Of these there came fifty ships, and in each one embarked young men of the Boiotians an hundred and twenty. And they that dwelt in Aspledon and Orchomenos of the Minyai were led of Askalaphos and Ialmenos, sons of Ares, whom Astyoche conceived of the mighty god in the palace of Aktor son of Azeus, having entered her upper chamber, a stately maiden; for mighty Ares lay with her privily. And with them sailed thirty hollow ships.

And the Phokians were led of Schedios and Epistrophos, sons of great-hearted Iphitos son of Naubolos; these were they that possessed Kyparissos and rocky Pytho and sacred Krisa and Daulis and Panopeus, and they that dwelt about Anemoreia and Hyampolis, yea, and they that lived by the goodly river Kephisos and possessed Lilaia by Kephisos' springs. And with them followed thirty black ships. So they marshalled the ranks of the Phokians diligently, and had their station hard by the Boiotians on the left.

And of the Lokrians the fleet son of Oileus was captain, Aias the less, that was not so great as was the Telamonian Aias but far less. Small was he, with linen corslet, but with the spear he far outdid all the Hellenes and Achaians. These were they that dwelt in Kynos and Opus and Kalliaros and Bessa and Skarphe and lovely Augeiai and Tarphe and Thronion, about the streams of Boagrios. And with Aias followed forty black ships of the Lokrians that dwell over against holy Euboia.

And the Abantes breathing fury, they that possessed Euboia and Chalkis and Eiretria and Histiaia rich in vines, and Kerinthos by the sea and the steep fortress of Dios and they that possessed Karytos, and they that dwelt in Styra, all these again were led of Elephenor of the stock of Ares, even the son of Chalkodon, and captain of the proud Abantes. And with him followed the fleet Abantes with hair flowing behind, spearmen eager with ashen shafts outstretched to tear the corslets on the breasts of the foes. And with him forty black ships followed.

And they that possessed the goodly citadel of Athens, the domain of Erechtheus the high-hearted, whom erst Athene daughter of Zeus fostered when Earth, the grain-giver, brought him to birth;—and she gave him a resting-place in Athens in her own rich sanctuary; and there the sons of the Athenians worship him with bulls and rams as the years turn in their courses—these again were led of Menestheus son of Peteos. And there was no man upon the face of earth that was like him for the marshalling of horsemen and warriors that bear the shield. Only Nestor rivalled him, for he was the elder by birth. And with him rivalled him, for he was the elder by birth. And with him fifty black ships followed.

And Aias led twelve ships from Salamis, [and brought them and set them where the battalions of the Athenians stood.]

And they that possessed Argos and Tiryns of the great walls, Hermione and Asine that enfold the deep gulf, Troizen and Eionai and Epidauros full of vines, and the youths of the Achaians that possessed Aigina and Mases, these were led of Diomedes of the loud war-cary and Sthenelos, dear son of famous Kapaneus. And the third with them came Euryalos, a godlike warrior, the son of king Mekisteus son of Talaos. But Diomedes of the loud war-cry was lord over all. And with them eighty black ships followed.

And of them that possessed the stablished fortress of Mykene and wealthy Corinth and stablished Kleonai, and dwelt in Orneiai and lovely Araithyrea and Sikyon, wherein Adrestos was king at the first; and of them that possessed Hyperesie and steep Gonoessa and Pellene, and dwelt about Aigion and through all the coast-land and about broad Helike, of them did lord Agamemnon son of Atreus lead an hundred ships. With him followed most and goodliest folk by far; and in their midst himself was clad in flashing bronze, all glorious, and was pre-eminent amid all warriors, because he was goodliest and led folk far greatest in number.

And of them that possessed Lakedaimon lying low amid the rifted hills, and Pharis and Sparta and Messe, the haunt of doves, and dwelt in Bryseiai and lovely Augeiai, and of them too that possessed Amyklai and the sea-coast fortress of Helos, and that possessed Laas and dwelt about Oitylos, of these was the king's brother leader, even Menelaos of the loud war-cry, leader of sixty ships, and these were arrayed apart. And himself marched among them confident in his zeal, urging his men to battle: and his heart most of all was set to take vengeance for his strivings and groans for Helen's sake [Or, "for Helen's searchings of heart and groans."].

And of them that dwelt in Pylos and lovely Arene and Thryon the fording-place of Alpheios, and in established Aipy, and were inhabitants of Kyparisseis and Amphigeneia and Pteleos and Helos and Dorion—where the Muses met Thamyris the Thracian, and made an end of his singing, as he was faring from Oichalia, from Eurytos the Oichalian; for he averred with boasting that he would conquer, even did the Muses themselves sing against him, the daughters of aegis-bearing Zeus; but they in their anger maimed him, moreover they took from him the high gift of song and made him to forget his harping—of all these was knightly Nestor of Gerenia leader, and with him sailed ninety hollow ships.

And of them that possessed Arkadia beneath the steep mountain of Kyllene, beside the tomb of Aipytos, where are warriors that fight hand to hand; and of them that dwelt in Pheneos and Orchomenos abounding in flocks, and Rhipe and Stratie and windy Enispe, and that possessed Tegea and lovely Mantineia, and possessed Stymphelos and dwelt in Parhasie, of these was Ankaios' son lord Agapenor leader, even of sixty ships; and in each ship embarked many Arkadian warriors skilled in fight. For Agamemnon king of men himself gave them benched ships wherewith to cross the wine-dark sea, even he the son of Atreus; for matters of seafaring concerned them not.

And they too that inhabited Bouprasion and goodly Elis, so much thereof as Hyrmine and Myrsinos upon the borders and the Olenian rock and Aleision bound between them, of these men there were four captains, and ten swift ships followed each one, and many Epeians embarked thereon. So some were led of Amphimachos and Thalpios, of the lineage of Aktor, sons one of Kteatos and one of Eurytos; and of some was stalwart Diores captain, son of Amarynkes; and of the fourth company godlike Polyxeinos was captain, son of king Agasthenes Augeias' son.

And them of Doulichion and the holy Echinean Isles that stand beyond the sea over against Elis, even these did Meges lead, the peer of Ares, Phyleides to wit, for he was begotten of knightly Phyleus dear to Zeus, him that erst changed his habitation to Doulichion for anger against his father. And with him followed forty black ships.

And Odysseus led the great-hearted Kephallenians, them that possessed Ithaka and Neriton with quivering leafage, and dwelt in Krokyleia and rugged Aigilips, and them that possessed Zakynthos and that dwelt in Samos, and possessed the mainland and dwelt in the parts over against the isles. Them did Odysseus lead, the peer of Zeus in counsel, and with him followed twelve ships with vermillion prow.

And of the Aitolians Thoas was captain, the son of Andraimon, even of them that dwelt in Pleuron and Olenos and Pylene, and Chalkis on the sea-shore and rocky Kalydon. For the sons of great-hearted Oineus were no more, neither did he still live, and golden-haired Meleagros was dead, to whose hands all had been committed, for him to be king of the Aitolians. And with Thoas there followed forty black ships.

And of the Cretans Idomeneus the famous spearman was leader, even of them that possessed Knosos and Gortys of the great walls, Lyktos and Miletos and chalky Lykastos and Phaistos and Rhytion, stablished cities all; and of all others that dwelt in Crete of the hundred cities. Of these men was Idomeneus the famous spearman leader, and Meriones peer of the man-slaying war-god. With these followed eighty black ships.

And Tlepolemmos, Herakles' son goodly and tall, led from Rhodes nine ships of the lordly Rhodians, that dwelt in Rhodes in threefold ordering, in Lindos and Ialysos and chalky Kameiros. These were led of Tlepolemos the famous spearman, that was born to great Herakles by Astyocheia, whom he had brought away from Ephyre by the river Selleeis, when he laid waste many cities of strong men, fosterlings of Zeus. Now when Tlepolemos had grown to manhood within the strong palace walls, anon he slew his own father's dear uncle, an old man now, Likymnios of the stock of Ares. Then with speed built he ships and gathered much folk together, and went fleeing across the deep, because the other sons and grandsons of great Herakles threatened him. So he came to Rhodes a wanderer, enduring hardships, and his folk settled by kinship in three tribes, and were loved of Zeus that is king among gods and men; and Kronion poured upon them exceeding great wealth.

Nireus, moreover, led three trim ships from Syme, Nireus son of Aglaia and king Charopos, Nireus the most beauteous man that came up under Ilios of all the Danaans, after the noble son of Peleus. Howbeit he was a weakling, and a scanty host followed him.

And of them that possessed Nisyros and Krapathos and Kasos and Kos the city of Eurypylos, and the Kalydnian Isles, of them Pheidippos and Antiphos were leaders, the two sons of king Thessalos son of Herakles. With them were arrayed thirty hollow ships.

Now all moreover that dwelt in the Pelasgian Argos and inhabited Alos and Alope and Trachis and possessed Phthia and Hellas the home of fair women, and were called Myrmidons and Hellenes and Achaians; of all these, even fifty ships, Achilles was captain. But these took no thought of noisy war; for there was no man to array them in line of battle. For fleet-footed goodly Achilles lay idle amid the ships, wroth for the sake of a damsel, Briseis of the lovely hair, whom he had won from Lyrnessos and the walls of Thebe, and overthrew Mynes and Epistrophos, warriors that bare the spear, sons of king Euenos Selepos' son. For her sake lay Achilles sorrowing; but soon was he to arise again.

And of them that possessed Phylake and flowery Pyrasos, Demeter's sanctuary, and Iton mother of flocks, and Antron by the sea-shore and Pteleos couched in grass, of all these was warlike Protesilaos leader while yet he lived; but now ere this the black earth held him fast. His wife with marred visage was left alone in Phylake, yea, and his bridal chamber half builded; for a Dardanian warrior slew him as he leapt from his ship far first of the Achaians. Yet neither were his men leaderless, though they sorrowed for their leader; for Podarkes of the stock of Ares marshalled them, son of Phylakos' son Iphiklos was he, the lord of many flocks, own brother of great-hearted Protesilaos, and younger-born than he: but the other was alike the elder and the braver, even Protesilaos, that mighty man of war. Yet did not the host lack at all a leader, only they yearned for the noble dead. With him followed forty black ships.

And of them that dwelt in Pherai by the Boibeian mere, in Boibe and Glaphyre and stablished Iolkos, of them, even eleven ships, Admetos' dear son was leader, Eumelos whom Alkestis, fair among women, bare to Admetos, she that was most beauteous to look upon of the daughters of Pelias.

And of them that dwelt in Methone and Thaumakie, and possessed Meliboia and rugged Olizon, of these, even seven ships, was Philoktetes leader, the cunning archer; and in each ship sailed fifty oarsmen skilled to fight amain with the bow. But their captain lay enduring sore pain in the isle of goodly Lemnos, where the sons of the Achaians left him sick of a grievous wound from a deadly water-snake. There lay he pining; yet were the Argives soon to bethink them beside their ships of king

Philoktetes. Yet neither were his men leaderless, only they sorrowed for their leader; but Medon marshalled them, Oileus' bastard son, whom Rhene bare to Oileus waster of cities.

And of them that possessed Trikke and terraced ithome and that possessed Oichalia city of Eurytos the Oichalian, of these again Asklepios' two sons were leaders, the cunning leeches Podaleirios and Machaon. And with them were arrayed thirty hollow ships.

And of them that possessed Ormenios and the fountain of Hypereia, and possessed Asterion and the white crests of Titanos, of these was Eurypylos leader, Euaimon's glorious son; and with him, forty black ships followed.

And of them that possessed Argissa and dwelt in Gyrtona, Orthe and Elone and the white city of Olooson, of these was captain unflinching Polypoites, son of Peirithoos that immortal Zeus begat: and Polypoites did famed Hippodameia conceive of Peirithoos on that day when he took vengeance of the shaggy wild folk, and thrust them forth from Pelion and drave them to the Aithikes. And Polypoites ruled not alone, but with him was Leonteus of the stock of Ares, son of high-hearted Koronos Kaineus' son. And with them forty black ships followed.

And Gouneus from Kyphos led two-and-twenty ships, and with him followed the Enienes and unflinching Peraibians that had pitched their homes about wintry Dodona, and dwelt on the tilth about lovely Titaresios that poureth his fair-flowing stream into Peneios. Yet doth he not mingle with the silver eddies of Peneios, but floweth on over him like unto oil, seeing that he is an offspring from the water of Styx, the dread river of the oath.

And the Magnetes were led of Prothoos son of Tenthredon, even they that dwelt about Peneios and Pelion with trembling leafage. These did fleet Prothoos lead, and with him forty black ships followed.

So these were the leaders of the Danaans and their captains. Now tell me, O Muse, who among them was first and foremost, of warriors alike and horses that followed the sons of Atreus. Of horses they of Pheres' son were far goodliest, those that Eumelos drave, swift as birds, like of coat, like of age, matched to the measure of a levelling line across their backs. These were reared in Peraia by Apollo of the silver bow, two mares carrying onward the terror of battle. But of warriors far best was the Telamonian Aias, while the wrath of Achilles yet endured; for he was greatest of all, he and his horses that bore him, even Peleus' noble son. But he lay idle among his seafaring ships, in sore wrath against Agamemnon Atreus' son, shepherd of the host; and his folk along the sea-shore sported with quoits and with casting of javelins and archery; and the horses each beside his own chariot stood idle, champing clover and parsley of the marsh, and their lords' chariots lay well covered up within the huts, while the men yearned for their warrior chief, and wandered hither and thither through the camp and fought not.

So marched they then as though all the land were consuming with fire; and the earth groaned beneath them as at the wrath of Zeus whose joy is in the thunder, when he lasheth the earth about Typhoeus in the country of the Arimoi, where men say is Typhoeus' couch. Even so groaned the earth aloud at their tread as they went: and with speed advanced they across the plain.

Now fleet Iris the wind-footed went to the Trojans, a messenger from aegis-bearing Zeus, with a grievous message. These were holding assembly at Priam's gate, being gathered all together both young men and old. And fleet-footed Iris stood hard by and spake to them; and she made her voice like to the voice of Polites son of Priam, who was the sentinel of the Trojans and was wont to sit trusting in his fleetness upon the barrow of Aisyetes of old, and on the top thereof wait the sallying of the Achaians forth from their ships. Even in his likeness did fleet-footed Iris speak to Priam: "Old man, words beyond number are still pleasant to thee as erst in the days of peace; but war without respite is upon us. Of a truth have I very oft ere now entered into battles of the warriors, yet have I never seen so goodly a host and so great; for in the very likeness of the leaves of the forest or the sands of the sea are they marching along the plain to fight against the city. But Hector, thee do I charge beyond all to do even as I shall say. Seeing that the allies are very many throughout Priam's great city, and diverse men, being scattered abroad, have diverse tongues; therefore let each one give the word to those whose chieftain he is, and them let him lead forth and have the ordering of his countrymen."

So spake she, and Hector failed not to know the voice of the goddess, and straightway dismissed the assembly, and they rushed to arms. And the gates were thrown open wide, and the host issued forth, footmen and horsemen, and mighty din arose.

Now there is before the city a certain steep mound apart in the plain, with a clear way about it on this side and on that; and men indeed call this "Batieia," but the immortals call it "The tomb of lithe Myrine." There did the Trojans and their allies divide their companies.

Amid the Trojans great Hector of the glancing helm was leader, the son of Priam; with him the greatest hosts by far and the goodliest were arrayed, eager warriors of the spear.

But the Dardanians were led of the princely son of Anchises, Aineias, whom bright Aphrodite conceived to Anchises amids the spurs of Ida, a goddess wedded to a mortal. Neither was he alone; with him were Antenor's two sons, Archelochos and Akamas, well skilled in all the ways of war.

And of them that dwelt in Zeleia beneath the nethermost foot of Ida, the men of substance that drink the dark waters of Aisepos, even the Troes; of these Lykaon's glorious son was leader, Pandaros, to whom Apollo himself gave the bow.

And of them that possessed Adresteia and the land of Apaisos and possessed Pityeia and the steep hill of Tereia, of these Adrestos was captain, and Amphios of the linen corslet, the two sons of Merops of Perkote, that beyond all men knew soothsaying, and would have hindered his children marching to murderous war. But they gave him no heed, for the fates of black death led them on.

And they that dwelt about Perkote and Praktios and possessed Sestos and Abydos and bright Arisbe, these were led of Hyrtakos' son Asios, a prince of men, Asios son of Hyrtakos, whom his tall sorrel steeds brought from Arisbe, from the river Selleeis.

And Hippothoos led the tribes of the Pelasgians that fight with spears, them that inhabited deep-soiled Larisa. These were led of Hippothoos and Pylaios of the stock of Ares, twain sons of Pelasgian Lethos son of Teutamos.

And the Thracians were led of Akamas and hero Peiroos, even all they that the strong stream of Hellespont shutteth in. And Euphemos was captain of the Kikonian spearmen, the son of Troizenos Keos' son, fosterling of Zeus.

But Pyraichmes led the Paionians with curving bows, from far away in Amydon, from the broad stream of Axios, Axios whose water is the fairest that floweth over the face of the earth.

And Pylaimenes of rugged heart led the Paphlagonians from the land of the Eneti, whence is the breed of wild mules. This folk were they that possessed Kytoros and dwelt about Sesamon, and inhabited their famed dwellings round the river Parthenios and Kromna and Aigialos and lofty Erythini.

And the Alizones were led of Odios and Epistrophos, from far away in Alybe, where is the birthplace of silver.

And the Mysians were led of Chromis and Ennomos the augur, yet with all his auguries warded he not black fate from him, but was vanguished by the hand of fleet-footed Aiakides in the river, when he made havoc of the Trojans there and of the rest.

And Phorkys and godlike Askanios led the Phrygians from far Askania, and these were eager to fight in the battle-throng.

And the Maionians were commanded of Mesthles and Antiphos, Talaimenes' two sons, whose mother was the Gygaian mere. So these led the Maionians, whose birthplace was under Tmolos.

But Nastes led the Karians, uncouth of speech, that possessed Miletos and the mountain of Phthires, of leafage numberless, and the streams of Maiandros and the steep crest of Mykale. These were led of Amphimachos and Nastes: Nastes and Amphimachos the glorious children of Nomion. And he came, forsooth, to battle with golden attire like a girl—fond man: that held not back in any wise grievous destruction, but he was vanguished by the hands of fleet-footed Aiakides in the river, and wise-hearted Achilles carried away his gold.

And Sarpedon and blameless Glaukos led the Lykians from far away in Lykia by eddying Xanthos.

BOOK III.

How Menelaos and Paris fought in single combat; and Aphrodite rescued Paris. And how Helen and Priam beheld the Achaian host from the walls of Troy.

Now when they were arrayed, each company with their captains, the Trojans marched with clamour and with shouting like unto birds, even as when there goeth up before heaven a clamour of cranes which flee from the coming of winter and sudden rain, and fly with clamour towards the streams of ocean, bearing slaughter and fate to the Pigmy men, and in early morn offer cruel battle. But on the other side marched the Achaians in silence breathing courage, eager at heart to give succour man to man.

Even as when the south wind sheddeth mist over the crests of a mountain, mist unwelcome to the shepherd, but to the robber better than night, and a man can see no further than he casteth a stone; even so thick arose the gathering dust-clouds at their tread as they went; and with all speed they advanced across the plain.

So when they were now come nigh in onset on each other, godlike Alexandros played champion to the Trojans, wearing upon his shoulders panther-skin and curved bow and sword; and he brandished two bronze-headed spears and challenged all the chieftains of the Argives to fight him man to man in deadly combat. But when Menelaos dear to Ares marked him coming in the forefront of the multitude with long strides, then even as a lion is glad when he lighteth upon a great carcase, a horned stag, or a wild goat that he hath found, being an hungered; and so he devoureth it amain, even though the fleet hounds and lusty youths set upon him; even thus was Menelaos glad when his eyes beheld godlike Alexandros; for he thought to take vengeance upon the sinner. So straightway he leap in his armour from his chariot to the ground.

But when godlike Alexandros marked him appear amid the champions, his heart was smitten, and he shrank back into the host of his comrades, avoiding death. And even as a man that hath seen a serpent in a mountain glade starteth backward and trembling seizeth his feet beneath him, and he retreateth back again, and paleness hath hold of his cheeks, even so did godlike Alexandros for fear of Atreus' son shrink back into the throng of lordly Trojans. But Hector beheld and upbraided him with scornful words: "Ill Paris, most fair in semblance, thou deceiver woman-mad, would thou hadst been unborn and died unwed. Yea, that were my desire, and it were far better than thus to be our shame and looked at askance of all men. I ween that the flowing-haired Achaians laugh, deeming that a prince is our champion only because a goodly favour is his; but in his heart is there no strength nor any courage. Art thou indeed such an one that in thy seafaring ships thou didst sail over the deep with the company of thy trusty comrades, and in converse with strangers didst bring back a fair woman from a far country, one that was by marriage daughter to warriors that bear the spear, that she might be a sore mischief to they father and city and all the realm, but to our foes a rejoicing, and to thyself a hanging of the head? And canst thou not indeed abide Menelaos dear to Ares? Thou mightest see what sort of warrior is he whose lovely wife thou hast. Thy lyre will not avail thee nor the gifts of Aphrodite, those thy locks and fair favour, when thou grovellest in the dust. But the Trojans are very cowards: else ere this hadst thou donned a robe of stone [i.e., been stoned by the people] for all the ill thou hast wrought."

And godlike Alexandros made answer to him again: "Hector, since in measure thou chidest me and not beyond measure—they heart is ever keen, even as an axe that pierceth a beam at the hand of a man that shapeth a ship's timber with skill, and thereby is the man's blow strengthened; even such is thy heart undaunted in thy breast. Cast not in my teeth the lovely gifts of golden Aphrodite; not to be flung aside are the gods' glorious gifts that of their own good will they give; for by his desire can no man win them. But now if thou wilt have me do battle and fight, make the other Trojans sit down and all the Achaians, and set ye me in the midst, and Menelaos dear to Ares, to fight for Helen and all her wealth. And whichsoever shall vanquish and gain the upper hand, let him take all the wealth aright, and the woman, and bear them home. And let the rest pledge friendship and sure oaths; so may ye dwell in deep-soiled Troy, and let them depart to Argos pasture-land of horses, and Achaia home of fair women."

So spake he, and Hector rejoiced greatly to hear his saying, and went into the midst and restrained the battalions of the Trojans, with his spear grasped by the middle; and they all sate them down. But the flowing-haired Achaians kept shooting at him, aiming with arrows and casting stones. But Agamemnon king of men cried aloud: "Refrain, ye Argives; shoot not, ye sons of the Achaians; for Hector of the glancing helm hath set himself to say somewhat."

So spake he, and they refrained from battle and made silence speedily. And Hector spake between the two hosts, "Hear of me, Trojans and well-greaved Achaians, the saying of Alexandros, for whose sake strife hath come about. He biddeth the other Trojans and all the Achaians to lay down their goodly armour on the bounteous earth, and himself in the midst and Menelaos dear to Ares to fight alone for Helen and all her wealth. And whichsoever shall vanquish and gain the upper hand, let him take all the wealth aright, and the woman, and bear them home; but let all of us pledge friendship and sure oaths."

So spake he, and they all kept silence and were still. Then in their midst spake Menelaos of the loud war-cry: "Hearken ye now to me, too; for into my heart most of all is grief entered; and I deem that the parting of Argives and Trojans hath come at last; seeing ye have endured many ills because of my quarrel and the first sin of Alexandros. And for whichsoever of us death and fate are prepared, let him lie dead: and be ye all parted with speed. Bring ye two lambs, one white ram and one black ewe, for earth and sun; and let us bring one for Zeus. And call hither great Priam, that he may pledge the oath himself, seeing he hath sons that are overweening and faithless, lest any by transgression do violence to the oath of Zeus; for young men's hearts are ever lifted up. But wheresoever an old man entereth in, he looketh both before and after, whereby the best issue shall come for either side."

So spake he, and Achaians and Trojans were glad, deeming that they should have rest from grievous war. So they refrained their chariots to the ranks, and themselves alighted and doffed their arms. And these they laid upon the earth each close to each, and there was but small space between. And Hector sent two heralds to the city will all speed, to bring the lambs, and to call Priam. And lord Agamemnon sent forth Talthybios to go to the hollow ships, and bade him bring a ram; and he was not disobedient to noble Agamemnon.

Now Iris went with a message to white-armed Helen in the likeness of her husband's sister, the spouse of Antenor's son, even her that lord Helikaon Antenor's son had to wife, Laodike fairest favoured of Priam's daughters. And in the hall she found Helen weaving a great purple web of double fold, and embroidering thereon many battles of horse-taming Trojans and mail-clad Achaians, that they had endured for her sake at the hands of Ares. So fleet-footed Iris stood by her side and said: "Come hither, dear sister, that thou mayest see the wondrous doings of horse-taming Trojans and mail-clad Achaians. They that erst waged tearful war upon each other in the plain, eager for deadly battle, even they sit now in silence, and the tall spears are planted by their sides. But Alexandros and Menelaos dear to Ares will fight with their tall spears for thee; and thou wilt be declared the dear wife of him that conquereth."

So spake the goddess, and put into her heart sweet longing for her former husband and her city and parents.

Forthwith she veiled her face in shining linen, and hastened from her chamber, letting fall a round tear; not unattended, for there followed with her two handmaidens, Aithre daughter of Pittheus and ox-eyed Klymene. Then came she straightway to the place of the Skaian gates. And they that were with Priam and Panthoos and Thymoites and Lampos and Klytios and Hiketaon of the stock of Ares, Oukalegon withal and Antenor, twain sages, being elders of the people, sat at the Skaian gates. These had now ceased from battle for old age, yet were they right good orators, like grasshoppers that in a forest sit upon a tree and utter their lily-like [supposed to mean "delicate" or "tender"] voice; even so sat the elders of the Trojans upon the tower. Now when they saw Helen coming to the tower they softly spake winged words one to the other: "Small blame is it that Trojans and well-greaved Achaians should for such a woman long time suffer hardships; marvellously like is she to the immortal goddesses to look upon. Yet even so, though she be so goodly, let her go upon their ships and not stay to vex us and our children after us."

So said they, and Priam lifted up his voice and called to Helen: "Come hither, dear child, and sit before me, that thou mayest see thy former husband and they kinsfolk and thy friends. I hold thee not to blame; nay, I hold the gods to blame who brought on me the dolorous war of the Achaians—so mayest thou now tell me who is this huge hero, this Achaian warrior so goodly and great. Of a truth there are others even taller by a head; yet mine eyes never behold a man so beautiful nor so royal; for he is like unto one that is a king."

And Helen, fair among women, spake and answered him: "Reverend art thou to me and dread, dear father of my lord; would that sore death had been my pleasure when I followed thy son hither, and left my home and my kinsfolk and my daughter in her girlhood and the lovely company of mine age-fellows. But that was not so, wherefore I pine with weeping. Now will I tell thee that whereof thou askest me and enquirest. This is Atreides, wide-ruling Agamemnon, one that is both a goodly king and mighty spearman. And he was my husband's brother to me, ah shameless me; if ever such an one there was."

So said she, and the old man marvelled at him, and said: "Ah, happy Atreides, child of fortune, blest of heaven; now know I that many sons of the Achaians are subject to thee. Erewhile fared I to Phrygia, the land of vines, and there saw I that the men of Phrygia, they of the nimble steeds, were very many, even the hosts of Otreus and godlike Mygdon, that were then encamped along the banks of Sangarios. For I too being their ally was numbered among them on the day that the Amazons came, the peers of men. Yet were not even they so many as are the glancing-eyed Achaians."

And next the old man saw Odysseus, and asked: "Come now, tell me of this man too, dear child, who is he, shorter by a head than Agamemnon son of Atreus, but broader of shoulder and of chest to behold? His armour lieth upon the bounteous earth, and himself like a bell-wether rangeth the ranks of warriors. Yea, I liken him to a thick-fleeced ram ordering a great flock of ewes."

Then Helen sprung of Zeus made answer to him: "Now this is Laertes' son, crafty Odysseus, that was reared in the realm of Ithaka, rugged though it be, and skilled in all the ways of wile and cunning device."

Then sage Antenor made answer to her: "Lady, verily the thing thou sayest is true indeed, for erst came goodly Odysseus hither also on an embassage for thee, in the company of Menelaos dear to Ares; and I gave them entertainment and welcomed them in my halls, and learnt the aspect of both and their wise devices. Now when they mingled with the Trojans in the assembly, while all stood up Menelaos overpassed them all by the measure of his broad shoulders; but when both sat down, Odysseus was the more stately. And when they began to weave the web of words and counsel in the face of all, then Menelaos harangued fluently, in few words, but very clearly, seeing he was not long of speech, neither random, though in years he was the younger. But whenever Odysseus full of wiles rose up, he stood and looked down, with eyes fixed upon the ground, and waved not his staff whether backwards or forwards, but held it stiff, like to a man of no understanding; one would deem him to be churlish, and naught but a fool. But when he uttered his great voice from his chest, and words like unto the snowflakes of winter, then could no mortal man contend with Odysseus; then marvelled we not thus to behold Odysseus' aspect."

And thirdly the old man say Aias, and asked: "Who then is this other Achaian warrior, goodly and great, preeminent among the Archives by the measure of his head and broad shoulders?"

And long-robed Helen, fair among women, answered: "This is huge Aias, bulwark of the Achaians. And on the other side amid the Cretans standeth Idomeneus like a god, and about him are gathered the captains of the Cretans. Oft did Menelaos dear to Ares entertain him in our house whene'er he came from Crete. And now behold I all the other glancing-eyed Achaians, whom well I could discern and tell their names; but two captains of the host can I not see, even Kastor tamer of horses and Polydeukes the skilful boxer, mine own brethren, whom the same mother bare. Either they came not in the company from lovely Lakedaimon; or they came hither indeed in their seafaring ships, but now will not enter into the battle of the warriors, for fear of the many scornings and revilings that are mine."

So said she; but them the life-giving earth held fast there in Lakedaimon, in their dear native land.

Meanwhile were the heralds bearing through the city the holy oath-offerings, two lambs and strong-hearted wine, the fruit of the earth, in a goat-skin bottle. And the herald Idaios bare the shining bowl and golden cups; and came to the old man and summoned him and said: "Rise, thou son of Laomedon. The chieftains of the horse-taming Trojans and mail-clad Achaians call on thee to go down into the plain, that ye may pledge a trusty oath. But Alexandros and Menelaos dear to Ares will fight with their long spears for the lady's sake; and let lady and treasure go with him that shall conquer. And may we that are left pledge friendship and trusty oaths and dwell in deep-soiled Troy, and they shall depart to Argos pasture-land of horses and Achaia home of fair women."

So said he, and the old man shuddered and base his companions yoke the horses; and they with speed obeyed. Then Priam mounted and drew back the reins, and by his side Antenor mounted the splendid chariot. So the two drave the fleet horses through the Skaian gates to the plain. And when they had come even to the Trojans and Achaians, they went down from the chariots upon the bounteous earth, and marched into the midst of Trojans and Achaians. Then forthwith rose up Agamemnon king of men, and up rose Odysseus the man of wiles; and the lordly heralds gathered together the holy oath-offerings of the gods, and mingled the wine in a bowl, and poured water over the princes' hands. And Atreides put forth his hand and drew his knife that hung ever beside his sword's great sheath, and cut the hair from off the lambs' heads; and then the heralds portioned it among the chief of the Trojans and Achaians. Then in their midst Atreus' son lifted up his hands and prayed aloud: "Father Zeus, that rulest from Ida, most glorious, most great, and thou Sun that seest all things and hearest all things, and ye Rivers and thou Earth, and ye that in the underworld punish men outworn, whosoever sweareth falsely; be ye witnesses, and watch over the faithful oath. If Alexandros slay Menelaos, then let him have Helen to himself and all her possessions; and we will depart on our seafaring ships. But if golden-haired Menelaos slay Alexandros, then let the Trojans give back Helen and all her possessions and pay the Argives the recompense that is seemly, such as shall live among men that shall be hereafter. But if so be that Priam and Priam's sons will not pay the recompense unto me when Alexandros falleth, then will I fight on thereafter for the price of sin, and abide here till I compass the end of war."

So said he, and cut the lambs' throats with the pitiless knife. Them he laid gasping upon the ground, failing of breath, for the knife had taken their strength from them; and next they drew the wine from the bowl into the cups, and poured it forth and prayed to the gods that live for ever. And thus would say many an one of Achaians and Trojans: "Zeus most glorious, most great, and all ye immortal gods, which folk soe'er be first to sin against the oaths, may their brains be so poured forth upon the earth even as this wine, theirs and their children's; and let their wives be made subject unto strangers."

So spake they, but the son of Kronos vouchsafed not yet fulfilment. And in their midst Priam of the seed of Dardanos uttered his saying: "Hearken to me, Trojans and well-greaved Achaians. I verily will return back to windy Ilios, seeing that I can in no wise bear to behold with mine eyes my dear son fighting with Menelaos dear to Ares. But Zeus knoweth, and all the immortal gods, for whether of the twain the doom of death is appointed."

So spake the godlike man, and laid the lambs in his chariot, and entered in himself, and drew back the reins; and by his side Antenor mounted the splendid chariot. So they departed back again to Ilios; and Hector son of Priam and goodly Odysseus first meted out a space, and then they took the lots, and shook them in a bronze-bound helmet, to know whether of the twain should first cast his spear of bronze. And the people prayed and lifted up their hands to the gods; and thus would say many an one of Achaians and Trojans: "Father Zeus, that rulest from Ida, most glorious, most great; whichsoe'er it be that brought this trouble upon both peoples, vouchsafe that he may die and enter the house of Hades; that so for us peace may be assured and trusty oaths."

So said they; and great Hector of the glancing plume shook the helmet, looking behind him; and quickly leapt forth the lot of Paris. Then the people sat them down by ranks where each man's high-stepping horses and inwrought armour lay. And upon his shoulders goodly Alexandros donned his beauteous armour, even he that was lord to Helen of the lovely hair. First upon his legs set he his greaves, beautiful, fastened with silver ankle-clasps; next upon his breast he donned the corslet of his brother Lykaon, and fitted it upon himself. And over his shoulders cast he his silver-studded sword of bronze, and then a shield great and sturdy. And on his mighty head he set a wrought helmet of horse-hair crest, whereover the plume nodded terribly, and he took him a strong spear fitted to his grasp. And in like wise warlike Menelaos donned his armour.

So when they had armed themselves on either side in the throng, they strode between Trojans and Achaians, fierce of aspect, and wonder came on them that beheld, both on the Trojans tamers of horses and on the well-greaved Achaians. Then took they their stand near together in the measured space, brandishing their spears in wrath each against other. First Alexandros hurled his far shadowing spear, and smote on Atreides' round shield; but the bronze brake not through, for its point was turned in the stout shield. Next Menelaos son of Atreus lifted up his hand to cast, and made prayer to father Zeus: "King Zeus, grant me revenge on him that was first to do me wrong, even on goodly Alexandros, and subdue thou him at my hands; so that many an one of men that shall be hereafter may shudder to wrong his host that hath shown him kindness."

So said he, and poised his far-shadowing spear, and hurled, and smote on the round shield of the son of Priam. Through the bright shield went the ponderous spear and through the inwrought breastplate it pressed on; and straight beside his flank the spear rent the tunic, but he swerved and escaped black death. Then Atreides drew his silver-studded sword, and lifted up his hand and smote the helmet-ridge; but the sword shattered upon it into three, yea four, and fell from his hand. Thereat Atreides looked up to the wide heaven and cried: "Father Zeus, surely none of the gods is crueller than thou. Verily I thought to have gotten vengeance on Alexandros for his wickedness, but now my sword breaketh in my hand, and my spear sped from my grasp in vain, and I have not smitten him."

So saying, he leapt upon him and caught him by his horse-hair crest, and swinging him round dragged him towards the well-greaved Achaians; and he was strangled by the embroidered strap beneath his soft throat, drawn tight below his chin to hold his helm. Now would Menelaos have dragged him away and won glory unspeakable, but that Zeus' daughter Aphrodite was swift to mark, and tore asunder for him the strap of slaughtered ox's hide; so the helmet came away empty in his stalwart hand. Thereat Menelaos cast it with a swing toward the well-greaved Achaians, and his trusty comrades took it up; and himself sprang back again eager to slay him with spear of bronze. But Aphrodite snatched up Paris, very easily as a goddess may, and hid him in thick darkness, and sent him down in his fragrant perfumed chamber; and herself went to summon Helen. Her she found on the high tower, and about her the Trojan women thronged. So with her hand she plucked her perfumed raiment and shook it and spake to her in the likeness of an aged dame, a wool-comber that was wont to work for her fair wool when she dwelt in Lakedaimon, whom too she greatly loved. Even in her likeness fair Aphrodite spake: "Come hither; Alexandros summoneth thee to go homeward. There is he in his chamber and inlaid bed, radiant in beauty and vesture; nor wouldst thou deem him to be come from fighting his foe, but rather to be faring to the dance, or from the dance to be just resting and set down."

So said she, and stirred Helen's soul within her breast; and when now she marked the fair neck and lovely breast and sparkling eyes of the goddess, she marvelled straightway and spake a word and called upon her name: "Strange queen, why art thou desirous now to beguile me? Verily thou wilt lead me further on to some one of the people cities of Phrygia or lovely Maionia, if there too thou hast perchance some other darling among mortal men, because even now Menelaos hath conquered goodly Alexandros, and will lead me, accursed me, to his home. Therefore thou comest hither with guileful intent. Go and sit thou by his side and depart from the way of the gods; neither let thy feet ever bear thee back to Olympus, but still be vexed for his sake and guard him till he make thee his wife or perchance his slave. But thither will I not go— that were a sinful thing—to array the bed of him; all the women of Troy will blame me thereafter; and I have griefs untold within my soul."

Then in wrath bright Aphrodite spake to her: "Provoke me not, rash woman, lest in mine anger I desert thee, and hate thee even as now I love thee beyond measure, and lest I devise grievous enmities between both, even betwixt Trojans and Achaians, and so thou perish in evil wise."

So said she, and Helen sprung of Zeus was afraid, and went wrapped in her bright radiant vesture, silently, and the Trojan women marked her not; and the goddess led the way.

Now when they were come to the beautiful house of Alexandros the handmaidens turned straightway to their tasks, and the fair lady went to the high-roofed chamber; and laughter-loving Aphrodite took for her a chair and brought it, even she the goddess, and set it before the face of Paris. There Helen took her seat, the child of aegis-bearing Zeus, and with eyes turned askance spake and chode her lord: "Thou comest back from battle; would thou hadst perished there, vanquished of that great warrior that was my former husband. Verily it was once thy boast that thou wast a better man than Menelaos dear to Ares, in the might of thine arm and thy spear. But go now, challenge Menelaos, dear to Ares to fight thee again face to face. Nay, but I, even I, bid thee refrain, nor fight a fight with golden-haired Menelaos man to man, neither attack him recklessly, lest perchance thou fall to his spear anon."

And Paris made answer to her and said: "Chide not my soul, lady, with cruel taunts. For now indeed hath Menelaos vanquished me with Athene's aid, but another day may I do so unto him; for we too have gods with us. But come now, let us have joy of love upon our couch; for never yet hath love so enwrapped my heart—not even then when first I snatched thee from lovely Lakedaimon and sailed with thee on my sea-faring ships, and in the isle of Kranae had converse with thee upon thy couch in love—as I love thee now and sweet desire taketh hold upon me." So saying he led the way to the couch, and the lady followed with him.

Thus laid they them upon their fretted couch; but Atreides the while strode through the host like to a wild beast, if anywhere he might set eyes on godlike Alexandros. But none of the Trojans or their famed allies could discover Alexandros to Menelaos dear to Ares. Yet surely did they in no wise hide him for kindliness, could any have seen him; for he was hated of all even as black death. So Agamemnon king of men spake among them there: "Hearken to me, Trojans and Dardanians and allies. Now is victory declared for Menelaos dear to Ares; give ye back Helen of Argos and the possessions with her, and pay ye the recompense such as is seemly, that it may live even among men that shall be hereafter." So said Atreides, and all the Achaians gave assent.

BOOK IV.

How Pandaros wounded Menelaos by treachery; and Agamemnon exhorted his chief captains to battle.

Now the gods sat by Zeus and held assembly on the golden floor, and in the midst the lady Hebe poured them their nectar: they with golden goblets pledged one another, and gazed upon the city of the Trojans. Then did Kronos' son essay to provoke Hera with vexing words, and spake maliciously: "Twain goddesses hath Menelaos for his helpers, even Hera of Argos and Alalkomenean Athene. Yet these sit apart and take there pleasure in beholding; but beside that other ever standeth laughter-loving Aphrodite and wardeth off fate from him, and now hath she saved him as he thought to perish. But of a truth the victory is to Menelaos dear to Ares; so let us take thought how these things shall be; whether once more we shall arouse ill war and the dread battle-din, or put friendship between the foes. Moreover if this were welcome to all and well pleasing, may the city of king Priam yet be an habitation, and Menelaos take back Helen of Argos."

So said he, but Athene and Hera murmured thereat, who were sitting by him and devising ills for the Trojans. Now Athene held her peace and said not anything, for wrath at father Zeus, and fierce anger gat hold upon her: But Hera's breast contained not her anger, and she spake: "Most dread son of Kronos, what word is this thou hast spoken? How hast thou the will to make my labour void and of none effect, and the sweat of my toil that I sweated, when my horses were wearied with my summoning of the host, to be the plague of Priam and his sons? Do as thou wilt; but we other gods do not all approve thee."

Then in sore anger Zeus the cloud-gatherer spake to her: "Good lack, how have Priam and Priam's sons done thee such great wrong that thou art furiously minded to sack the established citadel of Ilios? Perchance wert thou to enter within the gates and long walls and devour Priam raw, and Priam's sons and all the Trojans, then mightest thou assuage thine anger. Do as thou art minded, only let not this quarrel hereafter be to me and thee a sore strife between us both. And this moreover will I say to thee, and do thou lay it to they heart; whene'er I too be of eager mind to lay waste to a city where is the race of men that are dear to thee, hinder thou not my wrath, but let me be, even as I yield to thee of free will, yet with soul unwilling. For all cities beneath sun and starry heaven that are the dwelling of mortal men, holy Ilios was most honoured of my heart, and Priam and the folk of Priam of the good ashen spear. For never did mine altar lack the seemly feast, even drink-offering and burnt-offering, the worship that is our due."

Then Helen the ox-eyed queen made answer to him: "Of a surety three cities are there that are dearest far to me, Argos and Sparta and wide-wayed Mykene; these lay thou waste whene'er they are found hateful to thy heart; not for them will I stand forth, nor do I grudge thee them. For even if I be jealous and would forbid thee to overthrow them, yet will my jealousy not avail, seeing that thou art stronger far than I. Still must my labour too not be made of none effect; for I also am a god, and my lineage is even as thine, and Kronos the crooked counsellor begat me to the place of honour in double wise, by birthright, and because I am named thy spouse, and thou art king among all the immortals. Let us indeed yield each to other herein, I to thee and thou to me, and the rest of the immortal gods will follow with us; and do thou with speed charge Athene to betake her to the fierce battle din of Trojans and Achaians, and to essay that the Trojans may first take upon them to do violence to the Achaians in their triumph, despite the oaths."

So said she, and the father of men and gods disregarded not; forthwith he spake to Athene winged words: "Betake thee with all speed to the host, to the midst of Trojans and Achaians, and essay that the Trojans may first take upon them to do violence to the Achaians in their triumph, despite the oaths."

So spake he, and roused Athene that already was set thereon; and from Olympus' heights she darted down. Even as the son of Kronos the crooked counsellor sendeth a star, a portent for mariners or a wide host of men, bright shining, and therefrom are scattered sparks in multitude; even in such guise sped Pallas Athene to earth, and leapt into their midst; and astonishment came on them that beheld, on horse-taming Trojans and well-greaved Achaians. And thus would many an one say, looking at his neighbor: "Of a surety either shall sore war and the fierce battle din return again; or else Zeus doth stablish peace between the foes, even he that is men's dispenser of battle."

Thus would many an one of Achaians and Trojans say. Then the goddess entered the throng of Trojans in the likeness of a man, even Antenor's son Laodokos, a stalwart warrior, and sought for godlike Pandaros, if haply she might find him. Lykaon's son found she, the noble and stalwart, standing, and about him the stalwart ranks of the shield-bearing host that followed him from the streams of Aisepos. So she came near and spake winged words: "Wilt thou now hearken to me, thou wise son of Lykaon? Then wouldst thou take heart to shoot a swift arrow at Menelaos, and wouldst win favour and glory before all the Trojans, and before king Alexandros most of all. Surely from him first of any wouldst thou receive glorious gifts, if perchance he see Menelaos, Atreus' warrior son, vanquished by thy dart and brought to the grievous pyre. Go to now, shoot at glorious Menelaos, and vow to Apollo, the son of light [Or, perhaps, "the Wolf-born"], the lord of archery, to sacrifice a goodly hecatomb of firstling lambs when thou art returned to thy home, in the city of holy Zeleia."

So spake Athene, and persuaded his fool's heart. Forthwith he unsheathed his polished bow of horn of a wild ibex that he himself had erst smitten beneath the breast as it came forth from a rock, the while he awaited in a lurking-place; and had pierced it in the chest, so that it fell backward on the rock. Now from its head sprang there horns of sixteen palms; these the artificer, even the worker in horn, joined cunningly together, and polished them all well and set the top of gold thereon. So he laid it down when he had well strung it, by resting it upon the ground; and his staunch comrades held their shields before him, lest the warrior sons of the Achaians should first set on them, ere Menelaos, Atreus' son, were smitten. Then opened he the lid of his quiver and took forth a feathered arrow, never yet shot, a source of grievous pangs; and anon he laid the bitter dart upon the string and vowed to Apollo, the son of light, the lord of archery, to sacrifice a goodly hecatomb of firstling lambs when he should have returned to his home in the city of holy Zeleia. Then he took the notch and string of oxes' sinew together, and drew, bringing to his breast the string, and to the bow the iron head. So when he had now bent the great bow into a round, the horn twanged, and the string sang aloud, and the keen arrow leapt eager to wing his way amid the throng.

But the blessed gods immortal forgat not thee, Menelaos; and before all the daughter of Zeus, the driver of the spoil, who stood before thee and warded off the piercing dart. She turned it just aside from the flesh, even as a mother driveth a fly from her child that lieth in sweet slumber; and with her own hand guided it where the golden buckles of the belt were clasped and the doubled breastplate met them. So the bitter arrow lighted upon the firm belt; through the inwrought belt it sped and through the curiously wrought breastplate it pressed on and through the taslet [and apron or belt set with metal, worn below the corslet] he wore to shield his flesh, a barrier against darts; and this best shielded him, yet it passed on even through this. Then did the arrow graze the warrior's outermost flesh, and forthwith the dusky blood flowed from the wound.

As when some woman of Maionia or Karia staineth ivory with purple, to make a cheek-piece for horses, and it is laid up in the treasure chamber, and many a horseman prayeth for it to wear; but it is laid up to be a king's boast, alike an adornment for his horse and a glory for his charioteer; even in such wise, Menelaos, were thy shapely thighs stained with blood and thy legs and thy fair ankles beneath.

Thereat shuddered Agamemnon king of men when he saw the black blood flowing from the wound. And Menelaos dear to Ares likewise shuddered; but when he saw how thread [by which the iron head was attached to the shaft] and bards were without, his spirit was gathered in his breast again. Then lord Agamemnon moaned deep, and spake among them, holding Menelaos by the hand; and his comrades made moan the while: "Dear brother, to thy death, meseemeth, pledged I these oaths, setting thee forth to fight the Trojans alone before the face of the Achaians; seeing that the Trojans have so smitten thee, and trodden under floor the trusty oaths. Yet in no wise is and oath of none effect, and the blood of lambs and pure drink-offerings and the right hands of fellowship wherein we trusted. For even if the Olympian bring not about the fulfilment forthwith, yet doth he fulfil at last, and men make dear amends, even with their own heads and their wives and little ones. Yea of a surety I know this in heart and soul; the day shall come for holy Ilios to be laid low, and Priam and the folk of Priam of the good ashen spear; and Zeus the son of Kronos enthroned on high, that dwelleth in the heaven, himself shall brandish over them all his lowring aegis, in indignation at this deceit. Then shall all this not be void; yet shall I have sore sorrow for thee, Menelaos, if thou die and fulfil the lot of life. Yea in utter shame should I return to thirsty Argos, seeing that the Achaians will forthwith bethink them of their native land, and so should we leave to Priam and the Trojans their boast, even Helen of Argos. And the earth shall rot thy bones as thou liest in Troy with thy task unfinished: and thus shall many an overweening Trojan say as he leapeth upon the tomb of glorious Menelaos: 'Would to God Agamemnon might so fulfil his wrath in every matter, even as now he led hither the host of the Achaians for naught, and hath gone home again to his dear native land with empty ships, and hath left noble Menelaos behind.' Thus shall men say hereafter: in that day let the wide earth gape for me."

But golden-haired Menelaos encouraged him and said: "Be of good courage, neither dismay at all the host of the Achaians. The keen dart lighted not upon a deadly spot; my glistening belt in front stayed it, and the kirtle of mail beneath, and the taslet that the coppersmiths fashioned."

Then lord Agamemnon answered him and said: "Would it may be so, dear Menelaos. But the leech shall feel the wound, and lay thereon drugs that shall assuage thy dire pangs."

So saying he spake to godlike Talthybios, his herald: "Talthybios, with all speed call Machaon hither, the hero son of Asklepios the noble leech, to see Menelaos, Atreus' warrior son, whom one well skilled in archery, some Trojan or Lykian, hath wounded with a bow-shot, to his glory and our grief."

So said he, and the herald heard him and disregarded not, and went his way through the host of mail-clad Achaians to spy out the hero Machaon. Him he found standing, and about him the stalwart ranks of the shield-bearing host that followed him from Trike, pasture land of horses. So he came near and spake his winged words: "Arise, thou son of Asklepios. Lord Agamemnon calleth thee to see Menelaos, captain of the Achaians, whom one well skilled in archery, some Trojan or Lykian, hath wounded with a bow-shot, to his glory and our grief."

So saying he aroused his spirit in his breast, and they went their way amid the throng, through the wide host of the Achaians. And when they were now come where was golden-haired Menelaos wounded, and all as many as were chieftains gathered around him in a circle, the godlike hero came and stood in their midst, and anon drew forth the arrow from the clasped belt; and as it was drawn forth the keen barbs were broken backwards. Then he loosed the glistering belt and kirtle of mail beneath and taslet that the coppersmiths fashioned; and when he saw the wound where the bitter arrow had lighted, he sucked out the blood and cunningly spread thereon soothing drugs, such as Cheiron of his good will had imparted to his sire.

While these were tending Menelaos of the loud war-cry, the ranks of shield-bearing Trojans came on; so the Achaians donned their arms again, and bethought them of the fray. Now wouldest thou not see noble Agamemnon slumbering, nor cowering, unready to fight, but very eager for glorious battle. He left his horses and his chariot adorned with bronze; and his squire, even Eurymedon son of Ptolemaios Peiraieus' son, kept apart the snorting steeds; and he straitly charged him to have them at hand whenever weariness should come upon his limbs with marshalling so many; and thus on foot ranged he through the ranks of warriors. And whomsoever of all the fleet-horsed Danaans he found eager, he stood by them and by his words encouraged them: "Ye Argives, relax not in any wise your impetuous valour; for father Zeus will be no helper of liars, but as these were first to transgress against the oaths, so shall their own tender flesh be eaten of the vultures, and we shall bear away their dear wives and little children in our ships, when once we take the stronghold."

But whomsoever he found shrinking from hateful battle, these he chode sore with angry words: "Ye Argives, warriors of the bow, ye men of dishonour, have ye no shame? Why stand ye thus dazed like fawns that are weary with running over the long plain and so stand still, and no valour is found in their hearts at all? Even thus stand ye dazed, and fight not. Is it that ye wait for the Trojans to come near where your good ships' sterns are drawn up on the shore of the grey sea, to see if Kronion will stretch his arm over you indeed?"

So masterfully ranged he through the ranks of warriors. Then came he to the Cretans as he went through the throng of warriors; and these were taking arms around wise Idomeneus; Idomeneus amid the foremost, valiant as a wild boar, and Meriones the while was hastening his hindermost battalions. Then Agamemnon king of men rejoiced to see them, and anon spake to Idomeneus with kindly words: "Idomeneus, more than all the fleet-horsed Danaans do I honour thee, whether in war or in task of other sort or in the feast, when the chieftains of the Argives mingle in the bowl the gleaming wine of the counsellor. For even though all the other flowing-haired Achaians drink one allotted portion, yet thy cup standeth ever full even as mine, to drink as oft as they soul biddeth thee. Now arouse thee to war like such an one as thou avowest thyself to be of old."

And Idomeneus the captain of the Cretans made answer to him: "Atreides, of very truth will I be to thee a trusty comrade even as at the first I promised and gave my pledge; but do thou urge on all the flowing-haired Achaians, that we may fight will all speed, seeing the Trojans have disannulled the oaths. But for all that death and sorrow hereafter shall be their lot, because they were the first to transgress against the oaths."

So said he, and Agamemnon passed on glad at heart. Then came he to the Aiantes as he went through the throng of warriors; and these twain were arming, and a cloud of footmen followed with them. Even as when a goatherd from a place of outlook seeth a cloud coming across the deep before the blast of the west wind; and to him being afar it seemeth ever blacker, even as pitch, as it goeth along the deep, and bringeth a great whirlwind, and he shuddereth to see it and driveth his flock beneath a cave; even in such wise moved the serried battalions of young men, the fosterlings of Zeus, by the side of the Aiantes into furious war, battalions dark of line, bristling with shields and spears. And lord Agamemnon rejoiced to see them and spake to them winged words, and said: "Aiantes, leaders of the mail-clad Argives, to you twain, seeing it is not seemly to urge you, give I no charge; for of your own selves ye do indeed bid your folk to fight amain. Ah, father Zeus and Athene and Apollo, would that all had like spirit in their breasts; then would king Priam's city soon bow captive and wasted beneath our hands."

So saying he left them there, and went to others. Then found he Nestor, the clear-voiced orator of the Pylians, arraying his comrades, and urging them to fight, around great Pelegon and Alastor and Chromios and lord Haimon and Bias shepherd of the host. And first he arrayed the horsemen with horses and chariots, and behind them the footmen many and brave, to be a bulwark of battle; but the cowards he drave into the midst, that every man, even though he would not, yet of necessity must fight. First he laid charge upon the horsemen; these he bade hold in their horses nor be entangled in the throng. "Neither let any man, trusting in his horsemanship and manhood, be eager to fight the Trojans alone and before the rest, nor yet let him draw back, for so will ye be enfeebled. But whomsoever a warrior from the place of his own car can come at a chariot of the foe, let him thrust forth with his spear; even so is the far better way. Thus moreover did men of old time lay low cities and walls, because they had this mind and spirit in their breasts."

So did the old man charge them, being well skilled of yore in battles. And lord Agamemnon rejoiced to see him, and spake to him winged words, and said: "Old man, would to god that, even as thy spirit is in thine own breast, thy limbs might obey and thy strength be unabated. But the common lot of age is heavy upon thee; would that it had come upon some other man, and thou wert amid the young."

Then knightly Nestor of Gerenia answered him: "Atreides, I verily, even I too, would wish to be as on the day when I slew noble Ereuthalion. But the gods in no wise grant men all things at once. As I was then a youth, so doth old age now beset me. Yet even so will I abide among the horsemen and urge them by counsel and words; for that is the right of elders. But the young men shall wield the spear, they that are more youthful than I and have confidence in their strength."

So spake he, and Atreides passed on glad at heart. He found Menestheus the charioteer, the son of Peteos, standing still, and round him were the Athenians, masters of the battle-cry. And hard by stood crafty Odysseus, and round about him the ranks of Kephallenians, no feeble folk, stood still; for their host had not yet heard the battle-cry, seeing the battalions of horse-taming Trojans and Achaians had but just bestirred them to move; so these stood still tarrying till some other column of the Achaians should advance to set upon the Trojans and begin the battle. But when Agamemnon king of men saw it, he upbraided them, and spake to them winged words, saying: "O son of king Peteos fosterling of Zeus, and thou skilled in evil wiles, thou cunning of mind, why stand ye shrinking apart, and tarry for others? You beseemeth it to stand in your place amid the foremost and to front the fiery battle; for ye are the first to hear my bidding to the feast, as oft as we Achaians prepare a feast for the counsellors. Then are ye glad to eat roast meat and drink your cups of honey-sweet wine as long as ye will. But now would ye gladly behold it, yea, if ten columns of Achaians in front of you were fighting with the pitiless sword."

But Odysseus of many counsels looked fiercely at him and said: "Atreides, what word is this that hath escaped the barrier of thy lips? How sayest thou that we are slack in battle? When once our [Or, "that we are slack in battle, when once we Achaians," putting the note of interrogation after "tamers of horses."] Achaians launch furious war on the Trojans, tamers of horses, then shalt thou, if thou wilt, and if thou hast any care therefor, behold Telemachos' dear father mingling with the champions of the Trojans, the tamers of horses. But that thou sayest is empty as air."

Then lord Agamemnon spake to him smiling, seeing how he was wroth, and took back his saying: "Heaven-sprung son of Laertes, Odysseus full of devices, neither do I chide thee beyond measure nor urge thee; for I know that thy heart within thy breast is kindly disposed; for thy thoughts are as my thoughts. Go to, we will make amends hereafter, if any ill word hath been spoken now; may the gods bring it all to none effect."

So saying he left them there and went on to others. The son of Tydeus found he, high-hearted Diomedes, standing still with horses and chariot well compact; and by him stood Sthenelos son of Kapaneus. Him lord Agamemnon saw and upbraided, and spake to him winged words, and said: "Ah me, thou son of wise Tydeus tamer of horses, why shrinkest thou, why gazest thou at the highways of the battle? Not thus was Tydeus wont to shrink, but rather to fight his enemies far in front of his dear comrades, as they say that beheld him at the task; for never did I meet him nor behold him, but men say that he was preeminent amid all. Of a truth he came to Mykene, not in enmity, but as a guest with godlike Polyneikes, to raise him an army for the war that they were levying against the holy walls of Thebes; and they besought earnestly that valiant allies might be given them, and our folk were fain to grant them and made assent to their entreaty, only Zeus showed omens of ill and turned their minds. So when these were departed and were come on their way, and had attained to Asopos deep in rushes, that maketh his bed in grass, there did the Achaians appoint Tydeus to be their ambassador. So he went and found the multitude of the sons of Kadmos feasting in the palace of mighty Eteokles. Yet was knightly Tydeus, even though a stranger, not afraid, being alone amid the multitude of the Kadmeians, but challenged them all to feats of strength, and in every one vanquished he them easily; so present a helper was Athene unto him. But the Kadmeians, the urgers of horses, were wroth, and as he fared back again they brought and set a strong ambush, even fifty young men, whose leaders were twain, Maion son of Haimon, like to the immortals, and Autophonos' son Polyphontes staunch in battle. Still even on the Tydeus brought shameful death; he slew them all, save one that he sent home alone; Maion to wit he sent away in obedience to the omens of heaven. Such was Tydeus of Aitolia; but he begat a son that in battle is worse than he; only in harangue is he the better."

So said he, and stalwart Diomedes made no answer, but had respect to the chiding of the king revered. But the son of glorious Kapaneus answered him: "Atreides, utter not falsehood, seeing thou knowest how to speak truly. We avow ourselves to be better men by far than our fathers were: we did take the seat of Thebes the seven gated, though we led a scantier host against a stronger wall, because we followed the omens of the gods and the salvation of Zeus; but they perished by their own iniquities. Do not thou therefore in any wise have our fathers in like honour with us."

But stalwart Diomedes looked sternly at him, and said: "Brother, sit silent and obey my saying. I grudge not that Agamemnon shepherd of the host should urge on the well-greaved Achaians to fight; for him the glory will attend if the Achaians lay the Trojans low and take holy Ilios; and his will be the great sorrow if the Achaians be laid low. Go to now, let us too bethink us of impetuous valour."

He spake and leapt in his armour from the chariot to earth, and terribly rang the bronze upon the chieftain's breast as he moved; thereat might fear have come even upon one stout-hearted.

As when on the echoing beach the sea-wave lifteth up itself in close array before the driving of the west wind; out on the deep doth it first raise its head, and then breaketh upon the land and belloweth aloud and goeth with arching crest about the promontories, and speweth the foaming brine afar; even so in close array moved the battalions of the Danaans without pause to battle. Each captain gave his men the word, and the rest went silently; thou wouldest not deem that all the great host following them had any voice within their breasts; in silence feared they their captains. On every man glittered the inwrought armour wherewith they went clad. But for the Trojans, like sheep beyond number that stand in the courtyard of a man of great substance, to be milked of their white milk, and bleat without ceasing to hear their lambs' cry, even so arose the clamour of the Trojans through the wide host. For they had not all like speech nor one language, but their tongues were mingled, and they were brought from many lands. These were urged on of Ares, and those of bright-eyed Athene, and Terror and Rout, and Strife whose fury wearieth not, sister and friend of murderous Ares; her crest is but lowly at the first, but afterward she holdeth up her head in heaven and her feet walk upon the earth. She now cast common discord in their midst, as she fared through the throng and made the lamentation of men to wax.

Now when they were met together and come unto one spot, then clashed they targe and spear and fury of bronze-clad warrior; the bossed shields pressed each on each and mighty din arose. Then were heard the voice of groaning and the voice of triumph together of the slayers and the slain, and the earth streamed with blood. As when two winter torrents flow down the mountains to a watersmeet and join their furious flood within the ravine from their great springs, and the shepherd heareth the roaring far off among the hills: even so from the joining of battle came there forth shouting and travail. Antilochos first slew a Trojan warrior in full array, valiant amid the champions, Echepolos son of Thalysios; him was he first to smite upon the ridge of his crested helmet, and he drave the spear into his brow and the point of bronze passed within the bone; darkness clouded his eyes, and he crashed like a tower amid the press of fight. As he fell lord Elephenor caught him by the foot, Chalkodon's son, captain of the great-hearted Abantes, and dragged him from beneath the darts, eager with all speed to despoil him of his armour. Yet but for a little endured his essay; great-hearted Agenor saw him haling away the corpse, and where his side was left uncovered of his buckler as he bowed him down, there smote he him with bronze-tipped spear-shaft and unstrung his limbs. So his life departed from him, and over his corpse the task of Trojans and Achaians grew hot; like wolves leapt they one at another, and man lashed at man.

Next Telamonian Aias smote Anthemion's son, the lusty stripling Simoeisios, whose erst is mother bare beside the banks of Simoeis on the way down from Ida whither she had followed with her parents to see their flocks. Therefore they called him Simoeisios, but he repaid not his dear parents the recompense of his nurture; scanty was his span of life by reason of the spear of great-hearted Aias that laid him low. For as he went he first was smitten on his right breast beside the pap; straight though his shoulder passed the spear of bronze, and he fell to the ground in the dust like a poplar-tree, that hath grown up smooth in the lowland of a great marsh, and its branches grow upon the top thereof; this hath a wainwright felled with gleaming steel, to bend him a felloe for a goodly chariot, and so it lies drying by a river's banks. In such a fashion did heaven-sprung Aias slay Simoeisios son of Anthemion; then at him Antiphos of the glancing corslet, Priam's son, made a cast with his keen javelin across the throng. Him he missed, but smote Odysseus' valiant comrade Leukos in the groin as he drew the corpse his way, so that he fell upon it and the body dropped from his hands. Then Odysseus was very wroth at heart for the slaying of him, and strode through the forefront of the battle harnessed in flashing bronze, and went and stood hard by and glanced around him, and cast his bright javelin; and the Trojans shrank before the casting of the hero. He sped not the dart in vain, but smote Demokoon, Priam's bastard son that had come to him from tending his fleet mares in Abydos. Him Odysseus, being wroth for his comrade's sake, smote with his javelin on one temple; and through both temples passed the point of bronze, and darkness clouded his eyes, and he fell with a crash and his armour clanged upon him. Then the forefighters and glorious Hector yielded, and the Argives shouted aloud, and drew the bodies unto them, and pressed yet further onward. But Apollo looked down from Pergamos, and had indignation, and with a shout called to the Trojans: "Arise, ye Trojans, tamers of horses; yield not to the Argives in fight; not of stone nor iron is their flesh, that it should resist the piercing bronze when they are smitten. Moreover Achilles, son of Thetis of the fair tresses, fighteth not, but amid the ships broodeth on his bitter anger."

So spake the dread god from the city; and the Achaians likewise were urged on of Zeus' daughter the Triton-born, most glorious, as she passed through the throng wheresoever she beheld them slackening.

Next was Diores son of Amrynkeus caught in the snare of fate; for he was smitten by a jagged stone on the right leg hard by the ankle, and the caster thereof was captain of the men of Thrace, Peirros son of Imbrasos that had come from Ainos. The pitiless stone crushed utterly the two sinews and the bones; back fell he in the dust, and stretched out both his hands to his dear comrades, gasping out his soul. Then he that smote him, even Peiroos, sprang at him and pierced him with a spear beside the navel; so all his bowels gushed forth upon the ground, and darkness clouded his eyes. But even as Peiroos departed from him Thoas of Aitolia smote with a spear his chest above the pap, and the point fixed in his lung. Then Thoas came close, and plucked out from his breast the ponderous spear, and drew his sharp sword, wherewith he smote his belly in the midst, and took his life. Yet he stripped not off his armour; for his comrades, the men of Thrace that wear the top-knot, stood around, their long spears in their hands, and albeit he was great and valiant and proud they drave him off from them and he gave ground reeling. So were the two captains stretched in the dust side by side, he of the Thracians and he of the mail-clad Epeians; and around them were many others likewise slain.

Now would none any more enter in and make light of the battle, could it be that a man yet unwounded by dart or thrust of keen bronze might roam in the midst, being led of Pallas Athene by the hand, and by her guarded from the flying shafts. For many Trojans that day and many Achaians were laid side by side upon their faces in the dust.

BOOK V

How Diomedes by his great valour made havoc of the Trojans, and wounded even Aphrodite and Ares by the help of Athene.

But now to Tydeus' son Diomedes Athene gave might and courage, for him to be pre-eminent amid all the Argives and win glorious renown. She kindled flame unwearied from his helmet and shield, like to the star of summer that above all others glittereth bright after he hath bathed in the ocean stream. In such wise kindled she flame from his head and shoulders and sent him into the midst, where men thronged the thickest.

Now there was amid the Trojans one Dares, rich and noble, priest of Hephaistos; and he had two sons, Phegeus and Idaios, well skilled in all the art of battle. These separated themselves and assailed him face to face, they setting on him from their car and he on foot upon the ground. And when they were now come near in onset on each other, first Phegeus hurled his far-shadowing spear; and over Tydeides' left shoulder the spear point passed, and smote not his body. Then next Tydeides made a spear-cast, and the javelin sped not from his hand in vain, but smote his breast between the nipples, and thrust him from the chariot. So Idaios sprang away, leaving his beautiful car, and dared not to bestride his slain brother; else had neither he himself escaped black fate: but Hephaistos guarded him and saved him in a veil of darkness, that he might not have his aged priest all broken with sorrow. And the son of great-hearted Tydeus drave away the horses and gave them to his men to take to the hollow ships. But when the great-hearted Trojans beheld the sons of Dares, how one was fled, and one was slain beside his chariot, the spirit of all was stirred. But bright-eyed Athene took impetuous Ares by the hand and spake to him and said: "Ares, Ares, blood-stained bane of mortals, thou stormer of walls, can we not now leave the Trojans and Achaians to fight, on whichsoever it be that father Zeus bestoweth glory? But let us twain give place, and escape the wrath of Zeus."

So saying she led impetuous Ares from thc battle. Then she made him sit down beside loud Skamandros, and the Danaans pushed the Trojans back.

So they laboured in the violent mellay; but of Tydeides man could not tell with whom he were joined, whether he consorted with Trojans or with Achaians. For he stormed across the plain like a winter torrent at the full, that in swift course scattereth the causeys [Causeways.]; neither can the long lines of causeys hold it in, nor the fences of fruitful orchards stay its sudden coming when the rain of heaven driveth it; and before it perish in multitudes the fair works of the sons of men. Thus before Tydeides the serried battalions of the Trojans were overthrown, and they abode him not for all they were so many.

But when Lykaon's glorious son marked him storming across the plain, overthrowing battalions before him, anon he bent his crooked bow against Tydeides, and smote him as he sped onwards, hitting hard by his right shoulder the plate of his corslet; the bitter arrow flew through and held straight upon its way, and the corslet was dabbled with blood. Over him then loudly shouted Lykaon's glorious son: "Bestir you, great-hearted Trojans, urgers of horses; the best man of the Achaians is wounded, and I deem that he shall not for long endure the violent dart."

So spake he boasting; yet was the other not vanquished of the swift dart, only he gave place and stood before his horses and his chariot and spake to Sthenelos son of Kapaneus: "Haste thee, dear son of Kapaneus; descend from thy chariot, to draw me from my shoulder the bitter arrow."

So said he, and Sthenelos leapt from his chariot to earth and stood beside him and drew the swift shaft right through, out of his shoulder; and the blood darted up through the pliant tunic. Then Diomedes of the loud war-cry prayed thereat: "Hear me, daughter of aegis-bearing Zeus, unwearied maiden! If ever in kindly mood thou stoodest by my father in the heat of battle, even so now be thou likewise kind to me, Athene. Grant me to slay this man, and bring within my spear-cast him that took advantage to shoot me, and boasteth over me, deeming that not for long shall I see the bright light of the sun."

So spake he in prayer, and Pallas Athene heard him, and made his limbs nimble, his feet and his hands withal, and came near and spake winged words: "Be of good courage now, Diomedes, to fight the Trojans; for in thy breast I have set thy father's courage undaunted, even as it was in knightly Tydeus, wielder of the buckler. Moreover I have taken from thine eyes the mist that erst was on them, that thou mayest well discern both god and man. Therefore if any god come hither to make trial of thee, fight not thou face to face with any of the immortal gods; save only if Aphrodite daughter of Zeus enter into the battle, her smite thou with the keen bronze."

So saying bright-eyed Athene went her way and Tydeides returned and entered the forefront of the battle; even though erst his soul was eager to do battle with the Trojans, yet now did threefold courage come upon him, as upon a lion whom some shepherd in the field guarding his fleecy sheep hath wounded, being sprung into the fold, yet hath not vanquished him; he hath roused his might, and then cannot beat him back, but lurketh amid the steading, and his forsaken flock is affrighted; so the sheep are cast in heaps, one upon the other, and the lion in his fury leapeth out of the high fold; even so in fury mingled mighty Diomedes with the Trojans.

Him Aineias beheld making havoc of the ranks of warriors, and went his way along the battle and amid the hurtling of spears, seeking godlike Pandaros, if haply he might find him. Lykaon's son he found, the noble and stalwart, and stood before his face, and spake a word unto him. "Pandaros, where now are thy bow and thy winged arrows, and the fame wherein no man of this land rivalleth thee, nor any in Lykia boasteth to be thy better? Go to now, lift thy hands in prayer to Zeus and shoot thy dart at this fellow, whoe'er he be that lordeth it here and hath already wrought the Trojans much mischief, seeing he hath unstrung the knees of many a brave man; if indeed it be not some god wroth with the Trojans, in anger by reason of sacrifices; the wrath of god is a sore thing to fall on men."

And Lykaon's glorious son made answer to him: "Aineias, counsellor of the mail-clad Trojans, in everything liken I him to the wise son of Tydeus; I discern him by his shield and crested helmet, and by the aspect of his horses; yet know I not surely if it be not a god. But if it be the man I deem, even the wise son of Tydeus, then not without help of a god is he thus furious, but some immortal standeth beside him with a cloud wrapped about his shoulders and turned aside from him my swift dart even as it lighted. For already have I shot my dart at him and smote his right shoulder right through the breastplate of his corslet, yea and I thought to hurl him headlong to Aidoneus, yet I vanquished him not; surely it is some wrathful god. Already have I aimed at two princes, Tydeus' and Atreus' sons, and both I smote and surely drew forth blood, yet only roused them the more. Therefore in an evil hour I took from the peg my curved bow on that day when I led my Trojans to lovely Ilios, to do noble Hector pleasure. But if I return and mine eyes behold my native land and wife and great palace lofty-roofed, then may an alien forthwith cut my head from me if I break not this bow with mine hands and cast it upon the blazing fire; worthless is its service to me as air."

Then Aineias captain of the Trojans answered him: "Nay, talk not thus; naught shall be mended before that we with horses and chariot have gone to face this man, and made trial of him in arms. Come then, mount upon my car that thou mayest see of what sort are the steeds of Tros, well skilled for following or for fleeing hither or thither very fleetly across the plain; they will e'en bring us to the city safe and sound, even though Zeus hereafter give victory to Diomedes son of Tydeus. Come therefore, take thou the lash and shining reins, and I will stand upon the car to fight; or else withstand thou him, and to the horses will I look."

To him made answer Lykaon's glorious son: "Aineias, take thou thyself the reins and thine own horses; better will they draw the curved car for their wonted charioteer, if perchance it hap that we must flee from Tydeus' son; lest they go wild for fear and will not take us from the fight, for lack of thy voice, and so the son of great-hearted Tydeus attack us and slay us both and drive away the whole-hooved horses. So drive thou thyself thy chariot and thy horses, and I will await his onset with my keen spear." So saying mounted they upon the well dight chariot, and eagerly drave the fleet horses against Tydeides, And Sthenelos, the glorious son of Kapaneus, saw them, and anon spake to Tydeides winged words: "Diomedes son of Tydeus, dear to mine heart, I behold two stalwart warriors eager to fight against thee, endued with might beyond measure. The one is well skilled in the bow, even Pandaros, and he moreover boasteth him to be Lykaon's son; and Aineias boasteth himself to be born son of great-hearted Anchises, and his mother is Aphrodite. Come now, let us give place upon the chariot, neither rage thou thus, I pray thee, in the forefront of battle, lest perchance thou lose thy life."

Then stalwart Diomedes looked sternly at him and said: "Speak to me no word of flight, for I ween that thou shalt not at all persuade me; not in my blood is it to fight a skulking fight or cower down; my force is steadfast still. I have no mind to mount the chariot, nay, even as I am will I go to face them; Pallas Athene biddeth me not be afraid. And as for these, their fleet horses shall not take both back from us again, even if one or other escape. And this moreover tell I thee, and lay thou it to heart: if Athene rich in counsel grant me this glory, to slay them both, then refrain thou here these my fleet horses, and bind the reins tight to the chariot rim; and be mindful to leap upon Aineias' horses, and drive them forth from the Trojans amid the well-greaved Achaians. For they are of that breed whereof farseeing Zeus gave to Tros recompense for Ganymede his child, because they were the best of all horses beneath the daylight and the sun."

In such wise talked they one to the other, and anon those other twain came near, driving their fleet horses. First to him spake Lykaon's glorious son: "O thou strong-souled and cunning, son of proud Tydeus, verily my swift dart vanquished thee not, the bitter arrow; so now will I make trial with my spear if I can hit thee."

He spake and poised and hurled his far-shadowing spear, and smote upon Tydeides' shield; right through it sped the point of bronze and reached the breastplate. So over him shouted loudly Lykaon's glorious son: "Thou art smitten on the belly right through, and I ween thou shalt not long hold up thine head; so thou givest me great renown."

But mighty Diomedes unaffrighted answered him: "Thou hast missed, and not hit; but ye twain I deem shall not cease till one or other shall have fallen and glutted with blood Ares the stubborn god of war."

So spake he and hurled; and Athene guided the dart upon his nose beside the eye, and it pierced through his white teeth. So the hard bronze cut through his tongue at the root and the point issued forth by the base of the chin. He fell from his chariot, and his splendid armour gleaming clanged upon him, and the fleet-footed horses swerved aside; so there his soul and strength were unstrung.

Then Aineias leapt down with shield and long spear, fearing lest perchance the Achaians might take from him the corpse; and strode over him like a lion confident in his strength, and held before him his spear and the circle of his shield, eager to slay whoe'er should come to face him, crying his terrible cry. Then Tydeides grasped in his hand a stone—a mighty deed—such as two men, as men now are, would not avail to lift; yet he with ease wielded it all alone. Therewith he smote Aineias on the hip where the thigh turneth in the hip joint, and this men call the "cup-bone." So he crushed his cup-bone, and brake both sinews withal, and the jagged stone tore apart the skin. Then the hero stayed fallen upon his knees and with stout hand leant upon the earth; and the darkness of night veiled his eyes. And now might Aineias king of men have perished, but that Aphrodite daughter of Zeus was swift to mark. About her dear son wound she her white arms, and spread before his face a fold of her radiant vesture, to be a covering from the darts, lest any of the fleet-horsed Danaans might hurl the spear into his breast and take away his life.

So was she bearing her dear son away from battle; but the son of Kapaneus forgat not the behest that Diomedes of the loud war-cry had laid upon him; he refrained his own whole-hooved horses away from the tumult, binding the reins tight to the chariot-rim, and leapt on the sleek-coated horses of Aineias, and drave them from the Trojans to the well-greaved Achaians, and gave them to Deipylos his dear comrade whom he esteemed above all that were his age-fellows, because he was like-minded with himself; and bade him drive them to the hollow ships. Then did the hero mount his own chariot and take the shining reins and forthwith drive his strong-hooved horses in quest of Tydeides, eagerly. Now Tydeides had made onslaught with pitiless weapon on Kypris [Aphrodite], knowing how she was a coward goddess and none of those that have mastery in battle of the warriors. Now when he had pursued her through the dense throng and come on her, then great-hearted Tydeus' son thrust with his keen spear, and leapt on her and wounded the skin of her weak hand; straight through the ambrosial raiment that the Graces themselves had woven her pierced the dart into the flesh, above the springing of the palm. Then flowed the goddess's immortal blood, such ichor as floweth in the blessed gods; for they eat no bread neither drink they gleaming wine, wherefore they are bloodless and are named immortals. And she with a great cry let fall her son: him Phoebus Apollo took into his arms and saved him in a dusky cloud, lest any of the fleet-horsed Danaans might hurl the spear into his breast and take away his life. But over her Diomedes of the loud war-cry shouted afar: "Refrain thee, thou daughter of Zeus, from war and fighting. Is it not enough that thou beguilest feeble women? But if in battle thou wilt mingle, verily I deem that thou shalt shudder at the name of battle, if thou hear it even afar off"

So spake he, and she departed in amaze and was sore troubled: and wind-footed Iris took her and led her from the throng tormented with her pain, and her fair skin was stained. There found she impetuous Ares sitting, on the battle's left; and his spear rested upon a cloud, and his fleet steeds. Then she fell on her knees and with instant prayer besought of her dear brother his golden-frontleted steeds: "Dear brother, save me and give me thy steeds, that I may win to Olympus, where is the habitation of the immortals. Sorely am I afflicted with a wound wherewith a mortal smote me, even Tydeides, who now would fight even with father Zeus."

So spake she, and Ares gave her his golden-frontleted steeds, and she mounted on the chariot sore at heart. By her side mounted Iris, and in her hands grasped the reins and lashed the horses to start them; and they flew onward nothing loth. Thus soon they came to the habitation of the gods, even steep Olympus. There wind-footed fleet Iris loosed the horses from the chariot and stabled them, and set ambrosial forage before them; but fair Aphrodite fell upon Dione's knees that was her mother. She took her daughter in her arms and stroked her with her hand, and spake and called upon her name: "Who now of the sons of heaven, dear child, hath entreated thee thus wantonly, as though thou wert a wrong-doer in the face of all?"

Then laughter-loving Aphrodite made answer to her: "Tydeus' son wounded me, high-hearted Diomedes, because I was saving from the battle my dear son Aineias, who to me is dearest far of all men. For no more is the fierce battle-cry for Trojans and Achaians, but the Danaans now are fighting even the immortals."

Then the fair goddess Dione answered her: "Be of good heart, my child, and endure for all thy pain; for many of us that inhabit the mansions of Olympus have suffered through men, in bringing grievous woes one upon another."

So saying with both hands she wiped the ichor from the arm; her arm was comforted, and the grievous pangs assuaged. But Athene and Hera beheld, and with bitter words provoked Zeus the son, of Kronos. Of them was the bright-eyed goddess Athene first to speak: "Father Zeus, wilt thou indeed be wroth with me whate'er I say? Verily I ween that Kypris was urging some woman of Achaia to join her unto the Trojans whom she so marvellously loveth; and stroking such an one of the fair-robed women of Achaia, she tore upon the golden brooch her delicate hand."

So spake she, and the father of gods and men smiled, and called unto him golden Aphrodite and said: "Not unto thee, my child, are given the works of war; but follow thou after the loving tasks of wedlock, and to all these things shall fleet Ares and Athene look."

Now while they thus spake in converse one with the other, Diomedes of the loud war-cry leapt upon Aineias, knowing full well that Apollo himself had spread his arms over him; yet reverenced he not even the great god, but still was eager to slay Aineias and strip from him his glorious armour. So thrice he leapt on him, fain to slay him, and thrice Apollo beat back his glittering shield. And when the fourth time he sprang at him like a god, then Apollo the Far-darter spake to him with terrible shout: "Think, Tydeides, and shrink, nor desire to match thy spirit with gods; seeing there is no comparison of the race of immortal gods and of men that walk upon the earth."

So said he, and Tydeides shrank a short space backwards, to avoid the wrath of Apollo the Far-darter. Then Apollo set Aineias away from the throng in holy Pergamos where his temple stood. There Leto and Archer Artemis healed him in the mighty sanctuary, and gave him glory; but Apollo of the silver bow made a wraith like unto Aineias' self, and in such armour as his; and over the wraith Trojans and goodly Achaians each hewed the others' bucklers on their breasts, their round shields and fluttering targes.

Then to impetuous Ares said Phoebus Apollo: "Ares, Ares, blood-stained bane of mortals, thou stormer of walls, wilt thou not follow after this man and withdraw him from the battle, this Tydeides, who now would fight even with father Zeus? First in close fight he wounded Kypris in her hand hard by the wrist, and then sprang he upon myself like unto a god."

So saying he sate himself upon the height of Pergamos, and baleful Ares entered among the Trojan ranks and aroused them in the likeness of fleet Akamas, captain of the Thracians. On the heaven-nurtured sons of Priam he called saying: "O ye sons of Priam, the heaven-nurtured king, how long will ye yet suffer your host to be slain of the Achaians? Shall it be even until they fight about our well-builded gates? Low lieth the warrior whom we esteemed like unto goodly Hector, even Aineias son of Anchises great of heart. Go to now, let us save from the tumult our valiant comrade."

So saying he aroused the spirit and soul of every man. Thereat Sarpedon sorely chode noble Hector: "Hector, where now is the spirit gone that erst thou hadst? Thou saidst forsooth that without armies or allies thou wouldest hold the city, alone with thy sisters' husbands and thy brothers; but now can I not see any of these neither perceive them, but they are cowering like hounds about a lion; and we are fighting that are but allies among you."

So spake Sarpedon, and his word stung Hector to the heart, Forthwith he leapt from his chariot in his armour to the earth, and brandishing two keen spears went everywhere through the host, urging them to fight, and roused the dread battle-cry. So they were rallied and stood to face the Achaians: and the Argives withstood them in close array and fled not. Even as a wind carrieth the chaff about the sacred threshing-floors when men are winnowing, and the chaff-heaps grow white—so now grew the Achaians white with falling dust which in their midst the horses' hooves beat up into the brazen heaven, as fight was joined again, and the charioteers wheeled round. Thus bare they forward the fury of their hands: and impetuous Ares drew round them a veil of night to aid the Trojans in the battle, ranging everywhere. And Apollo himself sent forth Aineias from his rich sanctuary and put courage in the heart of him, shepherd of the hosts. So Aineias took his place amid his comrades, and they were glad to see him come among them alive and sound and full of valiant spirit. Yet they questioned him not at all, for all the toil forbade them that the god of the silver bow was stirring and Ares bane of men and Strife raging insatiably.

And on the other side the two Aiantes and Odysseus and Diomedes stirred the Danaans to fight; yet these of themselves feared neither the Trojans' violence nor assaults, but stood like mists that Kronos' son setteth in windless air on the mountain tops, at peace, while the might of the north wind sleepeth and of all the violent winds that blow with keen breath and scatter apart the shadowing clouds. Even so the Danaans withstood the Trojans steadfastly and fled not. And Atreides ranged through the throng exhorting instantly: "My friends, quit you like men and take heart of courage, and shun dishonour in one another's eyes amid the stress of battle. Of men that shun dishonour more are saved than slain, but for them that flee is neither glory found nor any safety."

So saying he darted swiftly with his javelin and smote a foremost warrior, even great-hearted Aineias' comrade Deikoon son of Pergasos, whom the Trojans held in like honour with Priam's sons, because he was swift to do battle amid the foremost. Him lord Agamemnon smote with his dart upon the shield, and it stayed not the spear, but the point passed through, so that he drave it through the belt into his nethermost belly: and he fell with a crash and his armour clanged upon him.

Then did Aineias slay two champions of the Danaans, even the sons of Diokles, Krethon and Orsilochos. Like them, two lions on the mountain tops are nurtured by their dam in the deep forest thickets; and these harry the kine and goodly sheep and make havoc of the farmsteads of men, till in their turn they too are slain at men's hands with the keen bronze; in such wise were these twain vanquished at Aineias' hands and fell like tall pine-trees.

But Menelaos dear to Ares had pity of them in their fall, and strode through the forefront, harnessed in flashing bronze, brandishing his spear; and Ares stirred his courage, with intent that he might fall beneath Aineias' hand. But Antilochos, great-hearted Nestor's son, beheld him, and strode through the forefront; because he feared exceedingly for the shepherd of the host, lest aught befall him and disappoint them utterly of their labour. So those two were now holding forth their hands and sharp spears each against the other, eager to do battle; when Antilochos came and stood hard by the shepherd of the host. But Aineias faced them not, keen warrior though he was, when he beheld two men abiding side by side; so these haled away the corpses to the Achaians' host, and laid the hapless twain in their comrades' arms, and themselves turned back and fought on amid the foremost.

But Hector marked them across the ranks, and sprang on them with a shout, and the battalions of the Trojans followed him in their might: and Ares led them on and dread Enyo, she bringing ruthless turmoil of war, the while Ares wielded in his hands his monstrous spear, and ranged now before Hector's face, and now behind.

Then Diomedes of the loud war-cry shuddered to behold him; and even as a shiftless man crossing a great plain cometh on a swift-streaming river flowing on to the sea, and seeing it boil with foam springeth backwards, even so now Tydeides shrank back and spake to the host: "Friends, how marvel we that noble Hector is a spearman and bold man of war! Yet ever is there beside him some god that wardeth off destruction; even as now

Ares is there by him in likeness of a mortal man. But with faces towards the Trojans still give ground backwards, neither be desirous to fight amain with gods."

Now the Argives before the face of Ares and mail-clad Hector neither turned them round about toward their black ships, nor charged forward in battle, but still fell backward, when they heard of Ares amid the Trojans. But when the white-armed goddess Hera marked them making havoc of the Argives in the press of battle, anon she spake winged words to Athene: "Out on it, thou daughter of aegis-bearing Zeus, unwearied maiden! Was it for naught we pledged our word to Menelaos, that he should not depart till he had laid waste well-walled Ilios,—if thus we let baleful Ares rage? Go to now, let us twain also take thought of impetuous valour."

So said she, and the bright-eyed goddess Athene disregarded not. So Hera the goddess queen, daughter of Kronos, went her way to harness the gold-frontleted steeds. And Athene, daughter of aegis-bearing Zeus, cast down at her father's threshold her woven vesture many-coloured, that herself had wrought and her hands had fashioned, and put on her the tunic of Zeus the cloud-gatherer, and arrayed her in her armour for dolorous battle. About her shoulders cast she the tasselled aegis terrible, whereon is Panic as a crown all round about, and Strife is therein and Valour and horrible Onslaught withal, and therein is the dreadful monster's Gorgon head, dreadful and grim, portent of aegis-bearing Zeus. Upon her head set she the two-crested golden helm with fourfold plate, bedecked with men-at-arms of a hundred cities. Upon the flaming chariot set she her foot, and grasped her heavy spear, great and stout, wherewith she vanquisheth the ranks of men, even of heroes with whom she of the awful sire is wroth. Then Hera swiftly smote the horses with the lash; self-moving groaned upon their hinges the gates of heaven whereof the Hours are warders, to whom is committed great heaven and Olympus, whether to throw open the thick cloud or set it to. There through the gates guided they their horses patient of the lash. And they found the son of Kronos sitting apart from all the gods on the topmost peak of many-ridged Olympus. Then the white-armed goddess Hera stayed her horses and questioned the most high Zeus, the son of Kronos, and said: "Father Zeus, hast thou no indignation with Ares for these violent deeds? How great and goodly a company of Achaians hath he destroyed recklessly and in unruly wise, unto my sorrow. But here in peace Kypris and Apollo of the silver bow take their pleasure, having set on this mad one that knoweth not any law. Father Zeus, wilt thou at all be wroth with me if I smite Ares and chase him from the battle in sorry plight?"

And Zeus the cloud-gatherer answered and said to her: "Go to now, set upon him Athene driver of the spoil, who most is wont to bring sore pain upon him."

So spake he, and the white-armed goddess Hera disregarded not, and lashed her horses; they nothing loth flew on between earth and starry heaven. As far as a man seeth with his eyes into the haze of distance as he sitteth on a place of outlook and gazeth over the wine-dark sea, so far leap the loudly neighing horses of the gods. Now when they came to Troy and the two flowing rivers, even to where Simoeis and Skamandros join their streams, there the white-armed goddess Hera stayed her horses and loosed them from the car and poured thick mist round about them, and Simoeis made ambrosia spring up for them to graze. So the goddesses went their way with step like unto turtle-doves, being fain to bring succour to the men of Argos. And when they were now come where the most and most valiant stood, thronging about mighty Diomedes tamer of horses, in the semblance of ravening lions or wild boars whose strength is nowise feeble, then stood the white-armed goddess Hera and shouted in the likeness of great-hearted Stentor with voice of bronze, whose cry was loud as the cry of fifty other men: "Fie upon you, Argives, base things of shame, so brave in semblance! While yet noble Achilles entered continually into battle, then issued not the Trojans even from the Dardanian gate; for they had dread of his terrible spear. But now fight they far from the city at the hollow ships."

So saying she aroused the spirit and soul of every man. And to Tydeides' side sprang the bright-eyed goddess Athene. That lord she found beside his horses and chariot, cooling the wound that Pandaros with his dart had pierced, for his sweat vexed it by reason of the broad baldrick of his round shield; therewith was he vexed and his arm grew weary, so he was lifting up the baldrick and wiping away the dusky blood. Then the goddess laid her hand on his horses' yoke, and said: "Of a truth Tydeus begat a son little after his own likeness. Tydeus was short of stature, but a man of war."

And stalwart Diomedes made answer to her and said: "I know thee, goddess daughter of aegis-bearing Zeus: therefore with my whole heart will I tell thee my thought and hide it not. Neither hath disheartening terror taken hold upon me, nor any faintness, but I am still mindful of thy behest that thou didst lay upon me. Thou forbadest me to fight face to face with all the blessed gods, save only if Zeus' daughter Aphrodite should enter into battle, then to wound her with the keen bronze. Therefore do I now give ground myself and have bidden all the Argives likewise to gather here together; for I discern Ares lording it in the fray."

Then the bright-eyed goddess Athene answered him: "Diomedes son of Tydeus, thou joy of mine heart, fear thou, for that, neither Ares nor any other of the immortals; so great a helper am I to thee. Go to now, at Ares first guide thou thy whole-hooved horses, and smite him hand to hand, nor have any awe of impetuous Ares, raving here, a curse incarnate, the renegade that of late in converse with me and Hera pledged him to fight against the Trojans and give succour to the Argives, but now consorteth with the Trojans and hath forgotten these."

So speaking, with her hand she drew back Sthenelos and thrust him from the chariot to earth, and instantly leapt he down; so the goddess mounted the car by noble Diomedes' side right eagerly. The oaken axle creaked loud with its burden, bearing the dread goddess and the man of might. Then Athene grasped the whip and reins; forthwith against Ares first guided she the whole-hooved horses. Now he was stripping huge Periphas, most valiant far of the Aitolians, Ochesios' glorious son. Him was blood-stained Ares stripping; and Athene donned the helm of Hades, that terrible Ares might not behold her. Now when Ares scourge of mortals beheld noble Diomedes, he left huge Periphas lying there, where at the first he had slain him and taken away his life, and made straight at Diomedes tamer of horses. Now when they were come nigh in onset on one another, first Ares thrust over the yoke and horse's reins with spear of bronze, eager to take away his life. But the bright-eyed goddess Athene with her hand seized the spear and thrust it up over the car, to spend itself in vain. Next Diomedes of the loud war-cry attacked with spear of bronze; and Athene drave it home against Ares' nethermost belly, where his taslets were girt about him. There smote he him and wounded him, rending through his fair skin, and plucked forth the spear again. Then brazen Ares bellowed loud as nine thousand warriors or ten thousand cry in battle as they join in strife and fray. Thereat trembling gat hold of Achaians and Trojans for fear, so mightily bellowed Ares insatiate of battle.

Even as gloomy mist appeareth from the clouds when after beat a stormy wind ariseth, even so to Tydeus' son Diomedes brazen Ares appeared amid clouds, faring to wide heaven. Swiftly came he to the gods' dwelling, steep Olympus, and sat beside Zeus son of Kronos with grief at heart, and shewed the immortal blood flowing from the wound, and piteously spake to him winged words: "Father Zeus, hast thou no indignation to behold these violent deeds? For ever cruelly suffer we gods by one another's devices, in shewing men grace. With thee are we all at variance, because thou didst beget that reckless maiden and baleful, whose thought is ever of iniquitous deeds. For all the other gods that are in Olympus hearken to thee, and we are subject every one; only her thou chastenest not, neither in deed nor word, but settest her on, because this pestilent one is thine own offspring. Now hath she urged on Tydeus' son, even overweening Diomedes, to rage furiously against the immortal gods. Kypris first he wounded in close fight, in the wrist of her hand, and then assailed he me, even me, with the might of a god. Howbeit my swift feet bare me away; else had I long endured anguish there amid the grisly heaps of dead, or else had lived strengthless from the smitings of the spear."

Then Zeus the cloud-gatherer looked sternly at him and said: "Nay, thou renegade, sit not by me and whine. Most hateful to me art thou of all gods that dwell in Olympus: thou ever lovest strife and wars and battles. Truly thy mother's spirit is intolerable, unyielding, even Hera's; her can I scarce rule with words. Therefore I deem that by her prompting thou art in this plight. Yet will I no longer endure to see thee in anguish; mine offspring art thou, and to me thy mother bare thee."

So spake he and bade Paieon heal him. And Paieon laid assuaging drugs upon the wound. Even as fig juice maketh haste to thicken white milk, that is liquid but curdleth speedily as a man stirreth, even so swiftly healed he impetuous Ares. And Hebe bathed him, and clothed him in gracious raiment, and he sate him down by Zeus son of Kronos, glorying in his might.

Then fared the twain back to the mansion of great Zeus, even Hera and Athene, having stayed Ares scourge of mortals from his man-slaying.

BOOK VI

How Diomedes and Glaukos, being about to fight, were known to each other, and parted in friendliness. And how Hector returning to the city bade farewell to Andromache his wife.

So was the dread fray of Trojans and Achaians left to itself, and the battle swayed oft this way and that across the plain, as they aimed against each other their bronze-shod javelins, between Simoeis and the streams of Xanthos.

Now had the Trojans been chased again by the Achaians, dear to Ares, up into Ilios, in their weakness overcome, but that Priam's son Helenos, far best of augurs, stood by Aineias' side and Hector's, and spake to them: "Aineias and Hector, seeing that on you lieth the task of war in chief of Trojans and Lykians, because for every issue ye are foremost both for fight and counsel, stand ye your ground, and range the host everywhither to rally them before the gates, ere yet they fall fleeing in their women's arms, and be made a rejoicing to the foe. Then when ye have aroused all our battalions we will abide here and fight the Danaans, though in sore weariness; for necessity presseth us hard: but thou, Hector, go into the city, and speak there to thy mother and mine; let her gather the aged wives to bright-eyed Athene's temple in the upper city, and with her key open the doors of the holy house; and let her lay the robe, that seemeth to her the most gracious and greatest in her hall and far dearest unto herself, upon the knees of beauteous-haired Athene; and vow to her to sacrifice in her temple twelve sleek kine, that have not felt the goad, if she will have mercy on the city and the Trojans' wives and little children. So may she perchance hold back Tydeus' son from holy Ilios, the furious spearman, the mighty deviser of rout, whom in good sooth I deem to have proved himself mightiest of the Achaians. Never in this wise feared we Achilles, prince of men, who they say is born of a goddess; nay, but he that we see is beyond measure furious; none can match him for might."

So spake he, and Hector disregarded not his brother's word, but leapt forthwith from his chariot in his armour to earth, and brandishing two sharp spears passed everywhere through the host, rousing them to battle, and stirred the dread war-cry. So they were rallied and stood to face the Achaians, and the Argives gave ground and ceased from slaughter, and deemed that some immortal had descended from starry heaven to bring the Trojans succour, in such wise rallied they. Then Hector called to the Trojans with far-reaching shout: "O high-souled Trojans and ye far-famed allies, quit you like men, my friends, and take thought of impetuous courage, while I depart to Ilios and bid the elders of the council and our wives pray to the gods and vow them hecatombs."

So saying Hector of the glancing helm departed, and the black hide beat on either side against his ankles and his neck, even the rim that ran uttermost about his bossed shield.

Now Glaukos son of Hippolochos and Tydeus' son met in the mid-space of the foes, eager to do battle. Thus when the twain were come nigh in onset on each other, to him first spake Diomedes of the loud war-cry: "Who art thou, noble sir, of mortal men? For never have I beheld thee in glorious battle ere this, yet now hast thou far outstripped all men in thy hardihood, seeing thou abidest my far-shadowing spear. Luckless are the fathers whose children face my might. But if thou art some immortal come down from heaven, then will not I fight with heavenly gods. But if thou art of men that eat the fruit of the field, come nigh, that anon thou mayest enter the toils of destruction."

Then Hippolochos' glorious son made answer to him: "Great-hearted Tydeides, why enquirest thou of my generation? Even as are the generations of leaves such are those likewise of men; the leaves that be the wind scattereth on the earth, and the forest buddeth and putteth forth more again, when the season of spring is at hand; so of the generations of men one putteth forth and another ceaseth. Yet if thou wilt, have thine answer, that thou mayest well know our lineage, whereof many men have knowledge. Hippolochos, son of Bellerophon, begat me, and of him do I declare me to be sprung; he sent me to Troy and bade me very instantly to be ever the best and to excel all other men, nor put to shame the lineage of my fathers that were of noblest blood in Ephyre and in wide Lykia. This is the lineage and blood whereof I avow myself to be."

So said he, and Diomedes of the loud war-cry was glad. He planted his spear in the bounteous earth and with soft words spake to the shepherd of the host: "Surely then thou art to me a guest-friend of old times through my father: for goodly Oineus of yore entertained noble Bellerophon in his halls and kept him twenty days. Moreover they gave each the other goodly gifts of friendship; Oineus gave a belt bright with purple, and Bellerophon a gold two-handled cup. Therefore now am I to thee a dear guest-friend in midmost Argos, and thou in Lykia, whene'er I fare to your land. So let us shun each other's spears, even amid the throng; Trojans are there in multitudes and famous allies for me to slay, whoe'er it be that God vouchsafeth me and my feet overtake; and for thee are there Achaians in multitude, to slay whome'er thou canst. But let us make exchange of arms between us, that these also may know how we avow ourselves to be guest-friends by lineage."

So spake the twain, and leaping from their cars clasped each the other by his hand, and pledged their faith. But now Zeus son of Kronos took from Glaukos his wits, in that he made exchange with Diomedes Tydeus' son of golden armour for bronze, the price of five score oxen for the price of nine.

Now when Hector came to the Skaian gates and to the oak tree, there came running round about him the Trojans' wives and daughters, enquiring of sons and brethren and friends and husbands. But he bade them thereat all in turn pray to the gods; but sorrow hung over many.

But when he came to Priam's beautiful palace, adorned with polished colonnades—and in it were fifty chambers of polished stone, builded hard by one another, wherein Priam's sons slept beside their wedded wives; and for his daughters over against them on the other side within the courtyard were twelve roofed chambers of polished stone builded hard by one another, wherein slept Priam's sons-in-law beside their chaste wives—then came there to meet him his bountiful mother, leading with her Laodike, fairest of her daughters to look on; and she clasped her hand in his, and spake, and called upon his name: "My son, why hast thou left violent battle to come hither. Surely the sons of the Achaians—name of evil!—press thee hard in fight about thy city, and so thy spirit hath brought thee hither, to come and stretch forth thy hands to Zeus from the citadel. But tarry till I bring thee honey-sweet wine, that thou mayest pour libation to Zeus and all the immortals first, and then shalt thou thyself also be refreshed if thou wilt drink. When a man is awearied wine greatly maketh his strength to wax, even as thou art awearied in fighting for thy fellows."

Then great Hector of the glancing helm answered her: "Bring me no honey-hearted wine, my lady mother, lest thou cripple me of my courage and I be forgetful of my might. But go thou to the temple of Athene, driver of the spoil, with offerings, and gather the aged wives together; and the robe that seemeth to thee the most gracious and greatest in thy palace, and dearest unto thyself, that lay thou upon the knees of beauteous-haired Athene, and vow to her to sacrifice in her temple twelve sleek kine, that have not felt the goad, if she will have mercy on the city and the Trojans' wives and little children. So go thou to the temple of Athene, driver of the spoil; and I will go after Paris, to summon him, if perchance he will hearken to my voice. Would that the earth forthwith might swallow him up! The Olympian fostered him to be a sore bane to the Trojans and to great-hearted Priam, and to Priam's sons. If I but saw him going down to the gates of death, then might I deem that my heart had forgotten its sorrows."

So said he, and she went unto the hall, and called to her handmaidens, and they gathered the aged wives throughout the city. Then she herself went down to her fragrant chamber where were her embroidered robes, the work of Sidonian women, whom godlike Alexandros himself brought from Sidon, when he sailed over the wide sea, that journey wherein he brought home high-born Helen. Of these Hekabe took one to bear for an offering to Athene, the one that was fairest for adornment and greatest, and shone like a star, and lay nethermost of all. Then went she her way and the multitude of aged wives hasted after her. And Hector was come to Alexandros' fair palace, that himself had builded with them that were most excellent carpenters then in deep-soiled Troy-land; these made him his chamber and hall and courtyard hard by to Priam and Hector, in the upper city. There entered in Hector dear to Zeus, and his hand bare his spear, eleven cubits long: before his face glittered the bronze spear-point, and a ring of gold ran round about it. And he found Paris in his chamber busied with his beauteous arms, his shield and breastplate, and handling his curved bow; and Helen of Argos sate among her serving-women and appointed brave handiwork for her handmaidens. Then when Hector saw him he rebuked him with scornful words: "Good sir, thou dost not well to cherish this rancour in thy heart. The folk are perishing about the city and high wall in battle, and for thy sake the battle-cry is kindled and war around this city; yes thyself wouldest thou fall out with another, didst thou see him shrinking from hateful war. Up then, lest the city soon be scorched with burning fire."

And godlike Alexandros answered him: "Hector, since in measure thou chidest me and not beyond measure, therefore will I tell thee; lay thou it to thine heart and hearken to me. Not by reason so much of the Trojans, for wrath and indignation, sate I me in my chamber, but fain would I yield me to my sorrow. Even now my wife hath persuaded me with soft words, and urged me into battle; and I moreover, even I, deem that it will be better so; for victory shifteth from man to man. Go to then, tarry awhile, let me put on my armour of war; or else fare thou forth, and I will follow; and I think to overtake thee."

So said he, but Hector of the glancing helm answered him not a word. But Helen spake to him with gentle words: "My brother, even mine that am a dog, mischievous and abominable, would that on the day when my mother bare me at the first, an evil storm-wind had caught me away to a mountain or a billow of the loud-sounding sea, where the billow might have swept me away before all these things came to pass. Howbeit, seeing the gods devised all these ills in this wise, would that then I had been mated with a better man, that felt dishonour and the multitude of men's reproachings. But as for him, neither hath he now sound heart, nor ever will have; thereof deem I moreover that he will reap the fruit. But now come, enter in and sit thee here upon this bench, my brother, since thy heart chiefly trouble hath encompassed, for the sake of me, that am a dog, and for Alexandros' sin; on whom Zeus bringeth evil doom, that even in days to come we may be a song in the ears of men that shall be hereafter."

Then great Hector of the glancing helm answered her: "Bid me not sit, Helen, of thy love; thou wilt not persuade me. Already my heart is set to succour the men of Troy, that have great desire for me that am not with them. But rouse thou this fellow, yea let himself make speed, to overtake me yet within the city. For I shall go into mine house to behold my housefolk and my dear wife, and infant boy; for I know not if I shall return home to them again, or if the gods will now overthrow me at the hands of the Achaians."

So spake Hector of the glancing helm and departed; and anon he came to his well-stablished house. But he found not white-armed Andromache in the halls; she with her boy and fair-robed handmaiden had taken her stand upon the tower, weeping and wailing. And when Hector found not his noble wife within, he came and stood upon the threshold and spake amid the serving women: "Come tell me now true, my serving women. Whither went white-armed Andromache forth from the hall? Hath she gone out to my sisters or unto my brothers' fair-robed wives, or to Athene's temple, where all the fair-tressed Trojan women propitiate the awful goddess?"

Then a busy housedame spake in answer to him: "Hector, seeing thou straitly chargest us tell thee true, neither hath she gone out to any of thy sisters or thy brothers' fair-robed wives, neither to Athene's temple, where all the fair-tressed Trojan women are propitiating the awful goddess; but she went to the great tower of Ilios, because she heard the Trojans were hard pressed, and great victory was for the Achaians. So hath she come in haste to the wall, like unto one frenzied; and the nurse with her beareth the child."

So spake the housedame, and Hector hastened from his house back by the same way down the well-builded streets. When he had passed through the great city and was come to the Skaian gates, whereby he was minded to issue upon the plain, then came his dear-won wife, running to meet him, even Andromache daughter of great-hearted Eetion. So she met him now, and with her went the handmaid bearing in her bosom the tender boy, the little child, Hector's loved son, like unto a beautiful star. Him Hector called Skamandrios, but all the folk Astyanax [Astyanax = "City King."]; for only Hector guarded Ilios. So now he smiled and gazed at his boy silently, and Andromache stood by his side weeping, and clasped her hand in his, and spake and called upon his name. "Dear my lord, this thy hardihood will undo thee, neither hast thou any pity for thine infant boy, nor for me forlorn that soon shall be thy widow; for soon will the Achaians all set upon thee and slay thee. But it were better for me to go down to the grave if I lose thee; for never more will any comfort be mine, when once thou, even thou, hast met thy fate, but only sorrow. Nay, Hector, thou art to me father and lady mother, yea and brother, even as thou art my goodly husband. Come now, have pity and abide here upon the tower, lest thou make thy child an orphan and thy wife a widow."

Then great Hector of the glancing helm answered her: "Surely I take thought for all these things, my wife; but I have very sore shame of the Trojans and Trojan dames with trailing robes, if like a coward I shrink away from battle. Moreover mine own soul forbiddeth me, seeing I have learnt ever to be valiant and fight in the forefront of the Trojans, winning my father's great glory and mine own. Yea of a surety I know this in heart and soul; the day shall come for holy Ilios to be laid low, and Priam and the folk of Priam of the good ashen spear. Yet doth the anguish of the Trojans hereafter not so much trouble me, neither Hekabe's own, neither king Priam's, neither my brethren's, the many and brave that shall fall in the dust before their foemen, as doth thine anguish in the day when some mail-clad Achaian shall lead thee weeping and rob thee of the light of freedom. So shalt thou abide in Argos and ply the loom at another woman's bidding, and bear water from fount Messeis or Hypereia, being grievously entreated, and sore constraint shall be laid upon thee. And then shall one say that beholdeth thee weep: 'This is the wife of Hector, that was foremost in battle of the horse-taming Trojans when men fought about Ilios.' Thus shall one say hereafter, and fresh grief will be thine for lack of such an husband as thou hadst to ward off the day of thraldom. But me in death may the heaped-up earth be covering, ere I hear thy crying and thy carrying into captivity."

So spake glorious Hector, and stretched out his arm to his boy. But the child shrunk crying to the bosom of his fair-girdled nurse, dismayed at his dear father's aspect, and in dread at the bronze and horse-hair crest that he beheld nodding fiercely from the helmet's top. Then his dear father laughed aloud, and his lady mother; forthwith glorious Hector took the helmet from his head, and laid it, all gleaming, upon the earth; then kissed he his dear son and dandled him in his arms, and spake in prayer to Zeus and all the gods, "O Zeus and all ye gods, vouchsafe ye that this my son may likewise prove even as I, pre-eminent amid the Trojans, and as valiant in might, and be a great king of Ilios. Then may men say of him, 'Far greater is he than his father' as he returneth home from battle; and may he bring with him blood-stained spoils from the foeman he hath slain, and may his mother's heart be glad."

So spake he, and laid his son in his dear wife's arms; and she took him to her fragrant bosom, smiling tearfully. And her husband had pity to see her, and caressed her with his hand, and spake and called upon her name: "Dear one, I pray thee be not of oversorrowful heart; no man against my fate shall hurl me to Hades; only destiny, I ween, no man hath escaped, be he coward or be he valiant, when once he hath been born. But go thou to thine house and see to thine own tasks, the loom and distaff, and bid thine handmaidens ply their work; but for war shall men provide, and I in chief of all men that dwell in Ilios."

So spake glorious Hector, and took up his horse-hair crested helmet; and his dear wife departed to her home, oft looking back, and letting fall big tears. Anon she came to the well-stablished house of man-slaying Hector, and found therein her many handmaidens, and stirred lamentation in them all. So bewailed they Hector, while yet he lived, within his house: for they deemed that he would no more come back to them from battle, nor escape the fury of the hands of the Achaians.

Neither lingered Paris long in his lofty house, but clothed on him his brave armour, bedight with bronze, and hasted through the city, trusting to his nimble feet. Even as when a stalled horse, full-fed at the manger, breaketh his tether and speedeth at the gallop across the plain, being wont to bathe him in the fair-flowing stream, exultingly; and holdeth his head on high, and his mane floateth about his shoulders, and he trusteth in his glory, and nimbly his limbs bear him to the haunts and pasturages of mares; even so Priam's son Paris, glittering in his armour like the shining sun, strode down from high Pergamos laughingly, and his swift feet bare him. Forthwith he overtook his brother noble Hector, even as he was on the point to turn him away from the spot where he had dallied with his wife. To him first spake godlike Alexandros: "Sir, in good sooth I have delayed thee in thine haste by my tarrying, and came not rightly as thou badest me."

And Hector of the glancing helm answered him and said: "Good brother, no man that is rightminded could make light of thy doings in fight, seeing thou art strong: but thou art wilfully remiss and hast no care; and for this my heart is grieved within me, that I hear shameful words concerning thee in the Trojans' mouths, who for thy sake endure much toil. But let us be going; all this will we make good hereafter, if Zeus ever vouchsafe us to set before the heavenly gods that are for everlasting the cup of deliverance in our halls, when we have chased out of Troy-land the well-greaved Achaians."

BOOK VII

Of the single combat between Alas and Hector, and of the burying of the dead, and the building of a wall about the Achaian ships.

So spake glorious Hector and issued from the gates, and with him went his brother Alexandros; and both were eager of soul for fight and battle. Even as God giveth to longing seamen fair wind when they have grown weary of beating the main with polished oars, and their limbs are fordone with toil, even so appeared these to the longing Trojans.

Now when the goddess bright-eyed Athene marked them making havoc of the Argives in the press of battle, she darted down from the crests of Olympus to holy Ilios. But Apollo rose to meet her, for he beheld her from Pergamos, and would have victory for the Trojans. So the twain met each the other by the oak-tree. To her spake first king Apollo son of Zeus: "Why now art thou come thus eagerly from Olympus, thou daughter of great Zeus, and why hath thy high heart sent thee? Surely it is to give the Danaans unequal victory in battle! seeing thou hast no mercy on the Trojans, that perish. But if thou wouldest hearken to me—and it were far better so—let us now stay battle and warring for the day; hereafter shall they fight again, till they reach the goal of Ilios, since thus it seemeth good to your hearts, goddesses immortal, to lay waste this city."

And the goddess bright-eyed Athene made answer to him: "So be it, Far-darter; in this mind I likewise came from Olympus to the midst of Trojans and Achaians. But come, how thinkest thou to stay the battle of the warriors?"

And king Apollo, son of Zeus, made answer to her: "Let us arouse the stalwart spirit of horse-taming Hector, if so be he will challenge some one of the Danaans in single fight man to man to meet him in deadly combat. So shall the bronze-greaved Achaians be jealous and stir up one to fight singly with goodly Hector." So spake he and the bright-eyed goddess Athene disregarded not. Now Helenos Priam's dear son understood in spirit their resolve that the gods in counsel had approved; and he went to Hector and stood beside him, and spake a word to him: "Hector son of Priam, peer of Zeus in counsel, wouldest thou now hearken at all to me? for I am thy brother. Make the other Trojans sit, and all the Achaians, and thyself challenge him that is best of the Achaians to meet thee man to man in deadly combat. It is not yet thy destiny to die and meet thy doom; for thus heard I the voice of the gods that are from everlasting." So said he, and Hector rejoiced greatly to hear his saying, and went into the midst and refrained the battalions of the Trojans with his spear grasped by the middle; and they all sate them down: and Agamemnon made the well-greaved Achaians sit. And Athene withal and Apollo of the silver bow, in the likeness of vulture birds, sate them upon a tall oak holy to aegis-bearing father Zeus, rejoicing in their warriors; and the ranks of all of them sate close together, bristling with shields and plumes and spears. Even as there spreadeth across the main the ripple of the west wind newly risen, and the sea grows black beneath it, so sate the ranks of Achaians and Trojans upon the plain. And Hector spake between both hosts: "Hearken to me, Trojans and well-greaved Achaians, that I may speak what my mind within my breast biddeth me. Our oaths of truce Kronos' son, enthroned on high, accomplished not; but evil is his intent and ordinance for both our hosts, until either ye take fair-towered Troy or yourselves be vanquished beside your seafaring ships. But in the midst of you are the chiefest of all the Achaians; therefore now let the man whose heart biddeth him fight with me come hither from among you all to be your champion against goodly Hector. And this declare I, and be Zeus our witness thereto; if that man slay me with the long-edged sword, let him spoil me of my armour and bear it to the hollow ships, but give back my body to my home, that Trojans and Trojans' wives may give me my due of burning in my death. But if I slay him and Apollo vouchsafe me glory, I will spoil him of his armour and bear it to holy Ilios and hang it upon the temple of far-darting Apollo, but his corpse will I render back to the well-decked ships, that the flowing-haired Achaians may entomb him, and build him a barrow beside wide Hellespont. So shall one say even of men that be late born, as he saileth in his benched ship over the wine-dark sea: 'This is the barrow of a man that died in days of old, a champion whom glorious Hector slew.' So shall a man say hereafter, and this my glory shall never die."

So spake he and they all were silent and held their peace; to deny him they were ashamed, and feared to meet him. But at the last stood up Menelaos and spake amid them and chiding upbraided them, and groaned deep at heart: "Ah me, vain threateners, ye women of Achaia and no more men, surely all this shall be a shame, evil of evil, if no one of the Danaans now goeth to meet Hector. Nay, turn ye all to earth and water, sitting there each man disheartened, helplessly inglorious; against him will I myself array me; and from on high the threads of victory are guided of the immortal gods."

So spake he and donned his fair armour. And now, O Menelaos, had the end of life appeared for thee at Hector's hands, seeing he was stronger far, but that the princes of the Achaians started up and caught thee. And Atreus' son himself, wide-ruling Agamemnon, took him by his right hand and spake a word and called upon his name: "Thou doest madly, Menelaos fosterling of Zeus; yet is it no time for this thy madness. Draw back, though it be with pain, nor think for contention's sake to fight with one better than thou, with Hector Priam's son, whom others beside thee abhor. Yea, this man even Achilles dreadeth to meet in battle, wherein is the warrior's glory; and Achilles is better far than thou. Go therefore now and sit amid the company of thy fellows; against him shall the Achaians put forth another champion. Fearless though he be and insatiate of turmoil, I ween that he shall be fain to rest his knees, if he escape from the fury of war and terrible fray."

So spake the hero and persuaded his brother's heart with just counsel; and he obeyed. So his squires thereat with gladness took his armour from his shoulders; and Nestor stood up and spake amid the Argives: "Fie upon it, verily sore lamentation cometh on the land of Achaia. Verily old Peleus driver of chariots would groan sore, that goodly counsellor of the Myrmidons and orator, who erst questioned me in his house, and rejoiced greatly, inquiring of the lineage and birth of all the Argives. If he heard now of those that all were cowering before Hector, then would he lift his

hands to the immortals, instantly praying that his soul might depart from
his limbs down to the house of Hades. Would to God I were thus young
and my strength were sound; then would Hector of the glancing helm soon
find his combat. But of those of you that be chieftains of the host of the
Achaians, yet desireth no man of good heart to meet Hector face to face."
So the old man upbraided them, and there stood up nine in all. Far first
arose Agamemnon king of men, and after him rose Tydeus' son stalwart
Diomedes, and after them the Aiantes clothed with impetuous might, and
after them Idomeneus and Idomeneus' brother-in-arms Meriones, peer of
Enyalios slayer of men, and after them Eurypylos Euaimon's glorious son;
and up rose Thoas Andraimon's son and goodly Odysseus. So all these
were fain to fight with goodly Hector. And among them spake again
knightly Nestor of Gerenia: "Now cast ye the lot from the first unto the
last, for him that shall be chosen: for he shall in truth profit the
well-greaved Achaians, yea and he shall have profit of his own soul, if he
escape from the fury of war and terrible fray."

So said he, and they marked each man his lot and cast them in the
helmet of Agamemnon Atreus' son; and the hosts prayed and lifted up
their hands to the gods. And thus would one say, looking up to wide
heaven: "O father Zeus, vouchsafe that the lot fall upon Aias or Tydeus'
son, or else on the king of Mykene rich in gold."

So spake they, and knightly Nestor of Gerenia shook the helmet, and
there leapt forth the lot that themselves desired, even the lot of Aias. And
Aias saw and knew the token upon the lot, and rejoiced in heart, and
spake: "My friends, verily the lot is mine, yea and myself am glad at heart,
because I deem that I shall vanquish goodly Hector. But come now, while
I clothe me in my armour of battle, pray ye the while to Kronos' son king
Zeus, in silence to yourselves, that the Trojans hear you not—nay rather,
openly if ye will, for we have no fear of any man soever. For none by force
shall chase me, he willing me unwilling, neither by skill; seeing I hope
that not so skill-less, either, was I born in Salamis nor nurtured."

So said he, and they prayed to Kronos' son, king Zeus; and thus would
one speak, looking up to wide heaven: "O father Zeus that rulest from Ida,
most glorious, most great, vouchsafe to Aias victory and the winning of
great glory. But if thou so lovest Hector indeed, and carest for him, grant
unto either equal prowess and renown."

So said they, while Aias arrayed him in flashing bronze. And when he
had now clothed upon his flesh all his armour, then marched he as huge
Ares coming forth, when he goeth to battle amid heroes whom Kronos' son
setteth to fight in fury of heart-consuming strife. So rose up huge Aias,
bulwark of the Achaians, with a smile on his grim face: and went with
long strides of his feet beneath him, shaking his far-shadowing spear.
Then moreover the Argives rejoiced to look upon him, but sore trembling
came upon the Trojans, on the limbs of every man, and Hector's own heart
beat within his breast. But in no wise could he now flee nor shrink back

into the throng of the host, seeing he had challenged him to battle. And Aias came near bearing his tower-like shield of bronze, with sevenfold ox-hide, and stood near to Hector, and spake to him threatening: "Hector, now verily shalt thou well know, man to man, what manner of princes the Danaans likewise have among them, even after Achilles, render of men, the lion-hearted. But he amid his beaked seafaring ships lieth in sore wrath with Agamemnon shepherd of the host; yet are we such as to face thee, yea and many of us. But make thou beginning of war and battle."

And great Hector of the glancing helm answered him: "Aias of the seed of Zeus, son of Telamon, chieftain of the host, tempt not thou me like some puny boy or woman that knoweth not deeds of battle. But I well know wars and slaughterings. To right know I, to left know I the wielding of my tough targe; therein I deem is stalwart soldiership. And I know how to charge into the mellay of fleet chariots, and how in close battle to join in furious Ares' dance. Howbeit, I have no mind to smite thee, being such an one as thou art, by spying thee unawares; but rather openly, if perchance I may hit thee."

He spake, and poised his far-shadowing spear, and hurled and smote Aias' dread shield of sevenfold hide upon the uttermost bronze, the eighth layer that was thereon. Through six folds went the stubborn bronze cleaving, but in the seventh hide it stayed. Then heaven-sprung Aias hurled next his far-shadowing spear, and smote upon the circle of the shield of Priam's son. Through the bright shield passed the violent spear, and through the curiously wrought corslet pressed it on; and straight forth beside the flank the spear rent his doublet; but he swerved aside and escaped black death. Then both together with their hands plucked forth their long spears and fell to like ravening lions or wild boars whose might is nowise feeble. Then Priam's son smote the shield's midst with his dart, but the bronze brake not through, for the point turned back; but Aias leapt on him and pierced his buckler, and straight through went the spear and staggered him in his onset, and cleft its way unto his neck, so that the dark blood gushed up. Yet even then did not Hector of the glancing helm cease from fight, but yielded ground and with stout hand seized a stone lying upon the plain, black and rugged and great; therewith hurled he and smote Aias' dread shield of sevenfold ox-hide in the midst upon the boss, and the bronze resounded. Next Aias lifted a far greater stone, and swung and hurled it, putting might immeasurable therein. So smote he the buckler and burst it inwards with the rock like unto a millstone, and beat down his knees; and he was stretched upon his back, pressed into his shield; but Apollo straightway raised him up. And now had they been smiting hand to hand with swords, but that the heralds, messengers of gods and men, came, one from the Trojans, one from the mail-clad Achaians, even Talthybios and Idaios, both men discreet. Between the two held they their staves, and herald Idaios spake a word, being skilled in wise counsel: "Fight ye no more, dear sons, neither do battle; seeing Zeus the cloud-gatherer loveth you both, and both are men of war; that verily know we all. But night already is upon us: it is well withal to obey the hest [behest] of night."

Then Telamonian Aias answered and said to him: "Idaios, bid ye Hector to speak those words; of his own self he challenged to combat all our best. Let him be first, and I will surely follow as he saith."

Then great Hector of the glancing helm said to him: "Aias, seeing God gave thee stature and might and wisdom, and with the spear thou art excellent above all the Achaians, let us now cease from combat and battle for the day; but hereafter will we fight until God judge between as, giving to one of us the victory: But come, let us give each the other famous gifts, that men may thus say, Achaians alike and Trojans: 'These, having fought for sake of heart-consuming strife, parted again reconciled in friendship.'"

So said he, and gave him his silver-studded sword, with scabbard and well-cut baldrick; and Aias gave his belt bright with purple. So they parted, and one went to the Achaian host, and one betook him to the throng of Trojans. And these rejoiced to behold him come to them alive and sound, escaped from the fury of Aias and his hands unapproachable; and they brought him to the city saved beyond their hope. And Aias on their side the well-greaved Achaians brought to noble Agamemnon, exulting in his victory.

So when these were come unto the huts of Atreides, then did Agamemnon king of men slay them an ox, a male of five years old, for the most mighty son of Kronos. This they flayed and made ready, and divided it all, and minced it cunningly, and pierced it through with spits, and roasted it carefully, and drew all off again. Then as soon as they had rest from the task and had made ready the meal, they began the feast, nor was their soul aught stinted of the equal banquet. And the hero son of Atreus, wide-ruling Agamemnon, gave to Aias slices of the chine's full length for his honour. And when they had put from them the desire of meat and drink, then first the old man began to weave the web of counsel, even Nestor whose rede [counsel] of old time was proved most excellent. He made harangue among them and said: "Son of Atreus and ye other princes of the Achaians, seeing that many flowing-haired Achaians are dead, and keen Ares hath spilt their dusky blood about fair-flowing Skamandros, and their souls have gone down to the house of Hades; therefore it behoveth thee to make the battle of the Achaians cease with daybreak; and we will assemble to wheel hither the corpses with oxen and mules; so let us burn them; and let us heap one barrow about the pyre, rearing it from the plain for all alike; and thereto build with speed high towers, a bulwark for our ships and for ourselves. In the midst thereof let us make gates well compact, that through them may be a way for chariot-driving. And without let us dig a deep foss hard by, to be about it and to hinder horses and footmen, lest the battle of the lordly Trojans be heavy on us hereafter."

So spake he and all the chiefs gave assent. But meanwhile there was in the high town of Ilios an assembly of the Trojans, fierce, confused, beside Priam's gate. To them discreet Antenor began to make harangue: "Hearken to me, Trojans and Dardanians and allies, that I may tell you that my soul within my breast commandeth me. Lo, go to now, let us give Helen of Argos and the wealth with her for the sons of Atreus to take away. Now fight we in guilt against the oaths of faith; therefore is there no profit for us that I hope to see fulfilled, unless we do thus."

So spake he and sate him down; and there stood up among them noble Alexandros, lord of Helen beautiful-haired; he made him answer and spake winged words: "Antenor, these words from thee are no longer to my pleasure; yet thou hast it in thee to devise other sayings more excellent than this. But if indeed thou sagest this in earnest, then verily the gods themselves have destroyed thy wit. But I will speak forth amid the horse-taming Trojans, and declare outright; my wife will I not give back; but the wealth I brought from Argos to our home, all that I have a mind to give, and add more of mine own substance."

So spake he and sate him down, and there stood up among them Priam of the seed of Dardanos, the peer of gods in counsel; he made harangue to them, and said: "Hearken to me, Trojans and Dardanians and allies, that I may tell you that my soul within my breast commandeth me. Now eat your supper throughout the city as of old, and take thought to keep watch, and be wakeful every man. And at dawn let Idaios fare to the hollow ships to tell to Atreus' sons Agamemnon and Menelaos the saying of Alexandros, for whose sake strife is come about: and likewise to ask them this wise word, whether they are minded to refrain from noisy war till we have burned our dead; afterwards will we fight again, till heaven part us and give one or other victory."

So spake he, and they hearkened diligently to him and obeyed: and at dawn Idaios fared to the hollow ships. He found the Danaans in assembly, the men of Ares' company, beside the stern of Agamemnon's ship; and so the loud-voiced herald stood in their midst and said unto them: "Atreides and ye other princes of the Achaians, Priam and all the noble Trojans bade me tell you-if perchance it might find favour and acceptance with you-the saying of Alexandros, for whose sake strife hath come about. The wealth that Alexandros brought in his hollow ships to Troy-would he had perished first!-all that he hath a mind to give, and to add more thereto of his substance. But the wedded wife of glorious Menelaos he saith he will not give; yet verily the Trojans bid him do it. Moreover they bade me ask this thing of you; whether ye are minded to refrain from noisy war until we have burned our dead; afterwards will we fight again, till heaven part us and give one or other victory."

So said he and they all kept silence and were still. But at the last spake Diomedes of the loud war-cry in their midst: "Let no man now accept Alexandros' substance, neither Helen's self; known is it, even to him that hath no wit at all, how that the issues of destruction hang already over the Trojans."

So spake he, and all the sons of the Achaians shouted, applauding the saying of horse-taming Diomedes. And then lord Agamemnon spake to Idaios: "Idaios, thyself thou hearest the saying of the Achaians, how they answer thee; and the like seemeth good to me. But as concerning the dead, I grudge you not to burn them; for dead corpses is there no stinting; when they once are dead, of the swift propitiation of fire. And for the oaths let Zeus be witness, the loud-thundering lord of Hera."

So saying he lifted up his sceptre in the sight of all the gods, and Idaios departed back to holy Ilios. Now Trojans and Dardanians sate in assembly, gathered all together to wait till Idaios should come; and he came and stood in their midst and declared his message. Then they made them ready very swiftly for either task, some to bring the dead, and some to seek for wood. And on their part the Argives hasted from their well-decked ships, some to bring the dead and some to seek for wood.

Now the sun was newly beating on the fields as he climbed heaven from the deep stream of gently-flowing Ocean, when both sides met together. Then was it a hard matter to know each man again; but they washed them with water clean of clotted gore, and with shedding of hot tears lifted them upon the wains. But great Priam bade them not wail aloud; so in silence heaped they the corpses on the pyre, stricken at heart; and when they had burned them with fire departed to holy Ilios. And in like manner on their side the well-greaved Achaians heaped the corpses on the pyre, stricken at heart, and when they had burned them with fire departed to the hollow ships.

And when day was not yet, but still twilight of night, then was the chosen folk of the Achaians gathered together around the pyre, and made one barrow about it, rearing it from the plain for all alike; and thereto built they a wall and lofty towers, a bulwark for their ships and for themselves. In the midst thereof made they gates well-compacted, that through them might be a way for chariot-driving. And without they dug a deep foss beside it, broad and great, and planted a palisade therein.

Thus toiled the flowing-haired Achaians: and the gods sate by Zeus, the lord of lightning, and marvelled at the great work of the mail-clad Achaians. And Poseidon shaker of earth spake first to them: "O father Zeus, is there any man throughout the boundless earth that will any more declare to the immortals his mind and counsel? Seest thou not how the flowing-haired Achaians have now again built them a wall before their ships, and drawn a foss around it, but gave not excellent hecatombs to the gods? Verily the fame thereof shall reach as far as the dawn spreadeth, and men will forget the wall that I and Phoebus Apollo built with travail for the hero Laomedon."

And Zeus the cloud-gatherer said to him, sore troubled: "Out on it, far-swaying Shaker of earth, for this thing thou sayest. Well might some other god fear this device, one that were far feebler than thou in the might of his hands: but thine shall be the fame as far as the dawn spreadeth. Go to now, hereafter when the flowing-haired Achaians be departed upon their ships to their dear native land, then burst thou this wall asunder and scatter it all into the sea, and cover the great sea-beach over with sand again, that the great wall of the Achaians be brought to naught."

BOOK VIII

How Zeus bethought him of his promise to avenge Achilles' wrong on Agamemnon; and therefore bade the gods refrain from war, and gave victory to the Trojans.

Now Dawn the saffron-robed was spreading over all the earth, and Zeus whose joy is in the thunder let call an assembly of the gods upon the topmost peak of many-ridged Olympus, and himself made harangue to them and all the gods gave ear: "Hearken to me, all gods and all ye goddesses, that I may tell you what my heart within my breast commandeth me. One thing let none essay, be it goddess or be it god, to wit, to thwart my saying; approve ye it all together, that with all speed I may accomplish these things. Whomsoever I shall perceive minded to go, apart from the gods, to succour Trojans or Danaans, chastened in no seemly wise shall he return to Olympus, or I will take and cast him into misty Tartaros, right far away, where is the deepest gulf beneath the earth; there are the gate of iron and threshold of bronze, as far beneath Hades as heaven is high above the earth: then shall he know how far I am mightiest of all gods. Go to now, ye gods, make trial that ye all may know. Fasten ye a rope of gold from heaven, and all ye gods lay hold thereof and all goddesses; yet could ye not drag from heaven to earth Zeus, counsellor supreme, not though ye toiled sore. But once I likewise were minded to draw with all my heart, then should I draw you up with very earth and sea withal. Thereafter would I bind the rope about a pinnacle of Olympus, and so should all those things be hung in air. By so much am I beyond gods and beyond men."

So saying he let harness to his chariot his bronze-shod horses, fleet of foot, with flowing manes of gold; and himself clad him with gold upon his flesh, and grasped the whip of gold, well wrought, and mounted upon his car, and lashed the horses to start them; they nothing loth sped on between earth and starry heaven. So fared he to many-fountained Ida, mother of wild beasts, even unto Gargaros, where is his demesne and fragrant altar. There did the father of men and gods stay his horses, and unloose them from the car, and cast thick mist about them; and himself sate on the mountain-tops rejoicing in his glory, to behold the city of the Trojans and ships of the Achaians.

Now the flowing-haired Achaians took meat hastily among the huts and thereafter arrayed themselves. Likewise the Trojans on their side armed them throughout the town—a smaller host, yet for all that were they eager to fight in battle, of forceful need, for their children's sake and their wives'. And the gates were opened wide and the host issued forth, footmen and horsemen; and mighty din arose.

So when they were met together and come unto one spot, then clashed they targe and spear and fury of bronze-clad warrior; the bossed shields pressed each on each, and mighty din arose. Then were heard the voice of groaning and the voice of triumph together of the slayers and the slain, and the earth streamed with blood.

Now while it yet was morn and the divine day waxed, so long from either side lighted the darts amain and the people fell. But when the sun bestrode mid-heaven, then did the Father balance his golden scales, and put therein two fates of death that layeth men at their length, one for horse-taming Trojans, one for mail-clad Achaians; and he took the scale-yard by the midst and lifted it, and the Achaians' day of destiny sank down. So lay the Achaians' fates on the bounteous earth, and the Trojans' fates were lifted up towards wide heaven. And the god thundered aloud from Ida, and sent his blazing flash amid the host of the Achaians; and they saw and were astonished, and pale fear gat hold upon all.

Then had Idomeneus no heart to stand, neither Agamemnon, neither stood the twain Aiantes, men of Ares' company. Only Nestor of Gerenia stood his ground, he the Warden of the Achaians; neither he of purpose, but his horse was fordone, which noble Alexandros, beauteous-haired Helen's lord, had smitten with an arrow upon the top of the crest where the foremost hairs of horses grow upon the skull; and there is the most deadly spot. So the horse leapt up in anguish and the arrow sank into his brain, and he brought confusion on the steeds as he writhed upon the dart. While the old man leapt forth and with his sword began to hew the traces, came Hector's fleet horses through the tumult, bearing a bold charioteer, even Hecktor. And now had the old man lost his life, but that Diomedes of the loud war-cry was swift to mark. Terribly shouted he, summoning Odysseus: "Heaven-born son of Laertes, Odysseus of many wiles, whither fleest thou with thy back turned, like a coward in the throng? Beware lest as thou fleest one plant a spear between thy shoulders. Nay, stand thy ground, till we thrust back from the old man his furious foe."

So spake he, but much-enduring noble Odysseus heard him not, but hastened by to the hollow ships of the Achaians. Yet Tydeides, though but one, mingled amid the fighters in the forefront, and took his stand before the steeds of the old man, Neleus' son, and spake to him winged words, and said: "Old man, of a truth young warriors beset thee hard; and thy force is abated, and old age is sore upon thee, and thy squire is but a weakling, and thy steeds are slow. Come then, mount upon my car, that thou mayest see of what sort are the steeds of Tros, well skilled for following or fleeing hither or thither very fleetly across the plain, even those that erst I took from Aineias inspirer of fear. Thine let our squires tend, and these let us guide straight against the horse-taming Trojans, that even Hector may know whether my spear also rageth in my hands."

So said he, and knightly Nestor of Gerenia disregarded not. Then the two squires tended Nestor's horses, even Sthenelos the valiant and kindly Eurymedon: and the other twain both mounted upon Diomedes' car. And Nestor took into his hands the shining reins, and lashed the horses; and soon they drew nigh Hector. Then Tydeus' son hurled at him as he charged straight upon them: him missed he, but his squire that drave his chariot, Eniopeus, high-hearted Thebaios' son, even him as he held the reins, he smote upon the breast beside the nipple. So he fell from out the car, and his fleet-footed horses swerved aside; and there his soul and spirit were unstrung. Then sore grief encompassed Hector's soul for sake of his charioteer. Yet left he him there lying, though he sorrowed for his comrade, and drave in quest of a bold charioteer; and his horses lacked not long a master, for anon he found Iphitos' son, bold Archeptolemos, and him he made mount behind his fleet horses, and gave the reins into his hands.

Then had destruction come and deeds beyond remedy been wrought, and so had they been penned in Ilios like lambs, had not the father of gods and men been swift to mark. So he thundered terribly and darted his white lightning and hurled it before Diomedes' steeds to earth; and there arose a terrible flame of sulphur burning, and the two horses were affrighted and cowered beneath the car. And the shining reins dropped from Nestor's hands, and he was afraid at heart and spake to Diomedes: "Come now Tydeides, turn back thy whole-hooved horses to flight: seest thou not that victory from Zeus attendeth not on thee? Now doth Kronos' son vouchsafe glory to this Hector, for the day; hereafter shall he grant it us likewise, if he will. A man may not at all ward off the will of Zeus, not though one be very valiant; he verily is mightier far."

Then Diomedes of the loud war-cry answered him: "Yea verily, old man, all this thou sayest is according unto right. But this is the sore grief that entereth my heart and soul: Hector some day shall say as he maketh harangue amid the Trojans: 'Tydeides betook him to the ships in flight before my face.' So shall he boast—in that day let the wide earth yawn for me."

So spake he and turned the whole-hooved horses to flight, back through the tumult; and the Trojans and Hector with wondrous uproar poured upon them their dolorous darts. And over him shouted loudly great Hector of the glancing helm: "Tydeides, the fleet-horsed Danaans were wont to honour thee with the highest place, and meats, and cups brimful, but now will they disdain thee; thou art after all no better than a woman. Begone, poor puppet; not for my flinching shalt thou climb on our towers, neither carry our wives away upon thy ships; ere that will I deal thee thy fate."

So said he, and Tydeides was of divided mind, whether to wheel his horses and fight him face to face. Thrice doubted he in heart and soul, and thrice from Ida's mountains thundered Zeus the lord of counsel, and gave to the Trojans a sign, the turning of the course of battle. And Hector with loud shout called to the Trojans: "Trojans and Lykians and Dardanians that love close fight, be men, my friends, and bethink you of impetuous valour. I perceive that of good will Kronion vouchsafest me victory and great glory, and to the Danaans destruction. Fools, that devised these walls weak and of none account; they shall not withhold our fury, and lightly shall our steeds overleap the delved foss. But when I be once come amid the hollow ships, then be thought taken of consuming fire, that with fire I may burn the ships and slay the men."

So spake he and shouted to his steeds, and said: "Xanthos, and thou Podargos, and Aithon and goodly Lampos, now pay me back your tending, even the abundance that Andromache, great-hearted Eetion's daughter, set before you of honey-hearted wheat, and mingled wine to drink at the heart's bidding. Pursue ye now and haste, that we may seize Nestor's shield, the fame whereof now reacheth unto heaven, how that it is of gold throughout, armrods and all; and may seize moreover from horse-taming Diomedes' shoulders his richly dight breastplate that Hephaistos wrought cunningly. Could we but take these, then might I hope this very night to make the Achaians to embark on their fleet ships."

And now had he burned the trim ships with blazing fire, but that queen Hera put it in Agamemnon's heart himself to bestir him and swiftly arouse the Achaians. So he went his way along the huts and ships of the Achaians, holding a great cloak of purple in his stalwart hand, and stood by Odysseus' black ship of mighty burden, that was in the midst, so that a voice could be heard to either end. Then shouted he in a piercing voice, and called to the Danaans aloud: "Fie upon you, Argives, ye sorry things of shame, so brave in semblance! Whither are gone our boastings when we said that we were bravest, the boasts ye uttered vaingloriously when in Lemnos, as ye ate your fill of flesh of tall-horned oxen and drank goblets crowned with wine, and said that every man should stand in war to face fivescore yea tenscore Trojans? yet now can we not match one, even this Hector that anon will burn our ships with flame of fire. O Father Zeus, didst ever thou blind with such a blindness any mighty king, and rob him of great glory? Nay, Zeus, this hope fulfil thou me; suffer that we ourselves at least flee and escape, neither suffer that the Achaians be thus vanquished of the Trojans."

So spake he, and the Father had pity on him as he wept, and vouchsafed him that his folk should be saved and perish not. Forthwith sent he an eagle—surest sign among winged fowl—holding in his claws a fawn, the young of a fleet hind; beside the beautiful altar of Zeus he let fall the fawn, where the Achaians did sacrifice unto Zeus lord of all oracles. So when they saw that the bird was come from Zeus, they sprang the more upon the Trojans and bethought them of the joy of battle.

Now could no man of the Danaans, for all they were very many, boast that he before Tydeus' son had guided his fleet horses forth, and driven them across the trench and fought man to man; first by far was Tydeides to slay a warrior of the Trojans in full array, even Agelaos son of Phradmon. Now he had turned his steeds to flee; but as he wheeled the other plunged the spear into his back between his shoulders, and drave it through his breast. So fell he from his chariot, and his armour clanged upon him.

And after him came Atreus' sons, even Agamemnon and Menelaos, and after them the Aiantes clothed upon with impetuous valour, and after them Idomeneus and Idomeneus' brother in arms Meriones, peer of Enyalios slayer of men, and after them Eurypylos, Euaimon's glorious son. And ninth came Teukros, stretching his back-bent bow, and took his stand beneath the shield of Aias son of Telamon. And so Aias would stealthily withdraw the shield, and Teukros would spy his chance; and when he had shot and smitten one in the throng, then fell such an one and gave up the ghost, and Teukros would return, and as a child beneath his mother, so gat he him to Aias; who hid him with the shining shield.

And Agamemnon king of men rejoiced to behold him making havoc with his stalwart bow of the battalions of the Trojans, and he came and stood by his side and spake to him, saying: "Teukros, dear heart, thou son of Telamon, prince of the host, shoot on in this wise, if perchance thou mayest be found the salvation of the Danaans and glory of thy father Telamon."

And noble Teukros made answer and said to him: "Most noble son of Atreus, why urgest thou me that myself am eager? Verily with such strength as is in me forbear I not, but ever since we drave them towards Ilios I watch with my bow to slay the foemen. Eight long-barbed arrows have I now sped, and all are buried in the flesh of young men swift in battle; only this mad dog can I not smite."

He said, and shot another arrow from the string right against Hector; and his heart was fain to smite him. Yet missed he once again, for Apollo turned the dart away; but Archeptolemos, Hector's bold charioteer, he smote on the breast beside the nipple as he hasted into battle: so he fell from his car and his fleet-footed horses swerved aside; and there his soul and spirit were unstrung. Then sore grief encompassed Hector's soul for his charioteer's sake; yet left he him, though he sorrowed for his comrade, and bade Kebriones his own brother, being hard by, take the chariot reins; and he heard and disregarded not. And himself he leapt to earth from the resplendent car, with a terrible shout; and in his hand he caught a stone, and made right at Teukros, and his heart bade him smite him. Now Teukros had plucked forth from his quiver a keen arrow, and laid it on the string; but even as he drew it back, Hector of the glancing helm smote him with the jagged stone, as he aimed eagerly against him, even beside his shoulder, where the collar-bone fenceth off neck and breast, and where is the most deadly spot; and he brake the bowstring, and his hand from the wrist grew numb, and he stayed fallen upon his knee, and his bow dropped from his hand. But Aias disregarded not his brother's fall, but ran and strode across him and hid him with his shield. Then two trusty comrades bent down to him, even Mekisteus son of Echios and goodly Alastor, and bare him, groaning sorely, to the hollow ships. And once again the Olympian aroused the spirit of the Trojans. So they drove the Achaians straight toward the deep foss, and amid the foremost went Hector exulting in his strength. And even as when a hound behind wild boar or lion, with swift feet pursuing snatcheth at him, at flank or buttock, and watcheth for him as he wheeleth, so Hector pressed hard on the flowing-haired Achaians, slaying ever the hindmost, and they fled on. But when they were passed in flight through palisade and foss, and many were fallen beneath the Trojans' hands, then halted they and tarried beside the ships, calling one upon another, and lifting up their hands to all the gods prayed each one instantly. But Hector wheeled round his beauteous-maned steeds this way and that, and his eyes were as the eyes of Gorgon or Ares bane of mortals.

Now at the sight of them the white-armed goddess Hera had compassion, and anon spake winged words to Athene: "Out on it, thou child of aegis-bearing Zeus, shall not we twain any more take thought for the Danaans that perish, if only for this last time? Now will they fill up the measure of evil destiny and perish by one man's onslaught; seeing that he is furious now beyond endurance, this Hector son of Priam, and verily hath wrought many a deed of ill."

And the bright-eyed goddess Athene made answer to her, "Yea in good sooth, may this fellow yield up strength and life, and perish at the Argives' hands in his native land; only mine own sire is furious, with no good intent, headstrong, ever sinful, the foiler of my purposes. But now make thou ready our whole-hooved horses, while I enter into the palace of aegis-bearing Zeus and gird me in my armour for battle, that I may see if Priam's son, Hector of the glancing helm, shall be glad at the appearing of us twain amid the highways of the battle. Surely shall many a Trojan likewise glut dogs and birds with fat and flesh, fallen dead at the ships of the Achaians."

So said she, and the white-armed goddess Hera disregarded not. But when father Zeus beheld from Ida, he was sore wroth, and sped Iris golden-winged to bear a message: "Go thy way, fleet Iris, turn them back, neither suffer them to face me; for in no happy wise shall we join in combat. For thus will I declare, and even so shall the fulfilment be; I will maim their fleet horses in the chariot, and them will I hurl out from the car, and will break in pieces the chariot; neither within the courses of ten years shall they heal them of the wounds the thunderbolt shall tear; that the bright-eyed one may know the end when she striveth against her father. But with Hera have I not so great indignation nor wrath: seeing it ever is her wont to thwart me, whate'er I have decreed."

So said he, and whirlwind-footed Iris arose to bear the message, and departed from the mountains of Ida unto high Olympus. And even at the entrance of the gates of Olympus many-folded she met them and stayed them, and told them the saying of Zeus.

And father Zeus drave from Ida his fair-wheeled chariot and horses unto Olympus, and came unto the session of the gods. For him also the noble Shaker of Earth unyoked the steeds, and set the car upon the stand, and spread a cloth thereover; and far-seeing Zeus himself sate upon his golden throne, and beneath his feet great Olympus quaked. Only Athene and Hera sate apart from Zeus, and spake no word to him neither questioned him. But he was ware thereof in his heart, and said, "Why are ye thus vexed, Athene and Hera? Surely ye are not wearied of making havoc in glorious battle of the Trojans, for whom ye cherish bitter hate! Howsoever, seeing that my might is so great and my hands invincible, all the gods that are in Olympus could not turn me: and for you twain, trembling erst gat hold upon your bright limbs ere that ye beheld war and war's fell deeds. For thus will I declare, and even so had the fulfilment been—never had ye, once smitten with the thunderbolt, fared on your chariots back unto Olympus where is the habitation of the immortals."

So spake he, and Athene and Hera murmured, that were sitting by him and devising ills for the Trojans. Now Athene held her peace, and said not anything, for wrath at father Zeus, and fierce anger gat hold upon her; but Hera's heart contained not her anger, and she spake: "Most dread son of Kronos, what word is this thou hast said? Well know we, even we, that thy might is no wise puny; yet still have we pity for the Danaan spearmen, that now shall perish and fill up the measure of grievous fate."

And Zeus the cloud-gatherer answered and said: "At morn shalt thou behold most mighty Kronion, if thou wilt have it so, O Hera, ox-eyed queen, making yet more havoc of the vast army of Argive spearmen; for headlong Hector shall not refrain from battle till that Peleus' son fleet of foot have arisen beside the ships, that day when these shall fight amid the sterns in most grievous stress, around Patroklos fallen. Such is the doom of heaven. And for thine anger reck I not, not even though thou go to the nethermost bounds of earth and sea, where sit Iapetos and Kronos and have no joy in the beams of Hyperion the Sun-god, neither in any breeze, but deep Tartaros is round about them. Though thou shouldest wander till thou come even thither, yet reck I not of thy vexation, seeing there is no thing more unabashed than thou."

So said he, but white-armed Hera spake him no word. And the sun's bright light dropped into Ocean, drawing black night across Earth the grain-giver. Against the Trojans' will daylight departed, but welcome, thrice prayed for, to the Achaians came down the murky night.

Now glorious Hector made an assembly of the Trojans, taking them apart from the ships, beside the eddying river, in an open space where was found a spot clear of dead. And they came down from their chariots to the ground to hear the word that Hector, dear unto Zeus, proclaimed. He in his hand held his spear eleven cubits long; before his face gleamed the spearhead of bronze, and a ring of gold ran round about it. Thereon he leaned and spake to the Trojans, saying: "Hearken to me, Trojans and Dardanians and allies. I thought but now to make havoc of the ships and all the Achaians and depart back again to windy Ilios; but dusk came too soon, and that in chief hath now saved the Argives and the ships beside the beach of the sea. So let us now yield to black night, and make our supper ready; unyoke ye from the chariots your fair-maned horses, and set fodder beside them. And from the city bring kine and goodly sheep with speed; and provide you with honey-hearted wine, and corn from your houses, and gather much wood withal, that all night long until early-springing dawn we may burn many fires, and the gleam may reach to heaven; lest perchance even by night the flowing-haired Achaians strive to take flight over the broad back of the sea. Verily must they not embark upon their ships unvexed, at ease: but see ye that many a one of them have a wound to nurse even at home, being stricken with arrow or keen-pointed spear as he leapeth upon his ship; that so many another man may dread to wage dolorous war on the horse-taming men of Troy. And let the heralds dear to Zeus proclaim throughout the city that young maidens and old men of hoary heads camp round the city on the battlements builded of the gods; and let the women folk burn a great fire each in her hall; and let there be a sure watch set, lest an ambush enter the city when the host is absent. Howbeit for the night will we guard our own selves, and at morn by daybreak, arrayed in our armour, let us awake keen battle at the hollow ships. I will know whether Tydeus' son stalwart Diomedes shall thrust me from the ships back to the wall, or I shall lay him low with my spear and bear away his gory spoils. To-morrow shall he prove his valour, whether he can abide the onslaught of my spear. Would that I were immortal and ageless all my days and honoured like as Athene is honoured and Apollo, so surely as this day bringeth the Argives ill."

So Hector made harangue, and the Trojans clamoured applause. And they loosed their sweating steeds from the yoke, and tethered them with thongs, each man beside his chariot; and from the city they brought kine and goodly sheep with speed, and provided them with honey-hearted wine and corn from their houses, and gathered much wood withal. And from the plain the winds bare into heaven the sweet savour. But these with high hopes sate them all night along the highways of the battle, and their watchfires burned in multitude. Even as when in heaven the stars about the bright moon shine clear to see, when the air is windless, and all the peaks appear and the tall headlands and glades, and from heaven breaketh open the infinite air, and all stars are seen, and the shepherd's heart is glad; even in like multitude between the ships and the streams of Xanthos appeared the watchfires that the Trojans kindled in front of Ilios. A thousand fires burned in the plain and by the side of each sate fifty in the gleam of blazing fire. And the horses champed white barley and spelt, and standing by their chariots waited for the throned Dawn.

BOOK IX

How Agamemnon sent an embassage to Achilles, beseeching him to be appeased; and how Achilles denied him.

Thus kept the Trojans watch; but the Achaians were holden of heaven-sent panic, handmaid of palsying fear, and all their best were stricken to the heart with grief intolerable. Like as two winds stir up the main, the home of fishes, even the north wind and the west wind that blow from Thrace, coming suddenly; and the dark billow straightway lifteth up its crest and casteth much tangle out along the sea; even so was the Achaians' spirit troubled in their breast.

But Atreides was stricken to the heart with sore grief, and went about bidding the clear-voiced heralds summon every man by name to the assembly, but not to shout aloud; and himself he toiled amid the foremost. So they sat sorrowful in assembly, and Agamemnon stood up weeping like unto a fountain of dark water that from a beetling cliff poureth down its black stream; even so with deep groaning he spake amid the Argives and said: "My friends, leaders and captains of the Argives, Zeus son of Kronos hath bound me with might in grievous blindness of soul; hard of heart is he, for that erewhile he promised and gave his pledge that not till I had laid waste well-walled Ilios should I depart, but now hath planned a cruel wile, and biddeth me return in dishonour to Argos with the loss of many of my folk. Such meseemeth is the good pleasure of most mighty Zeus, that hath laid low the heads of many cities, yea and shall lay low; for his is highest power. So come, even as I shall bid let us all obey; let us flee with our ships to our dear native land, for now shall we never take wide-wayed Troy."

So said he, and they all held their peace and kept silence. Long time were the sons of the Achaians voiceless for grief, but at the last Diomedes of the loud war-cry spake amid them and said: "Atreides: with thee first in thy folly will I contend, where it is just, O king, even in the assembly; be not thou wroth therefor. My valour didst thou blame in chief amid the Danaans, and saidst that I was no man of war but a coward; and all this know the Argives both young and old. But the son of crooked-counselling Kronos hath endowed thee but by halves; he granted thee to have the honour of the sceptre above all men, but valour he gave thee not, wherein is highest power. Sir, deemest thou that the sons of the Achaians are thus indeed cowards and weaklings as thou sayest? If thine own heart be set on departing, go thy way; the way is before thee, and thy ships stand beside the sea, even the great multitude that followed thee from Mykene. But all the other flowing-haired Achaians will tarry here until we lay waste Troy. Nay, let them too flee on their ships to their dear native land; yet will we twain, even I and Sthenelos, fight till we attain the goal of Ilios; for in God's name are we come."

So said he, and all the sons of the Achaians shouted aloud, applauding the saying of horse-taming Diomedes. Then knightly Nestor arose and said amid them: "Tydeides, in battle art thou passing mighty, and in council art thou best among thine equals in years; none of all the Achaians will make light of thy word nor gainsay it. Now let us yield to black night and make ready our meal; and let the sentinels bestow them severally along the deep-delved foss without the wall. This charge give I to the young men; and thou, Atreides, lead then the way, for thou art the most royal. Spread thou a feast for the councillors; that is thy place and seemly for thee. Thy huts are full of wine that the ships of the Achaians bring thee by day from Thrace across the wide sea; all entertainment is for thee, being king over many. In the gathering of many shalt thou listen to him that deviseth the most excellent counsel; sore need have all the Achaians of such as is good and prudent, because hard by the ships our foemen are burning their watch-fires in multitude; what man can rejoice thereat? This night shall either destroy or save the host."

So said he, and they gladly hearkened to him and obeyed. Forth sallied the sentinels in their harness. Seven were the captains of the sentinels, and with each went fivescore young men bearing their long spears in their hands; and they took post midway betwixt foss and wall, and kindled a fire and made ready each man his meal.

Then Atreides gathered the councillors of the Achaians, and led them to his hut, and spread before them an abundant feast. So they put forth their hands to the good cheer that lay before them. And when they had put away from them the desire of meat and drink, then the old man first began to weave his counsel, even Nestor, whose rede of old time was approved the best. He spake to them and said: "Most noble son of Atreus, Agamemnon king of men, in thy name will I end and with thy name begin, because thou art king over many hosts, and to thy hand Zeus hath entrusted sceptre and law, that thou mayest take counsel for thy folk. Thee therefore more than any it behoveth both to speak and hearken, and to accomplish what another than thou may say. No other man shall have a more excellent thought than this that I bear in mind from old time even until now, since the day when thou, O heaven-sprung king, didst go and take the damsel Briseis from angry Achilles' hut by no consent of ours. Nay, I right heartily dissuaded thee; but thou yieldedst to thy proud spirit, and dishonouredst a man of valour whom even the immortals honoured; for thou didst take and keepest from him his meed of valour. Still let us even now take thought how we may appease him and persuade him with gifts of friendship and kindly words."

And Agamemnon king of men answered and said to him: "Old sir, in no false wise hast thou accused my folly. Fool was I, I myself deny it not. Worth many hosts is he whom Zeus loveth in his heart, even as now he honoureth this man and destroyeth the host of the Achaians. But seeing I was a fool in that I yielded to my sorry passion, I will make amends and give a recompense beyond telling. In the midst of you all I will name the excellent gifts; seven tripods untouched of fire, and ten talents of gold and twenty gleaming caldrons, and twelve stalwart horses, winners in the race, that have taken prizes by their speed. No lackwealth were that man whose substance were as great as the prizes my whole-hooved steeds have borne me off. And seven women will I give, skilled in excellent handiwork, Lesbians whom I chose me from the spoils the day that he himself took stablished Lesbos, surpassing womankind in beauty. These will I give him, and with them shall be she whom erst I took from him, even the daughter of Briseus. All these things shall be set straightway before him; and if hereafter the gods grant us to lay waste the great city of Priam, then let him enter in when we Achaians be dividing the spoil, and lade his ship full of gold and bronze, and himself choose twenty Trojan women, the fairest that there be after Helen of Argos. And if we win to the richest of lands, even Achaian Argos, he shall be my son and I will hold him in like honour with Orestes, my stripling boy that is nurtured in all abundance. Three daughters are mine in my well-builded hall, Chrysothemis and Laodike and Iphianassa; let him take of them which he will, without gifts of wooing, to Peleus' house; and I will add a great dower such as no man ever yet gave with his daughter. And seven well-peopled cities will I give him, Kardamyle and Enope and grassy Hire and holy Pherai and Antheia deep in meads, and fair Aipeia and Pedasos land of vines. And all are nigh to the salt sea, on the uttermost border of sandy Pylos; therein dwell men abounding in flocks and kine, men that shall worship him like a god with gifts, and beneath his sway fulfil his prosperous ordinances. All this will I accomplish so he but cease from wrath. Let him yield; Hades I ween is not to be softened neither overcome, and therefore is he hatefullest of all gods to mortals. Yea, let him be ruled by me, inasmuch as I am more royal and avow me to be the elder in years."

Then knightly Nestor of Gerenia answered and said: "Most noble son of Atreus, Agamemnon king of men, now are these gifts not lightly to be esteemed that thou offerest king Achilles. Come therefore, let us speed forth picked men to go with all haste to the hut of Peleus' son Achilles. Lo now, whomsoever I appoint let them consent. First let Phoinix dear to Zeus lead the way, and after him great Aias and noble Odysseus; and for heralds let Odios and Eurybates be their companions. And now bring water for our hands, and bid keep holy silence, that we may pray unto Zeus the son of Kronos, if perchance he will have mercy upon us."

So said he, and spake words that were well-pleasing unto all. Forthwith the heralds poured water on their hands, and the young men crowned the bowls with drink and gave each man his portion after they had poured the libation in the cups. And when they had made libation and drunk as their heart desired, they issued forth from the hut of Agamemnon son of Atreus. And knightly Nestor of Gerenia gave them full charge, with many a glance to each, and chiefest to Odysseus, how they should essay to prevail on Peleus' noble son.

So the twain went along the shore of the loud-sounding sea, making instant prayer to the earth-embracer, the Shaker of the Earth, that they might with ease prevail on Aiakides' great heart. So they came to the huts and ships of the Myrmidons, and found their king taking his pleasure of a loud lyre, fair, of curious work, with a silver cross-bar upon it. Therein he was delighting his soul, and singing the glories of heroes. And over against him sate Patroklos alone in silence, watching till Aiakides should cease from singing. So the twain came forward, and noble Odysseus led the way, and they stood before his face; and Achilles sprang up amazed with the lyre in his hand, and left the seat where he was sitting, and in like manner Patroklos when he beheld the men arose. Then Achilles fleet of foot greeted them and said: "Welcome; verily ye are friends that are come—sore indeed is the need—even ye that are dearest of the Achaians to me even in my wrath."

So spake noble Achilles and led them forward, and made them sit on settles and carpets of purple; and anon he spake to Patroklos being near: "Bring forth a greater bowl, thou son of Menoitios; mingle stronger drink, and prepare each man a cup, for dearest of men are these that are under my roof."

Then put they forth their hands to the good cheer lying before them. And when they had put from them the desire of meat and drink, Aias nodded to Phoinix. But noble Odysseus marked it, and filled a cup with wine and pledged Achilles: "Hail, O Achilles! The fair feast lack we not either in the hut of Agamemnon son of Atreus neither now in thine; for feasting is there abundance to our heart's desire, but our thought is not for matters of the delicious feast; nay, we behold very sore destruction, thou fosterling of Zeus, and are afraid. Now is it in doubt whether we save the benched ships or behold them perish, if thou put not on thy might. Nigh unto ships and wall have the high-hearted Trojans and famed allies pitched their camp, and kindled many fires throughout their host, and ween that they shall no more be withheld but will fall on our black ships. And Zeus son of Kronos sheweth them signs upon the right by lightning, and Hector greatly exulteth in his might and rageth furiously, trusting in Zeus, and recketh not of god nor man, for mighty madness hath possessed him. He prayeth bright Dawn to shine forth with all speed, for he hath passed his word to smite off from the ships the ensigns' tops, and to fire the hulls with devouring flame, and hard thereby to make havoc of the Achaians confounded by the smoke. Therefore am I sore afraid in my heart lest the gods fulfil his boastings, and it be fated for us to perish here in Troy-land, far from Argos pasture-land of horses. Up then! if thou art minded even at the last to save the failing sons of the Achaians from the war-din of the Trojans. Eschew thy grievous wrath; Agamemnon offereth thee worthy gifts, so thou wilt cease from anger. Lo now, hearken thou to me, and I will tell thee all the gifts that in his hut Agamemnon promised thee. But if Agamemnon be too hateful to thy heart, both he and his gifts, yet have thou pity on all the Achaians that faint throughout the host; these shall honour thee as a god, for verily thou wilt earn exceeding great glory at their hands. Yea now mightest thou slay Hector, for he would come very near thee in his deadly madness, because he deemeth that there is no man like unto him among the Danaans that the ships brought hither."

And Achilles fleet of foot answered and said unto him: "Heaven-sprung son of Laertes, Odysseus of many wiles, in openness must I now declare unto you my saying, even as I am minded and as the fulfilment thereof shall be, that ye may not sit before me and coax this way and that. For hateful to me even as the gates of hell is he that hideth one thing in his heart and uttereth another: but I will speak what meseemeth best. Not me, I ween, shall Agamemnon son of Atreus persuade, nor the other Danaans, seeing we were to have no thank for battling with the foemen ever without respite. He that abideth at home hath equal share with him that fighteth his best, and in like honour are held both the coward and the brave; death cometh alike to the untoiling and to him that hath toiled long. Neither have I any profit for that I endured tribulation of soul, ever staking my life in fight. Even as a hen bringeth her unfledged chickens each morsel as she winneth it, and with herself it goeth hard, even so I was wont to watch out many a sleepless night and pass through many bloody days of battle, warring with folk for their women's sake. Twelve cities of men have I laid waste from ship-board, and from land eleven, throughout deep-soiled Troy-land; out of all these took I many goodly treasures and would bring and give them all to Agamemnon son of Atreus, and he staying behind amid the fleet ships would take them and portion out some few but keep the most. Now some he gave to be meeds of honour to the princes and the kings, and theirs are left untouched; only from me of all the Achaians took he my darling lady and keepeth her. But why must the Argives make war on the Trojans? why hath Atreides gathered his host and led them hither? is it not for lovely-haired Helen's sake? Do then the sons of Atreus alone of mortal men love their wives? surely whatsoever man is good and sound of mind loveth his own and cherisheth her, even as I too loved mine with all my heart, though but the captive of my spear. But now that he hath taken my meed of honour from mine arms and hath deceived me, let him not tempt me that know him full well; he shall not prevail. Nay, Odysseus, let him take counsel with thee and all the princes to ward from the ships the consuming fire. Verily without mine aid he hath wrought many things, and built a wall and dug a foss about it wide and deep, and set a palisade therein; yet even so can he not stay murderous Hector's might. But so long as I was fighting amid the Achaians, Hector had no mind to array his battle far from the wall, but scarce came unto the Skaian gates and to the oak-tree; there once he awaited me alone and scarce escaped my onset. But now, seeing I have no mind to fight with noble Hector, I will to-morrow do sacrifice to Zeus and all the gods, and store well my ships when I have launched them on the salt sea—then shalt thou see, if thou wilt and hast any care therefor, my ships sailing at break of day over Hellespont, the fishes' home, and my men right eager at the oar; and if the great Shaker of the Earth grant me good journey, on the third day should I reach deep-soiled Phthia. There are my great possessions that I left when I came hither to my hurt; and yet more gold and ruddy bronze shall I bring from hence, and fair-girdled women and grey iron, all at least that were mine by lot; only my meed of honour hath he that gave it me taken back in his despitefulness, even lord Agamemnon son of Atreus. To him declare ye everything even as I charge you, openly, that all the Achaians likewise may have indignation, if haply he hopeth to beguile yet some other Danaan, for that he is ever clothed in shamelessness. Verily not in my face would he dare to look, though he have the front of a dog. Neither will I devise counsel with him nor any enterprise, for utterly he hath deceived me and done wickedly; but never again shall he beguile me with fair speech—let this suffice him. Let him begone in peace; Zeus the lord of counsel hath taken away his wits. Hateful to me are his gifts, and I hold him at a straw's worth. Not even if he gave me ten times, yea twenty, all that now is his, and all that may come to him otherwhence, even all the revenue of Orchomenos or Egyptian Thebes where the treasure-houses are stored fullest—Thebes of the hundred gates, whence sally forth two hundred warriors through each with horses and chariots—nay, nor gifts in number as sand or dust; not even so shall Agamemnon persuade my soul till he have paid me back all the bitter despite. And the daughter of Agamemnon son of Atreus will I not wed, not were she rival of golden Aphrodite for fairness and for handiwork matched bright-eyed Athene—not even then will I wed her; let him choose him of the Achaians another that is his peer and is more royal than I. For if the gods indeed preserve me and I come unto my home, then will Peleus himself seek me a wife. Many Achaian maidens are there throughout Hellas and Phthia, daughters of princes that ward their cities; whomsoever of these I wish will I make my dear lady. Very often was my high soul moved to take me there a wedded wife, a help meet for me, and have joy of the possessions that the old man Peleus possesseth. For not of like worth with life hold I even all the wealth that men say was possessed of the well-peopled city of Ilios in days of peace gone by, before the sons of the Achaians came; neither all the treasure that the stone threshold of the archer Phoebus Apollo encompasseth in rocky Pytho. For kine and goodly flocks are to be had for the harrying, and tripods and chestnut horses for the purchasing; but to bring back man's life neither harrying nor earning availeth when once it hath passed the barrier of his lips. For thus my goddess mother telleth me, Thetis the silver-footed, that twain fates are bearing me to the issue of death. If I abide here and besiege the Trojans' city, then my returning home is taken from me, but my fame shall be imperishable; but if I go home to my dear native land, my high fame is taken from me, but my life shall endure long while, neither shall the issue of death soon reach me. Moreover I would counsel you all to set sail homeward, seeing ye shall never reach your goal of steep Ilios; of a surety far-seeing Zeus holdeth his hand over her and her folk are of good courage. So go your way and tell my answer to the princes of the Achaians, even as is the office of elders, that they may devise in their hearts some other better counsel, such as shall save them their ships and the host of the Achaians amid the hollow ships: since this counsel availeth them naught that they have now devised, by reason of my fierce wrath. But let Phoinix now abide with us and lay him to rest, that he may follow with me on my ships to our dear native land to-morrow, if he will; for I will not take him perforce."

So spake he, and they all held their peace and were still, and marvelled at his saying; for he denied them very vehemently. But at the last spake to them the old knight Phoinix, bursting into tears, because he was sore afraid for the ships of the Achaians: "If indeed thou ponderest departure in thy heart, glorious Achilles, and hast no mind at all to save the fleet ships from consuming fire, because that wrath bath entered into thy heart; how can I be left of thee, dear son, alone thereafter? To thee did the old knight Peleus send me the day he sent thee to Agamemnon forth from Phthia, a stripling yet unskilled in equal war and in debate wherein men wax pre-eminent. Therefore sent he me to teach thee all these things, to be both a speaker of words and a doer of deeds. Yea, I reared thee to this greatness, thou godlike Achilles, with my heart's love; for with none other wouldest thou go unto the feast, neither take meat in the hall, till that I had set thee upon my knees and stayed thee with the savoury morsel cut first for thee, and put the wine-cup to thy lips. Oft hast thou stained the doublet on my breast with sputtering of wine in thy sorry helplessness. Thus I suffered much with thee, and much I toiled, being mindful that the gods in nowise created any issue of my body; but I made thee my son, thou godlike Achilles, that thou mayest yet save me from grievous destruction. Therefore, Achilles, rule thy high spirit; neither beseemeth it thee to have a ruthless heart. Nay, even the very gods can bend, and theirs withal is loftier majesty and honour and might. Nay, come for the gifts; the Achaians shall honour thee even as a god. But if without gifts thou enter into battle the bane of men, thou wilt not be held in like honour, even though thou avert the fray."

And Achilles fleet of foot made answer and said to him: "Phoinix my father, thou old man fosterling of Zeus, such honour need I in no wise; for I deem that I have been honoured by the judgment of Zeus, which shall abide upon me amid my beaked ships as long as breath tarrieth in my body and my limbs are strong. Moreover I will say this thing to thee and lay thou it to thine heart; trouble not my soul by weeping and lamentation, to do the pleasure of warrior Atreides; neither beseemeth it thee to cherish him, lest thou be hated of me that cherish thee. It were good that thou with me shouldest vex him that vexeth me. Be thou king even as I, and share my sway by halves, but these shall bear my message. So tarry thou here and lay thee to rest in a soft bed, and with break of day will we consider whether to depart unto our own, or to abide."

He spake, and nodded his brow in silence unto Patroklos to spread for Phoinix a thick couch, that the others might bethink them to depart from the hut with speed. Then spake to them Aias, Telamon's godlike son, and said: "Heaven-sprung son of Laertes, Odysseus of many wiles, let us go hence; for methinks the purpose of our charge will not by this journey be accomplished; and we must tell the news, though it be no wise good, with all speed unto the Danaans, that now sit awaiting. But Achilles hath wrought his proud soul to fury within him—stubborn man, that recketh naught of his comrades' love, wherein we worshipped him beyond all men amid the ships—unmerciful! Yet doth a man accept recompense of his brother's murderer or for his dead son; and so the man-slayer for a great price abideth in his own land, and the kinsman's heart is appeased, and his proud soul, when he hath taken the recompense. But for thee, the gods have put within thy breast a spirit implacable and evil, by reason of one single damsel. And now we offer thee seven damsels, far best of all, and many other gifts besides; entertain thou then a kindly spirit, and have respect unto thine home; because we are guests of thy roof, sent of the multitude of Danaans, and we would fain be nearest to thee and dearest beyond all other Achaians, as many as there be."

And Achilles fleet of foot made answer and said to him: "Aias sprung of Zeus, thou son of Telamon, prince of the folk, thou seemest to speak all this almost after mine own mind; but my heart swelleth with wrath as oft as I bethink me of those things, how Atreides entreated me arrogantly among the Argives, as though I were some worthless sojourner. But go ye and declare my message; I will not take thought of bloody war until that wise Priam's son, noble Hector, come to the Myrmidons' huts and ships, slaying the Argives, and smirch the ships with fire. But about mine hut and black ship I ween that Hector, though he be very eager for battle, shall be refrained."

So said he, and they took each man a two-handled cup, and made libation and went back along the line of ships; and Odysseus led the way.

And Patroklos bade his fellows and handmaidens spread with all speed a thick couch for Phoinix; and they obeyed and spread a couch as he ordained, fleeces and rugs and fine flock of linen. Then the old man laid him down and tarried for bright Dawn.

Now when those were come unto Atreides' huts, the sons of the Achaians stood up on this side and on that, and pledged them in cups of gold, and questioned them; and Agamemnon king of men asked them first: "Come now, tell me, Odysseus full of praise, thou great glory of the Achaians; will he save the ships from consuming fire, or said he nay, and hath wrath yet hold of his proud spirit?"

And steadfast goodly Odysseus answered him: "Most noble son of Atreus, Agamemnon king of men, he yonder hath no mind to quench his wrath, but is yet more filled of fury, and spurneth thee and thy gifts. He biddeth thee take counsel for thyself amid the Argives, how to save the ships and folk of the Achaians. And for himself he threateneth that at break of day he will launch upon the sea his trim well-benched ships. Moreover he said that he would counsel all to sail for home, because ye now shall never reach your goal of steep Ilios; surely far-seeing Zeus holdeth his hand over her and her folk are of good courage. Even so said he, and here are also these to tell the tale that were my companions, Aias and the two heralds, both men discreet. But the old man Phoinix laid him there to rest, even as Achilles bade him, that he may follow with him on his ships to his dear native land to-morrow, if he will; for he will not take him perforce."

So said he, and they all held their peace and were still, marvelling at his saying, for he harangued very vehemently. Long were the sons of the Achaians voiceless for grief, but at the last Diomedes of the loud war-cry spake amid them: "Most noble son of Atreus, Agamemnon king of men, would thou hadst never besought Peleus' glorious son with offer of gifts innumerable; proud is he at any time, but now hast thou yet far more encouraged him in his haughtiness. Howbeit we will let him bide, whether he go or tarry; hereafter he shall fight, whenever his heart within him biddeth and god arouseth him. Come now, even as I shall say let us all obey. Go ye now to rest, full to your hearts' desire of meat and wine, wherein courage is and strength; but when fair rosy-fingered Dawn appeareth, array thou with all speed before the ships thy folk and horsemen, and urge them on; and fight thyself amid the foremost."

So said he, and all the princes gave assent, applauding the saying of Diomedes tamer of horses. And then they made libation and went every man to his hut, and there laid them to rest and took the boon of sleep.

Book X

How Diomedes and Odysseus slew Dolon, a spy of the Trojans, and themselves spied on the Trojan camp, and took the horses of Rhesos, the Thracian king.

Now beside the ships the other leaders of the whole Achaian host were sleeping all night long, by soft Sleep overcome, but Agamemnon son of Atreus, shepherd of the host, sweet Sleep held not, so many things he debated in his mind. And even as when the lord of fair-tressed Hera lighteneth, fashioning either a mighty rain unspeakable, or hail, or snow, when the flakes sprinkle all the ploughed lands, or fashioning perchance the wide mouth of bitter war, even so oft in his breast groaned Agamemnon, from the very deep of his heart, and his spirits trembled within him. And whensoever he looked toward that Trojan plain, he marvelled at the many fires that blazed in front of Ilios, and at the sound of flutes and pipes, and the noise of men; but whensoever to the ships he glanced and the host of the Achaians, then rent he many a lock clean forth from his head, to Zeus that is above, and greatly groaned his noble heart.

And this in his soul seemed to him the best counsel, to go first of all to Nestor son of Neleus, if perchance he might contrive with him some right device that should be for the warding off of evil from all the Danaans.

Then he rose, and did on his doublet about his breast, and beneath his shining feet he bound on fair sandals, and thereafter clad him in the tawny skin of a lion fiery and great, a skin that reached to the feet, and he grasped his spear.

And even in like wise did trembling fear take hold on Menelaos, (for neither on his eyelids did Sleep settle down,) lest somewhat should befall the Argives, who verily for his sake over wide waters were come to Troy-land, with fierce war in their thoughts.

With a dappled pard's akin first he covered his broad shoulders, and he raised and set on his head a casque of bronze, and took a spear in his strong hand. Then went he on his way to rouse his brother, that mightily ruled over all the Argives, and as a god was honoured by the people. Him found he harnessing his goodly gear about his shoulders, by the stern of the ship, and glad to his brother was his coming. Then Menelaos of the loud war-cry first accosted him: "Wherefore thus, dear brother, art thou arming? Wilt thou speed forth any of thy comrades to spy on the Trojans? Nay, terribly I fear lest none should undertake for thee this deed, even to go and spy out the foeman alone through the ambrosial night; needs must he be a man right hardy of heart."

Then the lord Agamemnon answered him and spake: "Need of good counsel have I and thou, Menelaos fosterling of Zeus, of counsel that will help and save the Argives and the ships, since the heart of Zeus hath turned again. Surely on the sacrifices of Hector hath he set his heart rather than on ours. For never did I see, nor heard any tell, that one man devised so many terrible deeds in one day, as Hector, dear to Zeus, hath wrought on the sons of the Achaians, unaided; though no dear son of a goddess is he, nor of a god. He hath done deeds that methinks will be a sorrow to the Argives, lasting and long, such evils hath he devised against the Achaians. But go now, run swiftly by the ships, and summon Aias and Idomeneus, but I will betake me to noble Nestor, and bid him arise, if perchance he will be fain to go to the sacred company of the sentinels and lay on them his command. For to him above others would they listen, for his own son is chief among the sentinels, he and the brother in arms of Idomeneus, even Meriones, for to them above all we entrusted this charge."

Then Menelaos of the loud war-cry answered him: "How meanest thou this word wherewith thou dost command and exhort me? Am I to abide there with them, waiting till thou comest, or run back again to thee when I have well delivered to them thy commandment?"

Then the king of men, Agamemnon, answered him again: "There do thou abide lest we miss each other as we go, for many are the paths through the camp. But call aloud, wheresoever thou goest, and bid men awake, naming each man by his lineage, and his father's name, and giving all their dues of honour, nor be thou proud of heart. Nay rather let us ourselves be labouring, for even thus did Zeus from our very birth dispense to us the heaviness of toil."

So he spake, and sent his brother away, having clearly laid on him his commandment. Then went he himself after Nestor, the shepherd of the host, whom he found by his hut and black ship, in his soft bed: beside him lay his arms, a shield, and two spears, and a shining helmet. Beside him lay his glittering girdle wherewith the old man was wont to gird himself when he harnessed him for war, the bane of men, and led on the host, for he yielded not to grievous old age. Then he raised him on his elbow, lifting his head, and spake to the son of Atreus, inquiring of him with this word: "Who art thou that farest alone by the ships, through the camp in the dark night, when other mortals are sleeping? Seekest thou one of thy mules, or of thy comrades? speak, and come not silently upon me. What need hast thou?"

Then the king of men, Agamemnon, answered him: "O Nestor, son of Neleus, great glory of the Achaians, thou shalt know Agamemnon, son of Atreus, whom above all men Zeus hath planted for ever among labours, while my breath abides within my breast, and my knees move. I wander thus, for that sweet sleep rests not on mine eyes, but war is my care, and the troubles of the Achaians. Yea, greatly I fear for the sake of the Danaans, nor is my heart firm, but I am tossed to and fro, and my heart is leaping from my breast, and my good knees tremble beneath me. But if thou wilt do aught, since neither on thee cometh sleep, let us go thither to the sentinels, that we may see them, lest they be fordone with toil, and so are slumbering, and have quite forgotten to keep watch. And hostile men camp hard by, nor know we at all but that they are keen to do battle in the night."

Then knightly Nestor of Gerenia answered him: "Verily will I follow after thee, but let us also rouse others again, both the son of Tydeus, spearman renowned, and Odysseus, and swift Aias, and the strong son of Phyleus. But well it would be if one were to go and call those also, the godlike Aias, and Idomeneus the prince; for their ships are furthest of all, and nowise close at hand. But Menelaos will I blame, dear as he is and worshipful, yea, even if thou be angry with me, nor will I hide my thought, for that he slumbereth, and to thee alone hath left the toil; now should he be toiling among all the chiefs and beseeching them, for need no longer tolerable is coming upon us."

And the king of men, Agamemnon, answered him again: "Old man, another day I even bid thee blame him, for often is he slack, and willeth not to labour, yielding neither to unreadiness nor heedlessness of heart, but looking toward me, and expecting mine instance. But now he awoke far before me, and came to me, and him I sent forward to call those concerning whom thou inquirest. But let us be gone, and them shall we find before the gates, among the sentinels, for there I bade them gather."

Then knightly Nestor of Gerenia answered him: "So will none of the Argives be wroth with him or disobey him, when soever he doth urge any one, and give him his commands."

So spake he, and did on his doublet about his breast, and beneath his bright feet he bound goodly shoon, and all around him buckled a purple cloak, with double folds and wide, and thick down all over it.

And he took a strong spear, pointed with sharp bronze, and he went among the ships of the mail-clad Achaians. Then Odysseus first, the peer of Zeus in counsel, did knightly Gerenian Nestor arouse out of sleep, with his voice, and quickly the cry came all about his heart, and he came forth from the hut and spake to them saying: "Wherefore thus among the ships and through the camp do ye wander alone, in the ambrosial night; what so great need cometh upon you?"

Then knightly Nestor of Gerenia answered him: "Laertes' son, be not wroth, for great trouble besetteth the Achaians. Nay follow, that we may arouse others too, even all that it behoveth to take counsel, whether we should fly, or fight."

So spake he, and Odysseus of the many counsels came to the hut, and cast a shield about his shoulders, and went after them.

And they went to seek Diomedes, son of Tydeus, and him they found outside his hut, with his arms, and around him his comrades were sleeping with their shields beneath their heads, but their spears were driven into the ground erect on the spikes of the butts, and afar shone the bronze, like the lightning of father Zeus. Now that hero was asleep, and under him was strewn the hide of an ox of the field, but beneath his head was stretched a shining carpet. Beside him went and stood knightly

Nestor of Gerenia and stirred him with a touch of his foot, and aroused him, chiding him to his face, saying: "Wake, son of Tydeus, why all night long dost thou sleep? Knowest thou not that the Trojans on the high place of the plain are camped near the ships, and but a little space holdeth them apart?"

So spake he, and Diomedes sprang swiftly up out of sleep, and spake to him winged words: "Hard art thou, old man, and from toil thou never ceasest. Now are there not other younger sons of the Achaians, who might rouse when there is need each of the kings, going all around the host? but thou, old man, art indomitable."

And him knightly Nestor of Gerenia answered again, "Nay verily, my son, all this that thou sayest is according unto right. Noble sons have I, and there be many of the host, of whom each man might go and call the others. But a right great need hath assailed the Achaians. For now to all of us it standeth on a razor's edge, either pitiful ruin for the Achaians, or life. But come now, if indeed thou dost pity me, rouse swift Aias, and the son of Phyleus, for thou art younger than I."

So spake he, and Diomedes cast round his shoulders the skin of a great fiery lion, that reached to his feet, and he grasped his spear, and started on his way, and roused the others from their place and led them on.

Now when they had come among the assembled sentinels, they found not the leaders of the sentinels asleep, but they all sat wide awake with their arms. And even as hounds keep difficult guard round the sheep in a fold, having heard a hardy wild beast that cometh through the wood among the hills, and much clamour riseth round him of hounds and men, and sleep perisheth from them, even so sweet sleep did perish from their eyes, as they watched through the wicked night, for ever were they turning toward the plains, when they heard the Trojans moving.

And that old man was glad when he saw them, and heartened them with his saying, and calling out to them he spake winged words: "Even so now, dear children, do ye keep watch, nor let sleep take any man, lest we become a cause of rejoicing to them that hate us."

So saying he sped through the moat, and they followed with him, the kings of the Argives, who had been called to the council. And with them went Meriones, and the glorious son of Nestor, for they called them to share their counsel. So they went clean out of the delved foss, and sat down in the open, where the mid-space was clear of dead men fallen, where fierce Hector had turned again from destroying the Argives, when night covered all. There sat they down, and declared their saying each to the other, and to them knightly Nestor of Gerenia began discourse: "O friends, is there then no man that would trust to his own daring spirit, to go among the great-hearted Trojans, if perchance he might take some straggler of the enemy, yea, or hear perchance some rumour among the Trojans, and what things they devise among themselves, whether they are fain to abide there by the ships, away from the city, or will retreat again to the city, now that they have conquered the Achaians? All this might such an one learn, and back to us come scathless: great would be his fame under heaven among all men, and a goodly gift will be given him. For all the best men that bear sway by the ships, each and all of them will give him a black ewe, with her lamb at her foot, and ever will he be present at feasts and clan-drinkings."

So spake he, and thereon were they all silent, holding their peace, but to them spake Diomedes of the loud war-cry: "Nestor, my heart and manful spirit urge me to enter the camp of the foemen hard by, even of the Trojans: and if some other man will follow with me, more comfort and more courage will there be. If two go together, one before another perceiveth a matter, how there may be gain therein; but if one alone perceive aught, even so his wit is shorter, and weak his device."

So spake he, and many were they that wished to follow Diomedes. The two Aiantes were willing, men of Ares' company, and Meriones was willing, and right willing the son of Nestor, and the son of Atreus, Menelaos, spearman renowned, yea and the hardy Odysseus was willing to steal into the throng of Trojans, for always daring was his heart within him. But among them spake the king of men, Agamemnon: "Diomedes son of Tydeus, joy of mine heart, thy comrade verily shalt thou choose, whomsoever thou wilt, the best of them that be here, for many are eager. But do not thou, out of reverent heart, leave the better man behind, and give thyself the worse companion, yielding to regard for any, and looking to their lineage, even if one be more kingly born."

So spake he, but was in fear for the sake of fair-haired Menelaos. But to them again answered Diomedes of the loud war-cry: "If indeed ye bid me choose myself a comrade, how then could I be unmindful of godlike Odysseus, whose heart is passing eager, and his spirit so manful in all manner of toils; and Athene loveth him. But while he cometh with me, even out of burning fire might we both return, for he excelleth in understanding."

Then him again answered the steadfast noble Odysseus: "Son of Tydeus, praise me not overmuch, neither blame me aught, for thou speakest thus among the Argives that themselves know all. But let us be going, for truly the night is waning, and near is the dawn, and the stars have gone onward, and the night has advanced more than two watches, but the third watch is yet left."

So spake they, and harnessed them in their dread armour. To the son of Tydeus did Thrasymedes steadfast in war give a two-edged sword (for his own was left by his ship) and a shield, and about his head set a helm of bull's hide, without cone or crest, that is called a skull-cap, and keeps the heads of stalwart youths. And Meriones gave Odysseus a bow and a quiver, and a sword, and on his head set a helm made of leather, and with many a thong was it stiffly wrought within, while without the white teeth of a boar of flashing tusks were arrayed thick set on either side, well and cunningly, and in the midst was fixed a cap of felt.

So when these twain had harnessed them in their dread armour, they set forth to go, and left there all the best of the host. And to them did Pallas Athene send forth an omen on the right, a heron hard by the way, and they beheld it not with their eyes, through the dark night, but they heard its shrill cry. And Odysseus was glad in the omen of the bird, and prayed to Athene: "Listen to me, thou child of aegis-bearing Zeus, that ever in all toils dost stand by me, nor doth any motion of mine escape thee: but now again above all be thou friendly to me, Athene, and grant that we come back with renown to the ships, having wrought a great work, that shall be sorrow to the Trojans."

Next again prayed Diomedes of the loud war-cry: "Listen now likewise to me, thou child of Zeus, unwearied maiden, and follow with me as when with my father thou didst follow, even noble Tydeus, into Thebes, when he went forth as a messenger from the Achaians. Even so now stand thou by me willingly, and protect me. And to thee will I sacrifice a yearling heifer, broad of brow, unbroken, that never yet hath man led below the yoke. Her will I sacrifice to thee, and gild her horns with gold."

So spake they in their prayer, and Pallas Athene heard them. And when they had prayed to the daughter of mighty Zeus, they went forth on their way, like two lions, through the dark night, amid the slaughter, amid the slain men, through the arms and the black blood.

Nay, nor the stout-hearted Trojans did Hector suffer to sleep, but he called together all the best of them, all that were chiefs and leaders of the Trojans, them did he call together, and contrived a crafty counsel: "Who is there that would promise and perform for me this deed, for a great gift? yea his reward shall be sufficient. For I will give him a chariot, and two horses of arching neck, the best that be at the swift ships of the Achaians, to whosoever shall dare the deed, and for himself shall win glory. And the deed is this; to go near the swift-faring ships, and seek out whether the swift ships are guarded, as of old, or whether already, being subdued beneath our hands, the foes are devising of flight among themselves, and have no care to watch through the night, being fordone with dread weariness."

So spake he, but they were all silent and held their peace. Now there was among the Trojans one Dolon, the son of Eumedes the godlike herald, and he was rich in gold, and rich in bronze: and verily he was ill favoured to look upon, but swift of foot. So he spake then a word to the Trojans and to Hector: "Hector, my heart and manful spirit urge me to go near the swift-faring ships, and spy out all. But come, I pray thee, hold up the staff, and swear to me, that verily thou wilt give me the horses and the chariots bedight with bronze that bear the noble son of Peleus. But to thee I will prove no vain spy, nor disappoint thy hope. For I will go straight to the camp, until I may come to the ship of Agamemnon, where surely the chiefs are like to hold council, whether to fight or flee."

So spake he, and Hector took the staff in his hand, and sware to him: "Now let Zeus himself be witness, the loud-thundering lord of Hera, that no other man of the Trojans shall mount those horses, but thou, I declare, shalt rejoice in them for ever."

So spake he, and sware a bootless oath thereto, and aroused Dolon to go. And straightway he cast on his shoulders his crooked bow, and did on thereover the skin of a grey wolf, and on his head a helm of ferret-skin, and took a sharp javelin, and went on his way to the ships from the host. But he was not like to come back from the ships and bring word to Hector.

But when he had left the throng of men and horses, he went forth eagerly on the way, and Odysseus of the seed of Zeus was ware of him as he approached, and said unto Diomedes: "Lo, here is some man, Diomedes, coming from the camp, I know not whether as a spy to our ships, or to strip certain of the dead men fallen. But let us suffer him to pass by us a little way on the plain, and thereafter may we rush on him and take him speedily, and if it chance that he outrun us by speed of foot, ever do thou hem him in towards the ships and away from the camp, rushing on him with thy spear, lest in any wise he escape towards the city."

So they spake, and turning out of the path they lay down among the bodies of the dead; and swiftly Dolon ran past them in his witlessness. But when he was as far off as is the length of the furrow made by mules, these twain ran after him, and he stood still when he heard the sound, supposing in his heart that they were friends come from among the Trojans to turn him back, at the countermand of Hector. But when they were about a spear-cast off, or even less, he knew them for foe-men, and stirred his swift limbs to fly, and speedily they started in pursuit.

And as when two sharp-toothed hounds, well skilled in the chase, press ever hard on a doe or a hare through a wooded land, and it runs screaming before them, even so Tydeus' son and Odysseus the sacker of cities cut Dolon off from the host, and ever pursued hard after him. But when he was just about to come among the sentinels, in his flight towards the ships, then Athene poured strength into the son of Tydeus, that none of the mail-clad Achaians might boast himself the first to smite, and he come second. And strong Diomedes leaped upon him with the spear, and said: "Stand, or I shall overtake thee with the spear, and methinks that thou shalt not long avoid sheer destruction at my hand."

So spake he, and threw his spear, but of his own will he missed the man, and passing over his right shoulder the point of the polished spear stuck fast in the ground: and Dolon stood still, in great dread and trembling, and the teeth chattered in his mouth, and he was green with fear. Then the twain came up with him, panting, and gripped his hands, and weeping he spake: "Take me alive, and I will ransom myself, for within our house there is bronze, and gold, and smithied iron, wherefrom my father would do you grace with ransom untold, if he should learn that I am alive among the ships of the Achaians."

Then Odysseus of the many counsels answered him and said: "Take courage, let not death be in thy mind, but come speak and tell me truly all the tale, why thus from the host lost thou come all alone among the ships, through the black night, when other mortals are sleeping? Comest thou to strip certain of the dead men fallen, or did Hector send thee forth to spy out everything at the hollow ships, or did thine own spirit urge thee on?"

Then Dolon answered him, his limbs trembling beneath him: "With many a blind hope did Hector lead my wits astray, who vowed to give me the whole-hooved horses of the proud son of Peleus, and his car bedight with bronze: and he bade me fare through the swift black night, and draw nigh the foemen, and seek out whether the swift ships are guarded, as of old, or whether, already, being subdued beneath our hands, they are devising of flight among themselves, and have no care to watch through the night, being fordone with dread weariness."

And smiling thereat did Odysseus of the many counsels make him answer: "Verily now thy soul was set on great rewards, even the horses of the wise son of Aiakos, but hard are they for mortal men to master, and hard to drive, for any but Achilles only, whom a deathless mother bare. But come, tell me all this truly, all the tale: where when thou camest hither didst thou leave Hector, shepherd of the host, and where lie his warlike gear, and where his horses? And how are disposed the watches, and the beds of the other Trojans? And what counsel take they among themselves; are they fain to abide there nigh the ships afar from the city, or will they return to the city again, seeing that they have subdued unto them the Achaiana?"

Then Dolon son of Eumedes made him answer again: "Lo, now all these things will I recount to thee most truly. Hector with them that are counsellors holdeth council by the barrow of godlike Ilos, apart from the din, but as for the guards whereof thou askest, oh hero, no chosen watch nor guard keepeth the host. As for all the watch fires of the Trojans—on them is necessity, so that they watch and encourage each other to keep guard; but, for the allies called from many lands, they are sleeping and to the Trojans they leave it to keep watch, for no wise near dwell the children and wives of the allies." Then Odysseus of the many counsels answered him and said: "How stands it now, do they sleep amidst the horse-taming Trojans, or apart? tell me clearly, that I may know."

Then answered him Dolon son of Eumedes: "Verily all this likewise will I recount to thee truly. Towards the sea lie the Karians, and Paionians of the bended bow, and the Leleges and Kaukones, and noble Pelasgoi. And towards Thymbre the Lykians have their place, and the haughty Mysians, and the Phrygians that fight from chariots, and Maionians lords of chariots. But wherefore do ye inquire of me throughly concerning all these things? for if ye desire to steal into the throng of Trojans, lo, there be those Thracians, new comers, at the furthest point apart from the rest, and among them their king Rhesos, son of Eioneus. His be the fairest horses that ever I beheld, and the greatest, whiter than snow, and for speed like the winds. And his chariot is fashioned well with gold and silver, and golden is his armour that he brought with him, marvellous, a wonder to behold; such as it is in no wise fit for mortal men to bear, but for the deathless gods. But bring me now to the swift ships, or leave me here, when ye have bound me with a ruthless bond, that ye may go and make trial of me whether I have spoken to you truth, or lies."

Then strong Diomedes, looking grimly on him, said: "Put no thought of escape, Dolon, in thy heart, for all the good tidings thou hast brought, since once thou halt come into our hands. For if now we release thee or let thee go, on some later day wilt thou come to the swift ships of the Achaians, either to play the spy, or to fight in open war, but if subdued beneath my hands thou lose thy life, never again wilt thou prove a bane to the Argives."

He spake, and that other with strong hand was about to touch his chin, and implore his mercy, but Diomedes smote him on the midst of the neck, rushing on him with the sword, and cut through both the sinews, and the head of him still speaking was mingled with the dust. And they stripped him of the casque of ferret's skin from off his head, and of his wolf-skin, and his bended bow, and his long spear, and these to Athene the Giver of Spoil did noble Odysseus hold aloft in his hand, and he prayed and spake a word: "Rejoice, O goddess, in these, for to thee first of all the immortals in Olympus will we call for aid; nay, but yet again send us on against the horses and the sleeping places of the Thracian men."

So spake he aloud, and lifted from him the spoils on high, and set them on a tamarisk bush, and raised thereon a mark right plain to see, gathering together reeds, and luxuriant shoots of tamarisk, lest they should miss the place as they returned again through the swift dark night.

So the twain went forward through the arms, and the black blood, and quickly they came to the company of Thracian men. Now they were slumbering, fordone with toil, but their goodly weapons lay by them on the ground, all orderly, in three rows, and by each man his pair of steeds. And Rhesos slept in the midst, and beside him his swift horses were bound with thongs to the topmost rim of the chariot. Him Odysseus spied from afar, and showed him unto Diomedes: "Lo, Diomedes, this is the man, and these are the horses whereof Dolon that we slew did give us tidings. But come now, put forth thy great strength; it doth not behove thee to stand idle with thy weapons: nay, loose the horses; or do thou slay the men, and of the horses will I take heed."

So spake he, and into that other bright-eyed Athene breathed might, and he began slaying on this side and on that, and hideously went up their groaning, as they were smitten with the sword, and the earth was reddened with blood. And like as a lion cometh on flocks without a herdsman, on goats or sheep, and leaps upon them with evil will, so set the son of Tydeus on the men of Thrace, till he had slain twelve. But whomsoever the son of Tydeus drew near and smote with the sword, him did Odysseus of the many counsels seize by the foot from behind, and drag him out of the way, with this design in his heart, that the fair-maned horses might lightly issue forth, and not tremble in spirit, when they trod over the dead; for they were not yet used to dead men. But when the son of Tydeus came upon the king, he was the thirteenth from whom he took sweet life away, as he was breathing hard, for an evil dream stood above his head that night through the device of Athens. Meanwhile the hardy Odysseus loosed the whole-hooved horses, and bound them together with thongs, and drave them out of the press, smiting them with his bow, since he had not taken thought to lift the shining whip with his hands from the chariot; then he whistled for a sign to noble Diomedes.

But Diomedes stood and pondered what most daring deed he might do, whether he should take the chariot, where lay the armour, and drag it out by the pole, or lift it upon high, and so bear it forth, or whether he should take the life away from yet more of the Thracians. And while he was pondering this in his heart, then Athene drew near, and stood, and spake to noble Diomedes: "Bethink thee of returning, O son of great-hearted Tydeus, to the hollow ships, lest perchance thou come thither in flight, and perchance another god rouse up the Trojans likewise."

So spake she, and he observed the voice of the utterance of the goddess, and swiftly he sprang upon the steeds, and Odysseus smote them with his bow, and they sped to the swift ships of the Achaians.

Nay, nor a vain watch kept Apollo of the silver bow, when he beheld Athene caring for the son of Tydeus; in wrath against her he stole among the crowded press of Trojans, and aroused a counsellor of the Thracians, Hippokoon, the noble kinsman of Rhesos. And he started out of sleep, when he beheld the place desolate where the swift horses had stood, and beheld the men gasping in the death struggle; then he groaned aloud, and called out by name to his comrade dear. And a clamour arose and din unspeakable of the Trojans hasting together, and they marvelled at the terrible deeds, even all that the heroes had wrought, and had gone thereafter to the hollow ships.

But when those others came to the place where they had slain the spy of Hector, there Odysseus, dear to Zeus, checked the swift horses, and Tydeus' son, leaping to the ground, set the bloody spoil in the hands of Odysseus, and again mounted, and lashed the horses, and they sped onward nothing loth. But Nestor first heard the sound, and said: "O friends, leaders and counsellors of the Argives, shall I be wrong or speak sooth? for my heart bids me speak. The sound of swift-footed horses strikes upon mine ears. Would to god that Odysseus and that strong

Diomedes may even instantly be driving the whole-hooved horses from among the Trojans; but terribly I fear in mine heart lest the bravest of the Argives suffer aught through the Trojans' battle din."

Not yet was his whole word spoken, when they came themselves, and leaped down to earth, but gladly the others welcomed them with hand-clasping, and with honeyed words. And first did knightly Nestor of Gerenia make question: "Come, tell me now, renowned Odysseus, great glory of the Achaians, how ye twain took those horses? Was it by stealing into the press of Trojans? Or did some god meet you, and give you them? Wondrous like are they to rays of the sun. Ever with the Trojans do I mix in fight, nor methinks do I tarry by the ships, old warrior as I am. But never yet saw I such horses, nor deemed of such. Nay, methinks some god must have encountered you and given you these. For both of you doth Zeus the cloud-gatherer love, and the maiden of aegis-bearing Zeus, bright-eyed Athene."

And him answered Odysseus of the many counsels: "O Nestor, son of Neleus, great glory of the Achaians, lightly could a god, if so he would, give even better steeds than these, for the gods are far stronger than we. But as for these new-come horses, whereof, old man, thou askest me, they are Thracian, but their lord did brave Diomedes slay, and beside him all the twelve best men of his company. The thirteenth man was a spy we took near the ships, one that Hector and the other haughty Trojans sent forth to pry upon our camp."

So spake he, and drave the whole-hooved horses through the foss, laughing; and the other Achaians went with him joyfully. But when they had come to the well-built hut of the son of Tydeus, they bound the horses with well-cut thongs, at the mangers where the swift horses of Diomedes stood eating honey-sweet barley.

And Odysseus placed the bloody spoils of Dolon in the stern of the ship, that they might make ready a sacred offering to Athene. But for themselves, they went into the sea, and washed off the thick sweat from shins, and neck, and thighs. But when the wave of the sea had washed the thick sweat from their skin, and their hearts revived again, they went into polished baths, and were cleansed.

And when they had washed, and anointed them with olive oil, they sat down at supper, and from the full mixing bowl they drew off the honey-sweet wine, and poured it forth to Athene.

BOOK XI

Despite the glorious deeds of Agamemnon, the Trojans press hard on the Achaians, and the beginning of evil comes on Patroklos.

Now Dawn arose from her couch beside proud Tithonos, to bring light to the immortals and to mortal men. But Zeus sent forth fierce Discord unto the fleet ships of the Achaians, and in her hands she held the signal of war. And she stood upon the huge black ship of Odysseus, that was in the midst, to make her voice heard on either side, both to the huts of Aias, son of Telamon, and to the huts of Achilles, for these twain, trusting in their valour and the might of their hands, had drawn up their trim ships at the two ends of the line. There stood the goddess and cried shrilly in a great voice and terrible, and mighty strength she set in the heart of each of the Achaians, to war and fight unceasingly. And straightway to them war grew sweeter than to depart in the hollow ships to their dear native land.

Then each man gave in charge his horses to his charioteer, to hold them in by the foss, well and orderly, and themselves as heavy men at arms were hasting about, being harnessed in their gear, and unquenchable the cry arose into the Dawn. And long before the charioteers were they arrayed at the foss, but after them a little way came up the drivers. And among them the son of Kronos aroused an evil din, and from above rained down dew danked with blood out of the upper air, for that he was about to send many strong men down to Hades.

But the Trojans on the other side, on the high ground of the plain, gathered them around great Hector, and noble Polydamus, and Aineias that as a god was honoured by the people of the Trojans, and the three sons of Antenor, Polybos, and noble Agenor, and young Akamas like unto the immortals. And Hector in the foremost rank bare the circle of his shield. And as from amid the clouds appeareth glittering a baneful star, and then again sinketh within the shadowy clouds, even so Hector would now appear among the foremost ranks, and again would be giving command in the rear, and all in bronze he shone, like the lightning of aegis-bearing father Zeus.

And even as when reapers over against each other drive their swaths through a rich man's field of wheat or barley, and thick fall the handfuls, even so the Trojans and Achaians leaped upon each other, destroying, and neither side took thought of ruinous flight; and equal heads had the battle, and they rushed on like wolves. And woful Discord was glad at the sight, for she alone of the gods was with them in the war; for the other gods were not beside them, but in peace they sat within their halls, where the goodly mansion of each was builded in the folds of Olympus. And they all were blaming the son of Kronos, lord of the storm-cloud, for that he willed to give glory to the Trojans. But of them took the father no heed, but aloof from the others he sat apart, glad in his glory, looking toward the city of the Trojans, and the ships of the Achaians, and the glitter of bronze, and the slayers and the slain.

So long as morning was, and the sacred day still waxed, so long did the shafts of both hosts strike, and the folk fell, but about the hour when a woodman maketh ready his meal, in the dells of a mountain, when he hath tired his hands with felling tall trees, and weariness cometh on his soul, and desire of sweet food taketh his heart, even then the Danaans by their valour brake the battalions, and called on their comrades through the lines. And in rushed Agamemnon first of all, where thickest clashed the battalions, there he set on, and with him all the well-greaved Achaians. Footmen kept slaying footmen as they were driven in flight, and horsemen slaying horsemen with the sword, and from beneath them rose up the dust from the plain, stirred by the thundering hooves of horses. And the lord Agamemnon, ever slaying, followed after, calling on the Argives. And as when ruinous fire falleth on dense woodland, and the whirling wind beareth it everywhere, and the thickets fall utterly before it, being smitten by the onset of the fire, even so beneath Agamemnon son of Atreus fell the heads of the Trojans as they fled; and many strong-necked horses rattled empty cars along the highways of the battle, lacking their noble charioteers; but they on the earth were lying, far more dear to the vultures than to their wives. But Hector did Zeus draw forth from the darts and the dust, from the man-slaying, and the blood, and the din, and the son of Atreus followed on, crying eagerly to the Danaans. And past the tomb of ancient Ilos, son of Dardanos, across the mid plain, past the place of the wild fig-tree they sped, making for the city, and ever the son of Atreus followed shouting, and his invincible hands were defiled with gore. But when they were come to the Skaian gates, and the oak-tree, there then they halted, and awaited each other. But some were still in full flight through the mid plain, like kine that a lion hath scattered, coming on them in the dead of night; all hath he scattered, but to one sheer death appeareth instantly, and he breaketh her neck first, seizing her with strong teeth, and thereafter swalloweth greedily the blood and all the guts; even so lord Agamemnon son of Atreus followed hard on the Trojans, ever slaying the hindmost man, and they were scattered in flight, and on face or back many of them fell from their chariots beneath the hands of Agamemnon, for mightily he raged with the spear. But when he was nowabout coming below the city, and the steep wall, then did the father of men and gods sit him down on the crests of many-fountained Ida, from heaven descending, with the thunderbolt in his hands.

Then sent he forth Iris of the golden wings, to bear his word: "Up and go, swift Iris, and tell this word unto Hector: So long as he sees Agamemnon, shepherd of the host, raging among the foremost fighters, and ruining the ranks of men, so long let him hold back, but bid the rest of the host war with the foe in strong battle. But when, or smitten with the spear or wounded with arrow shot, Agamemnon leapeth into his chariot, then will I give Hector strength to slay till he come even to the well-timbered ships, and the sun go down, and sacred darkness draw on."

So swift-footed Iris spake to Hector the words of Zeus and departed, but Hector with his harness leaped from the chariot to the ground, and, shaking his sharp spears went through all the host, stirring up his men to fight, and he roused the dread din of battle. And they wheeled round, and stood and faced the Achaians, while the Argives on the other side strengthened their battalions. And battle was made ready, and they stood over against each other, and Agamemnon first rushed in, being eager to fight far in front of all.

Tell me now, ye Muses that inhabit mansions in Olympus, who was he that first encountered Agamemnon, whether of the Trojans themselves, or of their allies renowned? It was Iphidamas, son of Antenor, great and mighty, who was nurtured in Thrace rich of soil, the mother of sheep; he it was that then encountered Agamemnon son of Atreus. And when they were come near in onset against each other, Atreus' son missed, and his spear was turned aside, but Iphidamas smote him on the girdle, below the corslet, and himself pressed on, trusting to his heavy hand, but pierced not the gleaming girdle, for long ere that the point struck on the silver, and was bent like lead. Then wide-ruling Agamemnon caught the spear with his hand and drew it toward him furiously, like a lion, and snatched it out of the hand of Iphidamas, and smote his neck with the sword, and unstrung his limbs. So even there he fell, and slept a sleep of bronze most piteously. Then did Agamemnon son of Atreus strip him, and went bearing his goodly harness into the throng of the Achaians.

Now when Koon beheld him, Koon Antenor's eldest son, illustrious among men, strong sorrow came on him, covering his eyes, for his brother's fall: and he stood on one side with his spear, and unmarked of noble Agamemnon smote him on the mid-arm, beneath the elbow, and clean through went the point of the shining spear. Then Agamemnon king of men shuddered, yet not even so did he cease from battle and war, but rushed against Koon, grasping his wind-nurtured spear. Verily then Koon seized right lustily by the foot Iphidamas, his brother, and his father's son, and called to all the best of his men; but him, as he dragged the dead through the press, beneath his bossy shield Agamemnon wounded with a bronze-shod spear, and unstrung his limbs, and drew near and cut off his head over Iphidamas. There the sons of Antenor, at the hands of Agamemnon the king, filled up the measure of their fate, and went down within the house of Hades.

But Agamemnon ranged among the ranks of men, with spear, and sword, and great stones for throwing, while yet the blood welled warm from his wound. But when the wound waxed dry, and the blood ceased to flow, then keen pangs came on the might of the son of Atreus. Then leaped he into his chariot, and bade his charioteer drive to the hollow ships, for he was sore vexed at heart. And he called in a piercing voice, and shouted to the Danaans: "O friends, leaders and counsellors of the Argives, do ye now ward from the seafaring ships the harsh din of battle, for Zeus the counsellor suffers me not all day to war with the Trojans."

So spake he, and his charioteer lashed the fair-maned steeds toward the hollow ships, and they flew onward nothing loth, and their breasts were covered with foam, and their bellies were stained with dust, as they bore the wounded king away from the war.

But Hector, when he beheld Agamemnon departed, cried to the Trojans and Lykians with a loud shout: "Ye Trojans and Lykians, and Dardanians that war in close fight, be men, my friends, and be mindful of your impetuous valour. The best man of them hath departed and to me hath Zeus, the son of Kronos, given great renown. But straightway drive ye the whole-hooved horses against the mighty Danaans, that ye may be the masters and bear away the higher glory."

So spake he, and aroused the might and spirit of every man. Himself with high thoughts he fared among the foremost, and fell upon the fight; like a roaring blast, that leapeth down and stirreth the violet-coloured deep. There whom first, whom last did he slay, even Hector, son of Priam, when Zeus vouchsafed him renown?

Asaios first, and Autonoos, and Opites, and Dolops, son of Klytios, and Opheltios, and Agelaos, and Aisymnos, and Oros, and Hipponoos steadfast in the fight; these leaders of the Danaans he slew, and thereafter smote the multitude, even as when the West Wind driveth the clouds of the white South Wind, smiting with deep storm, and the wave swelleth huge, rolling onward, and the spray is scattered on high beneath the rush of the wandering wind; even so many heads of the host were smitten by Hector.

There had ruin begun, and deeds remedeless been wrought, and now would all the Achaians have fled and fallen among the ships, if Odysseus had not called to Diomedes, son of Tydeus: "Tydeus' son, what ails us that we forget our impetuous valour? Nay, come hither, friend, and take thy stand by me, for verily it will be shame if Hector of the glancing helm take the ships."

And to him strong Diomedes spake in answer: "Verily will I abide and endure, but short will be all our profit, for Zeus, the cloud-gatherer, clearly desireth to give victory to the Trojans rather than to us."

He spake, and drave Thymbraios from his chariot to the ground, smiting him with the spear in the left breast, and Odysseus smote Molion the godlike squire of that prince. These then they let be, when they had made them cease from war, and then the twain fared through the crowd with a din, as when two boars full of valour fall on the hunting hounds; so rushed they on again, and slew the Trojans, while gladly the Achaians took breath again in their flight from noble Hector.

But Hector quickly spied them among the ranks, and rushed upon them shouting, and with him followed the battalions of the Trojans. And beholding him, Diomedes of the loud war-cry shuddered, and straightway spake to Odysseus that was hard by: "Lo, on us this ruin, even mighty Hector, is rolling: let us stand, and await him, and ward off his onset."

So spake he, and swayed and sent forth his far-shadowing spear, and smote him nor missed, for he aimed at the head, on the summit of the crest, and bronze by bronze was turned, nor reached his fair flesh, for it was stopped by the threefold helm with its socket, that Phoebus Apollo to Hector gave. But Hector sprang back a wondrous way, and mingled with the throng, and he rested, fallen on his knee, and leaned on the ground with his stout hand, and dark night veiled his eyes.

But while Tydeus' son was following after his spear-cast, far through the foremost fighters, where he saw it sink into the earth, Hector gat breath again, and leaping back into his chariot drave out into the throng, and avoided black Fate. Then rushing on with his spear mighty Diomedes spake to him: "Dog, thou art now again escaped from death; yet came ill very nigh thee: but now hath Phoebus Apollo saved thee, to whom thou must surely pray when thou goest amid the clash of spears. Verily I will slay thee yet when I meet thee hereafter, if any god is helper of me too. Now will I make after the rest, whomsoever I may seize."

So spake he, and stripped the son of Paeon, spearman renowned. But Alexandros, the lord of fair-tressed Helen, aimed with his arrows at Tydeides, shepherd of the host; leaning as he aimed against a pillar on the barrow, by men fashioned, of Ilos, son of Dardanos, an elder of the people in time gone by. Now Diomedes was stripping the shining corslet of strong Agastrophos from about his breast, and the shield from his shoulders, and his strong helmet, when Paris drew the centre of his bow; nor vainly did the shaft fly from his hand, for he smote the flat of the right foot of Diomedes, and the arrow went clean through, and stood fixed in the earth; and right sweetly laughing Paris leaped up from his lair, and boasted, and said: "Thou art smitten, nor vainly hath the dart flown forth; would that I had smitten thee in the nether belly, and taken thy life away. So should the Trojans have breathed again from their trouble, they that shudder at thee, as bleating goats at a lion."

But him answered strong Diomedes, no wise dismayed: "Bowman, reviler, proud in thy bow of horn, thou gaper after girls, verily if thou madest trial in full harness, man to man, thy bow and showers of shafts would nothing avail thee, but now thou boastest vainly, for that thou hast grazed the sole of my foot. I care not, more than if a woman had struck me or a senseless boy, for feeble is the dart of a craven man and a worthless. In other wise from my hand, yea, if it do but touch, the sharp shaft flieth, and straightway layeth low its man, and torn are the cheeks of his wife, and fatherless his children, and he, reddening the earth with his blood, doth rot away, more birds than women round him."

So spake he, and Odysseus, spearman renowned, drew near, and stood in front of him, and Diomedes sat down behind him, and drew the sharp arrow from his foot, and a sore pang passed through his flesh. Then sprang he into his car, and bade his charioteer drive back to the hollow ships, for he was hurt at heart. Then Odysseus, spearman renowned, was left alone, nor did one of the Argives abide by him, for fear had fallen on them all. Then in heaviness he spoke to his own great-hearted spirit: "Ah me, what thing shall befall me! A great evil it is if I flee, in dread of the throng; yet worse is this, if I be taken all alone, for the other Danaans bath Kronion scattered in flight. But wherefore doth my heart thus converse with herself? for I know that they are cowards, who flee the fight, but whosoever is a hero in war, him it mainly behoves to stand stubbornly, whether he be smitten, or whether he smite another."

While he pondered thus in heart and spirit, the ranks came on of the Trojans under shield, and hemmed him in the midst, setting among them their own bane. And even as when hounds and young men in their bloom press round a boar, and he cometh forth from his deep lair, whetting his white tusk between crooked jaws, and round him they rush, and the sound of the gnashing of tusks ariseth, and straightway they await his assault, so dread as he is, even so then round Odysseus, dear to Zeus, rushed the Trojans. And first he wounded noble Deiopites, from above, in the shoulder, leaping on him with sharp spear, and next he slew Thoon and Ennomos, and next Chersidamas, being leapt down from his chariot, he smote with the spear on the navel beneath the bossy shield, and he fell in the dust and clutched the ground with the hollow of his hand. These left he, and wounded Charops, son of Hippasos, with the spear, the brother of high-born Sokos. And to help him came Sokos, a godlike man, and stood hard by him, and spake saying: "O renowned Odysseus, insatiable of craft and toil, to-day shalt thou either boast over two sons of Hippasos, as having slain two such men of might, and stripped their harness, or smitten by my spear shaft lose thy life."

So spake he, and smote him on the circle of his shield; through the shining shield passed the strong spear, and through the fair-dight corslet it was thrust, and tore clean off the flesh of the flanks, but Pallas Athens did not suffer it to mingle with the bowels of the hero, and Odysseus knew that the dart had in nowise lighted on a deadly spot, and drawing backward, he spake unto Sokos "Ah, wretched one, verily sheer destruction is come upon thee. Surely thou hast made me to cease from warring among the Trojans, but here to thee I declare that slaying and black Fate will be upon thee this day, and beneath my spear overthrown shalt thou give glory to me, and thy soul to Hades of the noble steeds."

He spake, and the other turned, and started to flee, and in his back as he turned he fixed the spear, between the shoulders, and drave it through the breast. Then he fell with a crash, and noble Odysseus boasted over him: "Ah, Sokos, son of wise-hearted Hippasos the tamer of horses, the end of death hath come upon and caught thee, nor hast thou avoided. Ah, wretch, thy father and lady mother shall not close thine eyes in death, but birds that eat flesh raw shall tear thee, shrouding thee in the multitude of their wings. But to me, if I die, the noble Achaians will yet give due burial."

So spake he, and drew the mighty spear of wise-hearted Sokos forth from his flesh, and from his bossy shield, and his blood flowed forth when the spear was drawn away, and afflicted his spirit. And the great-hearted

Trojans when they beheld the blood of Odysseus, with clamour through the throng came all together against him. But he gave ground, and shouted unto his comrades: thrice he shouted then, as loud as man's mouth might cry, and thrice did Menelaos dear to Zeus hear his call, and quickly he spake to Aias that was hard by him: "Aias, of the seed of Zeus, child of Telamon, lord of the hosts, the shout of Odysseus of the hardy heart rings round me, like as though the Trojans were oppressing him alone among them, and had cut him off in the strong battle. Nay, let us speed into the throng, for better it is to rescue him. I fear lest he suffer some evil, being alone among the Trojans, so brave as he is, and lest great sorrow for his loss come upon the Danaans."

So spake he, and led the way, and the other followed him, a godlike man. Then found they Odysseus dear to Zeus, and the Trojans beset him like tawny jackals from the hills round a wounded horned stag, that a man hath smitten with an arrow from the bow-string, and the stag hath fled from him by speed of foot, as long as the blood is warm and his limbs are strong, but when the swift arrow hath overcome him, then do the ravening jackals rend him in the hills, in a dark wood, and then god leadeth a murderous lion thither, and the jackals flee before him, but he rendeth them, so then, round wise-hearted Odysseus of the crafty counsels, did the Trojans gather, many and mighty, but that hero thrusting on with the spear held off the pitiless day. Then Aias drew near, bearing his shield like a tower, and stood thereby, and the Trojans fled from him, where each man might. Then warlike Menelaos led Odysseus out of the press, holding him by the hand, till the squire drave up the horses.

Then Aias leaped on the Trojans, and slew Doyrklos, bastard son of Priam, and thereafter wounded he Pandokos, and he wounded Lysandros, and Pyrasos, and Pylartes. And as when a brimming river cometh down upon the plain, in winter flood from the hills, swollen by the rain of Zeus, and many dry oaks and many pines it sucketh in, and much soil it casteth into the sea, even so renowned Aias charged them, pursuing through the plain, slaying horses and men. Nor wist Hector thereof at all, for he was fighting on the left of all the battle, by the banks of the river Skamandros, whereby chiefly fell the heads of men, and an unquenchable cry arose, around great Nestor and warlike Idomeneus. And Hector with them was warring, and terrible things did he, with the spear and in horsemanship, and he ravaged the battalions of the young men. Nor would the noble Achaians have yet given ground from the path, if Alexandros, the lord of fair-tressed Helen, had not stayed Machaon shepherd of the host in his valorous deeds, and smitten him on the right shoulder with a three-barbed arrow. Therefore were the Achaians, breathing valour, in great fear, lest men should seize Machaon in the turning of the fight.

Then Idomeneus spake to noble Nestor: "O Nestor, son of Neleus, great glory of the Achaians, arise, get thee up into thy chariot, and with thee let

Machaon go, and swiftly drive to the ships the whole-hooved horses. For a leech is worth many other men, to cut out arrows, and spread soothing medicaments."

So spake he, nor did knightly Nestor of Gerenia disobey him, but straightway gat up into his chariot, and with him went Machaon, son of Asklepios the good leech, and he lashed the horses, and willingly flew they forward to the hollow ships, where they desired to be.

But Kebriones, the charioteer of Hector, beheld the Trojans driven in flight, and spake to him, and said: "Hector, here do we contend with the Danaans, at the limit of the wailful war, but, lo, the other Trojans are driven in flight confusedly, men and horses. And Aias son of Telamon is driving them; well I know him, for wide is the shield round his shoulders. Nay, let us too urge thither the horses and chariot, there where horsemen and footmen thickest in the forefront of evil strife are slaying each other, and the cry goes up unquenchable."

So spake he, and smote the fair-maned horses with the shrill-sounding whip, and they felt the lash, and fleetly bore the swift chariot among the Trojans and Achaians, treading on the dead, and the shields, and with blood was sprinkled all the axle-tree beneath, and the rims round the car with the drops from the hooves of the horses, and with drops from the tires about the wheels. And Hector was eager to enter the press of men, and to leap in and break through, and evil din of battle he brought among the Danaans, and brief space rested he from smiting with the spear. Nay, but he ranged among the ranks of other men, with spear, and sword, and with great stones, but he avoided the battle of Aias son of Telamon.

Now father Zeus, throned in the highest, roused dread in Aias, and he stood in amaze, and cast behind him his sevenfold shield of bull's hide, and gazed round in fear upon the throng, like a wild beast, turning this way and that, and slowly retreating step by step. And as when hounds and country folk drive a tawny lion from the mid-fold of the kine, and suffer him not to carry away the fattest of the herd; all night they watch, and he in great desire for the flesh maketh his onset, but takes nothing thereby, for thick the darts fly from strong hands against him, and the burning brands, and these he dreads for all his fury, and in the dawn he departeth with vexed heart; even so at that time departed Aias, vexed at heart, from among the Trojans, right unwillingly, for he feared sore for the ships of the Achaians. And as when a lazy ass going past a field hath the better of the boys with him, an ass that hath had many a cudgel broken about his sides, and he fareth into the deep crop, and wasteth it, while the boys smite him with cudgels, and feeble is the force of them, but yet with might and main they drive him forth, when he hath had his fill of fodder, even so did the high-hearted Trojans and allies, called from many lands, smite great Aias, son of Telamon, with darts on the centre of his shield, and ever followed after him. And Aias would now be mindful of his impetuous valour, and turn again, and hold at bay the battalions of the horse-taming Trojans, and once more he would turn him again to flee. Yet he hindered them all from making their way to the fleet ships, and himself stood and smote between the Trojans and the Achaians, and the spears from strong hands stuck some of them in his great shield, fain to win further, and many or ever they reached his white body stood fast halfway in the earth, right eager to sate themselves with his flesh.

So they fought like unto burning fire.

But the mares of Neleus all sweating bare Nestor out of the battle, and also carried they Machaon, shepherd of the host. Then the noble Achilles, swift of foot, beheld and was ware of him, for Achilles was standing by the stern of his great ship, watching the dire toil, and the woful rout of battle. And straightway he spake to his own comrade, Patroklos, calling to him from beside the ship, and he heard, and from the hut he came, like unto Ares; and this to him was the beginning of evil. Then the strong son of Menoitios spake first to Achilles: "Why dost thou call me, Achilles, what need hast thou of me?"

Then swift-footed Achilles answered him and spake: "Noble son of Menoitios, dear to my heart, now methinks that the Achaians will stand in prayer about my knees, for need no longer tolerable cometh upon them. But go now, Patroklos dear to Zeus, and ask Nestor who is this that he bringeth wounded from the war. Verily from behind he is most like Machaon, that child of Asklepios, but I beheld not the eyes of the man, for the horses sped past me, straining forward eagerly."

So spake he and Patroklos obeyed his dear comrade, and started and ran past the ships, and the huts of the Achaians.

Now when they came to the hut of the son of Neleus, they lighted down on the bounteous earth, and the squire, Eurymedon, loosed the horses of that old man from the car, and they dried the sweat from their doublets, standing before the breeze, by the shore of the sea, and thereafter came they to the hut, and sat them down on chairs. And fair-tressed Hekamede mixed for them a mess, Hekamede that the old man won from Tenedos, when Achilles sacked it, and she was the daughter of great-hearted Arsinoos, and her the Achaians chose out for him, because always in counsel he excelled them all. First she drew before them a fair table, polished well, with feet of cyanus, and thereon a vessel of bronze, with onion, for relish to the drink, and pale honey, and the grain of sacred barley, and beside it a right goodly cup, that the old man brought from home, embossed with studs of gold, and four handles there were to it, and round each two golden doves were feeding, and to the cup were two feet below. Another man could scarce have lifted the cup from the table, when it was full, but Nestor the Old raised it easily. In this cup the woman, like unto the goddesses, mixed a mess for them, with Pramnian wine, and therein grated cheese of goats' milk, with a grater of bronze, and scattered white barley thereover, and bade them drink, whenas she had made ready the mess.

So when the twain had drunk, and driven away parching thirst, they took their pleasure in discourse, speaking each to the other. Now Patroklos stood at the doors, a godlike man, and when the old man beheld him, he arose from his shining chair, and took him by the hand, and led him in, and bade him be seated. But Patroklos, from over against him, was for refusing, and spake and said: "No time to sit have I, old man, fosterling of Zeus, nor wilt thou persuade me. Revered and dreaded is he that sent me forth to ask thee who this man is that thou bringest home wounded. Nay, but I know myself, for I see Machaon, shepherd of the host. And now will I go back again, a messenger, to speak a word to Achilles. And well dost thou know, old man, fosterling of Zeus, how terrible a man he is; lightly would he blame even one that is blameless."

Then knightly Nestor of Gerenia answered him again: "Wherefore is Achilles thus sorry for the sons of the Achaians, for as many as are wounded with darts? He knoweth not at all what grief hath arisen in the camp: for the best men lie in the ships, wounded by shaft or smitten by spear. Wounded with the shaft is strong Diomedes, son of Tydeus, and smitten is Odysseus, spearman renowned, and Agamemnon, and this other have I but newly carried out of battle, wounded with an arrow from the bowstring. But Achilles, for all his valiance, careth not for the Danaans, nor pities them at all. Doth he wait till the fleet ships hard by the shore shall burn in the consuming fire, and till we be slain one upon another? Nay, but even now speak thou thus and thus to wise-hearted Achilles, if perchance he will obey thee. Who knows but that, God helping, thou mightst stir his spirit with thy persuading? and good is the persuasion of a friend. But if in his heart he be shunning some oracle of God, and his lady mother hath told him somewhat from Zeus, natheless let him send forth thee, and let the rest of the host of the Myrmidons follow with thee, if perchance any light shall arise from thee to the Danaans; and let him give thee his fair harness, to bear into the war, if perchance the Trojans may take thee for him, and withhold them from the strife, and the warlike sons of the Achaians might take breath, being wearied; for brief is the breathing time in battle. And lightly might ye, being unwearied, drive men wearied in the war unto the city, away from the ships and the huts."

So spake he, and roused his heart within his breast, and he started and ran by the ships to Achilles of the seed of Aiakos.

BOOK XII

How the Trojans and allies broke within the wall of the Achaians.

So in the huts the strong son of Menortios was tending the wounded Eurypylos, but still they fought confusedly, the Argives and Trojans. Nor were the fosse of the Danaans and their wide wall above long to protect them, the wall they had builded for defence of the ships, and the fosse they had drawn round about; for neither had they given goodly hecatombs to the gods, that it might guard with its bounds their swift ships and rich spoil. Nay, maugre the deathless gods was it builded, wherefore it abode steadfast for no long time. While Hector yet lived, and yet Achilles kept his wrath, and unsacked was the city of Priam the king, so long the great wall of the Achaians likewise abode steadfast. But when all the bravest of the Trojans died, and many of the Argives,—some were taken, and some were left,—and the city of Priam was sacked in the tenth year, and the Argives had gone back in their ships to their own dear country, then verily did Poseidon and Apollo take counsel to wash away the wall, bringing in the might of the rivers, of all that flow from the hills of Ida to the sea. Rhesos there was, and Heptaporos, and Karesos, and Rhodios, Grenikos, and Aisepos, and goodly Skamandros, and Simoeis, whereby many shields and helms fell in the dust, and the generation of men half divine; the mouths of all these waters did Phoebus Apollo turn together, and for nine days he drave their stream against the wall; and still Zeus rained unceasingly, that the quicker he might mingle the wall with the salt sea. And the Shaker of the earth, with his trident in his hands, was himself the leader, and sent forth into the waves all the foundations of beams and stones that the Achaians had laid with toil, and made all smooth by the strong current of the Hellespont, and covered again the great beach with sand, when he had swept away the wall, and turned the rivers back to flow in their channel, where of old they poured down their fair flow of water.

So were Poseidon and Apollo to do in the aftertime; but then war and the din of war sounded about the well-builded wall, and the beams of the towers rang beneath the strokes; while the Argives, subdued by the scourge of Zeus, were penned and driven in by the hollow ships, in dread of Hector, the mighty maker of flight, but he, as aforetime, fought like a whirlwind. And as when, among hounds and hunting men, a boar or lion wheeleth him about, raging in his strength, and these array themselves in fashion like a tower, and stand up against him, casting many javelins from their hands; but never is his stout heart confused nor afraid, and his courage is his bane, and often he wheeleth him about, and maketh trial of the ranks of men, and wheresoever he maketh onset there the ranks of men give way, even so Hector went and besought his comrades through the press, and spurred them on to cross the dyke. But his swift-footed horses dared not, but loud they neighed, standing by the sheer edge, for the wide fosse affrighted them, neither easy to leap from hard by, nor to cross, for overhanging banks stood round about it all on either hand, and above it was furnished with sharp stakes that the sons of the Achaians had planted there, thick set and great, a bulwark against hostile men. Thereby not lightly might a horse enter, drawing a well-wheeled chariot; but the footmen were eager, if they might accomplish it. Then Polydamas drew near valiant Hector, and spake to him: "Hector and ye other leaders of the Trojans and allies, foolishly do we drive our fleet horses through the dyke; nay right hard it is to cross, for sharp stakes stand in it, and over against them the wall of the Achaians. Thereby none may go down and fight in chariots, for strait is the place wherein, methinks, we might come by a mischief. For if Zeus that thunders on high is utterly to destroy them in his evil will, and is minded to help the Trojans, verily then I too would desire that even instantly this might be, that the Achaians should perish here nameless far from Argos: but and if they turn again, and we flee back from among the ships, and rush into the delved ditch, then methinks that not even one from among us to bear the tidings will win back to the city before the force of the Achaians when they rally. But come as I declare, let us all obey. Let our squires hold the horses by the dyke, while we being harnessed in our gear as foot soldiers follow all together with Hector, and the Achaians will not withstand us, if indeed the bands of death be made fast upon them."

So spake Polydamas, and his wise word pleased Hector well, and straightway in his harness he leaped from his chariot to the ground. Nor were the other Trojans gathered upon the chariots, but they all leaped forth, when they beheld goodly Hector. There each gave it into the charge of his own charioteer, to keep the horses orderly there by the fosse. And they divided, and arrayed themselves, and ordered in five companies they followed with the leaders.

Now they that went with Hector and noble Polydamas, these were most, and bravest, and most were eager to break the wall, and fight by the hollow ships; and with them followed Kebriones for the third, for Hector had left another man with his chariot, a weaker warrior than Kebriones. The second company Paris led, and Alkathoos, and Agenor: and the third company Helenos led, and godlike Deiphobos,—two sons of Priam,—the third was the warrior Asios, Asios Hyrtakos' son, whom his tall sorrel steeds brought out of Arisbe, from the river Selleeis. And of the fourth company was the brave son of Anchises leader, even Aineias; and with him were two sons of Antenor, Archelochos and Akamas, both well skilled in all warfare.

And Sarpedon led the glorious allies, and to be with him he chose Glaukos and warlike Asteropaios, for they seamed to him to be manifestly the bravest of all after himself but he was excellent, yea, above all the host. And these when they had arrayed one another with well-fashioned shields of bulls' hide, went straight and eager against the Danaans, nor deemed that they could longer resist them, but that themselves should fall on the black ships.

Then the rest of the Trojans and the far-famed allies obeyed the counsel of blameless Polydamas, but Asios, son of Hyrtakos, leader of men, willed not to leave his horses there, and his squire the charioteer, but with them he drew near the swift ships, fond man! for never was he, avoiding evil

Fates, to return, rejoicing in his horses and chariot, back from the ships to windy Ilios. Nay, ere that the Fate of ill name over-shadowed him, by the spear of Idomeneus, the haughty son of Deukalion. For Asios went against the left flank of the ships, whereby the Achaians returned out of the plain with chariots and horses: there he drave through his horses and his car, nor found he the doors shut on the gates, and the long bar, but men were holding them open if perchance they might save any of their comrades fleeing out of the battle towards the ships. Straight thereby held he his horses with unswerving aim, and his men followed him, crying shrilly, for they deemed that the Achaians could no longer hold them off, but that themselves would fall on the black ships: fools, for in the gates they found two men of the bravest, the high-hearted sons of the warrior Lapithae, one the son of Peirithoos, strong Polypoites, and one Leonteus, peer of Ares the bane of men. These twain stood in front of the lofty gates, like high-crested oak trees in the hills, that for ever abide the wind and rain, firm fixed with roots great and long; even so these twain, trusting to the mightiness of their hands, abode the coming of great Asios, and fled not. But straight came the Trojans against the well-builded wall, holding their shields of dry bulls' hide on high, with mighty clamour, round the prince Asios, and Iamenos, and Orestes, and Adamas, son of Asios, and Thoon, and Oinomaos. But the other twain for a while, being within the wall, urged the well-greaved Achaians to fight for the ships; but when they saw the Trojans assailing the wall, while the Danaans cried and turned in flight, then forth rushed the twain, and fought in front of the gates like wild boars that in the mountains abide the assailing crew of men and dogs, and charging on either flank they crush the wood around them, cutting it at the root, and the clatter of their tusks wages loud, till one smite them and take their life away: so clattered the bright bronze on the breasts of the twain, as they were smitten in close fight, for right hardily they fought, trusting to the host above them, and to their own strength.

For the men above were casting with stones from the well-builded towers, in defence of themselves and of the huts, and of the swift-faring ships. And like snowflakes the stones fell earthward, flakes that a tempestuous wind, as it driveth the dark clouds, rains thickly down on the bounteous earth: so thick fell the missiles from the hands of Achaians and Trojans alike, and their helms rang harsh and their bossy shields, being smitten with mighty stones. Verily then Asios, son of Hyrtakos, groaned and smote both his thighs, and indignantly he spake: "Zeus, verily thou too dost greatly love a lie, for I deemed not that the Achaian heroes could withstand our might and our hands invincible. But they like wasps of nimble body, or bees that have made their dwellings in a rugged path, and leave not their hollow hold, but abide and keep the hunters at bay for the sake of their little ones, even so these men have no will to give ground from the gates, though they are but two, ere they slay or be slain."

So spake he, nor with his speech did he persuade the mind of Zeus, for his will was to give renown to Hector.

But the others were fighting about the other gates, and hard it were for me like a god to tell all these things, for everywhere around the wall of stone rose the fire divine; the Argives, for all their sorrow, defending the ships of necessity; and all the gods were grieved at heart, as many as were defenders of the Danaans in battle. And together the Lapithae waged war and strife.

There the son of Peirithoos, mighty Polypoites, smote Damasos with the spear, through the helmet with cheekpieces of bronze; nor did the bronze helm stay the spear, but the point of bronze brake clean through the bone, and all the brain within was scattered, and the spear overcame him in his eagerness. Thereafter he slew Pylon and Ormenos. And Leonteus of the stock of Ares smote Hippomachos, son of Antimachos, with the spear, striking him on the girdle. Then again he drew his sharp sword from the sheath, and smote Antiphates first in close fight, rushing on him through the throng, that he fell on his back on the ground; and thereafter he brought down Menon, and Iamenos, and Orestes one after the other, to the bounteous earth.

While they were stripping from these the shining arms, the young men who followed with Polydamas and Hector, they that were most in number and bravest, and most were eager to break the wall and set the ships on fire, these still stood doubtful by the fosse, for as they were eager to pass over a bird had appeared to them, an eagle of lofty flight, skirting the host on the left hand. In its talons it bore a blood-red monstrous snake, alive, and struggling still; yea, not yet had it forgotten the joy of battle, but writhed backward and smote the bird that held it on the breast, beside the neck, and the bird cast it from him down to the earth, in sore pain, and dropped it in the midst of the throng; then with a cry sped away down the gusts of the wind. And the Trojans shuddered when they saw the gleaming snake lying in the midst of them; an omen of aegis-bearing Zeus.

Then verily Polydamas stood by brave Hector, and spake: "Hector, ever dost thou rebuke me in the assemblies, though I counsel wisely; since it by no means beseemeth one of the people to speak contrary to thee, in council or in war, but always to increase thy power; but now again will I say all that seemeth to me to be best. Let us not advance and fight with the Danaans for the ships. For even thus, methinks, the end will be, if indeed this bird hath come for the Trojans when they were eager to cross the dyke, this eagle of lofty flight, skirting the host on the left hand, bearing in his talons a blood-red monstrous snake, yet living; then straightway left he hold of him, before he reached his own nest, nor brought him home in the end to give to his nestlings. Even so shall we, though we burst with mighty force the gates and wall of the Achaians, and the Achaians give ground, even so we shall return in disarray from the ships by the way we came; for many of the Trojans shall we leave behind, whom the Achaians will slay with the sword, in defence of the ships. Even so would a soothsayer interpret that in his heart had clear knowledge of omens, and whom the people obeyed."

Then Hector of the glancing helm lowered on him and said: "Polydamas, that thou speakest is no longer pleasing to me; yea, thou knowest how to conceive another counsel better than this. But if thou verily speakest thus in earnest, then the gods themselves have utterly destroyed thy wits; thou that bidst us forget the counsels of loud-thundering Zeus, that himself promised me, and confirmed with a nod of his head! But thou bidst us be obedient to birds long of wing, whereto I give no heed, nor take any care thereof, whether they fare to the right, to the dawn and to the sun, or to the left, to mist and darkness. Nay, for us, let us trust to the counsel of mighty Zeus, who is king over all mortals and immortals. One omen is best, to fight for our own country. And wherefore dost thou fear war and battle? For if all the rest of us be slain by the ships of the Argives, yet needst thou not fear to perish, for thy heart is not warlike, nor enduring in battle. But if thou dost hold aloof from the fight, or winnest any other with thy words to turn him from war, straightway by my spear shalt thou be smitten, and lose thy life."

So spake he, and led on, and they followed with a wondrous din; and Zeus that joyeth in the thunder roused from the hills of Ida, a blast of wind, which bare the dust straight against the ships; and he made weak the heart of the Achaians, but gave renown to the Trojans and to Hector. Trusting then in his omens, and their might, they strove to break the great wall of the Achaians. They dragged down the machicolations [projecting galleries] of the towers, and overthrew the battlements, and heaved up the projecting buttresses, that the Achaians set first in the earth, to be the props of the towers. These they overthrew, and hoped to break the wall of the Achaians. Nor even now did the Danaans give ground from the path, but closed up the battlements with shields of bulls' hides, and cast from them at the foemen as they went below the walls.

Now the two Aiantes went everywhere on the towers, ever urging, and arousing the courage of the Achaians. One they would accost with honeyed words, another with hard words they would rebuke, whomsoever they saw utterly giving ground from the fight: "O friends, whosoever is eminent, or whosoever is of middle station among the Argives, ay, or lower yet, for in no wise are all men equal in war, now is there work for all, and this yourselves well know. Let none turn back to the ships, for that he hath heard one threatening aloud; nay, get ye forward, and cheer another on, if perchance Olympian Zeus, the lord of lightning, will grant us to drive back the assault, and push the foe to the city."

So these twain shouted in the front, and aroused the battle of the Achaians. But as flakes of snow fall thick on a winter day, when Zeus the Counsellor hath begun to snow, showing forth these arrows of his to men, and he hath lulled the winds, and he snoweth continually, till he hath covered the crests of the high hills, and the uttermost headlands, and the grassy plains, and rich tillage of men; and the snow is scattered over the havens and shores of the grey sea, and only the wave as it rolleth in keeps off the snow, but all other things are swathed over, when the shower of Zeus cometh heavily, so from both sides their stones flew thick, some towards the Trojans, and some from the Trojans against the Achaians, while both sides were smitten, and over all the wall the din arose.

Yet never would the Trojans, then, and renowned Hector have broken the gates of the wall, and the long bar, if Zeus the Counsellor had not roused his son Sarpedon against the Argives, like a lion against the kine of crooked horn. Straightway he held forth his fair round shield, of hammered bronze, that the bronze-smith had hammered out, and within had stitched many bulls' hides with rivets of gold, all round the circle, this held he forth, and shook two spears; and sped on his way, like a mountain-nurtured lion, that long lacketh meat, and his brave spirit urgeth him to make assail on the sheep, and come even against a well-builded homestead. Nay, even if he find herdsmen thereby, guarding the sheep with hounds and spears, yet hath he no mind to be driven without an effort from the steading, but he either leapeth on a sheep, and seizeth it, or himself is smitten in the foremost place with a dart from a strong hand. So did his heart then urge on the godlike Sarpedon to rush against the wall, and break through the battlements. And instantly he spake to Glaukos, son of Hippolochos: "Glaukos, wherefore have we twain the chiefest honour,—seats of honour, and messes, and full cups in Lykia, and all men look on us as gods? And wherefore hold we a great demesne by the banks of Xanthos, a fair demesne of orchard-land, and wheat-bearing tilth? Therefore now it behoveth us to take our stand in the first rank of the Lykians, and encounter fiery battle, that certain of the well-corsleted Lykians may say, 'Verily our kings that rule Lykia be no inglorious men, they that eat fat sheep, and drink the choice wine honey-sweet: nay, but they are also of excellent might, for they war in the foremost ranks of the Lykians.' Ah, friend, if once escaped from this battle we were for ever to be ageless and immortal, neither would I fight myself in the foremost ranks, nor would I send thee into the war that giveth men renown, but now—for assuredly ten thousand fates of death do every way beset us, and these no mortal may escape nor avoid—now let us go forward, whether we shall give glory to other men, or others to us."

So spake he, and Glaukos turned not apart, nor disobeyed him, and they twain went straight forward, leading the great host of the Lykians.

Then Menestheus son of Peteos shuddered when he beheld them, for against his tower they went, bringing with them ruin; and he looked along the tower of the Achaians if perchance he might see any of the leaders, that would ward off destruction from his comrades, and he beheld the two Aiantes, insatiate of war, standing there, and Teukros hard by, newly come from his hut; but he could not cry to be heard of them, so great was the din, and the noise went up unto heaven of smitten shields and helms with horse-hair crests, and of the gates, for they had all been shut, and the Trojans stood beside them, and strove by force to break them, and enter in. Swiftly then to Aias he sent the herald Thootes: "Go, noble Thootes, and run, and call Aias: or rather the twain, for that will be far the best of all, since quickly here will there be wrought utter ruin. For hereby press the leaders of the Lykians, who of old are fierce in strong battle. But if beside them too war and toil arise, yet at least let the strong Telamonian Aias come alone and let Teukros the skilled bowman follow with him."

So spake he, and the herald listened and disobeyed him not, but started and ran by the wall of the mail-clad Achaians, and came, and stood by the Aiantes, and straightway spake: "Ye twain Aiantes, leaders of the mail-clad Achaians, the dear son of Peteos, fosterling of Zeus, biddeth you go thither, that, if it be but for a little while, ye may take your part in battle: both of you he more desireth, for that will be far the best of all, since quickly there will there be wrought utter ruin. For thereby press the leaders of the Lykians, who of old are fierce in strong battle. But if beside you too war and toil arise, yet at least let the strong Telamonian Aias come alone, and let Teukros the skilled bowman follow with him."

So spake he, nor did the strong Telamonian Aias disobey, but instantly spake winged words to the son of Oileus: "Aias, do ye twain stand here, thyself and strong Lykomedes, and urge the Danaans to war with all their might; but I go thither, to take my part in battle, and quickly will I come again, when I have well aided them."

So spake Telamonian Aias and departed, and Teukros went with him, his brother by the same father, and with them Pandion bare the bended bow of Teukros.

Now when they came to the tower of great-hearted Menestheus, passing within the wall,—and to men sore pressed they came,—the foe were climbing upon the battlements, like a dark whirlwind, even the strong leaders and counsellors of the Lykians; and they hurled together into the war and the battle-cry arose. Now first did Aias Telamon's son slay a man, Epikles great of heart, the comrade of Sarpedon. With a jagged stone he smote him, a great stone that lay uppermost within the wall, by the battlements. Not lightly could a man hold it in both hands, however strong in his youth, of such mortals as now are, but Aias lifted it, and cast it from above, and shattered the helm of fourfold crest, and broke the bones of the head, and he fell like a diver from the lofty tower, and his life left his bones. And Teukros smote Glaukos, the strong son of Hippolochos, as he came on, with an arrow from the lofty wall; even where he saw his shoulder bare he smote him, and made him cease from delight in battle. Back from the wall he leapt secretly, lest any of the Achaians should see him smitten, and speak boastfully. But sorrow came on Sarpedon when Glaukos departed, so soon as he was aware thereof, but he forgot not the joy of battle. He aimed at Alkmaon, son of Thestor, with the spear, and smote him, and drew out the spear. And Alkmaon following the spear fell prone, and his bronze-dight arms rang round him. Then Sarpedon seized with strong hands the battlement, and dragged, and it all gave way together, while above the wall was stripped bare, and made a path for many.

Then Aias and Teukros did encounter him: Teukros smote him with an arrow, on the bright baldric of his covering shield, about the breast, but Zeus warded off the Fates from his son, that he should not be overcome beside the ships' sterns. Then Aias leaped on and smote his shield, nor did the spear pass clean through, yet shook he Sarpedon in his eagerness. He gave ground a little way from the battlement, yet retreated not wholly, since his heart hoped to win renown. Then he turned and cried to the godlike Lykians: "O Lykians, wherefore thus are ye slack in impetuous valour. Hard it is for me, stalwart as I am, alone to break through, and make a path to the ships, nay, follow hard after me, for the more men, the better work."

So spake he, and they, dreading the rebuke of their king, pressed on the harder around the counsellor and king. And the Argives on the other side made strong their battalions within the wall, and mighty toil began for them. For neither could the strong Lykians burst through the wall of the Danaans, and make a way to the ships, nor could the warlike Danaans drive back the Lykians from the wall, when once they had drawn near thereto. But as two men contend about the marches of their land, with measuring rods in their hands, in a common field, when in narrow space they strive for equal shares, even so the battlements divided them, and over those they smote the round shields of ox hide about the breasts of either side, and the fluttering bucklers. And many were wounded in the flesh with the ruthless bronze, whensoever the back of any of the warriors was laid bare as he turned, ay, and many clean through the very shield. Yea, everywhere the towers and battlements swam with the blood of men shed on either side, by Trojans and Achaians. But even so they could not put the Argives to rout, but they held their ground, as an honest woman that laboureth with her hands holds the balance, and raises the weight and the wool together, balancing them, that she may win scant wages for her children; so evenly was strained their war and battle, till the moment when Zeus gave the greater renown to Hector, son of Priam, who was the first to leap within the wall of the Achaians. In a piercing voice he cried aloud to the Trojans: "Rise, ye horse-taming Trojans, break the wall of the Argives, and cast among the ships fierce blazing fire."

So spake he, spurring them on, and they all heard him with their ears, and in one mass rushed straight against the wall, and with sharp spears in their hands climbed upon the machicolations of the towers. And Hector seized and carried a stone that lay in front of the gates, thick in the hinder part, but sharp at point: a stone that not the two best men of the people, such as mortals now are, could lightly lift from the ground on to a wain, but easily he wielded it alone, for the son of crooked-counselling Kronos made it light for him. And as when a shepherd lightly beareth the fleece of a ram, taking it in one hand, and little doth it burden him, so Hector lifted the stone, and bare it straight against the doors that closely guarded the stubborn-set portals, double gates and tall, and two cross bars held them within, and one bolt fastened them. And he came, and stood hard by, and firmly planted himself, and smote them in the midst, setting his legs well apart, that his cast might lack no strength. And he brake both the hinges, and the stone fell within by reason of its weight, and the gates rang loud around, and the bars held not, and the doors burst this way and that beneath the rush of the stone. Then glorious Hector leaped in, with face like the sudden night, shining in wondrous mail that was clad about his body, and with two spears in his hands. No man that met him could have held him back when once he leaped within the gates: none but the gods, and his eyes shone with fire. Turning towards the throng he cried to the Trojans to overleap the wall, and they obeyed his summons, and speedily some overleaped the wall, and some poured into the fair-wrought gateways, and the Danaans fled in fear among the hollow ships, and a ceaseless clamour arose.

BOOK XIII

Poseidon stirreth up the Achaians to defend the ships. The valour of Idomeneus.

Now Zeus, after that he had brought the Trojans and Hector to the ships, left them to their toil and endless labour there, but otherwhere again he turned his shining eyes, and looked upon the land of the Thracian horsebreeders, and the Mysians, fierce fighters hand to hand, and the proud Hippemolgoi that drink mare's milk, and the Abioi, the most righteous of men. To Troy no more at all he turned his shining eyes, for he deemed in his heart that not one of the Immortals would draw near, to help either Trojans or Danaans.

But the mighty Earth-shaker held no blind watch, who sat and marvelled on the war and strife, high on the topmost crest of wooded Samothrace, for thence all Ida was plain to see; and plain to see were the city of Priam, and the ships of the Achaians. Thither did he go from the sea and sate him down, and he had pity on the Achaians, that they were subdued to the Trojans, and strong was his anger against Zeus.

Then forthwith he went down from the rugged hill, faring with swift steps, and the high hills trembled, and the woodland, beneath the immortal footsteps of Poseidon as he moved. Three strides he made, and with the fourth he reached his goal, even Aigae, and there was his famous palace in the deeps of the mere, his glistering golden mansions builded, imperishable for ever. Thither went he, and let harness to the car his bronze-hooved horses, swift of flight, clothed with their golden manes. He girt his own golden array about his body, and seized the well-wrought lash of gold, and mounted his chariot, and forth he drove across the waves. And the sea beasts frolicked beneath him, on all sides out of the deeps, for well they knew their lord, and with gladness the sea stood asunder, and swiftly they sped, and the axle of bronze was not wetted beneath, and the bounding steeds bare him on to the ships of the Achaians.

Now there is a spacious cave in the depths of the deep mere, between Tenedos and rugged Imbros; there did Poseidon, the Shaker of the earth, stay his horses, and loosed them out of the chariot, and cast before them ambrosial food to graze withal, and golden tethers he bound about their hooves, tethers neither to be broken nor loosed, that there the horses might continually await their lord's return. And he went to the host of the Achaians.

Now the Trojans like flame or storm-wind were following in close array, with fierce intent, after Hector, son of Priam. With shouts and cries they came, and thought to take the ships of the Achaians, and to slay thereby all the bravest of the host. But Poseidon, that girdleth the world, the Shaker of the earth, was urging on the Argives, and forth he came from the deep salt sea, in form and untiring voice like unto Kalchas. First he spake to the two Aiantes, that themselves were eager for battle: "Ye Aiantes twain, ye shall save the people of the Achaians, if ye are mindful of your might, and reckless of chill fear. For verily I do not otherwhere dread the invincible hands of the Trojans, that have climbed the great wall in their multitude, nay, the well-greaved Achaians will hold them all at bay; but hereby verily do I greatly dread lest some evil befall us, even here where that furious one is leading like a flame of fire, Hector, who boasts him to be son of mighty Zeus. Nay, but here may some god put it into the hearts of you twain, to stand sturdily yourselves, and urge others to do the like; thereby might ye drive him from the fleet-faring ships, despite his eagerness, yea, even if the Olympian himself is rousing him to war."

Therewith the Shaker of the world, the girdler of the earth, struck the twain with his staff, and filled them with strong courage, and their limbs he made light, and their feet, and their hands withal. Then, even as a swift-winged hawk speeds forth to fly, poised high above a tall sheer rock, and swoops to chase some other bird across the plain, even so Poseidon sped from them, the Shaker of the world. And of the twain Oileus' son, the swift-footed Aias, was the first to know the god, and instantly he spake to Aias, son of Telamon: "Aias, since it is one of the gods who hold Olympus, that in the semblance of a seer commands us now to fight beside the ships-not Kalchas is he, the prophet and sooth-sayer, for easily I knew the tokens of his feet and knees as he turned away, and the gods are easy to discern—lo, then mine own heart within my breast is more eagerly set on war and battle, and my feet beneath and my hands above are lusting for the fight."

Then Aias, son of Telamon, answered him saying: "Even so, too, my hands invincible now rage about the spear-shaft, and wrath has risen within me, and both my feet are swift beneath me; yea, I am keen to meet, even in single fight, the ceaseless rage of Hector son of Priam."

So they spake to each other, rejoicing in the delight of battle, which the god put in their heart. Then the girdler of the earth stirred up the Achaians that were in the rear and were renewing their strength beside the swift ships. Their limbs were loosened by their grievous toil, yea, and their souls filled with sorrow at the sight of the Trojans, that had climbed over the great wall in their multitude. And they looked on them, and shed tears beneath their brows, thinking that never would they escape destruction. But the Shaker of the earth right easily came among them, and urged on the strong battalions of warriors. Teukros first he came and summoned, and Leitos, and the hero Peneleos, and Thoas, and Deipyros, and Meriones, and Antilochos, lords of the war-cry, all these he spurred on with winged words: "Shame on you, Argives, shame, ye striplings, in your battle had I trusted for the salvation of our ships. But if you are to withdraw from grievous war, now indeed the day doth shine that shall see us conquered by the Trojans. Out on it, for verily a great marvel is this that mine eyes behold, a terrible thing that methought should never come to pass, the Trojans advancing against our ships! Of yore they were like fleeting hinds, that in the wild wood are the prey of jackals, and pards, and wolves, and wander helpless, strengthless, empty of the joy of battle. Even so the Trojans of old cared never to wait and face the wrath and the hands of the Achaians, not for a moment. But now they are fighting far from the town, by the hollow ships, all through the baseness of our leader and the remissness of the people, who, being at strife with the chief, have no heart to defend the swift-faring ships, nay, thereby they are slain. But if indeed and in truth the hero Agamemnon, the wide-ruling son of Atreus, is the very cause of all, for that he did dishonour the swift-footed son of Peleus, not even so may we refrain in any wise from war. Nay, let us right our fault with speed, for easily righted are the hearts of the brave. No longer do ye well to refrain from impetuous might, all ye that are the best men of the host. I myself would not quarrel with one that, being a weakling, abstained from war, but with you I am heartily wroth. Ah, friends, soon shall ye make the mischief more through this remissness,—but let each man conceive shame in his heart, and indignation, for verily great is the strife that hath arisen. Lo, the mighty Hector of the loud war-cry is fighting at the ships, and the gates and the long bar he hath burst in sunder."

On this wise did the Earth-enfolder call to and spur on the Achaians. And straightway they made a stand around the two Aiantes, strong bands that Ares himself could not enter and make light of, nor Athene that

marshals the host. Yea, they were the chosen best that abode the Trojans
and goodly Hector, and spear on spear made close-set fence, and shield on
serried shield, buckler pressed on buckler, and helm on helm, and man on
man. The horse-hair crests on the bright helmet-ridges touched each other
as they nodded, so close they stood each by other, and spears brandished
in bold hands were interlaced; and their hearts were steadfast and lusted
for battle.

Then the Trojans drave forward in close array, and Hector led them,
pressing straight onwards, like a rolling rock from a cliff, that the
winter-swollen water thrusteth from the crest of a hill, having broken the
foundations of the stubborn rock with its wondrous flood; leaping aloft it
flies, and the wood echoes under it, and unstayed it runs its course, till it
reaches the level plain, and then it rolls no more for all its
eagerness,—even so Hector for a while threatened lightly to win to the sea
through the huts and the ships of the Achaians, slaying as he came, but
when he encountered the serried battalions, he was stayed when he drew
near against them. But they of the other part, the sons of the Achaians,
thrust with their swords and double-pointed spears, and drave him forth
from them, that he gave ground and reeled backward. Then he cried with
a piercing voice, calling on the Trojans: "Trojans, and Lykians, and
close-fighting Dardanians, hold your ground, for the Achaians will not
long ward me off, nay, though they have arrayed themselves in fashion
like a tower. Rather, methinks, they will flee back before the spear, if
verily the chief of gods has set me on, the loud-thundering lord of Hera."

Therewith he spurred on the heart and spirit of each man; and
Deiphobos, the son of Priam, strode among them with high thoughts, and
held in front of him the circle of his shield, and lightly he stepped with his
feet, advancing beneath the cover of his shield. Then Meriones aimed at
him with a shining spear, and struck, and missed not, but smote the circle
of the bulls-hide shield, yet no whit did he pierce it; nay, well ere that
might be, the long spear-shaft snapped in the socket. Now Deiphobos was
holding off from him the bulls-hide shield, and his heart feared the lance
of wise Meriones, but that hero shrunk back among the throng of his
comrades, greatly in wrath both for the loss of victory, and of his spear,
that he had shivered. So he set forth to go to the huts and the ships of the
Achaians, to bring a long spear, that he had left in his hut.

Meanwhile the others were fighting on, and there arose an
inextinguishable cry. First Teukros, son of Telamon, slew a man, the
spearman Imbrios, the son of Mentor rich in horses. In Pedaion he dwelt,
before the coming of the sons of the Achaians, and he had for wife a
daughter of Priam, born out of wedlock, Medesikaste; but when the curved
ships of the Danaans came, he returned again to Ilios, and was
pre-eminent among the Trojans, and dwelt with Priam, who honoured
him like his own children. Him the son of Telemon pierced below the ear
with his long lance, and plucked back the spear. Then he fell like an ash

that on the crest of a far-seen hill is smitten with the axe of bronze, and brings its delicate foliage to the ground; even so he fell, and round him rang his armour bedight with bronze. Then Teukros rushed forth, most eager to strip his armour, and Hector cast at him as he came with his shining spear. But Teukros, steadily regarding him, avoided by a little the spear of bronze; so Hector struck Amphimachos, son of Kteatos, son of Aktor, in the breast with the spear, as he was returning to the battle. With a crash he fell, and his armour rang upon him.

Then Hector sped forth to tear from the head of great-hearted Amphimachos the helmet closely fitted to his temples, but Aias aimed at Hector as he came, with a shining spear, yet in no wise touched his body, for he was all clad in dread armour of bronze; but he smote the boss of his shield, and drave him back by main force, and he gave place from behind the two dead men, and the Achaians drew them out of the battle. So Stichios and goodly Menestheus, leaders of the Athenians, conveyed Amphimachos back among the host of the Achaians, but Imbrios the two Aiantes carried, with hearts full of impetuous might. And as when two lions have snatched away a goat from sharp-toothed hounds, and carry it through the deep thicket, holding the body on high above the ground in their jaws, so the two warrior Aiantes held Imbrios aloft and spoiled his arms. Then the son of Oileus cut his head from his delicate neck, in wrath for the sake of Amphimachos, and sent it rolling like a ball through the throng, and it dropped in the dust before the feet of Hector.

Then verily was Poseidon wroth at heart, when his son's son fell in the terrible fray. [Kteatos, father of Amphimachos, was Poseidon's son.] So he set forth to go by the huts and the ships of the Achaians, to spur on the Danaans, and sorrows he was contriving for the Trojans. Then Idomeneus, spearman renowned, met him on his way from his comrade that had but newly returned to him out of the battle, wounded on the knee with the sharp bronze. Him his comrades carried forth, and Idomeneus gave charge to the leeches, and so went on to his hut, for he still was eager to face the war. Then the mighty Shaker of the earth addressed him, in the voice of Thoas, son of Andraimon, that ruled over the Aitolians in all Pleuron, and mountainous Kalydon, and was honoured like a god by the people: "Idomeneus, thou counsellor of the Cretans, say, whither have thy threats fared, wherewith the sons of the Achaians threatened the Trojans?"

Then Idomeneus, leader of the Cretans, answered him again: "O Thaos, now is there no man to blame, that I wot of, for we all are skilled in war. Neither is there any man that spiritless fear holds aloof, nor any that gives place to cowardice, and shuns the cruel war, nay, but even thus, methinks, must it have seemed good to almighty Kronion, even that the Achaians should perish nameless here, far away from Argos. But Thoas, seeing that of old thou wert staunch, and dost spur on some other man, wheresoever thou mayst see any give ground, therefore slacken not now, but call aloud to every warrior."

Then Poseidon, the Shaker of the earth, answered him again: "Idomeneus, never may that man go forth out of Troy-land, but here may he be the sport of dogs, who this day wilfully is slack in battle. Nay, come, take thy weapons and away: herein we must play the man together, if any avail there may be, though we are no more than two. Ay, and very cowards get courage from company, but we twain know well how to battle even with the brave."

Therewith the god went back again into the strife of men, but Idomeneus, so soon as he came to his well-builded hut, did on his fair armour about his body, and grasped two spears, and set forth like the lightning that Kronion seizes in his hand and brandishes from radiant Olympus, showing forth a sign to mortal men, and far seen are the flames thereof. Even so shone the bronze about the breast of Idomeneus as he ran, and Meriones, his good squire, met him, while he was still near his hut,—he was going to bring his spear of bronze,—and mighty Idomeneus spake to him: "Meriones son of Molos, fleet of foot, dearest of my company, wherefore hast thou come hither and left the war and strife? Art thou wounded at all, and vexed by a dart's point, or dost thou come with a message for me concerning aught? Verily I myself have no desire to sit in the huts, but to fight."

Then wise Meriones answered him again, saying: "I have come to fetch a spear, if perchance thou hast one left in the huts, for that which before I carried I have shivered in casting at the shield of proud Deiphobos."

Then Idomeneus, leader of the Cretans, answered him again: "Spears, if thou wilt, thou shalt find, one, ay, and twenty, standing in the hut, against the shining side walls, spears of the Trojans whereof I have spoiled their slain. Yea, it is not my mood to stand and fight with foemen from afar, wherefore I have spears, and bossy shields, and helms, and corslets of splendid sheen."

Then wise Meriones answered him again: "Yea, and in mine own hut and my black ship are many spoils of the Trojans, but not ready to my hand. Nay, for methinks that neither am I forgetful of valour; but stand forth among the foremost to face the glorious war, whensoever ariseth the strife of battle. Any other, methinks, of the mail-clad Achaians should sooner forget my prowess, but thou art he that knoweth it."

Then Idomeneus, leader of the Cretans, answered him again: "I know what a man of valour thou art, wherefore shouldst thou tell me thereof? Nay, if now beside the ships all the best of us were being chosen for an ambush—wherein the valour of men is best discerned; there the coward, and the brave man most plainly declare themselves: for the colour of the coward changes often, and his spirit cannot abide firm within him, but now he kneels on one knee, now on the other, and rests on either foot, and his heart beats noisily in his breast, as he thinks of doom, and his teeth chatter loudly. But the colour of the brave man does not change, nor is he greatly afraid, from the moment that he enters the ambush of heroes, but his prayer is to mingle instantly in woeful war. Were we being chosen for such an ambush, I say, not even then would any man reckon lightly of thy courage and thy strength. Nay, and even if thou wert stricken in battle from afar, or smitten in close fight, the dart would not strike thee in the hinder part of the neck, nor in the back, but would encounter thy breast or belly, as thou dost press on, towards the gathering of the foremost fighters. But come, no more let us talk thus, like children, loitering here, lest any man be vehemently wroth, but go thou to the hut, and bring the strong spear."

Thus he spake, and Meriones, the peer of swift Ares, quickly bare the spear of bronze from the hut, and went after Idomeneus, with high thoughts of battle. And even as Ares, the bane of men, goes forth into the war, and with him follows his dear son Panic, stark and fearless, that terrifies even the hardy warrior; and these twain leave Thrace, and harness them for fight with the Ephyri, or the great-hearted Phlegyans, yet hearken not to both peoples, but give honour to one only; like these gods did Meriones and Idomeneus, leaders of men, set forth into the fight, harnessed in gleaming bronze. And Meriones spake first to Idomeneus saying: "Child of Deukalion, whither art thou eager to enter into the throng: on the right of all the host, or in the centre, or on the left? Ay, and no other where, methinks, are the flowing-haired Achaians so like to fail in fight."

Then Idomeneus, the leader of the Cretans, answered him again: "In the centre of the ships there are others to bear the brunt, the two Aiantes, and Teukros, the best bowman of the Achaians, ay, and a good man in close fight; these will give Hector Priam's son toil enough, howsoever keen he be for battle; yea, though he be exceeding stalwart. Hard will he find it, with all his lust for war, to overcome their strength and their hands invincible, and to fire the ships, unless Kronion himself send down on the swift ships a burning brand. But not to a man would he yield, the great Telamonian Aias, to a man that is mortal and eateth Demeter's grain, and may be chosen with the sword of bronze, and with hurling of great stones. Nay, not even to Achilles the breaker of the ranks of men would he give way, not in close fight; but for speed of foot none may in any wise strive with Achilles. But guide us twain, as thou sayest, to the left hand of the host, that speedily we may learn whether we are to win glory from others, or other men from us."

So he spake, and Meriones, the peer of swift Ares, led the way, till they came to the host, in that place whither he bade him go.

And when the Trojans saw Idomeneus, strong as flame, and his squire with him, and their glorious armour, they all shouted and made for him through the press. Then their mellay began, by the sterns of the ships. And as the gusts speed on, when shrill winds blow, on a day when dust lies thickest on the roads, and the winds raise together a great cloud of dust, even so their battle clashed together, and all were fain of heart to slay each other in the press with the keen bronze. And the battle, the bane of men, bristled with the long spears, the piercing spears they grasped, and the glitter of bronze from gleaming helmets dazzled the eyes, and the sheen of new-burnished corslets, and shining shields, as the men thronged all together. Right hardy of heart would he have been that joyed and sorrowed not at the sight of this labour of battle.

Thus the two mighty sons of Kronos, with contending will, were contriving sorrow and anguish for the heroes. Zeus desired victory for the Trojans and Hector, giving glory to swift-footed Achilles; yet he did not wish the Achaian host to perish utterly before Ilios, but only to give renown to Thetis and her strong-hearted son. But Poseidon went among the Argives and stirred them to war, stealing secretly forth from the grey salt sea: for he was sore vexed that they were overcome by the Trojans, and was greatly in wrath against Zeus. Verily both were of the same lineage and the same place of birth, but Zeus was the elder and the wiser. Therefore also Poseidon avoided to give open aid, but secretly ever he spurred them on, throughout the host, in the likeness of a man. These twain had strained the ends of the cords of strong strife and equal war, and had stretched them over both Trojans and Achaians, a knot that none might break nor undo, for the loosening of the knees of many.

Even then Idomeneus, though his hair was flecked with grey, called on the Danaans, and leaping among the Trojans, roused their terror. For he slew Othryoneus of Kabesos, a sojourner there, who but lately had followed after the rumour of war, and asked in marriage the fairest of the daughters of Priam, Kassandra, without gifts of wooing, but with promise of mighty deed, namely that he would drive perforce out of Troy-land the sons of the Achaians. To him the old man Priam had promised and appointed that he would give her, so he fought trusting in his promises. And Idomeneus aimed at him with a bright spear, and cast and smote him as he came proudly striding on, and the corslet of bronze that he wore availed not, but the lance struck in the midst of his belly. And he fell with a crash, and Idomeneus boasted over him, and lifted up his voice, saying: "Othryoneus, verily I praise thee above all mortal men, if indeed thou shalt accomplish all that thou hast promised Priam, son of Dardanos, that promised thee again his own daughter. Yea, and we likewise would promise as much to thee, and fulfil it, and would give thee the fairest daughter of the son of Atreus, and bring her from Argos, and wed her to thee, if only thou wilt aid us to take the fair-set citadel of Ilios. Nay, follow us that we may make a covenant of marriage by the seafaring ships, for we are no hard exacters of gifts of wooing."

Therewith the hero Idomeneus dragged him by the foot across the fierce mellay. But Asios came to his aid, on foot before his horses that the charioteer guided so that still their breath touched the shoulders of Asios.

And the desire of his heart was to cast at Idomeneus, who was beforehand with him, and smote him with the spear in the throat, below the chin, and drove the point straight through. And he fell as an oak falls, or a poplar, or tall pine tree, that craftsmen have felled on the hills with new whetted axes, to be a ship's timber; even so he lay stretched out before the horses and the chariot, groaning, and clutching the bloody dust. And the charioteer was amazed, and kept not his wits, as of old, and dared not turn his horses and avoid out of the hands of foemen; and Antilochos the steadfast in war smote him, and pierced the middle of his body with a spear. Nothing availed the corslet of bronze he was wont to wear, but he planted the spear fast in the midst of his belly. Therewith he fell gasping from the well-wrought chariot, and Antilochos, the son of great-hearted Nestor, drave the horses out from the Trojans, among the well-greaved Achaians. Then Deiphobos, in sorrow for Asios, drew very nigh Idomeneus, and cast at him with his shining spear. But Idomeneus steadily watching him, avoided the spear of bronze, being hidden beneath the circle of his shield, the shield covered about with ox-hide and gleaming bronze, that he allows bore, fitted with two arm-rods: under this he crouched together, and the spear of bronze flew over. And his shield rang sharply, as the spear grazed thereon. Yet it flew not vainly from the heavy hand of Deiphobos, but smote Hypsenor, son of Hippasos, the shepherd of the hosts, in the liver, beneath the midriff, and instantly unstrung his knees. And Deiphobos boasted over him terribly, crying aloud: "Ah, verily, not unavenged lies Asios, nay, methinks, that even on his road to Hades, strong Warden of the gate, he will rejoice at heart, since, lo, I have sent him escort for the way!"

So spake he, but grief came on the Argives by reason of his boast, and stirred above all the soul of the wise-hearted Antilochos, yet, despite his sorrow, he was not heedless of his dear comrade, but ran and stood over him, and covered him with his buckler. Then two trusty companions, Mekisteus, son of Echios, and goodly Alastor, stooped down and lifted him, and with heavy groaning bare him to the hollow ships.

And Idomeneus relaxed not his mighty force, but ever was striving, either to cover some one of the Trojans with black night, or himself to fall in warding off death from the Achaians. There the dear son of Aisyetes, fosterling of Zeus, even the hero Alkathoos, was slain, who was son-in-law of Anchises, and had married the eldest of his daughters, Hippodameia, whom her father and her lady mother dearly loved in the halls, for she excelled all the maidens of her age in beauty, and skill, and in wisdom, wherefore the best man in wide Troy took her to wife. This Alkathoos did Poseidon subdue to Idomeneus, throwing a spell over his shining eyes, and snaring his glorious limbs; so that he might neither flee backwards, nor avoid the stroke, but stood steady as a pillar, or a tree with lofty crown of leaves, when the hero Idomeneus smote him in the midst of the breast with the spear, and rent the coat of bronze about him, that aforetime warded death from his body, but now rang harsh as it was rent by the spear. And he fell with a crash, and the lance fixed in his heart, that, still beating, shook the butt-end of the spear. Then at length mighty Ares spent its fury there; but Idomeneus boasted terribly, and cried aloud: "Deiphobos, are we to deem it fair acquittal that we have slain three men for one, since thou boastest thus? Nay, sir, but stand thou up also thyself against me, that thou mayst know what manner of son of Zeus am I that have come hither! For Zeus first begat Minos, the warden of Crete, and Minos got him a son, the noble Deukalion, and Deukalion begat me, a prince over many men in wide Crete, and now have the ships brought me hither, a bane to thee and thy father, and all the Trojans."

Thus he spake, but the thoughts of Deiphobos were divided, whether be should retreat, and call to his aid some one of the great-hearted Trojans, or should try the adventure alone. And on this wise to his mind it seemed the better, to go after Aineias, whom he found standing the last in the press, for Aineias was ever wroth against goodly Priam, for that Priam gave him no honour, despite his valour among men. So Deiphobos stood by him, and spake winged words to him: "Aineias, thou counsellor of the Trojans, now verily there is great need that thou shouldst succour thy sister's husband, if any care for kin doth touch thee. Nay follow, let us succour Alkathoos, thy sister's husband, who of old did cherish thee in his hall, while thou wert but a little one, and now, lo, spear-famed Idomeneus hath stripped him of his arms!"

So he spake, and roused the spirit in the breast of Aineias, who went to seek Idomeneus, with high thoughts of war. But fear took not hold upon Idomeneus, as though he had been some tender boy, but he stood at bay, like a boar on the hills that trusteth to his strength, and abides the great assailing throng of men in a lonely place, and he bristles up his back, and his eyes shine with fire, while he whets his tusks, and is right eager to keep at bay both men and hounds. Even so stood spear-famed Idomeneus at bay against Aineias, that came to the rescue, and gave ground no whit, but called on his comrades, glancing to Askalaphos, and Aphareus, and Deipyros, and Meriones, and Antilochos, all masters of the war-cry; them he spurred up to battle, and spake winged words: "Hither, friends, and rescue me, all alone as I am, and terribly I dread the onslaught of swift-footed Aineias, that is assailing me; for he is right strong to destroy men in battle, and he hath the flower of youth, the greatest avail that may be. Yea, if he and I were of like age, and in this spirit whereof now we are, speedily should he or I achieve high victory."

So he spake, and they all, being of one spirit in their hearts, stood hard by each other, with buckler laid on shoulder. But Aineias, on the other side, cried to his comrades, glancing to Deiphobos, and Paris, and noble Agenor, that with him were leaders of the Trojans; and then the hosts followed them, as sheep follow their leader to the water from the pasture, and the shepherd is glad at heart; even so the heart of Aineias was glad in his breast, when he saw the hosts of the people following to aid him.

Then they rushed in close fight around Alkathoos with their long spears, and round their breasts the bronze rang terribly, as they aimed at each other in the press, while two men of war beyond the rest, Aineias and Idomeneus, the peers of Ares, were each striving to hew the flesh of the other with the pitiless bronze. Now Aineias first cast at Idomeneus, who steadily watching him avoided the spear of bronze, and the point of Aineias went quivering in the earth, since vainly it had flown from his stalwart hand. But Idomeneus smote Oinomaos in the midst of the belly, and brake the plate of his corslet, and the bronze let forth the bowels through the corslet, and he fell in the dust and clutched the earth in his palms. And Idomeneus drew forth the far-shadowing spear from the dead, but could not avail to strip the rest of the fair armour from his shoulders, for the darts pressed hard on him. Nay, and his feet no longer served him firmly in a charge, nor could he rush after his own spear, nor avoid the foe. Wherefore in close fight he still held off the pitiless day of destiny, but in retreat: his feet no longer bore him swiftly from the battle. And as he was slowly departing, Deiphobos aimed at him with his shining spear, for verily he ever cherished a steadfast hatred against Idomeneus. But this time, too, he missed him, and smote Askalapbos, the son of Enyalios, with his dart, and the strong spear passed through his shoulder, and he fell in the dust, and clutched the earth in his outstretched hand. But loud-voiced awful Ares was not yet aware at all that his son had fallen in strong battle, but he was reclining on the peak of Olympus, beneath the golden clouds, being held there by the design of Zeus, where also were the other deathless gods, restrained from the war.

Now the people rushed in close fight around Askalaphos, and Deiphobos tore from Askalaphos his shining helm, but Meriones, the peer of swift Ares, leaped forward and smote the arm of Deiphobos with his spear, and from his hand the vizored casque fell clanging to the ground. And Meriones sprang forth instantly, like a vulture, and drew the strong spear from the shoulder of Deiphobos, and fell back among the throng of his comrades. But the own brother of Deiphobos, Polites, stretched his hands round his waist, and led him forth from the evil din of war, even till he came to the swift horses, that waited for him behind the battle and the fight, with their charioteer, and well-dight chariot. These bore him heavily groaning to the city, worn with his hurt, and the blood ran down from his newly wounded arm.

But the rest still were fighting, and the war-cry rose unquenched. There Aineias rushed on Aphareus, son of Kaletor, and struck his throat, that chanced to be turned to him, with the keen spear, and his head dropped down and his shield and helm fell with him, and death that slays the spirit overwhelmed him. And Antilochos watched Thoon as he turned the other way, and leaped on him, and wounded him, severing all the vein that runs up the back till it reaches the neck; this he severed clean, and Thoon fell on his back in the dust, stretching out both his hands to his comrades dear. Then Antilochos rushed on, and stripped the armour from his shoulders, glancing around while the Trojans gathered from here and there, and smote his wide shining shield, yet did not avail to graze, behind the shield, the delicate flesh of Antilochos with the pitiless bronze. For verily Poseidon, the Shaker of the earth, did guard on every side the son of Nestor, even in the midst of the javelins. And never did Antilochos get free of the foe, but turned him about among them, nor ever was his spear at rest, but always brandished and shaken, and the aim of his heart was to smite a foeman from afar, or to set on him at close quarters. But as he was aiming through the crowd, he escaped not the ken of Adamas, son of Asios, who smote the midst of his shield with the sharp bronze, setting on nigh at hand; but Poseidon of the dark locks made his shaft of no avail, grudging him the life of Antilochos. And part of the spear abode there, like a burned stake, in the shield of Antilochos, and half lay on the earth, and back retreated Adamas to the ranks of his comrades, avoiding Fate. But Meriones following after him as he departed, smote him with a spear between the privy parts and the navel, where a wound is most baneful to wretched mortals. Even there he fixed the spear in him and he fell, and writhed about the spear, even as a bull that herdsmen on the hills drag along perforce when they have bound him with withes, so he when he was smitten writhed for a moment, not for long, till the hero Meriones came near, and drew the spear out of his body. And darkness covered his eyes.

And Helenos in close fight smote Deipyros on the temple, with a great Thracian sword, and tore away the helm, and the helm, being dislodged, fell on the ground, and one of the Achaians in the fight picked it up as it rolled between his feet. But dark night covered the eyes of Deipyros.

Then grief took hold of the son of Atreus, Menelaos of the loud war-cry, and he went with a threat against the warrior Helenos, the prince, shaking his sharp spear, while the other drew the centre-piece of his bow. And both at once were making ready to let fly, one with his sharp spear, the other with the arrow from the string. Then the son of Priam smote Menelaos on the breast with his arrow, on the plate of the corslet, and off flew the bitter arrow. Even as from a broad shovel in a great threshing floor, fly the black-skinned beans and pulse, before the whistling wind, and the stress of the winnower's shovel, even so from the corslet of the renowned Menelaos flew glancing far aside the bitter arrow. But the son of Atreus, Menelaos of the loud war-cry, smote the hand of Helenos wherein he held the polished bow, and into the bow, clean through the hand, was driven the spear of bronze. Back he withdrew to the ranks of his comrades, avoiding Fate, with his hand hanging down at his side, for the ashen spear dragged after him. And the great-hearted Agenor drew the spear from his hand, and himself bound up the hand with a band of twisted sheep's-wool, a sling that a squire carried for him, the shepherd of the host.

Then Peisandros made straight for renowned Menelaos, but an evil Fate was leading him to the end of Death; by thee, Menelaos, to be overcome in the dread strife of battle. Now when the twain had come nigh in onset upon each other, the son of Atreus missed, and his spear was turned aside, but Peisandros smote the shield of renowned Menelaos, yet availed not to drive the bronze clean through, for the wide shield caught it, and the spear brake in the socket, yet Peisandros rejoiced in his heart, and hoped for the victory. But the son of Atreus drew his silver-studded sword, and leaped upon Peisandros. And Peisandros, under his shield, clutched his goodly axe of fine bronze, with long and polished haft of olive-wood, and the twain set upon each other. Then Peisandros smote the crest of the helmet shaded with horse hair, close below the very plume, but Menelaos struck the other, as he came forward, on the brow, above the base of the nose, and the bones cracked, and the eyes, all bloody, fell at his feet in the dust. Then he bowed and fell, and Menelaos set his foot on his breast, and stripped him of his arms, and triumphed, saying: "Even thus then surely, ye will leave the ships of the Danaans of the swift steeds, ye Trojans overweening, insatiate of the dread din of war. Yea, and ye shall not lack all other reproof and shame, wherewith ye made me ashamed, ye hounds of evil, having no fear in your hearts of the strong wrath of loud-thundering Zeus, the god of guest and host, who one day will destroy your steep citadel. O ye that wantonly carried away my wedded wife and many of my possessions, when ye were entertained by her, now again ye are fain to throw ruinous fire on the seafaring ships, and to slay the Achaian heroes. Nay, but ye will yet refrain you from battle, for as eager as ye be. O Zeus, verily they say that thou dost excel in wisdom all others, both gods and men, and all these things are from thee. How wondrously art thou favouring men of violence, even the Trojans, whose might is ever iniquitous, nor can they have their fill of the din of equal war. Of all things there is satiety, yea, even of love and sleep, and of sweet song, and dance delectable, whereof a man would sooner have his fill than of war, but the Trojans are insatiable of battle."

Thus noble Menelaos spake, and stripped the bloody arms from the body, and gave them to his comrades, and instantly himself went forth again, and mingled in the forefront of the battle. Then Harpalion, the son of king Pylaimenes, leaped out against him, Harpalion that followed his dear father to Troy, to the war, nor ever came again to his own country. He then smote the middle of the shield of Atreus' son with his spear, in close fight, yet availed not to drive the bronze clean through, but fell back into the host of his comrades, avoiding Fate, glancing round every way, lest one should wound his flesh with the bronze. But Meriones shot at him as he retreated with a bronze-shod arrow, and smote him in the right buttock, and the arrow went right through the bladder and came out under the bone. And sitting down, even there, in the arms of his dear comrades, he breathed away his soul, lying stretched like a worm on the earth, and out flowed the black blood, and wetted the ground. And the Paphlagonians great of heart, tended him busily, and set him in a chariot, and drove him to sacred Ilios sorrowing, and with them went his father, shedding tears, and there was no atonement for his dead son.

Now Paris was very wroth at heart by reason of his slaying, for he had been his host among the many Paphlagonions, wherefore, in wrath for his sake, he let fly a bronze-shod arrow. Now there was a certain Euchenor, the son of Polyidos the seer, a rich man and a good, whose dwelling was in Corinth. And well he knew his own ruinous fate, when he went on ship-board, for often would the old man, the good Polyidos, tell him, that he must either perish of a sore disease in his halls, or go with the ships of the Achaians, and be overcome by the Trojans. Wherefore he avoided at once the heavy war-fine of the Achaians, and the hateful disease, that so he might not know any anguish. This man did Paris smite beneath the jaw and under the ear, and swiftly his spirit departed from his limbs, and, lo, dread darkness overshadowed him.

So they fought like flaming fire, but Hector, beloved of Zeus had not heard nor knew at all that, on the left of the ships, his host was being subdued by the Argives, and soon would the Achaians have won renown, so mighty was the Holder and Shaker of the earth that urged on the Argives; yea, and himself mightily defended them. But Hector kept where at first he had leaped within the walls and the gate, and broken the serried ranks of shield-bearing Danaans, even where were the ships of Aias and Protesilaos, drawn up on the beach of the hoary sea, while above the wall was builded lowest, and thereby chiefly the heroes and their horses were raging in battle.

There the Boiotians, and Ionians with trailing tunics, and Lokrians and Phthians and illustrious Epeians scarcely availed to stay his onslaught on the ships, nor yet could they drive back from them noble Hector, like a flame of fire. And there were the picked men of the Athenians; among them Menestheus son of Peteos was the leader; and there followed with him Pheidas and Stichios, and brave Bias, while the Epeians were led by Meges, son of Phyleus, and Amphion and Drakios, and in front of the Phthians were Medon, and Podarkes resolute in war. Now the one, Medon, was the bastard son of noble Oileus, and brother of Aias, and he dwelt in Phylake, far from his own country, for that he had slain a man, the brother of his stepmother Eriopis, wife of Oileus. But the other, Podarkes, was the son of Iphiklos son of Phylakos, and they in their armour, in the van of the great-hearted Phthians, were defending the ships, and fighting among the Boiotians.

Now never at all did Aias, the swift son of Oileus, depart from the side of Aias, son of Telamon, nay, not for an instant, but even as in fallow land two wine-dark oxen with equal heart strain at the shapen plough, and round the roots of their horns springeth up abundant sweat, and nought sunders them but the polished yoke, as they labour through the furrow, till the end of the furrow brings them up, so stood the two Aiantes close by each other. Now verily did many and noble hosts of his comrades follow with the son of Telamon, and bore his shield when labour and sweat came upon his limbs. But the Lokrians followed not with the high-hearted son of Oileus, for their hearts were not steadfast in close brunt of battle, seeing that they had no helmets of bronze, shadowy with horse-hair plumes, nor round shields, nor ashen spears, but trusting in bows and well-twisted slings of sheep's wool, they followed with him to Ilios. Therewith, in the war, they shot thick and fast, and brake the ranks of the Trojans. So the one party in front contended with the Trojans, and with Hector arrayed in bronze, while the others from behind kept shooting from their ambush, and the Trojans lost all memory of the joy of battle, for the arrows confounded them.

There then right ruefully from the ships and the huts would the Trojans have withdrawn to windy Ilios, had not Polydamas come near valiant Hector and said: "Hector, thou art hard to be persuaded by them that would counsel thee; for that god has given thee excellence in the works of war, therefore in council also thou art fain to excel other men in knowledge. But in nowise wilt thou be able to take everything on thyself. For to one man has god given for his portion the works of war, [to another the dance, to another the lute and song,] but in the heart of yet another hath far-seeing Zeus placed an excellent understanding, whereof many men get gain, yea he saveth many an one, and himself best knoweth it. But, lo, I will speak even as it seemeth best to me. Behold all about thee the circle of war is blazing, but the great-hearted Trojans, now that they have got down the wall, are some with their arms standing aloof and some are fighting, few men against a host, being scattered among the ships. Nay, withdraw thee, and call hither all the best of the warriors. Thereafter shall we take all counsel carefully, whether we should fall on the ships of many benches, if indeed god willeth to give us victory, or after counsel held, should return unharmed from the ships. For verily I fear lest the Achaians repay their debt of yesterday, since by the ships there tarrieth a man insatiate of war, and never, methinks, will he wholly stand aloof from battle."

So spake Polydamas, and his safe counsel pleased Hector well, who spake to him winged words and said: "Polydamas, do thou stay here all the best of the host, but I will go thither to face the war, and swiftly will return again, when I have straitly laid on them my commands."

So he spake, and set forth, in semblance like a snowy mountain, and shouting aloud he flew through the Trojans and allies. And they all sped to Polydamas, the kindly son of Panthoos, when they heard the voice of Hector. But he went seeking Deiphobos, and the strong prince Helenos, and Adamas son of Asios, and Asios son of Hyrtakos, among the warriors

in the foremost line, if anywhere he might find them. But them he found
not at all unharmed, nor free of bane, but, lo, some among the sterns of
the ships of the Achaians lay lifeless, slain by the hands of the Argives,
and some were within the wall wounded by thrust or cast. But one he
readily found, on the left of the dolorous battle, goodly Alexandros, the
lord of fair-tressed Helen, heartening his comrades and speeding them to
war. And he drew near to him, and addressed him with words of shame:
"Thou evil Paris, fairest of face, thou that lustest for women, thou seducer,
where, prithee, are Deiphobos, and the strong prince Helenos, and
Adamas son of Asios, and Asios son of Hyrtakos, and where is
Othryoneus? Now hath all high Ilios perished utterly. Now, too, thou
seest, is sheer destruction sure."

Then godlike Alexandros answered him again saying: "Hector, since thy
mind is to blame one that is blameless, some other day might I rather
withdraw me from the war, since my mother bare not even me wholly a
coward. For from the time that thou didst gather the battle of thy
comrades about the ships, from that hour do we abide here, and war with
the Danaans ceaselessly; and our comrades concerning whom thou
inquirest are slain. Only Deiphobos and the strong prince Helenos have
both withdrawn, both of them being wounded in the hand with long
spears, for Kronion kept death away from them. But now lead on,
wheresoever thy heart and spirit bid thee, and we will follow with thee
eagerly, nor methinks shall we lack for valour, as far as we have strength;
but beyond his strength may no man fight, howsoever eager he be."

So spake the hero, and persuaded his brother's heart, and they went
forth where the war and din were thickest, round Kebriones, and noble
Polydamas, and Phalkes, and Orthaios, and godlike Polyphetes, and
Palmys, and Askanios, and Morys, son of Hippotion, who had come in
their turn, out of deep-soiled Askanie, on the morn before, and now Zeus
urged them to fight. And these set forth like the blast of violent winds,
that rushes earthward beneath the thunder of Zeus, and with marvellous
din doth mingle with the salt sea, and therein are many swelling waves
of the loud roaring sea, arched over and white with foam, some vanward,
others in the rear; even so the Trojans arrayed in van and rear and
shining with bronze, followed after their leaders.

And Hector son of Priam was leading them, the peer of Ares, the bane
of men. In front he held the circle of his shield, thick with hides, and
plates of beaten bronze, and on his temples swayed his shining helm. And
everywhere he went in advance and made trial of the ranks, if perchance
they would yield to him as he charged under cover of his shield. But he
could not confound the heart within the breast of the Achaians. And Aias,
stalking with long strides, challenged him first: "Sir, draw nigh, wherefore
dost thou vainly try to dismay the Argives? We are in no wise ignorant of
war, but by the cruel scourge of Zeus are we Achaians vanquished. Surely
now thy heart hopes utterly to spoil the ships, but we too have hands

presently to hold our own. Verily your peopled city will long ere that beneath our hands be taken and sacked. But for thee, I tell thee that the time is at hand, when thou shalt pray in thy flight to Zeus, and the other immortal gods, that thy fair-maned steeds may be fleeter than falcons: thy steeds that are to bear thee to the city, as they storm in dust across the plain."

And even as he spake, a bird flew forth on the right hand, an eagle of lofty flight, and the host of the Achaians shouted thereat, encouraged by the omen, but renowned Hector answered: "Aias, thou blundering boaster, what sayest thou! Would that indeed I were for ever as surely the son of aegis-bearing Zeus, and that my mother were lady Hera, and that I were held in such honour as Apollo and Athene, as verily this day is to bring utter evil on all the Argives! And thou among them shalt be slain, if thou hast the heart to await my long spear, which shall rend thy lily skin, and thou shalt glut with thy fat and flesh the birds and dogs of the Trojans, falling among the ships of the Achaians."

So he spake and led the way, and they followed with wondrous din, and the whole host shouted behind. And the Argives on the other side answered with a shout, and forgot not their valiance, but abode the onslaught of the bravest of the Trojans. And the cry of the two hosts went up through the higher air, to the splendour of Zeus.

BOOK XIV

How Sleep and Hera beguiled Zeus to slumber on the heights of Ida, and Poseidon spurred on the Achaians to resist Hector, and how Hector was wounded.

Yet the cry of battle escaped not Nestor, albeit at his wine, but he spake winged words to the son of Asklepios: "Bethink thee, noble Machaon, what had best be done; lo, louder waxes the cry of the strong warriors by the ships. Nay, now sit where thou art, and drink the bright wine, till Hekamede of the fair tresses shall heat warm water for the bath, and wash away the clotted blood, but I will speedily go forth and come to a place of outlook."

Therewith he took the well-wrought shield of his son, horse-taming Thrasymedes, which was lying in the hut, all glistering with bronze, for the son had the shield of his father. And he seized a strong spear, with a point of keen bronze, and stood outside the hut, and straightway beheld a deed of shame, the Achaians fleeing in rout, and the high-hearted Trojans driving them, and the wall of the Achaians was overthrown. And as when the great sea is troubled with a dumb wave, and dimly bodes the sudden paths of the shrill winds, but is still unmoved nor yet rolled forward or to either side, until some steady gale comes down from Zeus, even so the old man pondered,—his mind divided this way and

that,—whether he should fare into the press of the Danaans of the swift
steeds, or go after Agamemnon, son of Atreus, shepherd of the host. And
thus as he pondered, it seemed to him the better counsel to go to the son
of Atreus. Meanwhile they were warring and slaying each other, and the
stout bronze rang about their bodies as they were thrust with swords and
double-pointed spears.

Now the kings, the fosterlings of Zeus, encountered Nestor, as they
went up from the ships, even they that were wounded with the bronze,
Tydeus' son, and Odysseus, and Agamemnon, son of Atreus. For far apart
from the battle were their ships drawn up, on the shore of the grey sea, for
these were the first they had drawn up to the plain, but had builded the
wall in front of the hindmost. For in no wise might the beach, wide as it
was, hold all the ships, and the host was straitened. Wherefore they drew
up the ships row within row, and filled up the wide mouth of all the shore
that the headlands held between them. Therefore the kings were going
together, leaning on their spears, to look on the war and fray, and the
heart of each was sore within his breast. And the old man met them, even
Nestor, and caused the spirit to fail within the breasts of the Achaians.

And mighty Agamemnon spake and accosted him: "O Nestor, son of
Neleus, great glory of the Achaians, wherefore dost thou come hither and
hast deserted the war, the bane of men? Lo, I fear the accomplishment of
the word that dread Hector spake, and the threat wherewith he
threatened us, speaking in the assembly of the Trojans, namely, that
never would he return to Ilios from the ships, till he had burned the ships
with fire, and slain the men. Even so he spake, and, lo, now all these
things are being fulfilled. Alas, surely even the other well-greaved
Achaians store wrath against me in their hearts, like Achilles, and have
no desire to fight by the rearmost ships."

Then Nestor of Gerenia the knight answered him saying "Verily these
things are now at hand, and being accomplished, nor otherwise could Zeus
himself contrive them, he that thundereth on high. For, lo, the wall is
overthrown, wherein we trusted that it should be an unbroken bulwark
of the ships and of our own bodies. But let us take counsel, bow these
things may best be done, if wit may do aught: but into the war I counsel
not that we should go down, for in no wise may a wounded man do battle."

Then Agamemnon king of men answered him again: "Nestor, for that
they are warring by the rearmost ships, and the well-builded wall hath
availed not, nor the trench, whereat the Achaians endured so much
labour, hoping in their hearts that it should be the unbroken bulwark of
the ships, and of their own bodies—such it seemeth must be the will of
Zeus supreme, [that the Achaians should perish here nameless far from
Argos]. For I knew it when he was forward to aid the Danaans, and now
I know that he is giving to the Trojans glory like that of the blessed gods,
and hath bound our hands and our strength. But come, as I declare, let us
all obey. Let us drag down the ships that are drawn up in the first line

near to the sea, and speed them all forth to the salt sea divine, and moor them far out with stones, till the divine night comes, if even at night the Trojans will refrain from war, and then might we drag down all the ships. For there is no shame in fleeing from ruin, yea, even in the night. Better doth he fare who flees from trouble, than he that is overtaken."

Then, looking on him sternly, spake Odysseus of many counsels: "Atreus' son, what word hath passed the door of thy lips? Man of mischief, sure thou shouldst lead some other inglorious army, not be king among us, to whom Zeus hath given it, from youth even unto age, to wind the skein of grievous wars, till every man of us perish. Art thou indeed so eager to leave the wide-wayed city of the Trojans, the city for which we endure with sorrow so many evils? Be silent, lest some other of the Achaians hear this word, that no man should so much as suffer to pass through his mouth, none that understandeth in his heart how to speak fit counsel, none that is a sceptred king, and hath hosts obeying him so many as the Argives over whom thou reignest. And now I wholly scorn thy thoughts, such a word as thou hast uttered, thou that, in the midst of war and battle, dost bid us draw down the well-timbered ships to the sea, that even more than ever the Trojans may possess their desire, albeit they win the mastery even now, and sheer destruction fall upon us. For the Achaians will not make good the war, when the ships are drawn down to the salt sea, but will look round about to flee, and withdraw from battle. There will thy counsel work a mischief, O marshal of the host!"

Then the king of men, Agamemnon, answered him: "Odysseus, right sharply hast thou touched my heart with thy stern reproof: nay, I do not bid the sons of the Achaians to drag, against their will, the well-timbered ships to the salt sea. Now perchance there may be one who will utter a wiser counsel than this of mine,—a young man or an old,—welcome would it be to me."

Then Diomedes of the loud war-cry spake also among them: "The man is near,—not long shall we seek him, if ye be willing to be persuaded of me, and each of you be not resentful at all, because in years I am the youngest among you. Nay, but I too boast me to come by lineage of a noble sire, Tydeus, whom in Thebes the piled-up earth doth cover. For Portheus had three well-born children, and they dwelt in Pleuron, and steep Kalydon, even Agrios and Melas, and the third was Oineus the knight, the father of my father, and in valour he excelled the others. And there he abode, but my father dwelt at Argos, whither he had wandered, for so Zeus and the other gods willed that it should be. And he wedded one of the daughters of Adrastos, and dwelt in a house full of livelihood, and had wheat-bearing fields enow, and many orchards of trees apart, and many sheep were his, and in skill with the spear he excelled all the Achaians: these things ye must have heard, if I speak sooth. Therefore ye could not say that I am weak and a coward by lineage, and so dishonour my spoken counsel, that well I may speak. Let us go down to the battle, wounded as we are, since we needs must; and then might we hold ourselves aloof from the battle, beyond the range of darts, lest any take wound upon wound; but the others will we spur on, even them that aforetime gave place to their passion, and stand apart, and fight not."

So he spake, and they all heard him readily, and obeyed him. And they set forth, led by Agamemnon the king of men.

Now the renowned Earth-shaker held no vain watch, but went with them in the guise of an ancient man, and he seized the right hand of Agamemnon, Atreus' son, and uttering winged words he spake to him, saying: "Atreides, now methinks the ruinous heart of Achilles rejoices in his breast, as he beholds the slaughter and flight of the Achaians, since he hath no wisdom, not a grain. Nay, even so may he perish likewise, and god mar him. But with thee the blessed gods are not utterly wroth, nay, even yet methinks the leaders and rulers of the Trojans will cover the wide plain with dust, and thyself shalt see them fleeing to the city from the ships and the huts."

So spake he, and shouted mightily, as he sped over the plain. And loud as nine thousand men, or ten thousand cry in battle, when they join the strife of war, so mighty was the cry that the strong Shaker of the earth sent forth from his breast, and great strength he put into the heart of each of the Achaians, to strive and war unceasingly.

Now Hera of the golden throne stood on the peak of Olympus, and saw with her eyes, and anon knew him that was her brother and her lord's going to and fro through the glorious fight, and she rejoiced in her heart. And she beheld Zeus sitting on the topmost crest of many-fountained Ida, and to her heart he was hateful. Then she took thought, the ox-eyed lady Hera, how she might beguile the mind of aegis-bearing Zeus. And this seemed to her in her heart to be the best counsel, namely to fare to Ida, when she had well adorned herself, if perchance a sweet sleep and a kindly she could pour on his eye lids and his crafty wits. And she set forth to her bower, that her dear son Hephaistos had fashioned, and therein had made fast strong doors on the pillars, with a secret bolt, that no other god might open. There did she enter in and closed the shining doors. With ambrosia first did she cleanse every stain from her winsome body, and anointed her with olive oil, ambrosial, soft, and of a sweet savour; if it were but shaken, in the bronze-floored mansion of Zeus, the savour thereof went right forth to earth and heaven. Therewith she anointed her fair body, and combed her hair, and with her hands plaited her shining tresses, fair and ambrosial, flowing from her immortal head. Then she clad her in her fragrant robe that Athene wrought delicately for her, and therein set many things beautifully made, and fastened it over her breast with clasps of gold. And she girdled it with a girdle arrayed with a hundred tassels, and she set earrings in her pierced ears, earrings of three drops, and glistering, therefrom shone grace abundantly. And with a veil over all the peerless goddess veiled herself, a fair new veil, bright as the sun, and beneath her shining feet she bound goodly sandals. But when she had adorned her body with all her array, she went forth from her bower, and called Aphrodite apart from the other gods, and spake to her, saying: "Wilt thou obey me, dear child, in that which I shall tell thee? or wilt thou refuse, with a grudge in thy heart, because I succour the Danaans, and thou the Trojans?"

Then Aphrodite the daughter of Zeus answered her: "Hera, goddess queen, daughter of mighty Kronos, say the thing that is in thy mind, my heart bids me fulfil it, if fulfil it I may, and if it may be accomplished."

Then with crafty purpose the lady Hera answered her: "Give me now Love and Desire wherewith thou dost overcome all the Immortals, and mortal men. For I am going to visit the limits of the bountiful Earth, and Okeanos, father of the gods, and mother Tethys, who reared me well and nourished me in their halls, having taken me from Rhea, when far-seeing Zeus imprisoned Kronos beneath the earth and the unvintaged sea. Them am I going to visit, and their endless strife will I loose, for already this long time they hold apart from each other, since wrath hath settled in their hearts. If with words I might persuade their hearts, and bring them back to love, ever should I be called dear to them and worshipful."

Then laughter-loving Aphrodite answered her again: "It may not be, nor seemly were it, to deny that thou askest, for thou sleepest in the arms of Zeus, the chief of gods."

Therewith from her breast she loosed the broidered girdle, fair-wrought, wherein are all her enchantments; therein are love, and desire, and loving converse, that steals the wits even of the wise. This girdle she laid in her hands, and spake, and said: "Lo now, take this girdle and lay it up in thy bosom, this fair-wrought girdle, wherein all things are fashioned; methinks thou wilt not return with that unaccomplished, which in thy heart thou desirest."

So spake she, and the ox-eyed lady Hera smiled, and smiling laid up the zone within her breast.

Then the daughter of Zeus, Aphrodite, went to her house, and Hera, rushing down, left the peak of Olympus, and sped' over the snowy hills of the Thracian horsemen, even over the topmost crests, nor grazed the ground with her feet, and from Athos she fared across the foaming sea, and came to Lemnos, the city of godlike Thoas. There she met Sleep, the brother of Death, and clasped her hand in his, and spake and called him by name: "Sleep, lord of all gods and of all men, if ever thou didst hear my word, obey me again even now, and I will be grateful to thee always. Lull me, I pray thee, the shining eyes of Zeus beneath his brows. And gifts I will give to thee, even a fair throne, imperishable for ever, a golden throne, that Hephaistos the Lame, mine own child, shall fashion skilfully, and will set beneath it a footstool for the feet, for thee to set thy shining feet upon, when thou art at a festival. Nay come, and I will give thee one of the younger of the Graces, to wed and to be called thy wife."

So she spake, and Sleep was glad, and answered and said:—"Come now, swear to me by the inviolable water of Styx, and with one of thy hands grasp the bounteous earth, and with the other the shining sea, that all may be witnesses to us, even all the gods below that are with Kronos, that verily thou wilt give me one of the younger of the Graces, even Pasithea, that myself do long for all my days."

So spake he, nor did she disobey, the white-armed goddess Hera; she sware as he bade her, and called all the gods by name, even those below Tartaros that are called Titans. But when she had sworn and ended that oath, the twain left the citadel of Lemnos, and of Imbros, clothed on in mist, and swiftly they accomplished the way. To many-fountained Ida they came, the mother of wild beasts, to Lekton, where first they left the sea, and they twain fared above the dry land, and the topmost forest waved beneath their feet. There Sleep halted, ere the eyes of Zeus beheld him, and alighted on a tall pine tree, the loftiest pine that then in all Ida rose through the nether to the upper air. But Hera swiftly drew nigh to topmost Gargaros, the highest crest of Ida, and Zeus the cloud-gatherer beheld her. And as he saw her, so love came over his deep heart, and he stood before her, and spoke, and said: "Hera, with what desire comest thou thus hither from Olympus, and thy horses and chariot are not here, whereon thou mightst ascend?"

Then with crafty purpose lady Hera answered him: "I am going to visit the limits of the bountiful Earth, and Okeanos, father of the gods, and mother Tethys, who reared me well and cherished me in their halls. Them am I going to visit, and their endless strife will I loose, for already this long time they hold apart from each other, since wrath hath settled in their hearts. But my horses are standing at the foot of many-fountained Ida, my horses that shall bear me over wet and dry. And now it is because of thee that I am thus come hither, down from Olympus, lest perchance thou mightest be wroth with me hereafter, if silently I were gone to the mansion of deep-flowing Okeanos."

Then Zeus, the gatherer of the clouds, answered her and said: "Hera, thither mayst thou go on a later day. For never once as thus did the love of goddess or woman so mightily overflow and conquer the heart within my breast."

Thus slept the Father in quiet on the crest of Gargaros, by Sleep and love overcome. But sweet Sleep started and ran to the ships of the Achaians, to tell his tidings to the god that holdeth and shaketh the earth. And he stood near him, and spake winged words: "Eagerly now, Poseidon, do thou aid the Danaans, and give them glory for a little space, while yet Zeus sleepeth, for over him have I shed soft slumber, and Hera hath beguiled him."

So he spake, and passed to the renowned tribes of men, and still the more did he set on Poseidon to aid the Danaans, who straightway sprang far afront of the foremost, and called to them: "Argives, are we again to yield the victory to Hector, son of Priam, that he may take our ships and win renown? Nay, even so he saith and declareth that he will do, for that Achilles by the hollow ships abides angered at heart. But for him there will be no such extreme regret, if we spur us on to aid each the other. Nay come, as I command, let us all obey. Let us harness us in the best shields that are in the host, and the greatest, and cover our heads with shining helms, and take the longest spears in our hands, and so go forth. Yea, and I will lead the way, and methinks that Hector, son of Priam, will not long await us, for all his eagerness. And whatsoever man is steadfast in battle, and hath a small buckler on his shoulder, let him give it to a worse man, and harness him in a larger shield."

So spake he, and they heard him eagerly and obeyed him. And them the kings themselves arrayed, wounded as they were, Tydeus' son, and Odysseus, and Agamemnon, son of Atreus. They went through all the host, and made exchange of weapons of war. The good arms did the good warrior harness him in, the worse he gave to the worse. But when they had done on the shining bronze about their bodies, they started on the march, and Poseidon led them, the Shaker of the earth, with a dread sword of fine edge in his strong hand, like unto lightning; wherewith it is not permitted that any should mingle in woful war, but fear holds men afar therefrom. But the Trojans on the other side was renowned Hector arraying. Then did they now strain the fiercest strife of war, even dark-haired Poseidon and glorious Hector, one succouring the Trojans, the other with the Argives. And the sea washed up to the huts and ships of the Argives, and they gathered together with a mighty cry. Not so loudly bellows the wave of the sea against the land, stirred up from the deep by the harsh breath of the north wind, nor so loud is the roar of burning fire in the glades of a mountain, when it springs to burn up the forest, nor calls the wind so loudly in the high leafy tresses of the trees, when it rages and roars its loudest, as then was the cry of the Trojans and Achaians, shouting dreadfully as they rushed upon each other.

First glorious Hector cast with his spear at Aias, who was facing him full, and did not miss, striking him where two belts were stretched across his breast, the belt of his shield, and of his silver-studded sword; these guarded his tender flesh. And Hector was enraged because his swift spear had flown vainly from his hand, and he retreated into the throng of his fellows, avoiding Fate.

Then as he was departing the great Telamonian Aias smote him with a huge stone; for many stones, the props of swift ships, were rolled among the feet of the fighters; one of these he lifted, and smote Hector on the breast, over the shield-rim, near the neck, and made him spin like a top with the blow, that he reeled round and round. And even as when an oak falls uprooted beneath the stroke of father Zeus, and a dread savour of brimstone arises therefrom, and whoso stands near and beholds it has no more courage, for dread is the bolt of great Zeus, even so fell mighty

Hector straightway in the dust. And the spear fell from his hand, but his shield and helm were made fast to him, and round him rang his arms adorned with bronze.

Then with a loud cry they ran up, the sons of the Achaians, hoping to drag him away, and they cast showers of darts. But not one availed to wound or smite the shepherd of the host, before that might be the bravest gathered about him, Polydamas, and Aineias, and goodly Agenor, and Sarpedon, leader of the Lykians, and noble Glaukos, and of the rest not one was heedless of him, but they held their round shields in front of him, and his comrades lifted him in their arms, and bare him out of the battle, till he reached his swift horses that were standing waiting for him, with the charioteer and the fair-dight chariot at the rear of the combat and the war. These toward the city bore him heavily moaning. Now when they came to the ford of the fair-flowing river, of eddying Xanthos, that immortal Zeus begat, there they lifted him from the chariot to the ground, and poured water over him, and he gat back his breath, and looked up with his eyes, and sitting on his heels kneeling, he vomited black blood. Then again he sank back on the ground, and black night covered his eyes, the stroke still conquering his spirit.

BOOK XV

Zeus awakening, biddeth Apollo revive Hector, and restore the fortunes of the Trojans. Fire is thrown on the ship of Protesilaos.

Now when they had sped in flight across the palisade and trench, and many were overcome at the hands of the Danaans, the rest were stayed, and abode beside the chariots in confusion, and pale with terror, and Zeus awoke, on the peaks of Ida, beside Hera of the golden throne. Then he leaped up, and stood, and beheld the Trojans and Achaians, those in flight, and these driving them on from the rear, even the Argives, and among them the prince Poseidon. And Hector he saw lying on the plain, and around him sat his comrades, and he was gasping with difficult breath, and his mind wandering, and was vomiting blood, for it was not the weakest of the Achaians that had smitten him. Beholding him, the father of men and gods had pity on him, and terribly he spoke to Hera, with fierce look: "O thou ill to deal with, Hera, verily it is thy crafty wile that has made noble Hector cease from the fight, and has terrified the host. Nay, but yet I know not whether thou mayst not be the first to reap the fruits of thy cruel treason, and I beat thee with stripes. Dost thou not remember, when thou wert hung from on high, and from thy feet I suspended two anvils, and round thy hands fastened a golden bond that might not be broken? And thou didst hang in the clear air and the clouds, and the gods were wroth in high Olympus, but they could not come round and unloose thee."

So spake he, and the ox-eyed lady Hera shuddered, and spake unto him winged words, saying: "Let earth now be witness hereto, and wide heaven above, and that falling water of Styx, the greatest oath and the most terrible to the blessed gods, and thine own sacred head, and our own bridal bed, whereby never would I forswear myself, that not by my will does earth-shaking Poseidon trouble the Trojans and Hector, and succour them of the other part. Nay, it is his own soul that urgeth and commandeth him, and he had pity on the Achaians, when he beheld them hard pressed beside the ships. I would even counsel him also to go even where thou, lord of the storm-cloud, mayst lead him."

So spake she, and the father of gods and men smiled, and answering her he spake winged words: "If thou, of a truth, O ox-eyed lady Hera, wouldst hereafter abide of one mind with me among the immortal gods, thereon would Poseidon, howsoever much his wish be contrariwise, quickly turn his mind otherwhere, after thy heart and mine. But if indeed thou speakest the truth and soothly, go thou now among the tribes of the gods, and call Iris to come hither, and Apollo, the renowned archer, that Iris may go among the host of mail-clad Achaians and tell Poseidon the prince to cease from the war, and get him unto his own house. But let Phoebus Apollo spur Hector on to the war, and breathe strength into him again, and make him forget his anguish, that now wears down his heart, and drive the Achaians back again, when he hath stirred in them craven fear. Let them flee and fall among the many-benched ships of Achilles son of Peleus, and he shall rouse his own comrade, Patroklos; and him shall renowned Hector slay with the spear, in front of Ilios, after that he has slain many other youths, and among them my son, noble Sarpedon. In wrath therefor shall goodly Achilles slay Hector. From that hour verily will I cause a new pursuit from the ships, that shall endure continually, even until the Achaians take steep Ilios, through the counsels of Athene. But before that hour neither do I cease in my wrath, nor will I suffer any other of the Immortals to help the Danaans there, before I accomplish that desire of the son of Peleus, as I promised him at the first, and confirmed the same with a nod of my head, on that day when the goddess Thetis clasped my knees, imploring me to honour Achilles, the sacker of cities."

So spake he, nor did the white-armed goddess Hera disobey him, and she sped down from the hills of Ida to high Olympus, and went among the gathering of the immortal gods. And she called Apollo without the hall and Iris, that is the messenger of the immortal gods, and she spake winged words, and addressed them, saying: "Zeus bids you go to Ida as swiftly as may be, and when ye have gone, and looked on the face of Zeus, do ye whatsoever he shall order and command."

And these twain came before the face of Zeus the cloud gatherer, and stood there, and he was nowise displeased at heart when he beheld them, for that speedily they had obeyed the words of his dear wife. And to Iris first he spake winged words: "Go, get thee, swift Iris, to the prince Poseidon, and tell him all these things, nor be a false messenger. Command him to cease from war and battle, and to go among the tribes of the gods, or into the bright sea. But if he will not obey my words, but will hold me in no regard, then let him consider in his heart and mind, lest he dare not for all his strength to abide me when I come against him, since I deem me to be far mightier than he, and elder born."

So spake he, nor did the wind-footed fleet Iris disobey him, but went down the hills of Ida to sacred Ilios. And as when snow or chill hail fleets from the clouds beneath the stress of the North Wind born in the clear air, so fleetly she fled in her eagerness, swift Iris, and drew near the renowned Earth-shaker and spake to him the message of Zeus. And he left the host of the Achaians, and passed to the sea, and sank, and sorely they missed him, the heroes of the Achaians.

Then Zeus, the gatherer of the clouds, spake to Apollo, saying: "Go now, dear Phoebus, to Hector of the helm of bronze. Let glorious Hector be thy care, and rouse in him great wrath even till the Achaians come in their flight to the ships, and the Hellespont. And from that moment will I devise word and deed wherewithal the Achaians may take breath again from their toil."

So spake he, nor was Apollo deaf to the word of the Father, but he went down the hills of Ida like a fleet falcon, the bane of doves, that is the swiftest of flying things. And he found the son of wise-hearted Priam, noble Hector, sitting up, no longer lying, for he had but late got back his life, and knew the comrades around him, and his gasping and his sweat had ceased, from the moment when the will of aegis-bearing Zeus began to revive him. Then far-darting Apollo stood near him, and spake to him: "Hector, son of Priam, why dost thou sit fainting apart from the others? Is it perchance that some trouble cometh upon thee?"

Then, with faint breath answered him Hector of the glancing helm: "Nay, but who art thou, best of the gods, who enquirest of me face to face? Dost thou not know that by the hindmost row of the ships of the Achaians, Aias of the loud war-cry smote me on the breast with a stone, as I was slaying his comrades, and made me cease from mine impetuous might? And verily I deemed that this very day I should pass to the dead, and the house of Hades, when I had gasped my life away."

Then prince Apollo the Far-darter answered him again: "Take courage now, so great an ally hath the son of Kronos sent thee out of Ida, to stand by thee and defend thee, even Phoebus Apollo of the golden sword, me who of old defend thee, thyself and the steep citadel. But come now, bid thy many charioteers drive their swift steeds against the hollow ships, and I will go before and make smooth all the way for the chariots, and will put to flight the Achaian heroes."

So he spake, and breathed great might into the shepherd of the host, and even as when a stalled horse, full fed at the manger, breaks his tether and speedeth at the gallop over the plain exultingly, being wont to bathe in the fair-flowing stream, and holds his head on high, and the mane floweth about his shoulders, and he trusteth in his glory, and nimbly his knees bear him to the haunts and pasture of the mares, even so Hector lightly moved his feet and knees, urging on his horsemen, when he heard the voice of the god. But as when hounds and country folk pursue a horned stag, or a wild goat, that steep rock and shady wood save from them, nor is it their lot to find him, but at their clamour a bearded lion hath shown himself on the way, and lightly turned them all despite their eagerness, even so the Danaans for a while followed on always in their companies, smiting with swords and double-pointed spears, but when they saw Hector going up and down the ranks of men, then were they afraid, and the hearts of all fell to their feet.

Then to them spake Thoas, son of Andraimon, far the best of the Aitolians, skilled in throwing the dart, and good in close fight, and in council did few of the Achaians surpass him, when the young men were striving in debate; he made harangue and spake among them: "Alas, and verily a great marvel is this I behold with mine eyes, how he hath again arisen, and hath avoided the Fates, even Hector. Surely each of us hoped in his heart, that he had died beneath the hand of Aias, son of Telamon. But some one of the gods again hath delivered and saved Hector, who verily hath loosened the knees of many of the Danaans, as methinks will befall even now, for not without the will of loud-thundering Zeus doth he rise in the front ranks, thus eager for battle. But come, as I declare let us all obey. Let us bid the throng turn back to the ships, but let us as many as avow us to be the best in the host, take our stand, if perchance first we may meet him, and hold him off with outstretched spears, and he, methinks, for all his eagerness, will fear at heart to enter into the press of the Danaans."

So spake he, and they heard him eagerly, and obeyed him. They that were with Aias and the prince Idomeneus, and Teukros, and Neriones, and Meges the peer of Ares, called to all the best of the warriors and sustained the fight with Hector and the Trojans, but behind them the multitude returned to the ships of the Achaians.

Now the Trojans drave forward in close ranks, and with long strides Hector led them, while in front of him went Phoebus Apollo, his shoulders wrapped in cloud, and still he held the fell aegis, dread, circled with a shaggy fringe, and gleaming, that Hephaistos the smith gave to Zeus, to bear for the terror of men; with this in his hands did he lead the host.

Now the Argives abode them in close ranks, and shrill the cry arose on both sides, and the arrows leaped from the bow-strings, and many spears from stalwart hands, whereof some stood fast in the flesh of young men swift in fight, but many halfway, ere ever they reached the white flesh, stuck in the ground, longing to glut themselves with flesh. Now so long as Phoebus Apollo held the aegis unmoved in his hands, so long the darts smote either side amain, and the folk fell. But when he looked face to face on the Danaans of the swift steeds, and shook the aegis, and himself shouted mightily, he quelled their heart in their breast, and they forgot their impetuous valour. And as when two wild beasts drive in confusion a herd of kine, or a great flock of sheep, in the dark hour of black night, coming swiftly on them when the herdsman is not by, even so were the Achaians terror-stricken and strengthless, for Apollo sent a panic among them, but still gave renown to the Trojans and Hector.

And Hector smote his horses on the shoulder with the lash, and called aloud on the Trojans along the ranks. And they all cried out, and level with his held the steeds that drew their chariots, with a marvellous din, and in front of them Phoebus Apollo lightly dashed down with his feet the banks of the deep ditch, and cast them into the midst thereof, making a bridgeway long and wide as is a spear-cast, when a man throws to make trial of his strength. Thereby the Trojans poured forward in their battalions, while in their van Apollo held the splendid aegis. And most easily did he cast down the wall of the Achaians, as when a boy scatters the sand beside the sea, first making sand buildings for sport in his childishness, and then again, in his sport, confounding them with his feet and hands; even so didst thou, archer Apollo, confound the long toil and labour of the Argives, and among them rouse a panic fear.

So they were halting, and abiding by the ships, calling each to other; and lifting their hands to all the gods did each man pray vehemently, and chiefly prayed Nestor, the Warden of the Achaians, stretching his hand towards the starry heaven: "O father Zeus, if ever any one of us in wheat-bearing Argos did burn to thee fat thighs of bull or sheep, and prayed that he might return, and thou didst promise and assent thereto, of these things be thou mindful, and avert, Olympian, the pitiless day, nor suffer the Trojans thus to overcome the Achaians."

So spake he in his prayer, and Zeus, the Lord of counsel, thundered loudly, hearing the prayers of the ancient son of Neleus.

But the Trojans when they heard the thunder of aegis-bearing Zeus, rushed yet the more eagerly upon the Argives, and were mindful of the joy of battle. And as when a great wave of the wide sea sweeps over the bulwarks of a ship, the might of the wind constraining it, which chiefly swells the waves, even so did the Trojans with a great cry bound over the wall, and drave their horses on, and at the hindmost row of the ships were fighting hand to hand with double-pointed spears, the Trojans from the chariots, but the Achaians climbing up aloft, from the black ships with long pikes that they had lying in the ships for battle at sea, jointed pikes shod at the head with bronze.

Now the Trojans, like ravening lions, rushed upon the ships, fulfilling the behests of Zeus, that ever was rousing their great wrath, but softened the temper of the Argives, and took away their glory, while he spurred on the others. For the heart of Zeus was set on giving glory to Hector, the son of Priam, that withal he might cast fierce-blazing fire, unwearied, upon the beaked ships, and so fulfil all the presumptuous prayer of Thetis; wherefore wise-counselling Zeus awaited, till his eyes should see the glare of a burning ship. For even from that hour was he to ordain the backward chase of the Trojans from the ships, and to give glory to the Danaans. With this design was he rousing Hector, Priam's son, that himself was right eager, against the hollow ships. For short of life was he to be, yea, and already Pallas Athene was urging against him the day of destiny, at the hand of the son of Peleus. And fain he was to break the ranks of men, trying them wheresoever he saw the thickest press, and the goodliest harness. Yet not even so might he break them for all his eagerness. Nay, they stood firm, and embattled like a steep rock and a great, hard by the hoary sea, a rock that abides the swift paths of the shrill winds, and the swelling waves that roar against it. Even so the Danaans steadfastly abode the Trojans and fled not away. But Hector shining with fire on all sides leaped on the throng, and fell upon them, as when beneath the storm-clouds a fleet wave reared of the winds falls on a swift ship, and she is all hidden with foam, and the dread blast of the wind roars against the sail, and the sailors fear, and tremble in their hearts, for by but a little way are they borne forth from death, even so the spirit was torn in the breasts of the Achaians.

So again keen battle was set by the ships. Thou wouldst deem that unwearied and unworn they met each other in war, so eagerly they fought. And in their striving they were minded thus; the Achaians verily deemed that never would they flee from the danger, but perish there, but the heart of each Trojan hoped in his breast, that they should fire the ships, and slay the heroes of the Achaians. With these imaginations they stood to each other, and Hector seized the stern of a seafaring ship, a fair ship, swift on the brine, that had borne Protesilaos to Troia, but brought him not back again to his own country. Now round his ship the Achaians and Trojans warred on each other hand to hand, nor far apart did they endure the flights of arrows, nor of darts, but standing hard each by other, with one heart, with sharp axes and hatchets they fought, and with great swords, and double-pointed spears. And many fair brands, dark-scabbarded and hilted, fell to the ground, some from the hands, some from off the shoulders of warring men, and the black earth ran with blood. But Hector, after that once he had seized the ship's stern, left not his hold, keeping the ensign in his hands, and he called to the Trojans: "Bring fire, and all with one voice do ye raise the war-cry; now hath Zeus given us the dearest day of all,—to take the ships that came hither against the will of the gods, and brought many woes upon us, by the cowardice of the elders, who withheld me when I was eager to fight at the sterns of the ships, and kept back the host. But if even then far-seeing Zeus did harm our wits, now he himself doth urge and command us onwards." So spake he, and they set yet the fiercer on the Argives. And Aias no longer abode their onset, for he was driven back by the darts, but he withdrew a little,—thinking that now he should die,—on to the oarsman's bench of seven feet long, and he left the decks of the trim ship. There then he stood on the watch, and with his spear he ever drave the Trojans from the ships, whosoever brought unwearied fire, and ever he shouted terribly, calling to the Danaans: "O friends, Danaan heroes, men of Ares' company, play the man, my friends, and be mindful of impetuous valour. Do we deem that there be allies at our backs, or some wall stronger than this to ward off death from men? Verily there is not hard by any city arrayed with towers, whereby we might defend ourselves, having a host that could turn the balance of battle. Nay, but we are set down in the plain of the mailed men of Troy, with our backs against the sea, and far off from our own land. Therefore is safety in battle, and not in slackening from the fight." So spake he, and rushed on ravening for battle, with his keen spear. And whosoever of the Trojans was coming against the ship with blazing fire, to pleasure Hector at his urging, him would Aias wound, awaiting him with his long spear, and twelve men in front of the ships at close quarters did he wound.

BOOK XVI

How Patroklos fought in the armour of Achilles, and drove the Trojans from the ships, but was slain at last by Hector.

So they were warring round the well-timbered ship, but Patroklos drew near Achilles, shepherd of the host, and he shed warm tears, even as a fountain of dark water that down a steep cliff pours its cloudy stream. And noble swift-footed Achilles when he beheld him was grieved for his sake, and accosted him, and spake winged words, saying: "Wherefore weepest thou, Patroklos, like a fond little maid, that runs by her mother's side, and bids her mother take her up, snatching at her gown, and hinders her in her going, and tearfully looks at her, till the mother takes her up? like her, Patroklos, dost thou let fall soft tears. Hast thou aught to tell to the Myrmidons, or to me myself, or is it some tidings out of Phthia that thou alone hast beard? Or dost thou lament for the sake of the Argives,—how they perish by the hollow ships through their own transgression? Speak out, and hide it not within thy spirit, that we may both know all."

But with a heavy groan didst thou speak unto him, O knight Patroklos: "O Achilles, son of Peleus, far the bravest of the Achaians, be not wroth, seeing that so great calamity has beset the Achaians. For verily all of them that aforetime were the best are lying among the ships, smitten and wounded. Smitten is the son of Tydeus, strong Diomedes, and wounded is Odysseus, spearman renowned, and Agamemnon; and smitten is Eurypylos on the thigh with an arrow. And about them the leeches skilled in medicines are busy, healing their wounds, but thou art hard to reconcile, Achilles. Never then may such wrath take hold of me as that thou nursest; thou brave to the hurting of others. What other men later born shall have profit of thee, if thou dost not ward off base ruin from the Argives? Pitiless that thou art, the knight Peleus was not then thy father, nor Thetis thy mother, but the grey sea bare thee, and the sheer cliffs, so untoward is thy spirit. But if in thy heart thou art shunning some oracle, and thy lady mother hath told thee somewhat from Zeus, yet me do thou send forth quickly, and make the rest of the host of the Myrmidons follow me, if yet any light may arise from me to the Danaans. And give me thy harness to buckle about my shoulders, if perchance the Trojans may take me for thee, and so abstain from battle, and the warlike sons of the Achaians may take breath, wearied as they be, for brief is the breathing in war. And lightly might we that are fresh drive men wearied with the battle back to the citadel, away from the ships and the huts."

So he spake and besought him, in his unwittingness, for truly it was to be his own evil death and fate that he prayed for. Then to him in great heaviness spake swift-footed Achilles: "Ah me, Patroklos of the seed of Zeus, what word hast thou spoken? Neither take I heed of any oracle that I wot of, nor yet has my lady mother told me somewhat from Zeus, but this dread sorrow comes upon my heart and spirit, from the hour that a man wishes to rob me who am his equal, and to take away my prize, for that he excels me in power. A dread sorrow to me is this, after all the toils that my heart hath endured. The maiden that the sons of the Achaians chose out for me as my prize, and that I won with my spear when I sacked a well-walled city, her has mighty Agamemnon the son of Atreus taken back out of my hands, as though I were but some sojourner dishonourable. But we will let bygones be bygones. No man may be angry of heart for ever, yet verily I said that I would not cease from my wrath, until that time when to mine own ships should come the war-cry and the battle. But do thou on thy shoulders my famous harness, and lead the war-loving Myrmidons to the fight, to ward off destruction from the ships, lest they even burn the ships with blazing fire, and take away our desired return. But when thou hast driven them from the ships, return, and even if the loud-thundering lord of Hera grant thee to win glory, yet long not thou apart from me to fight with the war-loving Trojans; thereby wilt thou minish mine honour. Neither do thou, exulting in war and strife, and slaying the Trojans, lead on toward Ilios, lest one of the eternal gods from Olympus come against thee; right dearly doth Apollo the Far-darter love them. Nay, return back when thou halt brought safety to the ships, and suffer the rest to fight along the plain. For would, O father Zeus, and Athene, and Apollo, would that not one of all the Trojans might escape death, nor one of the Argives, but that we twain might avoid destruction, that alone we might undo the sacred coronal of Troy."

So spake they each to other, but Aias no longer abode the onset, for he was overpowered by darts; the counsel of Zeus was subduing him, and the shafts of the proud Trojans; and his bright helmet, being smitten, kept ringing terribly about his temples: for always it was smitten upon the fair-wrought cheek-pieces. Moreover his left shoulder was wearied, as steadfastly he held up his glittering shield, nor yet could they make him give ground, as they pressed on with their darts around him. And ever he was worn out with difficult breath, and much sweat kept running from all his limbs, nor had he a moment to draw breath, so on all sides was evil heaped on evil.

Tell me now, ye Muses that have mansions in Olympus, how first fire fell on the ships of the Achaians. Hector drew near, and the ashen spear of Aias he smote with his great sword, hard by the socket, behind the point, and shore it clean away, and the son of Telamon brandished in his hand no more than a pointless spear, and far from him the head of bronze fell ringing on the ground.

And Aias knew in his noble heart, and shuddered at the deeds of the gods, even how Zeus that thundereth on high did utterly cut off from him avail in war, and desired victory for the Trojans. Then Aias gave back out of the darts. But the Trojans cast on the swift ship unwearying fire, and instantly the inextinguishable flame streamed over her: so the fire begirt the stern, whereon Achilles smote his thighs, and spake to Patroklos: "Arise, Patroklos of the seed of Zeus, commander of the horsemen, for truly I see by the ships the rush of the consuming fire. Up then, lest they take the ships, and there be no more retreat; do on thy harness speedily, and I will summon the host."

So spake he, while Patroklos was harnessing him in shining bronze. His goodly greaves, fitted with silver clasps, he first girt round his legs, and next did on around his breast the well-dight starry corslet of the swift-footed son of Aiakos. And round his shoulders he cast a sword of bronze, with studs of silver, and next took the great and mighty shield, and on his proud head set a well-wrought helm with a horse-hair crest, and terribly nodded the crest from above. Then seized he two strong lances that fitted his grasp, only he took not the spear of the noble son of Aiakos, heavy, and huge, and stalwart, that none other of the Achaians could wield. And Patroklos bade Automedon to yoke the horses speedily, even Automedon whom most he honoured after Achilles, the breaker of the ranks of men, and whom he held trustiest in battle to abide his call. And for him Automedon led beneath the yoke the swift horses, Xanthos and Balios, that fly as swift as the winds, the horses that the harpy Podarge bare to the West Wind, as she grazed on the meadow by the stream of Okeanos. And in the side-traces he put the goodly Pedasos, that Achilles carried away, when he took the city of Eetion; and being but a mortal steed, he followed with the immortal horses.

Meanwhile Achilles went and harnessed all the Myrmidons in the huts with armour, and they gathered like ravening wolves with strength in their hearts unspeakable. And among them all stood warlike Achilles urging on the horses and the targeteers. And he aroused the heart and valour of each of them, and the ranks were yet the closer serried when they heard the prince. And as when a man builds the wall of a high house with close-set stones, to avoid the might of the winds, even so close were arrayed the helmets and bossy shields, and shield pressed on shield, helm on helm, and man on man, and the horse-hair crests on the bright helmet-ridges touched each other when they nodded, so close they stood by each other.

And straightway they poured forth like wasps that have their dwelling by the wayside, and that boys are ever wont to vex, always tormenting them in their nests beside the way in childish sport, and a common evil they make for many. With heart and spirit like theirs the Myrmidons poured out now from the ships, and a cry arose unquenchable, and Patroklos called on his comrades, shouting aloud: "Myrmidons, ye comrades of Achilles son of Peleus, be men, my friends, and be mindful of your impetuous valour, that so we may win honour for the son of Peleus, that is far the bravest of the Argives by the ships, and whose close-fighting squires are the best. And let wide-ruling Agamemnon the son of Atreus learn his own blindness of heart, in that he nothing honoured the best of the Achaians."

So spake he, and aroused each man's heart and courage, and all in a mass they fell on the Trojans, and the ships around echoed wondrously to the cry of the Achaians. But when the Trojans beheld the strong son of Menoitios, himself and his squire, shining in their armour, the heart was stirred in all of them, and the companies wavered, for they deemed that by the ships the swift-footed son of Peleus had cast away his wrath, and chosen reconcilement: then each man glanced round, to see where he might flee sheer destruction.

But Patroklos first with a shining spear cast straight into the press, where most men were thronging, even by the stern of the ship of great-hearted Protesilaos, and he smote Pyraichmes, who led his Paionian horsemen out of Amydon, from the wide water of Axios; him he smote on the right shoulder, and he fell on his back in the dust with a groan, and his comrades around him, the Paionians, were afraid, for Patroklos sent fear among them all, when he slew their leader that was ever the best in fight. Then he drove them out from the ships, and quenched the burning fire. And the half-burnt ship was left there, and the Trojans fled, with a marvellous din, and the Danaans poured in among the hollow ships, and ceaseless was the shouting. And as when from the high crest of a great hill Zeus, the gatherer of the lightning, hath stirred a dense cloud, and forth shine all the peaks, and sharp promontories, and glades, and from heaven the infinite air breaks open, even so the Danaans, having driven the blazing fire from the ships, for a little while took breath, but there was no pause in the battle. For not yet were the Trojans driven in utter rout by the Achaians, dear to Ares, from the black ships, but they still stood up against them, and only perforce gave ground from the ships. But even as robber wolves fall on the lambs or kids, choosing them out of the herds, when they are scattered on hills by the witlessness of the shepherd, and the wolves behold it, and speedily harry the younglings that have no heart of courage,—even so the Danaans fell on the Trojans, and they were mindful of ill-sounding flight, and forgot their impetuous valour.

But that great Aias ever was fain to cast his spear at Hector of the helm of bronze, but he, in his cunning of war, covered his broad shoulders with his shield of bulls' hide, and watched the hurtling of the arrows, and the noise of spears. And verily well he knew the change in the mastery of war, but even so he abode, and was striving to rescue his trusty comrades.

And as when from Olympus a cloud fares into heaven, from the sacred air, when Zeus spreadeth forth the tempest, even so from the ships came the war-cry and the rout, nor in order due did they cross the ditch again. But his swift-footed horses bare Hector forth with his arms, and he left the host of Troy, whom the delved trench restrained against their will. And in the trench did many swift steeds that draw the car break the fore-part of the pole, and leave the chariots of their masters.

But Patroklos followed after, crying fiercely to the Danaans, and full of evil will against the Trojans, while they with cries and flight filled all the ways, for they were scattered, and on high the storm of dust was scattered below the clouds, and the whole-hooved horses strained back towards the city, away from the ships and the huts.

But even where Patroklos saw the folk thickest in the rout, thither did he guide his horses with a cry, and under his axle-trees men fell prone from their chariots, and the cars were overturned with a din of shattering. But straight over the ditch, in forward flight, leaped the swift horses. And the heart of Patroklos urged him against Hector, for he was eager to smite him, but his swift steeds bore Hector forth and away. And even as beneath a tempest the whole black earth is oppressed, on an autumn day, when Zeus pours forth rain most vehemently, and all the rivers run full, and many a scaur the torrents tear away, and down to the dark sea they rush headlong from the hills, roaring mightily, and minished are the works of men, even so mighty was the roar of the Trojan horses as they ran.

Now Patroklos when he had cloven the nearest companies, drave them backward again to the ships, nor suffered them to approach the city, despite their desire, but between the ships, and the river, and the lofty wall, he rushed on them, and slew them, and avenged many a comrade slain. There first he smote Pronoos with a shining spear, where the shield left bare the breast, and loosened his limbs, and he fell with a crash. Then Thestor the son of Enops he next assailed, as he sat crouching in the polished chariot, for he was struck distraught, and the reins flew from his hands. Him he drew near, and smote with the lance on the right jaw, and clean pierced through his teeth. And Patroklos caught hold of the spear and dragged him over the rim of the car, as when a man sits on a jutting rock, and drags a sacred fish forth from the sea, with line and glittering hook of bronze; so on the bright spear dragged he Thestor gaping from the chariot, and cast him down on his face and life left him as he fell. Next, as Euryalos came on, he smote him on the midst of the head with a stone, and all his head was shattered within the strong helmet, and prone on the earth he fell, and death that slayeth the spirit overwhelmed him. Next Erymas, and Amphoteros, and Epaltes and Tlepolemos son of Damastor, and Echios and Pyris, and Ipheus and Euippos, and Polymelos son of Argeas, all these in turn he brought low to the bounteous earth. But when Sarpedon beheld his comrades with ungirdled doublets, subdued beneath the hands of Patroklos son of Menoitios, he cried aloud, upbraiding the godlike Lykians: "Shame, ye Lykians, whither do ye flee? Now be ye strong, for I will encounter this man that I may know who he is that conquers here, and verily many evils hath he wrought the Trojans, in that he hath loosened the knees of many men and noble."

So spake he, and leaped with his arms from the chariot to the ground. But Patroklos, on the other side, when he beheld him leaped from his chariot. And they, like vultures of crooked talons and curved beaks, that war with loud yells on some high cliff, even so they rushed with cries against each other. And beholding then the son of Kronos of the crooked counsels took pity on them, and he spake to Hera, his sister and wife: "Ah woe is me for that it is fated that Sarpedon, the best-beloved of men to me, shall be subdued under Patroklos son of Menoitios. And in two ways my heart within my breast is divided, as I ponder whether I should catch him up alive out of the tearful war, and set him down in the rich land of Lykia, or whether I should now subdue him beneath the hands of the son of Menoitios."

Then the ox-eyed lady Hera made answer to him: "Most dread son of Kronos, what word is this thou hast spoken? A mortal man long doomed to fate dost thou desire to deliver again from death of evil name? Work thy will, but all we other gods will in no wise praise thee. And another thing I will tell thee, and do thou lay it up in thy heart; if thou dost send Sarpedon living to his own house, consider lest thereon some other god likewise desire to send his own dear son away out of the strong battle. For round the great citadel of Priam war many sons of the Immortals, and among the Immortals wilt thou send terrible wrath. But if he be dear to thee, and thy heart mourns for him, truly then suffer him to be subdued in the strong battle beneath the hands of Patroklos son of Menoitios, but when his soul and life leave that warrior, send Death and sweet Sleep to bear him, even till they come to the land of wide Lykia, there will his kindred and friends bury him, with a barrow and a pillar, for this is the due of the dead."

So spake she, nor did the father of gods and men disregard her. But he shed bloody raindrops on the earth, honouring his dear son, that Patroklos was about to slay in the deep-soiled land of Troia, far off from his own country. Now when they were come near each other in onset, there verily did Patroklos smite the renowned Thrasymelos, the good squire of the prince Sarpedon, on the lower part of the belly, and loosened his limbs. But Sarpedon missed him with his shining javelin, as he in turn rushed on, but wounded the horse Pedasos on the right shoulder with the spear, and he shrieked as he breathed his life away, and fell crying in the dust, and his spirit fled from him. But the other twain reared this way and that, and the yoke creaked, and the reins were confused on them, when their trace-horse lay in the dust. But thereof did Automedon, the spearman renowned, find a remedy, and drawing his long-edged sword from his stout thigh, he leaped forth, and cut adrift the horse, with no delay, and the pair righted themselves, and strained in the reins, and they met again in life-devouring war.

Then again Sarpedon missed with his shining dart, and the point of the spear flew over the left shoulder of Patroklos and smote him not, but he in turn arose with the bronze, and his javelin flew not vainly from his hand, but struck Sarpedon even where the midriff clasps the beating heart. And he fell as falls an oak, or a silver poplar, or a slim pine tree, that on the hills the shipwrights fell with whetted axes, to be timber for ship-building; even so before the horses and chariot he lay at length, moaning aloud, and clutching at the bloody dust. And as when a lion hath fallen on a herd, and slain a bull, tawny and high of heart, among the kine of trailing gait, and he perishes groaning beneath the claws of the lion, even so under Patroklos did the leader of the Lykian shieldmen rage, even in death, and he called to his dear comrade: "Dear Glaukos, warrior among warlike men, now most doth it behove thee to be a spearman, and a hardy fighter: now let baneful war be dear to thee, if indeed thou art a man of might. First fare all about and urge on the heroes that be leaders of the Lykians, to fight for Sarpedon, and thereafter thyself do battle for me with the sword. For to thee even in time to come shall I be shame and disgrace for ever, all thy days, if the Achaians strip me of mine armour, fallen in the gathering of the ships. Nay, hold out manfully, and spur on all the host."

Even as he spake thus, the end of death veiled over his eyes and his nostrils, but Patroklos, setting foot on his breast drew the spear out of his flesh, and the midriff followed with the spear, so that he drew forth together the spear point, and the soul of Sarpedon; and the Myrmidons held there his panting steeds, eager to fly afar, since the chariot was reft of its lords.

Then dread sorrow came on Glaukos, when he heard the voice of Sarpedon, and his heart was stirred, that he availed not to succour him. And with his hand he caught and held his arm, for the wound galled him, the wound of the arrow wherewith, as he pressed on towards the lofty wall, Teukros had smitten him, warding off destruction from his fellows. Then in prayer spake Glaukos to far-darting Apollo: "Hear, O Prince that art somewhere in the rich land of Lykia, or in Troia, for thou canst listen everywhere to the man that is in need, as even now need cometh upon me. For I have this stark wound, and mine arm is thoroughly pierced with sharp pains, nor can my blood be stanched, and by the wound is my shoulder burdened, and I cannot hold my spear firm, nor go and fight against the enemy. And the best of men has perished, Sarpedon, the son of Zeus, and he succours not even his own child. But do thou, O Prince, heal me this stark wound, and lull my pains, and give me strength, that I may call on my Lykian kinsmen, and spur them to the war, and myself may fight about the dead man fallen."

So spake he in his prayer, and Phoebus Apollo heard him. Straightway he made his pains to cease, and in the grievous wound stanched the black blood, and put courage into his heart. And Glaukos knew it within him, and was glad, for that the great god speedily heard his prayer. First went he all about and urged on them that were leaders of the Lykians to fight around Sarpedon, and thereafter he went with long strides among the Trojans, to Polydamas son of Panthoos and noble Agenor, and he went after Aineias, and Hector of the helm of bronze, and standing by them spake winged words: "Hector, now surely art thou utterly forgetful of the allies, that for thy sake, far from their friends and their own country, breathe their lives away! but thou carest not to aid them! Sarpedon lies low, the leader of the Lykian shieldmen, he that defended Lykia by his dooms and his might, yea him hath mailed Ares subdued beneath the spear of Patroklos. But, friends, stand by him, and be angry in your hearts lest the Myrmidons strip him of his harness, and dishonour the dead, in wrath for the sake of the Danaans, even them that perished, whom we slew with spears by the swift ships."

So spake he, and sorrow seized the Trojans utterly, ungovernable and not to be borne; for Sarpedon was ever the stay of their city, all a stranger as he was, for many people followed with him, and himself the best warrior of them all. Then they made straight for the Danaans eagerly, and Hector led them, being wroth for Sarpedon's sake. But the fierce heart of Patrokloa son of Menoitios urged on the Achaians. And he spake first to the twain Aiantes that themselves were right eager: "Aiantes, now let defence be your desire, and be such as afore ye were among men, or even braver yet. That man lies low who first leaped on to the wall of the Achaians, even Sarpedon. Nay, let us strive to take him, and work his body shame, and strip the harness from his shoulders, and many a one of his comrades fighting for his sake let us subdue with the pitiless bronze."

So spake he, and they themselves were eager in defence. So on both sides they strengthened the companies, Trojans and Lykians, Myrmidons and Achaians, and they joined battle to fight around the dead man fallen;

terribly they shouted, and loud rang the harness of men. And as the din ariseth of woodcutters in the glades of a mountain, and the sound thereof is heard far away, so rose the din of them from the wide-wayed earth, the noise of bronze and of well-tanned bulls' hides smitten with swords and double-pointed spears. And now not even a clear-sighted man could any longer have known noble Sarpedon, for with darts and blood and dust was he covered wholly from head to foot. And ever men thronged about the dead, as in a steading flies buzz around the full milk-pails, in the season of spring, when the milk drenches the bowls, even so thronged they about the dead. Nor ever did Zeus turn from the strong fight his shining eyes, but ever looked down on them, and much in his heart he debated of the slaying of Patroklos, whether there and then above divine Sarpedon glorious Hector should slay him likewise in strong battle with the sword, and strip his harness from his shoulders, or whether to more men yet he should deal sheer labour of war. And thus to him as he pondered it seemed the better way, that the gallant squire of Achilles, Peleus' son, should straightway drive the Trojans and Hector of the helm of bronze towards the city, and should rob many of their life. And in Hector first he put a weakling heart, and leaping into his car Hector turned in flight, and cried on the rest of the Trojans to flee, for he knew the turning of the sacred scales of Zeus. Thereon neither did the strong Lykians abide, but fled all in fear, when they beheld their king stricken to the heart, lying in the company of the dead, for many had fallen above him, when Kronion made fierce the fight. Then the others stripped from the shoulders of Sarpedon his shining arms of bronze, and these the strong son of Menoitios gave to his comrades to bear to the hollow ships. Then Zeus that gathereth the clouds spake to Apollo: "Prithee, dear Phoebus, go take Sarpedon out of range of darts, and cleanse the black blood from him, and thereafter bear him far away, and bathe him in the streams of the river, and anoint him with ambrosia, and clothe him in garments that wax not old, and send him to be wafted by fleet convoy, by the twin brethren Sleep and Death, that quickly will set him in the rich land of wide Lykia. There will his kinsmen and clansmen give him burial, with barrow and pillar, for such is the due of the dead."

So spake he, nor was Apollo disobedient to his father. He went down the hills of Ida to the dread battle din, and straight way bore goodly Sarpedon out of the darts, and carried him far away and bathed him in the streams of the river, and anointed him with ambrosia, and clad him in garments that wax not old, and sent him to be wafted by fleet convoy, the twin brethren Sleep and Death, that swiftly set him down in the rich land of wide Lykia. But Patroklos cried to his horses and Automedon, and after the Trojans and Lykians went he, and so was blindly forgetful, in his witlessness, for if he had kept the saying of the son of Peleus, verily he should have escaped the evil fate of black death. But ever is the wit of Zeus stronger than the wit of men, so now he roused the spirit of

Patroklos in his breast. There whom first, whom last didst thou slay, Patroklos, when the gods called thee deathward? Adrestos first, and Autonoos, and Echeklos, and Perimos, son of Megas, and Epistor, and Melanippos, and thereafter Elasos, and Moulios, and Pylartes; these he slew, but the others were each man of them fain of flight. Then would the sons of the Achaians have taken high-gated Troy, by the hands of Patroklos, for around and before him he raged with the spear, but that Phoebus Apollo stood on the well-builded wall, with baneful thoughts towards Patroklos, and succouring the Trojans. Thrice clomb Patroklos on the corner of the lofty wall, and thrice did Apollo force him back and smote the shining shield with his immortal hands. But when for the fourth time he came on like a god, then cried far-darting Apollo terribly, and spake winged words: "Give back, Patroklos of the seed of Zeus! Not beneath thy spear is it fated that the city of the valiant Trojans shall fall, nay nor beneath Achilles, a man far better than thou."

So spake he, and Patroklos retreated far back, avoiding the wrath of far-darting Apollo. But Hector within the Skaian gates was restraining his whole-hooved horses, pondering whether he should drive again into the din and fight, or should call unto the host to gather to the wall. While thus he was thinking, Phoebus Apollo stood by him in the guise of a young man and a strong, Asios, who was the mother's brother of horse-taming Hector, being own brother of Hekabe, and son of Dymas, who dwelt in Phrygia, on the streams of Sangarios. In his guise spake Apollo, son of Zeus, to Hector: "Hector, wherefore dost thou cease from fight? It doth not behove thee. Would that I were as much stronger than thou as I am weaker, thereon quickly shouldst thou stand aloof from war to thy hurt. But come, turn against Patroklos thy strong-hooved horses, if perchance thou mayst slay him, and Apollo give thee glory."

So spake the god, and went back again into the moil of men. But renowned Hector bade wise-hearted Kebriones to lash his horses into the war. Then Apollo went and passed into the press, and sent a dread panic among the Argives, but to the Trojans and Hector gave he renown. And Hector let the other Argives be, and slew none of them, but against Patroklos he turned his strong-hooved horses, and Patroklos on the other side leaped from his chariot to the ground, with a spear in his left hand, and in his other hand grasped a shining jagged stone, that his hand covered. Firmly he planted himself and hurled it, nor long did he shrink from his foe, nor was his cast in vain, but he struck Kebriones the charioteer of Hector, the bastard son of renowned Priam, on the brow with the sharp stone, as he held the reins of the horses. Both his brows the stone drave together, and his bone held not, but his eyes fell to the ground in the dust, there, in front of his feet. Then he, like a diver, fell from the well-wrought car, and his spirit left his bones. Then taunting him didst thou address him, knightly Patroklos: "Out on it, how nimble a man, how lightly he diveth! Yea, if perchance he were on the teeming deep, this man would satisfy many by seeking for oysters, leaping from the ship, even if it were stormy weather, so lightly now he diveth from the chariot into the plain. Verily among the Trojans too there be diving men."

So speaking he set on the hero Kebriones with the rush of a lion, that while wasting the cattle-pens is smitten in the breast, and his own valour is his bane, even so against Kebriones, Patroklos, didst thou leap furiously. But Hector, on the other side, leaped from his chariot to the ground. And these twain strove for Kebriones like lions, that on the mountain peaks fight, both hungering, both high of heart, for a slain hind. Even so for Kebriones' sake these two masters of the war-cry, Patroklos son of Menoitios, and renowned Hector, were eager each to hew the other's flesh with the ruthless bronze.

Hector then seized him by the head, and slackened not hold, while Patroklos on the other side grasped him by the foot, and thereon the others, Trojans and Danaans, joined strong battle. And as the East wind and the South contend with one another in shaking a deep wood in the dells of a mountain, shaking beech, and ash, and smooth-barked cornel tree, that clash against each other their long boughs with marvellous din, and a noise of branches broken, so the Trojans and Achaians were leaping on each other and slaying, nor had either side any thought of ruinous flight. And many sharp darts were fixed around Kebriones, and winged arrows leaping from the bow-string, and many mighty stones smote the shields of them that fought around him. But he in the whirl of dust lay mighty and mightily fallen, forgetful of his chivalry.

Now while the sun was going about mid-heaven, so long the darts smote either side, and the host fell, but when the sun turned to the time of the loosing of oxen, lo, then beyond their doom the Achaians proved the better. The hero Kebriones drew they forth from the darts, out of the tumult of the Trojans, and stripped the harness from his shoulders, and with ill design against the Trojans, Patroklos rushed upon them. Three times then rushed he on, peer of swift Ares, shouting terribly, and thrice he slew nine men. But when the fourth time he sped on like a god, thereon to thee, Patroklos, did the end of life appear, for Phoebus met thee in the strong battle, in dreadful wise. And Patroklos was not ware of him coming through the press, for hidden in thick mist did he meet him, and stood behind him, and smote his back and broad shoulders with a down-stroke of his hand, and his eyes were dazed. And from his head Phoebus Apollo smote the helmet that rolled rattling away with a din beneath the hooves of the horses, the helm with upright socket, and the crests were defiled with blood and dust. And all the long-shadowed spear was shattered in the hands of Patroklos, the spear great and heavy and strong, and sharp, while from his shoulders the tasselled shield with the baldric fell to the ground.

And the prince Apollo, son of Zeus, loosed his corslet, and blindness seized his heart and his shining limbs were unstrung, and he stood in amaze, and at close quarters from behind a Dardanian smote him on the back, between the shoulders, with a sharp spear, even Euphorbos, son of Panthoos, who excelled them of his age in casting the spear, and in horsemanship, and in speed of foot.

Even thus, verily, had he cast down twenty men from their chariots, though then first had he come with his car to learn the lesson of war. He it was that first smote a dart into thee, knightly Patroklos, nor overcame thee, but ran back again and mingled with the throng, first drawing forth from the flesh his ashen spear, nor did he abide the onset of Patroklos, unarmed as he was, in the strife. But Patroklos, being overcome by the stroke of the god, and by the spear, gave ground, and retreated to the host of his comrades, avoiding Fate. But Hector, when he beheld great-hearted Patroklos give ground, being smitten with the keen bronze, came nigh unto him through the ranks, and wounded him with a spear, in the lowermost part of the belly, and drave the bronze clean through. And he fell with a crash, and sorely grieved the host of Achaians. And as when a lion hath overcome in battle an untiring boar, they twain fighting with high heart on the crests of a hill, about a little well, and both are desirous to drink, and the lion hath by force overcome the boar that draweth difficult breath; so after that he had slain many did Hector son of Priam take the life away from the strong son of Menoitios, smiting him at close quarters with the spear; and boasting over him he spake winged words: "Patroklos, surely thou saidst that thou wouldst sack my town, and from Trojan women take away the day of freedom, and bring them in ships to thine own dear country: fool! nay, in front of these were the swift horses of Hector straining their speed for the fight; and myself in wielding the spear excel among the war-loving Trojans, even I who ward from them the day of destiny: but thee shall vultures here devour. Ah, wretch, surely Achilles for all his valour, availed thee not, who straitly charged thee as thou camest, he abiding there, saying, 'Come not to me, Patroklos lord of steeds, to the hollow ships, till thou hast torn the gory doublet of man-slaying Hector about his breast;' so, surely, he spake to thee, and persuaded the wits of thee in thy witlessness."

Then faintly didst thou answer him, knightly Patroklos: "Boast greatly, as now, Hector, for to thee have Zeus, son of Kronos, and Apollo given the victory, who lightly have subdued me; for themselves stripped my harness from my shoulders. But if twenty such as thou had encountered me, here had they all perished, subdued beneath my spear. But me have ruinous Fate and the son of Leto slain, and of men Euphorbos, but thou art the third in my slaying. But another thing will I tell thee, and do thou lay it up in thy heart: verily thou thyself art not long to live, but already doth Death stand hard by thee, and strong Fate, that thou art to be subdued by the hands of noble Achilles, of the seed of Aiakos."

Even as so he spake the end of death overshadowed him. And his soul, fleeting from his limbs, went down to the house of Hades, wailing its own doom, leaving manhood and youth.

Then renowned Hector spake to him even in his death: "Patroklos, wherefore to me dolt thou prophesy sheer destruction? who knows but that Achilles, the child of fair-tressed Thetis, will first be smitten by my spear, and lose his life?"

So spake he, and drew the spear of bronze from the wound, setting his foot on the dead, and cast him off on his back from the spear. And straightway with the spear he went after Automedon, the godlike squire of the swift-footed Aiakides, for he was eager to smite him; but his swift-footed immortal horses bare him out of the battle, horses that the gods gave to Peleus, a splendid gift.

BOOK XVII

Of the battle around the body of Patroklos.

But Atreus' son, Menelaos dear to Ares, was not unaware of the slaying of Patroklos by the Trojans in the fray. He went up through the front of the fight harnessed in flashing bronze, and strode over the body as above a first-born calf standeth lowing its mother. Thus above Patroklos strode fair-haired Menelaos, and before him held his spear and the circle of his shield, eager to slay whoever should encounter him. Then was Panthoos' son of the stout ashen spear not heedless of noble Patroklos as he lay, and he smote on the circle of the shield of Menelaos, but the bronze spear brake it not, but the point was bent back in the stubborn shield. And Menelaos Atreus' son in his turn made at him with his bronze spear, having prayed unto father Zeus, and as he gave back pierced the nether part of his throat, and threw his weight into the stroke, following his heavy hand; and sheer through the tender neck went the point of the spear. And he fell with a crash, and his armour rang upon him. In blood was his hair drenched that was like unto the hair of the Graces, and his tresses closely knit with bands of silver and gold.

Then easily would the son of Atreus have borne off the noble spoils of Panthoos' son, had not Phoebus Apollo grudged it to him, and aroused against him Hector peer of swift Ares, putting on the semblance of a man, of Mentes chief of the Kikones. And he spake aloud to him winged words: "Hector, now art thou hasting after things unattainable, even the horses of wise Aiakides; for hard are they to be tamed or driven by mortal man, save only Achilles whom an immortal mother bare. Meanwhile hath warlike Menelaos Atreus' son stridden over Patroklos and slain the best of the Trojans there, even Panthoos' son Euphorbos, and hath stayed him in his impetuous might."

Thus saying the god went back into the strife of men, but dire grief darkened Hectors inmost soul, and then he gazed searchingly along the lines, and straightway was aware of the one man stripping off the noble arms, and the other lying on the earth; and blood was flowing about the gaping wound. Then he went through the front of the fight harnessed in flashing bronze, crying a shrill cry, like unto Hephaistos' flame unquenchable. Not deaf to his shrill cry was Atreus' son, and sore troubled he spake to his great heart: "Ay me, if I shall leave behind me these goodly arms, and Patroklos who here lieth for my vengeance' sake, I fear lest some Danaan beholding it be wroth against me. But if for honour's sake I do battle alone with Hector and the Trojans, I fear lest they come about me many against one; for all the Trojans is bright-helmed Hector leading hither. But if I might somewhere find Aias of the loud war-cry, then both together would we go and be mindful of battle even were it against the power of heaven, if haply we might save his dead for Achilles Peleus' son: that were best among these ills."

While thus he communed with his mind and heart, therewithal the Trojan ranks came onward, and Hector at their head. Then Menelaos gave backward, and left the dead man, turning himself ever about like a deep-waned lion which men and dogs chase from a fold with spears and cries; and his strong heart within him groweth chill, and loth goeth he from the steading; so from Patroklos went fair-haired Menelaos, and turned and stood, when he came to the host of his comrades, searching for mighty Aias Telamon's son. Him very speedily he espied on the left of the whole battle, cheering his comrades and rousing them to fight, for great terror had Phoebus Apollo sent on them; and he hasted him to run, and straightway stood by him and said: "This way, beloved Aias; let us bestir us for the dead Patroklos, if haply his naked corpse at least we may carry to Achilles, though his armour is held by Hector of the glancing helm."

Thus spake he, and aroused the heart of wise Aias. And he went up through the front of the fight, and with him fair-haired Menelaos. Now Hector, when he had stripped from Patroklos his noble armour, was dragging him thence that he might cut off the head from the shoulders with the keen bronze and carry his body to give to the dogs of Troy. But Aias came anigh, and the shield that he bare was as a tower; then Hector gave back into the company of his comrades, and sprang into his chariot; and the goodly armour he gave to the Trojans to carry to the city, to be great glory unto him. But Aias spread his broad shield over the son of Menoitios and stood as it were a lion before his whelps when huntsmen in a forest encounter him as he leadeth his young. And by his side stood Atreus' son, Menelaos dear to Ares, nursing great sorrow in his breast.

Then Hector called on the Trojans with a mighty shout; "Trojans and Lykians and Dardanians that fight hand to hand, be men, my friends, and bethink you of impetuous valour, until I do on me the goodly arms of noble Achilles that I stripped from brave Patroklos when I slew him."

Thus having spoken went Hector of the glancing helm forth out of the strife of war, and ran and speedily with fleet feet following overtook his comrades, not yet far off, who were bearing to the city Peleides' glorious arms. And standing apart from the dolorous battle he changed his armour; his own he gave the warlike Trojans to carry to sacred Ilios, and he put on the divine arms of Achilles, Peleus' son.

But when Zeus that gathereth the clouds beheld from afar off Hector arming him in the armour of Peleus' godlike son, he shook his head and spake thus unto his soul: "Ah, hapless man, no thought is in thy heart of death that yet draweth nigh unto thee; thou doest on thee the divine armour of a peerless man before whom the rest have terror. His comrade, gentle and brave, thou hast slain, and unmeetly hast stripped the armour from his head and shoulders; yet now for a while at least I will give into thy hands great might, in recompense for this, even that nowise shalt thou come home out of the battle, for Andromache to receive from thee Peleides' glorious arms."

Thus spake the son of Kronos, and bowed his dark brows therewithal.

But the armour fitted itself unto Hectors body, and Ares the dread war-god entered into him, and his limbs were filled within with valour and strength. Then he sped among the noble allies with a mighty cry, and in the flashing of his armour he seemed to all of them like unto Peleus' great-hearted son. And he came to each and encouraged him with his words—Mesthles and Glaukos and Medon and Thersilochos and Asteropaios and Deisenor and Hippothoos and Phorkys and Chromios and the augur Ennomos—these encouraged he and spake to them winged words: "Listen, ye countless tribes of allies that dwell round about. It was not for mere numbers that I sought or longed when I gathered each of you from your cities, but that ye might zealously guard the Trojans' wives and infant little ones from the war-loving Achaians. For this end am I wearying my people by taking gifts and food from them, and nursing thereby the courage of each of you. Now therefore let all turn straight against the foe and live or die, for such is the dalliance of war. And whoso shall drag Patroklos, dead though he be, among the horse-taming men of Troy, and make Aias yield, to him will I award half the spoils and keep half myself; so shall his glory be great as mine."

Thus spake he, and they against the Danaans charged with all their weight, levelling their spears, and their hearts were high of hope to drag the corpse from under Aias, Telamon's son. Fond men! from full many reft he life over that corpse. And then spake Aias to Menelaos of the loud war-cry: "Dear Menelaos, fosterling of Zeus, no longer count I that we two of ourselves shall return home out of the war. Nor have I so much dread for the corpse of Patroklos, that shall soon glut the dogs and birds of the men of Troy, as for thy head and mine lest some evil fall thereon, for all is shrouded by a storm-cloud of war, even by Hector, and sheer doom stareth in our face. But come, call thou to the best men of the Danaans, if haply any hear."

Thus spake he, and Menelaos of the loud war-cry disregarded him not, but shouted unto the Danaans, crying a far-heard cry: "O friends, ye leaders and counsellors of the Argives, who by the side of the sons of Atreus, Agamemnon and Menelaos, drink at the common cost and are all commanders of the host, on whom wait glory and honour from Zeus, hard is it for me to distinguish each chief amid the press—such blaze is there of the strife of war. But let each go forward of himself and be wroth at heart that Patroklos should become a sport among the dogs of Troy."

Thus spake he, and Oileus' son fleet Aias heard him clearly, and was first to run along the mellay to meet him, and after him Idomeneus, and Idomeneus' brother-in-arms, Meriones, peer of the man-slaying war-god.

And who shall of his own thought tell the names of the rest, even of all that after these aroused the battle of the Achaians?

Now the Trojans charged forward in close array, and Hector led them. And as when at the mouth of some heaven-born river a mighty wave roareth against the stream, and arouseth the high cliffs' echo as the salt sea belloweth on the beach, so loud was the cry wherewith the Trojans came. But the Achaians stood firm around Menoitios' son with one soul all, walled in with shields of bronze. And over their bright helmets the son of Kronos shed thick darkness, for in the former time was Menoitios' son not unloved of him, while he was yet alive and squire of Aiakides. So was Zeus loth that he should become a prey of the dogs of his enemies at Troy, and stirred his comrades to do battle for him.

Now first the Trojans thrust back the glancing-eyed Achaians, who shrank before them and left the dead, yet the proud Trojans slew not any of them with spears, though they were fain, but set to hale the corpse. But little while would the Achaians hold back therefrom, for very swiftly Aias rallied them, Aias the first in presence and in deeds of all the Danaans after the noble son of Peleus. Right through the fighters in the forefront rushed he like a wild boar in his might that in the mountains when he turneth at bay scattereth lightly dogs and lusty young men through the glades. Thus did proud Telamon's son the glorious Aias press on the Trojan battalions and lightly scatter them, as they had bestrode Patroklos and were full fain to drag him to their city and win renown.

Then would the Trojans in their turn in their weakness overcome have been driven back into Ilios by the Achaians dear to Ares, and the Argives would have won glory even against the appointment of Zeus by their power and might. But Apollo himself aroused Aineias, putting on the semblance of Periphas the herald, the son of Epytos, who grew old with his old father in his heraldship, of friendly thought toward Aineias. In his similitude spake Apollo, son of Zeus: "Aineias, how could ye ever guard high Ilios if it were against the will of God? Other men have I seen that trust in their own might and power and valour, and in their host, even though they have scant folk to lead. But here, albeit Zeus is fainer far to give victory to us than to the Danaans, yet ye are dismayed exceedingly and fight not."

Thus spake he, and Aineias knew far-darting Apollo when he looked upon his face, and spake unto Hector, shouting loud "Hector and ye other leaders of the Trojans and their allies, shame were this if in our weakness overcome we were driven back into Ilios by the Achaians dear to Ares. Nay, thus saith a god, who standeth by my side: Zeus, highest Orderer, is our helper in this fight. Therefore let us go right onward against the Danaans. Not easily at least let them take the dead Patroklos to the ships."

Thus spake he, and leapt forth far before the fighters in the front. And the Trojans rallied and stood up against the Achaians. Thus strove they as it had been fire, nor wouldst thou have thought there was still sun or moon, for over all the battle where the chiefs stood around the slain son of Menoitios they were shrouded in darkness, while the other Trojans and well-greaved Achaians fought at ease in the clear air, and piercing sunlight was spread over them, and on all the earth and hills there was no cloud seen; and they ceased fighting now sad again, avoiding each other's dolorous darts and standing far apart. But they who were in the midst endured affliction of the darkness and the battle, and all the best men of them were wearied by the pitiless weight of their bronze arms.

Thus all day long waxed the mighty fray of their sore strife; and unabatingly ever with the sweat of toil were the knees and legs and feet of each man and arms anal eyes bedewed as the two hosts did battle around the brave squire of fleet Aiakides. And as when a man giveth the hide of a great bull to his folk to stretch, all soaked in fat, and they take and stretch it standing in a circle, and straightway the moisture thereof departeth and the fat entereth in under the haling of many hands, and it is all stretched throughout,—thus they on both sides haled the dead man this way and that in narrow space, for their hearts were high of hope, the Trojans that they should drag him to Ilios and the Achaians to the hollow ships; and around him the fray waxed wild, nor might Ares rouser of hosts nor Athene despise the sight thereof, albeit their anger were exceeding great.

Such was the grievous travail of men and horses over Patroklos that Zeus on that day wrought. But not as yet knew noble Achilles aught of Patroklos' death, for far away from the swift ships they were fighting beneath the wall of the men of Troy. Therefore never deemed he in his heart that he was dead, but that he should come back alive, after that he had touched the gates; for neither that other thought had he anywise, that Patroklos should sack the stronghold without his aid.

Now the rest continually around the dead man with their keen spears made onset relentlessly and slew each the other. And thus would one speak among the mail-clad Achaians: "Friends, it were verily not glorious for us to go back to the hollow ships; rather let the black earth yawn for us all beneath our feet. Far better were that straightway for us if we suffer the horse-taming Trojans to hale this man to their city and win renown."

And thus on the other side would one of the great-hearted Trojans say: "Friends, though it were our fate that all together we be slain beside this man, let none yet give backward from the fray."

Thus would one speak, and rouse the spirit of each. So they fought on, and the iron din went up through the high desert air unto the brazen heaven. But the horses of Aiakides that were apart from the battle were weeping, since first they were aware that their charioteer was fallen in the dust beneath the hand of man-slaying Hector. Verily Automedon, Diores' valiant son, plied them oft with blows of the swift lash, and oft with gentle words he spake to them and oft with chiding, yet would they neither go back to the ships at the broad Hellespont nor yet to the battle after the Achaians, but as a pillar abideth firm that standeth on the tomb of a man or woman dead, so abode they immovably with the beautiful chariot, abasing their heads unto the earth. And hot tears flowed from their eyes to the ground as they mourned in sorrow for their charioteer, and their rich manes were soiled as they drooped from beneath the yoke-cushion on both sides beside the yoke. And when the son of Kronos beheld them mourning he had compassion on them, and shook his head and spake to his own heart: "Ah, hapless pair, why gave we you to king Peleus, a mortal man, while ye are deathless and ever young? Was it that ye should suffer sorrows among ill-fated men? For methinketh there is nothing more piteous than a man among all things that breathe and creep upon the earth. But verily Hector Priam's son shall not drive you and your deftly-wrought car; that will I not suffer. Is it a small thing that he holdeth the armour and vaunteth himself vainly thereupon? Nay, I will put courage into your knees and heart that ye may bring Automedon also safe out of the war to the hollow ships. For yet further will I increase victory to the men of Troy, so that they slay until they come unto the well-timbered ships, and the sun set and divine night come down."

Thus saying he breathed good courage into the horses. And they shook to earth the dust from their manes, and lightly bare the swift car amid Trojans and Achaians. And behind them fought Automedon, albeit in grief for his comrade, swooping with his chariot as a vulture on wild geese; for lightly he would flee out of the onset of the Trojans and lightly charge, pursuing them through the thick mellay. Yet could he not slay any man as he halted to pursue them, for it was impossible that being alone in his sacred car he should at once assail them with the spear and hold his fleet horses. Then at last espied him a comrade, even Alkimedon son of Laerkes, son of Haimon, and he halted behind the car and spake unto Automedon: "Automedon, what god hath put into thy breast unprofitable counsel and taken from thee wisdom, that thus alone thou art fighting against the Trojans in the forefront of the press? Thy comrade even now was slain, and Hector goeth proudly, wearing on his own shoulders the armour of Aiakides."

And Automedon son of Diores answered him, saying: "Alkimedon, what other Achaian hath like skill to guide the spirit of immortal steeds, save only Patroklos, peer of gods in counsel, while he yet lived? but now have death and fate overtaken him. But take thou the lash and shining reins, and I will get me down from my, horses, that I may fight."

Thus spake he, and Alkimedon leapt on the fleet war-chariot and swiftly took the lash and reins in his hands, and Automedon leapt down. And noble Hector espied them, and straightway spake unto Aineias as he stood near: "Aineias, counsellor of mail-clad Trojans, I espy here the two horses of fleet Aiakides come forth to battle with feeble charioteers.

Therefore might I hope to take them if thou in thy heart art willing, since they would not abide our onset and stand to do battle against us."

Thus spake he, and the brave son of Anchises disregarded him not. And they twain went right onward, their shoulders shielded by ox-hides dried and tough, and bronze thick overlaid. And with them went both Chromios and godlike Aretos, and their hearts were of high hope to slay the men and drive off the strong-necked horses—fond hope, for not without blood lost were they to get them back from Automedon. He praying to father Zeus was filled in his inmost heart with valour and strength. And straightway he spake to Alkimedon, his faithful comrade: "Alkimedon, hold the horses not far from me, but with their very breath upon my back; for I deem that Hector the son of Priam will not refrain him from his fury until he mount behind Achilles' horses of goodly manes after slaying us twain, and dismay the ranks of Argive men, or else himself fall among the foremost."

Thus said he, and called upon the Aiantes and Menelaos: "Aiantes, leaders of the Argives, and Menelaos, lo now, commit ye the corpse unto whoso may best avail to bestride it and resist the ranks of men, and come ye to ward the day of doom from us who are yet alive, for here in the dolorous war are Hector and Aineias, the best men of the Trojans, pressing hard. Yet verily these issues lie in the lap of the gods: I too will cast my spear, and the rest shall Zeus decide."

He said, and poised his far-shadowing spear and hurled it, and smote on the circle of the shield of Aretos, and the shield sustained not the spear, but right through went the bronze, and he forced it into his belly low down through his belt. And as when a strong man with a sharp axe smiting behind the horns of an ox of the homestead cleaveth the sinew asunder, and the ox leapeth forward and falleth, so leapt Aretos forward and fell on his back; and the spear in his entrails very piercingly quivering unstrung his limbs. And Hector hurled at Automedon with his bright spear, but he looked steadfastly on the bronze javelin as it came at him and avoided it, for he stooped forward, and the long spear fixed itself in the ground behind, and the javelin-butt quivered, and there dread Ares took away its force. And then had they lashed at each other with their swords hand to hand, had not the Aiantes parted them in their fury, when they were come through the mellay at their comrades' call. Before them Hector and Aineias and godlike Chromios shrank backward and gave ground and left Aretos wounded to the death as he lay. And Automedon, peer of swift Ares, stripped off the armour of the dead, and spake exultingly: "Verily, I have a little eased my heart of grief for the death of Menoitios' son, albeit a worse man than him have I slain."

Thus saying he took up the gory spoils and set them in his car, and gat him thereon, with feet and hands all bloody, as a lion that hath devoured a bull.

Now great-hearted Aias and Menelaos were aware of Zeus how he gave the Trojans their turn to victory. First of these to speak was great Aias son of Telamon: "Ay me, now may any man, even though he be a very fool, know that father Zeus himself is helping the Trojans. Come, let us ourselves devise some excellent means, that we may both hale the corpse away and ourselves return home to the joy of our friends, who grieve as they look hitherward and deem that no longer shall the fury of man-slaying Hector's unapproachable hand refrain itself, but fall upon the black ships. And would there were some comrade to carry tidings with all speed unto the son of Peleus, since I deem that he hath not even heard the grievous tidings, how his dear comrade is slain. But nowhere can I behold such an one among the Achaians, for themselves and their horses likewise are wrapped in darkness. O father Zeus, deliver thou the sons of the Achaians from the darkness, and make clear sky and vouchsafe sight unto our eyes. In the light be it that thou slayest us, since it is thy good pleasure that we die."

Then fair-haired Menelaos departed glancing everywhither, as an eagle which men say hath keenest sight of all birds under heaven, and though he be far aloft the fleet-footed hare eludeth him not by crouching beneath a leafy bush, but the eagle swoopeth thereon and swiftly seizeth her and taketh her life. Thus in that hour, Menelaos fosterling of Zeus, ranged thy shining eyes everywhither through the multitude of the host of thy comrades, if haply they might behold Nestor's son yet alive. Him quickly he perceived at the left of the whole battle, heartening his comrades and rousing them to fight. And fair-haired Menelaos came and stood nigh and said unto him: "Antilochos, fosterling of Zeus, come hither that thou mayest learn woful tidings—would it had never been. Ere now, I ween, thou too hast known by thy beholding that God rolleth mischief upon the Danaans, and with the Trojans is victory. And slain is the best man of the Achaians, Patroklos, and great sorrow is wrought for the Danaans. But run thou to the ships of the Achaians and quickly tell this to Achilles, if haply he may straightway rescue to his ship the naked corpse: but his armour is held by Hector of the glancing helmet."

Thus spake he, and Antilochos had horror of the word he heard. And long time speechlessness possessed him, and his eyes were filled with tears, and his full voice choked. Yet for all this disregarded he not the bidding of Menelaos, but set him to run, when he had given his armour to a noble comrade, Laodokos, who close anigh him was wheeling his whole-hooved horses.

So him his feet bare out of the battle weeping, to Achilles son of Peleus carrying an evil tale. But thy heart, Menelaos fosterling of Zeus, chose not to stay to aid the wearied comrades from whom Antilochos departed, and great sorrow was among the Pylians. But to them Menelaos sent noble Thrasymedes, and himself went again to bestride the hero Patroklos. And he hasted and stood beside the Aiantes and straightway spake to them:

"So have I sent that man to the swift ships to go to fleet-footed Achilles. Yet deem I not that he will now come, for all his wrath against noble Hector, for he could not fight unarmed against the men of Troy. But let us ourselves devise some excellent means, both how we may hale the dead away, and how we ourselves may escape death and fate amid the Trojans' battle-cry."

Then answered him great Aias Telamon's son, saying: "All this hast thou said well, most noble Menelaos. But do thou and Meriones put your shoulders beneath the dead and lift him and bear him swiftly out of the fray, while we twain behind you shall do battle with the Trojans and noble Hector, one in heart as we are in name, for from of old time we are wont to await fierce battle side by side."

Thus spake he, and the others took the dead man in their arms and lifted him mightily on high. But the Trojan host behind cried aloud when they saw the Achaians lifting the corpse, and charged like hounds that spring in front of hunter-youths upon a wounded wild boar, and for a while run in haste to rend him, but when he wheeleth round among them, trusting in his might, then they give ground and shrink back here and there. Thus for a while the Trojans pressed on with all their power, striking with swords and double-headed spears, but when the Aiantes turned about and halted over against them, then they changed colour, and none dared farther onset to do battle around the dead.

BOOK XVIII

How Achilles grieved for Patroklos, and how Thetis asked for him new armour of Hephaistos; and of the making of the armour.

Thus fought the rest in the likeness of blazing fire, while to Achilles came Antilochos, a messenger fleet of foot. Him found he in front of his ships of upright horns, boding in his soul the things which even now were accomplished. And sore troubled he spake to his great heart: "Ay me, wherefore again are the flowing-haired Achaians flocking to the ships and flying in rout over the plain? May the gods not have wrought against me the grievous fears at my heart, even as my mother revealed and told me that while I am yet alive the best man of the Myrmidons must by deed of the men of Troy forsake the light of the sun. Surely now must Menoitios' valiant son be dead—foolhardy! surely I bade him when he should have beaten off the fire of the foe to come back to the ships nor with Hector fight amain."

While thus he held debate in his heart and soul, there drew nigh unto him noble Nestor's son, shedding hot tears, and spake his grievous tidings: "Ay me, wise Peleus' son, very bitter tidings must thou hear, such as I would had never been. Fallen is Patroklos, and they are fighting around his body, naked, for his armour is held by Hector of the glancing helm."

Thus spake he, and a black cloud of grief enwrapped Achilles, and with both hands he took dark dust and poured it over his head and defiled his comely face, and on his fragrant doublet black ashes fell. And himself in the dust lay mighty and mightily fallen, and with his own hands tore and marred his hair. And the handmaidens, whom Achilles and Patroklos took captive, cried aloud in the grief of their hearts, and ran forth around valiant Achilles, and all beat on their breasts with their hands, and the knees of each of them were unstrung. And Antilochos on the other side wailed and shed tears, holding Achilles' hands while he groaned in his noble heart, for he feared lest he should cleave his throat with the sword. Then terribly moaned Achilles; and his lady mother heard him as she sate in the depths of the sea beside her ancient sire. And thereon she uttered a cry, and the goddesses flocked around her, all the daughters of Nereus that were in the deep of the sea. With these the bright cave was filled, and they all beat together on their breasts, and Thetis led the lament: "Listen, sister Nereids, that ye all hear and know well what sorrows are in my heart. Ay me unhappy, ay me that bare to my sorrow the first of men! For after I had borne a son noble and strong, the chief of heroes, and he shot up like a young branch, then when I had reared him as a plant in a very fruitful field I sent him in beaked ships to Ilios to fight against the men of Troy; but never again shall I welcome him back to his home, to the house of Peleus. And while he yet liveth in my sight and beholdeth the light of the sun, he sorroweth, neither can I help him any whit though I go unto him. But I will go, that I may look upon my dear child, and learn what sorrow hath come to him though he abide aloof from the war."

Thus spake she and left the cave; and the nymphs went with her weeping, and around them the surge of the sea was sundered. And when they came to deep-soiled Troy-land they went up upon the shore in order, where the ships of the Myrmidons were drawn up thickly around fleet Achilles. And as he groaned heavily his lady mother stood beside him, and with a shrill cry clasped the head of her child, and spake unto him winged words of lamentation: "My child, why weepest thou? what sorrow hath come to thy heart? Tell it forth, hide it not. One thing at least hath been accomplished of Zeus according to the prayer thou madest, holding up to him thy hands, that the sons of the Achaians should all be pent in at the ships, through lack of thee, and should suffer hateful things."

Then groaning heavily spake unto her Achilles fleet of foot: "My mother, that prayer truly hath the Olympian accomplished for me. But what delight have I therein, since my dear comrade is dead, Patroklos, whom I honoured above all my comrades as it were my very self! Him have I lost, and Hector that slew him hath stripped from him the armour great and fair, a wonder to behold, that the gods gave to Peleus a splendid gift, on the day when they laid thee in the bed of a mortal man. Would thou hadst abode among the deathless daughters of the sea, and Peleus had wedded a mortal bride! But now, that thou mayest have sorrow a thousand fold in thy heart for a dead son, never shalt thou welcome him back home, since my soul biddeth me also live no longer nor abide among men, if Hector be not first smitten by my spear and yield his life, and pay for his slaughter of Patroklos, Menoitios' son."

Then answered unto him Thetis shedding tears: "Short-lived, I ween, must thou be then, my child, by what thou sayest, for straightway after Hector is death appointed unto thee."

Then mightily moved spake unto her Achilles fleet of foot: "Straightway may I die, since I might not succour my comrade at his slaying. He hath fallen afar from his country and lacked my help in his sore need. Now therefore, since I go not back to my dear native land, neither have at all been succour to Patroklos nor to all my other comrades that have been slain by noble Hector, but I sit beside my ships a profitless burden of the earth, I that in war am such an one as is none else of the mail-clad Achaians, though in council are others better—may strife perish utterly among gods and men, and wrath that stirreth even a wise man to be vexed, wrath that far sweeter than trickling honey waxeth like smoke in the breasts of men, even as I was wroth even now against Agamemnon king of men. But bygones will we let be, for all our pain, curbing the heart in our breasts under necessity. Now go I forth, that I may light on the destroyer of him I loved, on Hector: then will I accept my death whensoever Zeus willeth to accomplish it and the other immortal gods. For not even the mighty Herakles escaped death, albeit most dear to Kronian Zeus the king, but Fate overcame him and Hera's cruel wrath. So also shall I, if my fate hath been fashioned likewise, lie low when I am dead. But now let me win high renown, let me set some Trojan woman, some deep-bosomed daughter of Dardanos, staunching with both hands the tears upon her tender cheeks and wailing bitterly; yea, let them know that I am come back, though I tarried long from the war. Hold not me then from the battle in thy love, for thou shalt not prevail with me."

Then Thetis the silver-footed goddess answered him, saying: "Yea verily, my child, no blame is in this, that thou ward sheer destruction from thy comrades in their distress. But thy fair glittering armour of bronze is held among the Trojans. Hector of the glancing helm beareth it on his shoulders in triumph, yet not for long, I ween, shall he glory therein, for death is hard anigh him. But thou, go not yet down into the mellay of war until thou see me with thine eyes come hither. In the morning will I return, at the coming up of the sun, bearing fair armour from the king Hephaistos."

Thus spake she and turned to go from her son, and as she turned she spake among her sisters of the sea: "Ye now go down within the wide bosom of the deep, to visit the Ancient One of the Sea and our father's

house, and tell him all. I am going to high Olympus to Hephaistos of noble
skill, if haply he will give unto my son noble armour shining gloriously."

Thus spake she, and they forthwith went down beneath the surge of the
sea. And the silver-footed goddess Thetis went on to Olympus that she
might bring noble armour to her son.

So her unto Olympus her feet bore. But the Achaians with terrible cries
were fleeing before man-slaying Hector till they came to the ships and to
the Hellespont. Nor might the well-greaved Achaians drag the corpse of
Patroklos Achilles' squire out of the darts, for now again overtook him the
host and the horses of Troy, and Hector son of Priam, in might as it were
a flame of fire. Thrice did glorious Hector seize him from behind by the
feet, resolved to drag him away, and mightily called upon the men of Troy.
Thrice did the two Aiantes, clothed on with impetuous might, beat him off
from the dead man, but he nathless, trusting in his might, anon would
charge into the press, anon would stand and cry aloud, but he gave
ground never a whit. As when shepherds in the field avail nowise to chase
a fiery lion in fierce hunger away from a carcase, so availed not the two
warrior Aiantes to scare Hector son of Priam from the dead. And now
would he have won the body and gained renown unspeakable, had not
fleet wind-footed Iris come speeding from Olympus with a message to the
son of Peleus to array him, unknown of Zeus and the other gods, for Hera
sent her. And she stood anigh and spake to him winged words: "Rouse
thee, son of Peleus, of all men most redoubtable! Succour Patroklos, for
whose body is terrible battle afoot before the ships. There slay they one
another, these guarding the dead corpse, while the men of Troy are fierce
to hale him unto windy Ilios, and chiefliest noble Hector is fain to drag
him, and his heart biddeth him fix the head on the stakes of the wall
when he hath sundered it from the tender neck. But arise, lie thus no
longer! let awe enter thy heart to forbid that Patroklos become the sport
of dogs of Troy. Thine were the shame if he go down mangled amid the
dead."

Then answered her fleet-footed noble Achilles: "Goddess Iris, what god
sent thee a messenger unto me?"

And to him again spake wind-footed fleet Iris: "It was Hera that sent
me, the wise wife of Zeus, nor knoweth the high-throned son of Kronos nor
any other of the Immortals that on snowy Olympus have their
dwelling-place."

And Achilles fleet of foot made answer to her and said: "And how may
I go into the fray? The Trojans hold my arms; and my dear mother bade
me forbear to array me until I behold her with my eyes returned, for she
promised to bring fair armour from Hephaistos. Other man know I none
whose noble armour I might put on, save it were the shield of Aias
Telamon's son. But himself, I ween, is in the forefront of the press, dealing
death with his spear around Patroklos dead."

Then again spake unto him wind-footed fleet Iris: "Well are we also aware that thy noble armour is held from thee. But go forth unto the trench as thou art and show thyself to the men of Troy, if haply they will shrink back and refrain them from battle, and the warlike sons of the Achaians take breath."

Thus spake fleet-footed Iris and went her way. But Achilles dear to Zeus arose, and around his strong shoulders Athene cast her tasselled aegis, and around his head the bright goddess set a crown of a golden cloud, and kindled therefrom a blazing flame. And as when a smoke issueth from a city and riseth up into the upper air, from an island afar off that foes beleaguer, while the others from their city fight all day in hateful war,—but with the going down of the sun blaze out the beacon-fires in line, and high aloft rusheth up the glare for dwellers round about to behold, if haply they may come with ships to help in need—thus from the head of Achilles soared that blaze toward the heavens. And he went and stood beyond the wall beside the trench, yet mingled not among the Achaians, for he minded the wise bidding of his mother. There stood he and shouted aloud, and afar off Pallas Athene uttered her voice, and spread terror unspeakable among the men of Troy. Clear as the voice of a clarion when it soundeth by reason of slaughterous foemen that beleaguer a city, so clear rang forth the voice of Aiakides. And when they heard the brazen voice of Aiakides, the souls of all of them were dismayed, and the horses of goodly manes were fain to turn the chariots backward, for they boded anguish in their hearts, And the charioteers were amazed when they saw the unwearying fire blaze fierce on the head of the great-hearted son of Peleus, for the bright-eyed goddess Athene made it blaze. Thrice from over the trench shouted mightily noble Achilles, and thrice were the men of Troy confounded and their proud allies. Yea there and then perished twelve men of their best by their own chariot wheels and spears. But the Achaians with joy drew Patroklos forth of the darts and laid him on a litter, and his dear comrades stood around lamenting him; and among them followed fleet-footed Achilles, shedding hot tears, for his true comrade he saw lying on the bier, mangled by the keen bronze. Him sent he forth with chariot and horses unto the battle, but home again welcomed never more.

Then Hera the ox-eyed queen sent down the unwearying Sun to be gone unwillingly unto the streams of Ocean. So the Sun set, and the noble Achaians made pause from the stress of battle and the hazardous war.

But the Achaians all night made moan in lamentation for Patroklos. And first of them in the loud lamentation was the son of Peleus, laying upon the breast of his comrade his man-slaying hands and moaning very sore, even as a deep-bearded lion whose whelps some stag-hunter hath snatched away out of a deep wood; and the lion coming afterward grieveth and through many glens he rangeth on the track of the footsteps of the man, if anywhere he might find him, for most bitter anger seizeth him;—thus Achilles moaning heavily spake among the Myrmidons: "Ay me, vain verily was the word I uttered on that day when I cheered the hero Menoitios in his halls and said that I would bring back to Opoeis his son in glory from the sack of Ilios with the share of spoil that should fall unto him. Not all the purposes of men doth Zeus accomplish for them. It is appointed that both of us redden the same earth with our blood here in Troy-land, for neither shall the old knight Peleus welcome me back home within his halls, nor my mother Thetis, but even here shall earth keep hold on me. Yet now, O Patroklos, since I follow thee under earth, I will not hold thy funeral till I have brought hither the armour and the head of Hector, thy high-hearted slayer, and before thy pyre I will cut the throats of twelve noble sons of the men of Troy, for mine anger thou art slain. Till then beside the beaked ships shalt thou lie as thou art, and around thee deep-bosomed women, Trojan and Dardanian, shall mourn thee weeping night and day, even they whom we toiled to win by our strength and, our long spears when we sacked rich cities of mortal men."

Thus spake noble Achilles, and bade his comrades set a great tripod on the fire, that with all speed they might wash from Patroklos the bloody gore. So they set a tripod of ablution on the burning fire, and poured therein water and took wood and kindled it beneath; and the fire wrapped the belly of the tripod, and the water grew hot. And when the water boiled in the bright bronze, then washed they him and anointed with olive oil, and filled his wounds with fresh ointment, and laid him on a bier and covered him with soft cloth from head to foot, and thereover a white robe. Then all night around Achilles fleet of foot the Myrmidons made lament and moan for Patroklos.

Meanwhile Zeus spake unto Hera his sister and wife: "Thou hast accomplished this, O Hera, ox-eyed queen, thou hast aroused Achilles fleet of foot. Verily of thine own children must the flowing-haired Achaians be."

Then answered unto him Hera the ox-eyed queen: "Most dread son of Kronos, what is this word thou hast said? Truly even a man, I ween, is to accomplish what he may for another man, albeit he is mortal and hath not wisdom as we. How then was I who avow me the first of goddesses both by birth and for that I am called thy wife, and thou art king among all Immortals—how was I not in mine anger to devise evil against the men of Troy?"

So debated they on this wise with one another. But Thetis of the silver feet came unto the house of Hephaistos, imperishable, starlike, far seen among the dwellings of Immortals, a house of bronze, wrought by the crook-footed god himself. Him found she sweating in toil and busy about his bellows, for he was forging tripods twenty in all to stand around the wall of his stablished hall, and beneath the base of each he had set golden wheels, that of their own motion they might enter the assembly of the gods and again return unto his house, a marvel to look upon. Thus much were they finished that not yet were away from the fire, and gathered all his gear wherewith he worked into a silver chest; and with a sponge he wiped his face and hands and sturdy neck and shaggy breast, and did on his doublet, and took a stout staff and went forth limping; but there were handmaidens of gold that moved to help their lord, the semblances of living maids. In them is understanding at their hearts, in them are voice and strength, and they have skill of the immortal gods. These moved beneath their lord, and he gat him haltingly near to where Thetis was, and set him on a bright seat, and clasped her hand in his and spake and called her by her name: "Wherefore, long-robed Thetis, comest thou to our house, honoured that thou art and dear? No frequent comer art thou hitherto. Speak what thou hast at heart; my soul is fain to accomplish it; if accomplish it I can, and if it be appointed for accomplishment."

Then answered unto him Thetis shedding tears: "Hephaistos, hath there verily been any of all goddesses in Olympus that hath endured so many grievous sorrows at heart as are the woes that Kronian Zeus hath laid upon me above all others? He chose me from among the sisters of the sea to enthrall me to a man, even Peleus Aiakos' son, and with a man I endured wedlock sore against my will. Now lieth he in his halls forspent with grievous age, but other griefs are mine. A son he gave me to bear and nourish, the chief of heroes, and he shot up like a young branch. Like a plant in a very fruitful field I reared him and sent him forth on beaked ships to Ilios to fight against the men of Troy, but never again shall I welcome him back to his home within the house of Peleus. And while he yet liveth in my sight and beholdeth the light of the sun, he sorroweth, neither can I help him any whit though I go unto him. The maiden whom the sons of the Achaians chose out to be his prize, her hath the lord Agamemnon taken back out of his hands. In grief for her wasted he his heart, while the men of Troy were driving the Achaians on their ships, nor suffered them to come forth. And the elders of the Argives entreated him, and told over many noble gifts. Then albeit himself he refused to ward destruction from them, he put his armour on Patroklos and sent him to the war, and much people with him. All day they fought around the Skaian gates and that same day had sacked the town, but that when now Menoitios' valiant son had wrought much harm, Apollo slew him in the forefront of the battle, and gave glory unto Hector. Therefore now come I a suppliant unto thy knees, if haply thou be willing to give my short-lived son shield and helmet, and goodly greaves fitted with ankle-pieces, and cuirass. For the armour that he had erst, his trusty comrade lost when he fell beneath the men of Troy; and my son lieth on the earth with anguish in his soul."

Then made answer unto her the lame god of great renown: "Be of good courage, let not these things trouble thy heart. Would that so might I avail to hide him far from dolorous death, when dread fate cometh upon him, as surely shall goodly armour be at his need, such as all men afterward shall marvel at, whatsoever may behold."

Thus saying he left her there and went unto his bellows and turned them upon the fire and bade them work. And the bellows, twenty in all, blew on the crucibles, sending deft blasts on every side, now to aid his labour and now anon howsoever Hephaistos willed and the work went on. And he threw bronze that weareth not into the fire, and tin and precious gold and silver, and next he set on an anvil-stand a great anvil, and took in his hand a sturdy hammer, and in the other he took the tongs.

First fashioned he a shield great and strong, adorning it all over, and set thereto a shining rim, triple, bright-glancing, and therefrom a silver baldric. Five were the folds of the shield itself; and therein fashioned he much cunning work from his wise heart.

There wrought he the earth, and the heavens, and the sea, and the unwearying sun, and the moon waxing to the full, and the signs every one wherewith the heavens are crowned, Pleiads and Hyads and Orion's might, and the Bear that men call also the Wain, her that turneth in her place and watcheth Orion, and alone hath no part in the baths of Ocean.

Also he fashioned therein two fair cities of mortal men. In the one were espousals and marriage feasts, and beneath the blaze of torches they were leading the brides from their chambers through the city, and loud arose the bridal song. And young men were whirling in the dance, and among them flutes and viols sounded high; and women standing each at her door were marvelling. But the folk were gathered in the assembly place; for there a strife was arisen, two men striving about the blood-price of a man slain; the one claimed to pay full atonement, expounding to the people, but the other denied him and would take naught. And the folk were cheering both, as they took part on either side. And heralds kept order among the folk, while the elders on polished stones were sitting in the sacred circle, and holding in their hands staves from the loud-voiced heralds. Then before the people they rose up and gave judgment each in turn. And in the midst lay two talents of gold, to be given unto him who should plead among them most righteously.

But around the other city were two armies in siege with glittering arms. And two counsels found favour among them, either to sack the town or to share all with the townsfolk even whatsoever substance the fair city held within. But the besieged were not yet yielding, but arming for an ambushment. On the wall there stood to guard it their dear wives and infant children, and with these the old men; but the rest went forth, and their leaders were Ares and Pallas Athene, both wrought in gold, and golden was the vesture they had on. Goodly and great were they in their armour, even as gods, far seen around, and the folk at their feet were smaller. And when they came where it seemed good to them to lay ambush, in a river bed where there was a common watering-place of herds, there they set them, clad in glittering bronze. And two scouts were posted by them afar off to spy the coming of flocks and of oxen with crooked horns. And presently came the cattle, and with them two herdsmen playing on pipes, that took no thought of the guile. Then the others when they beheld these ran upon them and quickly cut off the herds of oxen and fair flocks of white sheep, and slew the shepherds withal. But the besiegers, as they sat before the speech-places [from which the orators spoke] and heard much din among the oxen, mounted forthwith behind their high-stepping horses, and came up with speed. Then they arrayed their battle and fought beside the river banks, and smote one another with bronze-shod spears. And among them mingled Strife and Tumult, and fell Death, grasping one man alive fresh-wounded, another without wound, and dragging another dead through the mellay by the feet; and the raiment on her shoulders was red with the blood of men. Like living mortals they hurled together and fought, and haled the corpses each of the other's slain.

Furthermore he set in the shield a soft fresh-ploughed field, rich tilth and wide, the third time ploughed; and many ploughers therein drave their yokes to and fro as they wheeled about. Whensoever they came to the boundary of the field and turned, then would a man come to each and give into his hands a goblet of sweet wine, while others would be turning back along the furrows, fain to reach the boundary of the deep tilth. And the field grew black behind and seemed as it were a-ploughing, albeit of gold, for this was the great marvel of the work.

Furthermore he set therein the demesne-land of a king, where hinds were reaping with sharp sickles in their hands. Some armfuls along the swathe were falling in rows to the earth, whilst others the sheaf-binders were binding in twisted bands of straw. Three sheaf-binders stood over them, while behind boys gathering corn and bearing it in their arms gave it constantly to the binders; and among them the king in silence was standing at the swathe with his staff, rejoicing in his heart. And henchmen apart beneath an oak were making ready a feast, and preparing a great ox they had sacrificed; while the women were strewing much white barley to be a supper for the hinds.

Also he set therein a vineyard teeming plenteously with clusters, wrought fair in gold; black were the grapes, but the vines hung throughout on silver poles. And around it he ran a ditch of cyanus, and round that a fence of tin; and one single pathway led to it, whereby the vintagers might go when they should gather the vintage. And maidens and striplings in childish glee bare the sweet fruit in plaited baskets. And in the midst of them a boy made pleasant music on a clear-toned viol, and sang thereto a sweet Linos-song [probably a lament for departing summer] with delicate voice; while the rest with feet falling together kept time with the music and song.

Also he wrought therein a herd of kine with upright horns, and the kine were fashioned of gold and tin, and with lowing they hurried from the byre to pasture beside a murmuring river, beside the waving reed. And herdsmen of gold were following with the kine, four of them, and nine dogs fleet of foot came after them. But two terrible lions among the foremost kine had seized a loud-roaring bull that bellowed mightily as they haled him, and the dogs and the young men sped after him. The lions rending the great bull's hide were devouring his vitals and his black blood; while the herdsmen in vain tarred on their fleet dogs to set on, for they shrank from biting the lions but stood hard by and barked and swerved away.

Also the glorious lame god wrought therein a pasture in a fair glen, a great pasture of white sheep, and a steading, and roofed huts, and folds.

Also did the glorious lame god devise a dancing-place like unto that which once in wide Knosos Daidalos wrought for Ariadne of the lovely tresses. There were youths dancing and maidens of costly wooing, their hands upon one another's wrists. Fine linen the maidens had on, and the youths well-woven doublets faintly glistening with oil. Fair wreaths had the maidens, and the youths daggers of gold hanging from silver baldrics. And now would they run round with deft feet exceeding lightly, as when a potter sitting by his wheel that fitteth between his hands maketh trial of it whether it run: and now anon they would run in lines to meet each other. And a great company stood round the lovely dance in joy; and through the midst of them, leading the measure, two tumblers whirled.

Also he set therein the great might of the River of Ocean around the uttermost rim of the cunningly-fashioned shield.

Now when he had wrought the shield great and strong, then wrought he him a corslet brighter than a flame of fire, and he wrought him a massive helmet to fit his brows, goodly and graven, and set thereon a crest of gold, and he wrought him greaves of pliant tin.

So when the renowned lame god had finished all the armour, he took and laid it before the mother of Achilles. Then she like a falcon sprang down from snowy Olympus, bearing from Hephaistos the glittering arms.

BOOK XIX

How Achilles and Agamemnon were reconciled before the assembly of the Achaians, and Achilles went forth with them to battle.

Now Morning saffron-robed arose from the streams of Ocean to bring light to gods and men, and Thetis came to the ships, bearing his gift from the god. Her dear son she found fallen about Patroklos and uttering loud lament; and round him many of his company made moan. And the bright goddess stood beside him in their midst, and clasped her hand in his and spake and called upon his name: "My child, him who lieth here we must let be, for all our pain, for by the will of gods from the beginning was he brought low. But thou take from Hephaistos arms of pride, arms passing goodly, such as no man on his shoulders yet hath borne."

Thus spake the goddess and in front of Aehifies laid the arms, and they rang all again in their glory. And awe fell on all the Myrmidons, nor dared any to gaze thereon, for they were awe-stricken. But when Achilles looked thereon, then came fury upon him the more, and his eyes blazed terribly forth as it were a flame beneath their lids: glad was he as he held in his hands that splendid gift of a god. But when he had satisfied his soul in gazing on the glory of the arms, straightway to his mother spake he winged words: "My mother, the arms the god has given are such as it beseemeth that the work of Immortals should be, and that no mortal man should have wrought. Now therefore will I arm me in them, but I have grievous fear lest meantime on the gashed wounds of Menoitios' valiant son flies light and breed worms therein, and defile his corpse—for the life is slain out of him—and so all his flesh shall rot."

Then answered him Thetis, goddess of the silver feet: "Child, have no care for this within thy mind. I will see to ward from him the cruel tribes of flies which prey on men slain in fight: for even though he lie till a whole year's course be run, yet his flesh shall be sound continually, or better even than now. But call thou the Achaian warriors to the place of assembly, and unsay thy wrath against Agamemnon shepherd of the host, and then arm swiftly for battle, and clothe thee with thy strength."

Thus saying she filled him with adventurous might, while on Patroklos she shed ambrosia and red nectar through his nostrils, that his flesh might abide the same continually.

But noble Achilles went down the beach of the sea, crying his terrible cry, and roused the Achaian warriors. And they who before were wont to abide in the circle of the ships, and they who were helmsmen and kept the steerage of the ships, or were stewards there and dealt out food, even these came then to the place of assembly, because Achilles was come forth, after long ceasing from grievous war. Limping came two of Ares' company, Tydeus' son staunch in fight and noble Odysseus, each leaning on his spear, for their wounds were grievous still; and they went and sate them down in the forefront of the assembly. And last came Agamemnon king of men, with his wound upon him, for him too in the stress of battle Kooen Antenor's son had wounded with his bronze-tipped spear. But when all the Achaians were gathered, then uprose fleet-footed Achilles and spake in their midst: "Son of Atreus, was this in any wise the better way for both thee and me, what time with grief at our hearts we waxed fierce in soul-devouring strife for the sake of a girl? Would that Artemis had slain her with her arrow at the ships, on the day whereon I took her to me, when I had spoiled Lyrnessos; so should not then so many Achaians have bitten the wide earth beneath their enemies' hands, by reason of my exceeding wrath. It hath been well for Hector and the Trojans, but the Achaians I think shall long remember the strife that was betwixt thee and me. But bygones will we let be, for all our pain, and curb under necessity the spirit within our breasts. I now will stay my anger: it beseems me not implacably for ever to be wroth; but come rouse speedily to the fight the flowing-haired Achaians, that I may go forth against the men of Troy and put them yet again to the proof, if they be fain to couch hard by the ships. Methinks that some among them shall be glad to rest their knees when they are fled out of the fierceness of the battle, and from before our spear."

He spake, and the well-greaved Achaians rejoiced that the great-hearted son of Peleus had made renouncement of his wrath. Then among them spake Agamemnon king of men, speaking from the place where he sat, not arisen to stand forth in their midst: "O Danaan friends and heroes, men of Ares' company, seemly is it to listen to him who standeth up to speak, nor behoveth it to break in upon his words: even toward a skilled man that were hard. For amid the uproar of many men how should one listen, or yet speak? even the clearest-voiced speech is marred. To the son of Peleus I will declare myself, but ye other Argives give heed, and each mark well my word. Oft have the Achaians spoken thus to me, and upbraided me; but it is not I who am the cause, but Zeus and Destiny and Erinys that walketh in the darkness, who put into my soul fierce madness on the day when in the assembly I, even I, bereft Achilles of his meed. What could I do? it is God who accomplisheth all. Eldest daughter of Zeus is Ate who blindeth all, a power of bane: delicate are her feet, for not upon the earth she goeth, but walketh over the heads of men, making men fall; and entangleth this one or that. Ye even Zeus was blinded upon a time, he who they say is greatest among gods and men; yet even him Hera with a female wile deceived, on the day when Alkmene in fair-crowned Thebes was to bring forth the strength of Herakles. For then proclaimed he solemnly among the gods: 'Here me ye all, both gods and goddesses, while I utter the council of my soul within my heart. This day shall Eileithuia, the help of travailing women, bring to the light a man who shall be lord over all that dwell round about, among the raise of men who are sprung of me by blood.' And to him in subtlety queen Hera spake: 'Though wilt play the cheat and not accomplish thy word. Come now, Olympian, swear me a firm oath that verily and indeed shall that man be lord over all that dwell round about, who this day shall fall between a woman's feet, even he among all men who are of the lineage of thy blood.' So spake she, and Zeus no wise perceived her subtlety but sware a mighty oath, and therewith was he sore blinded. For Hera darted from Olympus' peak and came swiftly to Achaian Argus, were she knew was the stately wife of Sthenelos son of Perseus, who was also great with child, and her seventh month had come. Her son Hera brought to the light, though his tale of months was untold, but she stayed Alkmene's bearing and kept the Eileithuiai from her aid. Then she brought the tidings herself and to Kronos' son Zeus she spake: 'Father Zeus of the bright lightning, a word will I speak to thee for my heed. Today is born a man of valor who shall rule among the Archives, Eurystheus, son of Sthenelos the son of Perseus, of thy lineage; not unmeet is it that he be lord among Argives.' She said, but sharp pain smote him in the depths of his soul, and straightway he seized Ate by her bright-haired head in the anger of his soul, and sware a mighty oath that never again to Olympus and the starry heaven should Ate come, who blindeth all alike. He said, and whirling her in his hand flung her from the starry heaven, and quickly came she down among the works of men. Yet ever he groaned against her when he beheld his beloved son in cruel travail at Eurystheus' hest. Thus also I, what time great Hector of the glancing helm was slaying Argives at the sterns of our ships, could not be unmindful of Ate, who blinded me at the first. But since thus blinded was I, and Zeus bereft me of my wit, fain am I to make amends, and recompense manifold for the wrong. Only arise thou to the battle and rouse the rest of the host. Gifts am I ready to offer, even all that noble Odysseus went yesterday to promise in thy hut. So, if thou wilt, stay awhile, though eager, from battle, and squires shall take the gifts from my ship and carry them to thee, that thou mayest see that what I give sufficeth thee."

Then answered him Achilles swift of foot: "Most noble son of Atreus, Agamemnon king of men, for the gifts, to give them as it beseemeth, if so thou wilt, or to withhold, is in thy choice. But now let us bethink us of battle with all speed; this is no time to dally here with subtleties, for a great work is yet undone. Once more must Achilles be seen in the forefront of the battle, laying waste with his brazen spear the battalions of the men of Troy. Thereof let each of you think as he fighteth with his man."

Then Odysseus of many counsels answered him and said: "Nay yet, for all thy valour, godlike Achilles, not against Ilios lead thou the sons of Achaians fasting to fight the men of Troy, since not of short spell shall the battle be, when once the ranks of men are met, and God shall breathe valour into both. But bid the Achaians taste at the swift ships food and wine; for thence is vigour and might. For no man fasting from food shall be able to fight with the foe all day till the going down of the sun; for though his spirit be eager for battle yet his limbs unaware grow weary, and thirst besetteth him, and hunger, and his knees in his going fail. But the man who having his fill of food and wine fighteth thus all day against the enemy, his heart is of good cheer within him, nor anywise tire his limbs, ere all give back from battle. So come, disperse the host and bid them make ready their meal. And the gifts let Agamemnon king of men bring forth into the midst of the assembly, that all Achaians may behold them with their eyes, and thou be glad at heart. And let him swear to thee an oath, standing in the midst of the Argives, that he hath never gone up into the damsel's bed or lain with her, [O prince, as is the wont of man with woman]; and let thine own spirit be placable within thy breast. Then let him make thee a rich feast of reconcilement in his hut, that thou have nothing lacking of thy right. And thou, son of Atreus, toward others also shalt be more righteous hereafter; for no shame it is that a man that is a king should make amends if he have been the first to deal violently."

Then to him spake Agamemnon king of men: "Son of Laertes, I rejoice to listen to thy speech; for rightfully hast thou told over all. And the oath I am willing to swear, yea my heart biddeth it, nor will I forswear myself before God. Let Achilles abide for a space, eager for battle though he be, and all ye others abide together, until the gifts come forth from my hut, and we make faithful oath with sacrifice. But thee thyself I thus charge and bid. Choose thee young men, princes of the Achaian folk, and bear my gifts from my ship, even all that we promised yesterday to Achilles, and take with thee the women. And let Talthybios speedily make me ready a boar-swine in the midst of the wide Achaian host, to sacrifice to Zeus and to the Sun."

And to him in answer swift-footed Achilles spake: "Most noble son of Atreus, Agamemnon king of men, at some other time were it even better ye should be busied thus, when haply there shall be some pause of war, and the spirit within my breast shall be less fierce. But now they lie mangled on the field—even they whom Hector son of Priam slew, when Zeus gave him glory—and ye call men to their food. Verily for my part I would bid the sons of the Achaians to fight now unfed and fasting, and with the setting sun make ready a mighty meal, when we shall have avenged the shame. Till then down my throat at least nor food nor drink shall go, since my comrade is dead, who in my hut is lying mangled by the sharp spear, with his feet toward the door, and round him our comrades mourn, wherefore in my heart to no thought of those matters, but of slaying, and blood, and grievous moans of men."

Then answered him Odysseus of many counsels: "O Achilles, Peleus' son, mightiest of Achaians far, better and mightier not a little art thou than I with the spear, but in counsel I may surpass thee greatly, since I was born first and know more things: wherefore let thy heart endure to listen to my speech. Quickly have men surfeit of battle, of that wherein the sword streweth most straw yet is the harvest scantiest, [i.e., in a pitched battle there is little plunder, the hope of which might help to sustain men's efforts in storming a town] when Zeus inclineth his balance, who is disposer of the wars of men. But it cannot be that the Achaians fast to mourn a corpse; for exceeding many and thick fall such on every day; when then should there be rest from toil? Nay, it behoveth to bury him who is dead, steeling our hearts, when once we have wept him for a day; but such as are left alive from hateful war must take thought of meat and drink, that yet more against our foes we may fight relentlessly ever, clad in unyielding bronze. Then let none of the host hold back awaiting other summons; this is the summons, and ill shall it be for whoso is left behind at the Argive ships; but all together as one we will rouse against the horse-taming Trojans the fury of war."

He spoke, and took with him the sons of noble Nestor, and Meges son of Phyleus, and Thoas, and Meriones, and Lykomedes son of Kreiontes, and Melanippos. And they went on their way to the hut of Agamemnon, Atreus' son. Forthwith as the word was spoken so was the deed done. Seven tripods they bare from the hut, as he promised him, and twenty bright caldrons, and twelve horses, and anon they led forth women skilled in goodly arts, seven, and the eighth was fair-faced Briseis. Then Odysseus, having weighed ten talents of gold in all, led the way, and with him young men of the Achaians bare the gifts. These they set in the midst of the place of assembly, and Agamemnon rose up, and beside that shepherd of the host stood Talthybios, whose voice was like a god's, and held a boar between his hands. And the son of Atreus drawing with his hands his knife, which ever hung beside the mighty scabbard of his sword, cut off the first hairs from the boar, and lifting up his hands he prayed to Zeus, and all the Argives sat silent in their places, duly hearkening to the king. And he prayed aloud, looking up to the wide heaven: "Be Zeus before all witness, highest and best of the gods, and Earth, and Sun, and Erinyes, who under earth take vengeance upon men, whosoever for-sweareth himself, that never have I laid hand on the damsel Briseis, neither to lie with her nor anywise else, but she has abode untouched within my huts. And if aught that I swear be false, may the gods give me all sorrows manifold, that they send on him who sinneth against them in his oath."

He said, and cut the boar's throat with the pitiless knife. And the body Taithybios whirled and threw into the great wash of the hoary sea, to be the food of fishes; but Achilles arose up and spake in the midst of the warrior Argives: "Father Zeus, sore madness dealest thou verily to men. Never could the son of Atreus have stirred the soul within my breast, nor led off the damsel implacably against my will, had not Zeus willed that on many of the Achaians death should come. But now go forth to your meal, that we may join battle thereupon."

Thus he spake and dispersed the assembly with all speed. The rest were scattered each to his own ship, but the great-hearted Myrmidons took up the gifts, and bare them to the ship of godlike Achilles. And they laid them in the huts and set the women there, and gallant squires drave the horses among their troop.

But Briseis that was like unto golden Aphrodite, when she beheld Patroklos mangled by the keen spear, fell about him and made shrill lament, and tore with her hands her breast and tender neck, and beautiful face. And she spake amid her weeping, that woman like unto goddesses: "Patroklos, dearest to my hapless heart, alive I left thee when I left this hut, but now, O prince of the people, I am come back to find thee dead; thus evil ever followeth evil in my lot. My husband, unto whom my father and lady mother gave me, I beheld before our city mangled with the keen spear, and my three brothers whom my own mother bore, my near and dear, who all met their day of doom. But thou, when swift Achilles slew my husband and wasted godlike Mynes' city, wouldest ever that I should not even weep, and saidest that thou wouldst make me godlike Achilles' wedded wife, and that ye would take me in your ships to Phthia and make me a marriage feast among the Myrmidons. Therefore with all my soul I mourn thy death, for thou wert ever kind."

Thus spake she weeping, and thereon the women wailed, in semblance for Patroklos, but each for her own woe. But round Achilles gathered the elders of the Achaians, praying him that he would eat; but he denied them with a groan: "I pray you, if any kind comrade will hearken to me, bid me not sate my heart with meat and drink, since terrible grief is come upon me. Till the sun go down I will abide, and endure continually until then."

He spoke, and his speech made the other chiefs depart, but the two sons of Atreus stayed, and noble Odysseus, and Nestor and Idomeneus and Phoinox, ancient knight, soothing him in his exceeding sorrow, but he could no whit be soothed until he had entered the mouth of bloody war. And bethinking him he sighed very heavily and spake aloud: "Thou too, O hapless, dearest of my friends, thyself wouldst verily of yore set forth in out hut with ready speed a savoury meal, what time the Achaians hasted to wage against the horse-taming Trojans dolorous war. But now thou liest mangled, and my heart will none of meat and drink, that stand within, for desire of thee. Nought worse than this could I endure, not though I should hear of my father's death, who now I ween in Phthia is shedding big tears for lack of a son so dear, even me that in an alien land for sake of baleful Helen do battle with the men of Troy; nor though it were my beloved son who is reared for me in Skyros (if still at least is godlike Neoptolemos alive). For hitherto had my soul within me trusted that I alone should perish far from horse-pasturing Argos, here in the Trojan land, but that thou shouldest return to Phthia, so that thou mightest take me the child in thy swift black ship from Skyros and show him everything—my substance and servants, and high-roofed mighty hall. For Peleus I ween already must be dead and gone, or else in feeble life he hath sorrow of age, and of waiting ever for bitter news of me, till he hear that I am dead."

Thus spake he weeping, and the elders mourned with him, bethinking them what each had left at home. And when the son of Kronos beheld them sorrowing he pitied them, and forthwith to Athene spake he winged words: "My child, thou hast then left utterly the man of thy heart. Hath Achilles then no longer a place within thy thought? He before the steep-prowed ships sits mourning his dear comrade; the rest are gone to their meal, but he is fasting and unfed. But go, distil into his breast nectar and pleasant ambrosia, that no pains of hunger come on him."

Thus saying he sped forward Athene who before was fain. And she, like a falcon wide-winged and shrill-voiced, hurled herself forth from heaven through the upper air. So while the Achaians were arming presently throughout the camp, she in Achilles' breast distilled nectar and pleasant ambrosia, that grievous hunger might not assail his knees, and then herself was gone to the firm house of her mighty father. Then the Achaians poured forth from the swift ships. As when thick snowflakes flutter down from Zeus, chill beneath the blast of Boreas born in the upper air, so thick from the ships streamed forth bright glittering helms and bossy shields, strong-plaited cuirasses and ashen spears. And the sheen thereof went up to heaven and all the earth around laughed in the flash of bronze, and there went a sound beneath the feet of the men, and in the midst of them noble Achilles harnessed him. His teeth gnashed together, and his eyes blazed as it were the flame of a fire, for into his heart was intolerable anguish entered in. Thus wroth against the men of Troy he put on the gift of the god, which Hephaistos wrought him by his art. First on his legs he set the fair greaves fitted with silver ankle-pieces, and next he donned the cuirass about his breast. Then round his shoulders he slung the bronze sword silver-studded; then lastly he took the great and strong shield, and its brightness shone afar off as the moon's. Or as when over the sea there appeareth to sailors the brightness of a burning fire, and it burneth on high among the mountains in some lonely steading—sailors whom storm-blasts bear unwilling over the sea, the home of fishes, afar from them they love:— so from Achilles' goodly well-dight shield the brightness thereof shot up toward heaven. And he lifted the stout helmet and set it on his head, and like a star it shone, the horse-hair crested helmet, and around it waved plumes of gold that Hephaistos had set thick about the crest. Then noble Achilles proved him in his armour to know whether it fitted unto him, and whether his glorious limbs ran free; and it became to him as it were wings, and buoyed up the shepherd of hosts.

And forth from its stand he drew his father's spear, heavy and great and strong: that spear could none other of the Achaians wield, but Achilles alone awaited to wield it, the Pelian ashen spear that Cheiron gave to his father dear, from a peak of Pelion, to be the death of warriors. And Automedon and Alkimos went about to yoke the horses, and put on them fair breast-straps, and bits within their jaws, and stretched the reins behind to the firm-built chariot. Then Automedon took the bright lash, fitted to his hand, and sprang up behind the horses, and after him mounted Achilles armed, effulgent in his armour like bright Hyperion. And terribly he called upon the horses of his sire: "Xanthos and Balios, famed children of Podarge, in other sort take heed to bring your charioteer safe back to the Danaan host, when we have done with battle, and leave him not as ye left Patroklos to lie there dead."

Then the horse Xanthos of glancing feet made answer unto him from beneath the yoke;—and he bowed with his head, and all his mane fell from the yoke-cushion beside the yoke and touched the ground;—for the white-armed goddess Hera gave him speech: "Yea verily for this hour, dread Achilles, we will still bear thee safe, yet is thy death day nigh at hand, neither shall we be cause thereof, but a mighty god, and forceful Fate. For not through sloth or heedlessness of ours did the men of Troy from Patrokios' shoulders strip his arms, but the best of the gods, whom bright-haired Leto bore, slew him in the forefront of the battle, and to Hector gave renown. We even with the wind of Zephyr, swiftest, they say, of all winds, well might run; nathless to thee thyself it is appointed to be slain in fight by a god and by a man."

Now when he had thus spoken the Erinyes stayed his voice. And sore troubled did fleet-footed Achilles answer him: "Xanthos, why prophesiest thou my death? no wise behoveth it thee. Well know I of myself that it is appointed me to perish here, far from my father dear and mother; howbeit anywise I will not refrain till I give the Trojans surfeit of war."

He said, and with a cry among the foremost held on his whole-hooved steeds.

BOOK XX

How Achilles made havoc among the men of Troy.

So by the beaked ships around thee, son of Peleus, hungry for war, the Achaians armed; and over against them the men of Troy, upon the high ground of the plain.

But Zeus bade Themis call the gods to council from many-folded Olympus' brow; and she ranged all about and bade them to the house of Zeus. There was no River came not up, save only Ocean, nor any nymph, of all that haunt fair thickets and springs of rivers and grassy water-meadows. And they came to the house of Zeus who gathereth the clouds, and sat them down in the polished colonnades which Hephaistos in the cunning of his heart had wrought for father Zeus.

Thus gathered they within the doors of Zeus; nor was the Earthshaker heedless of the goddess' call, but from the salt sea came up after the rest, and set him in the midst, and inquired concerning the purpose of Zeus: "Wherefore, O Lord of the bright lightning, hast thou called the gods again to council? Say, ponderest thou somewhat concerning the Trojans and Achaians? for lo, the war and the fighting of them are kindled very nigh."

And Zeus, who gathered the clouds, answered him, saying: "Thou knowest, O Earthshaker, the purpose within my breast, wherefor I gathered you hither; even in their perishing have I regard unto them. But for me I will abide here, sitting within a fold of Olympus, where I will gladden my heart with gazing; but go all ye forth that ye come among the Trojans and Achaians and succour these or those, howsoever each of you hath a mind. For if Achilles alone shall fight against the Trojans, not even a little while shall they hold back the son of Peleus, the fleet of foot. Nay, but even aforetime they trembled when they looked upon him; now

therefore that his wrath for his friend is waxen terrible I fear me lest he
overleap the bound of fate, and storm the wall."

Thus spake the son of Kronos, and roused unabating war. For on this
side and on that the gods went forth to war: to the company of the ships
went Hera, and Pallas Athene, and Poseidon, Earth-enfolder, and the
Helper Hermes, pro-eminent in subtle thoughts; and with these went
Hephaistos in the greatness of his strength, halting, but his shrunk legs
moved nimbly under him: but to the Trojans went Ares of the glancing
helm, and with him Phoebus of the unshorn hair, and archer Artemis, and
Leto and Xanthos and laughter-loving Aphrodite.

Now for so long as gods were afar from mortal men, so long waxed the
Achaians glorious, for that Achilles was come forth among them, and his
long ceasing from grim battle was at an end. And the Trojans were
smitten with sore trembling in the limbs of every one of them, in terror
when they beheld the son of Peleus, fleet of foot, blazing in his arms, peer
of man-slaying Ares. But when among the mellay of men the Olympians
were come down, then leapt up in her might Strife, rouser of hosts, then
sent forth Athene a cry, now standing by the hollowed trench without the
wall, and now on the echoing shores she shouted aloud. And a shout
uttered Ares against her, terrible as the blackness of the storm, now from
the height of the city to the Trojans calling clear, or again along Simois
shore over Kallikolon he sped.

So urged the blessed gods both hosts to battle, then themselves burst
into fierce war. And terribly thundered the father of gods and men from
heaven above; and from beneath Poseidon made the vast earth shake and
the steep mountain tops. Then trembled all the spurs of many-fountained
Ida, and all her crests, and the city of the Trojans, and the ships of the
Achaians. And the Lord of the Underworld, Aiedoneus, had terror in hell,
and leapt from his throne in that terror and cried aloud, lest the world be
cloven above him by Poseidon, Shaker of earth, and his dwelling-place be
laid bare to mortals and immortals—grim halls, and vast, and lothly to
the gods. So loud the roar rose of that battle of gods. For against King
Poseidon stood Phoebus Apollo with his winged arrows, and against
Enyalios stood Athene, bright-eyed goddess, and against Hera she of the
golden shafts and echoing chase, even archer Artemis, sister of the
Far-darter; and against Leto the strong Helper Hermes, and against
Hephaistos the great deep-eddying River, whom gods call Xanthos and
men Skamandros.

Thus gods with gods were matched. Meanwhile Achilles yearned above
all to meet Hector, son of Priam, in the fray; for with that blood chiefliest
his spirit bade him sate Ares, stubborn lord of war. But straightway
Apollo, rouser of hosts, moved Aineias to go to meet the son of Peleus, and
filled him with brave spirit: and he made his own voice like the voice of
Lykaon the son of Priam; in his semblance spake Apollo, son of Zeus:
"Aineias, counsellor of Trojans, where now are thy threats wherewith thou

didst boast to the Trojan lords over thy wine, saying thou wouldest stand up in battle against Achilles, Peleus' son?"

And to him Aineias answered and said: "Son of Priam, why biddest thou me thus face the fierce son of Peleus in battle, though I be not fain thereto? Not for the first time now shall I match me with Achilles, fleet of foot; once before drave he me with his spear from Ida, when he harried our kine and wasted Lyrnessos and Pedasos; but Zeus delivered me out of his hand and put strength into my knees that they were swift. Else had I fallen beneath the hands of Achilles, and of Athene who went before and gave him light, and urged him to slay Leleges and Trojans with his spear of bronze. Therefore it is impossible for man to face Achilles in fight, for that ever some god is at his side to ward off death. Ay, and at any time his spear flieth straight, neither ceaseth till it have pierced through flesh of man. But if God once give us fair field of battle, not lightly shall he overcome me, not though he boast him made of bronze throughout."

And to him in answer spake Apollo son of Zeus: "Yea, hero, pray thou too to the everliving gods; for thou too, men say, wast born of Aphrodite daughter of Zeus, and Achilles' mother is of less degree among the gods. For thy mother is child of Zeus, his but of the Ancient One of the Sea. Come, bear up thy unwearying spear against him, let him no wise turn thee back with revilings and bitter words."

He said, and breathed high spirit into the shepherd of the host, and he went onward through the forefront of the fighting, harnessed in flashing bronze. But white-armed Hera failed not to discern Anchises' son as he went through the press of men to meet the son of Peleus, and gathering the gods about her she spake among them thus: "Consider ye twain, Poseidon and Athene, within your hearts, what shall come of these things that are done. Here is Aineias gone forth harnessed in flashing bronze, to meet the son of Peleus, and it is Phoebus Apollo that hath sent him. Come then, be it ours to turn him back straightway; or else let some one of us stand likewise beside Achilles and give him mighty power, so that he fail not in his spirit, but know that they who love him are the best of the Immortals, and that they who from of old ward war and fighting from the Trojans are vain as wind. All we from Olympus are come down to mingle in this fight that he take no hurt among the Trojans on this day—afterward he shall suffer whatsoever things Fate span for him with her thread, at his beginning, when his mother bare him. If Achilles learn not this from voice divine, then shall he be afraid when some god shall come against him in the battle; for gods revealed are hard to look upon."

Then to her made answer Poseidon, Shaker of the earth: "Hera, be not fierce beyond wisdom; it behoveth thee not. Not fain am I at least to match gods with gods in strife. Let us go now into some high place apart and seat us there to watch, and battle shall be left to men. Only if Ares or Phoebus Apollo fall to fighting, or put constraint upon Achilles and hinder him from fight, then straightway among us too shall go up the battle-cry of strife; right soon, methinks, shall they hie them from the issue of the fray back to Olympus to the company of the gods, overcome by the force of our hands."

Thus spake the blue-haired god, and led the way to the mounded wall of heaven-sprung Herakles, that lofty wall built him by the Trojans and Pallas Athene, that he might escape the monster and be safe from him, what time he should make his onset from the beach to the plain. There sate them down Poseidon and the other gods, and clothed their shoulders with impenetrable cloud. And they of the other part sat down on the brows of Kallikolon around thee, Archer Phoebus, and Ares waster of cities. Thus they on either side sat devising counsels, but shrank all from falling to grievous war, and Zeus from his high seat commanded them.

Meanwhile the whole plain was filled with men and horses and ablaze with bronze; and the earth rang with the feet of them as they rushed together in the fray. Two men far better than the rest were meeting in the midst between the hosts, eager for battle, Aineias, Anchises' son, and noble Achilles. First came on Aineias threateningly, tossing his strong helm; his rapid shield he held before his breast, and brandished his bronze spear. And on the other side the son of Peleus rushed to meet him like a lion, a ravaging lion whom men desire to slay, a whole tribe assembled: and first he goeth his way unheeding, but when some warrior youth hath smitten him with a spear, the he gathereth himself open-mouthed, and foam cometh forth about his teeth, and his stout spirit groaneth in his heart, and with his tail he scourgeth either side his ribs and flanks and goadeth himself on to fight, and glaring is borne straight on them by his passion, to try whether he shall slay some man of them, or whether himself shall perish in the forefront of the throng: thus was Achilles driven of his passion and valiant spirit to go forth to meet Aineias great of heart. And when they were come near against each other, then first to Aineias spake fleet-footed noble Achilles: "Aineias, wherefore hast thou so far come forward from the crowd to stand against me: doth thy heart bid thee fight with me in hope of holding Priam's honour and lordship among the horse-taming Trojans? Nay, though thou slay me, not for that will Priam lay his kingdom in thy hands, for he hath sons, and is sound and of unshaken mind. Or have the Trojans allotted thee some lot of ground more choice than all the rest, fair land of tilth and orchard, that thou mayest dwell therein, if thou slay me? But methinks thou wilt find the slaying hard; for once before, I ween, have I made thee flee before my spear. Host thou forgotten the day when thou wert alone with the kine, and I made thee run swift-footed down Ida's steeps in haste?—then didst thou not look behind thee in thy flight. Thence fleddest thou to Lernessos, but I wasted it, having fought against it with the help of Athene and of father Zeus, and carried away women captive, bereaving them of their day of freedom: only thee Zeus shielded, and other gods. But not this time, methinks, shall they shield thee, as thou imaginest in thy heart: therefore

I bid thee go back into the throng and come not forth against me, while as yet thou art unhurt—after the event even a fool is wise."

Then to him in answer again Aineias spake: "Son of Peleus, think not with words to affright me as a child, since I too well know myself how to speak taunts and unjust speech. We know each other's race and lineage in that we have heard the fame proclaimed by mortal men, but never hast thou set eyes on my parents, or I on thine. Thou, they say, art son of noble Peleus, and of Thetis of the fair tresses, the daughter of the sea: the sire I boast is Anchises great of heart, and my mother is Aphrodite. Of these shall one pair or the other mourn their dear son today; for verily not with idle words shall we two satisfy our strife and depart out of the battle. But, if thou wilt, learn also this, that thou mayest well know our lineage, known to full many men: First Zeus the cloud-gatherer begat Dardanos, and he stablished Dardania, for not yet was holy Ilios built upon the plain to be a city of mortal men, but still they dwelt on slopes of many-fountained Ida. Then Dardanos begat a son, king Erichthonios, who became richest of mortal men. Three thousand mares had he that pastured along the marsh meadow, rejoicing in their tender foals. Of them was Boreas enamoured as they grazed, and in semblance of a dark-maned horse he covered them: then they having conceived bare twelve fillies. These when they bounded over Earth the grain-giver would run upon the topmost ripened ears of corn and break them not; and when they bounded over the broad backs of the sea they would run upon the crests of the breakers of the hoary brine. Then Erichthonios begat Tros to be load over the Trojans, and to Tros three noble sons were born, Ilos and Assarakos and godlike Ganymedes, who became the most beautiful of mortal men. Him the gods caught up to be cupbearer to Zeus, for sake of his beauty, that he might dwell among immortals. Then Ilos again begat a son, noble Laomedon, and Laomedon begat Tithonos and Priam and Lamppos and Klytios and Hiketaon, of the stock of Ares. And Assarakos begat Kapys, and Kapys Anchises, and Anchises me; but Priam begat the goodly Hector.

"Lo then of this blood and lineage declare I myself unto thee. But for valour, Zeus increaseth it in men or minisheth it according as he will, for he is lord of all. But come, let us talk thus together no longer like children, standing in mid onset of war. For there are revilings in plenty for both of us to utter—a hundred-thwarted ship would not suffice for the load of them. Glib is the tongue of man, and many words are therein of every kind, and wide is the range of his speech hither and thither. Whatsoever word thou speak, such wilt thou hear in answer. But what need that we should bandy strife and wrangling each against each. Not by speech shalt thou turn me from the battle that I desire, until we have fought together, point to point: come then, and straightway we will each try the other with bronze-headed spears."

He said, and against that other's dread and mighty shield hurled his great spear, and the shield rang loud beneath the spear-point. And the son of Peleus held away the shield from him with his stout hand, in fear, for he thought that the far-shadowing spear of Aineias great of heart would lightly pierce it through—fond man, and knew not in his mind and heart that not lightly do the glorious gifts of gods yield to force of mortal men. So did not the great spear of wise Aineias pierce that shield, for the gold resisted it, even the gift of the god. Yet through two folds he drave it, but three remained, for five folds had the lame god welded, two bronze, and two inside of tin, and one of gold; therein was stayed the ashen spear.

Then Achilles in his turn hurled his far-shadowing spear, and smote upon the circle of the shield of Aineias, beneath the edge of the rim, where the bronze ran thinnest round, and the bull-hide was thinnest thereon; and right through sped the Pelian ashen spear, and the shield cracked under it. And Aineias crouched and held up the shield away from him in dread; and the spear flew over his back and fixed itself in the earth, having divided asunder the two circles of the sheltering shield. And having escaped the long spear he stood still, and a vast anguish drowned his eyes, affrighted that the spear was planted by him so nigh. But Achilles drew his sharp sword and furiously made at him, crying his terrible cry: then Aineias grasped in his hand a stone (a mighty deed) such as two men, as men now are, would not avail to lift, but he with ease wielded it all alone. Then would Aineias have smitten him with the stone as he charged, either on helm or shield, which had warded from him bitter death, and then would the son of Peleus have closed and slain him with his sword, had not Poseidon, Shaker of earth, marked it with speed, and straightway spoken among the immortal gods: "Alas, woe is me for Aineias great of heart, who quickly will go down to Hades slain by the son of Peleus, for that he will obey the words of Apollo the far-darter, fond man, but nowise shall the god help him from grievous death. But wherefore now is he to suffer ill in his innocence, causelessly for others' wickedness, yet welcome ever are his offerings to the gods who inhabit the spacious heaven? Come, let us guide him out of death's way, lest the son of Kronos be wroth, if Achilles slay him; for it is appointed to him to escape, that the race of Dardanos perish not without seed or sign, even Dardanos whom the son of Kronos loved above all the children born to him from the daughters of men. For the race of Priam hath Zeus already hated. But thus shall the might of Aineias reign among the Trojans, and his children's children, who shall be born in the aftertime."

And him then answered Hera the ox-eyed queen: "Shaker of earth, thyself with thine own mind take counsel, whether thou wilt save Aineias, or leave him [to be slain, brave though he be, by Achilles, Peleus' son]. For by many oaths among all the Immortals have we two sworn, even Pallas Athene and I, never to help the Trojans from their evil day, not even when all Troy shall burn in the burning of fierce fire, and they that burn her shall be the warlike sons of the Achaians."

Now when Poseidon Shaker of earth heard that, he went up amid the battle and the clash of spears, and came where Aineias and renowned Achilles were. Then presently he shed mist over the eyes of Achilles, Peleus' son, and drew the bronze-headed ashen spear from the shield of Aineias great of heart, and set it before Achilles' feet, and lifted Aineias and swung him high from off the earth. Over many ranks of warriors, of horses many, sprang Aineias soaring in the hand of the god, and lighted at the farthest verge of the battle of many onsets, where the Kaukones were arraying them for the fight. Then hard beside him came Poseidon, Shaker of earth, and spake aloud to him winged words: "Aineias, what god is it that biddeth thee fight infatuate against Peleus' vehement son, who is both a better man than thou and dearer to Immortals? Rather withdraw thee whensoever thou fallest in with him, lest even contrary to thy fate thou enter the house of Hades. But when Achilles shall have met his death and doom, then be thou of good courage to fight among the foremost, for there shall none other of the Achaians slay thee."

He spoke, and left him there, when he had shown him all these things. Then quickly from Achilles' eyes he purged the magic mist; and he stared with wide eyes, and in trouble spake unto his proud soul: "Ha! verily a great marvel behold I here with mine eyes. My spear lieth here upon the ground, nor can I anywise see the man at whom I hurled it with intent to slay him. Truly then is Aineias likewise dear to the immortal gods, howbeit I deemed that his boasting thereof was altogether vanity. Away with him! not again will he find heart to make trial of me, now that once more he has escaped death to his joy. But come, I will call on the warlike Danaans and go forth to make trial of some other Trojan face to face."

He said, and leapt along the lines, and called upon each man: "No longer stand afar from the men of Troy, noble Achaians, but come let man match man and throw his soul into the fight. Hard is it for me, though I be strong, to assail so vast a folk and fight them all: not even Ares, though an immortal god, nor Athene, could plunge into the jaws of such a fray and toil therein. But to my utmost power with hands and feet and strength no whit, I say, will I be slack, nay, never so little, but right through their line will I go forward, nor deem I that any Trojan shall be glad who shall come nigh my spear."

Thus spake he urging them. But to the Trojans glorious Hector called aloud, and proclaimed that he would go forth against Achilles: "High-hearted Trojans, fear not Peleus' son. I too in words could fight even Immortals, but with the spear it were hard, for they are stronger far. Neither shall Achilles accomplish all his talk, but part thereof he is to accomplish, and part to break asunder in the midst. And against him will I go forth, though the hands of him be even as fire, yea though his hands be as fire and his fierceness as the flaming steel."

Thus spake he urging them, and the Trojans raised their spears for battle; and their fierceness was mingled confusedly, and the battle-cry arose. Then Phoebus Apollo stood by Hector and spake to him: "Hector, no longer challenge Achilles at all before the lines, but in the throng await him and from amid the roar of the battle, lest haply he spear thee or come near and smite thee with his sword."

Thus spake he, and Hector again fell back into the crowd of men, for he was amazed when he heard the sound of a god's voice.

But Achilles sprang in among the Trojans, his heart clothed with strength, crying his terrible cry, and first he took Iphition, Otrynteus' valiant son, a leader of much people, born of a Naiad nymph to Otrynteus waster of cities, beneath snowy Tmolos, in Hyde's rich domain. Him as he came right on did goodly Achilles smite with his hurled spear, down through the midst of his head, and it was rent asunder utterly. And he fell with a crash, and goodly Achilles exulted over him; "here is thy death, thy birth was on the Gygaian lake, where is thy sire's demesne, by Hyllos rich in fish and eddying Hermos."

Thus spake he exultant, but darkness fell upon the eyes of Iphition: him the chariots of the Achaians clave with their tires asunder in the forefront of the battle, and over him Achilles pierced in the temples, through his bronze-cheeked helmet, Demoleon, brave stemmer of battle, Antenor's son. No stop made the bronze helmet, but therethrough sped the spear-head and clave the bone, and the brain within was all scattered: that stroke made ending of his zeal. Then Hippodamas, as he leapt from his chariot and fled before him, Achilles wounded in the back with his spear: and he breathed forth his spirit with a roar, as when a dragged bull roareth that the young men drag to the altar of the Lord of Helike; for in such hath the Earthshaker his delight: thus roared Hippodamas as from his bones fled forth his haughty spirit. But Achilles with his spear went on after godlike Polydoros, Priam's son. Him would his sire continually forbid to fight, for that among his children he was youngest born and best beloved, and overcame all in fleetness of foot. Just then in boyish folly, displaying the swiftness of his feet, he was rushing through the forefighters, until he lost his life. Him in the midst did fleet-footed noble Achilles smite with a javelin, in his back as he darted by, where his belt's golden buckles clasped, and the breast and back plates overlapped: and right through beside the navel went the spear-head, and he fell on his knee with a cry, and dark cloud covered him round about, and he clasped his bowels to him with his hands as he sank.

Then when Hector saw his brother Polydoros clasping his bowels with his hands, and sinking to the earth, a mist fell over his eyes, nor longer might he endure to range so far apart, but he came up against Achilles brandishing his sharp spear, and like flame of fire. And Achilles when he saw him, sprang up, and spake exultingly: "Behold the man who hath deepest stricken into my soul, who slew my dear-prized friend; not long shall we now shrink from each other along the highways of the war."

He said, and looking grimly spake unto goodly Hector: "Come thou near, that the sooner thou mayest arrive at the goal of death."

Then to him, unterrified, said Hector of the glancing helm: "Son of Peleus, think not with words to affright me as a child, since I too know myself how to speak taunts and unjust speech. And I know that thou art a man of might, and a far better man than I. Yet doth this issue lie in the lap of the gods, whether I though weaker shall take thy life with my hurled spear, for mine too hath been found keen ere now."

He said, and poised his spear and hurled it, and Athene with a breath turned it back from glorious Achilles, breathing very lightly; and it came back to goodly Hector, and fell there before his feet. Then Achilles set fiercely upon him, eager to slay him, crying his terrible cry. But Apollo caught Hector up, very easily, as a god may, and hid him in thick mist. Thrice then did fleet-footed noble Achilles make onset with his spear of bronze, and thrice smote the thick mist. [But when the fourth time he had come godlike on,] then with dread shout he spake to him winged words: "Dog, thou art now again escaped from death; yet came ill very nigh thee; but now hath Phoebus Apollo saved thee, to whom thou must surely pray when thou goest forth amid the clash of spears. Verily I will slay thee yet when I meet thee hereafter, if any god is helper of me too. Now will I make after the rest, whomsoever I may seize."

Thus speaking he pierced Dryops in the midst of his neck with his spear, and he fell down before his feet. But he left him where he lay, and hurled at Demuchos Philetor's son, a good man and a tall, and stayed him with a stroke upon his knees; then smote him with his mighty sword and reft him of life. Then springing on Laogonos and Dardanos, sons of Bias, he thrust both from their chariot to the ground, one with a spear-cast smiting and the other in close battle with his sword. Then Tros, Alastor's son—he came and clasped his knees to pray him to spare him, and let him live, and slay him not, having compassion on his like age, fond fool, and knew not that he might not gain his prayers; for nowise soft of heart or tender was that man, but of fierce mood—with his hands he touched Achilles' knees, eager to entreat him, but he smote him in the liver with his sword, and his liver fell from him, and black blood therefrom filled his bosom, and he swooned, and darkness covered his eyes. Then Achilles came near and struck Mulios in the ear, and right through the other ear went the bronze spear-head. Then he smote Agenor's son Echeklos on the midst of the head with his hilted sword, and all the sword grew hot thereat with blood; and dark death seized his eyes, and forceful fate. Then next Deukalion, just where the sinews of the elbow join, there pierced he him through the forearm with his bronze spear-head; so abode he with his arm weighed down, beholding death before him; and Achilles smiting the neck with his sword swept far both head and helm, and the marrow rose out of the backbone, and the corpse lay stretched upon the earth. Then went he onward after Peires' noble son, Rhigmos, who had come from deep-soiled Thrace: him in the midst he smote with his hurled javelin, and the point fixed in his lung, and he fell forth of his chariot. And Areithoos his squire, as he turned the horses round, he pierced in the back with his sharp spear, and thrust him from the car, and the horse ran wild with fear.

As through deep glens rageth fierce fire on some parched mountain-side, and the deep forest burneth, and the wind driving it whirleth every way the flame, so raged he every way with his spear, as it had been a god, pressing hard on the men he slew; and the black earth ran with blood. For even as when one yoketh wide-browed bulls to tread white barley in a stabled threshing-floor, and quickly is it trodden out beneath the feet of the loud-lowing bulls, thus beneath great-hearted Achilles his whole-hooved horses trampled corpses and shields together; and with blood all the axletree below was sprinkled and the rims that ran around the car, for blood-drops from the horses' hooves splashed them, and blood-drops from the tires of the wheels. But the son of Peleus pressed on to win him glory, flecking with gore his irresistible hands.

BOOK XXI.

How Achilles fought with the River, and chased the men of Troy within their gates.

But when now they came unto the ford of the fair-flowing river, even eddying Xanthos, whom immortal Zeus begat, there sundering them he chased the one part to the plain toward the city, even where the Achaians were flying in affright the day before, when glorious Hector was in his fury—thither poured some in flight, and Hera spread before them thick mist to hinder them :—but half were pent into the deep-flowing silver eddied river, and fell therein with a mighty noise, and the steep channel sounded, and the banks around rang loudly; for with shouting they swam therein hither and thither whirled round the eddies. And as when at the rush of fire locusts take wing to fly unto a river, and the unwearying fire flameth forth on them with sudden onset, and they huddle in the water; so before Achilles was the stream of deep-eddying Xanthos filled with the roar and the throng of horses and men.

Then the seed of Zeus left behind him his spear upon the bank, leant against tamarisk bushes, and leapt in, as it were a god, keeping his sword alone, and devised grim work at heart, and smote as he turned him every way about: and their groaning went up ghastly as they were stricken by the sword, and the water reddened with blood. As before a dolphin of huge maw fly other fish and fill the nooks of some fair-havened bay, in terror, for he devoureth amain whichsoever of them he may catch; so along the channels of that dread stream the Trojans crouched beneath the precipitous sides. And when his hands were weary of slaughter he chose twelve young men alive out of the river, an atonement for Patroklos, Menoitios' son that was dead. These brought he forth amazed like fawns, and bound behind them their hands with well-cut thongs, which they themselves wore on their pliant doublets, and gave them to his comrades to lead down to the hollow ships. Then again he made his onset, athirst for slaying.

There met he a son of Dardanid Priam, in flight out of the river, Lykaon, whom once himself he took and brought unwilling out of his father's orchard, in a night assault; he was cutting with keen bronze young shoots of a wild fig tree, to be hand-rails of a chariot; but to him an unlooked-for bane came goodly Achilles. And at that time he sold him into well-peopled Lemnos, sending him on ship board, and the son of Jason gave a price for him; and thence a guest friend freed him with a great ransom, Eetion of Imbros, and sent him to goodly Arisbe; whence flying secretly he came to his father's house. Eleven days he rejoiced among his friends after he was come from Lemnos, but on the twelfth once more God brought him into the hands of Achilles, who was to send him to the house of Hades though nowise fain to go. Him when fleet-footed noble Achilles saw bare of helm and shield, neither had he a spear, but had thrown all to the ground; for he sweated grievously as he tried to flee out of the river, and his knees were failing him for weariness: then in wrath spake Achilles to his great heart: "Ha! verily great marvel is this that I behold with my eyes. Surely then will the proud Trojans whom I have slain rise up again from beneath the murky gloom, since thus hath this man come back escaped from his pitiless fate, though sold into goodly Lemnos, neither hath the deep of the hoary sea stayed him, that holdeth many against their will. But come then, of our spear's point shall he taste, that I may see and learn in my mind whether likewise he shall come back even from beneath, or whether the life-giving Earth shall hold him down, she that holdeth so even the strong."

Thus pondered he in his place; but the other came near amazed, fain to touch his knees, for his soul longed exceedingly to flee from evil death and black destruction. Then goodly Achilles lifted his long spear with intent to smite him, but he stooped and ran under it and caught his knees; and the spear went over his back and stood in the ground, hungering for flesh of men. Then Lykaon besought him, with one hand holding his knees, while with the other he held the sharp spear and loosed it not, and spake to him winged words: "I cry thee mercy, Achilles; have thou regard and pity for me: to thee, O fosterling of Zeus, am I in the bonds of suppliantship. For at thy table first I tasted meal of Demeter on the day when thou didst take me captive in the well-ordered orchard, and didst sell me away from my father and my friends unto goodly Lemnos, and I fetched thee the price of a hundred oxen. And now have I been ransomed for thrice that, and this is my twelfth morn since I came to Ilios after much pain. Now once again hath ruinous fate delivered me unto thy hands; surely I must be hated of father Zeus, that he hath given me a second time unto thee; and to short life my mother bare me, Laothoe, old Altes' daughter—Altes who ruleth among the war-loving Leleges, holding steep Pedasos on the Satnioeis. His daughter Priam had to wife, with many others, and of her were we two born, and thou wilt butcher both. Him among the foremost of the foot-soldiers didst thou lay low, even godlike Polydoros, when thou smotest him with they sharp spear: and now will it go hard with me here, for no hope have I to escape thy hands, since God hath delivered me thereunto. Yet one thing will I tell thee, and do thou lay it to heart: slay me not, since I am not of the same mother as Hector, who slew thy comrade the gentle and brave."

Thus spake to him the noble son of Priam, beseeching him with words, but he heard a voice implacable: "Fond fool, proffer me no ransom, nor these words. Until Patroklos met his fated day, then was it welcomer to my soul to spare the men of Troy, and many I took alive and sold beyond the sea: but now there is none shall escape death, whomsoever before Ilios God shall deliver into my hands—yes, even among all Trojans, but chiefest among Priam's sons. Ay, friend, thou too must die: why lamentest thou? Patroklos is dead, who was better far than thou. Seest thou not also what manner of man am I for might and goodliness? and a good man was my father, and a goddess mother bare me. Yet over me too hang death and forceful fate. There cometh morn or eve or some noonday when my life too some man shall take in battle, whether with spear he smite or arrow from the string."

Thus spake he, and the other's knees and heart were unstrung. He let go Achilles' spear, and sat with both hands outspread. But Achilles drew his sharp sword and smote on the collar-bone beside the neck, and all the two-edged sword sank into him, and he lay stretched prone upon the earth, and blood flowed dark from him and soaked the earth. Him seized Achilles by the foot and sent him down the stream, and over him exulting spake winged words: "There lie thou among the fishes, which shall lick off thy wound's blood heedlessly, nor shall thy mother lay thee on a bed and mourn for thee, but Skamandros shall bear thee on his eddies into the broad bosom of the sea. Leaping along the wave shall many a fish dart up to the dark ripple to eat of the white flesh of Lykaon. So perish all, until we reach the citadel of sacred Ilios, ye flying and I behind destroying. Nor even the River, fair-flowing, silver-eddied, shall avail you, to whom long time forsooth ye sacrifice many bulls, and among his eddies throw whole-hooved horses down alive. For all this yet shall ye die the death, until ye pay all for Patroklos' slaying and the slaughter of Achaians whom at the swift ships ye slew while I tarried afar."

Thus spake he, but the River waxed ever more wroth in his heart, and sought in his soul how he should stay goodly Achilles from his work, and ward destruction from the Trojans. Meanwhile the son of Peleus with his far-shadowing spear leapt, fain to slay him, upon Asteropaios son of

Pelegon, whom wide-flowing Axios begat of Periboia eldest of the daughters of Akessamenos. Upon him set Achilles, and Asteropaios stood against him from the river, holding two spears; for Xanthos put courage into his heart, being angered for the slaughtered youths whom Achilles was slaughtering along the stream and had no pity on them. Then when the twain were come nigh in onset on each other, unto him first spake fleet-footed noble Achilles: "Who and whence art thou of men, that darest to come against me? Ill-fated are they whose children match them with my might."

And to him, made answer Pelegon's noble son: "High-hearted son of Peleus, why askest thou my lineage? I come from deep-soiled Paionia, a land far off, leading Paionian men with their long spears, and this now is the eleventh morn since I am come to Ilios. My lineage is of wide-flowing Axios, who begat Pelegon famous with the spear, and he, men say, was my father. Now fight we, noble Achilles!"

Thus spake he in defiance, and goodly Achilles lifted the Pelian ash: but the warrior Asteropaios hurled with both spears together, for he could use both hands alike, and with the one spear smote the shield, but pierced it not right through, for the gold stayed it, the gift of a god; and with the other he grazed the elbow of Achilles' right arm, and there leapt forth dark blood, but the point beyond him fixed itself in the earth, eager to batten on flesh. Then in his turn Achilles hurled on Asteropaios his straight-flying ash, fain to have slain him, but missed the man and struck the high bank, and quivering half its length in the bank he left the ashen spear. Then the son of Peleus drew his sharp sword from his thigh and leapt fiercely at him, and he availed not to draw with his stout hand Achilles' ashen shaft from the steep bank. Thrice shook he it striving to draw it forth, and thrice gave up the strain, but the fourth time he was fain to bend and break the ashen spear of the seed of Aiakos, but ere that Achilles closing on him reft him of life with his sword. For in the belly he smote him beside the navel, and all his bowels gushed out to the earth, and darkness covered his eyes as he lay gasping. Then Achilles trampling on his breast stripped off his armour and spake exultingly: "Lie there! It is hard to strive against children of Kronos' mighty son, even though one be sprung from a River-god. Thou truly declarest thyself the seed of a wide-flowing River, but I avow me of the linkage of great Zeus. My sire is a man ruling many Myrmidons, Peleus the son of Aiakos, and Aiakos was begotten of Zeus. As Zeus is mightier than seaward-murmuring rivers, so is the seed of Zeus made mightier than the seed of a river. Nay, there is hard beside thee a great river, if he may anywise avail; but against Zeus the son of Kronos it is not possible to fight. For him not even king Acheloios is match, nor yet the great strength of deep-flowing Ocean, from whom all rivers flow and every sea, and all springs and deep wells: yea, even he hath fear of the lightning of great Zeus and his dread thunder, when it pealeth out of heaven."

He said, and from the steep bank drew his bronze spear, and left there Asteropaios whom he had slain, lying in the sands, and the dark water flooded him. Around him eels and fishes swarmed, tearing and gnawing the fat about his kidneys. But Achilles went on after the charioted Paiones who still along the eddying river huddled in fear, when they saw their best man in the stress of battle slain violently by the hands and the sword of the son of Peleus. There slew he Thersilochos and Mydon and Astypylos and Mnesos and Thrasios and Ainios and Ophelestes; and more yet of the Paiones would swift Achilles have slain, had not the deep-eddying River called unto him in wrath, in semblance of a man, and from an eddy's depth sent forth a voice: "O Achilles, thy might and thy evil work are beyond the measure of men; for gods themselves are ever helping thee. If indeed the son of Kronos hath delivered thee all the Trojans to destroy, at least drive them forth from me and do thy grim deeds on the plain, for filled with dead men is my. pleasant bed, nor can I pour my stream to the great sea, being choked with dead, and thou slayest ruthlessly. Come then, let be; I am astonished, O captain of hosts."

And to him answered Achilles fleet of foot: "So be it, heaven-sprung Skamandros, even as thou biddest. But the proud Trojans I will not cease from slaying until I have driven them into their city, and have made trial with Hector face to face whether he is to vanquish me or I him."

Thus saying, he set upon the Trojans, like a god. Then unto Apollo spake the deep-eddying River: "Out on it, lord of the silver bow, child of Zeus, thou hast not kept the ordinance of Kronos' son, who charged thee straitly to stand by the Trojans and to help them, until eve come with light late-setting, and darken the deep-soiled earth."

He said, and spear-famed Achilles sprang from the bank and leapt into his midst; but he rushed on him in a furious wave, and stirred up all his streams in tumult, and swept down the many dead who lay thick in him, slain by Achilles; these out to land he cast with bellowing like a bull, and saved the living under his fair streams, hiding them within eddies deep and wide. But terribly around Achilles arose his tumultuous wave, and the stream smote violently against his shield, nor availed he to stand firm upon his feet. Then he grasped a tall fair-grown elm, and it fell uprooted and tore away all the bank, and reached over the fair river bed with its thick shoots, and stemmed the River himself, falling all within him: and Achilles, struggling out of the eddy, made haste to fly over the plain with his swift feet, for he was afraid. But the great god ceased not, but arose upon him with darkness on his crest, that he might stay noble Achilles from slaughter, and ward destruction from the men of Troy. And the son of Peleus rushed away a spear's throw, with the swoop of a black eagle, the mighty hunter, strongest at once and swiftest of winged birds. Like him he sped, and on his breast the bronze rang terribly as he fled from beneath the onset, and behind him the River rushed on with a mighty roar. As when a field-waterer from a dark spring leadeth water along a bed through crops and garden grounds, a mattock in his hands, casting forth hindrances from the ditch, and as it floweth all pebbles are swept down, and swiftly gliding it murmureth down a sloping place, and outrunneth him that is its guide:—thus ever the river wave caught up Achilles for all his speed; for gods are mightier than men. For whensoever fleet-footed noble Achilles struggled to stand against it, and know whether all immortals be upon him who inhabit spacious heaven, then would a great wave of the heaven-sprung River beat upon his shoulders from above, and he sprang upward with his feet, sore vexed at heart; and the River was wearying his knees with violent rush beneath, devouring the earth from under his feet. Then the son of Peleus cried aloud, looking up to the broad heaven: "Zeus, Father, how doth none of the gods take it on him in pity to save me from the River! after that let come to me what may. None other of the inhabitants of Heaven is chargeable so much, but only my dear mother, who beguiled me with false words, saying that under the wall of the mail-clad men of Troy I must die by the swift arrows of Apollo. Would that Hector had slain me, the best of men bred here: then brave had been the slayer, and a brave man had he slain. But now by a sorry death am I doomed to die, pent in this mighty river, like a swineherd boy whom a torrent sweepeth down as he essayeth to cross it in a storm."

Thus spake he, and quickly Poseidon and Athene came near and stood beside him, in the likeness of men, and taking his hands in theirs pledged him in words. And the first that spake was Poseidon, Shaker of the earth: "Son of Peleus, tremble not, neither be afraid; such helpers of thee are we from the gods, approved of Zeus, even Pallas Athene and I, for to be vanquished of a river is not appointed thee, but he will soon give back, and thou wilt thyself perceive it: but we will give thee wise counsel, if thou wilt obey it; hold not thy hand from hazardous battle until within Ilios' famous walls thou have pent the Trojan host, even all that flee before thee. But do thou, when thou hast taken the life of Hector, go back unto the ships; this glory we give unto thee to win."

They having thus spoken departed to the immortals, but he toward the plain—for the bidding of gods was strong upon him—went onward; and all the plain was filled with water-flood, and many beautiful arms and corpses of slain youths were drifting there. So upward sprang his knees as he rushed against the stream right on, nor stayed him the wide-flowing River, for Athene put great strength in him. Neither did Skamandros slacken his fierceness, but yet more raged against the son of Peleus, and he curled crestwise the billow of his stream, lifting himself on high, and on Simoeis he called with a shout: "Dear brother, the strength of this man let us both join to stay, since quickly he will lay waste the great city of king Priam, and the Trojans abide not in the battle. Help me with speed, and fill thy streams with water from thy springs, and urge on all thy torrents, and raise up a great wave, and stir huge roaring of tree-stumps and stones, that we may stay the fierce man who now is lording it, and deeming himself match for gods. For neither, I ween, will strength avail him nor comeliness anywise, nor that armour beautiful, which deep beneath the flood shall be o'erlaid with slime, and himself I will wrap him in my sands and pour round him countless shingle without stint, nor shall the Achaians know where to gather his bones, so vast a shroud of silt will I heap over them. Where he dieth there shall be his tomb, neither shall he have need of any barrow to be raised, when the Achaians make his funeral."

He said, and rushed in tumult on Achilles, raging from on high, thundering with foam and blood and bodies of dead men. Then did a dark wave of the heaven-sprung River stand towering up and overwhelm the son of Peleus. But Hera cried aloud in terror of Achilles, lest the great deep-eddying River sweep him away, and straightway she called to Hephaistos, her dear son: "Rise, lame god, O my son; it was against thee we thought that eddying Xanthos was matched in fight. Help with all speed, put forth large blast of flame. Then will I go to raise a strong storm out of the sea of the west wind and the white south which shall utterly consume the dead Trojans and their armour, blowing the angry flame. Thou along Xanthos' banks burn up his trees and wrap himself in fire, nor let him anywise turn thee back by soft words or by threat, nor stay thy rage—only when I cry to thee with my voice, then hold the unwearying fire."

Thus spake she, and Hephaistos made ready fierce-blazing fire. First on the plain fire blazed, and burnt the many dead who lay there thick, slain by Achilles; and all the plain was parched and the bright water stayed. And as when in late summer the north wind swiftly parcheth a new watered orchard, and he that tilleth it is glad, thus was the whole plain parched, and Hephaistos consumed the dead; then against the river he turned his gleaming flame. Elms burnt and willow trees and tamarisks, and lotos burnt and rush and galingale which round the fair streams of the river grew in multitude. And the eels and fishes beneath the eddies were afflicted, which through the fair streams tumbled this way and that, in anguish at the blast of crafty Hephaistos. And the strong River burned, and spake and called to him by name: "Hephaistos, there is no god can match with thee, nor will I fight thee thus ablaze with fire. Cease strife, yea, let noble Achilles drive the Trojans forthwith out of their city; what have I to do with strife and succour?"

Thus spake he, burnt with fire, for his fair streams were bubbling. And as a cauldron boileth within, beset with much fire, melting the lard of some fatted hog spurting up on all sides, and logs of firewood lie thereunder,—so burned his fair streams in the fire, and the water boiled. He had no mind to flow, but refrained him, for the breath of cunning Hephaistos violently afflicted him. Then unto Hera, earnestly beseeching her,' he spake winged words: "Hera, wherefore hath thy son assailed my stream to vex it above others? I am less chargeable than all the rest that are helpers of the Trojans. But lo, I will give over, if thou wilt, and let thy son give over too. And I further will swear even this, that never will I ward the day of evil from the Trojans, not even when all Troy is burning in the blaze of hungry fire, and the warlike sons of Achaians are the burners thereof."

Then when the white-armed goddess Hera heard his speech, straightway she spake unto Hephaistos her dear son: "Hephaistos, hold, famed son; it befitteth not thus for mortals' sake to do violence to an immortal god."

Thus said she and Hephaistos quenched the fierce-blazing fire, and the wave once more rolled down the fair river-bed.

So when the rage of Xanthos was overcome, both ceased, for Hera stayed them, though in wrath. But among the other gods fell grievous bitter strife, and their hearts were carried diverse in their breasts. And they clashed together with a great noise, and the wide earth groaned, and the clarion of great Heaven rang around. Zeus heard as he sate upon Olympus, and his heart within him laughed pleasantly when he beheld that strife of gods. Then no longer stood they asunder, for Ares piercer of shields began the battle and first made for Athene with his bronze spear, and spake a taunting word: "Wherefore, O dogfly, dost thou match gods with gods in strife, with stormy daring, as thy great spirit moveth thee? Rememberest thou not how thou movedst Diomedes Tydeus' son to wound me, and thyself didst take a visible spear and thrust it straight at me and pierce through my fair skin? Therefore deem I now that thou shalt pay me for all that thou hast done."

Thus saying he smote on the dread tasselled aegis that not even the lightning of Zeus can overcome—thereon smote bloodstained Ares with his long spear. But she, giving back, grasped with stout hand a stone that lay upon the plain, black, rugged, huge, which men of old time set to be the landmark of a field; this hurled she, and smote impetuous Ares on the neck, and unstrung his limbs. Seven roods he covered in his fall, and soiled his hair with dust, and his armour rang upon him. And Pallas Athene laughed, and spake to him winged words exultingly: "Fool, not even yet hast thou learnt how far better than thou I claim to be, that thus thou matchest thy might with mine. Thus shalt thou satisfy thy mother's curses, who deviseth mischief against thee in her wrath, for that thou hast left the Achaians and givest the proud Trojan's aid."

Thus having said she turned from him her shining eyes. Him did Aphrodite daughter of Zeus take by the hand and lead away, groaning continually, for scarce gathered he his spirit back to him. But when the white-armed goddess Hera was aware of them, straightway she spake unto Athene winged words: "Out on it, child of aegis-bearing Zeus, maiden invincible, lo there the dogfly is leading Ares destroyer of men out of the fray of battle down the throng—nay then, pursue her."

She said, and Athene sped after her with heart exultant, and made at her and smote her with stout hand upon the breast, and straightway her knees and heart were unstrung. So they twain lay on the bounteous earth, and she spake winged words exultingly: "Such let all be who give the Trojans aid when they fight against the mailed Argives. Be they even so bold and brave as Aphrodite when she came to succour Ares and defied my might. Then should we long ago have ceased from war, having laid waste the stablished citadel of Ilios."

[She said, and the white-armed goddess Hera smiled.] Then to Apollo spake the earth-shaking lord: "Phoebus, why stand we apart? It befitteth not after the rest have begun: that were the more shameful if without fighting we should go to Olympus to the bronze-thresholded house of Zeus. Begin, for thou art younger; it were not meet for me, since I was born first and know more. Fond god, how foolish is thy heart! Thou rememberest not all the ills we twain alone of gods endured at Ilios, when by ordinance of Zeus we came to proud Laomedon and served him through a year for promised recompense, and he laid on us his commands. I round their city built the Trojans a wall, wide and most fair, that the city might be unstormed, and thou Phoebus, didst herd shambling crook-horned kine among the spurs of woody many-folded Ida. But when the joyous seasons were accomplishing the term of hire, then redoubtable Laomedon robbed us of all hire, and sent us off with threats. He threatened that he would bind together our feet and hands and sell us into far-off isles, and the ears of both of us he vowed to shear off with the sword. So we went home with angry hearts, wroth for the hire he promised and gave us not. To his folk not thou showest favour, nor essayest with us how the proud Trojans may be brought low and perish miserably with their children and noble wives."

Then to him answered King Apollo the Far-darter: "Shaker of the earth, of no sound mind wouldst thou repute me if I should fight against thee for the sake of pitiful mortals, who like unto leaves now live in glowing life, consuming the fruit of the earth, and now again pine into death. Let us with all speed cease from combat, and let them do battle by themselves."

Thus saying he turned away, for he felt shame to deal in blows with his father's brother. But his sister upbraided him sore, the queen of wild beasts, huntress Artemis, and spake a taunting word: "So then thou fleest, Far-darter, hast quite yielded to Poseidon the victory, and given him glory for naught! Fond god, why bearest thou an ineffectual bow in vain? Let me not hear thee again in the halls of our sire boast as before among the immortal gods thou wouldst stand up to fight against Poseidon."

Thus spake she, but far-darting Apollo answered her not. But angrily the noble spouse of Zeus [upbraided the Archer Queen with taunting words:] "How now art thou fain, bold vixen, to set thyself against me? Hard were it for thee to match my might, bow-bearer though thou art, since against women Zeus made thee a lion, and giveth thee to slay whomso of them thou wilt. Truly it is better on the mountains to slay wild beasts and deer than to fight amain with mightier than thou. But if thou wilt, try war, that thou mayest know well how far stronger am I, since thou matchest thy might with mine."

She said, and with her left hand caught both the other's hands by the wrist, and with her right took the bow from off her shoulders, and therewith, smiling, beat her on the ears as she turned this way and that; and the swift arrows fell out of her quiver. And weeping from before her the goddess fled like a dove that from before a falcon flieth to a hollow rock, a cleft—for she was not fated to be caught;—thus Artemis fled weeping, and left her bow and arrows where they lay. Then to Leto spake the Guide, the slayer of Argus: "Leto, with thee will I no wise fight; a grievous thing it is to come to blows with wives of cloud-gathering Zeus; but boast to thy heart's content among the immortal gods that thou didst vanquish me by might and main."

Thus said he, and Leto gathered up the curved bow and arrows fallen hither and thither amid the whirl of dust: so taking her daughter's bow she went back. And the maiden came to Olympus, to the bronze-thresholded house of Zeus, and weeping set herself on her father's knee, while round her her divine vesture quivered: and her father, Kronos' son, took her to him and asked of her, laughing gently: "Who of the inhabitants of heaven, dear child, hath dealt with thee thus [hastily, as though thou hadst been doing some wrong thing openly]?"

And to him in answer spake the fair-crowned queen of the echoing chase: "It was thy wife that buffeted me, father, the white-armed Hera, from whom are strife and contention come upon the immortals."

Thus talked they unto one another. Then Phoebus Apollo entered into sacred Ilios, for he was troubled for the wall of the well-builded city, lest the Danaans waste it before its hour upon that day. But the other ever-living gods went to Olympus, some angry and some greatly triumphing, and sat down beside Zeus who hideth himself in dark clouds.

Now Achilles was still slaying the Trojans, both themselves and their whole-hooved horses. And as when a smoke goeth up to the broad heaven, when a city burneth, kindled by the wrath of gods, and causeth toil to all, and griefs to many, thus caused Achilles toil and griefs to the Trojans. And the old man Priam stood on the sacred tower, and was aware of dread Achilles, how before him the Trojans thronged in rout, nor was any succour found of them. Then with a cry he went down from the tower, to rouse the gallant warders along the walls: "Hold open the gates in your hands until the folk come to the city in their rout, for closely is Achilles chasing them—now trow I there will be deadly deeds. And when they are gathered within the wall and are taking breath, then again shut back the gate-wings firmly builded; for I fear lest that murderous man spring in within the wall."

Thus spake he, and they opened the gates and thrust back the bolts; and the gates flung back gave safety. Then Apollo leapt forth to the front that he might ward destruction from the Trojans. They straight for the city and the high wall were fleeing, parched with thirst and dust-grimed from the plain, and Achilles chased them vehemently with his spear, for strong frenzy possessed his heart continually, and he thirsted to win him renown. Then would the sons of the Achaians have taken high-gated Troy, had not Phoebus Apollo aroused goodly Agenor, Antenor's son, a princely man and strong. In his heart he put good courage, and himself stood by his side that he might ward off the grievous visitations of death, leaning against the oak, and he was shrouded in thick mist. So when Agenor was aware of Achilles waster of cities, he halted, and his heart much wavered as he stood; and in trouble he spake to his great heart: "Ay me, if I flee before mighty Achilles, there where the rest are driven terror-struck, nathless will he overtake me and slaughter me as a coward. Or what if I leave these to be driven before Achilles the son of Peleus, and flee upon my feet from the wall by another way to the Ileian plain, until I come to the spurs of Ida, and hide me in the underwood? So then at evening, having bathed in the river and refreshed me of sweat, I might return to Ilios. Nay, why doth my heart debate thus within me? Lest he might be aware of me as I get me from the city for the plain, and speeding after overtake me with swift feet; then will it no more be possible to avoid the visitation of death, for he is exceeding mighty above all mankind. What then if in front of the city I go forth to meet him? Surely his flesh too is penetrable by sharp bronze, and there is but one life within, and men say he is mortal, howbeit Zeus the son of Kronos giveth him renown."

Thus saying, he gathered himself to await Achilles, and within him his stout heart was set to strive and fight. As a leopardess goeth forth from a deep thicket to affront a huntsman, nor is afraid at heart, nor fleeth when she heareth the bay of hounds; for albeit the man first smite her with thrust or throw, yet even pierced through with the spear she ceaseth not from her courage until she either grapple or be slain, so noble Antenor's son, goodly Agenor, refused to flee till he should put Achilles to the proof, but held before him the circle of his shield, and aimed at him with his spear, and cried aloud: "Doubtless thou hopest in thy heart, noble Achilles, on this day to sack the city of the proud men of Troy. Fond man, there shall many woful things yet be wrought before it, for within it we are many men and staunch, who in front of our parents dear and wives and sons keep Ilios safe; but thou shalt here meet death, albeit so redoubtable and bold a man of war."

He said, and hurled his sharp spear with weighty hand, and smote him on the leg beneath the knee, nor missed his mark, and the greave of new-wrought tin rang terribly on him; but the bronze bounded back from him it smote, nor pierced him, for the god's gift drave it back. Then the son of Peleus in his turn made at godlike Agenor, but Apollo suffered him not to win renown, but caught away Agenor, and shrouded him in thick mist, and sent him in peace to be gone out of the war. Then by wile kept the son of Peleus away from the folk, for in complete semblance of Agenor himself he stood before the feet of Achilles, who hasted to run upon him and chase him. And while he chased him over the wheat-bearing plain, edging him toward the deep-eddying river Skamandros, as he ran but a little in front of him (for by wile Apollo beguiled him that he kept ever hoping to overtake him in the race), meantime the other Trojans in common rout came gladly unto their fastness, and the city was filled with the throng of them. Neither had they heart to await one another outside the city and wall, and to know who might have escaped and who had perished in the fight, but impetuously they poured into the city, whomsoever of them his feet and knees might save.

BOOK XXII

How Achilles fought with Hector, and slew him, and brought his body to the ships.

Thus they throughout the city, scared like fawns, were cooling their sweat and drinking and slaking their thirst, leaning on the fair battlements, while the Achaians drew near the wall, setting shields to shoulders. But Hector deadly fate bound to abide in his place, in front of Ilios and the Skaian gates. Then to the son of Peleus spake Phoebus Apollo: "Wherefore, son of Peleus, pursuest thou me with swift feet, thyself being mortal and I a deathless god? Thou hast not even yet known me, that I am a god, but strivest vehemently. Truly thou regardest not thy task among the affliction of the Trojans whom thou affrightedst, who now are gathered into the city, while thou heat wandered hither. Me thou wilt never slay, for I am not subject unto death."

Then mightily moved spake unto him Achilles fleet of foot: "Thou hast baulked me, Far-darter, most mischievous of all the gods, in that thou hast turned me hither from the wall: else should full many yet have bitten the dust or ever within Ilios had they come. Now hast thou robbed me of great renown, and lightly hast saved them, because thou hadst no vengeance to fear thereafter. Verily I would avenge me on thee, had I but the power."

Thus saying toward the city he was gone in pride of heart, rushing like some victorious horse in a chariot, that runneth lightly at full speed over the plain; so swiftly plied Achilles his feet and knees. Him the old man Priam first beheld as he sped across the plain, blazing as the star that cometh forth at harvest-time, and plain seen his rays shine forth amid the host of stars in the darkness of night, the star whose name men call Orion's Dog. Brightest of all is he, yet for an evil sign is he set, and bringeth much fever upon hapless men. Even so on Achilles' breast the bronze gleamed as he ran. And the old man cried aloud and beat upon his head with his hands, raising them on high, and with a cry called aloud beseeching his dear son; for he before the gates was standing, all hot for battle with Achilles. And the old man spake piteously unto him, stretching forth his hands: "Hector, beloved son, I pray thee await not this man alone with none beside thee, lest thou quickly meet thy doom, slain by the son of Peleus, since he is mightier far, a merciless man. Would the gods loved him even as do I! then quickly would dogs and vultures devour him on the field—thereby would cruel pain go from my heart—the man who hath bereft me of many valiant sons, slaying them and selling them captive into far-off isles. Ay even now twain of my children, Lykaon and Polydoros, I cannot see among the Trojans that throng into the fastness, sons whom Laothoe bare me, a princess among women. If they be yet alive amid the enemy's host, then will we ransom them with bronze and gold, for there is store within, for much goods gave the old man famous Altes to his child. If they be dead, then even in the house of Hades shall they be a sorrow to my soul and to their mother, even to us who gave them birth, but to the rest of the folk a briefer sorrow, if but thou die not by Achilles' hand. Nay, come within the wall, my child, that thou preserve the men and women of Troy, neither give great triumph to the son of Peleus, and be thyself bereft of sweet life. Have compassion also on me, the helpless one, who still can feel, ill-fated; whom the father, Kronos' son, will bring to naught by a grievous doom in the path of old age, having seen full many ills, his sons perishing and his daughters carried away captive, and his chambers laid waste and infant children hurled to the ground in terrible war, and his sons' wives dragged away by the ruinous hands of the Achaians. Myself then last of all at the street door will ravening dogs tear, when some one by stroke or throw of the sharp bronze hath bereft my limbs of life—even the dogs I reared in my halls about my table and to guard my door, which then having drunk my blood, maddened at heart shall lie in the gateway. A young man all beseemeth, even to be slain in war, to be torn by the sharp bronze and lie on the field; though he be dead yet is all honourable to him, whate'er be seen: but when dogs defile the hoary head and hoary beard of an old man slain, this is the most piteous thing that cometh upon hapless men."

Thus spake the old man, and grasped his hoary hairs, plucking them from his head, but he persuaded not Hector's soul. Then his mother in her turn wailed tearfully, loosening the folds of her robe, while with the other hand she showed her breast; and through her tears spake to him winged words: "Hector, my child, have regard unto this bosom and pity me, if ever I gave thee consolation of my breast. Think of it, dear child, and from this side the wall drive back the foe, nor stand in front to meet him. He is merciless; if he slay thee it will not be on a bed that I or thy wife shall bewail thee, my own dear child, but far away from us by the ships of the Argives will swift dogs devour thee."

Thus they with wailing spake to their dear son, beseeching him sore, yet they persuaded not Hector's soul, but he stood awaiting Achilles as he drew nigh in giant might. As a serpent of the mountains upon his den awaiteth a man, having fed on evil poisons, and fell wrath hath entered into him, and terribly he glared as he coileth himself about his den, so Hector with courage unquenchable gave not back, leaning his shining shield against a jutting tower. Then sore troubled he spake to his great heart: "Ay me, if I go within the gates and walls, Polydamas will be first to bring reproach against me, since he bade me lead the Trojans to the city during this ruinous night, when noble Achilles arose. But I regarded him not, yet surely it had been better far. And now that I have undone the host by my wantonness, I am ashamed before the men of Troy and women of trailing robes, lest at any time some worse man than I shall say: 'Hector by trusting his own might undid the host.' So will they speak; then to me would it be better far to face Achilles and either slay him and go home, or myself die gloriously before the city. Or what if I lay down my bossy shield and my stout helm, and lean my spear against the wall, and go of myself to meet noble Achilles and promise him that Helen, and with her all possessions that Alexandros brought in hollow ships to Troy, the beginning of strife, we will give to the Sons of Atreus to take away, and therewithal to divide in half with the Achaians all else that this city holdeth: and if thereafter I obtain from the Trojans an oath of the Elders that they will hide nothing but divide all in twain [whatever wealth the pleasant city hold within]? But wherefore doth my heart debate thus? I might come unto him and he would not pity or regard me at all, but presently slay me unarmed as it were but a woman, if I put off my armour. No time is it now to dally with him from oaktree or from rock, like youth with maiden, as youth and maiden hold dalliance one with another. Better is it to join battle with all speed: let us know upon which of us twain the Olympian shall bestow renown."

Thus pondered he as he stood, but nigh on him came Achilles, peer of Enyalios warrior of the waving helm, brandishing from his right shoulder the Pelian ash, his terrible spear; and all around the bronze on him flashed like the gleam of blazing fire or of the Sun as he ariseth. And trembling seized Hector as he was aware of him, nor endured he to abide in his place, but left the gates behind him and fled in fear. And the son of Peleus darted after him, trusting in his swift feet. As a falcon upon the mountains, swiftest of winged things, swoopeth fleetly after a trembling dove; and she before him fleeth, while he with shrill screams hard at hand still darteth at her, for his heart urgeth him to seize her; so Achilles in hot haste flew straight for him, and Hector fled beneath the Trojans' wall, and plied swift knees. They past the watch-place and wind-waved wild fig-tree sped ever, away from under the wall, along the waggon-track, and came to the two fair-flowing springs, where two fountains rise that feed deep-eddying Skamandros. The one floweth with warm water, and smoke goeth up therefrom around as it were from a blazing fire, while the other even in summer floweth forth like cold hail or snow or ice that water formeth. And there beside the springs are broad washing-troughs hard by, fair troughs of stone, where wives and fair daughters of the men of Troy were wont to wash bright raiment, in the old time of peace, before the sons of the Achaians came. Thereby they ran, he flying, he pursuing. Valiant was the flier but far mightier he who fleetly pursued him. For not for beast of sacrifice or for an oxhide were they striving, such as are prizes for men's speed of foot, but for the life of horse-taming Hector was their race. And as when victorious whole-hooved horses run rapidly round the turning-points, and some great prize lieth in sight, be it a tripod or a woman, in honour of a man that is dead, so thrice around Priam's city circled those twain with flying feet, and all the gods were gazing on them. Then among them spake first the father of gods and men: "Ay me, a man beloved I see pursued around the wall. My heart is woe for Hector, who hath burnt for me many thighs of oxen amid the crests of many-folded Ida, and other times on the city-height; but now is goodly Achilles pursuing him with swift feet round Priam's town. Come, give your counsel, gods, and devise whether we shall save him from death or now at last slay him, valiant though he be, by the hand of Achilles Peleus' son."

Then to him answered the bright-eyed goddess Athene: "O Father, Lord of the bright lightning and the dark cloud, what is this thou hast said? A man that is a mortal, doomed long ago by fate, wouldst thou redeem back from ill-boding death? Do it, but not all we other gods approve."

And unto her in answer spake cloud-gathering Zeus: "Be of good cheer, Trito-born, dear child: not in full earnest speak I, and I would fain be kind to thee. Do as seemeth good to thy mind, and draw not back."

Thus saying he roused Athene, that already was set thereon, and from the crests of Olympus she darted down.

But after Hector sped fleet Achilles chasing him vehemently. And as when on the mountains a hound hunteth the fawn of a deer, having started it from its covert, through glens and glades, and if it crouch to baffle him under a bush, yet scenting it out the hound runneth constantly until he find it; so Hector baffled not Peleus' fleet-footed son. Oft as he set himself to dart under the well-built walls over against the Dardanian gates, if haply from above they might succour him with darts, so oft would Achilles gain on him and turn him toward the plain, while himself he sped ever on the city-side. And as in a dream one faileth in chase of a flying man, the one faileth in his flight and the other in his chase—so failed Achilles to overtake him in the race, and Hector to escape. And thus would Hector have avoided the visitation of death, had not this time been utterly the last wherein Apollo came nigh to him, who nerved his strength and his swift knees. For to the host did noble Achilles sign with his head, and forbade them to hurl bitter darts against Hector, lest any smiting him should gain renown, and he himself come second. But when the fourth time they had reached the springs, then the Father hung his golden balances, and set therein two lots of dreary death, one of Achilles, one of horse-taming Hector, and held them by the midst and poised. Then Hector's fated day sank down, and fell to the house of Hades, and Phoebus Apollo left him. But to Peleus' son came the bright-eyed goddess Athene, and standing near spake to him winged words: "Now verily, glorious Achilles dear to Zeus, I have hope that we twain shall carry off great glory to the ships for the Achaians, having slain Hector, for all his thirst for fight. No longer is it possible for him to escape us, not even though far-darting Apollo should travail sore, grovelling before the Father, aegis-bearing Zeus. But do thou now stand and take breath, and I will go and persuade this man to confront thee in fight."

Thus spake Athene, and he obeyed, and was glad at heart, and stood leaning on his bronze-pointed ashen-spear. And she left him and came to noble Hector, like unto Deiphobos in shape and in strong voice, and standing near spake to him winged words: "Dear brother, verily fleet Achilles doth thee violence, chasing thee round Priam's town with swift feet: but come let us make a stand and await him on our defence."

Then answered her great Hector of the glancing helm: "Deiphobos, verily aforetime wert thou far dearest of my brothers, but now methinks I shall honour thee even more, in that thou hast dared for my sake, when thou sawest me, to come forth of the wall, while the others tarry within."

Then to him again spake the bright-eyed goddess Athene: "Dear brother, of a truth my father and lady mother and my comrades around besought me much, entreating me in turn, to tarry there, so greatly do they all tremble before him; but my heart within was sore with dismal grief. And now fight we with straight-set resolve and let there be no sparing of spears, that we may know whether Achilles is to slay us and carry our bloody spoils to the hollow ships, or whether he might be vanquished by thy spear."

Thus saying Athene in her subtlety led him on. And when they were come nigh in onset on one another, to Achilles first spake great Hector of the glancing helm: "No longer, son of Peleus, will I fly thee, as before I thrice ran round the great town of Priam, and endured not to await thy onset. Now my heart biddeth me stand up against thee; I will either slay or be slain. But come hither and let us pledge us by our gods, for they shall be best witnesses and beholders of covenants: I will entreat thee in no outrageous sort, if Zeus grant me to outstay thee, and if I take thy life, but when I have despoiled thee of thy glorious armour, O Achilles, I will give back thy dead body to the Achaians, and do thou the same."

But unto him with grim gaze spake Achilles fleet of foot: "Hector, talk not to me, thou madman, of covenants. As between men and lions there is no pledge of faith, nor wolves and sheep can be of one mind, but imagine evil continually against each other, so is it impossible for thee and me to be friends, neither shall be any pledge between us until one or other shall have fallen and glutted with blood Ares, the stubborn god of war. Bethink thee of all thy soldiership: now behoveth it thee to quit thee as a good spearman and valiant man of war. No longer is there way of escape for thee, but Pallas Athene will straightway subdue thee to my spear; and now in one hour shalt thou pay back for all my sorrows for my friends whom thou hast slain in the fury of thy spear."

He said, and poised his far-shadowing spear and hurled. And noble Hector watched the coming thereof and avoided it; for with his eye on it he crouched, and the bronze spear flew over him, and fixed itself in the earth; but Pallas Athene caught it up and gave it back to Achilles, unknown of Hector shepherd of hosts. Then Hector spake unto the noble son of Peleus: "Thou hast missed, so no wise yet, godlike Achilles, has thou known from Zeus the hour of my doom, though thou thoughtest it. Cunning of tongue art thou and a deceiver in speech, that fearing thee I might forget my valour and strength. Not as I flee shalt thou plant thy spear in my reins, but drive it straight through my breast as I set on thee, if God hath given thee to do it. Now in thy turn avoid my spear of bronze. O that thou mightst take it all into thy flesh! Then would the war be lighter to the Trojans, if but thou wert dead, for thou art their greatest bane."

He said, and poised his long-shadowed spear and hurled it, and smote the midst of the shield of Peleus' son, and missed him not: but far from the shield the spear leapt back. And Hector was wroth that his swift weapon had left his hand in vain, and he stood downcast, for he had no second ashen spear. And he called with a loud shout to Deiphobos of the white shield, and asked of him a long spear, but he was no wise nigh. Then Hector knew he truth in his heart, and spake and said: "Ay me, now verily the gods have summoned me to death. I deemed the warrior Deiphobos was by my side, but he is within the wall, and it was Athene who played me false. Now therefore is evil death come very nigh me, not far off, nor is there way of escape. This then was from of old the pleasure of Zeus and of the far-darting son of Zeus, who yet before were fain to succour me: but now my fate hath found me. At least let me not die without a struggle or ingloriously, but in some great deed of arms whereof men yet to be born shall hear."

Thus saying he drew his sharp sword that by his flank hung great and strong, and gathered himself and swooped like a soaring eagle that darteth to the plain through the dark clouds to seize a tender lamb or crouching hare. So Hector swooped, brandishing his sharp sword. And Achilles made at him, for his heart was filled with wild fierceness, and before his breast he made a covering with his fair graven shield, and tossed his bright four-plated helm; and round it waved fair golden plumes [that Hephaistos had set thick about the crest.]. As a star goeth among stars in the darkness of night, Hesperos, fairest of all stars set in heaven, so flashed there forth a light from the keen spear Achilles poised in his right hand, devising mischief against noble Hector, eyeing his fair flesh to find the fittest place. Now for the rest of him his flesh was covered by the fair bronze armour he stripped from strong Patroklos when he slew him, but there was an opening where the collar bones coming from the shoulders clasp the neck, even at the gullet, where destruction of life cometh quickliest; there, as he came on, noble Achilles drave at him with his spear, and right through the tender neck went the point. Yet the bronze-weighted ashen spear clave not the windpipe, so that he might yet speak words of answer to his foe. And he fell down in the dust, and noble Achilles spake exultingly: "Hector, thou thoughtest, whilst thou wert spoiling Patroklos, that thou wouldst be safe, and didst reck nothing of me who was afar, thou fool. But away among the hollow ships his comrade, a mightier far, even I, was left behind, who now have unstrung thy knees. Thee shall dogs and birds tear foully, but his funeral shall the Achaians make."

Then with faint breath spake unto him Hector of the glancing helm: "I pray thee by thy life and knees and parents leave me not for dogs of the Achaians to devour by the ships, but take good store of bronze and gold, gifts that my father and lady mother shall give to thee, and give them home my body back again, that the Trojans and Trojans' wives give me my due of fire after my death."

But unto him with grim gaze spake Achilles fleet of foot: "Entreat me not, dog, by knees or parents. Would that my heart's desire could so bid me myself to carve and eat raw thy flesh, for the evil thou hast wrought me, as surely is there none that shall keep the dogs from thee, not even should they bring ten or twenty fold ransom and here weigh it out, and promise even more, not even were Priam Dardanos' son to bid pay thy weight in gold, not even so shall thy lady mother lay thee on a bed to mourn her son, but dogs and birds shall devour thee utterly."

Then dying spake unto him Hector of the glancing helm: "Verily I know thee and behold thee as thou art, nor was I destined to persuade thee; truly thy heart is iron in thy breast. Take heed now lest I draw upon thee wrath of gods, in the day when Paris and Phoebus Apollo slay thee, for all thy valour, at the Skaian gate."

He ended, and the shadow of death came down upon him, and his soul flew forth of his limbs and was gone to the house of Hades, wailing her fate, leaving her vigour and youth. Then to the dead man spake noble Achilles: "Die: for my death, I will accept it whensoever Zeus and the other immortal gods are minded to accomplish it."

He said, and from the corpse drew forth his bronze spear, and set it aside, and stripped the bloody armour from the shoulders. And other sons of Achaians ran up around, who gazed upon the stature and marvellous goodliness of Hector. Nor did any stand by but wounded him, and thus would many a man say looking toward his neighbour: "Go to, of a truth far easier to handle is Hector now than when he burnt the ships with blazing fire." Thus would many a man say, and wound him as he stood hard by. And when fleet noble Achilles had despoiled him, he stood up among the Achaians and spake winged words: "Friends, chiefs and counsellors of the Argives, since the gods have vouchsafed us to vanquish this man who hath done us more evil than all the rest together, come let us make trial in arms round about the city, that we may know somewhat of the Trojans' purpose, whether since he hath fallen they will forsake the citadel, or whether they are minded to abide, albeit Hector is no more. But wherefore doth my heart debate thus? There lieth by the ships a dead man unbewailed, unburied, Patroklos; him will I not forget, while I abide among the living and my knees can stir. Nay if even in the house of Hades the dead forget their dead, yet will I even there be mindful of my dear comrade. But come, ye sons of the Achaians, let us now, singing our song of victory, go back to the hollow ships and take with us our foe. Great glory have we won; we have slain the noble Hector, unto whom the Trojans prayed throughout their city, as he had been a god."

He said, and devised foul entreatment of noble Hector. The tendons of both feet behind he slit from heel to ankle-joint, and thrust therethrough thongs of ox-hide, and bound him to his chariot, leaving his head to trail. And when he had mounted the chariot and lifted therein the famous armour, he lashed his horses to speed, and they nothing loth flew on. And dust rose around him that was dragged, and his dark hair flowed loose on either side, and in the dust lay all his once fair head, for now had Zeus given him over to his foes to entreat foully in his own native land.

Thus was his head all grimed with dust. But his mother when she beheld her son, tore her hair and cast far from her her shining veil, and cried aloud with an exceeding bitter cry. And piteously moaned his father, and around them the folk fell to crying and moaning throughout the town. Most like it seemed as though all beetling Ilios were burning utterly in fire. Scarcely could the folk keep back the old man in his hot desire to get him forth of the Dardanian gates. For he besought them all, casting himself down in the mire, and calling on each man by his name: "Hold, friends, and though you love me leave me to get me forth of the city alone and go unto the ships of the Achaians. Let me pray this accursed horror-working man, if haply he may feel shame before his age-fellows and pity an old man. He also hath a father such as I am, Peleus, who begat and reared him to be a bane of Trojans—and most of all to me hath he brought woe. So many sons of mine hath he slain in their flower—yet for all my sorrow for the rest I mourn them all less than this one alone, for whom my sharp grief will bring me down to the house of Hades—even Hector. Would that he had died in my arms; then would we have wept and wailed our fill, his mother who bore him to her ill hap, and I myself."

Thus spake he wailing, and all the men of the city made moan with him. And among the women of Troy, Hekabe led the wild lament: "My child, ah, woe is me! wherefore should I live in my pain, now thou art dead, who night and day wert my boast through the city, and blessing to all, both men and women of Troy throughout the town, who hailed thee as a god, for verily an exceeding glory to them wert thou in thy life:—now death and fate have overtaken thee."

Thus spake she wailing. But Hector's wife knew not as yet, for no true messenger had come to tell her how her husband abode without the gates, but in an inner chamber of the lofty house she was weaving a double purple web, and broidering therein manifold flowers. Then she called to her goodly-haired handmaids through the house to set a great tripod on the fire, that Hector might have warm washing when he came home out of the battle fond heart, and was unaware how, far from all washings, bright-eyed Athene had slain him by the hand of Achilles. But she heard shrieks and groans from the battlements, and her limbs reeled, and the shuttle fell from her hands to earth. Then again among her goodly-haired maids she spake: "Come two of ye this way with me that I may see what deeds are done. It was the voice of my husband's noble mother that I heard, and in my own breast my heart leapeth to my mouth and my knees are numbed beneath me: surely some evil thing is at hand against the children of Priam.

Would that such word might never reach my ear! yet terribly I dread lest noble Achilles have cut off bold Hector from the city by himself and chased him to the plain and ere this ended his perilous pride that possessed him, for never would he tarry among the throng of men but ran out before them far, yielding place to no man in his hardihood."

Thus saying she sped through the chamber like one mad, with beating heart, and with her went her handmaidens. But when she came to the battlements and the throng of men, she stood still upon the wall and gazed, and beheld him dragged before the city:—swift horses dragged him recklessly toward the hollow ships of the Achaians. Then dark night came on her eyes and shrouded her, and she fell backward and gasped forth her spirit. From off her head she shook the bright attiring thereof, frontlet and net and woven band, and veil, the veil that golden Aphrodite gave her on the day when Hector of the glancing helm led her forth of the house of Eetion, having given bride-gifts untold. And around her thronged her husband's sisters and his brothers' wives, who held her up among them, distraught even to death. But when at last she came to herself and her soul returned into her breast, then wailing with deep sobs she spake among the women of Troy: "O Hector, woe is me! to one fate then were we both born, thou in Troy in the house of Priam, and I in Thebe under woody Plakos, in the house of Eetion, who reared me from a little one—ill-fated sire of cruel-fated child. Ah, would he have begotten me not. Now thou to the house of Hades beneath the secret places of the earth departest, and me in bitter mourning thou leavest a widow in thy halls: and thy son is but an infant child—son of unhappy parents, thee and me—nor shalt thou profit him, Hector, since thou art dead, neither he thee. For even if he escape the Achaians' woful war, yet shall labour and sorrow cleave unto him hereafter, for other men shall seize his lands. The day of orphanage sundereth a child from his fellows, and his head is bowed down ever, and his cheeks are wet with tears. And in his need the child seeketh his father's friends, plucking this one by cloak and that by coat, and one of them that pity him holdeth his cup a little to his mouth, and moisteneth his lips, but his palate he moisteneth not. And some child unorphaned thrusteth him from the feast with blows and taunting words, 'Out with thee! no father of thine is at our board.' Then weeping to his widowed mother shall he return, even Astyanax, who erst upon his father's knee ate only marrow and fat flesh of sheep; and when sleep fell on him and he ceased from childish play, then in bed in his nurse's arms he would slumber softly nested, having satisfied his heart with good things; but now that he hath lost his father he will suffer many ills, Astyanax—that name the Trojans gave him, because thou only wet the defence of their gates and their long walls. But now by the beaked ships, far from thy parents, shall coiling worms devour thee when the dogs have had their fill, as thou liest naked; yet in these halls lieth raiment of thine, delicate and fair, wrought by the hands of women. But verily all these will I consume with burning fire—to thee no profit, since thou wilt never lie therein, yet that his be honour to thee from the men and the women of Troy."

Thus spake she wailing, and the women joined their moan.

BOOK XXIII

Of the funeral of Patroklos, and the funeral games.

Thus they throughout the city made moan: but the Achaians when they were come to the ships and to the Hellespont were scattered each to his own ship: only the Myrmidons Achilles suffered not to be scattered, but spake among his comrades whose delight was in war: "Fleet-horsed Myrmidons, my trusty comrades, let us not yet unyoke our whole-hooved steeds from their cars, but with horses and chariots let us go near and mourn Patroklos, for such is the honour of the dead. Then when we have our fill of grievous wailing, we will unyoke the horses and all sup here."

He said, and they with one accord made lamentation, and Achilles led their mourning. So thrice around the dead they drave their well-maned steeds, moaning; and Thetis stirred among them desire of wailing. Bedewed were the sands with tears, bedewed the warriors' arms; so great a lord of fear they sorrowed for. And Peleus' son led their loud wail, laying his man-slaying hands on his comrade's breast: "All hail, Patroklos, even in the house of Hades; for all that I promised thee before am I accomplishing, seeing I have dragged hither Hector to give raw unto dogs to devour, and twelve noble children of the Trojans to slaughter before thy pyre, because of mine anger at thy slaying."

He said, and devised foul entreatment of noble Hector, stretching him prone in the dust beside the bier of Menoitios' son. And the rest put off each his glittering bronze arms, and unyoked their high-neighing horses, and sate them down numberless beside the ship of fleet-footed Aiakides, and he gave them ample funeral feast. Many sleek oxen were stretched out, their throats cut with steel, and many sheep and bleating goats, and many white-tusked boars well grown in fat were spitted to singe in the flame of Hephaistos; so on all sides round the corpse in cupfuls blood was flowing.

But the fleet-footed prince, the son of Peleus, was brought to noble Agamemnon by the Achaian chiefs, hardly persuading him thereto, for his heart was wroth for his comrade. And when they were come to Agamemnon's hut, forthwith they bade clear-voiced heralds set a great tripod on the fire, if haply they might persuade the son of Peleus to wash from him the bloody gore. But he denied them steadfastly, and sware moreover an oath: "Nay, verily by Zeus, who is highest and best of gods, not lawful is it that water should come nigh my head or ever I shall have laid Patroklos on the fire, and heaped a barrow, and shaved my hair, since never again shall second grief thus reach my heart, while I remain among the living. Yet now for the present let us yield us to our mournful meal: but with the morning, O king of men Agamemnon, rouse the folk to bring wood and furnish all that it beseemeth a dead man to have when he goeth beneath the misty gloom, to the end that untiring fire may burn him quickly from sight, and the host betake them to their work."

Thus spake he, and they listened readily to him and obeyed, and eagerly making ready each his meal they supped, and no lack had their soul of equal feast. But when they had put off from them the desire of meat and drink, the rest went down each man to his tent to take his rest, but the son of Peleus upon the beach of the sounding sea lay groaning heavily, amid the host of Myrmidons, in an open place, where waves were breaking on the shore. Now when sleep took hold on him, easing the cares of his heart, deep sleep that fell about him, (for sore tired were his glorious knees with onset upon Hector toward windy Ilios), then came there unto him the spirit of hapless Patroklos, in all things like his living self, in stature, and fair eyes, and voice, and the raiment of his body was the same; and he stood above Achilles' head and spake to him: "Thou sleepest, and hast forgotten me, O Achilles. Not in my life wast thou ever unmindful of me, but in my death. Bury me with all speed, that I pass the gates of Hades. Far off the spirits banish me, the phantoms of men outworn, nor suffer me to mingle with them beyond the River, but vainly I wander along the wide-gated dwelling of Hades. Now give me, I pray pitifully of thee, thy hand, for never more again shall I come back from Hades, when ye have given me my due of fire. Never among the living shall we sit apart from our dear comrades and take counsel together, but me hath the harsh fate swallowed up which was appointed me even from my birth. Yea and thou too thyself, Achilles peer of gods, beneath the wall of the noble Trojans art doomed to die. Yet one thing will I say, and charge thee, if haply thou wilt have regard thereto. Lay not my bones apart from thine, Achilles, but together, even as we were nurtured in your house, when Menoitios brought me yet a little one from Opoeis to your country by reason of a grievous man-slaying, on the day when I slew Amphidamas' son, not willing it, in childish wrath over the dice. Then took me the knight Peleus into his house and reared me kindly and named me thy squire: so therefore let one coffer hide our bones [a golden coffer, two handled, thy lady mother's gift]."

Then made answer unto him Achilles fleet of foot: "Wherefore, O my brother, hast thou come hither, and chargest me everything that I should do? Verily I will accomplish all, and have regard unto thy bidding. But stand more nigh me; for one moment let us throw our arms around each other, and take our fill of dolorous lament."

He spake, and reached forth with his hands, but clasped him not; for like a vapour the spirit was gone beneath the earth with a faint shriek. And Achilles sprang up marvelling, and smote his hands together, and spake a word of woe: "Ay me, there remaineth then even in the house of Hades a spirit and phantom of the dead, albeit the life be not anywise therein: for all night long hath the spirit of hapless Patroklos stood over me, wailing and making moan, and charged me everything that I should do, and wondrous like his living self it seemed."

Thus said he, and stirred in all of them yearning to make lament; and rosy-fingered Morn shone forth on them while they still made moan around the piteous corpse. Then lord Agamemnon sped mules and men from all the huts to fetch wood; and a man of valour watched thereover, even Meriones, squire of kindly Idomeneus. And they went forth with wood-cutting axes in their hands and well-woven ropes, and before them went the mules, and uphill and downhill and sideways and across they went. But when they came to the spurs of many-fountained Ida, straightway they set them lustily to hew high-foliaged oaks with the long-edged bronze, and with loud noise fell the trees. Then splitting them asunder the Achaians bound them behind the mules, and they tore up the earth with their feet as they made for the plain through the thick underwood. And all the wood-cutters bare logs; for thus bade Meriones, squire of kindly Idomeneus. And on the Shore they threw them down in line, where Achilles purposed a mighty tomb for Patroklos and for himself.

Then when they had laid down all about great piles of wood, they sate them down all together and abode. Then straightway Achilles bade the warlike Myrmidons gird on their arms and each yoke the horses to his chariot; and they arose and put their armour on, and mounted their chariots, both fighting men and charioteers. In front were the men in chariots, and a cloud of footmen followed after, numberless; and in the midst his comrades bare Patroklos. And they heaped all the corpse with their hair that they cut off and threw thereon; and behind did goodly Achilles bear the head, sorrowing; for a noble comrade was he speeding forth unto the realm of Hades.

And when they came to the place where Achilles had bidden them, they set down the dead, and piled for him abundant wood. Then fleet-footed noble Achilles bethought him of one thing more: standing apart from the pyre he shore off a golden lock, the lock whose growth he nursed to offer unto the River Spercheios, and sore troubled spake be, looking forth over the wine-dark sea: "Spercheios, in other wise vowed my father Peleus unto thee that I returning thither to my native land should shear my hair for thee and offer a holy hecatomb, and fifty rams should sacrifice there above thy springs, where is the sacred close and altar burning spice. So vowed the old man, but thou hast not accomplished him his desire. And now since I return not to my dear native land, unto the hero Patroklos I may give this hair to take away."

Thus saying he set the hair in the hands of his dear comrade, and stirred in all of them yearning to make lament. And so would the light of the sun have gone down on their lamentation, had not Achilles said quickly to Agamemnon as be stood beside him: "Son of Atreus—for to thy words most will the host of the Achaians have regard—of lamentation they may sate them to the full. But now disperse them from the burning and bid them make ready their meal, and we to whom the dead is dearest will take pains for these things; yet let the chiefs tarry nigh unto us."

Then when Agamemnon king of men heard that, he forthwith dispersed the host among the trim ships, but the nearest to the dead tarried there and piled the wood, and made a pyre a hundred feet this way and that, and on the pyre's top set the corpse, with anguish at their hearts. And many lusty sheep and shambling crook-horned oxen they flayed and made ready before the pyre; and taking from all of them the fat, great hearted Achilles wrapped the corpse therein from head to foot, and heaped the flayed bodies round. And he set therein two-handled jars of honey and oil, leaning them against the bier; and four strong-necked horses he threw swiftly on the pyre, and groaned aloud. Nine house-dogs had the dead chief: of them did Achilles slay twain and throw them on the pyre. And twelve valiant sons of great-hearted Trojans he slew with the sword—for he devised mischief in his heart and he set to the merciless might of the fire, to feed thereon. Then moaned he aloud, and called on his dear comrade by his name: "All hail to thee, O Patroklos, even in the house of Hades, for all that I promised thee before am I now accomplishing. Twelve valiant sons of great-hearted Trojans, behold these all in company with thee the fire devoureth: but Hector son of Priam will I nowise give to the fire to feed upon, but to dogs."

Thus spake he threatening, but no dogs might deal with Hector, for day and night Aphrodite daughter of Zeus kept off the dogs, and anointed him with rose-sweet oil ambrosial that Achilles might not tear him when he dragged him. And over him Phoebus Apollo brought a dark cloud from heaven to earth and covered all that place whereon the dead man lay, lest meanwhile the sun's strength shrivel his flesh round about upon his sinews and limbs.

But the pyre of dead Patroklos kindled not. Then fleet-footed noble Achilles had a further thought: standing aside from the pyre he prayed to the two Winds of North and West, and promised them fair offerings, and pouring large libations from a golden cup besought them to come, that the corpses might blaze up speedily in the fire, and the wood make haste to be enkindled. Then Iris, when she heard his prayer, went swiftly with the message to the Winds. They within the house of the gusty West Wind were feasting all together at meat, when Iris sped thither, and halted on the threshold of stone. And when they saw her with their eyes, they sprang up and called to her every one to sit by him. But she refused to sit, and spake her word: "No seat for me; I must go back to the streams of Ocean, to the Ethiopians' land where they sacrifice hecatombs to the immortal gods, that I too may feast at their rites. But Achilles is praying the North Wind and the loud West to come, and promising them fair offerings, that ye may make the pyre be kindled whereon lieth Patroklos, for whom all the Achaians are making moan."

She having thus said departed, and they arose with a mighty sound, rolling the clouds before them. And swiftly they came blowing over the sea, and the wave rose beneath their shrill blast; and they came to deep-soiled Troy, and fell upon the pile, and loudly roared the mighty fire. So all night drave they the flame of the pyre together, blowing shrill; and all night fleet Achilles, holding a two-handled cup, drew wine from a golden bowl, and poured it forth and drenched the earth, calling upon the spirit of hapless Patroklos. As a father waileth when he burneth the bones of his son, new-married, whose death is woe to his hapless parents, so wailed Achilles as he burnt the bones of his comrade, going heavily round the burning pile, with many moans.

But at the hour when the Morning star goeth forth to herald light upon the earth, the star that saffron-mantled Dawn cometh after, and spreadeth over the salt sea, then grew the burning faint, and the flame died down. And the Winds went back again to betake them home over the Thracian main, and it roared with a violent swell. Then the son of Peleus turned away from the burning and lay down wearied, and sweet sleep leapt on him. But they who were with Atreus' son gathered all together, and the noise and clash of their approach aroused him; and he sate upright and spake a word to them: "Son of Atreus and ye other chiefs of the Achaians, first quench with gleaming wine all the burning so far as the fire's strength hath reached, and then let us gather up the bones of Patroklos, Menoitios' son, singling them well, and easy are they to discern, for he lay in the middle of the pyre, while the rest apart at the edge burnt-confusedly, horses and men. And his bones let us put within a golden urn, and double-folded fat, until that I myself be hidden in Hades. But no huge barrow I bid you toil to raise—a seemly one, no more: then afterward do ye Achaians build it broad and high, whosoever of you after I am gone may be left in the benched ships."

Thus spake he, and they hearkened to the fleet-footed son of Peleus. First quenched they with gleaming wine the burning so far as the flame went, and the ash had settled deep: then with lamentation they gathered up the white bones of their gentle comrade into a golden urn and double-folded fat, and placed the urn in the hut and covered it with a linen veil. And they marked the circle of the barrow, and set the foundations thereof around the pyre, and straightway heaped thereon a heap of earth. Then when they had heaped up the barrow they were for going back. But Achilles stayed the folk in that place, and made them sit in wide assembly, and from his ships he brought forth prizes, caldrons and tripods, and horses and mules and strong oxen, and fair-girdled women, and grey iron.

First for fleet chariot-racers he ordained a noble prize, a woman skilled in fair handiwork for the winner to lead home, and an eared tripod that held two-and-twenty measures; these for the first man; and for the second he ordained a six-year-old mare unbroke with a mule foal in her womb;

and for the third he gave a goodly caldron yet untouched by fire, holding four measures, bright as when first made; and for the fourth he ordained two talents of gold; and for the fifth a two-handled urn untouched of fire, Then he stood up and spake a word among the Argives: "Son of Atreus and ye other well-greaved Achaians, for the chariot-racers these prizes lie awaiting them in the lists. If in some other's honour we Achaians were now holding our games, it would be I who should win the first prize and bear it to my hut; for ye know how far my pair of horses are first in excellence, for they are immortal and Poseidon gave them to my father Peleus, and he again to me. But verily I will abide, I and my whole-hooved horses, so glorious a charioteer have they lost, and one so kind, who on their manes full often poured smooth oil, when he had washed them in clear water. For him they stand and mourn, and their manes are trailing on the ground, and there stand they with sorrow at their hearts. But ye others throughout the host get ye to your places, whosoever of the Achaians hath trust in his horses and firm-jointed car."

Thus spake the son of Peleus, and the fleet chariot-racers were gathered. First of all arose up Eumelos king of men, Admetos' son, a skilful charioteer; and next to him arose Tydeus' son, valiant Diomedes, and yoked his horses of the breed of Tros, which on a time he seized from Aineias, when Apollo saved their lord. And after him arose Atreus' son, fair-haired heaven-sprung Menelaos, and yoked him a swift pair Aithe, Agamemnon's mare, and his own horse Podargos. Her unto Agamemnon did Anchises' son Echepolos give in fee, that he might escape from following him to windy Ilios and take his pleasure at home; for great wealth had Zeus given him, and he dwelt in Sikyon of spacious lawns:— so Menelaos yoked her, and she longed exceedingly for the race. And fourth, Antilochos made ready his fair-maned horses, even the noble son of Nestor, high-hearted king, who was the son of Neleus; and fleet horses bred at Pylos drew his car. And his father standing by his side spake counselling him to his profit, though himself was well advised: "Antilochos, verily albeit thou art young, Zeus and Poseidon have loved thee and taught thee all skill with horses; wherefore to teach thee is no great need, for thou well knowest how to wheel round the post; yet are thy horses very slow in the race: therefore methinks there will be sad work for thee. For the horses of the others are fleeter, yet the men know not more cunning than thou hast. So come, dear son, store thy mind with all manner of cunning, that the prize escape thee not. By cunning is a woodman far better than by force; by cunning doth a helmsman on the wine-dark deep steer his swift ship buffeted by winds; by cunning hath charioteer the better of charioteer. For whoso trusting in his horses and car alone wheeleth heedlessly and wide at either end, his horses swerve on the course, and he keepeth them not in hand. But whoso is of crafty mind, though he drive worse horses, he ever keeping his eye upon the post turneth closely by it, neither is unaware how far at first to force his horses by the ox-hide reins, but holdeth them safe in hand and watcheth the leader in the race. Now will I tell thee a certain sign, and it shall not escape thee. A fathom's height above the ground standeth a withered stump, whether of oak or pine: it decayeth not in the rain, and two white stones on either side thereof are fixed at the joining of the track, and all round it is smooth driving ground. Whether it be a monument of some man dead long ago, or have been made their goal in the race by ancient men, this now is the mark fixed by fleet-footed Achilles. Wherefore do thou drive close and bear thy horses and chariot hard thereon, and lean thy body on the well-knit car slightly to their left, and call upon the off-horse with voice and lash, and give him rein from thy hand. But let the near horse hug the post so that the nave of the well-wrought wheel seem to graze it—yet beware of touching the stone, lest thou wound the horses and break the chariot; so would that be triumph to the rest and reproach unto thyself. But, dear son, be wise and on thy guard; for if at the turning-post thou drive past the rest, there is none shall overtake thee from behind or pass thee by, not though he drave the goodly Arion in pursuit, the fleet horse of Adrastos, of divine descent, or the horses of Laomedon, best of all bred in this land."

Thus spake Neleian Nestor and sate him down again in his place, when he had told his son the sum of every matter.

And Meriones was the fifth to make ready his sleek-coated steeds. Then went they up into their chariots, and cast in the lots: and Achilles shook them, and forth leapt the lot of Antilochos Nestor's son, and the next lot had lord Eumelos, and next to him the son of Atreus, spear-famed Menelaos, and next to him drew Meriones his place; then lastly Tydeides, far the best of all, drew his lot for his chariot's place. Then they stood side by side, and Achilles showed to them the turning post, far off in the smooth plain; and beside it he placed an umpire, godlike Phoinix, his father's follower, that he might note the running and tell the truth thereof.

Then all together lifted the lash above their steeds, and smote them with the reins, and called on them eagerly with words: and they forthwith sped swiftly over the plain, leaving the ships behind; and beneath their breasts stood the rising dust like a cloud or whirlwind, and their manes waved on the blowing wind. And the chariots ran sometimes on the bounteous earth, and other whiles would bound into the air. And the drivers stood in the cars, and the heart of every man beat in desire of victory, and they called every man to his horses, that flew amid their dust across the plain.

But when the fleet horses were now running the last part of the course, back toward the grey sea, then was manifest the prowess of each, and the horses strained in the race; and presently to the front rushed the fleet mares of Pheres' grandson, and next to them Diomedes' stallions of the breed of Tros, not far apart, but hard anigh, for they seemed ever as they would mount Eumelos' car, and with their breath his back was warm and his broad shoulders, for they bent their heads upon him as they flew along. Thus would Tydeus' son have either outstripped the other or made it a dead heat, had not Phoebus Apollo been wroth with him and smitten from his hand the shining lash. Then from his eyes ran tears of anger, for that he saw the mares still at speed, even swiftlier than before, while his own horses were thrown out, as running without spur. But Athene was not unaware of Apollo's guile against Tydeides, and presently sped after the shepherd of hosts, and gave him back the lash, and put spirit into his steeds. Then in wrath after the son of Admetos was the goddess gone, and brake his steeds' yoke, and the mares ran sideways off the course, and the pole was twisted to the ground. And Eumelos was hurled out of the car beside the wheel, and his elbows and mouth and nose were flayed, and his forehead bruised above his eyebrows; and his eyes filled with tears and his lusty voice was choked. Then Tydeides held his whole-hooved horses on one side, darting far out before the rest, for Athene put spirit into his steeds and shed glory on himself. Now next after him came golden-haired Menelaos Atreus' son. But Antilochos called to his father's horses: "Go ye too in, strain to your fleetest pace. Truly I nowise bid you strive with those, the horses of wise Tydeides, unto which Athene hath now given speed, and shed glory on their charioteer. But overtake Atreides' horses with all haste, and be not outstripped by them, lest Aithe that is but a mare pour scorn on you. Why are ye outstripped, brave steeds? Thus will I tell you, and verily it shall be brought to pass—ye will find no tendance with Nestor shepherd of hosts, but straightway he will slay you with the edge of the sword if through heedlessness we win but the worse prize. Have after them at your utmost speed, and I for my part will devise a plan to pass them in the strait part of the course, and this shall fail me not."

Thus spake he, and they fearing the voice of the prince ran swiftlier some little while; and presently did the good warrior Antilochos espy a strait place in a sunk part of the way. There was a rift in the earth, where torrent water gathered and brake part of the track away, and hollowed all the place; there drave Menelaos, shunning the encounter of the wheels. But Antilochos turned his whole-hooved horses out of the track, and followed him a little at one side. And the son of Atreus took alarm and shouted to Antilochos: "Antilochos, thou art driving recklessly—hold in thy horses! The road is straitened, soon thou mayest pass me in a wider place, lest thou foul my chariot and undo us both."

Thus spake he, but Antilochos drave even fiercelier than before, plying his lash, as though he heard him not. As far as is the range of a disk swung from the shoulder when a young man hurleth it, making trial of his force, even so far ran they on; then the mares of Atreus' son gave back, for he ceased of himself to urge them on, lest the whole-hooved steeds should encounter on the track, and overset the well-knit cars, and the drivers fall in the dust in their zeal for victory. So upbraiding Antilochos spake golden-haired Menelaos: "Antilochos, no mortal man is more malicious than thou. Go thy mad way, since falsely have we Achaians called thee wise. Yet even so thou shalt not bear off the prize unchallenged to an oath."

Thus saying he called aloud to his horses: "Hold ye not back nor stand still with sorrow at heart. Their feet and knees will grow weary before yours, for they both lack youth."

Thus spake he, and they fearing the voice of the prince sped faster on, and were quickly close upon the others.

Now the Argives sitting in concourse were gazing at the horses, and they came flying amid their dust over the plain. And the first aware of them was Idomeneus, chief of the Cretans, for he was sitting outside the concourse in the highest place of view, and when he heard the voice of one that shouted, though afar off, he knew it; and he was aware of a horse showing plainly in the front, a chestnut all the rest of him, but in the forehead marked with a white star round like the moon. And he stood upright and spoke among the Argives: "Friends, chiefs, and counsellors of the Argives, is it I alone who see the horses, or do ye also? A new pair seem to me now to be in front, and a new charioteer appeareth; the mares which led in the outward course must have been thrown out there in the plain. For I saw them turning first the hither post, but now can see them nowhere, though my eyes are gazing everywhere along the Trojan plain. Did the reins escape the charioteer so that he could not drive aright round the post and failed in the turn? There, methinks, must he have been cast forth, and have broken his chariot, and the mares must have left the course, in the wildness of their heart. But stand up ye too and look, for myself I discern not certainly, but the first man seemeth to me one of Aitolian race, and he ruleth among Argives, the son of horse-taming Tydeus, stalwart Diomedes."

Then fleet Aias Oileus' son rebuked him in unseemly sort: "Idomeneus, why art thou a braggart of old? As yet far off the high-stepping mares are coursing over the wide plain. Neither art thou so far the youngest among the Argives, nor do thy eyes look so far the keenliest from thy head, yet continually braggest thou. It beseemeth thee not to be a braggart, for there are here better men. And the mares leading are they that led before, Eumelos' mares, and he standeth and holdeth the reins within the car."

Then wrathfully in answer spake the chief of Cretans: "Aias, master of railing, ill-counselled, in all else art thou behind other Argives, for thy mind is unfriendly. Come then let us wager a tripod or caldron, and make Agamemnon Atreus' son our umpire, which mares are leading, that thou mayest pay and learn."

Thus said he, and straightway fleet Aias Oileus' son arose angrily to answer with harsh words: and strife between the twain would have gone further, had not Achilles himself stood up and spake a word: "No longer answer each other with harsh words, Aias and Idomeneus, ill words, for it beseemeth not. Surely ye are displeased with any other who should do thus. Sit ye in the concourse and keep your eyes upon the horses; soon they in zeal for victory will come hither, and then shall ye know each of you the Argives' horses, which follow, and which lead."

He said, and the son of Tydeus came driving up, and with his lash smote now and again from the shoulder, and his horses were stepping high as they sped swiftly on their way. And sprinklings of dust smote ever the charioteer, and his chariot overlaid with gold and tin ran behind his fleet-footed steeds, and small trace was there of the wheel-tires behind in the fine dust, as they flew speeding on. Then he drew up in the mid concourse, and much sweat poured from the horses' heads and chests to the ground. And Diomedes leapt to earth from the shining car, and leant his lash against the yoke. Then stalwart Sthenelos tarried not, but promptly took the prize, and gave to his proud comrades the woman to lead and the eared tripod to bear away, and he loosed the horses from the yoke.

And next after him drave Neleian Antilochos his horses, by craft, not swiftness, having passed by Menelaos; yet even now Menelaos held his swift steeds hard anigh. As far as a horse is from the wheel, which draweth his master, straining with the car over the plain—his hindmost tail-hairs touch the tire, for the wheel runneth hard anigh nor is much space between, as he speedeth far over the plain—by so much was Menelaos behind high-born Antilochos, howbeit at first he was a whole disk-cast behind, but quickly he was catching Antilochos up, for the high mettle of Agamemnon's mare, sleek-coated Aithe, was rising in her. And if yet further both had had to run he would have passed his rival nor left it even a dead heat. But Meriones, stout squire of Idomeneus, came in a spear-throw behind famous Menelaos, for tardiest of all were his sleek-coated horses, and slowest he himself to drive a chariot in the race. Last of them all came Admetos' son, dragging his goodly car driving his steeds in front. Him when fleet-footed noble Achilles beheld he pitied him, and he stood up and spake winged words among the Argives: "Last driveth his whole-hooved horses the best man of them all. But come let us give him a prize, as is seemly, prize for the second place, but the first let the son of Tydeus take."

Thus spake he, and all applauded that he bade. And he would have given him the mare, for the Achaians applauded, had not Antilochos, son of great-hearted Nestor; risen up and answered Peleian Achilles on behalf of his right: "O Achilles, I shall be sore angered with thee if thou accomplish this word, for thou art minded to take away my prize, because thou thinkest of how his chariot and fleet steeds miscarried, and himself withal, good man though he be. Nay, it behoved him to pray to the Immortals, then would he not have come in last of all in the race. But if thou pitiest him and he be dear to thy heart, there is much gold in thy hut, bronze is there and sheep, hand-maids are there and whole-hooved

horses. Thereof take thou and give unto him afterward even a richer
prize, or even now at once, that the Achaians may applaud thee. But the
mare I will not yield; for her let what man will essay the battle at my
hands."

Thus spake he, and fleet-footed noble Achilles smiled, pleased with
Antilochos, for he was his dear comrade; and spake in answer to him
winged words: "Antilochos, if thou wouldst have me give Eumelos some
other thing beside from out my house, that also will I do. I will give unto
him a breast-plate that I took from Asteropaios, of bronze, whereon a
casting of bright tin is overlaid, and of great worth will it be to him." He
said, and bade his dear comrade Automedon bring it from the hut, and he
went and brought it. [Then he placed it in Eumelos' hands, and he
received it gladly.]

But Menelaos also arose among them, sore at heart, angered
exceedingly against Antilochos; and the herald set the staff in his hand,
and called for silence among the Argives; then spake among them that
godlike man: "Antilochos, who once wert wise, what thing is this thou hast
done? Thou hast shamed my skill and made my horses fail, thrusting
thine own in front that are far worse. Come now, ye chiefs and counsellors
of the Argives, give judgment between us both, and favour neither: lest
some one of the mail-clad Achaïans say at any time: 'By constraining
Antilochos through false words hath Menelaos gone off with the mare, for
his horses were far worse, howbeit he hath advantage in rank and power.'
Nay, I myself will bring the issue about, and I deem that none other of the
Danaans shall reproach me, for the trial shall be just. Antilochos,
fosterling of Zeus, come thou hither and as it is ordained stand up before
thy horses and chariot and take in thy hand the pliant lash wherewith
thou dravest erst, and touching thy horses swear by the Enfolder and
Shaker of the earth that not wilfully didst thou hinder my chariot by
guile."

Then answered him wise Antilochos: "Bear with me now, for far
younger am I than thou, king Menelaos, and thou art before me and my
better. Thou knowest how a young man's transgressions come about, for
his mind is hastier and his counsel shallow. So let thy heart suffer me,
and I will of myself give to thee the mare I have taken. Yea, if thou
shouldst ask some other greater thing from my house, I were fain to give
it thee straightway, rather than fall for ever from my place in thy heart,
O fosterling of Zeus, and become a sinner against the gods."

Thus spake great-hearted Nestor's son, and brought the mare and put
her in the hand of Menelaos. And his heart was gladdened as when the
dew cometh upon the ears of ripening harvest-corn, what time the fields
are bristling. So gladdened was thy soul, Menelaos, within thy heart. And
he spake unto Antilochos and uttered winged words: "Antilochos, now will
I of myself put away mine anger against thee, since no wise formerly wert
thou flighty or light-minded, howbeit now thy reason was overcome of

youthfulness. Another time be loth to outwit better men. Not easily should another of the Achaians have persuaded me, but thou hast suffered and toiled greatly, and thy brave father and brother, for my sake: therefore will I hearken to thy prayer, and will even give unto thee the mare, though she is mine, that these also may know that my heart was never overweening or implacable."

He said, and gave the mare to Noemon Antilochos' comrade to lead away, and then took the shining caldron. And Meriones took up the two talents of gold in the fourth place, as he had come in. So the fifth prize was left unclaimed, a two-handled cup; to Nester gave Achilles this, bearing it to him through the concourse of Argives, and stood by him and said: "Lo now for thee too, old man, be this a treasure, a memorial of Patroklos' burying; for no more shalt thou behold him among the Argives. Now give I thee this prize unwon, for not in boxing shalt thou strive, neither wrestle, nor enter on the javelin match, nor race with thy feet; for grim old age already weigheth on thee."

Thus saying he placed it in his hand, and Nestor received it gladly, and spake unto him winged words: "Ay, truly all this, my son, thou hast meetly said; for no longer are my limbs, friend, firm, nor my feet, nor do my arms at all swing lightly from my shoulders either side. Would that my youth were such and my force so firm as when the Epeians were burying lord Amarynkes at Buprasion, and his sons held the king's funeral games. Then was no man found like me, neither of the Epeians nor of the Pylians themselves or the great-hearted Aitolians. In boxing I overcame Klytomedes, son of Enops, and in wrestling Ankaios of Pleuron, who stood up against me, and in the foot-race I outran Iphiklos, a right good man, and with the spear outthrew Phyleus and Polydoros; only in the chariot-race the two sons of Aktor beat me [by crowding their horses in front of me, jealous for victory, because the chief prizes were left at home.] Now they were twins—one ever held the reins, the reins he ever held, the other called on the horses with the lash. Thus was I once, but now let younger men join in such feats; I must bend to grievous age, but then was I of mark among heroes. But come hold funeral for thy comrade too with with games. This gift do I accept with gladness, and my heart rejoiceth that thou rememberest ever my friendship to thee—(nor forget I thee)—and the honour wherewith it is meet that I be honoured among the Achaians. And may the gods for this grant thee due grace."

Thus spake he, and Peleides was gone down the full concourse of Achaians, when he had hearkened to all the thanks of Neleus' son. Then he ordained prizes of the violent boxing match; a sturdy mule he led forth and tethered amid the assembly, a six-year mule unbroken, hardest of all to break; and for the loser set a two-handled cup. Then he stood up and spake a word among the Argives: "Son of Atreus and ye other well-greaved Achaians, for these rewards we summon two men of the best to lift up their hands to box amain. He to whom Apollo shall grant endurance to the end, and all the Achaians acknowledge it, let him take the sturdy mule and return with her to his hut; and the loser shall take with him the two-handled-cup."

Thus spake he, and forthwith arose a man great and valiant and skilled in boxing, Epeios son of Panopeus, and laid his hand on the sturdy mule and said aloud: "Let one come nigh to bear off the two-handled cup; the mule I say none other of the Achaians shall take for victory with his fists, for I claim to be the best man here. Sufficeth it not that I fall short of you in battle? Not possible is it that in all arts a man be skilled. Thus proclaim I, and it shall be accomplished: I will utterly bruise mine adversary's flesh and break his bones, so let his friends abide together here to bear him forth when vanquished by my hands."

Thus spake he, and they all kept deep silence. And alone arose against him Euryalos, a godlike man, son of king Mekisteus the son of Talaos, Mekisteus, who came on a time to Thebes when Oedipus had fallen, to his burial, and there he overcame all the sons of Kadmos. Thus Tydeides famous with the spear made ready Euryalos for the fight, cheering him with speech, and greatly desired for him victory. And first he cast about him a girdle, and next gave him well-cut thongs of the hide of an ox of the field. And the two boxers being girt went into the midst of the ring, and both lifting up their stalwart hands fell to, and their hands joined battle grievously. Then was there terrible grinding of teeth, and sweat flowed from all their limbs. And noble Epeios came on, and as the other spied for an opening, smote him on the cheek, nor could he much more stand, for his limbs failed straightway under him. And as when beneath the North Wind's ripple a fish leapeth on a tangle-covered beach, and then the black wave hideth it, so leapt up Euryalos at that blow. But great-hearted Epeios took him in his hands and set him upright, and his dear comrades stood around him, and led him through the ring with trailing feet, spitting out clotted blood, drooping his head awry, and they set him down in his swoon among them and themselves went forth and fetched the two-handled cup.

Then Peleus' son ordained straightway the prizes for a third contest, offering them to the Danaans, for the grievous wrestling match: for the winner a great tripod for standing on the fire, prized by the Achaians among them at twelve oxens' worth; and for the loser he brought a woman into the midst, skilled in manifold work, and they prized her at four oxen. And he stood up and spake a word among the Argives: "Rise, ye who will essay this match."

Thus said he, and there arose great Aias son of Telamon, and Odysseus of many wiles stood up, the crafty-minded. And the twain being girt went into the midst of the ring, and clasped each the other in his arms with stalwart hands, like gable rafters of a lofty house which some famed craftsman joineth, that he may baffle the wind's force. And their backs creaked, gripped firmly under the vigorous hands, and sweat ran down in streams, and frequent weals along their ribs and shoulders sprang up, red with blood, while ever they strove amain for victory, to win the wrought tripod. Neither could Odysseus trip Aias and bear him to the ground, nor Aias him, for Odysseus' strength withheld him. But when they began to irk the well-greaved Achaians, then said to Odysseus great Aias, Telamon's son: "Heaven-sprung son of Laertes, Odysseus of many wiles, or lift thou me, or I will thee, and the issue shall be with Zeus."

Having thus said he lifted him, but Odysseus was not unmindful of his craft. He smote deftly from behind the hollow of Aias' knee, and loosed his limbs, and threw him down backward, and Odysseus fell upon his chest, and the folk gazed and marvelled. Then in his turn much-enduring noble Odysseus tried to lift, and moved him a little from the ground, but lifted him not, so he crooked his knee within the other's, and both fell on the ground nigh to each other, and were soiled with dust, And now starting up again a third time would they have wrestled, had not Achilles himself arisen and held them back: "No longer press each the other, nor wear you out with pain. Victory is with both; take equal prizes and depart, that other Achaians may contend."

Thus spake he, and they were fain to hear and to obey, and wiped the dust from them and put their doublets on.

Then straightway the son of Peleus set forth other prizes for fleetness of foot; a mixing-bowl of silver, chased; six measures it held, and in beauty it was far the best in all the earth, for artificers of Sidon wrought it cunningly, and men of the Phoenicians brought it over the misty sea, and landed it in harbour, and gave it a gift to Thoas; and Euneos son of Jason gave it to the hero Patroklos a ransom for Lykaon Priam's son. Now this cup did Achilles set forth as a prize in honour of his friend, for whoso should be fleetest in speed of foot. For the second he set an ox great and very fat, and for the last prize half a talent of gold. And he stood up and spake a word among the Argives: "Rise, ye who will essay this match."

Thus spake he, and straightway arose fleet Aias Oileus' son, and Odysseus of many wiles, and after them Nestor's son Antilochos, for he was best of all the youth in the foot-race. Then they stood side by side, and Achilles showed to them the goal. Right eager was the running from the start, but Oileus' son forthwith shot to the front, and close behind him came noble Odysseus, as close as is a weaving-rod to a fair-girdled woman's breast when she pulleth it deftly with her hands, drawing the spool along the warp, and holdeth the rod nigh her breast— so close ran Odysseus behind Aias and trod in his footsteps or ever the dust had settled there, and on his head fell the breath of noble Odysseus as he ran ever lightly on, and all the Achaians applauded his struggle for the victory and called on him as he laboured hard. But when they were running the last part of the course, forthwith Odysseus prayed in his soul to bright-eyed Athene: "Hearken, goddess, come thou a good helper of my feet."

Thus prayed he, and Pallas Athene hearkened to him, and made his limbs feel light, both feet and hands. But when they, were now nigh darting on the prize, then Aias slipped as he ran, for Athene marred his race, where filth was strewn from the slaughter of loud-bellowing oxen that fleet Achilles slew in honour of Patroklos: and Aias' mouth and nostrils were filled with that filth of oxen. So much-enduring noble Odysseus, as he came in first, took up the mixing-bowl, and famous Aias took the ox. And he stood holding in his hand the horn of the ox of the field, sputtering away the filth, and spake among the Argives: "Out on it, it was the goddess who marred my running, she who from of old like a mother standeth by Odysseus' side and helpeth him."

So spake he, but they all laughed pleasantly to behold him. Then Antilochos smiling bore off the last prize, and spake his word among the Argives: "Friends, ye will all bear me witness when I say that even herein also the immortals favour elder men. For Aias is a little older than I, but Odysseus of an earlier generation and earlier race of men. A green old age is his, they say, and hard were it for any Achaian to rival him in speed, save only Achilles."

Thus spake he, and gave honour to the fleet son of Peleus. And Achilles answered him and said: "Antilochos, not unheeded shall thy praise be given; a half-talent of gold I will give thee over and above." He said, and set it in his hands, and Antilochos received it gladly.

Then Peleus' son brought and set in the ring a far-shadowing spear and a chaldron that knew not the fire, an ox's worth, embossed with flowers; and men that were casters of the javelin arose up. There rose Atreus' son wide-ruling Agamemnon, and Meriones, Idomeneus' brave squire. And swift-footed noble Achilles spake among them: "Son of Atreus, for that we know how far thou excellest all, and how far the first thou art in the might of thy throw, take thou this prize with thee to the hollow ships, and to the hero Meriones let us give the spear, if thou art willing in thy heart: thus I at least advise."

Thus spake he, nor disregarded him Agamemnon king of men. So to Meriones he gave the spear of bronze, but to the herald Talthybios the hero gave the goodliest prize.

BOOK XXIV

How the body of Hector was ransomed, and of his funeral.

Then the assembly was broken up, and the tribes were scattered to betake them each to their own swift ships. The rest bethought them of supper and sweet sleep to have joy thereof; but Achilles wept, remembering his dear comrade, nor did sleep that conquereth all take hold on him, but he kept turning him to this side and to that, yearning for Patroklos' manhood and excellent valour, and all the toils he achieved with him and the woes he bare, cleaving the battles of men and the grievous waves. As he thought thereon be shed big tears, now lying on his side, now on his back, now on his face; and then anon he would arise upon his feet and roam wildly beside the beach of the salt sea. Nor would he be unaware of the Dawn when she arose over the sea and shores. But when he had yoked the swift steeds to his car he would bind Hector behind his chariot to drag him withal; and having thrice drawn him round the barrow of the dead son of Menoitios he rested again in his hut, and left Hector lying stretched on his face in the dust. But Apollo kept away all defacement from his flesh, for he had pity on him even in death, and covered him all with his golden aegis, that Achilles might not tear him when be dragged him.

Thus Achilles in his anger entreated noble Hector shamefully; but the blessed gods when they beheld him pitied him, and urged the clear-sighted slayer of Argus to steal the corpse away. So to all the others seemed it good, yet not to Hera or Poseidon or the bright-eyed Maiden, but they continued as when at the beginning sacred Ilios became hateful to them, and Priam and his people, by reason of the sin of Alexandros in that he contemned those goddesses when they came to his steading, and preferred her who brought him deadly lustfulness. But when the twelfth morn from that day arose, then spake among the Immortals Phœbus Apollo: "Hard of heart are ye, O gods, and cruel Hath Hector never burnt for you thigh-bones of unblemished bulls and goats? Now have ye not taken heart to rescue even his corpse for his wife to look upon and his mother and his child and his father Priam and his people, who speedily would burn him in the fire and make his funeral. But fell Achilles, O gods, ye are fain to abet, whose mind is nowise just nor the purpose in his breast to be turned away, but he is cruelly minded as a lion that in great strength and at the bidding of his proud heart goeth forth against men's flocks to make his meal; even thus Achilles hath cast out pity, neither hath he shame, that doth both harm and profit men greatly. It must be that many a man lose even some dearer one than was this, a brother of the same womb born or perchance a son; yet bringeth he his wailing and lamentation to an end, for an enduring soul have the Fates given unto men. But Achilles after bereaving noble Hector of his life bindeth him behind his horses and draggeth him around the tomb of his dear comrade: not, verily, is that more honourable or better for him. Let him take heed lest we wax wroth with him, good man though he be, for in his fury he is entreating shamefully the senseless clay."

Then in anger spake unto him white-armed Hera: "Even thus mightest thou speak, O Lord of the silver bow, if ye are to give equal honour to Achilles and to Hector. Hector is but a mortal and was suckled at a woman's breast, but Achilles is child of a goddess whom I myself bred up and reared and gave to a man to be his wife, even to Peleus who was dearest of all men to the Immortals' heart. And all ye gods came to her bridal, and thou among them wert feasting with thy lyre, O lover of ill company, faithless ever."

Then to her in answer spake Zeus who gathereth the clouds: "Hera, be not wroth utterly with the gods: for these men's honour is not to be the same, yet Hector also was dearest to the gods of all mortals that are in Ilios. So was he to me at least, for nowise failed he in the gifts I loved. Never did my altar lack seemly feast, drink-offering and the steam of sacrifice, even the honour that falleth to our due. But verily we will say no more of stealing away brave Hector, for it cannot be hidden from Achilles, for his mother abideth ever nigh to him night and day. But I were fain that some one of the gods would call Thetis to come near to me, that I may speak unto her a wise word, so that Achilles may take gifts from Priam and give Hector back." Thus spake he, and airy-footed Iris sped forth upon the errand and between Samothrace and rocky Imbros leapt into the black sea, and the waters closed above her with a noise. And she sped to the bottom like a weight of lead that mounted on horn of a field-ox goeth down bearing death to ravenous fishes. And she found Thetis in a hollow cave; about her sat gathered other goddesses of the seas and she in their midst was wailing for the fate of her noble son who must perish in deep-soiled Troy, far from his native land. And standing near, fleet-footed Iris spake to her: "Rise, Thetis; Zeus of immortal counsels calleth thee."

And to her made answer Thetis the silver-footed goddess: "Wherefore biddeth me that mighty god? I shrink from mingling among the Immortals, for I have countless woes at heart. Yet go I, nor shall his word be in vain, whatsoever he saith."

Thus having said the noble goddess took to her a dark-hued robe, no blacker raiment was there found than that. Then she went forth, and wind-footed swift Iris led the way before her, and around them the surge of the sea was sundered. And when they had come forth upon the shore they sped up to heaven, and found the far-seeing son of Kronos, and round him sat gathered all the other blessed gods that are for ever. Then she sat down beside father Zeus, and Athene gave her place. And Hera set a fair golden cup in her hand and cheered her with words, and Thetis drank, and gave back the cup. Then began speech to them the father of gods and men: "Thou art come to Olympus, divine Thetis, in thy sorrow, with violent grief at thy heart; I know it of myself. Nevertheless will I tell thee wherefore I called thee hither. Nine days hath dispute arisen among the Immortals concerning the corpse of Hector and Achilles waster of cities. Fain are they to send clear-sighted Hermes to steal the body away, but now hear what glory I accord herein to Achilles, that I may keep through times to come thy honour and good will. Go with all speed to the host and bear to thy son my bidding. Say to him that the gods are displeased at him, and that I above all Immortals am wroth, because with furious heart be holdeth Hector at the beaked ships and hath not given him back, if haply he may fear me and give Hector back. But I will send Iris to great-hearted Priam to bid him go to the ships of the Achaians to ransom his dear son, and carry gifts to Achilles that may gladden his heart."

Thus spake he, and Thetis the silver-footed goddess was not disobedient to his word, and sped darting upon her way down from the peaks of Olympus. And she came to her son's hut; there found she him making grievous moan, and his dear comrades round were swiftly making ready and furnishing their early meal, and a sheep great and fleecy was being sacrificed in the hut. Then his lady-mother sate her down close beside him, and stroked him with her hand and spake to him by his name: "My child, how long with lamentation and woe wilt thou devour thine heart, taking thought of neither food nor rest? good were even a woman's embrace, for not long shalt thou be left alive to me; already death and forceful fate are standing nigh thee. But hearken forthwith unto me, for I am the messenger of Zeus to thee. He saith that the gods are displeased at thee, and that himself above all Immortals is wroth, because with furious heart thou holdest Hector at the beaked ships and hast not given him back. But come restore him, and take ransom for the dead."

Then to her in answer spake fleet-footed Achilles: "So be it: whoso bringeth ransom let him take back the dead, if verily with heart's intent the Olympian biddeth it himself."

So they in the assembly of the ships, mother and son, spake to each other many winged words. But the son of Kronos thus bade Iris go to holy Ilios: "Go forth, fleet Iris, leave the abode of Olympus and bear my message within Ilios to great-hearted Priam that he go to the ships of the Achaians and ransom his dear son and carry gifts to Achilles that may gladden his heart; let him go alone, and no other man of the Trojans go with him. Only let some elder herald attend on him to guide the mules and smooth-wheeled waggon and carry back to the city the dead man whom noble Achilles slew. Let not death be in his thought nor any fear; such guide will we give unto him, even the slyer of Argus who shall lead him until his leading bring him to Achilles. And when he shall have led him within the hut, neither shall Achilles himself slay him nor suffer any other herein, for not senseless is he or unforeseeing or wicked, but with all courtesy he will spare a suppliant man."

Thus spake he, and airy-footed Iris sped forth upon the errand. And she came to the house of Priam, and found therein crying and moan. His children sitting around their father within the court were bedewing their raiment with their tears, and the old man in their midst was close wrapped all over in his cloak; and on his head and neck was much mire that he had gathered in his hands as he grovelled upon the earth. And his daughters and his sons' wives were wailing throughout the house, bethinking them of all those valiant men who had lost their lives at the hands of the Argives and were lying low. And the messenger of Zeus stood beside Priam and spake softly unto him, and trembling came upon his limbs: "Be of good cheer in thy heart, O Priam son of Dardanos, and be not dismayed for anything, for no evil come I hither to forebode to thee, but with good will. I am the messenger of Zeus to thee, who, though he be afar off, hath great care and pity for thee. The Olympian biddeth thee ransom noble Hector and carry gifts to Achilles that may gladden his heart: go thou alone, let none other of the Trojans go with thee. Only let some elder herald attend on thee to guide the mules and the smooth-wheeled waggon to carry back to the city the dead man whom noble Achilles slew. Let not death be in thy thought, nor any fear; such guide shall go with thee, even the slayer of Argus, who shall lead thee until his leading bring thee to Achilles. And when he shall have led thee into the hut, neither shall Achilles himself slay thee, nor suffer any other herein, for not senseless is he or unforeseeing or wicked, but with all courtesy he will spare a suppliant man."

Thus having spoken fleet Iris departed from him; and he bade his sons make ready the smooth-wheeled mule waggon, and bind the wicker carriage thereon. And himself he went down to his fragrant chamber, of cedar wood, high-roofed, that held full many jewels: and to Hekabe his wife he called and spake: "Lady, from Zeus hath an Olympian messenger come to me, that I go to the ships of the Achaians and ransom my dear son, and carry gifts to Achilles that may gladden his heart. Come tell me how seemeth it to thy mind, for of myself at least my desire and heart bid me mightily to go thither to the ships and enter the wide camp of the Achaians."

Thus spake he, but his wife lamented aloud and made answer to him: "Woe is me, whither is gone thy mind whereby aforetime thou wert famous among stranger men and among them thou rulest? How art thou fain to go alone to the ships of the Achaians, to meet the eyes of the man who hath slain full many of thy brave sons? of iron verily is thy heart. For if he light on thee and behold thee with his eyes, a savage and ill-trusted man is this, and he will not pity thee, neither reverence thee at all. Nay, now let us sit in the hall and make lament afar off. Even thus did forceful Fate erst spin for Hector with her thread at his beginning when I bare him, even I, that he should glut fleet-footed dogs, far from his parents, in the dwelling of a violent man whose inmost vitals I were fain to fasten and feed upon; then would his deeds against my son be paid again to him, for not playing the coward was he slain of him, but championing the men and deep-bosomed women of Troy, neither bethought he him of shelter or of flight."

The to her in answer spake the old man godlike Priam: "Stay me not, for I am fain to go, neither be thyself a bird of ill boding in my halls, for thou wilt not change my mind. Were it some other and a child of earth that bade me this, whether some seer or of the priests that divine from sacrifice, then would we declare it false and have no part therein; but now, since I have heard the voice of the goddess myself and looked upon her face, I will go forth, and her word shall not be void. And if it be my fate to die by the ships of the mail-clad Achaians, so would I have it; let Achilles slay me with all speed, when once I have taken in my arms my son, and have satisfied my desire with moan."

He spake, and opened fair lids of chests wherefrom he chose twelve very goodly women's robes and twelve cloaks of single fold and of coverlets a like number and of fair sheets, and of doublets thereupon. And he weighed and brought forth talents of gold ten in all, and two shining tripods and four caldrons, and a goblet exceeding fair that men of Thrace had given him when he went thither on an embassy, a chattel of great price, yet not that even did the old man grudge from his halls, for he was exceeding fain at heart to ransom his dear son. Then he drave out all the Trojans from the colonnade, chiding them with words of rebuke: "Begone, ye that dishonour and do me shame! Have ye no mourning of your own at home that ye come to vex me here? Think ye it a small thing that Zeus Kronos' son hath given me this sorrow, to lose him that was the best man of my sons? Nay, but ye too shall feel it, for easier far shall ye be to the Achaians to slay now he is dead. But for me, ere I behold with mine eyes the city sacked and wasted, let me go down into the house of Hades."

He said, and with his staff chased forth the men, and they went forth before the old man in his haste. Then he called unto his sons, chiding Helenos and Paris and noble Agathon and Pammon and Antiphonos, and Polites of the loud war-cry, and Deiphobos and Hippothoos and proud Dios; nine were they whom the old man called and bade unto him: "Haste ye, ill sons, my shame; would that ye all in Hector's stead had been slain at the swift ships! Woe is me all unblest, since I begat sons the best men in wide Troy-land, but none of them is left for me to claim, neither godlike Mestor, nor Troilos with his chariot of war, nor Hector who was a god among men, neither seemed he as the son of a mortal man but of a god:—all these hath Ares slain, and here are my shames all left to me, false-tongued, light-heeled, the heroes of dance, plunderers of your own people's sheep and kids. Will ye not make me ready a wain with all speed, and lay all these thereon, that we get us forward on our way?"

Thus spake he, and they fearing their father's voice brought forth the smooth-running mule chariot, fair and new, and bound the body thereof on the frame; and from its peg they took down the mule yoke, a boxwood yoke with knob well fitted with guiding-rings; and they brought forth the yoke-band of nine cubits with the yoke. The yoke they set firmly on the polished pole on the rest at the end thereof, and slipped the ring over the upright pin, which with three turns of the band they lashed to the knob, and then belayed it close round the pole and turned the tongue thereunder. Then they brought from the chamber and heaped on the polished wain the countless ransom of Hector's head, and yoked strong-hooved harness mules, which on a time the Mysians gave to Priam, a splendid gift. But to Priam's car they yoked the horses that the old man kept for his use and reared at the polished crib.

Thus in the high palace were Priam and the herald letting yoke their cars, with wise thoughts at their hearts, when nigh came Hekabe sore at heart, with honey-sweet wine in her right hand in a golden cup that they might make libation ere they went. And she stood before the horses and spake a word to Priam by name: "Lo now make libation to father Zeus and pray that thou mayest come back home from among the enemy, since thy heart speedeth thee forth to the ships, though fain were I thou wentest not. And next pray to Kronion of the Storm-cloud, the gods of Ida, that beholdeth all Troy-land beneath, and ask of him a bird of omen, even the swift messenger that is dearest of all birds to him and of mightiest strength, to appear upon thy right, that seeing the sign with thine own eyes thou mayest go in trust thereto unto the ships of the fleet-horsed Danaans. But if far-seeing Zeus shall not grant unto thee his messenger, I at least shall not bid thee on to go among the ships of the Achaians how fain soever thou mayest be."

Then answered and spake unto her godlike Priam: "Lady, I will not disregard this hest of thine, for good it is to lift up hands to Zeus, if haply he will have pity."

Thus spake the old man, and bade a house-dame that served him pour pure water on his hands; and she came near to serve him with water in a ewer to wash withal. And when he had washed his hands he took a goblet from his wife: then he stood in the midst of the court and prayed and poured forth wine as he looked up to heaven, and spake a word aloud: "Father Zeus that bearest sway from Ida, most glorious and most great, grant that I find welcome and pity under Achilles' roof, and send a bird of omen, even the swift messenger that is dearest of all birds to thee and of mightiest strength, to appear upon the right, that seeing this sign with mine eyes I may go trusting therein unto the ships of the fleet-horsed Danaans."

Thus spake he praying, and Zeus of wise counsels hearkened unto him, and straightway sent forth an eagle, surest omen of winged birds, the dusky hunter called of men the Black Eagle. Wide as the door, well locking, fitted close, of some rich man's high-roofed hall, so wide were his wings either way; and he appeared to them speeding on the right hand above the city. And when they saw the eagle they rejoiced and all their hearts were glad within their breasts.

Then the old man made haste to go up into his car, and drave forth from the doorway and the echoing portico. In front the mules drew the four-wheeled wain, and wise Idaios drave them; behind came the horses which the old man urged with the lash at speed along the city: and his friends all followed lamenting loud as though he were faring to his death. And when they were come down from the city and were now on the plain, then went back again to Ilios his sons and marriage kin. But the two coming forth upon the plain were not unbeheld of far-seeing Zeus. But he looked upon the old man and had compassion on him, and straightway spake unto Hermes his dear son: "Hermes, since unto thee especially is it dear to companion men, and thou hearest whomsoever thou wilt, go forth and so guide Priam to the hollow ships of the Achaians that no man behold or be aware of him, among all the Danaans' host, until he come to the son of Peleus."

Thus spake he, and the Messenger, the slayer of Argus, was not disobedient unto his word. Straightway beneath his feet he bound on his fair sandals, golden, divine, that bare him over wet sea and over the boundless land with the breathings of the wind. And he took up his wand wherewith he entranceth the eyes of such men as he will, and others he likewise waketh out of sleep: this did the strong slayer of Argus take in his hand, and flew. And quickly came he to Troy-land and the Hellespont, and went on his way in semblance as a young man that is a prince, with the new down on his chin, as when the youth of men is the comeliest.

Now the others, when they had driven beyond the great barrow of Ilios, halted the mules and horses at the river to drink; for darkness was come down over the earth. Then the herald beheld Hermes from hard by, and marked him, and spake and said to Priam: "Consider, son of Dardanos; this is matter of prudent thought. I see a man, methinks we shall full soon be rent in pieces. Come, let us flee in our chariot, or else at least touch his knees and entreat him that he have mercy on us."

Thus spake he, and the old man was confounded, and he was dismayed exceedingly, and the hair on his pliant limbs stood up, and he stood still amazed. But the Helper came nigh of himself and took the old man's hand, and spake and questioned him: "Whither, father, dost thou thus guide these horses and mules through the divine night, when other mortals are asleep? Hadst thou no fear of the fierce-breathing Achaians, thy bitter foes that are hard anigh thee? If one of them should espy thee carrying such treasures through the swift black night, what then would be thy thought? Neither art thou young thyself, and thy companion here is old, that ye should make defence against a man that should assail thee first. But I will no wise harm thee, yea I will keep any other from thy hurt: for the similitude of my dear father I see in thee."

And to him in answer spake the old man, godlike Priam: "Even so, kind son, are all these things as thou sayest. Nevertheless hath some god stretched forth his hand even over me in that he hath sent a wayfarer such as thou to meet me, a bearer of good luck, by the nobleness of thy form and semblance; and thou art wise of heart and of blessed parents art thou sprung."

And to him again spake the Messenger, the slayer of Argus: "All this, old sire, hast thou verily spoken aright. But come say this and tell me truly whether thou art taking forth a great and goodly treasure unto alien men, where it may abide for thee in safety, or whether by this ye are all forsaking holy Ilios in fear; so far the best man among you hath perished, even thy son; for of battle with the Achaians abated he never a jot."

And to him in answer spake the old man, godlike Priam, "Who art thou, noble sir, and of whom art born? For meetly hast thou spoken of the fate of my hapless son."

And to him again spake the Messenger, the slayer of Argus: "Thou art proving me, old sire, in asking me of noble Hector. Him have I full oft seen with mine eyes in glorious battle, and when at the ships he was slaying the Argives he drave thither, piercing them with the keen bronze, and we stood still and marvelled thereat, for Achilles suffered us not to fight, being wroth against Atreus' son. His squire am I, and came in the same well-wrought ship. From the Myrmidons I come, and my father is Polyktor. Wealthy is he, and an old man even as thou, and six other sons hath he, and I am his seventh. With the others I cast lots, and it fell to me to fare hither with the host. And now am I come from the ships to the plain, for at day-break the glancing-eyed Achaians will set the battle in array around the town. For it chafeth them to be sitting here, nor can the Achaian lords hold in their fury for the fray."

And the old man, godlike Priam, answered him, saying: "If verily thou art a squire of Achilles Peleus' son, come tell me all the truth, whether still my son is by the ships, or whether ere now Achilles hath riven him limb from limb and cast him to the dogs."

Then to him again spake the Messenger the slayer of Argus: "Old sire, not yet have dogs or birds devoured him, but there lieth he still by Achilles' ship, even as he fell, among the huts, and the twelfth morn now hath risen upon him, nor doth his flesh corrupt at all, neither worms consume it, such as devour men slain in war. Truly Achilles draggeth him recklessly around the barrow of his dear comrade so oft as divine day dawneth, yet marreth he him not; thou wouldst marvel if thou couldst go see thyself how dewy fresh he lieth, and is washed clean of blood, nor anywhere defiled; and all his wounds wherewith he was stricken are closed; howbeit many of thy son, though he be but a dead corpse, for they held him dear at heart."

Thus spake he, and the old man rejoiced, and answered him, saying: "My son, it is verily a good thing to give due offerings withal to the Immortals, for never did my child—if that child indeed I had—forget in our halls the gods who inhabit Olympus. Therefore have they remembered this for him, albeit his portion is death. But come now take from me this goodly goblet, and guard me myself and guide me, under Heaven, that I may come unto the hut of Peleus' son."

Then spake unto him again the Messenger the slayer of Argus: "Thou art proving me, old sire, who am younger than thou, but thou wilt not prevail upon me, in that thou biddest me take gifts from thee without Achilles' privity. I were afraid and shamed at heart to defraud him, lest some evil come to pass on me hereafter. But as thy guide I would go even unto famous Argos, accompanying thee courteously in swift ship or on foot. Not from scorn of thy guide would any assail thee then."

Thus spake the Helper, and leaping on the chariot behind the horses he swiftly took lash and reins into his hand, and breathed brave spirit into horses and mules. But when they were come to the towers and trench of the ships, there were the sentinels just busying them about their supper. Then the Messenger, the slayer of Argus, shed sleep upon them all, and straightway opened the gates and thrust back the bars, and brought within Priam and the splendid gifts upon his wain. And they came to the lofty hut of the son of Peleus, which the Myrmidons made for their king and hewed therefor timber of the pine, and thatched it with downy thatching-rush that they mowed in the meadows, and around it made for him their lord a great court with close-set palisades; and the door was barred by a single bolt of pine that three Achaians wont to drive home, and three drew back that mighty bar—three of the rest, but Achilles by himself would drive it home. Then opened the Helper Hermes the door for the old man, and brought in the splendid gifts for Peleus' fleet-footed son, and descended from the chariot to the earth and spake aloud: "Old sire, I that have come to thee am an immortal god, even Hermes, for my father sent me to companion thee on thy way. But now will I depart from thee nor come within Achilles' sight; it were cause of wrath that an immortal god should thus show favour openly unto mortals. But thou go in and clasp the knees of Peleus' son and entreat him for his father's sake and his mother's of the lovely hair and for his child's sake that thou mayest move his soul."

Thus Hermes spake, and departed unto high Olympus. But Priam leapt from the car to the earth, and left Idaios in his place; he stayed to mind the horses and mules; but the old man made straight for the house where Achilles dear to Zeus was wont to sit. And therein he found the man himself, and his comrades sate apart: two only, the hero Automedon and Alkimos, of the stock of Ares, were busy in attendance; and he was lately ceased from meat, even from eating and drinking: and still the table stood beside him. But they were unaware of great Priam as he came in, and so stood he anigh and clasped in his hands the knees of Achilles, and kissed his hands, terrible, man-slaying, that slew many of Priam's sons. And as when a grievous curse cometh upon a man who in his own country hath slain another and escapeth to a land of strangers, to the house of some rich man, and wonder possesseth them that look on him—so Achilles wondered when he saw godlike Priam, and the rest wondered likewise, and looked upon one another. Then Priam spake and entreated him, saying: "Bethink thee, O Achilles like to gods, of thy father that is of like years with me, on the grievous pathway of old age. Him haply are the dwellers round about entreating evilly, nor is there any to ward from him ruin and bane. Nevertheless while he heareth of thee as yet alive he rejoiceth in his heart, and hopeth withal day after day that he shall see his dear son returning from Troy-land. But I, I am utterly unblest, since I begat sons the best men in wide Troy-land, but declare unto thee that none of them is left. Fifty I had, when the sons of the Achaians came; nineteen were born to me of one mother, and concubines bare the rest within my halls. Now of the more part had impetuous Ares unstrung the knees, and he who was yet left and guarded city and men, him slewest thou but now as he fought for his country, even Hector. For his sake come I unto the ships of the Achaians that I may win him back from thee, and I bring with me untold ransom. Yea, fear thou the gods, Achilles, and have compassion on me, even me, bethinking thee of thy father. Lo, I am yet more piteous than he, and have braved what none other man on earth hath braved before, to stretch forth my hand toward the face of the slayer of my sons."

Thus spake he, and stirred within Achilles desire to make lament for his father. And he touched the old man's hand and gently moved him back. And as they both bethought them of their dead, so Priam for man-slaying Hector wept sore as he was fallen before Achilles' feet, and Achilles wept for his own father, and now again for Patroklos, and their moan went up throughout the house. But when noble Achilles had satisfied him with lament, and the desire thereof departed from his heart and limbs, straightway he sprang from his seat and raised the old man by his hand, pitying his hoary head and hoary beard, and spake unto him winged words and said: "Ah hapless! many ill things verily thou hast endured in thy heart. How durst thou come alone to the ships of the Achaians and to meet the eyes of the man who hath slain full many of the brave sons? of iron verily is thy heart. But come then set thee on a seat, and we will let our sorrows lie quiet in our hearts for all our pain, for no avail cometh of chill lament. This is the lot the gods have spun for miserable men, that they should live in pain; yet themselves are sorrowless. For two urns stand upon the floor of Zeus filled with his evil gifts, and one with blessings. To whomsoever Zeus whose joy is in the lightning dealeth a mingled lot, that man chanceth now upon ill and now again on good, but to whom he giveth but of the bad kind him he bringeth to scorn, and evil famine chaseth him over the goodly earth, and he is a wanderer honoured of neither gods nor men. Even thus to Peleus gave the gods splendid gifts from his birth, for he excelled all men in good fortune and wealth, and was king of the Myrmidons, and mortal though he was the gods gave him a goddess to be his bride. Yet even on him God brought evil, seeing that there arose to him no offspring of princely sons in his halls, save that he begat one son to an untimely death. Neither may I tend him as he groweth old, since very far from my country I am dwelling in Troy-land, to vex thee and thy children. And of thee, old sire, we have heard how of old time thou wert happy, even how of all that Lesbos, seat of Makar, boundeth to the north thereof and Phrygia farther up and the vast Hellespont—of all these folk, men say, thou wert the richest in wealth and in sons, but after that the Powers of Heaven brought this bane on thee, ever are battles and man-slayings around thy city. Keep courage, and lament not unabatingly in thy heart. For nothing wilt thou avail by grieving for thy son, neither shalt thou bring him back to life or ever some new evil come upon thee."

Then made answer unto him the old man, godlike Priam: "Bid me not to a seat, O fosterling of Zeus, so long as Hector lieth uncared for at the huts, but straightway give him back that I may behold him with mine eyes; and accept thou the great ransom that we bring. So mayest thou have pleasure thereof, and come unto thy native land, since thou hast spared me from the first."

Then fleet-footed Achilles looked sternly upon him and said: "No longer chafe me, old sire; of myself am I minded to give Hector back to thee, for there came to me a messenger from Zeus, even my mother who bare me, daughter of the Ancient One of the Sea. And I know, O Priam, in my mind, nor am unaware that some god it is that hath guided thee to the swift ships of the Achaians. For no mortal man, even though in prime of youth, would dare to come among the host, for neither could he escape the watch, nor easily thrust back the bolt of our doors. Therefore now stir my heart no more amid my troubles, lest I leave not even thee in peace, old sire, within my hut, albeit thou art my suppliant, and lest I transgress the commandment of Zeus."

Thus spake he, and the old man feared, and obeyed his word. And the son of Peleus leapt like a lion through the door of the house, not alone, for with him went two squires, the hero Automedon and Alkimos, they whom above all his comrades Achilles honoured, save only Patroklos that was dead. They then loosed from under the yoke the horses and mules, and led in the old man's crier-herald and set him on a chair, and from the wain of goodly felloes they took the countless ransom set on Hector's head. But they left two robes and a well-spun doublet, that Achilles might wrap the dead therein when he gave him to be carried home. And he called forth handmaids and bade them wash and anoint him when they had borne him apart, so that Priam should not look upon his son, lest he should not refrain the wrath at his sorrowing heart when he should look upon his son, and lest Achilles' heart be vexed thereat and he slay him and transgress the commandment of Zeus. So when the handmaids had washed the body and anointed it with oil, and had thrown over it a fair robe and a doublet, then Achilles himself lifted it and laid it on a bier, and his comrades with him lifted it on to the polished waggon. Then he groaned aloud and called on his dear comrade by his name: "Patroklos, be not vexed with me if thou hear even in the house of Hades that I have given back noble Hector unto his dear father, for not unworthy is the ransom he hath given me, whereof I will deal to thee again thy rightful share."

Thus spake noble Achilles, and went back into the hut, and sate him down on the cunningly-wrought couch whence he had arisen by the opposite wall, and spake a word to Priam: "Thy son, old sire, is given back as thou wouldest and lieth on a bier, and with the break of day thou shalt see him thyself as thou carriest him. But now bethink we us of supper. For even fair-haired Niobe bethought her of meat, she whose twelve children perished in her halls, six daughters and six lusty sons. The sons Apollo, in his anger against Niobe, slew with arrows from his silver bow, and the daughters archer Artemis, for that Niobe matched herself against fair-cheeked Leto, saying that the goddess bare but twain but herself many children: so they though they were but twain destroyed the other all. Nine days they lay in their blood, nor was there any to bury them, for Kronion turned the folk to stones. Yet on the tenth day the gods of heaven buried them, and she then bethought her of meat, when she was wearied out with weeping tears. And somewhere now among the cliffs, on the lonely mountains, even on Sipylos, where they say are the couching-places of nymphs that dance around Acheloos, there she, albeit a stone, broodeth still over her troubles from the gods. But come let us too, noble father, take thought of meat, and afterward thou shalt mourn over thy dear son as thou carriest him to Ilios; and many tears shall be his due."

Thus spake fleet Achilles, and sprang up, and slew a pure white sheep, and his comrades skinned and made it ready in seemly fashion, and divided it cunningly and pierced it with spits, and roasted it carefully and drew all off. And Automedon took bread and served it on a table in fair baskets, while Achilles dealt out the flesh. And they stretched forth their hands to the good cheer lying ready before them. But when they had put off the desire of meat and drink, then Priam son of Dardanos marvelled at Achilles to see how great he was and how goodly, for he was like a god to look upon. And Achilles marvelled at Priam son of Dardanos, beholding his noble aspect and hearkening to his words. But when they had gazed their fill upon one another, then first spake the old man, godlike Priam, to Achilles: "Now presently give me whereon to lie, fosterling of Zeus, that of sweet sleep also we may now take our fill at rest: for never yet have mine eyes closed beneath their lids since at thy hands my son lost his life, but I continually mourn and brood over countless griefs, grovelling in the courtyard-close amid the mire. Now at last have I tasted bread and poured bright wine down my throat, but till now I had tasted naught."

He said, and Achilles bade his comrades and handmaids to set a bedstead beneath the portico, and to cast thereon fair shining rugs and spread coverlets above and thereon to lay thick mantles to be a clothing over all. And the maids went forth from the inner hail with torches in their hands, and quickly spread two beds in haste. Then with bitter meaning [in his reference to Agamemnon] said fleet-footed Achilles unto Priam: "Lie thou without, dear sire, lest there come hither one of the counsellors of the Achaians, such as ever take counsel with me by my side, as custom is. If any of such should behold thee through the swift black night, forthwith he might haply tell it to Agamemnon shepherd of the host, and thus would there be delay in giving back the dead. But come say this to me and tell it true, how many days' space thou art fain to make funeral for noble Hector, so that for so long I may myself abide and may keep back the host."

And the old man, godlike Priam, answered him, saying: "If thou art verily willing that I accomplish noble Hector's funeral, by doing as thou sayest, O Achilles, thou wilt do me grace. For thou knowest how we are pent within the city, and wood from the mountain is far to fetch, and the Trojans are much in fear. Nine days will we make moan for him in our halls, and on the tenth we will hold funeral and the folk shall feast, and on the eleventh we will make, a barrow over him, and on the twelfth we will do battle if need be."

Then again spake the fleet noble Achilles unto him, saying: "All this, O ancient Priam, shall be as thou biddest; for I will hold back the battle even so long a time as thou tellest me."

Thus speaking he clasped the old man's right hand at the wrist, lest he should be anywise afraid at heart. So they in the forepart of the house laid them down, Priam and the herald, with wise thoughts at their hearts, but Achilles slept in a recess of the firm-wrought hut, and beside him lay fair-cheeked Briseis.

Now all other gods and warriors lords of chariots slumbered all night, by soft sleep overcome. But not on the Helper Hermes did sleep take hold as he sought within his heart how he should guide forth king Priam from the ships unespied of the trusty sentinels. And he stood above his head and spake a word to him: "Old sire, no thought then hast thou of any evil, seeing thou yet sleepest among men that are thine enemies, for that Achilles spared thee. Truly now hast thou won back thy dear son, and at great price. But for thy life will thy sons thou hast left behind be offering threefold ransom, if but Agamemnon Atreus' son be aware of thee, and aware be all the Achaians."

Thus spake he, and the old man feared, and roused the herald. And Hermes yoked the horses and mules for them, and himself drave them lightly through the camp, and none was aware of them.

But when they came to the ford of the fair-flowing river, [even eddying Xanthos, begotten of immortal Zeus,] then Hermes departed up to high Olympus, and Morning of the saffron robe spread over all the earth. And they with wail and moan drave the horses to the city, and the mules drew the dead. Nor marked them any man or fair-girdled woman until Kassandra, peer of golden Aphrodite, having gone up upon Pergamos, was aware of her dear father as he stood in the car, and the herald that was crier to the town. Then beheld she him that lay upon the bier behind the mules, and thereat she wailed and cried aloud throughout all the town: "O men and women of Troy, come ye hither and look upon Hector, if ever while he was alive ye rejoiced when he came back from battle, since great joy was he to the city and all the folk."

Thus spake she, nor was man or woman left within the city, for upon all came unendurable grief. And near the gates they met Priam bringing home the dead. First bewailed him his dear wife and lady mother, as they cast them on the fair-wheeled wain and touched his head; and around them stood the throng and wept. So all day long unto the setting of the sun they had lamented Hector in tears without the gate, had not the old man spoken from the car among the folk: "Give me place for the mules to pass through; hereafter ye shall have your fill of wailing, when I have brought him unto his home."

Thus spake he, and they parted asunder and gave place to the wain. And the others when they had brought him to the famous house, laid him on a fretted bed, and set beside him minstrel leaders of the dirge, who wailed a mournful lay, while the women made moan with them. And among the women white-armed Andromache led the lamentation, while in her hands she held the head of Hector slayer of men: "Husband, thou art gone young from life, and leavest me a widow in thy halls. And the child is yet but a little one, child of ill-fated parents, thee and me; nor methinks shall he grow up to manhood, for ere then shall this city be utterly destroyed. For thou art verily perished who didst watch over it, who guardedst it and keptest safe its noble wives and infant little ones. These soon shall be voyaging in the hollow ships, yea and I too with them, and thou, my child, shalt either go with me unto a place where thou shalt toil at unseemly tasks, labouring before the face of some harsh lord, or else some Achaian will take thee by the arm and hurl thee from the battlement, a grievous death, for that he is wroth because Hector slew his brother or father or son, since full many of the Achaians in Hector's hands have bitten the firm earth. For no light hand had thy father in the grievous fray. Therefore the folk lament him throughout the city, and woe unspeakable and mourning hast thou left to thy parents, Hector, but with me chiefliest shall grievous pain abide. For neither didst thou stretch thy hands to me from a bed in thy death, neither didst speak to me some memorable word that I might have thought on evermore as my tears fall night and day."

Thus spake she wailing, and the women joined their moan. And among them Hekabe again led the loud lament: "Hector, of all my children far dearest to my heart, verily while thou wert alive dear wert thou to the gods, and even in thy doom of death have they had care for thee. For other sons of mine whom he took captive would fleet Achilles sell beyond the unvintaged sea unto Samos and Imbros and smoking Lemnos, but when with keen-edged bronze he had bereft thee of thy life he was fain to drag thee oft around the tomb of his comrade, even Patroklos whom thou slewest, yet might he not raise him up thereby. But now all dewy and fresh thou liest in our halls, like one on whom Apollo, lord of the silver bow, hath descended and slain him with his gentle darts."

Thus spake she wailing, and stirred unending moan. Then thirdly Helen led their sore lament: "Hector, of all my brethren of Troy far dearest to my heart! Truly my lord is godlike Alexandros who brought me to Troy-land—would I had died ere then. For this is now the twentieth year since I went thence and am gone from my own native land, but never yet heard I evil or despiteful word from thee; nay, if any other haply upbraided me in the palace-halls, whether brother or sister of thine or brother's fair-robed wife, or thy mother—but thy father is ever kind to me as he were my own—then wouldst thou soothe such with words and refrain them, by the gentleness of thy spirit and by thy gentle words. Therefore bewail I thee with pain at heart, and my hapless self with thee, for no more is any left in wide Troy-land to be my friend and kind to me, but all men shudder at me."

Thus spake she wailing, and therewith the great multitude of the people groaned. But the old man Priam spake a word among the folk: "Bring wood, men of Troy, unto the city, and be not anywise afraid at heart of a crafty ambush of the Achaians; for this message Achilles gave me when he sent me from the black ships, that they should do us no hurt until the twelfth morn arise."

Thus spake he, and they yoked oxen and mules to wains, and quickly then they flocked before the city. So nine days they gathered great store of wood. But when the tenth morn rose with light for men, then bare they forth brave Hector, weeping tears, and on a lofty pyre they laid the dead man, and thereon cast fire.

But when the daughter of Dawn, rosy-fingered Morning, shone forth, then gathered the folk around glorious Hector's pyre. First quenched they with bright wine all the burning, so far as the fire's strength went, and then his brethren and comrades gathered his white bones lamenting, and big tears flowed down their cheeks. And the bones they took and laid in a golden urn, shrouding them in soft purple robes, and straightway laid the urn in a hollow grave and piled thereon great close-set stones, and heaped with speed a barrow, while watchers were set everywhere around, lest the well-greaved Achaians should make onset before the time. And when they had heaped the barrow they went back, and gathered them together and feasted right well in noble feast at the palace of Priam, Zeus-fostered king.

Thus held they funeral for Hector tamer of horses.

The Odyssey

BOOK I

The gods in council—Miverva's visit to Ithaca—the challenge from Telemachus to the suitors.

Tell me, O Muse, of that ingenious hero who travelled far and wide after he had sacked the famous town of Troy. Many cities did he visit, and many were the nations with whose manners and customs he was acquainted; moreover he suffered much by sea while trying to save his own life and bring his men safely home; but do what he might he could not save his men, for they perished through their own sheer folly in eating the cattle of the Sun-god Hyperion; so the god prevented them from ever reaching home. Tell me, too, about all these things, oh daughter of Jove, from whatsoever source you may know them.

So now all who escaped death in battle or by shipwreck had got safely home except Ulysses, and he, though he was longing to return to his wife and country, was detained by the goddess Calypso, who had got him into a large cave and wanted to marry him. But as years went by, there came a time when the gods settled that he should go back to Ithaca; even then, however, when he was among his own people, his troubles were not yet over; nevertheless all the gods had now begun to pity him except Neptune, who still persecuted him without ceasing and would not let him get home.

Now Neptune had gone off to the Ethiopians, who are at the world's end, and lie in two halves, the one looking West and the other East. {1} He had gone there to accept a hecatomb of sheep and oxen, and was enjoying himself at his festival; but the other gods met in the house of Olympian Jove, and the sire of gods and men spoke first. At that moment he was thinking of Aegisthus, who had been killed by Agamemnon's son Orestes; so he said to the other gods:

"See now, how men lay blame upon us gods for what is after all nothing but their own folly. Look at Aegisthus; he must needs make love to Agamemnon's wife unrighteously and then kill Agamemnon, though he knew it would be the death of him; for I sent Mercury to warn him not to do either of these things, inasmuch as Orestes would be sure to take his revenge when he grew up and wanted to return home. Mercury told him this in all good will but he would not listen, and now he has paid for everything in full."

Then Minerva said, "Father, son of Saturn, King of kings, it served Aegisthus right, and so it would any one else who does as he did; but Aegisthus is neither here nor there; it is for Ulysses that my heart bleeds, when I think of his sufferings in that lonely sea-girt island, far away, poor man, from all his friends. It is an island covered with forest, in the very middle of the sea, and a goddess lives there, daughter of the magician Atlas, who looks after the bottom of the ocean, and carries the great columns that keep heaven and earth asunder. This daughter of Atlas has got hold of poor unhappy Ulysses, and keeps trying by every kind of blandishment to make him forget his home, so that he is tired of life, and thinks of nothing but how he may once more see the smoke of his own chimneys. You, sir, take no heed of this, and yet when Ulysses was before Troy did he not propitiate you with many a burnt sacrifice? Why then should you keep on being so angry with him?"

And Jove said, "My child, what are you talking about? How can I forget Ulysses than whom there is no more capable man on earth, nor more liberal in his offerings to the immortal gods that live in heaven? Bear in mind, however, that Neptune is still furious with Ulysses for having blinded an eye of Polyphemus king of the Cyclopes. Polyphemus is son to Neptune by the nymph Thoosa, daughter to the sea-king Phorcys; therefore though he will not kill Ulysses outright, he torments him by preventing him from getting home. Still, let us lay our heads together and see how we can help him to return; Neptune will then be pacified, for if we are all of a mind he can hardly stand out against us."

And Minerva said, "Father, son of Saturn, King of kings, if, then, the gods now mean that Ulysses should get home, we should first send Mercury to the Ogygian island to tell Calypso that we have made up our minds and that he is to return. In the meantime I will go to Ithaca, to put heart into Ulysses' son Telemachus; I will embolden him to call the Achaeans in assembly, and speak out to the suitors of his mother Penelope, who persist in eating up any number of his sheep and oxen; I will also conduct him to Sparta and to Pylos, to see if he can hear anything about the return of his dear father—for this will make people speak well of him."

So saying she bound on her glittering golden sandals, imperishable, with which she can fly like the wind over land or sea; she grasped the redoubtable bronze-shod spear, so stout and sturdy and strong, wherewith she quells the ranks of heroes who have displeased her, and down she darted from the topmost summits of Olympus, whereon forthwith she was in Ithaca, at the gateway of Ulysses' house, disguised as a visitor, Mentes, chief of the Taphians, and she held a bronze spear in her hand. There she found the lordly suitors seated on hides of the oxen which they had killed and eaten, and playing draughts in front of the house. Men-servants and pages were bustling about to wait upon them, some mixing wine with water in the mixing-bowls, some cleaning down the tables with wet sponges and laying them out again, and some cutting up great quantities of meat.

Telemachus saw her long before any one else did. He was sitting moodily among the suitors thinking about his brave father, and how he would send them flying out of the house, if he were to come to his own again and be honoured as in days gone by. Thus brooding as he sat among them, he caught sight of Minerva and went straight to the gate, for he was vexed that a stranger should be kept waiting for admittance. He took her right hand in his own, and bade her give him her spear. "Welcome," said he, "to our house, and when you have partaken of food you shall tell us what you have come for."

He led the way as he spoke, and Minerva followed him. When they were within he took her spear and set it in the spear-stand against a strong bearing-post along with the many other spears of his unhappy father, and he conducted her to a richly decorated seat under which he threw a cloth of damask. There was a footstool also for her feet,{2} and he set another seat near her for himself, away from the suitors, that she might not be annoyed while eating by their noise and insolence, and that he might ask her more freely about his father.

A maid servant then brought them water in a beautiful golden ewer and poured it into a silver basin for them to wash their hands, and she drew a clean table beside them. An upper servant brought them bread, and offered them many good things of what there was in the house, the carver fetched them plates of all manner of meats and set cups of gold by their side, and a manservant brought them wine and poured it out for them.

Then the suitors came in and took their places on the benches and seats. {3} Forthwith men servants poured water over their hands, maids went round with the bread-baskets, pages filled the mixing-bowls with wine and water, and they laid their hands upon the good things that were before them. As soon as they had had enough to eat and drink they wanted music and dancing, which are the crowning embellishments of a banquet, so a servant brought a lyre to Phemius, whom they compelled perforce to sing to them. As soon as he touched his lyre and began to sing Telemachus spoke low to Minerva, with his head close to hers that no man might hear.

"I hope, sir," said he, "that you will not be offended with what I am going to say. Singing comes cheap to those who do not pay for it, and all this is done at the cost of one whose bones lie rotting in some wilderness or grinding to powder in the surf. If these men were to see my father come back to Ithaca they would pray for longer legs rather than a longer purse, for money would not serve them; but he, alas, has fallen on an ill fate, and even when people do sometimes say that he is coming, we no longer heed them; we shall never see him again. And now, sir, tell me and tell me true, who you are and where you come from. Tell me of your town and parents, what manner of ship you came in, how your crew brought you to Ithaca, and of what nation they declared themselves to be—for you cannot have come by land. Tell me also truly, for I want to know, are you a stranger to this house, or have you been here in my father's time? In the old days we had many visitors for my father went about much himself."

And Minerva answered, "I will tell you truly and particularly all about it. I am Mentes, son of Anchialus, and I am King of the Taphians. I have come here with my ship and crew, on a voyage to men of a foreign tongue being bound for Temesa {4} with a cargo of iron, and I shall bring back copper. As for my ship, it lies over yonder off the open country away from the town, in the harbour Rheithron {5} under the wooded mountain Neritum. {6} Our fathers were friends before us, as old Laertes will tell you, if you will go and ask him. They say, however, that he never comes to town now, and lives by himself in the country, faring hardly, with an old woman to look after him and get his dinner for him, when he comes in tired from pottering about his vineyard. They told me your father was at home again, and that was why I came, but it seems the gods are still keeping him back, for he is not dead yet not on the mainland. It is more likely he is on some sea-girt island in mid ocean, or a prisoner among savages who are detaining him against his will. I am no prophet, and know very little about omens, but I speak as it is borne in upon me from heaven, and assure you that he will not be away much longer; for he is a man of such resource that even though he were in chains of iron he would find some means of getting home again. But tell me, and tell me true, can Ulysses really have such a fine looking fellow for a son? You are indeed wonderfully like him about the head and eyes, for we were close friends before he set sail for Troy where the flower of all the Argives went also. Since that time we have never either of us seen the other."

"My mother," answered Telemachus, "tells me I am son to Ulysses, but it is a wise child that knows his own father. Would that I were son to one who had grown old upon his own estates, for, since you ask me, there is no more ill-starred man under heaven than he who they tell me is my father."

And Minerva said, "There is no fear of your race dying out yet, while Penelope has such a fine son as you are. But tell me, and tell me true, what is the meaning of all this feasting, and who are these people? What is it all about? Have you some banquet, or is there a wedding in the family—for no one seems to be bringing any provisions of his own? And the guests—how atrociously they are behaving; what riot they make over the whole house; it is enough to disgust any respectable person who comes near them."

"Sir," said Telemachus, "as regards your question, so long as my father was here it was well with us and with the house, but the gods in their displeasure have willed it otherwise, and have hidden him away more closely than mortal man was ever yet hidden. I could have borne it better even though he were dead, if he had fallen with his men before Troy, or had died with friends around him when the days of his fighting were done; for then the Achaeans would have built a mound over his ashes, and I should myself have been heir to his renown; but now the storm-winds have spirited him away we know not whither; he is gone without leaving so much as a trace behind him, and I inherit nothing but dismay. Nor does the matter end simply with grief for the loss of my father; heaven has laid sorrows upon me of yet another kind; for the chiefs from all our islands, Dulichium, Same, and the woodland island of Zacynthus, as also all the principal men of Ithaca itself, are eating up my house under the pretext of paying their court to my mother, who will neither point blank say that she will not marry, {7} nor yet bring matters to an end; so they are making havoc of my estate, and before long will do so also with myself."

"Is that so?" exclaimed Minerva, "then you do indeed want Ulysses home again. Give him his helmet, shield, and a couple of lances, and if he is the man he was when I first knew him in our house, drinking and making merry, he would soon lay his hands about these rascally suitors, were he to stand once more upon his own threshold. He was then coming from Ephyra, where he had been to beg poison for his arrows from Ilus, son of Mermerus. Ilus feared the ever-living gods and would not give him any, but my father let him have some, for he was very fond of him. If Ulysses is the man he then was these suitors will have a short shrift and a sorry wedding.

"But there! It rests with heaven to determine whether he is to return, and take his revenge in his own house or no; I would, however, urge you to set about trying to get rid of these suitors at once. Take my advice, call the Achaean heroes in assembly to-morrow morning—lay your case before them, and call heaven to bear you witness. Bid the suitors take themselves off, each to his own place, and if your mother's mind is set on marrying again, let her go back to her father, who will find her a husband and provide her with all the marriage gifts that so dear a daughter may expect. As for yourself, let me prevail upon you to take the best ship you can get, with a crew of twenty men, and go in quest of your father who has so long been missing. Some one may tell you something, or (and people often hear things in this way) some heaven-sent message may direct you. First go to Pylos and ask Nestor; thence go on to Sparta and visit Menelaus, for he got home last of all the Achaeans; if you hear that your father is alive and on his way home, you can put up with the waste these suitors will make for yet another twelve months. If on the other hand you hear of his death, come home at once, celebrate his funeral rites with all due pomp, build a barrow to his memory, and make your mother marry again. Then, having done all this, think it well over in your mind how, by fair means or foul, you may kill these suitors in your own house. You are too old to plead infancy any longer; have you not heard how people are singing Orestes' praises for having killed his father's murderer Aegisthus? You are a fine, smart looking fellow; show your mettle, then, and make yourself a name in story. Now, however, I must go back to my ship and to my crew, who will be impatient if I keep them waiting longer; think the matter over for yourself, and remember what I have said to you."

"Sir," answered Telemachus, "it has been very kind of you to talk to me in this way, as though I were your own son, and I will do all you tell me; I know you want to be getting on with your voyage, but stay a little longer till you have taken a bath and refreshed yourself. I will then give you a present, and you shall go on your way rejoicing; I will give you one of great beauty and value—a keepsake such as only dear friends give to one another."

Minerva answered, "Do not try to keep me, for I would be on my way at once. As for any present you may be disposed to make me, keep it till I come again, and I will take it home with me. You shall give me a very good one, and I will give you one of no less value in return."

With these words she flew away like a bird into the air, but she had given Telemachus courage, and had made him think more than ever about his father. He felt the change, wondered at it, and knew that the stranger had been a god, so he went straight to where the suitors were sitting.

Phemius was still singing, and his hearers sat rapt in silence as he told the sad tale of the return from Troy, and the ills Minerva had laid upon the Achaeans. Penelope, daughter of Icarius, heard his song from her room upstairs, and came down by the great staircase, not alone, but attended by two of her handmaids. When she reached the suitors she stood by one of the bearing posts that supported the roof of the cloisters {8} with a staid maiden on either side of her. She held a veil, moreover, before her face, and was weeping bitterly.

"Phemius," she cried, "you know many another feat of gods and heroes, such as poets love to celebrate. Sing the suitors some one of these, and let them drink their wine in silence, but cease this sad tale, for it breaks my sorrowful heart, and reminds me of my lost husband whom I mourn ever without ceasing, and whose name was great over all Hellas and middle Argos." {9}

"Mother," answered Telemachus, "let the bard sing what he has a mind to; bards do not make the ills they sing of; it is Jove, not they, who makes them, and who sends weal or woe upon mankind according to his own good pleasure. This fellow means no harm by singing the ill-fated return of the Danaans, for people always applaud the latest songs most warmly. Make up your mind to it and bear it; Ulysses is not the only man who never came back from Troy, but many another went down as well as he. Go, then, within the house and busy yourself with your daily duties, your loom, your distaff, and the ordering of your servants; for speech is man's matter, and mine above all others {10}—for it is I who am master here."

She went wondering back into the house, and laid her son's saying in her heart. Then, going upstairs with her handmaids into her room, she mourned her dear husband till Minerva shed sweet sleep over her eyes. But the suitors were clamorous throughout the covered cloisters {11}, and prayed each one that he might be her bed fellow.

Then Telemachus spoke, "Shameless," he cried, "and insolent suitors, let us feast at our pleasure now, and let there be no brawling, for it is a rare thing to hear a man with such a divine voice as Phemius has; but in the morning meet me in full assembly that I may give you formal notice to depart, and feast at one another's houses, turn and turn about, at your own cost. If on the other hand you choose to persist in spunging upon one man, heaven help me, but Jove shall reckon with you in full, and when you fall in my father's house there shall be no man to avenge you."

The suitors bit their lips as they heard him, and marvelled at the boldness of his speech. Then, Antinous, son of Eupeithes, said, "The gods seem to have given you lessons in bluster and tall talking; may Jove never grant you to be chief in Ithaca as your father was before you."

Telemachus answered, "Antinous, do not chide with me, but, god willing, I will be chief too if I can. Is this the worst fate you can think of for me? It is no bad thing to be a chief, for it brings both riches and honour. Still, now that Ulysses is dead there are many great men in Ithaca both old and young, and some other may take the lead among them; nevertheless I will be chief in my own house, and will rule those whom Ulysses has won for me."

Then Eurymachus, son of Polybus, answered, "It rests with heaven to decide who shall be chief among us, but you shall be master in your own house and over your own possessions; no one while there is a man in Ithaca shall do you violence nor rob you. And now, my good fellow, I want to know about this stranger. What country does he come from? Of what family is he, and where is his estate? Has he brought you news about the return of your father, or was he on business of his own? He seemed a well to do man, but he hurried off so suddenly that he was gone in a moment before we could get to know him."

"My father is dead and gone," answered Telemachus, "and even if some rumour reaches me I put no more faith in it now. My mother does indeed sometimes send for a soothsayer and question him, but I give his prophecyings no heed. As for the stranger, he was Mentes, son of Anchialus, chief of the Taphians, an old friend of my father's." But in his heart he knew that it had been the goddess.

The suitors then returned to their singing and dancing until the evening; but when night fell upon their pleasuring they went home to bed each in his own abode. {12} Telemachus's room was high up in a tower {13} that looked on to the outer court; hither, then, he hied, brooding and full of thought. A good old woman, Euryclea, daughter of Ops, the son of Pisenor, went before him with a couple of blazing torches. Laertes had bought her with his own money when she was quite young; he gave the worth of twenty oxen for her, and shewed as much respect to her in his household as he did to his own wedded wife, but he did not take her to his bed for he feared his wife's resentment. {14} She it was who now lighted Telemachus to his room, and she loved him better than any of the other women in the house did, for she had nursed him when he was a baby. He opened the door of his bed room and sat down upon the bed; as he took off his shirt {15} he gave it to the good old woman, who folded it tidily up, and hung it for him over a peg by his bed side, after which she went out, pulled the door to by a silver catch, and drew the bolt home by means of the strap. {16} But Telemachus as he lay covered with a woollen fleece kept thinking all night through of his intended voyage and of the counsel that Minerva had given him.

BOOK II

Assembly of the people of Ithaca—speeches of Telemachus and of the suitors–Telemachus makes his preparations and starts for Pylos with minerva disguised as mentor.

Now when the child of morning, rosy-fingered Dawn, appeared Telemachus rose and dressed himself. He bound his sandals on to his comely feet, girded his sword about his shoulder, and left his room looking like an immortal god. He at once sent the criers round to call the people in assembly, so they called them and the people gathered thereon; then, when they were got together, he went to the place of assembly spear in hand—not alone, for his two hounds went with him. Minerva endowed him with a presence of such divine comeliness that all marvelled at him as he went by, and when he took his place in his father's seat even the oldest councillors made way for him.

Aegyptius, a man bent double with age, and of infinite experience, was the first to speak. His son Antiphus had gone with Ulysses to Ilius, land of noble steeds, but the savage Cyclops had killed him when they were all shut up in the cave, and had cooked his last dinner for him. {17} He had three sons left, of whom two still worked on their father's land, while the third, Eurynomus, was one of the suitors; nevertheless their father could not get over the loss of Antiphus, and was still weeping for him when he began his speech.

"Men of Ithaca," he said, "hear my words. From the day Ulysses left us there has been no meeting of our councillors until now; who then can it be, whether old or young, that finds it so necessary to convene us? Has he got wind of some host approaching, and does he wish to warn us, or would he speak upon some other matter of public moment? I am sure he is an excellent person, and I hope Jove will grant him his heart's desire."

Telemachus took this speech as of good omen and rose at once, for he was bursting with what he had to say. He stood in the middle of the assembly and the good herald Pisenor brought him his staff. Then, turning to Aegyptius, "Sir," said he, "it is I, as you will shortly learn, who have convened you, for it is I who am the most aggrieved. I have not got wind of any host approaching about which I would warn you, nor is there any matter of public moment on which I would speak. My grievance is purely personal, and turns on two great misfortunes which have fallen upon my house. The first of these is the loss of my excellent father; who

was chief among all you here present, and was like a father to every one
of you; the second is much more serious, and ere long will be the utter
ruin of my estate. The sons of all the chief men among you are pestering
my mother to marry them against her will. They are afraid to go to her
father Icarius, asking him to choose the one he likes best, and to provide
marriage gifts for his daughter, but day by day they keep hanging about
my father's house, sacrificing our oxen, sheep, and fat goats for their
banquets, and never giving so much as a thought to the quantity of wine
they drink. No estate can stand such recklessness; we have now no
Ulysses to ward off harm from our doors, and I cannot hold my own
against them. I shall never all my days be as good a man as he was, still
I would indeed defend myself if I had power to do so, for I cannot stand
such treatment any longer; my house is being disgraced and ruined. Have
respect, therefore, to your own consciences and to public opinion. Fear,
too, the wrath of heaven, lest the gods should be displeased and turn upon
you. I pray you by Jove and Themis, who is the beginning and the end of
councils, [do not] hold back, my friends, and leave me singlehanded
{18}—unless it be that my brave father Ulysses did some wrong to the
Achaeans which you would now avenge on me, by aiding and abetting
these suitors. Moreover, if I am to be eaten out of house and home at all,
I had rather you did the eating yourselves, for I could then take action
against you to some purpose, and serve you with notices from house to
house till I got paid in full, whereas now I have no remedy." {19}

With this Telemachus dashed his staff to the ground and burst into
tears. Every one was very sorry for him, but they all sat still and no one
ventured to make him an angry answer, save only Antinous, who spoke
thus:

"Telemachus, insolent braggart that you are, how dare you try to throw
the blame upon us suitors? It is your mother's fault not ours, for she is a
very artful woman. This three years past, and close on four, she had been
driving us out of our minds, by encouraging each one of us, and sending
him messages without meaning one word of what she says. And then
there was that other trick she played us. She set up a great tambour
frame in her room, and began to work on an enormous piece of fine
needlework. 'Sweet hearts,' said she, 'Ulysses is indeed dead, still do not
press me to marry again immediately, wait—for I would not have skill in
needlework perish unrecorded—till I have completed a pall for the hero
Laertes, to be in readiness against the time when death shall take him.
He is very rich, and the women of the place will talk if he is laid out
without a pall.'

"This was what she said, and we assented; whereon we could see her
working on her great web all day long, but at night she would unpick the
stitches again by torchlight. She fooled us in this way for three years and
we never found her out, but as time wore on and she was now in her
fourth year, one of her maids who knew what she was doing told us, and

we caught her in the act of undoing her work, so she had to finish it whether she would or no. The suitors, therefore, make you this answer, that both you and the Achaeans may understand-'Send your mother away, and bid her marry the man of her own and of her father's choice'; for I do not know what will happen if she goes on plaguing us much longer with the airs she gives herself on the score of the accomplishments Minerva has taught her, and because she is so clever. We never yet heard of such a woman; we know all about Tyro, Alcmena, Mycene, and the famous women of old, but they were nothing to your mother any one of them. It was not fair of her to treat us in that way, and as long as she continues in the mind with which heaven has now endowed her, so long shall we go on eating up your estate; and I do not see why she should change, for she gets all the honour and glory, and it is you who pay for it, not she. Understand, then, that we will not go back to our lands, neither here nor elsewhere, till she has made her choice and married some one or other of us."

Telemachus answered, "Antinous, how can I drive the mother who bore me from my father's house? My father is abroad and we do not know whether he is alive or dead. It will be hard on me if I have to pay Icarius the large sum which I must give him if I insist on sending his daughter back to him. Not only will he deal rigorously with me, but heaven will also punish me; for my mother when she leaves the house will call on the Erinyes to avenge her; besides, it would not be a creditable thing to do, and I will have nothing to say to it. If you choose to take offence at this, leave the house and feast elsewhere at one another's houses at your own cost turn and turn about. If, on the other hand, you elect to persist in spunging upon one man, heaven help me, but Jove shall reckon with you in full, and when you fall in my father's house there shall be no man to avenge you."

As he spoke Jove sent two eagles from the top of the mountain, and they flew on and on with the wind, sailing side by side in their own lordly flight. When they were right over the middle of the assembly they wheeled and circled about, beating the air with their wings and glaring death into the eyes of them that were below; then, fighting fiercely and tearing at one another, they flew off towards the right over the town. The people wondered as they saw them, and asked each other what all this might be; whereon Halitherses, who was the best prophet and reader of omens among them, spoke to them plainly and in all honesty, saying:

"Hear me, men of Ithaca, and I speak more particularly to the suitors, for I see mischief brewing for them. Ulysses is not going to be away much longer; indeed he is close at hand to deal out death and destruction, not on them alone, but on many another of us who live in Ithaca. Let us then be wise in time, and put a stop to this wickedness before he comes. Let the suitors do so of their own accord; it will be better for them, for I am not prophesying without due knowledge; everything has happened to Ulysses as I foretold when the Argives set out for Troy, and he with them. I said that after going through much hardship and losing all his men he should come home again in the twentieth year and that no one would know him; and now all this is coming true."

Eurymachus son of Polybus then said, "Go home, old man, and prophesy to your own children, or it may be worse for them. I can read these omens myself much better than you can; birds are always flying about in the sunshine somewhere or other, but they seldom mean anything. Ulysses has died in a far country, and it is a pity you are not dead along with him, instead of prating here about omens and adding fuel to the anger of Telemachus which is fierce enough as it is. I suppose you think he will give you something for your family, but I tell you—and it shall surely be—when an old man like you, who should know better, talks a young one over till he becomes troublesome, in the first place his young friend will only fare so much the worse—he will take nothing by it, for the suitors will prevent this—and in the next, we will lay a heavier fine, sir, upon yourself than you will at all like paying, for it will bear hardly upon you. As for Telemachus, I warn him in the presence of you all to send his mother back to her father, who will find her a husband and provide her with all the marriage gifts so dear a daughter may expect. Till then we shall go on harassing him with our suit; for we fear no man, and care neither for him, with all his fine speeches, nor for any fortune-telling of yours. You may preach as much as you please, but we shall only hate you the more. We shall go back and continue to eat up Telemachus's estate without paying him, till such time as his mother leaves off tormenting us by keeping us day after day on the tiptoe of expectation, each vying with the other in his suit for a prize of such rare perfection. Besides we cannot go after the other women whom we should marry in due course, but for the way in which she treats us."

Then Telemachus said, "Eurymachus, and you other suitors, I shall say no more, and entreat you no further, for the gods and the people of Ithaca now know my story. Give me, then, a ship and a crew of twenty men to take me hither and thither, and I will go to Sparta and to Pylos in quest of my father who has so long been missing. Some one may tell me something, or (and people often hear things in this way) some heaven-sent message may direct me. If I can hear of him as alive and on his way home I will put up with the waste you suitors will make for yet another twelve months. If on the other hand I hear of his death, I will return at once, celebrate his funeral rites with all due pomp, build a barrow to his memory, and make my mother marry again."

With these words he sat down, and Mentor {20} who had been a friend of Ulysses, and had been left in charge of everything with full authority over the servants, rose to speak. He, then, plainly and in all honesty addressed them thus:

"Hear me, men of Ithaca, I hope that you may never have a kind and well-disposed ruler any more, nor one who will govern you equitably; I hope that all your chiefs henceforward may be cruel and unjust, for there is not one of you but has forgotten Ulysses, who ruled you as though he were your father. I am not half so angry with the suitors, for if they choose to do violence in the naughtiness of their hearts, and wager their heads that Ulysses will not return, they can take the high hand and eat up his estate, but as for you others I am shocked at the way in which you all sit still without even trying to stop such scandalous goings on—which you could do if you chose, for you are many and they are few."

Leiocritus, son of Evenor, answered him saying, "Mentor, what folly is all this, that you should set the people to stay us? It is a hard thing for one man to fight with many about his victuals. Even though Ulysses himself were to set upon us while we are feasting in his house, and do his best to oust us, his wife, who wants him back so very badly, would have small cause for rejoicing, and his blood would be upon his own head if he fought against such great odds. There is no sense in what you have been saying. Now, therefore, do you people go about your business, and let his father's old friends, Mentor and Halitherses, speed this boy on his journey, if he goes at all—which I do not think he will, for he is more likely to stay where he is till some one comes and tells him something."

On this he broke up the assembly, and every man went back to his own abode, while the suitors returned to the house of Ulysses.

Then Telemachus went all alone by the sea side, washed his hands in the grey waves, and prayed to Minerva.

"Hear me," he cried, "you god who visited me yesterday, and bade me sail the seas in search of my father who has so long been missing. I would obey you, but the Achaeans, and more particularly the wicked suitors, are hindering me that I cannot do so."

As he thus prayed, Minerva came close up to him in the likeness and with the voice of Mentor. "Telemachus," said she, "if you are made of the same stuff as your father you will be neither fool nor coward henceforward, for Ulysses never broke his word nor left his work half done. If, then, you take after him, your voyage will not be fruitless, but unless you have the blood of Ulysses and of Penelope in your veins I see no likelihood of your succeeding. Sons are seldom as good men as their fathers; they are generally worse, not better; still, as you are not going to be either fool or coward henceforward, and are not entirely without some share of your father's wise discernment, I look with hope upon your undertaking. But mind you never make common cause with any of those foolish suitors, for they have neither sense nor virtue, and give no thought to death and to the doom that will shortly fall on one and all of them, so that they shall perish on the same day. As for your voyage, it shall not be long delayed; your father was such an old friend of mine that I will find you a ship, and will come with you myself. Now, however, return home, and go about among the suitors; begin getting provisions ready for your voyage; see everything well stowed, the wine in jars, and the barley meal, which is the staff of life, in leathern bags, while I go round the town and beat up volunteers at once. There are many ships in Ithaca both old and new; I will run my eye over them for you and will choose the best; we will get her ready and will put out to sea without delay."

Thus spoke Minerva daughter of Jove, and Telemachus lost no time in doing as the goddess told him. He went moodily home, and found the suitors flaying goats and singeing pigs in the outer court. Antinous came up to him at once and laughed as he took his hand in his own, saying, "Telemachus, my fine fire-eater, bear no more ill blood neither in word nor deed, but eat and drink with us as you used to do. The Achaeans will find you in everything—a ship and a picked crew to boot—so that you can set sail for Pylos at once and get news of your noble father."

"Antinous," answered Telemachus, "I cannot eat in peace, nor take pleasure of any kind with such men as you are. Was it not enough that you should waste so much good property of mine while I was yet a boy? Now that I am older and know more about it, I am also stronger, and whether here among this people, or by going to Pylos, I will do you all the harm I can. I shall go, and my going will not be in vain—though, thanks to you suitors, I have neither ship nor crew of my own, and must be passenger not captain."

As he spoke he snatched his hand from that of Antinous. Meanwhile the others went on getting dinner ready about the buildings, {21} jeering at him tauntingly as they did so.

"Telemachus," said one youngster, "means to be the death of us; I suppose he thinks he can bring friends to help him from Pylos, or again from Sparta, where he seems bent on going. Or will he go to Ephyra as well, for poison to put in our wine and kill us?"

Another said, "Perhaps if Telemachus goes on board ship, he will be like his father and perish far from his friends. In this case we should have plenty to do, for we could then divide up his property amongst us: as for the house we can let his mother and the man who marries her have that."

This was how they talked. But Telemachus went down into the lofty and spacious store-room where his father's treasure of gold and bronze lay heaped up upon the floor, and where the linen and spare clothes were kept in open chests. Here, too, there was a store of fragrant olive oil, while casks of old, well-ripened wine, unblended and fit for a god to drink, were ranged against the wall in case Ulysses should come home again after all. The room was closed with well-made doors opening in the middle; moreover the faithful old house-keeper Euryclea, daughter of Ops the son of Pisenor, was in charge of everything both night and day. Telemachus called her to the store-room and said:

"Nurse, draw me off some of the best wine you have, after what you are keeping for my father's own drinking, in case, poor man, he should escape death, and find his way home again after all. Let me have twelve jars, and see that they all have lids; also fill me some well-sewn leathern bags with barley meal—about twenty measures in all. Get these things put together at once, and say nothing about it. I will take everything away this evening as soon as my mother has gone upstairs for the night. I am going to Sparta and to Pylos to see if I can hear anything about the return of my dear father."

When Euryclea heard this she began to cry, and spoke fondly to him, saying, "My dear child, what ever can have put such notion as that into your head? Where in the world do you want to go to—you, who are the one hope of the house? Your poor father is dead and gone in some foreign country nobody knows where, and as soon as your back is turned these wicked ones here will be scheming to get you put out of the way, and will share all your possessions among themselves; stay where you are among your own people, and do not go wandering and worrying your life out on the barren ocean."

"Fear not, nurse," answered Telemachus, "my scheme is not without heaven's sanction; but swear that you will say nothing about all this to my mother, till I have been away some ten or twelve days, unless she hears of my having gone, and asks you; for I do not want her to spoil her beauty by crying."

The old woman swore most solemnly that she would not, and when she had completed her oath, she began drawing off the wine into jars, and getting the barley meal into the bags, while Telemachus went back to the suitors.

Then Minerva bethought her of another matter. She took his shape, and went round the town to each one of the crew, telling them to meet at the ship by sundown. She went also to Noemon son of Phronius, and asked him to let her have a ship—which he was very ready to do. When the sun had set and darkness was over all the land, she got the ship into the water, put all the tackle on board her that ships generally carry, and stationed her at the end of the harbour. Presently the crew came up, and the goddess spoke encouragingly to each of them.

Furthermore she went to the house of Ulysses, and threw the suitors into a deep slumber. She caused their drink to fuddle them, and made them drop their cups from their hands, so that instead of sitting over their wine, they went back into the town to sleep, with their eyes heavy and full of drowsiness. Then she took the form and voice of Mentor, and called Telemachus to come outside.

"Telemachus," said she, "the men are on board and at their oars, waiting for you to give your orders, so make haste and let us be off."

On this she led the way, while Telemachus followed in her steps. When they got to the ship they found the crew waiting by the water side, and Telemachus said, "Now my men, help me to get the stores on board; they are all put together in the cloister, and my mother does not know anything about it, nor any of the maid servants except one."

With these words he led the way and the others followed after. When they had brought the things as he told them, Telemachus went on board, Minerva going before him and taking her seat in the stern of the vessel, while Telemachus sat beside her. Then the men loosed the hawsers and took their places on the benches. Minerva sent them a fair wind from the West, {22} that whistled over the deep blue waves {23} whereon Telemachus told them to catch hold of the ropes and hoist sail, and they did as he told them. They set the mast in its socket in the cross plank, raised it, and made it fast with the forestays; then they hoisted their white sails aloft with ropes of twisted ox hide. As the sail bellied out with the wind, the ship flew through the deep blue water, and the foam hissed against her bows as she sped onward. Then they made all fast throughout the ship, filled the mixing bowls to the brim, and made drink offerings to the immortal gods that are from everlasting, but more particularly to the grey-eyed daughter of Jove.

BOOK III

Telemachus visits Nestor at Pylos.

Thus, then, the ship sped on her way through the watches of the night from dark till dawn, but as the sun was rising from the fair sea {24} into the firmament of heaven to shed light on mortals and immortals, they reached Pylos the city of Neleus. Now the people of Pylos were gathered on the sea shore to offer sacrifice of black bulls to Neptune lord of the Earthquake. There were nine guilds with five hundred men in each, and there were nine bulls to each guild. As they were eating the inward meats {25} and burning the thigh bones [on the embers] in the name of Neptune, Telemachus and his crew arrived, furled their sails, brought their ship to anchor, and went ashore.

Minerva led the way and Telemachus followed her. Presently she said, "Telemachus, you must not be in the least shy or nervous; you have taken this voyage to try and find out where your father is buried and how he came by his end; so go straight up to Nestor that we may see what he has got to tell us. Beg of him to speak the truth, and he will tell no lies, for he is an excellent person."

"But how, Mentor," replied Telemachus, "dare I go up to Nestor, and how am I to address him? I have never yet been used to holding long conversations with people, and am ashamed to begin questioning one who is so much older than myself."

"Some things, Telemachus," answered Minerva, "will be suggested to you by your own instinct, and heaven will prompt you further; for I am assured that the gods have been with you from the time of your birth until now."

She then went quickly on, and Telemachus followed in her steps till they reached the place where the guilds of the Pylian people were assembled. There they found Nestor sitting with his sons, while his company round him were busy getting dinner ready, and putting pieces of meat on to the spits {26} while other pieces were cooking. When they saw the strangers they crowded round them, took them by the hand and bade them take their places. Nestor's son Pisistratus at once offered his hand to each of them, and seated them on some soft sheepskins that were lying on the sands near his father and his brother Thrasymedes. Then he gave them their portions of the inward meats and poured wine for them into a golden cup, handing it to Minerva first, and saluting her at the same time.

"Offer a prayer, sir," said he, "to King Neptune, for it is his feast that you are joining; when you have duly prayed and made your drink offering, pass the cup to your friend that he may do so also. I doubt not that he too lifts his hands in prayer, for man cannot live without God in the world. Still he is younger than you are, and is much of an age with myself, so I will give you the precedence."

As he spoke he handed her the cup. Minerva thought it very right and proper of him to have given it to herself first; {27} she accordingly began praying heartily to Neptune. "O thou," she cried, "that encirclest the earth, vouchsafe to grant the prayers of thy servants that call upon thee. More especially we pray thee send down thy grace on Nestor and on his sons; thereafter also make the rest of the Pylian people some handsome return for the goodly hecatomb they are offering you. Lastly, grant Telemachus and myself a happy issue, in respect of the matter that has brought us in our ship to Pylos."

When she had thus made an end of praying, she handed the cup to Telemachus and he prayed likewise. By and by, when the outer meats were roasted and had been taken off the spits, the carvers gave every man his portion and they all made an excellent dinner. As soon as they had had enough to eat and drink, Nestor, knight of Gerene, began to speak.

"Now," said he, "that our guests have done their dinner, it will be best to ask them who they are. Who, then, sir strangers, are you, and from what port have you sailed? Are you traders? or do you sail the seas as rovers with your hand against every man, and every man's hand against you?"

Telemachus answered boldly, for Minerva had given him courage to ask about his father and get himself a good name.

"Nestor," said he, "son of Neleus, honour to the Achaean name, you ask whence we come, and I will tell you. We come from Ithaca under Neritum, {28} and the matter about which I would speak is of private not public import. I seek news of my unhappy father Ulysses, who is said to have sacked the town of Troy in company with yourself. We know what fate befell each one of the other heroes who fought at Troy, but as regards Ulysses heaven has hidden from us the knowledge even that he is dead at all, for no one can certify us in what place he perished, nor say whether he fell in battle on the mainland, or was lost at sea amid the waves of Amphitrite. Therefore I am suppliant at your knees, if haply you may be pleased to tell me of his melancholy end, whether you saw it with your own eyes, or heard it from some other traveller, for he was a man born to trouble. Do not soften things out of any pity for me, but tell me in all plainness exactly what you saw. If my brave father Ulysses ever did you loyal service, either by word or deed, when you Achaeans were harassed among the Trojans, bear it in mind now as in my favour and tell me truly all."

"My friend," answered Nestor, "you recall a time of much sorrow to my mind, for the brave Achaeans suffered much both at sea, while privateering under Achilles, and when fighting before the great city of king Priam. Our best men all of them fell there—Ajax, Achilles, Patroclus peer of gods in counsel, and my own dear son Antilochus, a man singularly fleet of foot and in fight valiant. But we suffered much more than this; what mortal tongue indeed could tell the whole story? Though you were to stay here and question me for five years, or even six, I could not tell you all that the Achaeans suffered, and you would turn homeward weary of my tale before it ended. Nine long years did we try every kind of stratagem, but the hand of heaven was against us; during all this time there was no one who could compare with your father in subtlety—if indeed you are his son—I can hardly believe my eyes—and you talk just like him too—no one would say that people of such different ages could speak so much alike. He and I never had any kind of difference from first to last neither in camp nor council, but in singleness of heart and purpose we advised the Argives how all might be ordered for the best.

"When, however, we had sacked the city of Priam, and were setting sail in our ships as heaven had dispersed us, then Jove saw fit to vex the Argives on their homeward voyage; for they had not all been either wise or understanding, and hence many came to a bad end through the displeasure of Jove's daughter Minerva, who brought about a quarrel between the two sons of Atreus.

"The sons of Atreus called a meeting which was not as it should be, for it was sunset and the Achaeans were heavy with wine. When they explained why they had called the people together, it seemed that Menelaus was for sailing homeward at once, and this displeased Agamemnon, who thought that we should wait till we had offered hecatombs to appease the anger of Minerva. Fool that he was, he might have known that he would not prevail with her, for when the gods have made up their minds they do not change them lightly. So the two stood bandying hard words, whereon the Achaeans sprang to their feet with a cry that rent the air, and were of two minds as to what they should do.

"That night we rested and nursed our anger, for Jove was hatching mischief against us. But in the morning some of us drew our ships into the water and put our goods with our women on board, while the rest, about half in number, stayed behind with Agamemnon. We—the other half—embarked and sailed; and the ships went well, for heaven had smoothed the sea. When we reached Tenedos we offered sacrifices to the gods, for we were longing to get home; cruel Jove, however, did not yet mean that we should do so, and raised a second quarrel in the course of which some among us turned their ships back again, and sailed away under Ulysses to make their peace with Agamemnon; but I, and all the ships that were with me pressed forward, for I saw that mischief was brewing. The son of Tydeus went on also with me, and his crews with him. Later on Menelaus joined us at Lesbos, and found us making up our minds about our course—for we did not know whether to go outside Chios by the island of Psyra, keeping this to our left, or inside Chios, over against the stormy headland of Mimas. So we asked heaven for a sign, and were shown one to the effect that we should be soonest out of danger if we headed our ships across the open sea to Euboea. This we therefore did, and a fair wind sprang up which gave us a quick passage during the night to Geraestus, {29} where we offered many sacrifices to Neptune for having helped us so far on our way. Four days later Diomed and his men stationed their ships in Argos, but I held on for Pylos, and the wind never fell light from the day when heaven first made it fair for me.

"Therefore, my dear young friend, I returned without hearing anything about the others. I know neither who got home safely nor who were lost but, as in duty bound, I will give you without reserve the reports that have reached me since I have been here in my own house. They say the Myrmidons returned home safely under Achilles' son Neoptolemus; so also did the valiant son of Poias, Philoctetes. Idomeneus, again, lost no men at sea, and all his followers who escaped death in the field got safe home with him to Crete. No matter how far out of the world you live, you will have heard of Agamemnon and the bad end he came to at the hands of Aegisthus—and a fearful reckoning did Aegisthus presently pay. See what a good thing it is for a man to leave a son behind him to do as Orestes did, who killed false Aegisthus the murderer of his noble father. You too, then—for you are a tall smart-looking fellow—show your mettle and make yourself a name in story."

"Nestor son of Neleus," answered Telemachus, "honour to the Achaean name, the Achaeans applaud Orestes and his name will live through all time for he has avenged his father nobly. Would that heaven might grant me to do like vengeance on the insolence of the wicked suitors, who are ill treating me and plotting my ruin; but the gods have no such happiness in store for me and for my father, so we must bear it as best we may."

"My friend," said Nestor, "now that you remind me, I remember to have heard that your mother has many suitors, who are ill disposed towards you and are making havoc of your estate. Do you submit to this tamely, or are public feeling and the voice of heaven against you? Who knows but what Ulysses may come back after all, and pay these scoundrels in full, either single-handed or with a force of Achaeans behind him? If Minerva were to take as great a liking to you as she did to Ulysses when we were fighting before Troy (for I never yet saw the gods so openly fond of any one as Minerva then was of your father), if she would take as good care of you as she did of him, these wooers would soon some of them forget their wooing."

Telemachus answered, "I can expect nothing of the kind; it would be far too much to hope for. I dare not let myself think of it. Even though the gods themselves willed it no such good fortune could befall me."

On this Minerva said, "Telemachus, what are you talking about? Heaven has a long arm if it is minded to save a man; and if it were me, I should not care how much I suffered before getting home, provided I could be safe when I was once there. I would rather this, than get home quickly, and then be killed in my own house as Agamemnon was by the treachery of Aegisthus and his wife. Still, death is certain, and when a man's hour is come, not even the gods can save him, no matter how fond they are of him."

"Mentor," answered Telemachus, "do not let us talk about it any more. There is no chance of my father's ever coming back; the gods have long since counselled his destruction. There is something else, however, about which I should like to ask Nestor, for he knows much more than any one else does. They say he has reigned for three generations so that it is like talking to an immortal. Tell me, therefore, Nestor, and tell me true; how did Agamemnon come to die in that way? What was Menelaus doing? And how came false Aegisthus to kill so far better a man than himself? Was Menelaus away from Achaean Argos, voyaging elsewhither among mankind, that Aegisthus took heart and killed Agamemnon?"

"I will tell you truly," answered Nestor, "and indeed you have yourself divined how it all happened. If Menelaus when he got back from Troy had found Aegisthus still alive in his house, there would have been no barrow heaped up for him, not even when he was dead, but he would have been thrown outside the city to dogs and vultures, and not a woman would have mourned him, for he had done a deed of great wickedness; but we were over there, fighting hard at Troy, and Aegisthus, who was taking his ease quietly in the heart of Argos, cajoled Agamemnon's wife Clytemnestra with incessant flattery.

"At first she would have nothing to do with his wicked scheme, for she was of a good natural disposition; {30} moreover there was a bard with her, to whom Agamemnon had given strict orders on setting out for Troy, that he was to keep guard over his wife; but when heaven had counselled her destruction, Aegisthus carried this bard off to a desert island and left him there for crows and seagulls to batten upon—after which she went willingly enough to the house of Aegisthus.

Then he offered many burnt sacrifices to the gods, and decorated many temples with tapestries and gilding, for he had succeeded far beyond his expectations.

"Meanwhile Menelaus and I were on our way home from Troy, on good terms with one another. When we got to Sunium, which is the point of Athens, Apollo with his painless shafts killed Phrontis the steersman of Menelaus' ship (and never man knew better how to handle a vessel in rough weather) so that he died then and there with the helm in his hand, and Menelaus, though very anxious to press forward, had to wait in order to bury his comrade and give him his due funeral rites. Presently, when he too could put to sea again, and had sailed on as far as the Malean heads, Jove counselled evil against him and made it blow hard till the waves ran mountains high. Here he divided his fleet and took the one half towards Crete where the Cydonians dwell round about the waters of the river Iardanus. There is a high headland hereabouts stretching out into the sea from a place called Gortyn, and all along this part of the coast as far as Phaestus the sea runs high when there is a south wind blowing, but after Phaestus the coast is more protected, for a small headland can make a great shelter. Here this part of the fleet was driven on to the rocks and wrecked; but the crews just managed to save themselves. As for the other five ships, they were taken by winds and seas to Egypt, where Menelaus gathered much gold and substance among people of an alien speech. Meanwhile Aegisthus here at home plotted his evil deed. For seven years after he had killed Agamemnon he ruled in Mycene, and the people were obedient under him, but in the eighth year Orestes came back from Athens to be his bane, and killed the murderer of his father. Then he celebrated the funeral rites of his mother and of false Aegisthus by a banquet to the people of Argos, and on that very day Menelaus came home, {31} with as much treasure as his ships could carry.

"Take my advice then, and do not go travelling about for long so far from home, nor leave your property with such dangerous people in your house; they will eat up everything you have among them, and you will have been on a fool's errand. Still, I should advise you by all means to go and visit Menelaus, who has lately come off a voyage among such distant peoples as no man could ever hope to get back from, when the winds had once carried him so far out of his reckoning; even birds cannot fly the distance in a twelve-month, so vast and terrible are the seas that they must cross. Go to him, therefore, by sea, and take your own men with you; or if you would rather travel by land you can have a chariot, you can have horses, and here are my sons who can escort you to Lacedaemon where Menelaus lives. Beg of him to speak the truth, and he will tell you no lies, for he is an excellent person."

As he spoke the sun set and it came on dark, whereon Minerva said, "Sir, all that you have said is well; now, however, order the tongues of the victims to be cut, and mix wine that we may make drink-offerings to Neptune, and the other immortals, and then go to bed, for it is bed time. People should go away early and not keep late hours at a religious festival."

Thus spoke the daughter of Jove, and they obeyed her saying. Men servants poured water over the hands of the guests, while pages filled the mixing-bowls with wine and water, and handed it round after giving every man his drink offering; then they threw the tongues of the victims into the fire, and stood up to make their drink offerings. When they had made their offerings and had drunk each as much as he was minded, Minerva and Telemachus were for going on board their ship, but Nestor caught them up at once and stayed them.

"Heaven and the immortal gods," he exclaimed, "forbid that you should leave my house to go on board of a ship. Do you think I am so poor and short of clothes, or that I have so few cloaks and as to be unable to find comfortable beds both for myself and for my guests? Let me tell you I have store both of rugs and cloaks, and shall not permit the son of my old friend Ulysses to camp down on the deck of a ship—not while I live—nor yet will my sons after me, but they will keep open house as I have done."

Then Minerva answered, "Sir, you have spoken well, and it will be much better that Telemachus should do as you have said; he, therefore, shall return with you and sleep at your house, but I must go back to give orders to my crew, and keep them in good heart. I am the only older person among them; the rest are all young men of Telemachus' own age, who have taken this voyage out of friendship; so I must return to the ship and sleep there. Moreover to-morrow I must go to the Cauconians where I have a large sum of money long owing to me. As for Telemachus, now that he is your guest, send him to Lacedaemon in a chariot, and let one of your sons go with him. Be pleased to also provide him with your best and fleetest horses."

When she had thus spoken, she flew away in the form of an eagle, and all marvelled as they beheld it. Nestor was astonished, and took Telemachus by the hand. "My friend," said he, "I see that you are going to be a great hero some day, since the gods wait upon you thus while you are still so young. This can have been none other of those who dwell in heaven than Jove's redoubtable daughter, the Trito-born, who shewed such favour towards your brave father among the Argives. Holy queen," he continued, "vouchsafe to send down thy grace upon myself, my good wife, and my children. In return, I will offer you in sacrifice a broad-browed heifer of a year old, unbroken, and never yet brought by man under the yoke. I will gild her horns, and will offer her up to you in sacrifice."

Thus did he pray, and Minerva heard his prayer. He then led the way to his own house, followed by his sons and sons in law. When they had got there and had taken their places on the benches and seats, he mixed them a bowl of sweet wine that was eleven years old when the housekeeper took the lid off the jar that held it. As he mixed the wine, he prayed much and made drink offerings to Minerva, daughter of Aegis-bearing Jove. Then, when they had made their drink offerings and had drunk each as much as he was minded, the others went home to bed each in his own abode; but Nestor put Telemachus to sleep in the room that was over the gateway along with Pisistratus, who was the only unmarried son now left him. As for himself, he slept in an inner room of the house, with the queen his wife by his side.

Now when the child of morning rosy-fingered Dawn appeared, Nestor left his couch and took his seat on the benches of white and polished marble that stood in front of his house. Here aforetime sat Neleus, peer of gods in counsel, but he was now dead, and had gone to the house of Hades; so Nestor sat in his seat sceptre in hand, as guardian of the public weal. His sons as they left their rooms gathered round him, Echephron, Stratius, Perseus, Aretus, and Thrasymedes; the sixth son was Pisistratus, and when Telemachus joined them they made him sit with them. Nestor then addressed them.

"My sons," said he, "make haste to do as I shall bid you. I wish first and foremost to propitiate the great goddess Minerva, who manifested herself visibly to me during yesterday's festivities. Go, then, one or other of you to the plain, tell the stockman to look me out a heifer, and come on here with it at once. Another must go to Telemachus' ship, and invite all the crew, leaving two men only in charge of the vessel. Some one else will run and fetch Laerceus the goldsmith to gild the horns of the heifer. The rest, stay all of you where you are; tell the maids in the house to prepare an excellent dinner, and to fetch seats, and logs of wood for a burnt offering. Tell them also to bring me some clear spring water."

On this they hurried off on their several errands. The heifer was brought in from the plain, and Telemachus's crew came from the ship; the goldsmith brought the anvil, hammer, and tongs, with which he worked his gold, and Minerva herself came to accept the sacrifice. Nestor gave out the gold, and the smith gilded the horns of the heifer that the goddess might have pleasure in their beauty. Then Stratius and Echephron brought her in by the horns; Aretus fetched water from the house in a ewer that had a flower pattern on it, and in his other hand he held a basket of barley meal; sturdy Thrasymedes stood by with a sharp axe, ready to strike the heifer, while Perseus held a bucket. Then Nestor began with washing his hands and sprinkling the barley meal, and he offered many a prayer to Minerva as he threw a lock from the heifer's head upon the fire.

When they had done praying and sprinkling the barley meal {32} Thrasymedes dealt his blow, and brought the heifer down with a stroke that cut through the tendons at the base of her neck, whereon the daughters and daughters in law of Nestor, and his venerable wife Eurydice (she was eldest daughter to Clymenus) screamed with delight. Then they lifted the heifer's head from off the ground, and Pisistratus cut her throat. When she had done bleeding and was quite dead, they cut her up. They cut out the thigh bones all in due course, wrapped them round in two layers of fat, and set some pieces of raw meat on the top of them; then Nestor laid them upon the wood fire and poured wine over them, while the young men stood near him with five-pronged spits in their hands. When the thighs were burned and they had tasted the inward meats, they cut the rest of the meat up small, put the pieces on the spits and toasted them over the fire.

Meanwhile lovely Polycaste, Nestor's youngest daughter, washed Telemachus. When she had washed him and anointed him with oil, she brought him a fair mantle and shirt, {33} and he looked like a god as he came from the bath and took his seat by the side of Nestor. When the outer meats were done they drew them off the spits and sat down to dinner where they were waited upon by some worthy henchmen, who kept pouring them out their wine in cups of gold. As soon as they had had enough to eat and drink Nestor said, "Sons, put Telemachus's horses to the chariot that he may start at once."

Thus did he speak, and they did even as he had said, and yoked the fleet horses to the chariot. The housekeeper packed them up a provision of bread, wine, and sweet meats fit for the sons of princes. Then Telemachus got into the chariot, while Pisistratus gathered up the reins and took his seat beside him. He lashed the horses on and they flew forward nothing loth into the open country, leaving the high citadel of Pylos behind them. All that day did they travel, swaying the yoke upon their necks till the sun went down and darkness was over all the land. Then they reached Pherae where Diocles lived, who was son to Ortilochus and grandson to Alpheus. Here they passed the night and Diocles entertained them hospitably. When the child of morning, rosy-fingered Dawn, appeared, they again yoked their horses and drove out through the gateway under the echoing gatehouse. {34} Pisistratus lashed the horses on and they flew forward nothing loth; presently they came to the corn lands of the open country, and in the course of time completed their journey, so well did their steeds take them. {35}

Book IV

The visit to King Menelaus, who tells his story—meanwhile the suitors in Ithaca plot against Telemachus.

Now when the sun had set and darkness was over the land, they reached the low lying city of Lacedaemon, where they drove straight to the abode of Menelaus {36} [and found him in his own house, feasting with his many clansmen in honour of the wedding of his son, and also of his daughter, whom he was marrying to the son of that valiant warrior Achilles. He had given his consent and promised her to him while he was still at Troy, and now the gods were bringing the marriage about; so he was sending her with chariots and horses to the city of the Myrmidons over whom Achilles' son was reigning. For his only son he had found a bride from Sparta, {37} the daughter of Alector. This son, Megapenthes, was born to him of a bondwoman, for heaven vouchsafed Helen no more children after she had borne Hermione, who was fair as golden Venus herself.

So the neighbours and kinsmen of Menelaus were feasting and making merry in his house. There was a bard also to sing to them and play his lyre, while two tumblers went about performing in the midst of them when the man struck up with his tune.] {38}

Telemachus and the son of Nestor stayed their horses at the gate, whereon Eteoneus servant to Menelaus came out, and as soon as he saw them ran hurrying back into the house to tell his Master. He went close up to him and said, "Menelaus, there are some strangers come here, two men, who look like sons of Jove. What are we to do? Shall we take their horses out, or tell them to find friends elsewhere as they best can?"

Menelaus was very angry and said, "Eteoneus, son of Boethous, you never used to be a fool, but now you talk like a simpleton. Take their horses out, of course, and show the strangers in that they may have supper; you and I have staid often enough at other people's houses before we got back here, where heaven grant that we may rest in peace henceforward."

So Eteoneus bustled back and bade the other servants come with him. They took their sweating steeds from under the yoke, made them fast to the mangers, and gave them a feed of oats and barley mixed. Then they leaned the chariot against the end wall of the courtyard, and led the way into the house. Telemachus and Pisistratus were astonished when they saw it, for its splendour was as that of the sun and moon; then, when they had admired everything to their heart's content, they went into the bath room and washed themselves.

When the servants had washed them and anointed them with oil, they brought them woollen cloaks and shirts, and the two took their seats by the side of Menelaus. A maid-servant brought them water in a beautiful golden ewer, and poured it into a silver basin for them to wash their hands; and she drew a clean table beside them. An upper servant brought them bread, and offered them many good things of what there was in the house, while the carver fetched them plates of all manner of meats and set cups of gold by their side.

Menelaus then greeted them saying, "Fall to, and welcome; when you have done supper I shall ask who you are, for the lineage of such men as you cannot have been lost. You must be descended from a line of sceptre-bearing kings, for poor people do not have such sons as you are."

On this he handed them {39} a piece of fat roast loin, which had been set near him as being a prime part, and they laid their hands on the good things that were before them; as soon as they had had enough to eat and drink, Telemachus said to the son of Nestor, with his head so close that no one might hear, "Look, Pisistratus, man after my own heart, see the gleam of bronze and gold—of amber, {40} ivory, and silver. Everything is so splendid that it is like seeing the palace of Olympian Jove. I am lost in admiration."

Menelaus overheard him and said, "No one, my sons, can hold his own with Jove, for his house and everything about him is immortal; but among mortal men—well, there may be another who has as much wealth as I have, or there may not; but at all events I have travelled much and have undergone much hardship, for it was nearly eight years before I could get home with my fleet. I went to Cyprus, Phoenicia and the Egyptians; I went also to the Ethiopians, the Sidonians, and the Erembians, and to Libya where the lambs have horns as soon as they are born, and the sheep lamb down three times a year. Every one in that country, whether master or man, has plenty of cheese, meat, and good milk, for the ewes yield all the year round. But while I was travelling and getting great riches among these people, my brother was secretly and shockingly murdered through the perfidy of his wicked wife, so that I have no pleasure in being lord of all this wealth. Whoever your parents may be they must have told you about all this, and of my heavy loss in the ruin {41} of a stately mansion fully and magnificently furnished. Would that I had only a third of what I now have so that I had stayed at home, and all those were living who perished on the plain of Troy, far from Argos. I often grieve, as I sit here in my house, for one and all of them. At times I cry aloud for sorrow, but presently I leave off again, for crying is cold comfort and one soon tires of it. Yet grieve for these as I may, I do so for one man more than for them all. I cannot even think of him without loathing both food and sleep, so miserable does he make me, for no one of all the Achaeans worked so hard or risked so much as he did. He took nothing by it, and has left a legacy of sorrow to myself, for he has been gone a long time, and we know not whether he is alive or dead. His old father, his long-suffering wife Penelope, and his son Telemachus, whom he left behind him an infant in arms, are plunged in grief on his account."

Thus spoke Menelaus, and the heart of Telemachus yearned as he bethought him of his father. Tears fell from his eyes as he heard him thus mentioned, so that he held his cloak before his face with both hands. When Menelaus saw this he doubted whether to let him choose his own time for speaking, or to ask him at once and find what it was all about.

While he was thus in two minds Helen came down from her high vaulted and perfumed room, looking as lovely as Diana herself. Adraste brought her a seat, Alcippe a soft woollen rug while Phylo fetched her the silver work-box which Alcandra wife of Polybus had given her. Polybus lived in Egyptian Thebes, which is the richest city in the whole world; he gave Menelaus two baths, both of pure silver, two tripods, and ten talents of gold; besides all this, his wife gave Helen some beautiful presents, to wit, a golden distaff, and a silver work box that ran on wheels, with a gold band round the top of it. Phylo now placed this by her side, full of fine spun yarn, and a distaff charged with violet coloured wool was laid upon the top of it. Then Helen took her seat, put her feet upon the footstool, and began to question her husband. {42}

"Do we know, Menelaus," said she, "the names of these strangers who have come to visit us? Shall I guess right or wrong?—but I cannot help saying what I think. Never yet have I seen either man or woman so like somebody else (indeed when I look at him I hardly know what to think) as this young man is like Telemachus, whom Ulysses left as a baby behind him, when you Achaeans went to Troy with battle in your hearts, on account of my most shameless self."

"My dear wife," replied Menelaus, "I see the likeness just as you do. His hands and feet are just like Ulysses; so is his hair, with the shape of his head and the expression of his eyes. Moreover, when I was talking about

Ulysses, and saying how much he had suffered on my account, tears fell from his eyes, and he hid his face in his mantle."

Then Pisistratus said, "Menelaus, son of Atreus, you are right in thinking that this young man is Telemachus, but he is very modest, and is ashamed to come here and begin opening up discourse with one whose conversation is so divinely interesting as your own. My father, Nestor, sent me to escort him hither, for he wanted to know whether you could give him any counsel or suggestion. A son has always trouble at home when his father has gone away leaving him without supporters; and this is how Telemachus is now placed, for his father is absent, and there is no one among his own people to stand by him."

"Bless my heart," replied Menelaus, "then I am receiving a visit from the son of a very dear friend, who suffered much hardship for my sake. I had always hoped to entertain him with most marked distinction when heaven had granted us a safe return from beyond the seas. I should have founded a city for him in Argos, and built him a house. I should have made him leave Ithaca with his goods, his son, and all his people, and should have sacked for them some one of the neighbouring cities that are subject to me. We should thus have seen one another continually, and nothing but death could have interrupted so close and happy an intercourse. I suppose, however, that heaven grudged us such great good fortune, for it has prevented the poor fellow from ever getting home at all."

Thus did he speak, and his words set them all a weeping. Helen wept, Telemachus wept, and so did Menelaus, nor could Pisistratus keep his eyes from filling, when he remembered his dear brother Antilochus whom the son of bright Dawn had killed. Thereon he said to Menelaus,

"Sir, my father Nestor, when we used to talk about you at home, told me you were a person of rare and excellent understanding. If, then, it be possible, do as I would urge you. I am not fond of crying while I am getting my supper. Morning will come in due course, and in the forenoon I care not how much I cry for those that are dead and gone. This is all we can do for the poor things. We can only shave our heads for them and wring the tears from our cheeks. I had a brother who died at Troy; he was by no means the worst man there; you are sure to have known him—his name was Antilochus; I never set eyes upon him myself, but they say that he was singularly fleet of foot and in fight valiant."

"Your discretion, my friend," answered Menelaus, "is beyond your years. It is plain you take after your father. One can soon see when a man is son to one whom heaven has blessed both as regards wife and offspring—and it has blessed Nestor from first to last all his days, giving him a green old age in his own house, with sons about him who are both well disposed and valiant. We will put an end therefore to all this weeping, and attend to our supper again. Let water be poured over our hands. Telemachus and I can talk with one another fully in the morning."

On this Asphalion, one of the servants, poured water over their hands and they laid their hands on the good things that were before them.

Then Jove's daughter Helen bethought her of another matter. She drugged the wine with an herb that banishes all care, sorrow, and ill humour. Whoever drinks wine thus drugged cannot shed a single tear all the rest of the day, not even though his father and mother both of them drop down dead, or he sees a brother or a son hewn in pieces before his very eyes. This drug, of such sovereign power and virtue, had been given to Helen by Polydamna wife of Thon, a woman of Egypt, where there grow all sorts of herbs, some good to put into the mixing bowl and others poisonous. Moreover, every one in the whole country is a skilled physician, for they are of the race of Paeeon. When Helen had put this drug in the bowl, and had told the servants to serve the wine round, she said:

"Menelaus, son of Atreus, and you my good friends, sons of honourable men (which is as Jove wills, for he is the giver both of good and evil, and can do what he chooses), feast here as you will, and listen while I tell you a tale in season. I cannot indeed name every single one of the exploits of Ulysses, but I can say what he did when he was before Troy, and you Achaeans were in all sorts of difficulties. He covered himself with wounds and bruises, dressed himself all in rags, and entered the enemy's city looking like a menial or a beggar, and quite different from what he did when he was among his own people. In this disguise he entered the city of Troy, and no one said anything to him. I alone recognised him and began to question him, but he was too cunning for me. When, however, I had washed and anointed him and had given him clothes, and after I had sworn a solemn oath not to betray him to the Trojans till he had got safely back to his own camp and to the ships, he told me all that the Achaeans meant to do. He killed many Trojans and got much information before he reached the Argive camp, for all which things the Trojan women made lamentation, but for my own part I was glad, for my heart was beginning to yearn after my home, and I was unhappy about the wrong that Venus had done me in taking me over there, away from my country, my girl, and my lawful wedded husband, who is indeed by no means deficient either in person or understanding."

Then Menelaus said, "All that you have been saying, my dear wife, is true. I have travelled much, and have had much to do with heroes, but I have never seen such another man as Ulysses. What endurance too, and what courage he displayed within the wooden horse, wherein all the bravest of the Argives were lying in wait to bring death and destruction upon the Trojans. {43} At that moment you came up to us; some god who wished well to the Trojans must have set you on to it and you had Deiphobus with you. Three times did you go all round our hiding place and pat it; you called our chiefs each by his own name, and mimicked all our wives—Diomed, Ulysses, and I from our seats inside heard what a noise you made. Diomed and I could not make up our minds whether to spring out then and there, or to answer you from inside, but Ulysses held us all in check, so we sat quite still, all except Anticlus, who was beginning to answer you, when Ulysses clapped his two brawny hands over his mouth, and kept them there. It was this that saved us all, for he muzzled Anticlus till Minerva took you away again."

"How sad," exclaimed Telemachus, "that all this was of no avail to save him, nor yet his own iron courage. But now, sir, be pleased to send us all to bed, that we may lie down and enjoy the blessed boon of sleep."

On this Helen told the maid servants to set beds in the room that was in the gatehouse, and to make them with good red rugs, and spread coverlets on the top of them with woollen cloaks for the guests to wear. So the maids went out, carrying a torch, and made the beds, to which a man-servant presently conducted the strangers. Thus, then, did Telemachus and Pisistratus sleep there in the forecourt, while the son of Atreus lay in an inner room with lovely Helen by his side.

When the child of morning, rosy-fingered Dawn appeared, Menelaus rose and dressed himself. He bound his sandals on to his comely feet, girded his sword about his shoulders, and left his room looking like an immortal god. Then, taking a seat near Telemachus he said:

"And what, Telemachus, has led you to take this long sea voyage to Lacedaemon? Are you on public, or private business? Tell me all about it."

"I have come, sir," replied Telemachus, "to see if you can tell me anything about my father. I am being eaten out of house and home; my fair estate is being wasted, and my house is full of miscreants who keep killing great numbers of my sheep and oxen, on the pretence of paying their addresses to my mother. Therefore, I am suppliant at your knees if haply you may tell me about my father's melancholy end, whether you saw it with your own eyes, or heard it from some other traveller; for he was a man born to trouble. Do not soften things out of any pity for myself, but tell me in all plainness exactly what you saw. If my brave father Ulysses ever did you loyal service either by word or deed, when you Achaeans were harassed by the Trojans, bear it in mind now as in my favour and tell me truly all."

Menelaus on hearing this was very much shocked. "So," he exclaimed, "these cowards would usurp a brave man's bed? A hind might as well lay her new born young in the lair of a lion, and then go off to feed in the forest or in some grassy dell: the lion when he comes back to his lair will make short work with the pair of them—and so will Ulysses with these suitors. By father Jove, Minerva, and Apollo, if Ulysses is still the man that he was when he wrestled with Philomeleides in Lesbos, and threw him so heavily that all the Achaeans cheered him—if he is still such and were to come near these suitors, they would have a short shrift and a sorry wedding. As regards your questions, however, I will not prevaricate nor deceive you, but will tell you without concealment all that the old man of the sea told me.

"I was trying to come on here, but the gods detained me in Egypt, for my hecatombs had not given them full satisfaction, and the gods are very strict about having their dues. Now off Egypt, about as far as a ship can sail in a day with a good stiff breeze behind her, there is an island called Pharos—it has a good harbour from which vessels can get out into open sea when they have taken in water—and here the gods becalmed me twenty days without so much as a breath of fair wind to help me forward. We should have run clean out of provisions and my men would have starved, if a goddess had not taken pity upon me and saved me in the person of Idothea, daughter to Proteus, the old man of the sea, for she had taken a great fancy to me.

"She came to me one day when I was by myself, as I often was, for the men used to go with their barbed hooks, all over the island in the hope of catching a fish or two to save them from the pangs of hunger. 'Stranger,' said she, 'it seems to me that you like starving in this way—at any rate it does not greatly trouble you, for you stick here day after day, without even trying to get away though your men are dying by inches.'

"'Let me tell you,' said I, 'whichever of the goddesses you may happen to be, that I am not staying here of my own accord, but must have offended the gods that live in heaven. Tell me, therefore, for the gods know everything, which of the immortals it is that is hindering me in this way, and tell me also how I may sail the sea so as to reach my home.'

"'Stranger,' replied she, 'I will make it all quite clear to you. There is an old immortal who lives under the sea hereabouts and whose name is Proteus. He is an Egyptian, and people say he is my father; he is Neptune's head man and knows every inch of ground all over the bottom of the sea. If you can snare him and hold him tight, he will tell you about your voyage, what courses you are to take, and how you are to sail the sea so as to reach your home. He will also tell you, if you so will, all that has been going on at your house both good and bad, while you have been away on your long and dangerous journey.'

"'Can you show me,' said I, 'some stratagem by means of which I may catch this old god without his suspecting it and finding me out? For a god is not easily caught—not by a mortal man.'

"'Stranger,' said she, 'I will make it all quite clear to you. About the time when the sun shall have reached mid heaven, the old man of the sea comes up from under the waves, heralded by the West wind that furs the water over his head. As soon as he has come up he lies down, and goes to sleep in a great sea cave, where the seals—Halosydne's chickens as they call them—come up also from the grey sea, and go to sleep in shoals all round him; and a very strong and fish-like smell do they bring with them. {44} Early to-morrow morning I will take you to this place and will lay you in ambush. Pick out, therefore, the three best men you have in your fleet, and I will tell you all the tricks that the old man will play you.

"'First he will look over all his seals, and count them; then, when he has seen them and tallied them on his five fingers, he will go to sleep among them, as a shepherd among his sheep. The moment you see that he is asleep seize him; put forth all your strength and hold him fast, for he will do his very utmost to get away from you. He will turn himself into every kind of creature that goes upon the earth, and will become also both fire and water; but you must hold him fast and grip him tighter and tighter, till he begins to talk to you and comes back to what he was when you saw him go to sleep; then you may slacken your hold and let him go; and you can ask him which of the gods it is that is angry with you, and what you must do to reach your home over the seas.'

"Having so said she dived under the waves, whereon I turned back to the place where my ships were ranged upon the shore; and my heart was clouded with care as I went along. When I reached my ship we got supper ready, for night was falling, and camped down upon the beach.

"When the child of morning rosy-fingered Dawn appeared, I took the three men on whose prowess of all kinds I could most rely, and went along by the sea-side, praying heartily to heaven. Meanwhile the goddess fetched me up four seal skins from the bottom of the sea, all of them just skinned, for she meant playing a trick upon her father. Then she dug four pits for us to lie in, and sat down to wait till we should come up. When we were close to her, she made us lie down in the pits one after the other, and threw a seal skin over each of us. Our ambuscade would have been intolerable, for the stench of the fishy seals was most distressing {45}—who would go to bed with a sea monster if he could help it?—but here, too, the goddess helped us, and thought of something that gave us great relief, for she put some ambrosia under each man's nostrils, which was so fragrant that it killed the smell of the seals. {46}

"We waited the whole morning and made the best of it, watching the seals come up in hundreds to bask upon the sea shore, till at noon the old man of the sea came up too, and when he had found his fat seals he went over them and counted them. We were among the first he counted, and he never suspected any guile, but laid himself down to sleep as soon as he had done counting. Then we rushed upon him with a shout and seized him; on which he began at once with his old tricks, and changed himself first into a lion with a great mane; then all of a sudden he became a dragon, a leopard, a wild boar; the next moment he was running water, and then again directly he was a tree, but we stuck to him and never lost hold, till at last the cunning old creature became distressed, and said, 'Which of the gods was it, Son of Atreus, that hatched this plot with you for snaring me and seizing me against my will? What do you want?'

"'You know that yourself, old man,' I answered, 'you will gain nothing by trying to put me off. It is because I have been kept so long in this island, and see no sign of my being able to get away. I am losing all heart; tell me, then, for you gods know everything, which of the immortals it is that is hindering me, and tell me also how I may sail the sea so as to reach my home?'

"'Then,' he said, 'if you would finish your voyage and get home quickly, you must offer sacrifices to Jove and to the rest of the gods before embarking; for it is decreed that you shall not get back to your friends, and to your own house, till you have returned to the heaven-fed stream of Egypt, and offered holy hecatombs to the immortal gods that reign in heaven. When you have done this they will let you finish your voyage.'

"I was broken hearted when I heard that I must go back all that long and terrible voyage to Egypt; {47} nevertheless, I answered, 'I will do all, old man, that you have laid upon me; but now tell me, and tell me true, whether all the Achaeans whom Nestor and I left behind us when we set sail from Troy have got home safely, or whether any one of them came to a bad end either on board his own ship or among his friends when the days of his fighting were done.'

"'Son of Atreus,' he answered, 'why ask me? You had better not know what I can tell you, for your eyes will surely fill when you have heard my story. Many of those about whom you ask are dead and gone, but many still remain, and only two of the chief men among the Achaeans perished during their return home. As for what happened on the field of battle—you were there yourself. A third Achaean leader is still at sea, alive, but hindered from returning. Ajax was wrecked, for Neptune drove him on to the great rocks of Gyrae; nevertheless, he let him get safe out of the water, and in spite of all Minerva's hatred he would have escaped death, if he had not ruined himself by boasting. He said the gods could not drown him even though they had tried to do so, and when Neptune heard this large talk, he seized his trident in his two brawny hands, and split the rock of Gyrae in two pieces. The base remained where it was, but the part on which Ajax was sitting fell headlong into the sea and carried Ajax with it; so he drank salt water and was drowned.

"'Your brother and his ships escaped, for Juno protected him, but when he was just about to reach the high promontory of Malea, he was caught by a heavy gale which carried him out to sea again sorely against his will, and drove him to the foreland where Thyestes used to dwell, but where Aegisthus was then living. By and by, however, it seemed as though he was to return safely after all, for the gods backed the wind into its old quarter and they reached home; whereon Agamemnon kissed his native soil, and shed tears of joy at finding himself in his own country.

"'Now there was a watchman whom Aegisthus kept always on the watch, and to whom he had promised two talents of gold. This man had been looking out for a whole year to make sure that Agamemnon did not give him the slip and prepare war; when, therefore, this man saw Agamemnon go by, he went and told Aegisthus, who at once began to lay a plot for him. He picked twenty of his bravest warriors and placed them in ambuscade on one side the cloister, while on the opposite side he prepared a banquet. Then he sent his chariots and horsemen to Agamemnon, and invited him to the feast, but he meant foul play. He got him there, all unsuspicious of the doom that was awaiting him, and killed him when the banquet was over as though he were butchering an ox in the shambles; not one of Agamemnon's followers was left alive, nor yet one of Aegisthus', but they were all killed there in the cloisters.'

"Thus spoke Proteus, and I was broken hearted as I heard him. I sat down upon the sands and wept; I felt as though I could no longer bear to live nor look upon the light of the sun. Presently, when I had had my fill of weeping and writhing upon the ground, the old man of the sea said, 'Son of Atreus, do not waste any more time in crying so bitterly; it can do no manner of good; find your way home as fast as ever you can, for Aegisthus may be still alive, and even though Orestes has been beforehand with you in killing him, you may yet come in for his funeral.'

"On this I took comfort in spite of all my sorrow, and said, 'I know, then, about these two; tell me, therefore, about the third man of whom you spoke; is he still alive, but at sea, and unable to get home? or is he dead? Tell me, no matter how much it may grieve me.'

"'The third man,' he answered, 'is Ulysses who dwells in Ithaca. I can see him in an island sorrowing bitterly in the house of the nymph Calypso, who is keeping him prisoner, and he cannot reach his home for he has no ships nor sailors to take him over the sea. As for your own end, Menelaus, you shall not die in Argos, but the gods will take you to the Elysian plain, which is at the ends of the world. There fair-haired Rhadamanthus reigns, and men lead an easier life than any where else in the world, for in Elysium there falls not rain, nor hail, nor snow, but Oceanus breathes ever with a West wind that sings softly from the sea, and gives fresh life to all men. This will happen to you because you have married Helen, and are Jove's son-in-law.'

"As he spoke he dived under the waves, whereon I turned back to the ships with my companions, and my heart was clouded with care as I went along. When we reached the ships we got supper ready, for night was falling, and camped down upon the beach. When the child of morning, rosy-fingered Dawn appeared, we drew our ships into the water, and put our masts and sails within them; then we went on board ourselves, took our seats on the benches, and smote the grey sea with our oars. I again stationed my ships in the heaven-fed stream of Egypt, and offered hecatombs that were full and sufficient. When I had thus appeased heaven's anger, I raised a barrow to the memory of Agamemnon that his name might live for ever, after which I had a quick passage home, for the gods sent me a fair wind.

"And now for yourself—stay here some ten or twelve days longer, and I will then speed you on your way. I will make you a noble present of a chariot and three horses. I will also give you a beautiful chalice that so long as you live you may think of me whenever you make a drink-offering to the immortal gods."

"Son of Atreus," replied Telemachus, "do not press me to stay longer; I should be contented to remain with you for another twelve months; I find your conversation so delightful that I should never once wish myself at home with my parents; but my crew whom I have left at Pylos are already impatient, and you are detaining me from them. As for any present you may be disposed to make me, I had rather that it should be a piece of plate. I will take no horses back with me to Ithaca, but will leave them to adorn your own stables, for you have much flat ground in your kingdom where lotus thrives, as also meadow-sweet and wheat and barley, and oats with their white and spreading ears; whereas in Ithaca we have neither open fields nor racecourses, and the country is more fit for goats than horses, and I like it the better for that. {48} None of our islands have much level ground, suitable for horses, and Ithaca least of all."

Menelaus smiled and took Telemachus's hand within his own. "What you say," said he, "shows that you come of good family. I both can, and will, make this exchange for you, by giving you the finest and most precious piece of plate in all my house. It is a mixing bowl by Vulcan's own hand, of pure silver, except the rim, which is inlaid with gold. Phaedimus, king of the Sidonians, gave it me in the course of a visit which I paid him when I returned thither on my homeward journey. I will make you a present of it."

Thus did they converse [and guests kept coming to the king's house. They brought sheep and wine, while their wives had put up bread for them to take with them; so they were busy cooking their dinners in the courts]. {49}

Meanwhile the suitors were throwing discs or aiming with spears at a mark on the levelled ground in front of Ulysses' house, and were behaving with all their old insolence. Antinous and Eurymachus, who were their ringleaders and much the foremost among them all, were sitting together when Noemon son of Phronius came up and said to Antinous,

"Have we any idea, Antinous, on what day Telemachus returns from Pylos? He has a ship of mine, and I want it, to cross over to Elis: I have twelve brood mares there with yearling mule foals by their side not yet broken in, and I want to bring one of them over here and break him."

They were astounded when they heard this, for they had made sure that Telemachus had not gone to the city of Neleus. They thought he was only away somewhere on the farms, and was with the sheep, or with the swineherd; so Antinous said, "When did he go? Tell me truly, and what young men did he take with him? Were they freemen or his own bondsmen—for he might manage that too? Tell me also, did you let him have the ship of your own free will because he asked you, or did he take it without your leave?"

"I lent it him," answered Noemon, "what else could I do when a man of his position said he was in a difficulty, and asked me to oblige him? I could not possibly refuse. As for those who went with him they were the best young men we have, and I saw Mentor go on board as captain—or some god who was exactly like him. I cannot understand it, for I saw Mentor here myself yesterday morning, and yet he was then setting out for Pylos."

Noemon then went back to his father's house, but Antinous and Eurymachus were very angry. They told the others to leave off playing, and to come and sit down along with themselves. When they came, Antinous son of Eupeithes spoke in anger. His heart was black with rage, and his eyes flashed fire as he said:

"Good heavens, this voyage of Telemachus is a very serious matter; we had made sure that it would come to nothing, but the young fellow has got away in spite of us, and with a picked crew too. He will be giving us trouble presently; may Jove take him before he is full grown. Find me a ship, therefore, with a crew of twenty men, and I will lie in wait for him in the straits between Ithaca and Samos; he will then rue the day that he set out to try and get news of his father."

Thus did he speak, and the others applauded his saying; they then all of them went inside the buildings.

It was not long ere Penelope came to know what the suitors were plotting; for a man servant, Medon, overheard them from outside the outer court as they were laying their schemes within, and went to tell his mistress. As he crossed the threshold of her room Penelope said: "Medon, what have the suitors sent you here for? Is it to tell the maids to leave their master's business and cook dinner for them? I wish they may neither woo nor dine henceforward, neither here nor anywhere else, but let this be the very last time, for the waste you all make of my son's estate. Did not your fathers tell you when you were children, how good Ulysses had been to them—never doing anything high-handed, nor speaking harshly to anybody? Kings may say things sometimes, and they may take a fancy to one man and dislike another, but Ulysses never did an unjust thing by anybody—which shows what bad hearts you have, and that there is no such thing as gratitude left in this world."

Then Medon said, "I wish, Madam, that this were all; but they are plotting something much more dreadful now—may heaven frustrate their design. They are going to try and murder Telemachus as he is coming home from Pylos and Lacedaemon, where he has been to get news of his father."

Then Penelope's heart sank within her, and for a long time she was speechless; her eyes filled with tears, and she could find no utterance. At last, however, she said, "Why did my son leave me? What business had he to go sailing off in ships that make long voyages over the ocean like sea-horses? Does he want to die without leaving any one behind him to keep up his name?"

"I do not know," answered Medon, "whether some god set him on to it, or whether he went on his own impulse to see if he could find out if his father was dead, or alive and on his way home."

Then he went downstairs again, leaving Penelope in an agony of grief. There were plenty of seats in the house, but she had no heart for sitting on any one of them; she could only fling herself on the floor of her own room and cry; whereon all the maids in the house, both old and young, gathered round her and began to cry too, till at last in a transport of sorrow she exclaimed,

"My dears, heaven has been pleased to try me with more affliction than any other woman of my age and country. First I lost my brave and lion-hearted husband, who had every good quality under heaven, and whose name was great over all Hellas and middle Argos, and now my darling son is at the mercy of the winds and waves, without my having heard one word about his leaving home. You hussies, there was not one of you would so much as think of giving me a call out of my bed, though you all of you very well knew when he was starting. If I had known he meant taking this voyage, he would have had to give it up, no matter how much he was bent upon it, or leave me a corpse behind him—one or other. Now, however, go some of you and call old Dolius, who was given me by my father on my marriage, and who is my gardener. Bid him go at once and tell everything to Laertes, who may be able to hit on some plan for enlisting public sympathy on our side, as against those who are trying to exterminate his own race and that of Ulysses."

Then the dear old nurse Euryclea said, "You may kill me, Madam, or let me live on in your house, whichever you please, but I will tell you the real truth. I knew all about it, and gave him everything he wanted in the way of bread and wine, but he made me take my solemn oath that I would not tell you anything for some ten or twelve days, unless you asked or happened to hear of his having gone, for he did not want you to spoil your beauty by crying. And now, Madam, wash your face, change your dress, and go upstairs with your maids to offer prayers to Minerva, daughter of Aegis-bearing Jove, for she can save him even though he be in the jaws of death. Do not trouble Laertes: he has trouble enough already. Besides, I cannot think that the gods hate the race of the son of Arceisius so much, but there will be a son left to come up after him, and inherit both the house and the fair fields that lie far all round it."

With these words she made her mistress leave off crying, and dried the tears from her eyes. Penelope washed her face, changed her dress, and went upstairs with her maids. She then put some bruised barley into a basket and began praying to Minerva.

"Hear me," she cried, "Daughter of Aegis-bearing Jove, unweariable. If ever Ulysses while he was here burned you fat thigh bones of sheep or heifer, bear it in mind now as in my favour, and save my darling son from the villainy of the suitors."

She cried aloud as she spoke, and the goddess heard her prayer; meanwhile the suitors were clamorous throughout the covered cloister, and one of them said:

"The queen is preparing for her marriage with one or other of us. Little does she dream that her son has now been doomed to die."

This was what they said, but they did not know what was going to happen. Then Antinous said, "Comrades, let there be no loud talking, lest some of it get carried inside. Let us be up and do that in silence, about which we are all of a mind."

He then chose twenty men, and they went down to their ship and to the sea side; they drew the vessel into the water and got her mast and sails inside her; they bound the oars to the thole-pins with twisted thongs of leather, all in due course, and spread the white sails aloft, while their fine servants brought them their armour. Then they made the ship fast a little way out, came on shore again, got their suppers, and waited till night should fall.

But Penelope lay in her own room upstairs unable to eat or drink, and wondering whether her brave son would escape, or be overpowered by the wicked suitors. Like a lioness caught in the toils with huntsmen hemming her in on every side she thought and thought till she sank into a slumber, and lay on her bed bereft of thought and motion.

Then Minerva bethought her of another matter, and made a vision in the likeness of Penelope's sister Iphthime daughter of Icarius who had married Eumelus and lived in Pherae. She told the vision to go to the house of Ulysses, and to make Penelope leave off crying, so it came into her room by the hole through which the thong went for pulling the door to, and hovered over her head saying,

"You are asleep, Penelope: the gods who live at ease will not suffer you to weep and be so sad. Your son has done them no wrong, so he will yet come back to you."

Penelope, who was sleeping sweetly at the gates of dreamland, answered, "Sister, why have you come here? You do not come very often, but I suppose that is because you live such a long way off. Am I, then, to leave off crying and refrain from all the sad thoughts that torture me? I, who have lost my brave and lion-hearted husband, who had every good quality under heaven, and whose name was great over all Hellas and middle Argos; and now my darling son has gone off on board of a ship—a foolish fellow who has never been used to roughing it, nor to going about among gatherings of men. I am even more anxious about him than about my husband; I am all in a tremble when I think of him, lest something should happen to him, either from the people among whom he has gone, or by sea, for he has many enemies who are plotting against him, and are bent on killing him before he can return home."

Then the vision said, "Take heart, and be not so much dismayed. There is one gone with him whom many a man would be glad enough to have stand by his side, I mean Minerva; it is she who has compassion upon you, and who has sent me to bear you this message."

"Then," said Penelope, "if you are a god or have been sent here by divine commission, tell me also about that other unhappy one—is he still alive, or is he already dead and in the house of Hades?"

And the vision said, "I shall not tell you for certain whether he is alive or dead, and there is no use in idle conversation."

Then it vanished through the thong-hole of the door and was dissipated into thin air; but Penelope rose from her sleep refreshed and comforted, so vivid had been her dream.

Meantime the suitors went on board and sailed their ways over the sea, intent on murdering Telemachus. Now there is a rocky islet called Asteris, of no great size, in mid channel between Ithaca and Samos, and there is a harbour on either side of it where a ship can lie. Here then the Achaeans placed themselves in ambush.

BOOK V

Calypso—Ulysses reaches Scheria on a raft.

And now, as Dawn rose from her couch beside Tithonus—harbinger of light alike to mortals and immortals—the gods met in council and with them, Jove the lord of thunder, who is their king. Thereon Minerva began to tell them of the many sufferings of Ulysses, for she pitied him away there in the house of the nymph Calypso.

"Father Jove," said she, "and all you other gods that live in everlasting bliss, I hope there may never be such a thing as a kind and well-disposed ruler any more, nor one who will govern equitably. I hope they will be all henceforth cruel and unjust, for there is not one of his subjects but has forgotten Ulysses, who ruled them as though he were their father. There he is, lying in great pain in an island where dwells the nymph Calypso, who will not let him go; and he cannot get back to his own country, for he can find neither ships nor sailors to take him over the sea. Furthermore, wicked people are now trying to murder his only son Telemachus, who is coming home from Pylos and Lacedaemon, where he has been to see if he can get news of his father."

"What, my dear, are you talking about?" replied her father, "did you not send him there yourself, because you thought it would help Ulysses to get home and punish the suitors? Besides, you are perfectly able to protect Telemachus, and to see him safely home again, while the suitors have to come hurry-skurrying back without having killed him."

When he had thus spoken, he said to his son Mercury, "Mercury, you are our messenger, go therefore and tell Calypso we have decreed that poor Ulysses is to return home. He is to be convoyed neither by gods nor men, but after a perilous voyage of twenty days upon a raft he is to reach fertile Scheria, {50} the land of the Phaeacians, who are near of kin to the gods, and will honour him as though he were one of ourselves. They will send him in a ship to his own country, and will give him more bronze and gold and raiment than he would have brought back from Troy, if he had had all his prize money and had got home without disaster. This is how we have settled that he shall return to his country and his friends."

Thus he spoke, and Mercury, guide and guardian, slayer of Argus, did as he was told. Forthwith he bound on his glittering golden sandals with which he could fly like the wind over land and sea. He took the wand with which he seals men's eyes in sleep or wakes them just as he pleases, and flew holding it in his hand over Pieria; then he swooped down through the firmament till he reached the level of the sea, whose waves he skimmed like a cormorant that flies fishing every hole and corner of the ocean, and drenching its thick plumage in the spray. He flew and flew over many a weary wave, but when at last he got to the island which was his journey's end, he left the sea and went on by land till he came to the cave where the nymph Calypso lived.

He found her at home. There was a large fire burning on the hearth, and one could smell from far the fragrant reek of burning cedar and sandal wood. As for herself, she was busy at her loom, shooting her golden shuttle through the warp and singing beautifully. Round her cave there was a thick wood of alder, poplar, and sweet smelling cypress trees, wherein all kinds of great birds had built their nests—owls, hawks, and chattering sea-crows that occupy their business in the waters. A vine loaded with grapes was trained and grew luxuriantly about the mouth of the cave; there were also four running rills of water in channels cut pretty close together, and turned hither and thither so as to irrigate the beds of violets and luscious herbage over which they flowed. {51} Even a god could not help being charmed with such a lovely spot, so Mercury stood still and looked at it; but when he had admired it sufficiently he went inside the cave.

Calypso knew him at once—for the gods all know each other, no matter how far they live from one another—but Ulysses was not within; he was on the sea-shore as usual, looking out upon the barren ocean with tears in his eyes, groaning and breaking his heart for sorrow. Calypso gave Mercury a seat and said: "Why have you come to see me, Mercury—honoured, and ever welcome—for you do not visit me often? Say what you want; I will do it for you at once if I can, and if it can be done at all; but come inside, and let me set refreshment before you."

As she spoke she drew a table loaded with ambrosia beside him and mixed him some red nectar, so Mercury ate and drank till he had had enough, and then said:

"We are speaking god and goddess to one another, and you ask me why I have come here, and I will tell you truly as you would have me do. Jove sent me; it was no doing of mine; who could possibly want to come all this way over the sea where there are no cities full of people to offer me sacrifices or choice hecatombs? Nevertheless I had to come, for none of us other gods can cross Jove, nor transgress his orders. He says that you have here the most ill-starred of all those who fought nine years before the city of King Priam and sailed home in the tenth year after having sacked it. On their way home they sinned against Minerva, {52} who raised both wind and waves against them, so that all his brave companions perished, and he alone was carried hither by wind and tide. Jove says that you are to let this man go at once, for it is decreed that he shall not perish here, far from his own people, but shall return to his house and country and see his friends again."

Calypso trembled with rage when she heard this, "You gods," she exclaimed, "ought to be ashamed of yourselves. You are always jealous and hate seeing a goddess take a fancy to a mortal man, and live with him in open matrimony. So when rosy-fingered Dawn made love to Orion, you precious gods were all of you furious till Diana went and killed him in Ortygia. So again when Ceres fell in love with Iasion, and yielded to him in a thrice-ploughed fallow field, Jove came to hear of it before so very long and killed Iasion with his thunderbolts. And now you are angry with me too because I have a man here. I found the poor creature sitting all alone astride of a keel, for Jove had struck his ship with lightning and sunk it in mid ocean, so that all his crew were drowned, while he himself was driven by wind and waves on to my island. I got fond of him and cherished him, and had set my heart on making him immortal, so that he should never grow old all his days; still I cannot cross Jove, nor bring his counsels to nothing; therefore, if he insists upon it, let the man go beyond the seas again; but I cannot send him anywhere myself for I have neither ships nor men who can take him. Nevertheless I will readily give him such advice, in all good faith, as will be likely to bring him safely to his own country."

"Then send him away," said Mercury, "or Jove will be angry with you and punish you".

On this he took his leave, and Calypso went out to look for Ulysses, for she had heard Jove's message. She found him sitting upon the beach with his eyes ever filled with tears, and dying of sheer home sickness; for he had got tired of Calypso, and though he was forced to sleep with her in the cave by night, it was she, not he, that would have it so. As for the day time, he spent it on the rocks and on the sea shore, weeping, crying aloud for his despair, and always looking out upon the sea. Calypso then went close up to him said:

"My poor fellow, you shall not stay here grieving and fretting your life out any longer. I am going to send you away of my own free will; so go, cut some beams of wood, and make yourself a large raft with an upper deck that it may carry you safely over the sea. I will put bread, wine, and water on board to save you from starving. I will also give you clothes, and will send you a fair wind to take you home, if the gods in heaven so will it—for they know more about these things, and can settle them better than I can."

Ulysses shuddered as he heard her. "Now goddess," he answered, "there is something behind all this; you cannot be really meaning to help me home when you bid me do such a dreadful thing as put to sea on a raft. Not even a well found ship with a fair wind could venture on such a distant voyage: nothing that you can say or do shall make me go on board a raft unless you first solemnly swear that you mean me no mischief."

Calypso smiled at this and caressed him with her hand: "You know a great deal," said she, "but you are quite wrong here. May heaven above and earth below be my witnesses, with the waters of the river Styx—and this is the most solemn oath which a blessed god can take—that I mean you no sort of harm, and am only advising you to do exactly what I should do myself in your place. I am dealing with you quite straightforwardly; my heart is not made of iron, and I am very sorry for you."

When she had thus spoken she led the way rapidly before him, and Ulysses followed in her steps; so the pair, goddess and man, went on and on till they came to Calypso's cave, where Ulysses took the seat that Mercury had just left. Calypso set meat and drink before him of the food that mortals eat; but her maids brought ambrosia and nectar for herself, and they laid their hands on the good things that were before them. When they had satisfied themselves with meat and drink, Calypso spoke, saying:

"Ulysses, noble son of Laertes, so you would start home to your own land at once? Good luck go with you, but if you could only know how much suffering is in store for you before you get back to your own country, you would stay where you are, keep house along with me, and let me make you immortal, no matter how anxious you may be to see this wife of yours, of whom you are thinking all the time day after day; yet I flatter myself that I am no whit less tall or well-looking than she is, for it is not to be expected that a mortal woman should compare in beauty with an immortal."

"Goddess," replied Ulysses, "do not be angry with me about this. I am quite aware that my wife Penelope is nothing like so tall or so beautiful as yourself. She is only a woman, whereas you are an immortal. Nevertheless, I want to get home, and can think of nothing else. If some god wrecks me when I am on the sea, I will bear it and make the best of it. I have had infinite trouble both by land and sea already, so let this go with the rest."

Presently the sun set and it became dark, whereon the pair retired into the inner part of the cave and went to bed.

When the child of morning rosy-fingered Dawn appeared, Ulysses put on his shirt and cloak, while the goddess wore a dress of a light gossamer fabric, very fine and graceful, with a beautiful golden girdle about her waist and a veil to cover her head. She at once set herself to think how she could speed Ulysses on his way. So she gave him a great bronze axe that suited his hands; it was sharpened on both sides, and had a beautiful olive-wood handle fitted firmly on to it. She also gave him a sharp adze, and then led the way to the far end of the island where the largest trees grew—alder, poplar and pine, that reached the sky—very dry and well seasoned, so as to sail light for him in the water. {53} Then, when she had shown him where the best trees grew, Calypso went home, leaving him to cut them, which he soon finished doing. He cut down twenty trees in all and adzed them smooth, squaring them by rule in good workmanlike fashion. Meanwhile Calypso came back with some augers, so he bored holes with them and fitted the timbers together with bolts and rivets. He made the raft as broad as a skilled shipwright makes the beam of a large vessel, and he fixed a deck on top of the ribs, and ran a gunwale all round it. He also made a mast with a yard arm, and a rudder to steer with. He fenced the raft all round with wicker hurdles as a protection against the waves, and then he threw on a quantity of wood. By and by Calypso brought him some linen to make the sails, and he made these too, excellently, making them fast with braces and sheets. Last of all, with the help of levers, he drew the raft down into the water.

In four days he had completed the whole work, and on the fifth Calypso sent him from the island after washing him and giving him some clean clothes. She gave him a goat skin full of black wine, and another larger one of water; she also gave him a wallet full of provisions, and found him in much good meat. Moreover, she made the wind fair and warm for him, and gladly did Ulysses spread his sail before it, while he sat and guided the raft skilfully by means of the rudder. He never closed his eyes, but kept them fixed on the Pleiads, on late-setting Bootes, and on the Bear—which men also call the wain, and which turns round and round where it is, facing Orion, and alone never dipping into the stream of Oceanus—for Calypso had told him to keep this to his left. Days seven and ten did he sail over the sea, and on the eighteenth the dim outlines of the mountains on the nearest part of the Phaeacian coast appeared, rising like a shield on the horizon.

But King Neptune, who was returning from the Ethiopians, caught sight of Ulysses a long way off, from the mountains of the Solymi. He could see him sailing upon the sea, and it made him very angry, so he wagged his head and muttered to himself, saying, "Good heavens, so the gods have been changing their minds about Ulysses while I was away in Ethiopia, and now he is close to the land of the Phaeacians, where it is decreed that he shall escape from the calamities that have befallen him. Still, he shall have plenty of hardship yet before he has done with it."

Thereon he gathered his clouds together, grasped his trident, stirred it round in the sea, and roused the rage of every wind that blows till earth, sea, and sky were hidden in cloud, and night sprang forth out of the heavens. Winds from East, South, North, and West fell upon him all at the same time, and a tremendous sea got up, so that Ulysses' heart began to fail him. "Alas," he said to himself in his dismay, "what ever will become of me? I am afraid Calypso was right when she said I should have trouble by sea before I got back home. It is all coming true. How black is Jove making heaven with his clouds, and what a sea the winds are raising from every quarter at once. I am now safe to perish. Blest and thrice blest were those Danaans who fell before Troy in the cause of the sons of Atreus. Would that I had been killed on the day when the Trojans were pressing me so sorely about the dead body of Achilles, for then I should have had due burial and the Achaeans would have honoured my name; but now it seems that I shall come to a most pitiable end."

As he spoke a sea broke over him with such terrific fury that the raft reeled again, and he was carried overboard a long way off. He let go the helm, and the force of the hurricane was so great that it broke the mast half way up, and both sail and yard went over into the sea. For a long time Ulysses was under water, and it was all he could do to rise to the surface again, for the clothes Calypso had given him weighed him down; but at last he got his head above water and spat out the bitter brine that was running down his face in streams. In spite of all this, however, he did not lose sight of his raft, but swam as fast as he could towards it, got hold of it, and climbed on board again so as to escape drowning. The sea took the raft and tossed it about as Autumn winds whirl thistledown round and round upon a road. It was as though the South, North, East, and West winds were all playing battledore and shuttlecock with it at once.

When he was in this plight, Ino daughter of Cadmus, also called Leucothea, saw him. She had formerly been a mere mortal, but had been since raised to the rank of a marine goddess. Seeing in what great distress Ulysses now was, she had compassion upon him, and, rising like a sea-gull from the waves, took her seat upon the raft.

"My poor good man," said she, "why is Neptune so furiously angry with you? He is giving you a great deal of trouble, but for all his bluster he will not kill you. You seem to be a sensible person, do then as I bid you; strip, leave your raft to drive before the wind, and swim to the Phaeacian coast where better luck awaits you. And here, take my veil and put it round your chest; it is enchanted, and you can come to no harm so long as you wear it. As soon as you touch land take it off, throw it back as far as you can into the sea, and then go away again." With these words she took off her veil and gave it him. Then she dived down again like a sea-gull and vanished beneath the dark blue waters.

But Ulysses did not know what to think. "Alas," he said to himself in his dismay, "this is only some one or other of the gods who is luring me to ruin by advising me to quit my raft. At any rate I will not do so at present, for the land where she said I should be quit of all troubles seemed to be still a good way off. I know what I will do—I am sure it will be best—no matter what happens I will stick to the raft as long as her timbers hold together, but when the sea breaks her up I will swim for it; I do not see how I can do any better than this."

While he was thus in two minds, Neptune sent a terrible great wave that seemed to rear itself above his head till it broke right over the raft, which then went to pieces as though it were a heap of dry chaff tossed about by a whirlwind. Ulysses got astride of one plank and rode upon it as if he were on horseback; he then took off the clothes Calypso had given him, bound Ino's veil under his arms, and plunged into the sea—meaning to swim on shore. King Neptune watched him as he did so, and wagged his head, muttering to himself and saying, "There now, swim up and down as you best can till you fall in with well-to-do people. I do not think you will be able to say that I have let you off too lightly." On this he lashed his horses and drove to Aegae where his palace is.

But Minerva resolved to help Ulysses, so she bound the ways of all the winds except one, and made them lie quite still; but she roused a good stiff breeze from the North that should lay the waters till Ulysses reached the land of the Phaeacians where he would be safe.

Thereon he floated about for two nights and two days in the water, with a heavy swell on the sea and death staring him in the face; but when the third day broke, the wind fell and there was a dead calm without so much as a breath of air stirring. As he rose on the swell he looked eagerly ahead, and could see land quite near. Then, as children rejoice when their dear father begins to get better after having for a long time borne sore affliction sent him by some angry spirit, but the gods deliver him from evil, so was Ulysses thankful when he again saw land and trees, and swam on with all his strength that he might once more set foot upon dry ground. When, however, he got within earshot, he began to hear the surf thundering up against the rocks, for the swell still broke against them with a terrific roar. Everything was enveloped in spray; there were no harbours where a ship might ride, nor shelter of any kind, but only headlands, low-lying rocks, and mountain tops.

Ulysses' heart now began to fail him, and he said despairingly to himself, "Alas, Jove has let me see land after swimming so far that I had given up all hope, but I can find no landing place, for the coast is rocky and surf-beaten, the rocks are smooth and rise sheer from the sea, with deep water close under them so that I cannot climb out for want of foot hold. I am afraid some great wave will lift me off my legs and dash me against the rocks as I leave the water—which would give me a sorry landing. If, on the other hand, I swim further in search of some shelving beach or harbour, a hurricane may carry me out to sea again sorely against my will, or heaven may send some great monster of the deep to attack me; for Amphitrite breeds many such, and I know that Neptune is very angry with me."

While he was thus in two minds a wave caught him and took him with such force against the rocks that he would have been smashed and torn to pieces if Minerva had not shown him what to do. He caught hold of the rock with both hands and clung to it groaning with pain till the wave retired, so he was saved that time; but presently the wave came on again and carried him back with it far into the sea—tearing his hands as the suckers of a polypus are torn when some one plucks it from its bed, and the stones come up along with it—even so did the rocks tear the skin from his strong hands, and then the wave drew him deep down under the water.

Here poor Ulysses would have certainly perished even in spite of his own destiny, if Minerva had not helped him to keep his wits about him. He swam seaward again, beyond reach of the surf that was beating against the land, and at the same time he kept looking towards the shore to see if he could find some haven, or a spit that should take the waves aslant. By and by, as he swam on, he came to the mouth of a river, and here he thought would be the best place, for there were no rocks, and it afforded shelter from the wind. He felt that there was a current, so he prayed inwardly and said:

"Hear me, O King, whoever you may be, and save me from the anger of the sea-god Neptune, for I approach you prayerfully. Any one who has lost his way has at all times a claim even upon the gods, wherefore in my distress I draw near to your stream, and cling to the knees of your riverhood. Have mercy upon me, O king, for I declare myself your suppliant."

Then the god staid his stream and stilled the waves, making all calm before him, and bringing him safely into the mouth of the river. Here at last Ulysses' knees and strong hands failed him, for the sea had completely broken him. His body was all swollen, and his mouth and nostrils ran down like a river with sea-water, so that he could neither breathe nor speak, and lay swooning from sheer exhaustion; presently, when he had got his breath and came to himself again, he took off the scarf that Ino had given him and threw it back into the salt {54} stream of the river, whereon Ino received it into her hands from the wave that bore it towards her. Then he left the river, laid himself down among the rushes, and kissed the bounteous earth.

"Alas," he cried to himself in his dismay, "what ever will become of me, and how is it all to end? If I stay here upon the river bed through the long watches of the night, I am so exhausted that the bitter cold and damp may make an end of me—for towards sunrise there will be a keen wind blowing from off the river. If, on the other hand, I climb the hill side, find shelter in the woods, and sleep in some thicket, I may escape the cold and have a good night's rest, but some savage beast may take advantage of me and devour me."

In the end he deemed it best to take to the woods, and he found one upon some high ground not far from the water. There he crept beneath two shoots of olive that grew from a single stock—the one an ungrafted sucker, while the other had been grafted. No wind, however squally, could break through the cover they afforded, nor could the sun's rays pierce them, nor the rain get through them, so closely did they grow into one another. Ulysses crept under these and began to make himself a bed to lie on, for there was a great litter of dead leaves lying about—enough to make a covering for two or three men even in hard winter weather. He was glad enough to see this, so he laid himself down and heaped the leaves all round him. Then, as one who lives alone in the country, far from any neighbor, hides a brand as fire-seed in the ashes to save himself from having to get a light elsewhere, even so did Ulysses cover himself up with leaves; and Minerva shed a sweet sleep upon his eyes, closed his eyelids, and made him lose all memories of his sorrows.

BOOK VI

The meeting between Nausicaa and Ulysses.

So here Ulysses slept, overcome by sleep and toil; but Minerva went off to the country and city of the Phaeacians—a people who used to live in the fair town of Hypereia, near the lawless Cyclopes. Now the Cyclopes were stronger than they and plundered them, so their king Nausithous moved them thence and settled them in Scheria, far from all other people. He surrounded the city with a wall, built houses and temples, and divided the lands among his people; but he was dead and gone to the house of Hades, and King Alcinous, whose counsels were inspired of heaven, was now reigning. To his house, then, did Minerva hie in furtherance of the return of Ulysses.

She went straight to the beautifully decorated bedroom in which there slept a girl who was as lovely as a goddess, Nausicaa, daughter to King Alcinous. Two maid servants were sleeping near her, both very pretty, one on either side of the doorway, which was closed with well made folding doors. Minerva took the form of the famous sea captain Dymas's daughter, who was a bosom friend of Nausicaa and just her own age; then, coming up to the girl's bedside like a breath of wind, she hovered over her head and said:

"Nausicaa, what can your mother have been about, to have such a lazy daughter? Here are your clothes all lying in disorder, yet you are going to be married almost immediately, and should not only be well dressed yourself, but should find good clothes for those who attend you. This is the way to get yourself a good name, and to make your father and mother proud of you. Suppose, then, that we make tomorrow a washing day, and start at daybreak. I will come and help you so that you may have everything ready as soon as possible, for all the best young men among your own people are courting you, and you are not going to remain a maid much longer. Ask your father, therefore, to have a waggon and mules ready for us at daybreak, to take the rugs, robes, and girdles, and you can ride, too, which will be much pleasanter for you than walking, for the washing-cisterns are some way from the town."

When she had said this Minerva went away to Olympus, which they say is the everlasting home of the gods. Here no wind beats roughly, and neither rain nor snow can fall; but it abides in everlasting sunshine and in a great peacefulness of light, wherein the blessed gods are illumined for ever and ever. This was the place to which the goddess went when she had given instructions to the girl.

By and by morning came and woke Nausicaa, who began wondering about her dream; she therefore went to the other end of the house to tell her father and mother all about it, and found them in their own room. Her mother was sitting by the fireside spinning her purple yarn with her maids around her, and she happened to catch her father just as he was going out to attend a meeting of the town council, which the Phaeacian aldermen had convened. She stopped him and said:

"Papa dear, could you manage to let me have a good big waggon? I want to take all our dirty clothes to the river and wash them. You are the chief man here, so it is only right that you should have a clean shirt when you attend meetings of the council. Moreover, you have five sons at home, two of them married, while the other three are good looking bachelors; you know they always like to have clean linen when they go to a dance, and I have been thinking about all this."

She did not say a word about her own wedding, for she did not like to, but her father knew and said, "You shall have the mules, my love, and whatever else you have a mind for. Be off with you, and the men shall get you a good strong waggon with a body to it that will hold all your clothes."

On this he gave his orders to the servants, who got the waggon out, harnessed the mules, and put them to, while the girl brought the clothes down from the linen room and placed them on the waggon. Her mother prepared her a basket of provisions with all sorts of good things, and a goat skin full of wine; the girl now got into the waggon, and her mother gave her also a golden cruse of oil, that she and her women might anoint themselves. Then she took the whip and reins and lashed the mules on, whereon they set off, and their hoofs clattered on the road. They pulled without flagging, and carried not only Nausicaa and her wash of clothes, but the maids also who were with her.

When they reached the water side they went to the washing cisterns, through which there ran at all times enough pure water to wash any quantity of linen, no matter how dirty. Here they unharnessed the mules and turned them out to feed on the sweet juicy herbage that grew by the water side. They took the clothes out of the waggon, put them in the water, and vied with one another in treading them in the pits to get the dirt out. After they had washed them and got them quite clean, they laid them out by the sea side, where the waves had raised a high beach of shingle, and set about washing themselves and anointing themselves with olive oil. Then they got their dinner by the side of the stream, and waited for the sun to finish drying the clothes. When they had done dinner they threw off the veils that covered their heads and began to play at ball, while Nausicaa sang for them. As the huntress Diana goes forth upon the mountains of Taygetus or Erymanthus to hunt wild boars or deer, and the wood nymphs, daughters of Aegis-bearing Jove, take their sport along with her (then is Leto proud at seeing her daughter stand a full head taller than the others, and eclipse the loveliest amid a whole bevy of beauties), even so did the girl outshine her handmaids.

When it was time for them to start home, and they were folding the clothes and putting them into the waggon, Minerva began to consider how Ulysses should wake up and see the handsome girl who was to conduct him to the city of the Phaeacians. The girl, therefore, threw a ball at one of the maids, which missed her and fell into deep water. On this they all shouted, and the noise they made woke Ulysses, who sat up in his bed of leaves and began to wonder what it might all be.

"Alas," said he to himself, "what kind of people have I come amongst? Are they cruel, savage, and uncivilised, or hospitable and humane? I seem to hear the voices of young women, and they sound like those of the nymphs that haunt mountain tops, or springs of rivers and meadows of green grass. At any rate I am among a race of men and women. Let me try if I cannot manage to get a look at them."

As he said this he crept from under his bush, and broke off a bough covered with thick leaves to hide his nakedness. He looked like some lion of the wilderness that stalks about exulting in his strength and defying both wind and rain; his eyes glare as he prowls in quest of oxen, sheep, or deer, for he is famished, and will dare break even into a well fenced homestead, trying to get at the sheep—even such did Ulysses seem to the young women, as he drew near to them all naked as he was, for he was in great want. On seeing one so unkempt and so begrimed with salt water, the others scampered off along the spits that jutted out into the sea, but the daughter of Alcinous stood firm, for Minerva put courage into her heart and took away all fear from her. She stood right in front of Ulysses, and he doubted whether he should go up to her, throw himself at her feet, and embrace her knees as a suppliant, or stay where he was and entreat her to give him some clothes and show him the way to the town. In the end he deemed it best to entreat her from a distance in case the girl should take offence at his coming near enough to clasp her knees, so he addressed her in honeyed and persuasive language.

"O queen," he said, "I implore your aid—but tell me, are you a goddess or are you a mortal woman? If you are a goddess and dwell in heaven, I can only conjecture that you are Jove's daughter Diana, for your face and figure resemble none but hers; if on the other hand you are a mortal and live on earth, thrice happy are your father and mother—thrice happy, too, are your brothers and sisters; how proud and delighted they must feel when they see so fair a scion as yourself going out to a dance; most happy, however, of all will he be whose wedding gifts have been the richest, and who takes you to his own home. I never yet saw any one so beautiful, neither man nor woman, and am lost in admiration as I behold you. I can only compare you to a young palm tree which I saw when I was at Delos growing near the altar of Apollo—for I was there, too, with much people after me, when I was on that journey which has been the source of all my troubles. Never yet did such a young plant shoot out of the ground as that was, and I admired and wondered at it exactly as I now admire and wonder at yourself. I dare not clasp your knees, but I am in great distress; yesterday made the twentieth day that I had been tossing about upon the sea. The winds and waves have taken me all the way from the Ogygian island, {55} and now fate has flung me upon this coast that I may endure still further suffering; for I do not think that I have yet come to the end of it, but rather that heaven has still much evil in store for me.

"And now, O queen, have pity upon me, for you are the first person I have met, and I know no one else in this country. Show me the way to your town, and let me have anything that you may have brought hither to wrap your clothes in. May heaven grant you in all things your heart's desire—husband, house, and a happy, peaceful home; for there is nothing better in this world than that man and wife should be of one mind in a house. It discomfits their enemies, makes the hearts of their friends glad, and they themselves know more about it than any one."

To this Nausicaa answered, "Stranger, you appear to be a sensible, well-disposed person. There is no accounting for luck; Jove gives prosperity to rich and poor just as he chooses, so you must take what he has seen fit to send you, and make the best of it. Now, however, that you have come to this our country, you shall not want for clothes nor for anything else that a foreigner in distress may reasonably look for. I will show you the way to the town, and will tell you the name of our people; we are called Phaeacians, and I am daughter to Alcinous, in whom the whole power of the state is vested."

Then she called her maids and said, "Stay where you are, you girls. Can you not see a man without running away from him? Do you take him for a robber or a murderer? Neither he nor any one else can come here to do us Phaeacians any harm, for we are dear to the gods, and live apart on a land's end that juts into the sounding sea, and have nothing to do with any other people. This is only some poor man who has lost his way, and we must be kind to him, for strangers and foreigners in distress are under Jove's protection, and will take what they can get and be thankful; so, girls, give the poor fellow something to eat and drink, and wash him in the stream at some place that is sheltered from the wind."

On this the maids left off running away and began calling one another back. They made Ulysses sit down in the shelter as Nausicaa had told them, and brought him a shirt and cloak. They also brought him the little golden cruse of oil, and told him to go and wash in the stream. But Ulysses said, "Young women, please to stand a little on one side that I may wash the brine from my shoulders and anoint myself with oil, for it is long enough since my skin has had a drop of oil upon it. I cannot wash as long as you all keep standing there. I am ashamed to strip {56} before a number of good looking young women."

Then they stood on one side and went to tell the girl, while Ulysses washed himself in the stream and scrubbed the brine from his back and from his broad shoulders. When he had thoroughly washed himself, and had got the brine out of his hair, he anointed himself with oil, and put on the clothes which the girl had given him; Minerva then made him look taller and stronger than before, she also made the hair grow thick on the top of his head, and flow down in curls like hyacinth blossoms; she glorified him about the head and shoulders as a skilful workman who has studied art of all kinds under Vulcan and Minerva enriches a piece of silver plate by gilding it—and his work is full of beauty. Then he went and sat down a little way off upon the beach, looking quite young and handsome, and the girl gazed on him with admiration; then she said to her maids:

"Hush, my dears, for I want to say something. I believe the gods who live in heaven have sent this man to the Phaeacians. When I first saw him I thought him plain, but now his appearance is like that of the gods who dwell in heaven. I should like my future husband to be just such another as he is, if he would only stay here and not want to go away. However, give him something to eat and drink."

They did as they were told, and set food before Ulysses, who ate and drank ravenously, for it was long since he had had food of any kind. Meanwhile, Nausicaa bethought her of another matter. She got the linen folded and placed in the waggon, she then yoked the mules, and, as she took her seat, she called Ulysses:

"Stranger," said she, "rise and let us be going back to the town; I will introduce you at the house of my excellent father, where I can tell you that you will meet all the best people among the Phaeacians. But be sure and do as I bid you, for you seem to be a sensible person. As long as we are going past the fields and farm lands, follow briskly behind the waggon along with the maids and I will lead the way myself. Presently, however, we shall come to the town, where you will find a high wall running all round it, and a good harbour on either side with a narrow entrance into the city, and the ships will be drawn up by the road side, for every one has a place where his own ship can lie. You will see the market place with a temple of Neptune in the middle of it, and paved with large stones bedded in the earth. Here people deal in ship's gear of all kinds, such as cables and sails, and here, too, are the places where oars are made, for the Phaeacians are not a nation of archers; they know nothing about bows and arrows, but are a sea-faring folk, and pride themselves on their masts, oars, and ships, with which they travel far over the sea.

"I am afraid of the gossip and scandal that may be set on foot against me later on; for the people here are very ill-natured, and some low fellow, if he met us, might say, 'Who is this fine-looking stranger that is going about with Nausicaa? Where did she find him? I suppose she is going to marry him. Perhaps he is a vagabond sailor whom she has taken from some foreign vessel, for we have no neighbours; or some god has at last come down from heaven in answer to her prayers, and she is going to live with him all the rest of her life. It would be a good thing if she would take herself off and find a husband somewhere else, for she will not look at one of the many excellent young Phaeacians who are in love with her.' This is the kind of disparaging remark that would be made about me, and I could not complain, for I should myself be scandalised at seeing any other girl do the like, and go about with men in spite of everybody, while her father and mother were still alive, and without having been married in the face of all the world.

"If, therefore, you want my father to give you an escort and to help you home, do as I bid you; you will see a beautiful grove of poplars by the road side dedicated to Minerva; it has a well in it and a meadow all round it. Here my father has a field of rich garden ground, about as far from the town as a man's voice will carry. Sit down there and wait for a while till the rest of us can get into the town and reach my father's house. Then, when you think we must have done this, come into the town and ask the way to the house of my father Alcinous. You will have no difficulty in finding it; any child will point it out to you, for no one else in the whole town has anything like such a fine house as he has. When you have got past the gates and through the outer court, go right across the inner court till you come to my mother. You will find her sitting by the fire and spinning her purple wool by firelight. It is a fine sight to see her as she leans back against one of the bearing-posts with her maids all ranged behind her. Close to her seat stands that of my father, on which he sits and topes like an immortal god. Never mind him, but go up to my mother, and lay your hands upon her knees if you would get home quickly. If you can gain her over, you may hope to see your own country again, no matter how distant it may be."

So saying she lashed the mules with her whip and they left the river. The mules drew well, and their hoofs went up and down upon the road. She was careful not to go too fast for Ulysses and the maids who were following on foot along with the waggon, so she plied her whip with judgement. As the sun was going down they came to the sacred grove of Minerva, and there Ulysses sat down and prayed to the mighty daughter of Jove.

"Hear me," he cried, "daughter of Aegis-bearing Jove, unweariable, hear me now, for you gave no heed to my prayers when Neptune was wrecking me. Now, therefore, have pity upon me and grant that I may find friends and be hospitably received by the Phaeacians."

Thus did he pray, and Minerva heard his prayer, but she would not show herself to him openly, for she was afraid of her uncle Neptune, who was still furious in his endeavors to prevent Ulysses from getting home.

BOOK VII

Reception of Ulysses at the palace of King Alcinous.

Thus, then, did Ulysses wait and pray; but the girl drove on to the town. When she reached her father's house she drew up at the gateway, and her brothers—comely as the gods—gathered round her, took the mules out of the waggon, and carried the clothes into the house, while she went to her own room, where an old servant, Eurymedusa of Apeira, lit the fire for her. This old woman had been brought by sea from Apeira, and had been chosen as a prize for Alcinous because he was king over the Phaeacians, and the people obeyed him as though he were a god. {57} She had been nurse to Nausicaa, and had now lit the fire for her, and brought her supper for her into her own room.

Presently Ulysses got up to go towards the town; and Minerva shed a thick mist all round him to hide him in case any of the proud Phaeacians who met him should be rude to him, or ask him who he was. Then, as he was just entering the town, she came towards him in the likeness of a little girl carrying a pitcher. She stood right in front of him, and Ulysses said:

"My dear, will you be so kind as to show me the house of king Alcinous? I am an unfortunate foreigner in distress, and do not know one in your town and country."

Then Minerva said, "Yes, father stranger, I will show you the house you want, for Alcinous lives quite close to my own father. I will go before you and show the way, but say not a word as you go, and do not look at any man, nor ask him questions; for the people here cannot abide strangers, and do not like men who come from some other place. They are a sea-faring folk, and sail the seas by the grace of Neptune in ships that glide along like thought, or as a bird in the air."

On this she led the way, and Ulysses followed in her steps; but not one of the Phaeacians could see him as he passed through the city in the midst of them; for the great goddess Minerva in her good will towards him had hidden him in a thick cloud of darkness. He admired their harbours, ships, places of assembly, and the lofty walls of the city, which, with the palisade on top of them, were very striking, and when they reached the king's house Minerva said:

"This is the house, father stranger, which you would have me show you. You will find a number of great people sitting at table, but do not be afraid; go straight in, for the bolder a man is the more likely he is to carry his point, even though he is a stranger. First find the queen. Her name is Arete, and she comes of the same family as her husband Alcinous. They both descend originally from Neptune, who was father to Nausithous by Periboea, a woman of great beauty. Periboea was the youngest daughter of Eurymedon, who at one time reigned over the giants, but he ruined his ill-fated people and lost his own life to boot.

"Neptune, however, lay with his daughter, and she had a son by him, the great Nausithous, who reigned over the Phaeacians. Nausithous had two sons Rhexenor and Alcinous; {58} Apollo killed the first of them while he was still a bridegroom and without male issue; but he left a daughter Arete, whom Alcinous married, and honours as no other woman is honoured of all those that keep house along with their husbands.

"Thus she both was, and still is, respected beyond measure by her children, by Alcinous himself, and by the whole people, who look upon her as a goddess, and greet her whenever she goes about the city, for she is a thoroughly good woman both in head and heart, and when any women are friends of hers, she will help their husbands also to settle their disputes. If you can gain her good will, you may have every hope of seeing your friends again, and getting safely back to your home and country."

Then Minerva left Scheria and went away over the sea. She went to Marathon {59} and to the spacious streets of Athens, where she entered the abode of Erechtheus; but Ulysses went on to the house of Alcinous, and he pondered much as he paused a while before reaching the threshold of bronze, for the splendour of the palace was like that of the sun or moon. The walls on either side were of bronze from end to end, and the cornice was of blue enamel. The doors were gold, and hung on pillars of silver that rose from a floor of bronze, while the lintel was silver and the hook of the door was of gold.

On either side there stood gold and silver mastiffs which Vulcan, with his consummate skill, had fashioned expressly to keep watch over the palace of king Alcinous; so they were immortal and could never grow old. Seats were ranged all along the wall, here and there from one end to the other, with coverings of fine woven work which the women of the house had made. Here the chief persons of the Phaeacians used to sit and eat and drink, for there was abundance at all seasons; and there were golden figures of young men with lighted torches in their hands, raised on pedestals, to give light by night to those who were at table. There are {60} fifty maid servants in the house, some of whom are always grinding rich yellow grain at the mill, while others work at the loom, or sit and spin, and their shuttles go backwards and forwards like the fluttering of aspen leaves, while the linen is so closely woven that it will turn oil. As the Phaeacians are the best sailors in the world, so their women excel all others in weaving, for Minerva has taught them all manner of useful arts, and they are very intelligent.

Outside the gate of the outer court there is a large garden of about four acres with a wall all round it. It is full of beautiful trees—pears, pomegranates, and the most delicious apples. There are luscious figs also, and olives in full growth. The fruits never rot nor fail all the year round, neither winter nor summer, for the air is so soft that a new crop ripens before the old has dropped. Pear grows on pear, apple on apple, and fig on fig, and so also with the grapes, for there is an excellent vineyard: on the level ground of a part of this, the grapes are being made into raisins; in another part they are being gathered; some are being trodden in the wine tubs, others further on have shed their blossom and are beginning to show fruit, others again are just changing colour. In the furthest part of the ground there are beautifully arranged beds of flowers that are in bloom all the year round. Two streams go through it, the one turned in ducts throughout the whole garden, while the other is carried under the ground of the outer court to the house itself, and the town's people draw water from it. Such, then, were the splendours with which the gods had endowed the house of king Alcinous.

So here Ulysses stood for a while and looked about him, but when he had looked long enough he crossed the threshold and went within the precincts of the house. There he found all the chief people among the Phaeacians making their drink offerings to Mercury, which they always did the last thing before going away for the night. {61} He went straight through the court, still hidden by the cloak of darkness in which Minerva had enveloped him, till he reached Arete and King Alcinous; then he laid his hands upon the knees of the queen, and at that moment the miraculous darkness fell away from him and he became visible. Every one was speechless with surprise at seeing a man there, but Ulysses began at once with his petition.

"Queen Arete," he exclaimed, "daughter of great Rhexenor, in my distress I humbly pray you, as also your husband and these your guests (whom may heaven prosper with long life and happiness, and may they leave their possessions to their children, and all the honours conferred upon them by the state) to help me home to my own country as soon as possible; for I have been long in trouble and away from my friends."

Then he sat down on the hearth among the ashes and they all held their peace, till presently the old hero Echeneus, who was an excellent speaker and an elder among the Phaeacians, plainly and in all honesty addressed them thus:

"Alcinous," said he, "it is not creditable to you that a stranger should be seen sitting among the ashes of your hearth; every one is waiting to hear what you are about to say; tell him, then, to rise and take a seat on a stool inlaid with silver, and bid your servants mix some wine and water that we may make a drink offering to Jove the lord of thunder, who takes all well disposed suppliants under his protection; and let the housekeeper give him some supper, of whatever there may be in the house."

When Alcinous heard this he took Ulysses by the hand, raised him from the hearth, and bade him take the seat of Laodamas, who had been sitting beside him, and was his favourite son. A maid servant then brought him water in a beautiful golden ewer and poured it into a silver basin for him to wash his hands, and she drew a clean table beside him; an upper servant brought him bread and offered him many good things of what there was in the house, and Ulysses ate and drank. Then Alcinous said to one of the servants, "Pontonous, mix a cup of wine and hand it round that we may make drink-offerings to Jove the lord of thunder, who is the protector of all well-disposed suppliants."

Pontonous then mixed wine and water, and handed it round after giving every man his drink-offering. When they had made their offerings, and had drunk each as much as he was minded, Alcinous said:

"Aldermen and town councillors of the Phaeacians, hear my words. You have had your supper, so now go home to bed. To-morrow morning I shall invite a still larger number of aldermen, and will give a sacrificial banquet in honour of our guest; we can then discuss the question of his escort, and consider how we may at once send him back rejoicing to his own country without trouble or inconvenience to himself, no matter how distant it may be. We must see that he comes to no harm while on his homeward journey, but when he is once at home he will have to take the luck he was born with for better or worse like other people. It is possible, however, that the stranger is one of the immortals who has come down from heaven to visit us; but in this case the gods are departing from their usual practice, for hitherto they have made themselves perfectly clear to us when we have been offering them hecatombs. They come and sit at our feasts just like one of our selves, and if any solitary wayfarer happens to stumble upon some one or other of them, they affect no concealment, for we are as near of kin to the gods as the Cyclopes and the savage giants are." {62}

Then Ulysses said: "Pray, Alcinous, do not take any such notion into your head. I have nothing of the immortal about me, neither in body nor mind, and most resemble those among you who are the most afflicted. Indeed, were I to tell you all that heaven has seen fit to lay upon me, you would say that I was still worse off than they are. Nevertheless, let me sup in spite of sorrow, for an empty stomach is a very importunate thing, and thrusts itself on a man's notice no matter how dire is his distress. I am in great trouble, yet it insists that I shall eat and drink, bids me lay aside all memory of my sorrows and dwell only on the due replenishing of itself. As for yourselves, do as you propose, and at break of day set about helping me to get home. I shall be content to die if I may first once more behold my property, my bondsmen, and all the greatness of my house." {63}

Thus did he speak. Every one approved his saying, and agreed that he should have his escort inasmuch as he had spoken reasonably. Then when they had made their drink offerings, and had drunk each as much as he was minded they went home to bed every man in his own abode, leaving Ulysses in the cloister with Arete and Alcinous while the servants were taking the things away after supper. Arete was the first to speak, for she recognised the shirt, cloak, and good clothes that Ulysses was wearing, as the work of herself and of her maids; so she said, "Stranger, before we go any further, there is a question I should like to ask you. Who, and whence are you, and who gave you those clothes? Did you not say you had come here from beyond the sea?"

And Ulysses answered, "It would be a long story Madam, were I to relate in full the tale of my misfortunes, for the hand of heaven has been laid heavy upon me; but as regards your question, there is an island far away in the sea which is called 'the Ogygian.' Here dwells the cunning and powerful goddess Calypso, daughter of Atlas. She lives by herself far from all neighbours human or divine. Fortune, however, brought me to her hearth all desolate and alone, for Jove struck my ship with his thunderbolts, and broke it up in mid-ocean. My brave comrades were drowned every man of them, but I stuck to the keel and was carried hither and thither for the space of nine days, till at last during the darkness of the tenth night the gods brought me to the Ogygian island where the great goddess Calypso lives. She took me in and treated me with the utmost kindness; indeed she wanted to make me immortal that I might never grow old, but she could not persuade me to let her do so.

"I stayed with Calypso seven years straight on end, and watered the good clothes she gave me with my tears during the whole time; but at last when the eighth year came round she bade me depart of her own free will, either because Jove had told her she must, or because she had changed her mind. She sent me from her island on a raft, which she provisioned with abundance of bread and wine. Moreover she gave me good stout clothing, and sent me a wind that blew both warm and fair. Days seven and ten did I sail over the sea, and on the eighteenth I caught sight of the first outlines of the mountains upon your coast—and glad indeed was I to set eyes upon them. Nevertheless there was still much trouble in store for me, for at this point Neptune would let me go no further, and raised a great storm against me; the sea was so terribly high that I could no longer keep to my raft, which went to pieces under the fury of the gale, and I had to swim for it, till wind and current brought me to your shores.

"There I tried to land, but could not, for it was a bad place and the waves dashed me against the rocks, so I again took to the sea and swam on till I came to a river that seemed the most likely landing place, for there were no rocks and it was sheltered from the wind. Here, then, I got out of the water and gathered my senses together again. Night was coming on, so I left the river, and went into a thicket, where I covered myself all over with leaves, and presently heaven sent me off into a very deep sleep. Sick and sorry as I was I slept among the leaves all night, and through the next day till afternoon, when I woke as the sun was westering, and saw your daughter's maid servants playing upon the beach, and your daughter among them looking like a goddess. I besought her aid, and she proved to be of an excellent disposition, much more so than could be expected from so young a person—for young people are apt to be thoughtless. She gave me plenty of bread and wine, and when she had had me washed in the river she also gave me the clothes in which you see me. Now, therefore, though it has pained me to do so, I have told you the whole truth."

Then Alcinous said, "Stranger, it was very wrong of my daughter not to bring you on at once to my house along with the maids, seeing that she was the first person whose aid you asked."

"Pray do not scold her," replied Ulysses; "she is not to blame. She did tell me to follow along with the maids, but I was ashamed and afraid, for I thought you might perhaps be displeased if you saw me. Every human being is sometimes a little suspicious and irritable."

"Stranger," replied Alcinous, "I am not the kind of man to get angry about nothing; it is always better to be reasonable; but by Father Jove, Minerva, and Apollo, now that I see what kind of person you are, and how much you think as I do, I wish you would stay here, marry my daughter, and become my son-in-law. If you will stay I will give you a house and an estate, but no one (heaven forbid) shall keep you here against your own wish, and that you may be sure of this I will attend tomorrow to the matter of your escort. You can sleep {64} during the whole voyage if you like, and the men shall sail you over smooth waters either to your own home, or wherever you please, even though it be a long way further off than Euboea, which those of my people who saw it when they took yellow-haired Rhadamanthus to see Tityus the son of Gaia, tell me is the furthest of any place—and yet they did the whole voyage in a single day without distressing themselves, and came back again afterwards. You will thus see how much my ships excel all others, and what magnificent oarsmen my sailors are."

Then was Ulysses glad and prayed aloud saying, "Father Jove, grant that Alcinous may do all as he has said, for so he will win an imperishable name among mankind, and at the same time I shall return to my country."

Thus did they converse. Then Arete told her maids to set a bed in the room that was in the gatehouse, and make it with good red rugs, and to spread coverlets on the top of them with woollen cloaks for Ulysses to wear. The maids thereon went out with torches in their hands, and when they had made the bed they came up to Ulysses and said, "Rise, sir stranger, and come with us for your bed is ready," and glad indeed was he to go to his rest.

So Ulysses slept in a bed placed in a room over the echoing gateway; but Alcinous lay in the inner part of the house, with the queen his wife by his side.

BOOK VIII

Banquet in the house of Alcinous—the games.

Now when the child of morning, rosy-fingered Dawn, appeared, Alcinous and Ulysses both rose, and Alcinous led the way to the Phaeacian place of assembly, which was near the ships. When they got there they sat down side by side on a seat of polished stone, while Minerva took the form of one of Alcinous' servants, and went round the town in order to help Ulysses to get home. She went up to the citizens, man by man, and said, "Aldermen and town councillors of the Phaeacians, come to the assembly all of you and listen to the stranger who has just come off a long voyage to the house of King Alcinous; he looks like an immortal god."

With these words she made them all want to come, and they flocked to the assembly till seats and standing room were alike crowded. Every one was struck with the appearance of Ulysses, for Minerva had beautified him about the head and shoulders, making him look taller and stouter than he really was, that he might impress the Phaeacians favourably as being a very remarkable man, and might come off well in the many trials of skill to which they would challenge him. Then, when they were got together, Alcinous spoke:

"Hear me," said he, "aldermen and town councillors of the Phaeacians, that I may speak even as I am minded. This stranger, whoever he may be, has found his way to my house from somewhere or other either East or West. He wants an escort and wishes to have the matter settled. Let us then get one ready for him, as we have done for others before him; indeed, no one who ever yet came to my house has been able to complain of me for not speeding on his way soon enough. Let us draw a ship into the sea—one that has never yet made a voyage—and man her with two and fifty of our smartest young sailors. Then when you have made fast your oars each by his own seat, leave the ship and come to my house to prepare a feast. {65} I will find you in everything. I am giving these instructions to the young men who will form the crew, for as regards you aldermen and town councillors, you will join me in entertaining our guest in the cloisters. I can take no excuses, and we will have Demodocus to sing to us; for there is no bard like him whatever he may choose to sing about."

Alcinous then led the way, and the others followed after, while a servant went to fetch Demodocus. The fifty-two picked oarsmen went to the sea shore as they had been told, and when they got there they drew the ship into the water, got her mast and sails inside her, bound the oars to the thole-pins with twisted thongs of leather, all in due course, and spread the white sails aloft. They moored the vessel a little way out from land, and then came on shore and went to the house of King Alcinous. The out houses, {66} yards, and all the precincts were filled with crowds of men in great multitudes both old and young; and Alcinous killed them a dozen sheep, eight full grown pigs, and two oxen. These they skinned and dressed so as to provide a magnificent banquet.

A servant presently led in the famous bard Demodocus, whom the muse had dearly loved, but to whom she had given both good and evil, for though she had endowed him with a divine gift of song, she had robbed him of his eyesight. Pontonous set a seat for him among the guests, leaning it up against a bearing-post. He hung the lyre for him on a peg over his head, and showed him where he was to feel for it with his hands.

He also set a fair table with a basket of victuals by his side, and a cup of wine from which he might drink whenever he was so disposed.

The company then laid their hands upon the good things that were before them, but as soon as they had had enough to eat and drink, the muse inspired Demodocus to sing the feats of heroes, and more especially a matter that was then in the mouths of all men, to wit, the quarrel between Ulysses and Achilles, and the fierce words that they heaped on one another as they sat together at a banquet. But Agamemnon was glad when he heard his chieftains quarrelling with one another, for Apollo had foretold him this at Pytho when he crossed the stone floor to consult the oracle. Here was the beginning of the evil that by the will of Jove fell both upon Danaans and Trojans.

Thus sang the bard, but Ulysses drew his purple mantle over his head and covered his face, for he was ashamed to let the Phaeacians see that he was weeping. When the bard left off singing he wiped the tears from his eyes, uncovered his face, and, taking his cup, made a drink-offering to the gods; but when the Phaeacians pressed Demodocus to sing further, for they delighted in his lays, then Ulysses again drew his mantle over his head and wept bitterly. No one noticed his distress except Alcinous, who was sitting near him, and heard the heavy sighs that he was heaving. So he at once said, "Aldermen and town councillors of the Phaeacians, we have had enough now, both of the feast, and of the minstrelsy that is its due accompaniment; let us proceed therefore to the athletic sports, so that our guest on his return home may be able to tell his friends how much we surpass all other nations as boxers, wrestlers, jumpers, and runners."

With these words he led the way, and the others followed after. A servant hung Demodocus's lyre on its peg for him, led him out of the cloister, and set him on the same way as that along which all the chief men of the Phaeacians were going to see the sports; a crowd of several thousands of people followed them, and there were many excellent competitors for all the prizes. Acroneos, Ocyalus, Elatreus, Nauteus, Prymneus, Anchialus, Eretmeus, Ponteus, Proreus, Thoon, Anabesineus, and Amphialus son of Polyneus son of Tecton. There was also Euryalus son of Naubolus, who was like Mars himself, and was the best looking man among the Phaeacians except Laodamas. Three sons of Alcinous, Laodamas, Halios, and Clytoneus, competed also.

The foot races came first. The course was set out for them from the starting post, and they raised a dust upon the plain as they all flew forward at the same moment. Clytoneus came in first by a long way; he left every one else behind him by the length of the furrow that a couple of mules can plough in a fallow field. {67} They then turned to the painful art of wrestling, and here Euryalus proved to be the best man. Amphialus excelled all the others in jumping, while at throwing the disc there was no one who could approach Elatreus. Alcinous's son Laodamas was the best boxer, and he it was who presently said, when they had all been diverted with the games, "Let us ask the stranger whether he excels in any of these sports; he seems very powerfully built; his thighs, calves, hands, and neck are of prodigious strength, nor is he at all old, but he has suffered much lately, and there is nothing like the sea for making havoc with a man, no matter how strong he is."

"You are quite right, Laodamas," replied Euryalus, "go up to your guest and speak to him about it yourself."

When Laodamas heard this he made his way into the middle of the crowd and said to Ulysses, "I hope, Sir, that you will enter yourself for some one or other of our competitions if you are skilled in any of them—and you must have gone in for many a one before now. There is nothing that does any one so much credit all his life long as the showing himself a proper man with his hands and feet. Have a try therefore at something, and banish all sorrow from your mind. Your return home will not be long delayed, for the ship is already drawn into the water, and the crew is found."

Ulysses answered, "Laodamas, why do you taunt me in this way? my mind is set rather on cares than contests; I have been through infinite trouble, and am come among you now as a suppliant, praying your king and people to further me on my return home."

Then Euryalus reviled him outright and said, "I gather, then, that you are unskilled in any of the many sports that men generally delight in. I suppose you are one of those grasping traders that go about in ships as captains or merchants, and who think of nothing but of their outward freights and homeward cargoes. There does not seem to be much of the athlete about you."

"For shame, Sir," answered Ulysses, fiercely, "you are an insolent fellow—so true is it that the gods do not grace all men alike in speech, person, and understanding. One man may be of weak presence, but heaven has adorned this with such a good conversation that he charms every one who sees him; his honeyed moderation carries his hearers with him so that he is leader in all assemblies of his fellows, and wherever he goes he is looked up to. Another may be as handsome as a god, but his good looks are not crowned with discretion. This is your case. No god could make a finer looking fellow than you are, but you are a fool. Your ill-judged remarks have made me exceedingly angry, and you are quite mistaken, for I excel in a great many athletic exercises; indeed, so long as I had youth and strength, I was among the first athletes of the age. Now, however, I am worn out by labour and sorrow, for I have gone through much both on the field of battle and by the waves of the weary sea; still, in spite of all this I will compete, for your taunts have stung me to the quick."

So he hurried up without even taking his cloak off, and seized a disc, larger, more massive and much heavier than those used by the Phaeacians when disc-throwing among themselves. {68} Then, swinging it back, he threw it from his brawny hand, and it made a humming sound in the air as he did so. The Phaeacians quailed beneath the rushing of its flight as it sped gracefully from his hand, and flew beyond any mark that had been made yet. Minerva, in the form of a man, came and marked the place where it had fallen. "A blind man, Sir," said she, "could easily tell your mark by groping for it—it is so far ahead of any other. You may make your mind easy about this contest, for no Phaeacian can come near to such a throw as yours."

Ulysses was glad when he found he had a friend among the lookers-on, so he began to speak more pleasantly. "Young men," said he, "come up to that throw if you can, and I will throw another disc as heavy or even heavier. If anyone wants to have a bout with me let him come on, for I am exceedingly angry; I will box, wrestle, or run, I do not care what it is, with any man of you all except Laodamas, but not with him because I am his guest, and one cannot compete with one's own personal friend. At least I do not think it a prudent or a sensible thing for a guest to challenge his host's family at any game, especially when he is in a foreign country. He will cut the ground from under his own feet if he does; but I make no exception as regards any one else, for I want to have the matter out and know which is the best man. I am a good hand at every kind of athletic sport known among mankind. I am an excellent archer. In battle I am always the first to bring a man down with my arrow, no matter how many more are taking aim at him alongside of me. Philoctetes was the only man who could shoot better than I could when we Achaeans were before Troy and in practice. I far excel every one else in the whole world, of those who still eat bread upon the face of the earth, but I should not like to shoot against the mighty dead, such as Hercules, or Eurytus the Oechalian—men who could shoot against the gods themselves. This in fact was how Eurytus came prematurely by his end, for Apollo was angry with him and killed him because he challenged him as an archer. I can throw a dart farther than any one else can shoot an arrow. Running is the only point in respect of which I am afraid some of the Phaeacians might beat me, for I have been brought down very low at sea; my provisions ran short, and therefore I am still weak."

They all held their peace except King Alcinous, who began, "Sir, we have had much pleasure in hearing all that you have told us, from which I understand that you are willing to show your prowess, as having been displeased with some insolent remarks that have been made to you by one of our athletes, and which could never have been uttered by any one who knows how to talk with propriety. I hope you will apprehend my meaning, and will explain to any one of your chief men who may be dining with yourself and your family when you get home, that we have an hereditary aptitude for accomplishments of all kinds. We are not particularly remarkable for our boxing, nor yet as wrestlers, but we are singularly fleet of foot and are excellent sailors. We are extremely fond of good dinners, music, and dancing; we also like frequent changes of linen, warm baths, and good beds, so now, please, some of you who are the best dancers set about dancing, that our guest on his return home may be able to tell his friends how much we surpass all other nations as sailors, runners, dancers, and minstrels. Demodocus has left his lyre at my house, so run some one or other of you and fetch it for him."

On this a servant hurried off to bring the lyre from the king's house, and the nine men who had been chosen as stewards stood forward. It was their business to manage everything connected with the sports, so they made the ground smooth and marked a wide space for the dancers. Presently the servant came back with Demodocus's lyre, and he took his place in the midst of them, whereon the best young dancers in the town began to foot and trip it so nimbly that Ulysses was delighted with the merry twinkling of their feet.

Meanwhile the bard began to sing the loves of Mars and Venus, and how they first began their intrigue in the house of Vulcan. Mars made Venus many presents, and defiled King Vulcan's marriage bed, so the sun, who saw what they were about, told Vulcan. Vulcan was very angry when he heard such dreadful news, so he went to his smithy brooding mischief, got his great anvil into its place, and began to forge some chains which none could either unloose or break, so that they might stay there in that place. {69} When he had finished his snare he went into his bedroom and festooned the bed-posts all over with chains like cobwebs; he also let many hang down from the great beam of the ceiling. Not even a god could see them so fine and subtle were they. As soon as he had spread the chains all over the bed, he made as though he were setting out for the fair state of Lemnos, which of all places in the world was the one he was most fond of. But Mars kept no blind look out, and as soon as he saw him start, hurried off to his house, burning with love for Venus.

Now Venus was just come in from a visit to her father Jove, and was about sitting down when Mars came inside the house, and said as he took her hand in his own, "Let us go to the couch of Vulcan: he is not at home, but is gone off to Lemnos among the Sintians, whose speech is barbarous."

She was nothing loth, so they went to the couch to take their rest, whereon they were caught in the toils which cunning Vulcan had spread for them, and could neither get up nor stir hand or foot, but found too late that they were in a trap. Then Vulcan came up to them, for he had turned back before reaching Lemnos, when his scout the sun told him what was going on. He was in a furious passion, and stood in the vestibule making a dreadful noise as he shouted to all the gods.

"Father Jove," he cried, "and all you other blessed gods who live for ever, come here and see the ridiculous and disgraceful sight that I will show you. Jove's daughter Venus is always dishonouring me because I am lame. She is in love with Mars, who is handsome and clean built, whereas I am a cripple—but my parents are to blame for that, not I; they ought never to have begotten me. Come and see the pair together asleep on my bed. It makes me furious to look at them. They are very fond of one another, but I do not think they will lie there longer than they can help, nor do I think that they will sleep much; there, however, they shall stay till her father has repaid me the sum I gave him for his baggage of a daughter, who is fair but not honest."

On this the gods gathered to the house of Vulcan. Earth-encircling Neptune came, and Mercury the bringer of luck, and King Apollo, but the goddesses staid at home all of them for shame. Then the givers of all good things stood in the doorway, and the blessed gods roared with inextinguishable laughter, as they saw how cunning Vulcan had been, whereon one would turn towards his neighbour saying:

"Ill deeds do not prosper, and the weak confound the strong. See how limping Vulcan, lame as he is, has caught Mars who is the fleetest god in heaven; and now Mars will be cast in heavy damages."

Thus did they converse, but King Apollo said to Mercury, "Messenger Mercury, giver of good things, you would not care how strong the chains were, would you, if you could sleep with Venus?"

"King Apollo," answered Mercury, "I only wish I might get the chance, though there were three times as many chains—and you might look on, all of you, gods and goddesses, but I would sleep with her if I could."

The immortal gods burst out laughing as they heard him, but Neptune took it all seriously, and kept on imploring Vulcan to set Mars free again. "Let him go," he cried, "and I will undertake, as you require, that he shall pay you all the damages that are held reasonable among the immortal gods."

"Do not," replied Vulcan, "ask me to do this; a bad man's bond is bad security; what remedy could I enforce against you if Mars should go away and leave his debts behind him along with his chains?"

"Vulcan," said Neptune, "if Mars goes away without paying his damages, I will pay you myself." So Vulcan answered, "In this case I cannot and must not refuse you."

Thereon he loosed the bonds that bound them, and as soon as they were free they scampered off, Mars to Thrace and laughter-loving Venus to Cyprus and to Paphos, where is her grove and her altar fragrant with burnt offerings. Here the Graces bathed her, and anointed her with oil of ambrosia such as the immortal gods make use of, and they clothed her in raiment of the most enchanting beauty.

Thus sang the bard, and both Ulysses and the seafaring Phaeacians were charmed as they heard him.

Then Alcinous told Laodamas and Halius to dance alone, for there was no one to compete with them. So they took a red ball which Polybus had made for them, and one of them bent himself backwards and threw it up towards the clouds, while the other jumped from off the ground and caught it with ease before it came down again. When they had done throwing the ball straight up into the air they began to dance, and at the same time kept on throwing it backwards and forwards to one another, while all the young men in the ring applauded and made a great stamping with their feet. Then Ulysses said:

"King Alcinous, you said your people were the nimblest dancers in the world, and indeed they have proved themselves to be so. I was astonished as I saw them."

The king was delighted at this, and exclaimed to the Phaeacians, "Aldermen and town councillors, our guest seems to be a person of singular judgement; let us give him such proof of our hospitality as he may reasonably expect. There are twelve chief men among you, and counting myself there are thirteen; contribute, each of you, a clean cloak, a shirt, and a talent of fine gold; let us give him all this in a lump down at once, so that when he gets his supper he may do so with a light heart. As for Euryalus he will have to make a formal apology and a present too, for he has been rude."

Thus did he speak. The others all of them applauded his saying, and sent their servants to fetch the presents. Then Euryalus said, "King Alcinous, I will give the stranger all the satisfaction you require. He shall have my sword, which is of bronze, all but the hilt, which is of silver. I will also give him the scabbard of newly sawn ivory into which it fits. It will be worth a great deal to him."

As he spoke he placed the sword in the hands of Ulysses and said, "Good luck to you, father stranger; if anything has been said amiss may the winds blow it away with them, and may heaven grant you a safe return, for I understand you have been long away from home, and have gone through much hardship."

To which Ulysses answered, "Good luck to you too my friend, and may the gods grant you every happiness. I hope you will not miss the sword you have given me along with your apology."

With these words he girded the sword about his shoulders and towards sundown the presents began to make their appearance, as the servants of the donors kept bringing them to the house of King Alcinous; here his sons received them, and placed them under their mother's charge. Then Alcinous led the way to the house and bade his guests take their seats.

"Wife," said he, turning to Queen Arete, "Go, fetch the best chest we have, and put a clean cloak and shirt in it. Also, set a copper on the fire and heat some water; our guest will take a warm bath; see also to the careful packing of the presents that the noble Phaeacians have made him; he will thus better enjoy both his supper and the singing that will follow. I shall myself give him this golden goblet—which is of exquisite workmanship—that he may be reminded of me for the rest of his life whenever he makes a drink offering to Jove, or to any of the gods." {70}

Then Arete told her maids to set a large tripod upon the fire as fast as they could, whereon they set a tripod full of bath water on to a clear fire;

they threw on sticks to make it blaze, and the water became hot as the flame played about the belly of the tripod. {71} Meanwhile Arete brought a magnificent chest from her own room, and inside it she packed all the beautiful presents of gold and raiment which the Phaeacians had brought. Lastly she added a cloak and a good shirt from Alcinous, and said to Ulysses:

"See to the lid yourself, and have the whole bound round at once, for fear any one should rob you by the way when you are asleep in your ship." {72}

When Ulysses heard this he put the lid on the chest and made it fast with a bond that Circe had taught him. He had done so before an upper servant told him to come to the bath and wash himself. He was very glad of a warm bath, for he had had no one to wait upon him ever since he left the house of Calypso, who as long as he remained with her had taken as good care of him as though he had been a god. When the servants had done washing and anointing him with oil, and had given him a clean cloak and shirt, he left the bath room and joined the guests who were sitting over their wine. Lovely Nausicaa stood by one of the bearing-posts supporting the roof of the cloister, and admired him as she saw him pass. "Farewell stranger," said she, "do not forget me when you are safe at home again, for it is to me first that you owe a ransom for having saved your life."

And Ulysses said, "Nausicaa, daughter of great Alcinous, may Jove the mighty husband of Juno, grant that I may reach my home; so shall I bless you as my guardian angel all my days, for it was you who saved me."

When he had said this, he seated himself beside Alcinous. Supper was then served, and the wine was mixed for drinking. A servant led in the favourite bard Demodocus, and set him in the midst of the company, near one of the bearing-posts supporting the cloister, that he might lean against it. Then Ulysses cut off a piece of roast pork with plenty of fat (for there was abundance left on the joint) and said to a servant, "Take this piece of pork over to Demodocus and tell him to eat it; for all the pain his lays may cause me I will salute him none the less; bards are honoured and respected throughout the world, for the muse teaches them their songs and loves them."

The servant carried the pork in his fingers over to Demodocus, who took it and was very much pleased. They then laid their hands on the good things that were before them, and as soon as they had had to eat and drink, Ulysses said to Demodocus, "Demodocus, there is no one in the world whom I admire more than I do you. You must have studied under the Muse, Jove's daughter, and under Apollo, so accurately do you sing the return of the Achaeans with all their sufferings and adventures. If you were not there yourself, you must have heard it all from some one who was. Now, however, change your song and tell us of the wooden horse which Epeus made with the assistance of Minerva, and which Ulysses got by stratagem into the fort of Troy after freighting it with the men who afterwards sacked the city. If you will sing this tale aright I will tell all the world how magnificently heaven has endowed you."

The bard inspired of heaven took up the story at the point where some of the Argives set fire to their tents and sailed away while others, hidden within the horse, {73} were waiting with Ulysses in the Trojan place of assembly. For the Trojans themselves had drawn the horse into their fortress, and it stood there while they sat in council round it, and were in three minds as to what they should do. Some were for breaking it up then and there; others would have it dragged to the top of the rock on which the fortress stood, and then thrown down the precipice; while yet others were for letting it remain as an offering and propitiation for the gods. And this was how they settled it in the end, for the city was doomed when it took in that horse, within which were all the bravest of the Argives waiting to bring death and destruction on the Trojans. Anon he sang how the sons of the Achaeans issued from the horse, and sacked the town, breaking out from their ambuscade. He sang how they overran the city hither and thither and ravaged it, and how Ulysses went raging like Mars along with Menelaus to the house of Deiphobus. It was there that the fight raged most furiously, nevertheless by Minerva's help he was victorious.

All this he told, but Ulysses was overcome as he heard him, and his cheeks were wet with tears. He wept as a woman weeps when she throws herself on the body of her husband who has fallen before his own city and people, fighting bravely in defence of his home and children. She screams aloud and flings her arms about him as he lies gasping for breath and dying, but her enemies beat her from behind about the back and shoulders, and carry her off into slavery, to a life of labour and sorrow, and the beauty fades from her cheeks—even so piteously did Ulysses weep, but none of those present perceived his tears except Alcinous, who was sitting near him, and could hear the sobs and sighs that he was heaving. The king, therefore, at once rose and said:

"Aldermen and town councillors of the Phaeacians, let Demodocus cease his song, for there are those present who do not seem to like it. From the moment that we had done supper and Demodocus began to sing, our guest has been all the time groaning and lamenting. He is evidently in great trouble, so let the bard leave off, that we may all enjoy ourselves, hosts and guest alike. This will be much more as it should be, for all these festivities, with the escort and the presents that we are making with so much good will are wholly in his honour, and any one with even a moderate amount of right feeling knows that he ought to treat a guest and a suppliant as though he were his own brother.

"Therefore, Sir, do you on your part affect no more concealment nor reserve in the matter about which I shall ask you; it will be more polite in you to give me a plain answer; tell me the name by which your father and mother over yonder used to call you, and by which you were known among your neighbours and fellow-citizens. There is no one, neither rich nor poor, who is absolutely without any name whatever, for people's fathers and mothers give them names as soon as they are born. Tell me also your country, nation, and city, that our ships may shape their purpose accordingly and take you there. For the Phaeacians have no pilots; their vessels have no rudders as those of other nations have, but the ships themselves understand what it is that we are thinking about and want; they know all the cities and countries in the whole world, and can traverse the sea just as well even when it is covered with mist and cloud, so that there is no danger of being wrecked or coming to any harm. Still I do remember hearing my father say that Neptune was angry with us for being too easy-going in the matter of giving people escorts. He said that one of these days he should wreck a ship of ours as it was returning from having escorted some one, {74} and bury our city under a high mountain. This is what my father used to say, but whether the god will carry out his threat or no is a matter which he will decide for himself.

"And now, tell me and tell me true. Where have you been wandering, and in what countries have you travelled? Tell us of the peoples themselves, and of their cities—who were hostile, savage and uncivilised, and who, on the other hand, hospitable and humane. Tell us also why you are made so unhappy on hearing about the return of the Argive Danaans from Troy. The gods arranged all this, and sent them their misfortunes in order that future generations might have something to sing about. Did you lose some brave kinsman of your wife's when you were before Troy? a son-in-law or father-in-law—which are the nearest relations a man has outside his own flesh and blood? or was it some brave and kindly-natured comrade—for a good friend is as dear to a man as his own brother?"

BOOK IX

Ulysses declares himself and begins his story—-the Cicons, Lotophagi, and Cyclopes.

And Ulysses answered, "King Alcinous, it is a good thing to hear a bard with such a divine voice as this man has. There is nothing better or more delightful than when a whole people make merry together, with the guests sitting orderly to listen, while the table is loaded with bread and meats, and the cup-bearer draws wine and fills his cup for every man. This is indeed as fair a sight as a man can see. Now, however, since you are inclined to ask the story of my sorrows, and rekindle my own sad memories in respect of them, I do not know how to begin, nor yet how to continue and conclude my tale, for the hand of heaven has been laid heavily upon me.

"Firstly, then, I will tell you my name that you too may know it, and one day, if I outlive this time of sorrow, may become my guests though I live so far away from all of you. I am Ulysses son of Laertes, renowned among mankind for all manner of subtlety, so that my fame ascends to heaven. I live in Ithaca, where there is a high mountain called Neritum, covered with forests; and not far from it there is a group of islands very near to one another—Dulichium, Same, and the wooded island of Zacynthus. It lies squat on the horizon, all highest up in the sea towards the sunset, while the others lie away from it towards dawn. {75} It is a rugged island, but it breeds brave men, and my eyes know none that they better love to look upon. The goddess Calypso kept me with her in her cave, and wanted me to marry her, as did also the cunning Aeaean goddess Circe; but they could neither of them persuade me, for there is nothing dearer to a man than his own country and his parents, and however splendid a home he may have in a foreign country, if it be far from father or mother, he does not care about it. Now, however, I will tell you of the many hazardous adventures which by Jove's will I met with on my return from Troy.

"When I had set sail thence the wind took me first to Ismarus, which is the city of the Cicons. There I sacked the town and put the people to the sword. We took their wives and also much booty, which we divided equitably amongst us, so that none might have reason to complain. I then said that we had better make off at once, but my men very foolishly would not obey me, so they staid there drinking much wine and killing great numbers of sheep and oxen on the sea shore. Meanwhile the Cicons cried out for help to other Cicons who lived inland. These were more in number, and stronger, and they were more skilled in the art of war, for they could fight, either from chariots or on foot as the occasion served; in the morning, therefore, they came as thick as leaves and bloom in summer, and the hand of heaven was against us, so that we were hard pressed. They set the battle in array near the ships, and the hosts aimed their bronze-shod spears at one another. {76} So long as the day waxed and it was still morning, we held our own against them, though they were more in number than we; but as the sun went down, towards the time when men loose their oxen, the Cicons got the better of us, and we lost half a dozen men from every ship we had; so we got away with those that were left.

"Thence we sailed onward with sorrow in our hearts, but glad to have escaped death though we had lost our comrades, nor did we leave till we had thrice invoked each one of the poor fellows who had perished by the hands of the Cicons. Then Jove raised the North wind against us till it blew a hurricane, so that land and sky were hidden in thick clouds, and night sprang forth out of the heavens. We let the ships run before the gale, but the force of the wind tore our sails to tatters, so we took them down for fear of shipwreck, and rowed our hardest towards the land.

There we lay two days and two nights suffering much alike from toil and distress of mind, but on the morning of the third day we again raised our masts, set sail, and took our places, letting the wind and steersmen direct our ship. I should have got home at that time unharmed had not the North wind and the currents been against me as I was doubling Cape Malea, and set me off my course hard by the island of Cythera.

"I was driven thence by foul winds for a space of nine days upon the sea, but on the tenth day we reached the land of the Lotus-eaters, who live on a food that comes from a kind of flower. Here we landed to take in fresh water, and our crews got their mid-day meal on the shore near the ships. When they had eaten and drunk I sent two of my company to see what manner of men the people of the place might be, and they had a third man under them. They started at once, and went about among the Lotus-eaters, who did them no hurt, but gave them to eat of the lotus, which was so delicious that those who ate of it left off caring about home, and did not even want to go back and say what had happened to them, but were for staying and munching lotus {77} with the Lotus-eaters without thinking further of their return; nevertheless, though they wept bitterly I forced them back to the ships and made them fast under the benches. Then I told the rest to go on board at once, lest any of them should taste of the lotus and leave off wanting to get home, so they took their places and smote the grey sea with their oars.

"We sailed hence, always in much distress, till we came to the land of the lawless and inhuman Cyclopes. Now the Cyclopes neither plant nor plough, but trust in providence, and live on such wheat, barley, and grapes as grow wild without any kind of tillage, and their wild grapes yield them wine as the sun and the rain may grow them. They have no laws nor assemblies of the people, but live in caves on the tops of high mountains; each is lord and master in his family, and they take no account of their neighbours.

"Now off their harbour there lies a wooded and fertile island not quite close to the land of the Cyclopes, but still not far. It is over-run with wild goats, that breed there in great numbers and are never disturbed by foot of man; for sportsmen—who as a rule will suffer so much hardship in forest or among mountain precipices—do not go there, nor yet again is it ever ploughed or fed down, but it lies a wilderness untilled and unsown from year to year, and has no living thing upon it but only goats. For the Cyclopes have no ships, nor yet shipwrights who could make ships for them; they cannot therefore go from city to city, or sail over the sea to one another's country as people who have ships can do; if they had had these they would have colonised the island, {78} for it is a very good one, and would yield everything in due season. There are meadows that in some places come right down to the sea shore, well watered and full of luscious grass; grapes would do there excellently; there is level land for ploughing, and it would always yield heavily at harvest time, for the soil is deep.

There is a good harbour where no cables are wanted, nor yet anchors, nor need a ship be moored, but all one has to do is to beach one's vessel and stay there till the wind becomes fair for putting out to sea again. At the head of the harbour there is a spring of clear water coming out of a cave, and there are poplars growing all round it.

"Here we entered, but so dark was the night that some god must have brought us in, for there was nothing whatever to be seen. A thick mist hung all round our ships; {79} the moon was hidden behind a mass of clouds so that no one could have seen the island if he had looked for it, nor were there any breakers to tell us we were close in shore before we found ourselves upon the land itself; when, however, we had beached the ships, we took down the sails, went ashore and camped upon the beach till daybreak.

"When the child of morning, rosy-fingered Dawn appeared, we admired the island and wandered all over it, while the nymphs Jove's daughters roused the wild goats that we might get some meat for our dinner. On this we fetched our spears and bows and arrows from the ships, and dividing ourselves into three bands began to shoot the goats. Heaven sent us excellent sport; I had twelve ships with me, and each ship got nine goats, while my own ship had ten; thus through the livelong day to the going down of the sun we ate and drank our fill, and we had plenty of wine left, for each one of us had taken many jars full when we sacked the city of the Cicons, and this had not yet run out. While we were feasting we kept turning our eyes towards the land of the Cyclopes, which was hard by, and saw the smoke of their stubble fires. We could almost fancy we heard their voices and the bleating of their sheep and goats, but when the sun went down and it came on dark, we camped down upon the beach, and next morning I called a council.

"'Stay here, my brave fellows,' said I, 'all the rest of you, while I go with my ship and exploit these people myself: I want to see if they are uncivilised savages, or a hospitable and humane race.'

"I went on board, bidding my men to do so also and loose the hawsers; so they took their places and smote the grey sea with their oars. When we got to the land, which was not far, there, on the face of a cliff near the sea, we saw a great cave overhung with laurels. It was a station for a great many sheep and goats, and outside there was a large yard, with a high wall round it made of stones built into the ground and of trees both pine and oak. This was the abode of a huge monster who was then away from home shepherding his flocks. He would have nothing to do with other people, but led the life of an outlaw. He was a horrid creature, not like a human being at all, but resembling rather some crag that stands out boldly against the sky on the top of a high mountain.

"I told my men to draw the ship ashore, and stay where they were, all but the twelve best among them, who were to go along with myself. I also took a goatskin of sweet black wine which had been given me by Maron, son of Euanthes, who was priest of Apollo the patron god of Ismarus, and lived within the wooded precincts of the temple. When we were sacking the city we respected him, and spared his life, as also his wife and child; so he made me some presents of great value—seven talents of fine gold, and a bowl of silver, with twelve jars of sweet wine, unblended, and of the most exquisite flavour. Not a man nor maid in the house knew about it, but only himself, his wife, and one housekeeper: when he drank it he mixed twenty parts of water to one of wine, and yet the fragrance from the mixing-bowl was so exquisite that it was impossible to refrain from drinking. I filled a large skin with this wine, and took a wallet full of provisions with me, for my mind misgave me that I might have to deal with some savage who would be of great strength, and would respect neither right nor law.

"We soon reached his cave, but he was out shepherding, so we went inside and took stock of all that we could see. His cheese-racks were loaded with cheeses, and he had more lambs and kids than his pens could hold. They were kept in separate flocks; first there were the hoggets, then the oldest of the younger lambs and lastly the very young ones {80} all kept apart from one another; as for his dairy, all the vessels, bowls, and milk pails into which he milked, were swimming with whey. When they saw all this, my men begged me to let them first steal some cheeses, and make off with them to the ship; they would then return, drive down the lambs and kids, put them on board and sail away with them. It would have been indeed better if we had done so but I would not listen to them, for I wanted to see the owner himself, in the hope that he might give me a present. When, however, we saw him my poor men found him ill to deal with.

"We lit a fire, offered some of the cheeses in sacrifice, ate others of them, and then sat waiting till the Cyclops should come in with his sheep. When he came, he brought in with him a huge load of dry firewood to light the fire for his supper, and this he flung with such a noise on to the floor of his cave that we hid ourselves for fear at the far end of the cavern. Meanwhile he drove all the ewes inside, as well as the she-goats that he was going to milk, leaving the males, both rams and he-goats, outside in the yards. Then he rolled a huge stone to the mouth of the cave—so huge that two and twenty strong four-wheeled waggons would not be enough to draw it from its place against the doorway. When he had so done he sat down and milked his ewes and goats, all in due course, and then let each of them have her own young. He curdled half the milk and set it aside in wicker strainers, but the other half he poured into bowls that he might drink it for his supper. When he had got through with all his work, he lit the fire, and then caught sight of us, whereon he said:

"'Strangers, who are you? Where do sail from? Are you traders, or do you sail the sea as rovers, with your hands against every man, and every man's hand against you?'

"We were frightened out of our senses by his loud voice and monstrous form, but I managed to say, 'We are Achaeans on our way home from Troy, but by the will of Jove, and stress of weather, we have been driven far out of our course. We are the people of Agamemnon, son of Atreus, who has won infinite renown throughout the whole world, by sacking so great a city and killing so many people. We therefore humbly pray you to show us some hospitality, and otherwise make us such presents as visitors may reasonably expect. May your excellency fear the wrath of heaven, for we are your suppliants, and Jove takes all respectable travellers under his protection, for he is the avenger of all suppliants and foreigners in distress.'

"To this he gave me but a pitiless answer, 'Stranger,' said he, 'you are a fool, or else you know nothing of this country. Talk to me, indeed, about fearing the gods or shunning their anger? We Cyclopes do not care about Jove or any of your blessed gods, for we are ever so much stronger than they. I shall not spare either yourself or your companions out of any regard for Jove, unless I am in the humour for doing so. And now tell me where you made your ship fast when you came on shore. Was it round the point, or is she lying straight off the land?'

"He said this to draw me out, but I was too cunning to be caught in that way, so I answered with a lie; 'Neptune,' said I, 'sent my ship on to the rocks at the far end of your country, and wrecked it. We were driven on to them from the open sea, but I and those who are with me escaped the jaws of death.'

"The cruel wretch vouchsafed me not one word of answer, but with a sudden clutch he gripped up two of my men at once and dashed them down upon the ground as though they had been puppies. Their brains were shed upon the ground, and the earth was wet with their blood. Then he tore them limb from limb and supped upon them. He gobbled them up like a lion in the wilderness, flesh, bones, marrow, and entrails, without leaving anything uneaten. As for us, we wept and lifted up our hands to heaven on seeing such a horrid sight, for we did not know what else to do; but when the Cyclops had filled his huge paunch, and had washed down his meal of human flesh with a drink of neat milk, he stretched himself full length upon the ground among his sheep, and went to sleep. I was at first inclined to seize my sword, draw it, and drive it into his vitals, but I reflected that if I did we should all certainly be lost, for we should never be able to shift the stone which the monster had put in front of the door. So we stayed sobbing and sighing where we were till morning came.

"When the child of morning, rosy-fingered dawn, appeared, he again lit his fire, milked his goats and ewes, all quite rightly, and then let each have her own young one; as soon as he had got through with all his work, he clutched up two more of my men, and began eating them for his morning's meal. Presently, with the utmost ease, he rolled the stone away from the door and drove out his sheep, but he at once put it back again—as easily as though he were merely clapping the lid on to a quiver full of arrows. As soon as he had done so he shouted, and cried 'Shoo, shoo,' after his sheep to drive them on to the mountain; so I was left to scheme some way of taking my revenge and covering myself with glory.

"In the end I deemed it would be the best plan to do as follows: The Cyclops had a great club which was lying near one of the sheep pens; it was of green olive wood, and he had cut it intending to use it for a staff as soon as it should be dry. It was so huge that we could only compare it to the mast of a twenty-oared merchant vessel of large burden, and able to venture out into open sea. I went up to this club and cut off about six feet of it; I then gave this piece to the men and told them to fine it evenly off at one end, which they proceeded to do, and lastly I brought it to a point myself, charring the end in the fire to make it harder. When I had done this I hid it under dung, which was lying about all over the cave, and told the men to cast lots which of them should venture along with myself to lift it and bore it into the monster's eye while he was asleep. The lot fell upon the very four whom I should have chosen, and I myself made five. In the evening the wretch came back from shepherding, and drove his flocks into the cave—this time driving them all inside, and not leaving any in the yards; I suppose some fancy must have taken him, or a god must have prompted him to do so. As soon as he had put the stone back to its place against the door, he sat down, milked his ewes and his goats all quite rightly, and then let each have her own young one; when he had got through with all this work, he gripped up two more of my men, and made his supper off them. So I went up to him with an ivy-wood bowl of black wine in my hands:

"'Look here, Cyclops,' said I, you have been eating a great deal of man's flesh, so take this and drink some wine, that you may see what kind of liquor we had on board my ship. I was bringing it to you as a drink-offering, in the hope that you would take compassion upon me and further me on my way home, whereas all you do is to go on ramping and raving most intolerably. You ought to be ashamed of yourself; how can you expect people to come see you any more if you treat them in this way?'

"He then took the cup and drank. He was so delighted with the taste of the wine that he begged me for another bowl full. 'Be so kind,' he said, 'as to give me some more, and tell me your name at once. I want to make you a present that you will be glad to have. We have wine even in this country, for our soil grows grapes and the sun ripens them, but this drinks like Nectar and Ambrosia all in one.'

"I then gave him some more; three times did I fill the bowl for him, and three times did he drain it without thought or heed; then, when I saw that the wine had got into his head, I said to him as plausibly as I could: 'Cyclops, you ask my name and I will tell it you; give me, therefore, the present you promised me; my name is Noman; this is what my father and mother and my friends have always called me.'

"But the cruel wretch said, 'Then I will eat all Noman's comrades before Noman himself, and will keep Noman for the last. This is the present that I will make him.'

"As he spoke he reeled, and fell sprawling face upwards on the ground. His great neck hung heavily backwards and a deep sleep took hold upon him. Presently he turned sick, and threw up both wine and the gobbets of human flesh on which he had been gorging, for he was very drunk. Then I thrust the beam of wood far into the embers to heat it, and encouraged my men lest any of them should turn faint-hearted. When the wood, green though it was, was about to blaze, I drew it out of the fire glowing with heat, and my men gathered round me, for heaven had filled their hearts with courage. We drove the sharp end of the beam into the monster's eye, and bearing upon it with all my weight I kept turning it round and round as though I were boring a hole in a ship's plank with an auger, which two men with a wheel and strap can keep on turning as long as they choose. Even thus did we bore the red hot beam into his eye, till the boiling blood bubbled all over it as we worked it round and round, so that the steam from the burning eyeball scalded his eyelids and eyebrows, and the roots of the eye sputtered in the fire. As a blacksmith plunges an axe or hatchet into cold water to temper it—for it is this that gives strength to the iron—and it makes a great hiss as he does so, even thus did the Cyclops' eye hiss round the beam of olive wood, and his hideous yells made the cave ring again. We ran away in a fright, but he plucked the beam all besmirched with gore from his eye, and hurled it from him in a frenzy of rage and pain, shouting as he did so to the other Cyclopes who lived on the bleak headlands near him; so they gathered from all quarters round his cave when they heard him crying, and asked what was the matter with him.

"'What ails you, Polyphemus,' said they, 'that you make such a noise, breaking the stillness of the night, and preventing us from being able to sleep? Surely no man is carrying off your sheep? Surely no man is trying to kill you either by fraud or by force?'

"But Polyphemus shouted to them from inside the cave, 'Noman is killing me by fraud; no man is killing me by force.'

"'Then,' said they, 'if no man is attacking you, you must be ill; when Jove makes people ill, there is no help for it, and you had better pray to your father Neptune.'

"Then they went away, and I laughed inwardly at the success of my clever stratagem, but the Cyclops, groaning and in an agony of pain, felt about with his hands till he found the stone and took it from the door; then he sat in the doorway and stretched his hands in front of it to catch anyone going out with the sheep, for he thought I might be foolish enough to attempt this.

"As for myself I kept on puzzling to think how I could best save my own life and those of my companions; I schemed and schemed, as one who knows that his life depends upon it, for the danger was very great. In the end I deemed that this plan would be the best; the male sheep were well grown, and carried a heavy black fleece, so I bound them noiselessly in threes together, with some of the withies on which the wicked monster used to sleep. There was to be a man under the middle sheep, and the two on either side were to cover him, so that there were three sheep to each man. As for myself there was a ram finer than any of the others, so I caught hold of him by the back, esconced myself in the thick wool under his belly, and hung on patiently to his fleece, face upwards, keeping a firm hold on it all the time.

"Thus, then, did we wait in great fear of mind till morning came, but when the child of morning, rosy-fingered Dawn, appeared, the male sheep hurried out to feed, while the ewes remained bleating about the pens waiting to be milked, for their udders were full to bursting; but their master in spite of all his pain felt the backs of all the sheep as they stood upright, without being sharp enough to find out that the men were underneath their bellies. As the ram was going out, last of all, heavy with its fleece and with the weight of my crafty self, Polyphemus laid hold of it and said:

"'My good ram, what is it that makes you the last to leave my cave this morning? You are not wont to let the ewes go before you, but lead the mob with a run whether to flowery mead or bubbling fountain, and are the first to come home again at night; but now you lag last of all. Is it because you know your master has lost his eye, and are sorry because that wicked Noman and his horrid crew has got him down in his drink and blinded him? But I will have his life yet. If you could understand and talk, you would tell me where the wretch is hiding, and I would dash his brains upon the ground till they flew all over the cave. I should thus have some satisfaction for the harm this no-good Noman has done me.'

"As he spoke he drove the ram outside, but when we were a little way out from the cave and yards, I first got from under the ram's belly, and then freed my comrades; as for the sheep, which were very fat, by constantly heading them in the right direction we managed to drive them down to the ship. The crew rejoiced greatly at seeing those of us who had escaped death, but wept for the others whom the Cyclops had killed. However, I made signs to them by nodding and frowning that they were to hush their crying, and told them to get all the sheep on board at once and put out to sea; so they went aboard, took their places, and smote the grey sea with their oars. Then, when I had got as far out as my voice would reach, I began to jeer at the Cyclops.

"'Cyclops,' said I, 'you should have taken better measure of your man before eating up his comrades in your cave. You wretch, eat up your visitors in your own house? You might have known that your sin would find you out, and now Jove and the other gods have punished you.'

"He got more and more furious as he heard me, so he tore the top from off a high mountain, and flung it just in front of my ship so that it was within a little of hitting the end of the rudder. {81} The sea quaked as the rock fell into it, and the wash of the wave it raised carried us back towards the mainland, and forced us towards the shore. But I snatched up a long pole and kept the ship off, making signs to my men by nodding my head, that they must row for their lives, whereon they laid out with a will. When we had got twice as far as we were before, I was for jeering at the Cyclops again, but the men begged and prayed of me to hold my tongue.

"'Do not,' they exclaimed, 'be mad enough to provoke this savage creature further; he has thrown one rock at us already which drove us back again to the mainland, and we made sure it had been the death of us; if he had then heard any further sound of voices he would have pounded our heads and our ship's timbers into a jelly with the rugged rocks he would have heaved at us, for he can throw them a long way.'

"But I would not listen to them, and shouted out to him in my rage, 'Cyclops, if any one asks you who it was that put your eye out and spoiled your beauty, say it was the valiant warrior Ulysses, son of Laertes, who lives in Ithaca.'

"On this he groaned, and cried out, 'Alas, alas, then the old prophecy about me is coming true. There was a prophet here, at one time, a man both brave and of great stature, Telemus son of Eurymus, who was an excellent seer, and did all the prophesying for the Cyclopes till he grew old; he told me that all this would happen to me some day, and said I should lose my sight by the hand of Ulysses. I have been all along expecting some one of imposing presence and superhuman strength, whereas he turns out to be a little insignificant weakling, who has managed to blind my eye by taking advantage of me in my drink; come here, then, Ulysses, that I may make you presents to show my hospitality, and urge Neptune to help you forward on your journey—for Neptune and I are father and son. He, if he so will, shall heal me, which no one else neither god nor man can do.'

"Then I said, 'I wish I could be as sure of killing you outright and sending you down to the house of Hades, as I am that it will take more than Neptune to cure that eye of yours.'

"On this he lifted up his hands to the firmament of heaven and prayed, saying, 'Hear me, great Neptune; if I am indeed your own true begotten son, grant that Ulysses may never reach his home alive; or if he must get back to his friends at last, let him do so late and in sore plight after losing all his men [let him reach his home in another man's ship and find trouble in his house.'] {82}

"Thus did he pray, and Neptune heard his prayer. Then he picked up a rock much larger than the first, swung it aloft and hurled it with prodigious force. It fell just short of the ship, but was within a little of hitting the end of the rudder. The sea quaked as the rock fell into it, and the wash of the wave it raised drove us onwards on our way towards the shore of the island.

"When at last we got to the island where we had left the rest of our ships, we found our comrades lamenting us, and anxiously awaiting our return. We ran our vessel upon the sands and got out of her on to the sea shore; we also landed the Cyclops' sheep, and divided them equitably amongst us so that none might have reason to complain. As for the ram, my companions agreed that I should have it as an extra share; so I sacrificed it on the sea shore, and burned its thigh bones to Jove, who is the lord of all. But he heeded not my sacrifice, and only thought how he might destroy both my ships and my comrades.

"Thus through the livelong day to the going down of the sun we feasted our fill on meat and drink, but when the sun went down and it came on dark, we camped upon the beach. When the child of morning rosy-fingered Dawn appeared, I bade my men on board and loose the hawsers. Then they took their places and smote the grey sea with their oars; so we sailed on with sorrow in our hearts, but glad to have escaped death though we had lost our comrades.

BOOK X

Aeolus, the Laestrygones, Circe.

"Thence we went on to the Aeolian island where lives Aeolus son of Hippotas, dear to the immortal gods. It is an island that floats (as it were) upon the sea, {83} iron bound with a wall that girds it. Now, Aeolus has six daughters and six lusty sons, so he made the sons marry the daughters, and they all live with their dear father and mother, feasting and enjoying every conceivable kind of luxury. All day long the atmosphere of the house is loaded with the savour of roasting meats till it groans again, yard and all; but by night they sleep on their well made bedsteads, each with his own wife between the blankets. These were the people among whom we had now come.

"Aeolus entertained me for a whole month asking me questions all the time about Troy, the Argive fleet, and the return of the Achaeans. I told him exactly how everything had happened, and when I said I must go, and asked him to further me on my way, he made no sort of difficulty, but set about doing so at once. Moreover, he flayed me a prime ox-hide to hold the ways of the roaring winds, which he shut up in the hide as in a sack—for Jove had made him captain over the winds, and he could stir or still each one of them according to his own pleasure. He put the sack in the ship and bound the mouth so tightly with a silver thread that not even a breath of a side-wind could blow from any quarter. The West wind which was fair for us did he alone let blow as it chose; but it all came to nothing, for we were lost through our own folly.

"Nine days and nine nights did we sail, and on the tenth day our native land showed on the horizon. We got so close in that we could see the stubble fires burning, and I, being then dead beat, fell into a light sleep, for I had never let the rudder out of my own hands, that we might get home the faster. On this the men fell to talking among themselves, and said I was bringing back gold and silver in the sack that Aeolus had given me. 'Bless my heart,' would one turn to his neighbour, saying, 'how this man gets honoured and makes friends to whatever city or country he may go. See what fine prizes he is taking home from Troy, while we, who have travelled just as far as he has, come back with hands as empty as we set out with—and now Aeolus has given him ever so much more. Quick—let us see what it all is, and how much gold and silver there is in the sack he gave him.'

"Thus they talked and evil counsels prevailed. They loosed the sack, whereupon the wind flew howling forth and raised a storm that carried us weeping out to sea and away from our own country. Then I awoke, and knew not whether to throw myself into the sea or to live on and make the best of it; but I bore it, covered myself up, and lay down in the ship, while the men lamented bitterly as the fierce winds bore our fleet back to the Aeolian island.

"When we reached it we went ashore to take in water, and dined hard by the ships. Immediately after dinner I took a herald and one of my men and went straight to the house of Aeolus, where I found him feasting with his wife and family; so we sat down as suppliants on the threshold. They were astounded when they saw us and said, 'Ulysses, what brings you here? What god has been ill-treating you? We took great pains to further you on your way home to Ithaca, or wherever it was that you wanted to go to.'

"Thus did they speak, but I answered sorrowfully, 'My men have undone me; they, and cruel sleep, have ruined me. My friends, mend me this mischief, for you can if you will.'

"I spoke as movingly as I could, but they said nothing, till their father answered, 'Vilest of mankind, get you gone at once out of the island; him whom heaven hates will I in no wise help. Be off, for you come here as one abhorred of heaven.' And with these words he sent me sorrowing from his door.

"Thence we sailed sadly on till the men were worn out with long and fruitless rowing, for there was no longer any wind to help them. Six days, night and day did we toil, and on the seventh day we reached the rocky stronghold of Lamus—Telepylus, the city of the Laestrygonians, where the shepherd who is driving in his sheep and goats [to be milked] salutes him who is driving out his flock [to feed] and this last answers the salute. In that country a man who could do without sleep might earn double wages, one as a herdsman of cattle, and another as a shepherd, for they work much the same by night as they do by day. {84}

"When we reached the harbour we found it land-locked under steep cliffs, with a narrow entrance between two headlands. My captains took all their ships inside, and made them fast close to one another, for there was never so much as a breath of wind inside, but it was always dead calm. I kept my own ship outside, and moored it to a rock at the very end of the point; then I climbed a high rock to reconnoitre, but could see no sign neither of man nor cattle, only some smoke rising from the ground. So I sent two of my company with an attendant to find out what sort of people the inhabitants were.

"The men when they got on shore followed a level road by which the people draw their firewood from the mountains into the town, till presently they met a young woman who had come outside to fetch water, and who was daughter to a Laestrygonian named Antiphates. She was going to the fountain Artacia from which the people bring in their water, and when my men had come close up to her, they asked her who the king of that country might be, and over what kind of people he ruled; so she directed them to her father's house, but when they got there they found his wife to be a giantess as huge as a mountain, and they were horrified at the sight of her.

"She at once called her husband Antiphates from the place of assembly, and forthwith he set about killing my men. He snatched up one of them, and began to make his dinner off him then and there, whereon the other two ran back to the ships as fast as ever they could. But Antiphates raised a hue-and-cry after them, and thousands of sturdy Laestrygonians sprang up from every quarter—ogres, not men. They threw vast rocks at us from the cliffs as though they had been mere stones, and I heard the horrid sound of the ships crunching up against one another, and the death cries of my men, as the Laestrygonians speared them like fishes and took them home to eat them. While they were thus killing my men within the harbour I drew my sword, cut the cable of my own ship, and told my men to row with all their might if they too would not fare like the rest; so they laid out for their lives, and we were thankful enough when we got into open water out of reach of the rocks they hurled at us. As for the others there was not one of them left.

"Thence we sailed sadly on, glad to have escaped death, though we had lost our comrades, and came to the Aeaean island, where Circe lives—a great and cunning goddess who is own sister to the magician Aeetes—for they are both children of the sun by Perse, who is daughter to Oceanus. We brought our ship into a safe harbour without a word, for some god guided us thither, and having landed we lay there for two days and two nights, worn out in body and mind. When the morning of the third day came I took my spear and my sword, and went away from the ship to reconnoitre, and see if I could discover signs of human handiwork, or hear the sound of voices. Climbing to the top of a high look-out I espied the smoke of Circe's house rising upwards amid a dense forest of trees, and when I saw this I doubted whether, having seen the smoke, I would not go on at once and find out more, but in the end I deemed it best to go back to the ship, give the men their dinners, and send some of them instead of going myself.

"When I had nearly got back to the ship some god took pity upon my solitude, and sent a fine antlered stag right into the middle of my path. He was coming down his pasture in the forest to drink of the river, for the heat of the sun drove him, and as he passed I struck him in the middle of the back; the bronze point of the spear went clean through him, and he lay groaning in the dust until the life went out of him. Then I set my foot upon him, drew my spear from the wound, and laid it down; I also gathered rough grass and rushes and twisted them into a fathom or so of good stout rope, with which I bound the four feet of the noble creature together; having so done I hung him round my neck and walked back to the ship leaning upon my spear, for the stag was much too big for me to be able to carry him on my shoulder, steadying him with one hand. As I threw him down in front of the ship, I called the men and spoke cheeringly man by man to each of them. 'Look here my friends,' said I, 'we are not going to die so much before our time after all, and at any rate we will not starve so long as we have got something to eat and drink on board.' On this they uncovered their heads upon the sea shore and admired the stag, for he was indeed a splendid fellow. Then, when they had feasted their eyes upon him sufficiently, they washed their hands and began to cook him for dinner.

"Thus through the livelong day to the going down of the sun we stayed there eating and drinking our fill, but when the sun went down and it came on dark, we camped upon the sea shore. When the child of morning, rosy-fingered Dawn, appeared, I called a council and said, 'My friends, we are in very great difficulties; listen therefore to me. We have no idea where the sun either sets or rises, {85} so that we do not even know East from West. I see no way out of it; nevertheless, we must try and find one. We are certainly on an island, for I went as high as I could this morning, and saw the sea reaching all round it to the horizon; it lies low, but towards the middle I saw smoke rising from out of a thick forest of trees.'

"Their hearts sank as they heard me, for they remembered how they had been treated by the Laestrygonian Antiphates, and by the savage ogre Polyphemus. They wept bitterly in their dismay, but there was nothing to be got by crying, so I divided them into two companies and set a captain over each; I gave one company to Eurylochus, while I took command of the other myself. Then we cast lots in a helmet, and the lot fell upon Eurylochus; so he set out with his twenty-two men, and they wept, as also did we who were left behind.

"When they reached Circe's house they found it built of cut stones, on a site that could be seen from far, in the middle of the forest. There were wild mountain wolves and lions prowling all round it—poor bewitched creatures whom she had tamed by her enchantments and drugged into subjection. They did not attack my men, but wagged their great tails, fawned upon them, and rubbed their noses lovingly against them. {86} As hounds crowd round their master when they see him coming from dinner—for they know he will bring them something—even so did these wolves and lions with their great claws fawn upon my men, but the men were terribly frightened at seeing such strange creatures. Presently they reached the gates of the goddess's house, and as they stood there they could hear Circe within, singing most beautifully as she worked at her loom, making a web so fine, so soft, and of such dazzling colours as no one but a goddess could weave. On this Polites, whom I valued and trusted more than any other of my men, said, 'There is some one inside working at a loom and singing most beautifully; the whole place resounds with it, let us call her and see whether she is woman or goddess.'

"They called her and she came down, unfastened the door, and bade them enter. They, thinking no evil, followed her, all except Eurylochus, who suspected mischief and staid outside. When she had got them into her house, she set them upon benches and seats and mixed them a mess with cheese, honey, meal, and Pramnian wine, but she drugged it with wicked poisons to make them forget their homes, and when they had drunk she turned them into pigs by a stroke of her wand, and shut them up in her pig-styes. They were like pigs—head, hair, and all, and they grunted just as pigs do; but their senses were the same as before, and they remembered everything.

"Thus then were they shut up squealing, and Circe threw them some acorns and beech masts such as pigs eat, but Eurylochus hurried back to tell me about the sad fate of our comrades. He was so overcome with dismay that though he tried to speak he could find no words to do so; his eyes filled with tears and he could only sob and sigh, till at last we forced his story out of him, and he told us what had happened to the others.

"'We went,' said he, 'as you told us, through the forest, and in the middle of it there was a fine house built with cut stones in a place that could be seen from far. There we found a woman, or else she was a goddess, working at her loom and singing sweetly; so the men shouted to her and called her, whereon she at once came down, opened the door, and invited us in. The others did not suspect any mischief so they followed her into the house, but I staid where I was, for I thought there might be some treachery. From that moment I saw them no more, for not one of them ever came out, though I sat a long time watching for them.'

"Then I took my sword of bronze and slung it over my shoulders; I also took my bow, and told Eurylochus to come back with me and shew me the way. But he laid hold of me with both his hands and spoke piteously, saying, 'Sir, do not force me to go with you, but let me stay here, for I know you will not bring one of them back with you, nor even return alive yourself; let us rather see if we cannot escape at any rate with the few that are left us, for we may still save our lives.'

"'Stay where you are, then,' answered I, 'eating and drinking at the ship, but I must go, for I am most urgently bound to do so.'

"With this I left the ship and went up inland. When I got through the charmed grove, and was near the great house of the enchantress Circe, I met Mercury with his golden wand, disguised as a young man in the hey-day of his youth and beauty with the down just coming upon his face. He came up to me and took my hand within his own, saying, 'My poor unhappy man, whither are you going over this mountain top, alone and without knowing the way? Your men are shut up in Circe's pigstyes, like so many wild boars in their lairs. You surely do not fancy that you can set them free? I can tell you that you will never get back and will have to stay there with the rest of them. But never mind, I will protect you and get you out of your difficulty. Take this herb, which is one of great virtue, and keep it about you when you go to Circe's house, it will be a talisman to you against every kind of mischief.

"'And I will tell you of all the wicked witchcraft that Circe will try to practice upon you. She will mix a mess for you to drink, and she will drug the meal with which she makes it, but she will not be able to charm you, for the virtue of the herb that I shall give you will prevent her spells from working. I will tell you all about it. When Circe strikes you with her wand, draw your sword and spring upon her as though you were going to kill her. She will then be frightened, and will desire you to go to bed with her; on this you must not point blank refuse her, for you want her to set your companions free, and to take good care also of yourself, but you must make her swear solemnly by all the blessed gods that she will plot no further mischief against you, or else when she has got you naked she will unman you and make you fit for nothing.'

"As he spoke he pulled the herb out of the ground and shewed me what it was like. The root was black, while the flower was as white as milk; the gods call it Moly, and mortal men cannot uproot it, but the gods can do whatever they like.

"Then Mercury went back to high Olympus passing over the wooded island; but I fared onward to the house of Circe, and my heart was clouded with care as I walked along. When I got to the gates I stood there and called the goddess, and as soon as she heard me she came down, opened the door, and asked me to come in; so I followed her—much troubled in my mind. She set me on a richly decorated seat inlaid with silver, there was a footstool also under my feet, and she mixed a mess in a golden goblet for me to drink; but she drugged it, for she meant me mischief. When she had given it me, and I had drunk it without its charming me, she struck me with her wand. 'There now,' she cried, 'be off to the pigstye, and make your lair with the rest of them.'

"But I rushed at her with my sword drawn as though I would kill her, whereon she fell with a loud scream, clasped my knees, and spoke piteously, saying, 'Who and whence are you? from what place and people have you come? How can it be that my drugs have no power to charm you? Never yet was any man able to stand so much as a taste of the herb I gave you; you must be spell-proof; surely you can be none other than the bold hero Ulysses, who Mercury always said would come here some day with his ship while on his way home from Troy; so be it then; sheathe your sword and let us go to bed, that we may make friends and learn to trust each other.'

"And I answered, 'Circe, how can you expect me to be friendly with you when you have just been turning all my men into pigs? And now that you have got me here myself, you mean me mischief when you ask me to go to bed with you, and will unman me and make me fit for nothing. I shall certainly not consent to go to bed with you unless you will first take your solemn oath to plot no further harm against me.'

"So she swore at once as I had told her, and when she had completed her oath then I went to bed with her.

"Meanwhile her four servants, who are her housemaids, set about their work. They are the children of the groves and fountains, and of the holy waters that run down into the sea. One of them spread a fair purple cloth over a seat, and laid a carpet underneath it. Another brought tables of silver up to the seats, and set them with baskets of gold. A third mixed some sweet wine with water in a silver bowl and put golden cups upon the tables, while the fourth brought in water and set it to boil in a large cauldron over a good fire which she had lighted. When the water in the cauldron was boiling, {87} she poured cold into it till it was just as I liked it, and then she set me in a bath and began washing me from the cauldron about the head and shoulders, to take the tire and stiffness out of my limbs. As soon as she had done washing me and anointing me with oil, she arrayed me in a good cloak and shirt and led me to a richly decorated seat inlaid with silver; there was a footstool also under my feet. A maid servant then brought me water in a beautiful golden ewer and poured it into a silver basin for me to wash my hands, and she drew a clean table beside me; an upper servant brought me bread and offered me many things of what there was in the house, and then Circe bade me eat, but I would not, and sat without heeding what was before me, still moody and suspicious.

"When Circe saw me sitting there without eating, and in great grief, she came to me and said, 'Ulysses, why do you sit like that as though you were dumb, gnawing at your own heart, and refusing both meat and drink? Is it that you are still suspicious? You ought not to be, for I have already sworn solemnly that I will not hurt you.'

"And I said, 'Circe, no man with any sense of what is right can think of either eating or drinking in your house until you have set his friends free and let him see them. If you want me to eat and drink, you must free my men and bring them to me that I may see them with my own eyes.'

"When I had said this she went straight through the court with her wand in her hand and opened the pigstye doors. My men came out like so many prime hogs and stood looking at her, but she went about among them and anointed each with a second drug, whereon the bristles that the bad drug had given them fell off, and they became men again, younger than they were before, and much taller and better looking. They knew me at once, seized me each of them by the hand, and wept for joy till the whole house was filled with the sound of their halloa-ballooing, and Circe herself was so sorry for them that she came up to me and said, 'Ulysses, noble son of Laertes, go back at once to the sea where you have left your ship, and first draw it on to the land. Then, hide all your ship's gear and property in some cave, and come back here with your men.'

"I agreed to this, so I went back to the sea shore, and found the men at the ship weeping and wailing most piteously. When they saw me the silly blubbering fellows began frisking round me as calves break out and gambol round their mothers, when they see them coming home to be milked after they have been feeding all day, and the homestead resounds with their lowing. They seemed as glad to see me as though they had got back to their own rugged Ithaca, where they had been born and bred. 'Sir,' said the affectionate creatures, 'we are as glad to see you back as though we had got safe home to Ithaca; but tell us all about the fate of our comrades.'

"I spoke comfortingly to them and said, 'We must draw our ship on to the land, and hide the ship's gear with all our property in some cave; then come with me all of you as fast as you can to Circe's house, where you will find your comrades eating and drinking in the midst of great abundance.'

"On this the men would have come with me at once, but Eurylochus tried to hold them back and said, 'Alas, poor wretches that we are, what will become of us? Rush not on your ruin by going to the house of Circe, who will turn us all into pigs or wolves or lions, and we shall have to keep guard over her house. Remember how the Cyclops treated us when our comrades went inside his cave, and Ulysses with them. It was all through his sheer folly that those men lost their lives.'

"When I heard him I was in two minds whether or no to draw the keen blade that hung by my sturdy thigh and cut his head off in spite of his being a near relation of my own; but the men interceded for him and said, 'Sir, if it may so be, let this fellow stay here and mind the ship, but take the rest of us with you to Circe's house.'

"On this we all went inland, and Eurylochus was not left behind after all, but came on too, for he was frightened by the severe reprimand that I had given him.

"Meanwhile Circe had been seeing that the men who had been left behind were washed and anointed with olive oil; she had also given them woollen cloaks and shirts, and when we came we found them all comfortably at dinner in her house. As soon as the men saw each other face to face and knew one another, they wept for joy and cried aloud till the whole palace rang again. Thereon Circe came up to me and said, 'Ulysses, noble son of Laertes, tell your men to leave off crying; I know how much you have all of you suffered at sea, and how ill you have fared among cruel savages on the mainland, but that is over now, so stay here, and eat and drink till you are once more as strong and hearty as you were when you left Ithaca; for at present you are weakened both in body and mind; you keep all the time thinking of the hardships you have suffered during your travels, so that you have no more cheerfulness left in you.'

"Thus did she speak and we assented. We stayed with Circe for a whole twelvemonth feasting upon an untold quantity both of meat and wine. But when the year had passed in the waning of moons and the long days had come round, my men called me apart and said, 'Sir, it is time you began to think about going home, if so be you are to be spared to see your house and native country at all.'

"Thus did they speak and I assented. Thereon through the livelong day to the going down of the sun we feasted our fill on meat and wine, but when the sun went down and it came on dark the men laid themselves down to sleep in the covered cloisters. I, however, after I had got into bed with Circe, besought her by her knees, and the goddess listened to what I had got to say. 'Circe,' said I, 'please to keep the promise you made me about furthering me on my homeward voyage. I want to get back and so do my men, they are always pestering me with their complaints as soon as ever your back is turned.'

"And the goddess answered, 'Ulysses, noble son of Laertes, you shall none of you stay here any longer if you do not want to, but there is another journey which you have got to take before you can sail homewards. You must go to the house of Hades and of dread Proserpine to consult the ghost of the blind Theban prophet Teiresias, whose reason is still unshaken. To him alone has Proserpine left his understanding even in death, but the other ghosts flit about aimlessly.'

"I was dismayed when I heard this. I sat up in bed and wept, and would gladly have lived no longer to see the light of the sun, but presently when I was tired of weeping and tossing myself about, I said, 'And who shall guide me upon this voyage—for the house of Hades is a port that no ship can reach.'

"'You will want no guide,' she answered; 'raise your mast, set your white sails, sit quite still, and the North Wind will blow you there of itself. When your ship has traversed the waters of Oceanus, you will reach the fertile shore of Proserpine's country with its groves of tall poplars and willows that shed their fruit untimely; here beach your ship upon the shore of Oceanus, and go straight on to the dark abode of Hades. You will find it near the place where the rivers Pyriphlegethon and Cocytus (which is a branch of the river Styx) flow into Acheron, and you will see a rock near it, just where the two roaring rivers run into one another.

"'When you have reached this spot, as I now tell you, dig a trench a cubit or so in length, breadth, and depth, and pour into it as a drink-offering to all the dead, first, honey mixed with milk, then wine, and in the third place water—sprinkling white barley meal over the whole. Moreover you must offer many prayers to the poor feeble ghosts, and promise them that when you get back to Ithaca you will sacrifice a barren heifer to them, the best you have, and will load the pyre with good things. More particularly you must promise that Teiresias shall have a black sheep all to himself, the finest in all your flocks.

"'When you shall have thus besought the ghosts with your prayers, offer them a ram and a black ewe, bending their heads towards Erebus; but yourself turn away from them as though you would make towards the river. On this, many dead men's ghosts will come to you, and you must tell your men to skin the two sheep that you have just killed, and offer them as a burnt sacrifice with prayers to Hades and to Proserpine. Then draw your sword and sit there, so as to prevent any other poor ghost from coming near the spilt blood before Teiresias shall have answered your questions. The seer will presently come to you, and will tell you about your voyage—what stages you are to make, and how you are to sail the sea so as to reach your home.'

"It was day-break by the time she had done speaking, so she dressed me in my shirt and cloak. As for herself she threw a beautiful light gossamer fabric over her shoulders, fastening it with a golden girdle round her waist, and she covered her head with a mantle. Then I went about among the men everywhere all over the house, and spoke kindly to each of them man by man: 'You must not lie sleeping here any longer,' said I to them, 'we must be going, for Circe has told me all about it.' And on this they did as I bade them.

"Even so, however, I did not get them away without misadventure. We had with us a certain youth named Elpenor, not very remarkable for sense or courage, who had got drunk and was lying on the house-top away from the rest of the men, to sleep off his liquor in the cool. When he heard the noise of the men bustling about, he jumped up on a sudden and forgot all about coming down by the main staircase, so he tumbled right off the roof and broke his neck, and his soul went down to the house of Hades.

"When I had got the men together I said to them, 'You think you are about to start home again, but Circe has explained to me that instead of this, we have got to go to the house of Hades and Proserpine to consult the ghost of the Theban prophet Teiresias.'

"The men were broken-hearted as they heard me, and threw themselves on the ground groaning and tearing their hair, but they did not mend matters by crying. When we reached the sea shore, weeping and lamenting our fate, Circe brought the ram and the ewe, and we made them fast hard by the ship. She passed through the midst of us without our knowing it, for who can see the comings and goings of a god, if the god does not wish to be seen?

BOOK XI

The visit to the dead. {88}

"Then, when we had got down to the sea shore we drew our ship into the water and got her mast and sails into her; we also put the sheep on board and took our places, weeping and in great distress of mind. Circe, that great and cunning goddess, sent us a fair wind that blew dead aft and staid steadily with us keeping our sails all the time well filled; so we did whatever wanted doing to the ship's gear and let her go as the wind and helmsman headed her. All day long her sails were full as she held her course over the sea, but when the sun went down and darkness was over all the earth, we got into the deep waters of the river Oceanus, where lie the land and city of the Cimmerians who live enshrouded in mist and darkness which the rays of the sun never pierce neither at his rising nor as he goes down again out of the heavens, but the poor wretches live in one long melancholy night. When we got there we beached the ship, took the sheep out of her, and went along by the waters of Oceanus till we came to the place of which Circe had told us.

"Here Perimedes and Eurylochus held the victims, while I drew my sword and dug the trench a cubit each way. I made a drink-offering to all the dead, first with honey and milk, then with wine, and thirdly with water, and I sprinkled white barley meal over the whole, praying earnestly to the poor feckless ghosts, and promising them that when I got back to Ithaca I would sacrifice a barren heifer for them, the best I had, and would load the pyre with good things. I also particularly promised that Teiresias should have a black sheep to himself, the best in all my flocks. When I had prayed sufficiently to the dead, I cut the throats of the two sheep and let the blood run into the trench, whereon the ghosts came trooping up from Erebus—brides, {89} young bachelors, old men worn out with toil, maids who had been crossed in love, and brave men who had been killed in battle, with their armour still smirched with blood; they came from every quarter and flitted round the trench with a strange kind of screaming sound that made me turn pale with fear. When I saw them coming I told the men to be quick and flay the carcasses of the two dead sheep and make burnt offerings of them, and at the same time to repeat prayers to Hades and to Proserpine; but I sat where I was with my sword drawn and would not let the poor feckless ghosts come near the blood till Teiresias should have answered my questions.

"The first ghost that came was that of my comrade Elpenor, for he had not yet been laid beneath the earth. We had left his body unwaked and unburied in Circe's house, for we had had too much else to do. I was very sorry for him, and cried when I saw him: 'Elpenor,' said I, 'how did you come down here into this gloom and darkness? You have got here on foot quicker than I have with my ship.'

"'Sir,' he answered with a groan, 'it was all bad luck, and my own unspeakable drunkenness. I was lying asleep on the top of Circe's house, and never thought of coming down again by the great staircase but fell right off the roof and broke my neck, so my soul came down to the house of Hades. And now I beseech you by all those whom you have left behind you, though they are not here, by your wife, by the father who brought you up when you were a child, and by Telemachus who is the one hope of your house, do what I shall now ask you. I know that when you leave this limbo you will again hold your ship for the Aeaean island. Do not go thence leaving me unwaked and unburied behind you, or I may bring heaven's anger upon you; but burn me with whatever armour I have, build a barrow for me on the sea shore, that may tell people in days to come what a poor unlucky fellow I was, and plant over my grave the oar I used to row with when I was yet alive and with my messmates.' And I said, 'My poor fellow, I will do all that you have asked of me.'

"Thus, then, did we sit and hold sad talk with one another, I on the one side of the trench with my sword held over the blood, and the ghost of my comrade saying all this to me from the other side. Then came the ghost of my dead mother Anticlea, daughter to Autolycus. I had left her alive when I set out for Troy and was moved to tears when I saw her, but even so, for all my sorrow I would not let her come near the blood till I had asked my questions of Teiresias.

"Then came also the ghost of Theban Teiresias, with his golden sceptre in his hand. He knew me and said, 'Ulysses, noble son of Laertes, why, poor man, have you left the light of day and come down to visit the dead in this sad place? Stand back from the trench and withdraw your sword that I may drink of the blood and answer your questions truly.'

"So I drew back, and sheathed my sword, whereon when he had drank of the blood he began with his prophecy.

"'You want to know,' said he, 'about your return home, but heaven will make this hard for you. I do not think that you will escape the eye of Neptune, who still nurses his bitter grudge against you for having blinded his son. Still, after much suffering you may get home if you can restrain yourself and your companions when your ship reaches the Thrinacian island, where you will find the sheep and cattle belonging to the sun, who sees and gives ear to everything. If you leave these flocks unharmed and think of nothing but of getting home, you may yet after much hardship reach Ithaca; but if you harm them, then I forewarn you of the destruction both of your ship and of your men. Even though you may yourself escape, you will return in bad plight after losing all your men, [in another man's ship, and you will find trouble in your house, which will be overrun by high-handed people, who are devouring your substance under the pretext of paying court and making presents to your wife.

"'When you get home you will take your revenge on these suitors; and after you have killed them by force or fraud in your own house, you must take a well made oar and carry it on and on, till you come to a country where the people have never heard of the sea and do not even mix salt with their food, nor do they know anything about ships, and oars that are as the wings of a ship. I will give you this certain token which cannot escape your notice. A wayfarer will meet you and will say it must be a winnowing shovel that you have got upon your shoulder; on this you must fix the oar in the ground and sacrifice a ram, a bull, and a boar to Neptune. {90} Then go home and offer hecatombs to all the gods in heaven one after the other. As for yourself, death shall come to you from the sea, and your life shall ebb away very gently when you are full of years and peace of mind, and your people shall bless you. All that I have said will come true].' {91}

"'This,' I answered, 'must be as it may please heaven, but tell me and tell me and tell me true, I see my poor mother's ghost close by us; she is sitting by the blood without saying a word, and though I am her own son she does not remember me and speak to me; tell me, Sir, how I can make her know me.'

"'That,' said he, 'I can soon do. Any ghost that you let taste of the blood will talk with you like a reasonable being, but if you do not let them have any blood they will go away again.'

"On this the ghost of Teiresias went back to the house of Hades, for his prophecyings had now been spoken, but I sat still where I was until my mother came up and tasted the blood. Then she knew me at once and spoke fondly to me, saying, 'My son, how did you come down to this abode of darkness while you are still alive? It is a hard thing for the living to see these places, for between us and them there are great and terrible waters, and there is Oceanus, which no man can cross on foot, but he must have a good ship to take him. Are you all this time trying to find your way home from Troy, and have you never yet got back to Ithaca nor seen your wife in your own house?'

"'Mother,' said I, 'I was forced to come here to consult the ghost of the Theban prophet Teiresias. I have never yet been near the Achaean land nor set foot on my native country, and I have had nothing but one long series of misfortunes from the very first day that I set out with Agamemnon for Ilius, the land of noble steeds, to fight the Trojans. But tell me, and tell me true, in what way did you die? Did you have a long illness, or did heaven vouchsafe you a gentle easy passage to eternity? Tell me also about my father, and the son whom I left behind me, is my property still in their hands, or has some one else got hold of it, who thinks that I shall not return to claim it? Tell me again what my wife intends doing, and in what mind she is; does she live with my son and guard my estate securely, or has she made the best match she could and married again?'

"My mother answered, 'Your wife still remains in your house, but she is in great distress of mind and spends her whole time in tears both night and day. No one as yet has got possession of your fine property, and Telemachus still holds your lands undisturbed. He has to entertain largely, as of course he must, considering his position as a magistrate, {92} and how every one invites him; your father remains at his old place in the country and never goes near the town. He has no comfortable bed nor bedding; in the winter he sleeps on the floor in front of the fire with the men and goes about all in rags, but in summer, when the warm weather comes on again, he lies out in the vineyard on a bed of vine leaves thrown any how upon the ground. He grieves continually about your never having come home, and suffers more and more as he grows older. As for my own end it was in this wise: heaven did not take me swiftly and painlessly in my own house, nor was I attacked by any illness such as those that generally wear people out and kill them, but my longing to know what you were doing and the force of my affection for you—this it was that was the death of me.' {93}

"Then I tried to find some way of embracing my poor mother's ghost. Thrice I sprang towards her and tried to clasp her in my arms, but each time she flitted from my embrace as it were a dream or phantom, and being touched to the quick I said to her, 'Mother, why do you not stay still when I would embrace you? If we could throw our arms around one another we might find sad comfort in the sharing of our sorrows even in the house of Hades; does Proserpine want to lay a still further load of grief upon me by mocking me with a phantom only?'

"'My son,' she answered, 'most ill-fated of all mankind, it is not Proserpine that is beguiling you, but all people are like this when they are dead. The sinews no longer hold the flesh and bones together; these perish in the fierceness of consuming fire as soon as life has left the body, and the soul flits away as though it were a dream. Now, however, go back to the light of day as soon as you can, and note all these things that you may tell them to your wife hereafter.'

"Thus did we converse, and anon Proserpine sent up the ghosts of the wives and daughters of all the most famous men. They gathered in crowds about the blood, and I considered how I might question them severally. In the end I deemed that it would be best to draw the keen blade that hung by my sturdy thigh, and keep them from all drinking the blood at once. So they came up one after the other, and each one as I questioned her told me her race and lineage.

"The first I saw was Tyro. She was daughter of Salmoneus and wife of Cretheus the son of Aeolus. {94} She fell in love with the river Enipeus who is much the most beautiful river in the whole world. Once when she was taking a walk by his side as usual, Neptune, disguised as her lover, lay with her at the mouth of the river, and a huge blue wave arched itself like a mountain over them to hide both woman and god, whereon he loosed her virgin girdle and laid her in a deep slumber. When the god had accomplished the deed of love, he took her hand in his own and said, 'Tyro, rejoice in all good will; the embraces of the gods are not fruitless, and you will have fine twins about this time twelve months. Take great care of them. I am Neptune, so now go home, but hold your tongue and do not tell any one.'

"Then he dived under the sea, and she in due course bore Pelias and Neleus, who both of them served Jove with all their might. Pelias was a great breeder of sheep and lived in Iolcus, but the other lived in Pylos. The rest of her children were by Cretheus, namely, Aeson, Pheres, and Amythaon, who was a mighty warrior and charioteer.

"Next to her I saw Antiope, daughter to Asopus, who could boast of having slept in the arms of even Jove himself, and who bore him two sons Amphion and Zethus. These founded Thebes with its seven gates, and built a wall all round it; for strong though they were they could not hold Thebes till they had walled it.

"Then I saw Alcmena, the wife of Amphitryon, who also bore to Jove indomitable Hercules; and Megara who was daughter to great King Creon, and married the redoubtable son of Amphitryon.

"I also saw fair Epicaste mother of king Oedipodes whose awful lot it was to marry her own son without suspecting it. He married her after having killed his father, but the gods proclaimed the whole story to the world; whereon he remained king of Thebes, in great grief for the spite the gods had borne him; but Epicaste went to the house of the mighty jailor Hades, having hanged herself for grief, and the avenging spirits haunted him as for an outraged mother—to his ruing bitterly thereafter.

"Then I saw Chloris, whom Neleus married for her beauty, having given priceless presents for her. She was youngest daughter to Amphion son of Iasus and king of Minyan Orchomenus, and was Queen in Pylos. She bore Nestor, Chromius, and Periclymenus, and she also bore that marvellously lovely woman Pero, who was wooed by all the country round; but Neleus would only give her to him who should raid the cattle of Iphicles from the grazing grounds of Phylace, and this was a hard task. The only man who would undertake to raid them was a certain excellent seer, {95} but the will of heaven was against him, for the rangers of the cattle caught him and put him in prison; nevertheless when a full year had passed and the same season came round again, Iphicles set him at liberty, after he had expounded all the oracles of heaven. Thus, then, was the will of Jove accomplished.

"And I saw Leda the wife of Tyndarus, who bore him two famous sons, Castor breaker of horses, and Pollux the mighty boxer. Both these heroes are lying under the earth, though they are still alive, for by a special dispensation of Jove, they die and come to life again, each one of them every other day throughout all time, and they have the rank of gods.

"After her I saw Iphimedeia wife of Aloeus who boasted the embrace of Neptune. She bore two sons Otus and Ephialtes, but both were short lived. They were the finest children that were ever born in this world, and the best looking, Orion only excepted; for at nine years old they were nine fathoms high, and measured nine cubits round the chest. They threatened to make war with the gods in Olympus, and tried to set Mount Ossa on the top of Mount Olympus, and Mount Pelion on the top of Ossa, that they might scale heaven itself, and they would have done it too if they had been grown up, but Apollo, son of Leto, killed both of them, before they had got so much as a sign of hair upon their cheeks or chin.

"Then I saw Phaedra, and Procris, and fair Ariadne daughter of the magician Minos, whom Theseus was carrying off from Crete to Athens, but he did not enjoy her, for before he could do so Diana killed her in the island of Dia on account of what Bacchus had said against her.

"I also saw Maera and Clymene and hateful Eriphyle, who sold her own husband for gold. But it would take me all night if I were to name every single one of the wives and daughters of heroes whom I saw, and it is time for me to go to bed, either on board ship with my crew, or here. As for my escort, heaven and yourselves will see to it."

Here he ended, and the guests sat all of them enthralled and speechless throughout the covered cloister. Then Arete said to them:—

"What do you think of this man, O Phaeacians? Is he not tall and good looking, and is he not clever? True, he is my own guest, but all of you share in the distinction. Do not be in a hurry to send him away, nor niggardly in the presents you make to one who is in such great need, for heaven has blessed all of you with great abundance."

Then spoke the aged hero Echeneus who was one of the oldest men among them, "My friends," said he, "what our august queen has just said to us is both reasonable and to the purpose, therefore be persuaded by it; but the decision whether in word or deed rests ultimately with King Alcinous."

"The thing shall be done," exclaimed Alcinous, "as surely as I still live and reign over the Phaeacians. Our guest is indeed very anxious to get home, still we must persuade him to remain with us until to-morrow, by which time I shall be able to get together the whole sum that I mean to give him. As regards his escort it will be a matter for you all, and mine above all others as the chief person among you."

And Ulysses answered, "King Alcinous, if you were to bid me to stay here for a whole twelve months, and then speed me on my way, loaded with your noble gifts, I should obey you gladly and it would redound greatly to my advantage, for I should return fuller-handed to my own people, and should thus be more respected and beloved by all who see me when I get back to Ithaca."

"Ulysses," replied Alcinous, "not one of us who sees you has any idea that you are a charlatan or a swindler. I know there are many people going about who tell such plausible stories that it is very hard to see through them, but there is a style about your language which assures me of your good disposition. Moreover you have told the story of your own misfortunes, and those of the Argives, as though you were a practiced bard; but tell me, and tell me true, whether you saw any of the mighty heroes who went to Troy at the same time with yourself, and perished there. The evenings are still at their longest, and it is not yet bed time—go on, therefore, with your divine story, for I could stay here listening till tomorrow morning, so long as you will continue to tell us of your adventures."

"Alcinous," answered Ulysses, "there is a time for making speeches, and a time for going to bed; nevertheless, since you so desire, I will not refrain from telling you the still sadder tale of those of my comrades who did not fall fighting with the Trojans, but perished on their return, through the treachery of a wicked woman.

"When Proserpine had dismissed the female ghosts in all directions, the ghost of Agamemnon son of Atreus came sadly up to me, surrounded by those who had perished with him in the house of Aegisthus. As soon as he had tasted the blood, he knew me, and weeping bitterly stretched out his arms towards me to embrace me; but he had no strength nor substance any more, and I too wept and pitied him as I beheld him. 'How did you come by your death,' said I, 'King Agamemnon? Did Neptune raise his winds and waves against you when you were at sea, or did your enemies make an end of you on the main land when you were cattle-lifting or sheep-stealing, or while they were fighting in defence of their wives and city?'

"'Ulysses,' he answered, 'noble son of Laertes, I was not lost at sea in any storm of Neptune's raising, nor did my foes despatch me upon the mainland, but Aegisthus and my wicked wife were the death of me between them. He asked me to his house, feasted me, and then butchered me most miserably as though I were a fat beast in a slaughter house, while all around me my comrades were slain like sheep or pigs for the wedding breakfast, or picnic, or gorgeous banquet of some great nobleman. You must have seen numbers of men killed either in a general engagement, or in single combat, but you never saw anything so truly pitiable as the way in which we fell in that cloister, with the mixing bowl and the loaded tables lying all about, and the ground reeking with our blood. I heard Priam's daughter Cassandra scream as Clytemnestra killed her close beside me. I lay dying upon the earth with the sword in my body, and raised my hands to kill the slut of a murderess, but she slipped away from me; she would not even close my lips nor my eyes when I was dying, for there is nothing in this world so cruel and so shameless as a woman when she has fallen into such guilt as hers was. Fancy murdering her own husband! I thought I was going to be welcomed home by my children and my servants, but her abominable crime has brought disgrace on herself and all women who shall come after—even on the good ones.'

"And I said, 'In truth Jove has hated the house of Atreus from first to last in the matter of their women's counsels. See how many of us fell for Helen's sake, and now it seems that Clytemnestra hatched mischief against you too during your absence.'

"'Be sure, therefore,' continued Agamemnon, 'and not be too friendly even with your own wife. Do not tell her all that you know perfectly well yourself. Tell her a part only, and keep your own counsel about the rest.

Not that your wife, Ulysses, is likely to murder you, for Penelope is a very admirable woman, and has an excellent nature. We left her a young bride with an infant at her breast when we set out for Troy. This child no doubt is now grown up happily to man's estate, {96} and he and his father will have a joyful meeting and embrace one another as it is right they should do, whereas my wicked wife did not even allow me the happiness of looking upon my son, but killed me ere I could do so. Furthermore I say—and lay my saying to your heart—do not tell people when you are bringing your ship to Ithaca, but steal a march upon them, for after all this there is no trusting women. But now tell me, and tell me true, can you give me any news of my son Orestes? Is he in Orchomenus, or at Pylos, or is he at Sparta with Menelaus—for I presume that he is still living.'

"And I said, 'Agamemnon, why do you ask me? I do not know whether your son is alive or dead, and it is not right to talk when one does not know.'

"As we two sat weeping and talking thus sadly with one another the ghost of Achilles came up to us with Patroclus, Antilochus, and Ajax who was the finest and goodliest man of all the Danaans after the son of Peleus. The fleet descendant of Aeacus knew me and spoke piteously, saying, 'Ulysses, noble son of Laertes, what deed of daring will you undertake next, that you venture down to the house of Hades among us silly dead, who are but the ghosts of them that can labour no more?'

"And I said, 'Achilles, son of Peleus, foremost champion of the Achaeans, I came to consult Teiresias, and see if he could advise me about my return home to Ithaca, for I have never yet been able to get near the Achaean land, nor to set foot in my own country, but have been in trouble all the time. As for you, Achilles, no one was ever yet so fortunate as you have been, nor ever will be, for you were adored by all us Argives as long as you were alive, and now that you are here you are a great prince among the dead. Do not, therefore, take it so much to heart even if you are dead.'

"'Say not a word,' he answered, 'in death's favour; I would rather be a paid servant in a poor man's house and be above ground than king of kings among the dead. But give me news about my son; is he gone to the wars and will he be a great soldier, or is this not so? Tell me also if you have heard anything about my father Peleus—does he still rule among the Myrmidons, or do they show him no respect throughout Hellas and Phthia now that he is old and his limbs fail him? Could I but stand by his side, in the light of day, with the same strength that I had when I killed the bravest of our foes upon the plain of Troy—could I but be as I then was and go even for a short time to my father's house, any one who tried to do him violence or supersede him would soon rue it.'

"'I have heard nothing,' I answered, 'of Peleus, but I can tell you all about your son Neoptolemus, for I took him in my own ship from Scyros with the Achaeans. In our councils of war before Troy he was always first to speak, and his judgement was unerring. Nestor and I were the only two who could surpass him; and when it came to fighting on the plain of Troy, he would never remain with the body of his men, but would dash on far in front, foremost of them all in valour. Many a man did he kill in battle—I cannot name every single one of those whom he slew while fighting on the side of the Argives, but will only say how he killed that valiant hero Eurypylus son of Telephus, who was the handsomest man I ever saw except Memnon; many others also of the Ceteians fell around him by reason of a woman's bribes. Moreover, when all the bravest of the Argives went inside the horse that Epeus had made, and it was left to me to settle when we should either open the door of our ambuscade, or close it, though all the other leaders and chief men among the Danaans were drying their eyes and quaking in every limb, I never once saw him turn pale nor wipe a tear from his cheek; he was all the time urging me to break out from the horse—grasping the handle of his sword and his bronze-shod spear, and breathing fury against the foe. Yet when we had sacked the city of Priam he got his handsome share of the prize money and went on board (such is the fortune of war) without a wound upon him, neither from a thrown spear nor in close combat, for the rage of Mars is a matter of great chance.'

"When I had told him this, the ghost of Achilles strode off across a meadow full of asphodel, exulting over what I had said concerning the prowess of his son.

"The ghosts of other dead men stood near me and told me each his own melancholy tale; but that of Ajax son of Telamon alone held aloof—still angry with me for having won the cause in our dispute about the armour of Achilles. Thetis had offered it as a prize, but the Trojan prisoners and Minerva were the judges. Would that I had never gained the day in such a contest, for it cost the life of Ajax, who was foremost of all the Danaans after the son of Peleus, alike in stature and prowess.

"When I saw him I tried to pacify him and said, 'Ajax, will you not forget and forgive even in death, but must the judgement about that hateful armour still rankle with you? It cost us Argives dear enough to lose such a tower of strength as you were to us. We mourned you as much as we mourned Achilles son of Peleus himself, nor can the blame be laid on anything but on the spite which Jove bore against the Danaans, for it was this that made him counsel your destruction—come hither, therefore, bring your proud spirit into subjection, and hear what I can tell you.'

"He would not answer, but turned away to Erebus and to the other ghosts; nevertheless, I should have made him talk to me in spite of his being so angry, or I should have gone on talking to him, {97} only that there were still others among the dead whom I desired to see.

"Then I saw Minos son of Jove with his golden sceptre in his hand sitting in judgement on the dead, and the ghosts were gathered sitting and standing round him in the spacious house of Hades, to learn his sentences upon them.

"After him I saw huge Orion in a meadow full of asphodel driving the ghosts of the wild beasts that he had killed upon the mountains, and he had a great bronze club in his hand, unbreakable for ever and ever.

"And I saw Tityus son of Gaia stretched upon the plain and covering some nine acres of ground. Two vultures on either side of him were digging their beaks into his liver, and he kept on trying to beat them off with his hands, but could not; for he had violated Jove's mistress Leto as she was going through Panopeus on her way to Pytho.

"I saw also the dreadful fate of Tantalus, who stood in a lake that reached his chin; he was dying to quench his thirst, but could never reach the water, for whenever the poor creature stooped to drink, it dried up and vanished, so that there was nothing but dry ground—parched by the spite of heaven. There were tall trees, moreover, that shed their fruit over his head—pears, pomegranates, apples, sweet figs and juicy olives, but whenever the poor creature stretched out his hand to take some, the wind tossed the branches back again to the clouds.

"And I saw Sisyphus at his endless task raising his prodigious stone with both his hands. With hands and feet he tried to roll it up to the top of the hill, but always, just before he could roll it over on to the other side, its weight would be too much for him, and the pitiless stone {98} would come thundering down again on to the plain. Then he would begin trying to push it up hill again, and the sweat ran off him and the steam rose after him.

"After him I saw mighty Hercules, but it was his phantom only, for he is feasting ever with the immortal gods, and has lovely Hebe to wife, who is daughter of Jove and Juno. The ghosts were screaming round him like scared birds flying all whithers. He looked black as night with his bare bow in his hands and his arrow on the string, glaring around as though ever on the point of taking aim. About his breast there was a wondrous golden belt adorned in the most marvellous fashion with bears, wild boars, and lions with gleaming eyes; there was also war, battle, and death. The man who made that belt, do what he might, would never be able to make another like it. Hercules knew me at once when he saw me, and spoke piteously, saying, 'My poor Ulysses, noble son of Laertes, are you too leading the same sorry kind of life that I did when I was above ground? I was son of Jove, but I went through an infinity of suffering, for I became bondsman to one who was far beneath me—a low fellow who set me all manner of labours. He once sent me here to fetch the hell-hound—for he did not think he could find anything harder for me than this, but I got the hound out of Hades and brought him to him, for Mercury and Minerva helped me.'

"On this Hercules went down again into the house of Hades, but I stayed where I was in case some other of the mighty dead should come to me. And I should have seen still other of them that are gone before, whom I would fain have seen—Theseus and Pirithous—glorious children of the gods, but so many thousands of ghosts came round me and uttered such appalling cries, that I was panic stricken lest Proserpine should send up from the house of Hades the head of that awful monster Gorgon. On this I hastened back to my ship and ordered my men to go on board at once and loose the hawsers; so they embarked and took their places, whereon the ship went down the stream of the river Oceanus. We had to row at first, but presently a fair wind sprang up.

BOOK XII

The Sirens, Scylla and Charybdis, the cattle of the sun.

"After we were clear of the river Oceanus, and had got out into the open sea, we went on till we reached the Aeaean island where there is dawn and sun-rise as in other places. We then drew our ship on to the sands and got out of her on to the shore, where we went to sleep and waited till day should break.

"Then, when the child of morning, rosy-fingered Dawn, appeared, I sent some men to Circe's house to fetch the body of Elpenor. We cut firewood from a wood where the headland jutted out into the sea, and after we had wept over him and lamented him we performed his funeral rites. When his body and armour had been burned to ashes, we raised a cairn, set a stone over it, and at the top of the cairn we fixed the oar that he had been used to row with.

"While we were doing all this, Circe, who knew that we had got back from the house of Hades, dressed herself and came to us as fast as she could; and her maid servants came with her bringing us bread, meat, and wine. Then she stood in the midst of us and said, 'You have done a bold thing in going down alive to the house of Hades, and you will have died twice, to other people's once; now, then, stay here for the rest of the day, feast your fill, and go on with your voyage at daybreak tomorrow morning. In the meantime I will tell Ulysses about your course, and will explain everything to him so as to prevent your suffering from misadventure either by land or sea.'

"We agreed to do as she had said, and feasted through the livelong day to the going down of the sun, but when the sun had set and it came on dark, the men laid themselves down to sleep by the stern cables of the ship. Then Circe took me by the hand and bade me be seated away from the others, while she reclined by my side and asked me all about our adventures.

"'So far so good,' said she, when I had ended my story, 'and now pay attention to what I am about to tell you—heaven itself, indeed, will recall it to your recollection. First you will come to the Sirens who enchant all who come near them. If any one unwarily draws in too close and hears the singing of the Sirens, his wife and children will never welcome him home again, for they sit in a green field and warble him to death with the sweetness of their song. There is a great heap of dead men's bones lying all around, with the flesh still rotting off them. Therefore pass these Sirens by, and stop your men's ears with wax that none of them may hear; but if you like you can listen yourself, for you may get the men to bind you as you stand upright on a cross piece half way up the mast, {99} and they must lash the rope's ends to the mast itself, that you may have the pleasure of listening. If you beg and pray the men to unloose you, then they must bind you faster.

"'When your crew have taken you past these Sirens, I cannot give you coherent directions {100} as to which of two courses you are to take; I will lay the two alternatives before you, and you must consider them for yourself. On the one hand there are some overhanging rocks against which the deep blue waves of Amphitrite beat with terrific fury; the blessed gods call these rocks the Wanderers. Here not even a bird may pass, no, not even the timid doves that bring ambrosia to Father Jove, but the sheer rock always carries off one of them, and Father Jove has to send another to make up their number; no ship that ever yet came to these rocks has got away again, but the waves and whirlwinds of fire are freighted with wreckage and with the bodies of dead men. The only vessel that ever sailed and got through, was the famous Argo on her way from the house of Aetes, and she too would have gone against these great rocks, only that Juno piloted her past them for the love she bore to Jason.

"'Of these two rocks the one reaches heaven and its peak is lost in a dark cloud. This never leaves it, so that the top is never clear not even in summer and early autumn. No man though he had twenty hands and twenty feet could get a foothold on it and climb it, for it runs sheer up, as smooth as though it had been polished. In the middle of it there is a large cavern, looking West and turned towards Erebus; you must take your ship this way, but the cave is so high up that not even the stoutest archer could send an arrow into it. Inside it Scylla sits and yelps with a voice that you might take to be that of a young hound, but in truth she is a dreadful monster and no one—not even a god—could face her without being terror-struck. She has twelve mis-shapen feet, and six necks of the most prodigious length; and at the end of each neck she has a frightful head with three rows of teeth in each, all set very close together, so that they would crunch any one to death in a moment, and she sits deep within her shady cell thrusting out her heads and peering all round the rock, fishing for dolphins or dogfish or any larger monster that she can catch, of the thousands with which Amphitrite teems. No ship ever yet got past her without losing some men, for she shoots out all her heads at once, and carries off a man in each mouth.

"'You will find the other rock lie lower, but they are so close together that there is not more than a bow-shot between them. [A large fig tree in full leaf {101} grows upon it], and under it lies the sucking whirlpool of Charybdis. Three times in the day does she vomit forth her waters, and three times she sucks them down again; see that you be not there when she is sucking, for if you are, Neptune himself could not save you; you must hug the Scylla side and drive ship by as fast as you can, for you had better lose six men than your whole crew.'

"'Is there no way,' said I, 'of escaping Charybdis, and at the same time keeping Scylla off when she is trying to harm my men?'

"'You dare devil,' replied the goddess, 'you are always wanting to fight somebody or something; you will not let yourself be beaten even by the immortals. For Scylla is not mortal; moreover she is savage, extreme, rude, cruel and invincible. There is no help for it; your best chance will be to get by her as fast as ever you can, for if you dawdle about her rock while you are putting on your armour, she may catch you with a second cast of her six heads, and snap up another half dozen of your men; so drive your ship past her at full speed, and roar out lustily to Crataiis who is Scylla's dam, bad luck to her; she will then stop her from making a second raid upon you.'

"'You will now come to the Thrinacian island, and here you will see many herds of cattle and flocks of sheep belonging to the sun-god—seven herds of cattle and seven flocks of sheep, with fifty head in each flock. They do not breed, nor do they become fewer in number, and they are tended by the goddesses Phaethusa and Lampetie, who are children of the sun-god Hyperion by Neaera. Their mother when she had borne them and had done suckling them sent them to the Thrinacian island, which was a long way off, to live there and look after their father's flocks and herds. If you leave these flocks unharmed, and think of nothing but getting home, you may yet after much hardship reach Ithaca; but if you harm them, then I forewarn you of the destruction both of your ship and of your comrades; and even though you may yourself escape, you will return late, in bad plight, after losing all your men.'

"Here she ended, and dawn enthroned in gold began to show in heaven, whereon she returned inland. I then went on board and told my men to loose the ship from her moorings; so they at once got into her, took their places, and began to smite the grey sea with their oars. Presently the great and cunning goddess Circe befriended us with a fair wind that blew dead aft, and staid steadily with us, keeping our sails well filled, so we did whatever wanted doing to the ship's gear, and let her go as wind and helmsman headed her.

"Then, being much troubled in mind, I said to my men, 'My friends, it is not right that one or two of us alone should know the prophecies that Circe has made me, I will therefore tell you about them, so that whether we live or die we may do so with our eyes open. First she said we were to keep clear of the Sirens, who sit and sing most beautifully in a field of flowers; but she said I might hear them myself so long as no one else did. Therefore, take me and bind me to the crosspiece half way up the mast; bind me as I stand upright, with a bond so fast that I cannot possibly break away, and lash the rope's ends to the mast itself. If I beg and pray you to set me free, then bind me more tightly still.'

"I had hardly finished telling everything to the men before we reached the island of the two Sirens, {102} for the wind had been very favourable. Then all of a sudden it fell dead calm; there was not a breath of wind nor a ripple upon the water, so the men furled the sails and stowed them; then taking to their oars they whitened the water with the foam they raised in rowing. Meanwhile I took a large wheel of wax and cut it up small with my sword. Then I kneaded the wax in my strong hands till it became soft, which it soon did between the kneading and the rays of the sun-god son of Hyperion. Then I stopped the ears of all my men, and they bound me hands and feet to the mast as I stood upright on the cross piece; but they went on rowing themselves. When we had got within earshot of the land, and the ship was going at a good rate, the Sirens saw that we were getting in shore and began with their singing.

"'Come here,' they sang, 'renowned Ulysses, honour to the Achaean name, and listen to our two voices. No one ever sailed past us without staying to hear the enchanting sweetness of our song—and he who listens will go on his way not only charmed, but wiser, for we know all the ills that the gods laid upon the Argives and Trojans before Troy, and can tell you everything that is going to happen over the whole world.'

"They sang these words most musically, and as I longed to hear them further I made signs by frowning to my men that they should set me free; but they quickened their stroke, and Eurylochus and Perimedes bound me with still stronger bonds till we had got out of hearing of the Sirens' voices. Then my men took the wax from their ears and unbound me.

"Immediately after we had got past the island I saw a great wave from which spray was rising, and I heard a loud roaring sound. The men were so frightened that they loosed hold of their oars, for the whole sea resounded with the rushing of the waters, {103} but the ship stayed where it was, for the men had left off rowing. I went round, therefore, and exhorted them man by man not to lose heart.

"'My friends,' said I, 'this is not the first time that we have been in danger, and we are in nothing like so bad a case as when the Cyclops shut us up in his cave; nevertheless, my courage and wise counsel saved us then, and we shall live to look back on all this as well. Now, therefore, let us all do as I say, trust in Jove and row on with might and main. As for you, coxswain, these are your orders; attend to them, for the ship is in your hands; turn her head away from these steaming rapids and hug the rock, or she will give you the slip and be over yonder before you know where you are, and you will be the death of us.'

"So they did as I told them; but I said nothing about the awful monster Scylla, for I knew the men would not go on rowing if I did, but would huddle together in the hold. In one thing only did I disobey Circe's strict instructions—I put on my armour. Then seizing two strong spears I took my stand on the ship's bows, for it was there that I expected first to see the monster of the rock, who was to do my men so much harm; but I could not make her out anywhere, though I strained my eyes with looking the gloomy rock all over and over.

"Then we entered the Straits in great fear of mind, for on the one hand was Scylla, and on the other dread Charybdis kept sucking up the salt water. As she vomited it up, it was like the water in a cauldron when it is boiling over upon a great fire, and the spray reached the top of the rocks on either side. When she began to suck again, we could see the water all inside whirling round and round, and it made a deafening sound as it broke against the rocks. We could see the bottom of the whirlpool all black with sand and mud, and the men were at their wits ends for fear. While we were taken up with this, and were expecting each moment to be our last, Scylla pounced down suddenly upon us and snatched up my six best men. I was looking at once after both ship and men, and in a moment I saw their hands and feet ever so high above me, struggling in the air as Scylla was carrying them off, and I heard them call out my name in one last despairing cry. As a fisherman, seated, spear in hand, upon some jutting rock {104} throws bait into the water to deceive the poor little fishes, and spears them with the ox's horn with which his spear is shod, throwing them gasping on to the land as he catches them one by one—even so did Scylla land these panting creatures on her rock and munch them up at the mouth of her den, while they screamed and stretched out their hands to me in their mortal agony. This was the most sickening sight that I saw throughout all my voyages.

"When we had passed the [Wandering] rocks, with Scylla and terrible Charybdis, we reached the noble island of the sun-god, where were the goodly cattle and sheep belonging to the sun Hyperion. While still at sea in my ship I could hear the cattle lowing as they came home to the yards, and the sheep bleating. Then I remembered what the blind Theban prophet Teiresias had told me, and how carefully Aeaean Circe had warned me to shun the island of the blessed sun-god. So being much troubled I said to the men, 'My men, I know you are hard pressed, but listen while I tell you the prophecy that Teiresias made me, and how carefully Aeaean Circe warned me to shun the island of the blessed sun-god, for it was here, she said, that our worst danger would lie. Head the ship, therefore, away from the island.'

"The men were in despair at this, and Eurylochus at once gave me an insolent answer. 'Ulysses,' said he, 'you are cruel; you are very strong yourself and never get worn out; you seem to be made of iron, and now, though your men are exhausted with toil and want of sleep, you will not let them land and cook themselves a good supper upon this island, but bid them put out to sea and go faring fruitlessly on through the watches of the flying night. It is by night that the winds blow hardest and do so much damage; how can we escape should one of those sudden squalls spring up from South West or West, which so often wreck a vessel when our lords the gods are unpropitious? Now, therefore, let us obey the behests of night and prepare our supper here hard by the ship; to-morrow morning we will go on board again and put out to sea.'

"Thus spoke Eurylochus, and the men approved his words. I saw that heaven meant us a mischief and said, 'You force me to yield, for you are many against one, but at any rate each one of you must take his solemn oath that if he meet with a herd of cattle or a large flock of sheep, he will not be so mad as to kill a single head of either, but will be satisfied with the food that Circe has given us.'

"They all swore as I bade them, and when they had completed their oath we made the ship fast in a harbour that was near a stream of fresh water, and the men went ashore and cooked their suppers. As soon as they had had enough to eat and drink, they began talking about their poor comrades whom Scylla had snatched up and eaten; this set them weeping and they went on crying till they fell off into a sound sleep.

"In the third watch of the night when the stars had shifted their places, Jove raised a great gale of wind that flew a hurricane so that land and sea were covered with thick clouds, and night sprang forth out of the heavens. When the child of morning, rosy-fingered Dawn, appeared, we brought the ship to land and drew her into a cave wherein the sea-nymphs hold their courts and dances, and I called the men together in council.

"'My friends,' said I, 'we have meat and drink in the ship, let us mind, therefore, and not touch the cattle, or we shall suffer for it; for these cattle and sheep belong to the mighty sun, who sees and gives ear to everything.' And again they promised that they would obey.

"For a whole month the wind blew steadily from the South, and there was no other wind, but only South and East. {105} As long as corn and wine held out the men did not touch the cattle when they were hungry; when, however, they had eaten all there was in the ship, they were forced to go further afield, with hook and line, catching birds, and taking whatever they could lay their hands on; for they were starving. One day, therefore, I went up inland that I might pray heaven to show me some means of getting away. When I had gone far enough to be clear of all my men, and had found a place that was well sheltered from the wind, I washed my hands and prayed to all the gods in Olympus till by and by they sent me off into a sweet sleep.

"Meanwhile Eurylochus had been giving evil counsel to the men, 'Listen to me,' said he, 'my poor comrades. All deaths are bad enough but there is none so bad as famine. Why should not we drive in the best of these cows and offer them in sacrifice to the immortal gods? If we ever get back to Ithaca, we can build a fine temple to the sun-god and enrich it with every kind of ornament; if, however, he is determined to sink our ship out of revenge for these homed cattle, and the other gods are of the same mind, I for one would rather drink salt water once for all and have done with it, than be starved to death by inches in such a desert island as this is.'

"Thus spoke Eurylochus, and the men approved his words. Now the cattle, so fair and goodly, were feeding not far from the ship; the men, therefore, drove in the best of them, and they all stood round them saying their prayers, and using young oak-shoots instead of barley-meal, for there was no barley left. When they had done praying they killed the cows and dressed their carcasses; they cut out the thigh bones, wrapped them round in two layers of fat, and set some pieces of raw meat on top of them. They had no wine with which to make drink-offerings over the sacrifice while it was cooking, so they kept pouring on a little water from time to time while the inward meats were being grilled; then, when the thigh bones were burned and they had tasted the inward meats, they cut the rest up small and put the pieces upon the spits.

"By this time my deep sleep had left me, and I turned back to the ship and to the sea shore. As I drew near I began to smell hot roast meat, so I groaned out a prayer to the immortal gods. 'Father Jove,' I exclaimed, 'and all you other gods who live in everlasting bliss, you have done me a cruel mischief by the sleep into which you have sent me; see what fine work these men of mine have been making in my absence.'

"Meanwhile Lampetie went straight off to the sun and told him we had been killing his cows, whereon he flew into a great rage, and said to the immortals, 'Father Jove, and all you other gods who live in everlasting bliss, I must have vengeance on the crew of Ulysses' ship: they have had the insolence to kill my cows, which were the one thing I loved to look upon, whether I was going up heaven or down again. If they do not square accounts with me about my cows, I will go down to Hades and shine there among the dead.'

"'Sun,' said Jove, 'go on shining upon us gods and upon mankind over the fruitful earth. I will shiver their ship into little pieces with a bolt of white lightning as soon as they get out to sea.'

"I was told all this by Calypso, who said she had heard it from the mouth of Mercury.

"As soon as I got down to my ship and to the sea shore I rebuked each one of the men separately, but we could see no way out of it, for the cows were dead already. And indeed the gods began at once to show signs and wonders among us, for the hides of the cattle crawled about, and the joints upon the spits began to low like cows, and the meat, whether cooked or raw, kept on making a noise just as cows do.

"For six days my men kept driving in the best cows and feasting upon them, but when Jove the son of Saturn had added a seventh day, the fury of the gale abated; we therefore went on board, raised our masts, spread sail, and put out to sea. As soon as we were well away from the island, and could see nothing but sky and sea, the son of Saturn raised a black cloud over our ship, and the sea grew dark beneath it. We did not get on much further, for in another moment we were caught by a terrific squall from the West that snapped the forestays of the mast so that it fell aft, while all the ship's gear tumbled about at the bottom of the vessel. The mast fell upon the head of the helmsman in the ship's stern, so that the bones of his head were crushed to pieces, and he fell overboard as though he were diving, with no more life left in him.

"Then Jove let fly with his thunderbolts, and the ship went round and round, and was filled with fire and brimstone as the lightning struck it. The men all fell into the sea; they were carried about in the water round the ship, looking like so many sea-gulls, but the god presently deprived them of all chance of getting home again.

"I stuck to the ship till the sea knocked her sides from her keel (which drifted about by itself) and struck the mast out of her in the direction of the keel; but there was a backstay of stout ox-thong still hanging about it, and with this I lashed the mast and keel together, and getting astride of them was carried wherever the winds chose to take me.

"[The gale from the West had now spent its force, and the wind got into the South again, which frightened me lest I should be taken back to the terrible whirlpool of Charybdis. This indeed was what actually happened, for I was borne along by the waves all night, and by sunrise had reached the rock of Scylla, and the whirlpool. She was then sucking down the salt sea water, {106} but I was carried aloft toward the fig tree, which I caught hold of and clung on to like a bat. I could not plant my feet anywhere so as to stand securely, for the roots were a long way off and the boughs that overshadowed the whole pool were too high, too vast, and too far apart for me to reach them; so I hung patiently on, waiting till the pool should discharge my mast and raft again—and a very long while it seemed. A jury-man is not more glad to get home to supper, after having been long detained in court by troublesome cases, than I was to see my raft beginning to work its way out of the whirlpool again. At last I let go with my hands and feet, and fell heavily into the sea, hard by my raft on to which I then got, and began to row with my hands. As for Scylla, the father of gods and men would not let her get further sight of me—otherwise I should have certainly been lost.] {107}

"Hence I was carried along for nine days till on the tenth night the gods stranded me on the Ogygian island, where dwells the great and powerful goddess Calypso. She took me in and was kind to me, but I need say no more about this, for I told you and your noble wife all about it yesterday, and I hate saying the same thing over and over again."

BOOK XIII

Ulysses leaves Scheria and returns to Ithaca.

Thus did he speak, and they all held their peace throughout the covered cloister, enthralled by the charm of his story, till presently Alcinous began to speak.

"Ulysses," said he, "now that you have reached my house I doubt not you will get home without further misadventure no matter how much you have suffered in the past. To you others, however, who come here night after night to drink my choicest wine and listen to my bard, I would insist as follows. Our guest has already packed up the clothes, wrought gold, {108} and other valuables which you have brought for his acceptance; let us now, therefore, present him further, each one of us, with a large tripod and a cauldron. We will recoup ourselves by the levy of a general rate; for private individuals cannot be expected to bear the burden of such a handsome present."

Every one approved of this, and then they went home to bed each in his own abode. When the child of morning, rosy-fingered Dawn, appeared they hurried down to the ship and brought their cauldrons with them. Alcinous went on board and saw everything so securely stowed under the ship's benches that nothing could break adrift and injure the rowers. Then they went to the house of Alcinous to get dinner, and he sacrificed a bull for them in honour of Jove who is the lord of all. They set the steaks to grill and made an excellent dinner, after which the inspired bard, Demodocus, who was a favourite with every one, sang to them; but Ulysses kept on turning his eyes towards the sun, as though to hasten his setting, for he was longing to be on his way. As one who has been all day ploughing a fallow field with a couple of oxen keeps thinking about his supper and is glad when night comes that he may go and get it, for it is all his legs can do to carry him, even so did Ulysses rejoice when the sun went down, and he at once said to the Phaeacians, addressing himself more particularly to King Alcinous:

"Sir, and all of you, farewell. Make your drink-offerings and send me on my way rejoicing, for you have fulfilled my heart's desire by giving me an escort, and making me presents, which heaven grant that I may turn to good account; may I find my admirable wife living in peace among friends, {109} and may you whom I leave behind me give satisfaction to your wives and children; {110} may heaven vouchsafe you every good grace, and may no evil thing come among your people."

Thus did he speak. His hearers all of them approved his saying and agreed that he should have his escort inasmuch as he had spoken reasonably. Alcinous therefore said to his servant, "Pontonous, mix some wine and hand it round to everybody, that we may offer a prayer to father Jove, and speed our guest upon his way."

Pontonous mixed the wine and handed it to every one in turn; the others each from his own seat made a drink-offering to the blessed gods that live in heaven, but Ulysses rose and placed the double cup in the hands of queen Arete.

"Farewell, queen," said he, "henceforward and for ever, till age and death, the common lot of mankind, lay their hands upon you. I now take my leave; be happy in this house with your children, your people, and with king Alcinous."

As he spoke he crossed the threshold, and Alcinous sent a man to conduct him to his ship and to the sea shore. Arete also sent some maidservants with him—one with a clean shirt and cloak, another to carry his strong box, and a third with corn and wine. When they got to the water side the crew took these things and put them on board, with all the meat and drink; but for Ulysses they spread a rug and a linen sheet on deck that he might sleep soundly in the stern of the ship. Then he too went on board and lay down without a word, but the crew took every man his place and loosed the hawser from the pierced stone to which it had been bound. Thereon, when they began rowing out to sea, Ulysses fell into a deep, sweet, and almost deathlike slumber. {111}

The ship bounded forward on her way as a four in hand chariot flies over the course when the horses feel the whip. Her prow curvetted as it were the neck of a stallion, and a great wave of dark blue water seethed in her wake. She held steadily on her course, and even a falcon, swiftest of all birds, could not have kept pace with her. Thus, then, she cut her way through the water, carrying one who was as cunning as the gods, but who was now sleeping peacefully, forgetful of all that he had suffered both on the field of battle and by the waves of the weary sea.

When the bright star that heralds the approach of dawn began to show, the ship drew near to land. {112} Now there is in Ithaca a haven of the old merman Phorcys, which lies between two points that break the line of the sea and shut the harbour in. These shelter it from the storms of wind and sea that rage outside, so that, when once within it, a ship may lie without being even moored. At the head of this harbour there is a large olive tree, and at no great distance a fine overarching cavern sacred to the nymphs who are called Naiads. {113} There are mixing bowls within it and wine-jars of stone, and the bees hive there. Moreover, there are great looms of stone on which the nymphs weave their robes of sea purple—very curious to see—and at all times there is water within it. It has two entrances, one facing North by which mortals can go down into the cave, while the other comes from the South and is more mysterious; mortals cannot possibly get in by it, it is the way taken by the gods.

Into this harbour, then, they took their ship, for they knew the place. {114} She had so much way upon her that she ran half her own length on to the shore; {115} when, however, they had landed, the first thing they did was to lift Ulysses with his rug and linen sheet out of the ship, and lay him down upon the sand still fast asleep. Then they took out the presents which Minerva had persuaded the Phaeacians to give him when he was setting out on his voyage homewards. They put these all together by the root of the olive tree, away from the road, for fear some passer by {116} might come and steal them before Ulysses awoke; and then they made the best of their way home again.

But Neptune did not forget the threats with which he had already threatened Ulysses, so he took counsel with Jove. "Father Jove," said he, "I shall no longer be held in any sort of respect among you gods, if mortals like the Phaeacians, who are my own flesh and blood, show such small regard for me. I said I would let Ulysses get home when he had suffered sufficiently. I did not say that he should never get home at all, for I knew you had already nodded your head about it, and promised that he should do so; but now they have brought him in a ship fast asleep and have landed him in Ithaca after loading him with more magnificent presents of bronze, gold, and raiment than he would ever have brought back from Troy, if he had had his share of the spoil and got home without misadventure."

And Jove answered, "What, O Lord of the Earthquake, are you talking about? The gods are by no means wanting in respect for you. It would be monstrous were they to insult one so old and honoured as you are. As regards mortals, however, if any of them is indulging in insolence and treating you disrespectfully, it will always rest with yourself to deal with him as you may think proper, so do just as you please."

"I should have done so at once," replied Neptune, "if I were not anxious to avoid anything that might displease you; now, therefore, I should like to wreck the Phaeacian ship as it is returning from its escort. This will stop them from escorting people in future; and I should also like to bury their city under a huge mountain."

"My good friend," answered Jove, "I should recommend you at the very moment when the people from the city are watching the ship on her way, to turn it into a rock near the land and looking like a ship. This will astonish everybody, and you can then bury their city under the mountain."

When earth-encircling Neptune heard this he went to Scheria where the Phaeacians live, and stayed there till the ship, which was making rapid way, had got close in. Then he went up to it, turned it into stone, and drove it down with the flat of his hand so as to root it in the ground. After this he went away.

The Phaeacians then began talking among themselves, and one would turn towards his neighbour, saying, "Bless my heart, who is it that can have rooted the ship in the sea just as she was getting into port? We could see the whole of her only a moment ago."

This was how they talked, but they knew nothing about it; and Alcinous said, "I remember now the old prophecy of my father. He said that

Neptune would be angry with us for taking every one so safely over the sea, and would one day wreck a Phaeacian ship as it was returning from an escort, and bury our city under a high mountain. This was what my old father used to say, and now it is all coming true. {117} Now therefore let us all do as I say; in the first place we must leave off giving people escorts when they come here, and in the next let us sacrifice twelve picked bulls to Neptune that he may have mercy upon us, and not bury our city under the high mountain." When the people heard this they were afraid and got ready the bulls.

Thus did the chiefs and rulers of the Phaeacians pray to king Neptune, standing round his altar; and at the same time {118} Ulysses woke up once more upon his own soil. He had been so long away that he did not know it again; moreover, Jove's daughter Minerva had made it a foggy day, so that people might not know of his having come, and that she might tell him everything without either his wife or his fellow citizens and friends recognising him {119} until he had taken his revenge upon the wicked suitors. Everything, therefore, seemed quite different to him—the long straight tracks, the harbours, the precipices, and the goodly trees, appeared all changed as he started up and looked upon his native land. So he smote his thighs with the flat of his hands and cried aloud despairingly.

"Alas," he exclaimed, "among what manner of people am I fallen? Are they savage and uncivilised or hospitable and humane? Where shall I put all this treasure, and which way shall I go? I wish I had staid over there with the Phaeacians; or I could have gone to some other great chief who would have been good to me and given me an escort. As it is I do not know where to put my treasure, and I cannot leave it here for fear somebody else should get hold of it. In good truth the chiefs and rulers of the Phaeacians have not been dealing fairly by me, and have left me in the wrong country; they said they would take me back to Ithaca and they have not done so: may Jove the protector of suppliants chastise them, for he watches over everybody and punishes those who do wrong. Still, I suppose I must count my goods and see if the crew have gone off with any of them."

He counted his goodly coppers and cauldrons, his gold and all his clothes, but there was nothing missing; still he kept grieving about not being in his own country, and wandered up and down by the shore of the sounding sea bewailing his hard fate. Then Minerva came up to him disguised as a young shepherd of delicate and princely mien, with a good cloak folded double about her shoulders; she had sandals on her comely feet and held a javelin in her hand. Ulysses was glad when he saw her, and went straight up to her.

"My friend," said he, "you are the first person whom I have met with in this country; I salute you, therefore, and beg you to be well disposed towards me. Protect these my goods, and myself too, for I embrace your knees and pray to you as though you were a god. Tell me, then, and tell me truly, what land and country is this? Who are its inhabitants? Am I on an island, or is this the sea board of some continent?"

Minerva answered, "Stranger, you must be very simple, or must have come from somewhere a long way off, not to know what country this is. It is a very celebrated place, and everybody knows it East and West. It is rugged and not a good driving country, but it is by no means a bad island for what there is of it. It grows any quantity of corn and also wine, for it is watered both by rain and dew; it breeds cattle also and goats; all kinds of timber grow here, and there are watering places where the water never runs dry; so, sir, the name of Ithaca is known even as far as Troy, which I understand to be a long way off from this Achaean country."

Ulysses was glad at finding himself, as Minerva told him, in his own country, and he began to answer, but he did not speak the truth, and made up a lying story in the instinctive wiliness of his heart.

"I heard of Ithaca," said he, "when I was in Crete beyond the seas, and now it seems I have reached it with all these treasures. I have left as much more behind me for my children, but am flying because I killed Orsilochus son of Idomeneus, the fleetest runner in Crete. I killed him because he wanted to rob me of the spoils I had got from Troy with so much trouble and danger both on the field of battle and by the waves of the weary sea; he said I had not served his father loyally at Troy as vassal, but had set myself up as an independent ruler, so I lay in wait for him with one of my followers by the road side, and speared him as he was coming into town from the country. It was a very dark night and nobody saw us; it was not known, therefore, that I had killed him, but as soon as I had done so I went to a ship and besought the owners, who were Phoenicians, to take me on board and set me in Pylos or in Elis where the Epeans rule, giving them as much spoil as satisfied them. They meant no guile, but the wind drove them off their course, and we sailed on till we came hither by night. It was all we could do to get inside the harbour, and none of us said a word about supper though we wanted it badly, but we all went on shore and lay down just as we were. I was very tired and fell asleep directly, so they took my goods out of the ship, and placed them beside me where I was lying upon the sand. Then they sailed away to Sidonia, and I was left here in great distress of mind."

Such was his story, but Minerva smiled and caressed him with her hand. Then she took the form of a woman, fair, stately, and wise, "He must be indeed a shifty lying fellow," said she, "who could surpass you in all manner of craft even though you had a god for your antagonist. Dare devil that you are, full of guile, unwearying in deceit, can you not drop your tricks and your instinctive falsehood, even now that you are in your own country again? We will say no more, however, about this, for we can both of us deceive upon occasion—you are the most accomplished counsellor and orator among all mankind, while I for diplomacy and subtlety have no equal among the gods. Did you not know Jove's daughter

Minerva—me, who have been ever with you, who kept watch over you in all your troubles, and who made the Phaeacians take so great a liking to you? And now, again, I am come here to talk things over with you, and help you to hide the treasure I made the Phaeacians give you; I want to tell you about the troubles that await you in your own house; you have got to face them, but tell no one, neither man nor woman, that you have come home again. Bear everything, and put up with every man's insolence, without a word."

And Ulysses answered, "A man, goddess, may know a great deal, but you are so constantly changing your appearance that when he meets you it is a hard matter for him to know whether it is you or not. This much, however, I know exceedingly well; you were very kind to me as long as we Achaeans were fighting before Troy, but from the day on which we went on board ship after having sacked the city of Priam, and heaven dispersed us—from that day, Minerva, I saw no more of you, and cannot ever remember your coming to my ship to help me in a difficulty; I had to wander on sick and sorry till the gods delivered me from evil and I reached the city of the Phaeacians, where you encouraged me and took me into the town. {120} And now, I beseech you in your father's name, tell me the truth, for I do not believe I am really back in Ithaca. I am in some other country and you are mocking me and deceiving me in all you have been saying. Tell me then truly, have I really got back to my own country?"

"You are always taking something of that sort in your head," replied Minerva, "and that is why I cannot desert you in your afflictions; you are so plausible, shrewd and shifty. Any one but yourself on returning from so long a voyage would at once have gone home to see his wife and children, but you do not seem to care about asking after them or hearing any news about them till you have exploited your wife, who remains at home vainly grieving for you, and having no peace night or day for the tears she sheds on your behalf. As for my not coming near you, I was never uneasy about you, for I was certain you would get back safely though you would lose all your men, and I did not wish to quarrel with my uncle Neptune, who never forgave you for having blinded his son. {121} I will now, however, point out to you the lie of the land, and you will then perhaps believe me. This is the haven of the old merman Phorcys, and here is the olive tree that grows at the head of it; [near it is the cave sacred to the Naiads;] {122} here too is the overarching cavern in which you have offered many an acceptable hecatomb to the nymphs, and this is the wooded mountain Neritum."

As she spoke the goddess dispersed the mist and the land appeared. Then Ulysses rejoiced at finding himself again in his own land, and kissed the bounteous soil; he lifted up his hands and prayed to the nymphs, saying, "Naiad nymphs, daughters of Jove, I made sure that I was never again to see you, now therefore I greet you with all loving salutations, and I will bring you offerings as in the old days, if Jove's redoubtable daughter will grant me life, and bring my son to manhood."

"Take heart, and do not trouble yourself about that," rejoined Minerva, "let us rather set about stowing your things at once in the cave, where they will be quite safe. Let us see how we can best manage it all."

Therewith she went down into the cave to look for the safest hiding places, while Ulysses brought up all the treasure of gold, bronze, and good clothing which the Phaeacians had given him. They stowed everything carefully away, and Minerva set a stone against the door of the cave. Then the two sat down by the root of the great olive, and consulted how to compass the destruction of the wicked suitors.

"Ulysses," said Minerva, "noble son of Laertes, think how you can lay hands on these disreputable people who have been lording it in your house these three years, courting your wife and making wedding presents to her, while she does nothing but lament your absence, giving hope and sending encouraging messages {123} to every one of them, but meaning the very opposite of all she says."

And Ulysses answered, "In good truth, goddess, it seems I should have come to much the same bad end in my own house as Agamemnon did, if you had not given me such timely information. Advise me how I shall best avenge myself. Stand by my side and put your courage into my heart as on the day when we loosed Troy's fair diadem from her brow. Help me now as you did then, and I will fight three hundred men, if you, goddess, will be with me."

"Trust me for that," said she, "I will not lose sight of you when once we set about it, and I imagine that some of those who are devouring your substance will then bespatter the pavement with their blood and brains. I will begin by disguising you so that no human being shall know you; I will cover your body with wrinkles; you shall lose all your yellow hair; I will clothe you in a garment that shall fill all who see it with loathing; I will blear your fine eyes for you, and make you an unseemly object in the sight of the suitors, of your wife, and of the son whom you left behind you. Then go at once to the swineherd who is in charge of your pigs; he has been always well affected towards you, and is devoted to Penelope and your son; you will find him feeding his pigs near the rock that is called Raven {124} by the fountain Arethusa, where they are fattening on beechmast and spring water after their manner. Stay with him and find out how things are going, while I proceed to Sparta and see your son, who is with Menelaus at Lacedaemon, where he has gone to try and find out whether you are still alive." {125}

"But why," said Ulysses, "did you not tell him, for you knew all about it? Did you want him too to go sailing about amid all kinds of hardship while others are eating up his estate?"

Minerva answered, "Never mind about him, I sent him that he might be well spoken of for having gone. He is in no sort of difficulty, but is staying quite comfortably with Menelaus, and is surrounded with abundance of every kind. The suitors have put out to sea and are lying in wait for him, for they mean to kill him before he can get home. I do not much think they will succeed, but rather that some of those who are now eating up your estate will first find a grave themselves."

As she spoke Minerva touched him with her wand and covered him with wrinkles, took away all his yellow hair, and withered the flesh over his whole body; she bleared his eyes, which were naturally very fine ones; she changed his clothes and threw an old rag of a wrap about him, and a tunic, tattered, filthy, and begrimed with smoke; she also gave him an undressed deer skin as an outer garment, and furnished him with a staff and a wallet all in holes, with a twisted thong for him to sling it over his shoulder.

When the pair had thus laid their plans they parted, and the goddess went straight to Lacedaemon to fetch Telemachus.

BOOK XIV

Ulysses in the hut with Eumaeus.

Ulysses now left the haven, and took the rough track up through the wooded country and over the crest of the mountain till he reached the place where Minerva had said that he would find the swineherd, who was the most thrifty servant he had. He found him sitting in front of his hut, which was by the yards that he had built on a site which could be seen from far. He had made them spacious {126} and fair to see, with a free run for the pigs all round them; he had built them during his master's absence, of stones which he had gathered out of the ground, without saying anything to Penelope or Laertes, and he had fenced them on top with thorn bushes. Outside the yard he had run a strong fence of oaken posts, split, and set pretty close together, while inside he had built twelve styes near one another for the sows to lie in. There were fifty pigs wallowing in each stye, all of them breeding sows; but the boars slept outside and were much fewer in number, for the suitors kept on eating them, and the swineherd had to send them the best he had continually. There were three hundred and sixty boar pigs, and the herdsman's four hounds, which were as fierce as wolves, slept always with them. The swineherd was at that moment cutting out a pair of sandals {127} from a good stout ox hide. Three of his men were out herding the pigs in one place or another, and he had sent the fourth to town with a boar that he had been forced to send the suitors that they might sacrifice it and have their fill of meat.

When the hounds saw Ulysses they set up a furious barking and flew at him, but Ulysses was cunning enough to sit down and loose his hold of the stick that he had in his hand: still, he would have been torn by them in his own homestead had not the swineherd dropped his ox hide, rushed full speed through the gate of the yard and driven the dogs off by shouting and throwing stones at them. Then he said to Ulysses, "Old man, the dogs were likely to have made short work of you, and then you would have got me into trouble. The gods have given me quite enough worries without that, for I have lost the best of masters, and am in continual grief on his account. I have to attend swine for other people to eat, while he, if he yet lives to see the light of day, is starving in some distant land. But come inside, and when you have had your fill of bread and wine, tell me where you come from, and all about your misfortunes."

On this the swineherd led the way into the hut and bade him sit down. He strewed a good thick bed of rushes upon the floor, and on the top of this he threw the shaggy chamois skin—a great thick one—on which he used to sleep by night. Ulysses was pleased at being made thus welcome, and said "May Jove, sir, and the rest of the gods grant you your heart's desire in return for the kind way in which you have received me."

To this you answered, O swineherd Eumaeus, "Stranger, though a still poorer man should come here, it would not be right for me to insult him, for all strangers and beggars are from Jove. You must take what you can get and be thankful, for servants live in fear when they have young lords for their masters; and this is my misfortune now, for heaven has hindered the return of him who would have been always good to me and given me something of my own—a house, a piece of land, a good looking wife, and all else that a liberal master allows a servant who has worked hard for him, and whose labour the gods have prospered as they have mine in the situation which I hold. If my master had grown old here he would have done great things by me, but he is gone, and I wish that Helen's whole race were utterly destroyed, for she has been the death of many a good man. It was this matter that took my master to Ilius, the land of noble steeds, to fight the Trojans in the cause of king Agamemnon."

As he spoke he bound his girdle round him and went to the styes where the young sucking pigs were penned. He picked out two which he brought back with him and sacrificed. He singed them, cut them up, and spitted them; when the meat was cooked he brought it all in and set it before Ulysses, hot and still on the spit, whereon Ulysses sprinkled it over with white barley meal. The swineherd then mixed wine in a bowl of ivy-wood, and taking a seat opposite Ulysses told him to begin.

"Fall to, stranger," said he, "on a dish of servant's pork. The fat pigs have to go to the suitors, who eat them up without shame or scruple; but the blessed gods love not such shameful doings, and respect those who do what is lawful and right. Even the fierce freebooters who go raiding on other people's land, and Jove gives them their spoil—even they, when they have filled their ships and got home again live conscience-stricken, and look fearfully for judgement; but some god seems to have told these people that Ulysses is dead and gone; they will not, therefore, go back to their own homes and make their offers of marriage in the usual way, but waste his estate by force, without fear or stint. Not a day or night comes out of heaven, but they sacrifice not one victim nor two only, and they take the run of his wine, for he was exceedingly rich. No other great man either in Ithaca or on the mainland is as rich as he was; he had as much as twenty men put together. I will tell you what he had. There are twelve herds of cattle upon the main land, and as many flocks of sheep, there are also twelve droves of pigs, while his own men and hired strangers feed him twelve widely spreading herds of goats. Here in Ithaca he runs even large flocks of goats on the far end of the island, and they are in the charge of excellent goat herds. Each one of these sends the suitors the best goat in the flock every day. As for myself, I am in charge of the pigs that you see here, and I have to keep picking out the best I have and sending it to them."

This was his story, but Ulysses went on eating and drinking ravenously without a word, brooding his revenge. When he had eaten enough and was satisfied, the swineherd took the bowl from which he usually drank, filled it with wine, and gave it to Ulysses, who was pleased, and said as he took it in his hands, "My friend, who was this master of yours that bought you and paid for you, so rich and so powerful as you tell me? You say he perished in the cause of King Agamemnon; tell me who he was, in case I may have met with such a person. Jove and the other gods know, but I may be able to give you news of him, for I have travelled much."

Eumaeus answered, "Old man, no traveller who comes here with news will get Ulysses' wife and son to believe his story. Nevertheless, tramps in want of a lodging keep coming with their mouths full of lies, and not a word of truth; every one who finds his way to Ithaca goes to my mistress and tells her falsehoods, whereon she takes them in, makes much of them, and asks them all manner of questions, crying all the time as women will when they have lost their husbands. And you too, old man, for a shirt and a cloak would doubtless make up a very pretty story. But the wolves and birds of prey have long since torn Ulysses to pieces, or the fishes of the sea have eaten him, and his bones are lying buried deep in sand upon some foreign shore; he is dead and gone, and a bad business it is for all his friends—for me especially; go where I may I shall never find so good a master, not even if I were to go home to my mother and father where I was bred and born. I do not so much care, however, about my parents now, though I should dearly like to see them again in my own country; it is the loss of Ulysses that grieves me most; I cannot speak of him without reverence though he is here no longer, for he was very fond of me, and took such care of me that wherever he may be I shall always honour his memory."

"My friend," replied Ulysses, "you are very positive, and very hard of belief about your master's coming home again, nevertheless I will not merely say, but will swear, that he is coming. Do not give me anything for my news till he has actually come, you may then give me a shirt and cloak of good wear if you will. I am in great want, but I will not take anything at all till then, for I hate a man, even as I hate hell fire, who lets his poverty tempt him into lying. I swear by king Jove, by the rites of hospitality, and by that hearth of Ulysses to which I have now come, that all will surely happen as I have said it will. Ulysses will return in this self same year; with the end of this moon and the beginning of the next he will be here to do vengeance on all those who are ill treating his wife and son."

To this you answered, O swineherd Eumaeus, "Old man, you will neither get paid for bringing good news, nor will Ulysses ever come home;

drink your wine in peace, and let us talk about something else. Do not keep on reminding me of all this; it always pains me when any one speaks about my honoured master. As for your oath we will let it alone, but I only wish he may come, as do Penelope, his old father Laertes, and his son Telemachus. I am terribly unhappy too about this same boy of his; he was running up fast into manhood, and bade fare to be no worse man, face and figure, than his father, but some one, either god or man, has been unsettling his mind, so he has gone off to Pylos to try and get news of his father, and the suitors are lying in wait for him as he is coming home, in the hope of leaving the house of Arceisius without a name in Ithaca. But let us say no more about him, and leave him to be taken, or else to escape if the son of Saturn holds his hand over him to protect him. And now, old man, tell me your own story; tell me also, for I want to know, who you are and where you come from. Tell me of your town and parents, what manner of ship you came in, how crew brought you to Ithaca, and from what country they professed to come—for you cannot have come by land."

And Ulysses answered, "I will tell you all about it. If there were meat and wine enough, and we could stay here in the hut with nothing to do but to eat and drink while the others go to their work, I could easily talk on for a whole twelve months without ever finishing the story of the sorrows with which it has pleased heaven to visit me.

"I am by birth a Cretan; my father was a well to do man, who had many sons born in marriage, whereas I was the son of a slave whom he had purchased for a concubine; nevertheless, my father Castor son of Hylax (whose lineage I claim, and who was held in the highest honour among the Cretans for his wealth, prosperity, and the valour of his sons) put me on the same level with my brothers who had been born in wedlock. When, however, death took him to the house of Hades, his sons divided his estate and cast lots for their shares, but to me they gave a holding and little else; nevertheless, my valour enabled me to marry into a rich family, for I was not given to bragging, or shirking on the field of battle. It is all over now; still, if you look at the straw you can see what the ear was, for I have had trouble enough and to spare. Mars and Minerva made me doughty in war; when I had picked my men to surprise the enemy with an ambuscade I never gave death so much as a thought, but was the first to leap forward and spear all whom I could overtake. Such was I in battle, but I did not care about farm work, nor the frugal home life of those who would bring up children. My delight was in ships, fighting, javelins, and arrows—things that most men shudder to think of; but one man likes one thing and another another, and this was what I was most naturally inclined to. Before the Achaeans went to Troy, nine times was I in command of men and ships on foreign service, and I amassed much wealth. I had my pick of the spoil in the first instance, and much more was allotted to me later on.

"My house grew apace and I became a great man among the Cretans, but when Jove counselled that terrible expedition, in which so many perished, the people required me and Idomeneus to lead their ships to Troy, and there was no way out of it, for they insisted on our doing so. There we fought for nine whole years, but in the tenth we sacked the city of Priam and sailed home again as heaven dispersed us. Then it was that Jove devised evil against me. I spent but one month happily with my children, wife, and property, and then I conceived the idea of making a descent on Egypt, so I fitted out a fine fleet and manned it. I had nine ships, and the people flocked to fill them. For six days I and my men made feast, and I found them many victims both for sacrifice to the gods and for themselves, but on the seventh day we went on board and set sail from Crete with a fair North wind behind us though we were going down a river. Nothing went ill with any of our ships, and we had no sickness on board, but sat where we were and let the ships go as the wind and steersmen took them. On the fifth day we reached the river Aegyptus; there I stationed my ships in the river, bidding my men stay by them and keep guard over them while I sent out scouts to reconnoitre from every point of vantage.

"But the men disobeyed my orders, took to their own devices, and ravaged the land of the Egyptians, killing the men, and taking their wives and children captive. The alarm was soon carried to the city, and when they heard the war cry, the people came out at daybreak till the plain was filled with horsemen and foot soldiers and with the gleam of armour. Then Jove spread panic among my men, and they would no longer face the enemy, for they found themselves surrounded. The Egyptians killed many of us, and took the rest alive to do forced labour for them. Jove, however, put it in my mind to do thus—and I wish I had died then and there in Egypt instead, for there was much sorrow in store for me—I took off my helmet and shield and dropped my spear from my hand; then I went straight up to the king's chariot, clasped his knees and kissed them, whereon he spared my life, bade me get into his chariot, and took me weeping to his own home. Many made at me with their ashen spears and tried to kill me in their fury, but the king protected me, for he feared the wrath of Jove the protector of strangers, who punishes those who do evil.

"I stayed there for seven years and got together much money among the Egyptians, for they all gave me something; but when it was now going on for eight years there came a certain Phoenician, a cunning rascal, who had already committed all sorts of villainy, and this man talked me over into going with him to Phoenicia, where his house and his possessions lay. I stayed there for a whole twelve months, but at the end of that time when months and days had gone by till the same season had come round again, he set me on board a ship bound for Libya, on a pretence that I was to take a cargo along with him to that place, but really that he might sell me as a slave and take the money I fetched. I suspected his intention, but went on board with him, for I could not help it.

"The ship ran before a fresh North wind till we had reached the sea that lies between Crete and Libya; there, however, Jove counselled their destruction, for as soon as we were well out from Crete and could see nothing but sea and sky, he raised a black cloud over our ship and the sea grew dark beneath it. Then Jove let fly with his thunderbolts and the ship went round and round and was filled with fire and brimstone as the lightning struck it. The men fell all into the sea; they were carried about in the water round the ship looking like so many sea-gulls, but the god presently deprived them of all chance of getting home again. I was all dismayed. Jove, however, sent the ship's mast within my reach, which saved my life, for I clung to it, and drifted before the fury of the gale. Nine days did I drift but in the darkness of the tenth night a great wave bore me on to the Thesprotian coast. There Pheidon king of the Thesprotians entertained me hospitably without charging me anything at all—for his son found me when I was nearly dead with cold and fatigue, whereon he raised me by the hand, took me to his father's house and gave me clothes to wear.

"There it was that I heard news of Ulysses, for the king told me he had entertained him, and shown him much hospitality while he was on his homeward journey. He showed me also the treasure of gold, and wrought iron that Ulysses had got together. There was enough to keep his family for ten generations, so much had he left in the house of king Pheidon. But the king said Ulysses had gone to Dodona that he might learn Jove's mind from the god's high oak tree, and know whether after so long an absence he should return to Ithaca openly, or in secret. Moreover the king swore in my presence, making drink-offerings in his own house as he did so, that the ship was by the water side, and the crew found, that should take him to his own country. He sent me off however before Ulysses returned, for there happened to be a Thesprotian ship sailing for the wheat-growing island of Dulichium, and he told those in charge of her to be sure and take me safely to King Acastus.

"These men hatched a plot against me that would have reduced me to the very extreme of misery, for when the ship had got some way out from land they resolved on selling me as a slave. They stripped me of the shirt and cloak that I was wearing, and gave me instead the tattered old clouts in which you now see me; then, towards nightfall, they reached the tilled lands of Ithaca, and there they bound me with a strong rope fast in the ship, while they went on shore to get supper by the sea side. But the gods soon undid my bonds for me, and having drawn my rags over my head I slid down the rudder into the sea, where I struck out and swam till I was well clear of them, and came ashore near a thick wood in which I lay concealed. They were very angry at my having escaped and went searching about for me, till at last they thought it was no further use and went back to their ship.

The gods, having hidden me thus easily, then took me to a good man's door—for it seems that I am not to die yet awhile."

To this you answered, O swineherd Eumaeus, "Poor unhappy stranger, I have found the story of your misfortunes extremely interesting, but that part about Ulysses is not right; and you will never get me to believe it. Why should a man like you go about telling lies in this way? I know all about the return of my master. The gods one and all of them detest him, or they would have taken him before Troy, or let him die with friends around him when the days of his fighting were done; for then the Achaeans would have built a mound over his ashes and his son would have been heir to his renown, but now the storm winds have spirited him away we know not whither.

"As for me I live out of the way here with the pigs, and never go to the town unless when Penelope sends for me on the arrival of some news about Ulysses. Then they all sit round and ask questions, both those who grieve over the king's absence, and those who rejoice at it because they can eat up his property without paying for it. For my own part I have never cared about asking anyone else since the time when I was taken in by an Aetolian, who had killed a man and come a long way till at last he reached my station, and I was very kind to him. He said he had seen Ulysses with Idomeneus among the Cretans, refitting his ships which had been damaged in a gale. He said Ulysses would return in the following summer or autumn with his men, and that he would bring back much wealth. And now you, you unfortunate old man, since fate has brought you to my door, do not try to flatter me in this way with vain hopes. It is not for any such reason that I shall treat you kindly, but only out of respect for Jove the god of hospitality, as fearing him and pitying you."

Ulysses answered, "I see that you are of an unbelieving mind; I have given you my oath, and yet you will not credit me; let us then make a bargain, and call all the gods in heaven to witness it. If your master comes home, give me a cloak and shirt of good wear, and send me to Dulichium where I want to go; but if he does not come as I say he will, set your men on to me, and tell them to throw me from yonder precipice, as a warning to tramps not to go about the country telling lies."

"And a pretty figure I should cut then," replied Eumaeus, "both now and hereafter, if I were to kill you after receiving you into my hut and showing you hospitality. I should have to say my prayers in good earnest if I did; but it is just supper time and I hope my men will come in directly, that we may cook something savoury for supper."

Thus did they converse, and presently the swineherds came up with the pigs, which were then shut up for the night in their styes, and a tremendous squealing they made as they were being driven into them. But Eumaeus called to his men and said, "Bring in the best pig you have, that I may sacrifice him for this stranger, and we will take toll of him ourselves. We have had trouble enough this long time feeding pigs, while others reap the fruit of our labour."

On this he began chopping firewood, while the others brought in a fine fat five year old boar pig, and set it at the altar. Eumaeus did not forget the gods, for he was a man of good principles, so the first thing he did was to cut bristles from the pig's face and throw them into the fire, praying to all the gods as he did so that Ulysses might return home again. Then he clubbed the pig with a billet of oak which he had kept back when he was chopping the firewood, and stunned it, while the others slaughtered and singed it. Then they cut it up, and Eumaeus began by putting raw pieces from each joint on to some of the fat; these he sprinkled with barley meal, and laid upon the embers; they cut the rest of the meat up small, put the pieces upon the spits and roasted them till they were done; when they had taken them off the spits they threw them on to the dresser in a heap. The swineherd, who was a most equitable man, then stood up to give every one his share. He made seven portions; one of these he set apart for Mercury the son of Maia and the nymphs, praying to them as he did so; the others he dealt out to the men man by man. He gave Ulysses some slices cut lengthways down the loin as a mark of especial honour, and Ulysses was much pleased. "I hope, Eumaeus," said he, "that Jove will be as well disposed towards you as I am, for the respect you are showing to an outcast like myself."

To this you answered, O swineherd Eumaeus, "Eat, my good fellow, and enjoy your supper, such as it is. God grants this, and withholds that, just as he thinks right, for he can do whatever he chooses."

As he spoke he cut off the first piece and offered it as a burnt sacrifice to the immortal gods; then he made them a drink-offering, put the cup in the hands of Ulysses, and sat down to his own portion. Mesaulius brought them their bread; the swineherd had brought this man on his own account from among the Taphians during his master's absence, and had paid for him with his own money without saying anything either to his mistress or Laertes. They then laid their hands upon the good things that were before them, and when they had had enough to eat and drink, Mesaulius took away what was left of the bread, and they all went to bed after having made a hearty supper.

Now the night came on stormy and very dark, for there was no moon. It poured without ceasing, and the wind blew strong from the West, which is a wet quarter, so Ulysses thought he would see whether Eumaeus, in the excellent care he took of him, would take off his own cloak and give it him, or make one of his men give him one. "Listen to me," said he, "Eumaeus and the rest of you; when I have said a prayer I will tell you something. It is the wine that makes me talk in this way; wine will make even a wise man fall to singing; it will make him chuckle and dance and say many a word that he had better leave unspoken; still, as I have begun, I will go on. Would that I were still young and strong as when we got up an ambuscade before Troy. Menelaus and Ulysses were the leaders, but I was in command also, for the other two would have it so. When we had come up to the wall of the city we crouched down beneath our armour and lay there under cover of the reeds and thick brushwood that grew about the swamp. It came on to freeze with a North wind blowing; the snow fell small and fine like hoar frost, and our shields were coated thick with rime. The others had all got cloaks and shirts, and slept comfortably enough with their shields about their shoulders, but I had carelessly left my cloak behind me, not thinking that I should be too cold, and had gone off in nothing but my shirt and shield. When the night was two-thirds through and the stars had shifted their places, I nudged Ulysses who was close to me with my elbow, and he at once gave me his ear.

"Ulysses,' said I, 'this cold will be the death of me, for I have no cloak; some god fooled me into setting off with nothing on but my shirt, and I do not know what to do.'

"Ulysses, who was as crafty as he was valiant, hit upon the following plan:

"'Keep still,' said he in a low voice, 'or the others will hear you.' Then he raised his head on his elbow.

"'My friends,' said he, 'I have had a dream from heaven in my sleep. We are a long way from the ships; I wish some one would go down and tell Agamemnon to send us up more men at once.'

"On this Thoas son of Andraemon threw off his cloak and set out running to the ships, whereon I took the cloak and lay in it comfortably enough till morning. Would that I were still young and strong as I was in those days, for then some one of you swineherds would give me a cloak both out of good will and for the respect due to a brave soldier; but now people look down upon me because my clothes are shabby."

And Eumaeus answered, "Old man, you have told us an excellent story, and have said nothing so far but what is quite satisfactory; for the present, therefore, you shall want neither clothing nor anything else that a stranger in distress may reasonably expect, but to-morrow morning you have to shake your own old rags about your body again, for we have not many spare cloaks nor shirts up here, but every man has only one. When Ulysses' son comes home again he will give you both cloak and shirt, and send you wherever you may want to go."

With this he got up and made a bed for Ulysses by throwing some goatskins and sheepskins on the ground in front of the fire. Here Ulysses lay down, and Eumaeus covered him over with a great heavy cloak that he kept for a change in case of extraordinarily bad weather.

Thus did Ulysses sleep, and the young men slept beside him. But the swineherd did not like sleeping away from his pigs, so he got ready to go outside, and Ulysses was glad to see that he looked after his property during his master's absence. First he slung his sword over his brawny shoulders and put on a thick cloak to keep out the wind. He also took the skin of a large and well fed goat, and a javelin in case of attack from men or dogs. Thus equipped he went to his rest where the pigs were camping under an overhanging rock that gave them shelter from the North wind.

BOOK XV

Minerva summons Telemachus from Lacedaemon—he meets with Theoclymenus at Pylos and brings him to Ithaca—on landing he goes to the hut of Eumaeus.

But Minerva went to the fair city of Lacedaemon to tell Ulysses' son that he was to return at once. She found him and Pisistratus sleeping in the forecourt of Menelaus's house; Pisistratus was fast asleep, but

Telemachus could get no rest all night for thinking of his unhappy father, so Minerva went close up to him and said:

"Telemachus, you should not remain so far away from home any longer, nor leave your property with such dangerous people in your house; they will eat up everything you have among them, and you will have been on a fool's errand. Ask Menelaus to send you home at once if you wish to find your excellent mother still there when you get back. Her father and brothers are already urging her to marry Eurymachus, who has given her more than any of the others, and has been greatly increasing his wedding presents. I hope nothing valuable may have been taken from the house in spite of you, but you know what women are—they always want to do the best they can for the man who marries them, and never give another thought to the children of their first husband, nor to their father either when he is dead and done with. Go home, therefore, and put everything in charge of the most respectable woman servant that you have, until it shall please heaven to send you a wife of your own. Let me tell you also of another matter which you had better attend to. The chief men among the suitors are lying in wait for you in the Strait {128} between Ithaca and Samos, and they mean to kill you before you can reach home. I do not much think they will succeed; it is more likely that some of those who are now eating up your property will find a grave themselves. Sail night and day, and keep your ship well away from the islands; the god who watches over you and protects you will send you a fair wind. As soon as you get to Ithaca send your ship and men on to the town, but yourself go straight to the swineherd who has charge of your pigs; he is well disposed towards you, stay with him, therefore, for the night, and then send him to Penelope to tell her that you have got back safe from Pylos."

Then she went back to Olympus; but Telemachus stirred Pisistratus with his heel to rouse him, and said, "Wake up Pisistratus, and yoke the horses to the chariot, for we must set off home." {129}

But Pisistratus said, "No matter what hurry we are in we cannot drive in the dark. It will be morning soon; wait till Menelaus has brought his presents and put them in the chariot for us; and let him say good bye to us in the usual way. So long as he lives a guest should never forget a host who has shown him kindness."

As he spoke day began to break, and Menelaus, who had already risen, leaving Helen in bed, came towards them. When Telemachus saw him he put on his shirt as fast as he could, threw a great cloak over his shoulders, and went out to meet him. "Menelaus," said he, "let me go back now to my own country, for I want to get home."

And Menelaus answered, "Telemachus, if you insist on going I will not detain you. I do not like to see a host either too fond of his guest or too rude to him. Moderation is best in all things, and not letting a man go when he wants to do so is as bad as telling him to go if he would like to stay. One should treat a guest well as long as he is in the house and speed him when he wants to leave it. Wait, then, till I can get your beautiful presents into your chariot, and till you have yourself seen them. I will tell the women to prepare a sufficient dinner for you of what there may be in the house; it will be at once more proper and cheaper for you to get your dinner before setting out on such a long journey. If, moreover, you have a fancy for making a tour in Hellas or in the Peloponnese, I will yoke my horses, and will conduct you myself through all our principal cities. No one will send us away empty handed; every one will give us something—a bronze tripod, a couple of mules, or a gold cup."

"Menelaus," replied Telemachus, "I want to go home at once, for when I came away I left my property without protection, and fear that while looking for my father I shall come to ruin myself, or find that something valuable has been stolen during my absence."

When Menelaus heard this he immediately told his wife and servants to prepare a sufficient dinner from what there might be in the house. At this moment Eteoneus joined him, for he lived close by and had just got up; so Menelaus told him to light the fire and cook some meat, which he at once did. Then Menelaus went down into his fragrant store room, {130} not alone, but Helen went too, with Megapenthes. When he reached the place where the treasures of his house were kept, he selected a double cup, and told his son Megapenthes to bring also a silver mixing bowl. Meanwhile Helen went to the chest where she kept the lovely dresses which she had made with her own hands, and took out one that was largest and most beautifully enriched with embroidery; it glittered like a star, and lay at the very bottom of the chest. {131} Then they all came back through the house again till they got to Telemachus, and Menelaus said, "Telemachus, may Jove, the mighty husband of Juno, bring you safely home according to your desire. I will now present you with the finest and most precious piece of plate in all my house. It is a mixing bowl of pure silver, except the rim, which is inlaid with gold, and it is the work of Vulcan. Phaedimus king of the Sidonians made me a present of it in the course of a visit that I paid him while I was on my return home. I should like to give it to you."

With these words he placed the double cup in the hands of Telemachus, while Megapenthes brought the beautiful mixing bowl and set it before him. Hard by stood lovely Helen with the robe ready in her hand.

"I too, my son," said she, "have something for you as a keepsake from the hand of Helen; it is for your bride to wear upon her wedding day. Till then, get your dear mother to keep it for you; thus may you go back rejoicing to your own country and to your home."

So saying she gave the robe over to him and he received it gladly. Then Pisistratus put the presents into the chariot, and admired them all as he did so. Presently Menelaus took Telemachus and Pisistratus into the house, and they both of them sat down to table. A maid servant brought them water in a beautiful golden ewer, and poured it into a silver basin for them to wash their hands, and she drew a clean table beside them; an upper servant brought them bread and offered them many good things of what there was in the house. Eteoneus carved the meat and gave them each their portions, while Megapenthes poured out the wine. Then they laid their hands upon the good things that were before them, but as soon as they had had enough to eat and drink Telemachus and Pisistratus yoked the horses, and took their places in the chariot. They drove out through the inner gateway and under the echoing gatehouse of the outer court, and Menelaus came after them with a golden goblet of wine in his right hand that they might make a drink-offering before they set out. He stood in front of the horses and pledged them, saying, "Farewell to both of you; see that you tell Nestor how I have treated you, for he was as kind to me as any father could be while we Achaeans were fighting before Troy."

"We will be sure, sir," answered Telemachus, "to tell him everything as soon as we see him. I wish I were as certain of finding Ulysses returned when I get back to Ithaca, that I might tell him of the very great kindness you have shown me and of the many beautiful presents I am taking with me."

As he was thus speaking a bird flew on his right hand—an eagle with a great white goose in its talons which it had carried off from the farm yard—and all the men and women were running after it and shouting. It came quite close up to them and flew away on their right hands in front of the horses. When they saw it they were glad, and their hearts took comfort within them, whereon Pisistratus said, "Tell me, Menelaus, has heaven sent this omen for us or for you?"

Menelaus was thinking what would be the most proper answer for him to make, but Helen was too quick for him and said, "I will read this matter as heaven has put it in my heart, and as I doubt not that it will come to pass. The eagle came from the mountain where it was bred and has its nest, and in like manner Ulysses, after having travelled far and suffered much, will return to take his revenge—if indeed he is not back already and hatching mischief for the suitors."

"May Jove so grant it," replied Telemachus, "if it should prove to be so, I will make vows to you as though you were a god, even when I am at home."

As he spoke he lashed his horses and they started off at full speed through the town towards the open country. They swayed the yoke upon their necks and travelled the whole day long till the sun set and darkness was over all the land. Then they reached Pherae, where Diocles lived who was son of Ortilochus, the son of Alpheus. There they passed the night and were treated hospitably. When the child of morning, rosy-fingered Dawn, appeared, they again yoked their horses and their places in the chariot. They drove out through the inner gateway and under the echoing gatehouse of the outer court. Then Pisistratus lashed his horses on and they flew forward nothing loath; ere long they came to Pylos, and then Telemachus said:

"Pisistratus, I hope you will promise to do what I am going to ask you. You know our fathers were old friends before us; moreover, we are both of an age, and this journey has brought us together still more closely; do not, therefore, take me past my ship, but leave me there, for if I go to your father's house he will try to keep me in the warmth of his good will towards me, and I must go home at once."

Pisistratus thought how he should do as he was asked, and in the end he deemed it best to turn his horses towards the ship, and put Menelaus's beautiful presents of gold and raiment in the stern of the vessel. Then he said, "Go on board at once and tell your men to do so also before I can reach home to tell my father. I know how obstinate he is, and am sure he will not let you go; he will come down here to fetch you, and he will not go back without you. But he will be very angry."

With this he drove his goodly steeds back to the city of the Pylians and soon reached his home, but Telemachus called the men together and gave his orders. "Now, my men," said he, "get everything in order on board the ship, and let us set out home."

Thus did he speak, and they went on board even as he had said. But as Telemachus was thus busied, praying also and sacrificing to Minerva in the ship's stern, there came to him a man from a distant country, a seer, who was flying from Argos because he had killed a man. He was descended from Melampus, who used to live in Pylos, the land of sheep; he was rich and owned a great house, but he was driven into exile by the great and powerful king Neleus. Neleus seized his goods and held them for a whole year, during which he was a close prisoner in the house of king Phylacus, and in much distress of mind both on account of the daughter of Neleus and because he was haunted by a great sorrow that dread Erinys had laid upon him. In the end, however, he escaped with his life, drove the cattle from Phylace to Pylos, avenged the wrong that had been done him, and gave the daughter of Neleus to his brother. Then he left the country and went to Argos, where it was ordained that he should reign over much people. There he married, established himself, and had two famous sons Antiphates and Mantius. Antiphates became father of Oicleus, and Oicleus of Amphiaraus, who was dearly loved both by Jove and by Apollo, but he did not live to old age, for he was killed in Thebes by reason of a woman's gifts. His sons were Alcmaeon and Amphilochus. Mantius, the other son of Melampus, was father to Polypheides and Cleitus. Aurora, throned in gold, carried off Cleitus for his beauty's sake, that he might dwell among the immortals, but Apollo made Polypheides the greatest seer in the whole world now that Amphiaraus was dead. He quarrelled with his father and went to live in Hyperesia, where he remained and prophesied for all men.

His son, Theoclymenus, it was who now came up to Telemachus as he was making drink-offerings and praying in his ship. "Friend," said he, "now that I find you sacrificing in this place, I beseech you by your sacrifices themselves, and by the god to whom you make them, I pray you also by your own head and by those of your followers tell me the truth and nothing but the truth. Who and whence are you? Tell me also of your town and parents."

Telemachus said, "I will answer you quite truly. I am from Ithaca, and my father is Ulysses, as surely as that he ever lived. But he has come to some miserable end. Therefore I have taken this ship and got my crew together to see if I can hear any news of him, for he has been away a long time."

"I too," answered Theoclymenus, "am an exile, for I have killed a man of my own race. He has many brothers and kinsmen in Argos, and they have great power among the Argives. I am flying to escape death at their hands, and am thus doomed to be a wanderer on the face of the earth. I am your suppliant; take me, therefore, on board your ship that they may not kill me, for I know they are in pursuit."

"I will not refuse you," replied Telemachus, "if you wish to join us. Come, therefore, and in Ithaca we will treat you hospitably according to what we have."

On this he received Theoclymenus' spear and laid it down on the deck of the ship. He went on board and sat in the stern, bidding Theoclymenus sit beside him; then the men let go the hawsers. Telemachus told them to catch hold of the ropes, and they made all haste to do so. They set the mast in its socket in the cross plank, raised it and made it fast with the forestays, and they hoisted their white sails with sheets of twisted ox hide. Minerva sent them a fair wind that blew fresh and strong to take the ship on her course as fast as possible. Thus then they passed by Crouni and Chalcis.

Presently the sun set and darkness was over all the land. The vessel made a quick passage to Pheae and thence on to Elis, where the Epeans rule. Telemachus then headed her for the flying islands, {132} wondering within himself whether he should escape death or should be taken prisoner.

Meanwhile Ulysses and the swineherd were eating their supper in the hut, and the men supped with them. As soon as they had had to eat and drink, Ulysses began trying to prove the swineherd and see whether he would continue to treat him kindly, and ask him to stay on at the station or pack him off to the city; so he said:

"Eumaeus, and all of you, to-morrow I want to go away and begin begging about the town, so as to be no more trouble to you or to your men. Give me your advice therefore, and let me have a good guide to go with me and show me the way. I will go the round of the city begging as I needs must, to see if any one will give me a drink and a piece of bread. I should like also to go to the house of Ulysses and bring news of her husband to Queen Penelope. I could then go about among the suitors and see if out of all their abundance they will give me a dinner. I should soon make them an excellent servant in all sorts of ways. Listen and believe when I tell you that by the blessing of Mercury who gives grace and good name to the works of all men, there is no one living who would make a more handy servant than I should—to put fresh wood on the fire, chop fuel, carve, cook, pour out wine, and do all those services that poor men have to do for their betters."

The swineherd was very much disturbed when he heard this. "Heaven help me," he exclaimed, "what ever can have put such a notion as that into your head? If you go near the suitors you will be undone to a certainty, for their pride and insolence reach the very heavens. They would never think of taking a man like you for a servant. Their servants are all young men, well dressed, wearing good cloaks and shirts, with well looking faces and their hair always tidy, the tables are kept quite clean and are loaded with bread, meat, and wine. Stay where you are, then; you are not in anybody's way; I do not mind your being here, no more do any of the others, and when Telemachus comes home he will give you a shirt and cloak and will send you wherever you want to go."

Ulysses answered, "I hope you may be as dear to the gods as you are to me, for having saved me from going about and getting into trouble; there is nothing worse than being always on the tramp; still, when men have once got low down in the world they will go through a great deal on behalf of their miserable bellies. Since, however, you press me to stay here and await the return of Telemachus, tell me about Ulysses' mother, and his father whom he left on the threshold of old age when he set out for Troy. Are they still living or are they already dead and in the house of Hades?"

"I will tell you all about them," replied Eumaeus, "Laertes is still living and prays heaven to let him depart peacefully in his own house, for he is terribly distressed about the absence of his son, and also about the death of his wife, which grieved him greatly and aged him more than anything else did. She came to an unhappy end {133} through sorrow for her son: may no friend or neighbour who has dealt kindly by me come to such an end as she did. As long as she was still living, though she was always grieving, I used to like seeing her and asking her how she did, for she brought me up along with her daughter Ctimene, the youngest of her children; we were boy and girl together, and she made little difference between us. When, however, we both grew up, they sent Ctimene to Same and received a splendid dowry for her. As for me, my mistress gave me a good shirt and cloak with a pair of sandals for my feet, and sent me off into the country, but she was just as fond of me as ever. This is all over now. Still it has pleased heaven to prosper my work in the situation which I now hold. I have enough to eat and drink, and can find something for any respectable stranger who comes here; but there is no getting a kind word or deed out of my mistress, for the house has fallen into the hands of wicked people. Servants want sometimes to see their mistress and have a talk with her; they like to have something to eat and drink at the house, and something too to take back with them into the country. This is what will keep servants in a good humour."

Ulysses answered, "Then you must have been a very little fellow, Eumaeus, when you were taken so far away from your home and parents. Tell me, and tell me true, was the city in which your father and mother lived sacked and pillaged, or did some enemies carry you off when you were alone tending sheep or cattle, ship you off here, and sell you for whatever your master gave them?"

"Stranger," replied Eumaeus, "as regards your question: sit still, make yourself comfortable, drink your wine, and listen to me. The nights are now at their longest; there is plenty of time both for sleeping and sitting up talking together; you ought not to go to bed till bed time, too much sleep is as bad as too little; if any one of the others wishes to go to bed let him leave us and do so; he can then take my master's pigs out when he has done breakfast in the morning. We too will sit here eating and drinking in the hut, and telling one another stories about our misfortunes; for when a man has suffered much, and been buffeted about in the world, he takes pleasure in recalling the memory of sorrows that have long gone by. As regards your question, then, my tale is as follows:

"You may have heard of an island called Syra that lies over above Ortygia, {134} where the land begins to turn round and look in another direction. {135} It is not very thickly peopled, but the soil is good, with much pasture fit for cattle and sheep, and it abounds with wine and wheat. Dearth never comes there, nor are the people plagued by any sickness, but when they grow old Apollo comes with Diana and kills them with his painless shafts. It contains two communities, and the whole country is divided between these two. My father Ctesius son of Ormenus, a man comparable to the gods, reigned over both.

"Now to this place there came some cunning traders from Phoenicia (for the Phoenicians are great mariners) in a ship which they had freighted with gewgaws of all kinds. There happened to be a Phoenician woman in my father's house, very tall and comely, and an excellent servant; these scoundrels got hold of her one day when she was washing near their ship, seduced her, and cajoled her in ways that no woman can resist, no matter how good she may be by nature. The man who had seduced her asked her who she was and where she came from, and on this she told him her father's name. 'I come from Sidon,' said she, 'and am daughter to Arybas, a man rolling in wealth. One day as I was coming into the town from the country, some Taphian pirates seized me and took me here over the sea, where they sold me to the man who owns this house, and he gave them their price for me.'

"The man who had seduced her then said, 'Would you like to come along with us to see the house of your parents and your parents themselves? They are both alive and are said to be well off.'

"'I will do so gladly,' answered she, 'if you men will first swear me a solemn oath that you will do me no harm by the way.'

"They all swore as she told them, and when they had completed their oath the woman said, 'Hush; and if any of your men meets me in the street or at the well, do not let him speak to me, for fear some one should go and tell my master, in which case he would suspect something. He would put me in prison, and would have all of you murdered; keep your own counsel therefore; buy your merchandise as fast as you can, and send me word when you have done loading. I will bring as much gold as I can lay my hands on, and there is something else also that I can do towards paying my fare. I am nurse to the son of the good man of the house, a funny little fellow just able to run about. I will carry him off in your ship, and you will get a great deal of money for him if you take him and sell him in foreign parts.'

"On this she went back to the house. The Phoenicians stayed a whole year till they had loaded their ship with much precious merchandise, and then, when they had got freight enough, they sent to tell the woman. Their messenger, a very cunning fellow, came to my father's house bringing a necklace of gold with amber beads strung among it; and while my mother and the servants had it in their hands admiring it and bargaining about it, he made a sign quietly to the woman and then went back to the ship, whereon she took me by the hand and led me out of the house. In the fore part of the house she saw the tables set with the cups of guests who had been feasting with my father, as being in attendance on him; these were now all gone to a meeting of the public assembly, so she snatched up three cups and carried them off in the bosom of her dress, while I followed her, for I knew no better. The sun was now set, and darkness was over all the land, so we hurried on as fast as we could till we reached the harbour, where the Phoenician ship was lying. When they had got on board they sailed their ways over the sea, taking us with them, and Jove sent then a fair wind; six days did we sail both night and day, but on the seventh day Diana struck the woman and she fell heavily down into the ship's hold as though she were a sea gull alighting on the water; so they threw her overboard to the seals and fishes, and I was left all sorrowful and alone. Presently the winds and waves took the ship to Ithaca, where Laertes gave sundry of his chattels for me, and thus it was that ever I came to set eyes upon this country."

Ulysses answered, "Eumaeus, I have heard the story of your misfortunes with the most lively interest and pity, but Jove has given you good as well as evil, for in spite of everything you have a good master, who sees that you always have enough to eat and drink; and you lead a good life, whereas I am still going about begging my way from city to city."

Thus did they converse, and they had only a very little time left for sleep, for it was soon daybreak. In the mean time Telemachus and his crew were nearing land, so they loosed the sails, took down the mast, and rowed the ship into the harbour. {136} They cast out their mooring stones and made fast the hawsers; they then got out upon the sea shore, mixed their wine, and got dinner ready. As soon as they had had enough to eat and drink Telemachus said, "Take the ship on to the town, but leave me here, for I want to look after the herdsmen on one of my farms. In the evening, when I have seen all I want, I will come down to the city, and to-morrow morning in return for your trouble I will give you all a good dinner with meat and wine." {137}

Then Theoclymenus said, 'And what, my dear young friend, is to become of me? To whose house, among all your chief men, am I to repair? or shall I go straight to your own house and to your mother?"

"At any other time," replied Telemachus, "I should have bidden you go to my own house, for you would find no want of hospitality; at the present moment, however, you would not be comfortable there, for I shall be away, and my mother will not see you; she does not often show herself even to the suitors, but sits at her loom weaving in an upper chamber, out of their way; but I can tell you a man whose house you can go to—I mean Eurymachus the son of Polybus, who is held in the highest estimation by every one in Ithaca. He is much the best man and the most persistent wooer, of all those who are paying court to my mother and trying to take Ulysses' place. Jove, however, in heaven alone knows whether or no they will come to a bad end before the marriage takes place."

As he was speaking a bird flew by upon his right hand—a hawk, Apollo's messenger. It held a dove in its talons, and the feathers, as it tore them off, {138} fell to the ground midway between Telemachus and the ship. On this Theoclymenus called him apart and caught him by the hand. "Telemachus," said he, "that bird did not fly on your right hand without having been sent there by some god. As soon as I saw it I knew it was an omen; it means that you will remain powerful and that there will be no house in Ithaca more royal than your own."

"I wish it may prove so," answered Telemachus. "If it does, I will show you so much good will and give you so many presents that all who meet you will congratulate you."

Then he said to his friend Piraeus, "Piraeus, son of Clytius, you have throughout shown yourself the most willing to serve me of all those who have accompanied me to Pylos; I wish you would take this stranger to your own house and entertain him hospitably till I can come for him."

And Piraeus answered, "Telemachus, you may stay away as long as you please, but I will look after him for you, and he shall find no lack of hospitality."

As he spoke he went on board, and bade the others do so also and loose the hawsers, so they took their places in the ship. But Telemachus bound on his sandals, and took a long and doughty spear with a head of sharpened bronze from the deck of the ship. Then they loosed the hawsers, thrust the ship off from land, and made on towards the city as they had been told to do, while Telemachus strode on as fast as he could, till he reached the homestead where his countless herds of swine were feeding, and where dwelt the excellent swineherd, who was so devoted a servant to his master.

BOOK XVI

Ulysses reveals himself to Telemachus.

Meanwhile Ulysses and the swineherd had lit a fire in the hut and were were getting breakfast ready at daybreak, for they had sent the men out with the pigs. When Telemachus came up, the dogs did not bark but fawned upon him, so Ulysses, hearing the sound of feet and noticing that the dogs did not bark, said to Eumaeus:

"Eumaeus, I hear footsteps; I suppose one of your men or some one of your acquaintance is coming here, for the dogs are fawning upon him and not barking."

The words were hardly out of his mouth before his son stood at the door. Eumaeus sprang to his feet, and the bowls in which he was mixing wine fell from his hands, as he made towards his master. He kissed his head and both his beautiful eyes, and wept for joy. A father could not be more delighted at the return of an only son, the child of his old age, after ten years' absence in a foreign country and after having gone through much hardship. He embraced him, kissed him all over as though he had come back from the dead, and spoke fondly to him saying:

"So you are come, Telemachus, light of my eyes that you are. When I heard you had gone to Pylos I made sure I was never going to see you any more. Come in, my dear child, and sit down, that I may have a good look at you now you are home again; it is not very often you come into the country to see us herdsmen; you stick pretty close to the town generally. I suppose you think it better to keep an eye on what the suitors are doing."

"So be it, old friend," answered Telemachus, "but I am come now because I want to see you, and to learn whether my mother is still at her old home or whether some one else has married her, so that the bed of Ulysses is without bedding and covered with cobwebs."

"She is still at the house," replied Eumaeus, "grieving and breaking her heart, and doing nothing but weep, both night and day continually."

As he spoke he took Telemachus' spear, whereon he crossed the stone threshold and came inside. Ulysses rose from his seat to give him place as he entered, but Telemachus checked him; "Sit down, stranger," said he,

"I can easily find another seat, and there is one here who will lay it for me."

Ulysses went back to his own place, and Eumaeus strewed some green brushwood on the floor and threw a sheepskin on top of it for Telemachus to sit upon. Then the swineherd brought them platters of cold meat, the remains from what they had eaten the day before, and he filled the bread baskets with bread as fast as he could. He mixed wine also in bowls of ivy-wood, and took his seat facing Ulysses. Then they laid their hands on the good things that were before them, and as soon as they had had enough to eat and drink Telemachus said to Eumaeus, "Old friend, where does this stranger come from? How did his crew bring him to Ithaca, and who were they?—for assuredly he did not come here by land."

To this you answered, O swineherd Eumaeus, "My son, I will tell you the real truth. He says he is a Cretan, and that he has been a great traveller. At this moment he is running away from a Thesprotian ship, and has taken refuge at my station, so I will put him into your hands. Do whatever you like with him, only remember that he is your suppliant."

"I am very much distressed," said Telemachus, "by what you have just told me. How can I take this stranger into my house? I am as yet young, and am not strong enough to hold my own if any man attacks me. My mother cannot make up her mind whether to stay where she is and look after the house out of respect for public opinion and the memory of her husband, or whether the time is now come for her to take the best man of those who are wooing her, and the one who will make her the most advantageous offer; still, as the stranger has come to your station I will find him a cloak and shirt of good wear, with a sword and sandals, and will send him wherever he wants to go. Or if you like you can keep him here at the station, and I will send him clothes and food that he may be no burden on you and on your men; but I will not have him go near the suitors, for they are very insolent, and are sure to ill treat him in a way that would greatly grieve me; no matter how valiant a man may be he can do nothing against numbers, for they will be too strong for him."

Then Ulysses said, "Sir, it is right that I should say something myself. I am much shocked about what you have said about the insolent way in which the suitors are behaving in despite of such a man as you are. Tell me, do you submit to such treatment tamely, or has some god set your people against you? May you not complain of your brothers—for it is to these that a man may look for support, however great his quarrel may be? I wish I were as young as you are and in my present mind; if I were son to Ulysses, or, indeed, Ulysses himself, I would rather some one came and cut my head off, but I would go to the house and be the bane of every one of these men. {139} If they were too many for me—I being single-handed—I would rather die fighting in my own house than see such disgraceful sights day after day, strangers grossly maltreated, and men dragging the women servants about the house in an unseemly way, wine drawn recklessly, and bread wasted all to no purpose for an end that shall never be accomplished."

And Telemachus answered, "I will tell you truly everything. There is no enmity between me and my people, nor can I complain of brothers, to whom a man may look for support however great his quarrel may be. Jove has made us a race of only sons. Laertes was the only son of Arceisius, and Ulysses only son of Laertes. I am myself the only son of Ulysses who left me behind him when he went away, so that I have never been of any use to him. Hence it comes that my house is in the hands of numberless marauders; for the chiefs from all the neighbouring islands, Dulichium, Same, Zacynthus, as also all the principal men of Ithaca itself, are eating up my house under the pretext of paying court to my mother, who will neither say point blank that she will not marry, nor yet bring matters to an end, so they are making havoc of my estate, and before long will do so with myself into the bargain. The issue, however, rests with heaven. But do you, old friend Eumaeus, go at once and tell Penelope that I am safe and have returned from Pylos. Tell it to herself alone, and then come back here without letting any one else know, for there are many who are plotting mischief against me."

"I understand and heed you," replied Eumaeus; "you need instruct me no further, only as I am going that way say whether I had not better let poor Laertes know that you are returned. He used to superintend the work on his farm in spite of his bitter sorrow about Ulysses, and he would eat and drink at will along with his servants; but they tell me that from the day on which you set out for Pylos he has neither eaten nor drunk as he ought to do, nor does he look after his farm, but sits weeping and wasting the flesh from off his bones."

"More's the pity," answered Telemachus, "I am sorry for him, but we must leave him to himself just now. If people could have everything their own way, the first thing I should choose would be the return of my father; but go, and give your message; then make haste back again, and do not turn out of your way to tell Laertes. Tell my mother to send one of her women secretly with the news at once, and let him hear it from her."

Thus did he urge the swineherd; Eumaeus, therefore, took his sandals, bound them to his feet, and started for the town. Minerva watched him well off the station, and then came up to it in the form of a woman—fair, stately, and wise. She stood against the side of the entry, and revealed herself to Ulysses, but Telemachus could not see her, and knew not that she was there, for the gods do not let themselves be seen by everybody. Ulysses saw her, and so did the dogs, for they did not bark, but went scared and whining off to the other side of the yards. She nodded her head and motioned to Ulysses with her eyebrows; whereon he left the hut and stood before her outside the main wall of the yards. Then she said to him:

"Ulysses, noble son of Laertes, it is now time for you to tell your son: do not keep him in the dark any longer, but lay your plans for the destruction of the suitors, and then make for the town. I will not be long in joining you, for I too am eager for the fray."

As she spoke she touched him with her golden wand. First she threw a fair clean shirt and cloak about his shoulders; then she made him younger and of more imposing presence; she gave him back his colour, filled out his cheeks, and let his beard become dark again. Then she went away and Ulysses came back inside the hut. His son was astounded when he saw him, and turned his eyes away for fear he might be looking upon a god.

"Stranger," said he, "how suddenly you have changed from what you were a moment or two ago. You are dressed differently and your colour is not the same. Are you some one or other of the gods that live in heaven? If so, be propitious to me till I can make you due sacrifice and offerings of wrought gold. Have mercy upon me."

And Ulysses said, "I am no god, why should you take me for one? I am your father, on whose account you grieve and suffer so much at the hands of lawless men."

As he spoke he kissed his son, and a tear fell from his cheek on to the ground, for he had restrained all tears till now. But Telemachus could not yet believe that it was his father, and said:

"You are not my father, but some god is flattering me with vain hopes that I may grieve the more hereafter; no mortal man could of himself contrive to do as you have been doing, and make yourself old and young at a moment's notice, unless a god were with him. A second ago you were old and all in rags, and now you are like some god come down from heaven."

Ulysses answered, "Telemachus, you ought not to be so immeasurably astonished at my being really here. There is no other Ulysses who will come hereafter. Such as I am, it is I, who after long wandering and much hardship have got home in the twentieth year to my own country. What you wonder at is the work of the redoubtable goddess Minerva, who does with me whatever she will, for she can do what she pleases. At one moment she makes me like a beggar, and the next I am a young man with good clothes on my back; it is an easy matter for the gods who live in heaven to make any man look either rich or poor."

As he spoke he sat down, and Telemachus threw his arms about his father and wept. They were both so much moved that they cried aloud like eagles or vultures with crooked talons that have been robbed of their half fledged young by peasants. Thus piteously did they weep, and the sun would have gone down upon their mourning if Telemachus had not suddenly said, "In what ship, my dear father, did your crew bring you to Ithaca? Of what nation did they declare themselves to be—for you cannot have come by land?"

"I will tell you the truth, my son," replied Ulysses. "It was the Phaeacians who brought me here. They are great sailors, and are in the habit of giving escorts to any one who reaches their coasts. They took me over the sea while I was fast asleep, and landed me in Ithaca, after giving me many presents in bronze, gold, and raiment. These things by heaven's mercy are lying concealed in a cave, and I am now come here on the suggestion of Minerva that we may consult about killing our enemies. First, therefore, give me a list of the suitors, with their number, that I may learn who, and how many, they are. I can then turn the matter over in my mind, and see whether we two can fight the whole body of them ourselves, or whether we must find others to help us."

To this Telemachus answered, "Father, I have always heard of your renown both in the field and in council, but the task you talk of is a very great one: I am awed at the mere thought of it; two men cannot stand against many and brave ones. There are not ten suitors only, nor twice ten, but ten many times over; you shall learn their number at once. There are fifty-two chosen youths from Dulichium, and they have six servants; from Same there are twenty-four; twenty young Achaeans from Zacynthus, and twelve from Ithaca itself, all of them well born. They have with them a servant Medon, a bard, and two men who can carve at table. If we face such numbers as this, you may have bitter cause to rue your coming, and your revenge. See whether you cannot think of some one who would be willing to come and help us."

"Listen to me," replied Ulysses, "and think whether Minerva and her father Jove may seem sufficient, or whether I am to try and find some one else as well."

"Those whom you have named," answered Telemachus, "are a couple of good allies, for though they dwell high up among the clouds they have power over both gods and men."

"These two," continued Ulysses, "will not keep long out of the fray, when the suitors and we join fight in my house. Now, therefore, return home early to-morrow morning, and go about among the suitors as before. Later on the swineherd will bring me to the city disguised as a miserable old beggar. If you see them ill treating me, steel your heart against my sufferings; even though they drag me feet foremost out of the house, or throw things at me, look on and do nothing beyond gently trying to make them behave more reasonably; but they will not listen to you, for the day of their reckoning is at hand. Furthermore I say, and lay my saying to your heart; when Minerva shall put it in my mind, I will nod my head to you, and on seeing me do this you must collect all the armour that is in the house and hide it in the strong store room. Make some excuse when the suitors ask you why you are removing it; say that you have taken it to be out of the way of the smoke, inasmuch as it is no longer what it was when Ulysses went away, but has become soiled and begrimed with soot. Add to this more particularly that you are afraid Jove may set them on to quarrel over their wine, and that they may do each other some harm which may disgrace both banquet and wooing, for the sight of arms sometimes tempts people to use them. But leave a sword and a spear apiece for yourself and me, and a couple of oxhide shields so that we can snatch them up at any moment; Jove and Minerva will then soon quiet these people. There is also another matter; if you are indeed my son and my blood runs in your veins, let no one know that Ulysses is within the house—neither Laertes, nor yet the swineherd, nor any of the servants, nor even Penelope herself. Let you and me exploit the women alone, and let us also make trial of some other of the men servants, to see who is on our side and whose hand is against us."

"Father," replied Telemachus, "you will come to know me by and by, and when you do you will find that I can keep your counsel. I do not think, however, the plan you propose will turn out well for either of us. Think it over. It will take us a long time to go the round of the farms and exploit the men, and all the time the suitors will be wasting your estate with impunity and without compunction. Prove the women by all means, to see who are disloyal and who guiltless, but I am not in favour of going round and trying the men. We can attend to that later on, if you really have some sign from Jove that he will support you."

Thus did they converse, and meanwhile the ship which had brought Telemachus and his crew from Pylos had reached the town of Ithaca. When they had come inside the harbour they drew the ship on to the land; their servants came and took their armour from them, and they left all the presents at the house of Clytius. Then they sent a servant to tell Penelope that Telemachus had gone into the country, but had sent the ship to the town to prevent her from being alarmed and made unhappy. This servant and Eumaeus happened to meet when they were both on the same errand of going to tell Penelope. When they reached the House, the servant stood up and said to the queen in the presence of the waiting women, "Your son, Madam, is now returned from Pylos"; but Eumaeus went close up to Penelope, and said privately all that her son had bidden him tell her. When he had given his message he left the house with its outbuildings and went back to his pigs again.

The suitors were surprised and angry at what had happened, so they went outside the great wall that ran round the outer court, and held a council near the main entrance. Eurymachus, son of Polybus, was the first to speak.

"My friends," said he, "this voyage of Telemachus's is a very serious matter; we had made sure that it would come to nothing. Now, however, let us draw a ship into the water, and get a crew together to send after the others and tell them to come back as fast as they can."

He had hardly done speaking when Amphinomus turned in his place and saw the ship inside the harbour, with the crew lowering her sails, and putting by their oars; so he laughed, and said to the others, "We need not send them any message, for they are here. Some god must have told them, or else they saw the ship go by, and could not overtake her."

On this they rose and went to the water side. The crew then drew the ship on shore; their servants took their armour from them, and they went up in a body to the place of assembly, but they would not let any one old or young sit along with them, and Antinous, son of Eupeithes, spoke first.

"Good heavens," said he, "see how the gods have saved this man from destruction. We kept a succession of scouts upon the headlands all day long, and when the sun was down we never went on shore to sleep, but waited in the ship all night till morning in the hope of capturing and killing him; but some god has conveyed him home in spite of us. Let us consider how we can make an end of him. He must not escape us; our affair is never likely to come off while he is alive, for he is very shrewd, and public feeling is by no means all on our side. We must make haste before he can call the Achaeans in assembly; he will lose no time in doing so, for he will be furious with us, and will tell all the world how we plotted to kill him, but failed to take him. The people will not like this when they come to know of it; we must see that they do us no hurt, nor drive us from our own country into exile. Let us try and lay hold of him either on his farm away from the town, or on the road hither. Then we can divide up his property amongst us, and let his mother and the man who marries her have the house. If this does not please you, and you wish Telemachus to live on and hold his father's property, then we must not gather here and eat up his goods in this way, but must make our offers to Penelope each from his own house, and she can marry the man who will give the most for her, and whose lot it is to win her."

They all held their peace until Amphinomus rose to speak. He was the son of Nisus, who was son to king Aretias, and he was foremost among all the suitors from the wheat-growing and well grassed island of Dulichium; his conversation, moreover, was more agreeable to Penelope than that of any of the other suitors, for he was a man of good natural disposition. "My friends," said he, speaking to them plainly and in all honestly, "I am not in favour of killing Telemachus. It is a heinous thing to kill one who is of noble blood. Let us first take counsel of the gods, and if the oracles of Jove advise it, I will both help to kill him myself, and will urge everyone else to do so; but if they dissuade us, I would have you hold your hands."

Thus did he speak, and his words pleased them well, so they rose forthwith and went to the house of Ulysses, where they took their accustomed seats.

Then Penelope resolved that she would show herself to the suitors. She knew of the plot against Telemachus, for the servant Medon had overheard their counsels and had told her; she went down therefore to the court attended by her maidens, and when she reached the suitors she stood by one of the bearing-posts supporting the roof of the cloister holding a veil before her face, and rebuked Antinous saying:

"Antinous, insolent and wicked schemer, they say you are the best speaker and counsellor of any man your own age in Ithaca, but you are nothing of the kind. Madman, why should you try to compass the death of Telemachus, and take no heed of suppliants, whose witness is Jove himself? It is not right for you to plot thus against one another. Do you not remember how your father fled to this house in fear of the people, who were enraged against him for having gone with some Taphian pirates and plundered the Thesprotians who were at peace with us? They wanted to tear him in pieces and eat up everything he had, but Ulysses stayed their hands although they were infuriated, and now you devour his property without paying for it, and break my heart by wooing his wife and trying to kill his son. Leave off doing so, and stop the others also."

To this Eurymachus son of Polybus answered, "Take heart, Queen Penelope daughter of Icarius, and do not trouble yourself about these matters. The man is not yet born, nor never will be, who shall lay hands upon your son Telemachus, while I yet live to look upon the face of the earth. I say—and it shall surely be—that my spear shall be reddened with his blood; for many a time has Ulysses taken me on his knees, held wine up to my lips to drink, and put pieces of meat into my hands. Therefore Telemachus is much the dearest friend I have, and has nothing to fear from the hands of us suitors. Of course, if death comes to him from the gods, he cannot escape it." He said this to quiet her, but in reality he was plotting against Telemachus.

Then Penelope went upstairs again and mourned her husband till Minerva shed sleep over her eyes. In the evening Eumaeus got back to Ulysses and his son, who had just sacrificed a young pig of a year old and were helping one another to get supper ready; Minerva therefore came up to Ulysses, turned him into an old man with a stroke of her wand, and clad him in his old clothes again, for fear that the swineherd might recognise him and not keep the secret, but go and tell Penelope.

Telemachus was the first to speak. "So you have got back, Eumaeus," said he. "What is the news of the town? Have the suitors returned, or are they still waiting over yonder, to take me on my way home?"

"I did not think of asking about that," replied Eumaeus, "when I was in the town. I thought I would give my message and come back as soon as I could. I met a man sent by those who had gone with you to Pylos, and he was the first to tell the news to your mother, but I can say what I saw with my own eyes; I had just got on to the crest of the hill of Mercury above the town when I saw a ship coming into harbour with a number of men in her. They had many shields and spears, and I thought it was the suitors, but I cannot be sure."

On hearing this Telemachus smiled to his father, but so that Eumaeus could not see him.

Then, when they had finished their work and the meal was ready, they ate it, and every man had his full share so that all were satisfied. As soon as they had had enough to eat and drink, they laid down to rest and enjoyed the boon of sleep.

BOOK XVII

Telemachus and his mother meet—Ulysses and Eumaeus come down to the town, and Ulysses is insulted by Melanthius—he is recognised by the dog Argos—he is insulted and presently struck by Antinous with a stool—Penelope desires that he shall be sent to her.

When the child of morning, rosy-fingered Dawn, appeared, Telemachus bound on his sandals and took a strong spear that suited his hands, for he wanted to go into the city. "Old friend," said he to the swineherd, "I will now go to the town and show myself to my mother, for she will never leave off grieving till she has seen me. As for this unfortunate stranger, take him to the town and let him beg there of any one who will give him a drink and a piece of bread. I have trouble enough of my own, and cannot be burdened with other people. If this makes him angry so much the worse for him, but I like to say what I mean."

Then Ulysses said, "Sir, I do not want to stay here; a beggar can always do better in town than country, for any one who likes can give him something. I am too old to care about remaining here at the beck and call of a master. Therefore let this man do as you have just told him, and take me to the town as soon as I have had a warm by the fire, and the day has got a little heat in it. My clothes are wretchedly thin, and this frosty morning I shall be perished with cold, for you say the city is some way off."

On this Telemachus strode off through the yards, brooding his revenge upon the suitors. When he reached home he stood his spear against a bearing-post of the cloister, crossed the stone floor of the cloister itself, and went inside.

Nurse Euryclea saw him long before any one else did. She was putting the fleeces on to the seats, and she burst out crying as she ran up to him; all the other maids came up too, and covered his head and shoulders with their kisses. Penelope came out of her room looking like Diana or Venus, and wept as she flung her arms about her son. She kissed his forehead and both his beautiful eyes, "Light of my eyes," she cried as she spoke fondly to him, "so you are come home again; I made sure I was never going to see you any more. To think of your having gone off to Pylos without saying anything about it or obtaining my consent. But come, tell me what you saw."

"Do not scold me, mother," answered Telemachus, "nor vex me, seeing what a narrow escape I have had, but wash your face, change your dress, go upstairs with your maids, and promise full and sufficient hecatombs to all the gods if Jove will only grant us our revenge upon the suitors. I must now go to the place of assembly to invite a stranger who has come back with me from Pylos. I sent him on with my crew, and told Piraeus to take him home and look after him till I could come for him myself."

She heeded her son's words, washed her face, changed her dress, and vowed full and sufficient hecatombs to all the gods if they would only vouchsafe her revenge upon the suitors.

Telemachus went through, and out of, the cloisters spear in hand—not alone, for his two fleet dogs went with him. Minerva endowed him with a presence of such divine comeliness that all marvelled at him as he went by, and the suitors gathered round him with fair words in their mouths and malice in their hearts; but he avoided them, and went to sit with Mentor, Antiphus, and Halitherses, old friends of his father's house, and they made him tell them all that had happened to him. Then Piraeus came up with Theoclymenus, whom he had escorted through the town to the place of assembly, whereon Telemachus at once joined them. Piraeus was first to speak: "Telemachus," said he, "I wish you would send some of your women to my house to take away the presents Menelaus gave you."

"We do not know, Piraeus," answered Telemachus, "what may happen. If the suitors kill me in my own house and divide my property among them, I would rather you had the presents than that any of those people should get hold of them. If on the other hand I managed to kill them, I shall be much obliged if you will kindly bring me my presents."

With these words he took Theoclymenus to his own house. When they got there they laid their cloaks on the benches and seats, went into the baths, and washed themselves. When the maids had washed and anointed them, and had given them cloaks and shirts, they took their seats at table. A maid servant then brought them water in a beautiful golden ewer, and poured it into a silver basin for them to wash their hands; and she drew a clean table beside them. An upper servant brought them bread and offered them many good things of what there was in the house. Opposite them sat Penelope, reclining on a couch by one of the bearing-posts of the cloister, and spinning. Then they laid their hands on the good things that were before them, and as soon as they had had enough to eat and drink Penelope said:

"Telemachus, I shall go upstairs and lie down on that sad couch, which I have not ceased to water with my tears, from the day Ulysses set out for Troy with the sons of Atreus. You failed, however, to make it clear to me before the suitors came back to the house, whether or no you had been able to hear anything about the return of your father."

"I will tell you then truth," replied her son. "We went to Pylos and saw Nestor, who took me to his house and treated me as hospitably as though I were a son of his own who had just returned after a long absence; so also did his sons; but he said he had not heard a word from any human being about Ulysses, whether he was alive or dead. He sent me, therefore, with a chariot and horses to Menelaus. There I saw Helen, for whose sake so many, both Argives and Trojans, were in heaven's wisdom doomed to suffer. Menelaus asked me what it was that had brought me to Lacedaemon, and I told him the whole truth, whereon he said, 'So, then, these cowards would usurp a brave man's bed? A hind might as well lay her new-born young in the lair of a lion, and then go off to feed in the forest or in some grassy dell. The lion, when he comes back to his lair, will make short work with the pair of them, and so will Ulysses with these suitors. By father Jove, Minerva, and Apollo, if Ulysses is still the man that he was when he wrestled with Philomeleides in Lesbos, and threw him so heavily that all the Greeks cheered him—if he is still such, and were to come near these suitors, they would have a short shrift and a sorry wedding. As regards your question, however, I will not prevaricate nor deceive you, but what the old man of the sea told me, so much will I tell you in full. He said he could see Ulysses on an island sorrowing bitterly in the house of the nymph Calypso, who was keeping him prisoner, and he could not reach his home, for he had no ships nor sailors to take him over the sea.' This was what Menelaus told me, and when I had heard his story I came away; the gods then gave me a fair wind and soon brought me safe home again."

With these words he moved the heart of Penelope. Then Theoclymenus said to her:

"Madam, wife of Ulysses, Telemachus does not understand these things; listen therefore to me, for I can divine them surely, and will hide nothing from you. May Jove the king of heaven be my witness, and the rites of hospitality, with that hearth of Ulysses to which I now come, that Ulysses himself is even now in Ithaca, and, either going about the country or staying in one place, is enquiring into all these evil deeds and preparing a day of reckoning for the suitors. I saw an omen when I was on the ship which meant this, and I told Telemachus about it."

"May it be even so," answered Penelope; "if your words come true, you shall have such gifts and such good will from me that all who see you shall congratulate you."

Thus did they converse. Meanwhile the suitors were throwing discs, or aiming with spears at a mark on the levelled ground in front of the house, and behaving with all their old insolence. But when it was now time for dinner, and the flock of sheep and goats had come into the town from all the country round, {140} with their shepherds as usual, then Medon, who was their favourite servant, and who waited upon them at table, said, "Now then, my young masters, you have had enough sport, so come inside that we may get dinner ready. Dinner is not a bad thing, at dinner time."

They left their sports as he told them, and when they were within the house, they laid their cloaks on the benches and seats inside, and then sacrificed some sheep, goats, pigs, and a heifer, all of them fat and well grown. {141} Thus they made ready for their meal. In the meantime Ulysses and the swineherd were about starting for the town, and the swineherd said, "Stranger, I suppose you still want to go to town to-day, as my master said you were to do; for my own part I should have liked you to stay here as a station hand, but I must do as my master tells me, or he will scold me later on, and a scolding from one's master is a very serious thing. Let us then be off, for it is now broad day; it will be night again directly and then you will find it colder." {142}

"I know, and understand you," replied Ulysses; "you need say no more. Let us be going, but if you have a stick ready cut, let me have it to walk with, for you say the road is a very rough one."

As he spoke he threw his shabby old tattered wallet over his shoulders, by the cord from which it hung, and Eumaeus gave him a stick to his liking. The two then started, leaving the station in charge of the dogs and herdsmen who remained behind; the swineherd led the way and his master followed after, looking like some broken down old tramp as he leaned upon his staff, and his clothes were all in rags. When they had got over the rough steep ground and were nearing the city, they reached the fountain from which the citizens drew their water. This had been made by Ithacus, Neritus, and Polyctor. There was a grove of water-loving poplars planted in a circle all round it, and the clear cold water came down to it from a rock high up, {143} while above the fountain there was an altar to the nymphs, at which all wayfarers used to sacrifice. Here Melanthius son of Dolius overtook them as he was driving down some goats, the best in his flock, for the suitors' dinner, and there were two shepherds with him. When he saw Eumaeus and Ulysses he reviled them with outrageous and unseemly language, which made Ulysses very angry.

"There you go," cried he, "and a precious pair you are. See how heaven brings birds of the same feather to one another. Where, pray, master swineherd, are you taking this poor miserable object? It would make any one sick to see such a creature at table. A fellow like this never won a prize for anything in his life, but will go about rubbing his shoulders against every man's door post, and begging, not for swords and cauldrons {144} like a man, but only for a few scraps not worth begging for. If you would give him to me for a hand on my station, he might do to clean out the folds, or bring a bit of sweet feed to the kids, and he could fatten his thighs as much as he pleased on whey; but he has taken to bad ways and will not go about any kind of work; he will do nothing but beg victuals all the town over, to feed his insatiable belly. I say, therefore—and it shall surely be—if he goes near Ulysses' house he will get his head broken by the stools they will fling at him, till they turn him out."

On this, as he passed, he gave Ulysses a kick on the hip out of pure wantonness, but Ulysses stood firm, and did not budge from the path. For a moment he doubted whether or no to fly at Melanthius and kill him with his staff, or fling him to the ground and beat his brains out; he resolved, however, to endure it and keep himself in check, but the swineherd looked straight at Melanthius and rebuked him, lifting up his hands and praying to heaven as he did so.

"Fountain nymphs," he cried, "children of Jove, if ever Ulysses burned you thigh bones covered with fat whether of lambs or kids, grant my prayer that heaven may send him home. He would soon put an end to the swaggering threats with which such men as you go about insulting people—gadding all over the town while your flocks are going to ruin through bad shepherding."

Then Melanthius the goatherd answered, "You ill conditioned cur, what are you talking about? Some day or other I will put you on board ship and take you to a foreign country, where I can sell you and pocket the money you will fetch. I wish I were as sure that Apollo would strike Telemachus dead this very day, or that the suitors would kill him, as I am that Ulysses will never come home again."

With this he left them to come on at their leisure, while he went quickly forward and soon reached the house of his master. When he got there he went in and took his seat among the suitors opposite Eurymachus, who liked him better than any of the others. The servants brought him a portion of meat, and an upper woman servant set bread before him that he might eat. Presently Ulysses and the swineherd came up to the house and stood by it, amid a sound of music, for Phemius was just beginning to sing to the suitors. Then Ulysses took hold of the swineherd's hand, and said:

"Eumaeus, this house of Ulysses is a very fine place. No matter how far you go, you will find few like it. One building keeps following on after another. The outer court has a wall with battlements all round it; the doors are double folding, and of good workmanship; it would be a hard matter to take it by force of arms. I perceive, too, that there are many people banqueting within it, for there is a smell of roast meat, and I hear a sound of music, which the gods have made to go along with feasting."

Then Eumaeus said, "You have perceived aright, as indeed you generally do; but let us think what will be our best course. Will you go inside first and join the suitors, leaving me here behind you, or will you wait here and let me go in first? But do not wait long, or some one may see you loitering about outside, and throw something at you. Consider this matter I pray you."

And Ulysses answered, "I understand and heed. Go in first and leave me here where I am. I am quite used to being beaten and having things thrown at me. I have been so much buffeted about in war and by sea that I am case-hardened, and this too may go with the rest. But a man cannot hide away the cravings of a hungry belly; this is an enemy which gives much trouble to all men; it is because of this that ships are fitted out to sail the seas, and to make war upon other people."

As they were thus talking, a dog that had been lying asleep raised his head and pricked up his ears. This was Argos, whom Ulysses had bred before setting out for Troy, but he had never had any work out of him. In the old days he used to be taken out by the young men when they went hunting wild goats, or deer, or hares, but now that his master was gone he was lying neglected on the heaps of mule and cow dung that lay in front of the stable doors till the men should come and draw it away to manure the great close; and he was full of fleas. As soon as he saw Ulysses standing there, he dropped his ears and wagged his tail, but he could not get close up to his master. When Ulysses saw the dog on the other side of the yard, he dashed a tear from his eyes without Eumaeus seeing it, and said:

"Eumaeus, what a noble hound that is over yonder on the manure heap: his build is splendid; is he as fine a fellow as he looks, or is he only one of those dogs that come begging about a table, and are kept merely for show?"

"This hound," answered Eumaeus, "belonged to him who has died in a far country. If he were what he was when Ulysses left for Troy, he would soon show you what he could do. There was not a wild beast in the forest that could get away from him when he was once on its tracks. But now he has fallen on evil times, for his master is dead and gone, and the women take no care of him. Servants never do their work when their master's hand is no longer over them, for Jove takes half the goodness out of a man when he makes a slave of him."

As he spoke he went inside the buildings to the cloister where the suitors were, but Argos died as soon as he had recognised his master.

Telemachus saw Eumaeus long before any one else did, and beckoned him to come and sit beside him; so he looked about and saw a seat lying near where the carver sat serving out their portions to the suitors; he picked it up, brought it to Telemachus's table, and sat down opposite him. Then the servant brought him his portion, and gave him bread from the bread-basket.

Immediately afterwards Ulysses came inside, looking like a poor miserable old beggar, leaning on his staff and with his clothes all in rags. He sat down upon the threshold of ash-wood just inside the doors leading from the outer to the inner court, and against a bearing-post of cypress-wood which the carpenter had skilfully planed, and had made to join truly with rule and line. Telemachus took a whole loaf from the bread-basket, with as much meat as he could hold in his two hands, and said to Eumaeus, "Take this to the stranger, and tell him to go the round of the suitors, and beg from them; a beggar must not be shamefaced."

So Eumaeus went up to him and said, "Stranger, Telemachus sends you this, and says you are to go the round of the suitors begging, for beggars must not be shamefaced."

Ulysses answered, "May King Jove grant all happiness to Telemachus, and fulfil the desire of his heart."

Then with both hands he took what Telemachus had sent him, and laid it on the dirty old wallet at his feet. He went on eating it while the bard was singing, and had just finished his dinner as he left off. The suitors applauded the bard, whereon Minerva went up to Ulysses and prompted him to beg pieces of bread from each one of the suitors, that he might see what kind of people they were, and tell the good from the bad; but come what might she was not going to save a single one of them. Ulysses, therefore, went on his round, going from left to right, and stretched out his hands to beg as though he were a real beggar. Some of them pitied him, and were curious about him, asking one another who he was and where he came from; whereon the goatherd Melanthius said, "Suitors of my noble mistress, I can tell you something about him, for I have seen him before. The swineherd brought him here, but I know nothing about the man himself, nor where he comes from."

On this Antinous began to abuse the swineherd. "You precious idiot," he cried, "what have you brought this man to town for? Have we not tramps and beggars enough already to pester us as we sit at meat? Do you think it a small thing that such people gather here to waste your master's property—and must you needs bring this man as well?"

And Eumaeus answered, "Antinous, your birth is good but your words evil. It was no doing of mine that he came here. Who is likely to invite a stranger from a foreign country, unless it be one of those who can do public service as a seer, a healer of hurts, a carpenter, or a bard who can charm us with his singing? Such men are welcome all the world over, but no one is likely to ask a beggar who will only worry him. You are always harder on Ulysses' servants than any of the other suitors are, and above all on me, but I do not care so long as Telemachus and Penelope are alive and here."

But Telemachus said, "Hush, do not answer him; Antinous has the bitterest tongue of all the suitors, and he makes the others worse."

Then turning to Antinous he said, "Antinous, you take as much care of my interests as though I were your son. Why should you want to see this stranger turned out of the house? Heaven forbid; take something and give it him yourself; I do not grudge it; I bid you take it. Never mind my mother, nor any of the other servants in the house; but I know you will not do what I say, for you are more fond of eating things yourself than of giving them to other people."

"What do you mean, Telemachus," replied Antinous, "by this swaggering talk? If all the suitors were to give him as much as I will, he would not come here again for another three months."

As he spoke he drew the stool on which he rested his dainty feet from under the table, and made as though he would throw it at Ulysses, but the other suitors all gave him something, and filled his wallet with bread and meat; he was about, therefore, to go back to the threshold and eat what the suitors had given him, but he first went up to Antinous and said:

"Sir, give me something; you are not, surely, the poorest man here; you seem to be a chief, foremost among them all; therefore you should be the better giver, and I will tell far and wide of your bounty. I too was a rich man once, and had a fine house of my own; in those days I gave to many a tramp such as I now am, no matter who he might be nor what he wanted. I had any number of servants, and all the other things which people have who live well and are accounted wealthy, but it pleased Jove to take all away from me. He sent me with a band of roving robbers to Egypt; it was a long voyage and I was undone by it. I stationed my ships in the river Aegyptus, and bade my men stay by them and keep guard over them, while I sent out scouts to reconnoitre from every point of vantage.

"But the men disobeyed my orders, took to their own devices, and ravaged the land of the Egyptians, killing the men, and taking their wives and children captives. The alarm was soon carried to the city, and when they heard the war-cry, the people came out at daybreak till the plain was filled with soldiers horse and foot, and with the gleam of armour. Then Jove spread panic among my men, and they would no longer face the enemy, for they found themselves surrounded. The Egyptians killed many of us, and took the rest alive to do forced labour for them; as for myself, they gave me to a friend who met them, to take to Cyprus, Dmetor by name, son of Iasus, who was a great man in Cyprus. Thence I am come hither in a state of great misery."

Then Antinous said, "What god can have sent such a pestilence to plague us during our dinner? Get out, into the open part of the court, {145} or I will give you Egypt and Cyprus over again for your insolence and importunity; you have begged of all the others, and they have given you lavishly, for they have abundance round them, and it is easy to be free with other people's property when there is plenty of it."

On this Ulysses began to move off, and said, "Your looks, my fine sir, are better than your breeding; if you were in your own house you would not spare a poor man so much as a pinch of salt, for though you are in another man's, and surrounded with abundance, you cannot find it in you to give him even a piece of bread."

This made Antinous very angry, and he scowled at him saying, "You shall pay for this before you get clear of the court." With these words he threw a footstool at him, and hit him on the right shoulder blade near the top of his back. Ulysses stood firm as a rock and the blow did not even stagger him, but he shook his head in silence as he brooded on his revenge. Then he went back to the threshold and sat down there, laying his well filled wallet at his feet.

"Listen to me," he cried, "you suitors of Queen Penelope, that I may speak even as I am minded. A man knows neither ache nor pain if he gets hit while fighting for his money, or for his sheep or his cattle; and even so Antinous has hit me while in the service of my miserable belly, which is always getting people into trouble. Still, if the poor have gods and avenging deities at all, I pray them that Antinous may come to a bad end before his marriage."

"Sit where you are, and eat your victuals in silence, or be off elsewhere," shouted Antinous. "If you say more I will have you dragged hand and foot through the courts, and the servants shall flay you alive."

The other suitors were much displeased at this, and one of the young men said, "Antinous, you did ill in striking that poor wretch of a tramp: it will be worse for you if he should turn out to be some god—and we know the gods go about disguised in all sorts of ways as people from foreign countries, and travel about the world to see who do amiss and who righteously." {146}

Thus said the suitors, but Antinous paid them no heed. Meanwhile Telemachus was furious about the blow that had been given to his father, and though no tear fell from him, he shook his head in silence and brooded on his revenge.

Now when Penelope heard that the beggar had been struck in the banqueting-cloister, she said before her maids, "Would that Apollo would so strike you, Antinous," and her waiting woman Eurynome answered, "If our prayers were answered not one of the suitors would ever again see the sun rise." Then Penelope said, "Nurse, {147} I hate every single one of them, for they mean nothing but mischief, but I hate Antinous like the darkness of death itself. A poor unfortunate tramp has come begging about the house for sheer want. Every one else has given him something to put in his wallet, but Antinous has hit him on the right shoulder-blade with a footstool."

Thus did she talk with her maids as she sat in her own room, and in the meantime Ulysses was getting his dinner. Then she called for the swineherd and said, "Eumaeus, go and tell the stranger to come here, I want to see him and ask him some questions. He seems to have travelled much, and he may have seen or heard something of my unhappy husband."

To this you answered, O swineherd Eumaeus, "If these Achaeans, Madam, would only keep quiet, you would be charmed with the history of his adventures. I had him three days and three nights with me in my hut, which was the first place he reached after running away from his ship, and he has not yet completed the story of his misfortunes. If he had been the most heaven-taught minstrel in the whole world, on whose lips all hearers hang entranced, I could not have been more charmed as I sat in my hut and listened to him. He says there is an old friendship between his house and that of Ulysses, and that he comes from Crete where the descendants of Minos live, after having been driven hither and thither by every kind of misfortune; he also declares that he has heard of Ulysses as being alive and near at hand among the Thesprotians, and that he is bringing great wealth home with him."

"Call him here, then," said Penelope, "that I too may hear his story. As for the suitors, let them take their pleasure indoors or out as they will, for they have nothing to fret about. Their corn and wine remain unwasted in their houses with none but servants to consume them, while they keep hanging about our house day after day sacrificing our oxen, sheep, and fat goats for their banquets, and never giving so much as a thought to the quantity of wine they drink. No estate can stand such recklessness, for we have now no Ulysses to protect us. If he were to come again, he and his son would soon have their revenge."

As she spoke Telemachus sneezed so loudly that the whole house resounded with it. Penelope laughed when she heard this, and said to Eumaeus, "Go and call the stranger; did you not hear how my son sneezed just as I was speaking? This can only mean that all the suitors are going to be killed, and that not one of them shall escape. Furthermore I say, and lay my saying to your heart: if I am satisfied that the stranger is speaking the truth I shall give him a shirt and cloak of good wear."

When Eumaeus heard this he went straight to Ulysses and said, "Father stranger, my mistress Penelope, mother of Telemachus, has sent for you; she is in great grief, but she wishes to hear anything you can tell her about her husband, and if she is satisfied that you are speaking the truth, she will give you a shirt and cloak, which are the very things that you are most in want of. As for bread, you can get enough of that to fill your belly, by begging about the town, and letting those give that will."

"I will tell Penelope," answered Ulysses, "nothing but what is strictly true. I know all about her husband, and have been partner with him in affliction, but I am afraid of passing through this crowd of cruel suitors, for their pride and insolence reach heaven. Just now, moreover, as I was going about the house without doing any harm, a man gave me a blow that hurt me very much, but neither Telemachus nor any one else defended me. Tell Penelope, therefore, to be patient and wait till sundown. Let her give me a seat close up to the fire, for my clothes are worn very thin—you know they are, for you have seen them ever since I first asked you to help me—she can then ask me about the return of her husband."

The swineherd went back when he heard this, and Penelope said as she saw him cross the threshold, "Why do you not bring him here, Eumaeus? Is he afraid that some one will ill-treat him, or is he shy of coming inside the house at all? Beggars should not be shamefaced."

To this you answered, O swineherd Eumaeus, "The stranger is quite reasonable. He is avoiding the suitors, and is only doing what any one else would do. He asks you to wait till sundown, and it will be much better, madam, that you should have him all to yourself, when you can hear him and talk to him as you will."

"The man is no fool," answered Penelope, "it would very likely be as he says, for there are no such abominable people in the whole world as these men are."

When she had done speaking Eumaeus went back to the suitors, for he had explained everything. Then he went up to Telemachus and said in his ear so that none could overhear him, "My dear sir, I will now go back to the pigs, to see after your property and my own business. You will look to what is going on here, but above all be careful to keep out of danger, for there are many who bear you ill will. May Jove bring them to a bad end before they do us a mischief."

"Very well," replied Telemachus, "go home when you have had your dinner, and in the morning come here with the victims we are to sacrifice for the day. Leave the rest to heaven and me."

On this Eumaeus took his seat again, and when he had finished his dinner he left the courts and the cloister with the men at table, and went back to his pigs. As for the suitors, they presently began to amuse themselves with singing and dancing, for it was now getting on towards evening.

BOOK XVIII

The fight with Irus—Ulysses warns Amphinomus—Penelope gets presents from the suitors—the braziers—Ulysses rebukes Eurymachus.

Now there came a certain common tramp who used to go begging all over the city of Ithaca, and was notorious as an incorrigible glutton and drunkard. This man had no strength nor stay in him, but he was a great hulking fellow to look at; his real name, the one his mother gave him, was Arnaeus, but the young men of the place called him Irus, {148} because he used to run errands for any one who would send him. As soon as he came he began to insult Ulysses, and to try and drive him out of his own house.

"Be off, old man," he cried, "from the doorway, or you shall be dragged out neck and heels. Do you not see that they are all giving me the wink, and wanting me to turn you out by force, only I do not like to do so? Get up then, and go of yourself, or we shall come to blows."

Ulysses frowned on him and said, "My friend, I do you no manner of harm; people give you a great deal, but I am not jealous. There is room enough in this doorway for the pair of us, and you need not grudge me things that are not yours to give. You seem to be just such another tramp as myself, but perhaps the gods will give us better luck by and by. Do not, however, talk too much about fighting or you will incense me, and old though I am, I shall cover your mouth and chest with blood. I shall have more peace tomorrow if I do, for you will not come to the house of Ulysses any more."

Irus was very angry and answered, "You filthy glutton, you run on trippingly like an old fish-fag. I have a good mind to lay both hands about you, and knock your teeth out of your head like so many boar's tusks. Get ready, therefore, and let these people here stand by and look on. You will never be able to fight one who is so much younger than yourself."

Thus roundly did they rate one another on the smooth pavement in front of the doorway, {149} and when Antinous saw what was going on he laughed heartily and said to the others, "This is the finest sport that you ever saw; heaven never yet sent anything like it into this house. The stranger and Irus have quarreled and are going to fight, let us set them on to do so at once."

The suitors all came up laughing, and gathered round the two ragged tramps. "Listen to me," said Antinous, "there are some goats' paunches down at the fire, which we have filled with blood and fat, and set aside for supper; he who is victorious and proves himself to be the better man shall have his pick of the lot; he shall be free of our table and we will not allow any other beggar about the house at all."

The others all agreed, but Ulysses, to throw them off the scent, said, "Sirs, an old man like myself, worn out with suffering, cannot hold his own against a young one; but my irrepressible belly urges me on, though I know it can only end in my getting a drubbing. You must swear, however that none of you will give me a foul blow to favour Irus and secure him the victory."

They swore as he told them, and when they had completed their oath Telemachus put in a word and said, "Stranger, if you have a mind to settle with this fellow, you need not be afraid of any one here. Whoever strikes you will have to fight more than one. I am host, and the other chiefs, Antinous and Eurymachus, both of them men of understanding, are of the same mind as I am."

Every one assented, and Ulysses girded his old rags about his loins, thus baring his stalwart thighs, his broad chest and shoulders, and his mighty arms; but Minerva came up to him and made his limbs even stronger still. The suitors were beyond measure astonished, and one would turn towards his neighbour saying, "The stranger has brought such a thigh out of his old rags that there will soon be nothing left of Irus."

Irus began to be very uneasy as he heard them, but the servants girded him by force, and brought him [into the open part of the court] in such a fright that his limbs were all of a tremble. Antinous scolded him and said, "You swaggering bully, you ought never to have been born at all if you are afraid of such an old broken down creature as this tramp is. I say, therefore—and it shall surely be—if he beats you and proves himself the better man, I shall pack you off on board ship to the mainland and send you to king Echetus, who kills every one that comes near him. He will cut off your nose and ears, and draw out your entrails for the dogs to eat."

This frightened Irus still more, but they brought him into the middle of the court, and the two men raised their hands to fight. Then Ulysses considered whether he should let drive so hard at him as to make an end of him then and there, or whether he should give him a lighter blow that should only knock him down; in the end he deemed it best to give the lighter blow for fear the Achaeans should begin to suspect who he was.

Then they began to fight, and Irus hit Ulysses on the right shoulder; but Ulysses gave Irus a blow on the neck under the ear that broke in the bones of his skull, and the blood came gushing out of his mouth; he fell groaning in the dust, gnashing his teeth and kicking on the ground, but the suitors threw up their hands and nearly died of laughter, as Ulysses caught hold of him by the foot and dragged him into the outer court as far as the gate-house. There he propped him up against the wall and put his staff in his hands. "Sit here," said he, "and keep the dogs and pigs off; you are a pitiful creature, and if you try to make yourself king of the beggars any more you shall fare still worse."

Then he threw his dirty old wallet, all tattered and torn over his shoulder with the cord by which it hung, and went back to sit down upon the threshold; but the suitors went within the cloisters, laughing and saluting him, "May Jove, and all the other gods," said they, "grant you whatever you want for having put an end to the importunity of this insatiable tramp. We will take him over to the mainland presently, to king Echetus, who kills every one that comes near him."

Ulysses hailed this as of good omen, and Antinous set a great goat's paunch before him filled with blood and fat. Amphinomus took two loaves out of the bread-basket and brought them to him, pledging him as he did so in a golden goblet of wine. "Good luck to you," he said, "father stranger, you are very badly off at present, but I hope you will have better times by and by."

To this Ulysses answered, "Amphinomus, you seem to be a man of good understanding, as indeed you may well be, seeing whose son you are. I have heard your father well spoken of; he is Nisus of Dulichium, a man both brave and wealthy. They tell me you are his son, and you appear to be a considerable person; listen, therefore, and take heed to what I am saying. Man is the vainest of all creatures that have their being upon earth. As long as heaven vouchsafes him health and strength, he thinks that he shall come to no harm hereafter, and even when the blessed gods bring sorrow upon him, he bears it as he needs must, and makes the best of it; for God almighty gives men their daily minds day by day. I know all about it, for I was a rich man once, and did much wrong in the stubbornness of my pride, and in the confidence that my father and my brothers would support me; therefore let a man fear God in all things always, and take the good that heaven may see fit to send him without vain glory. Consider the infamy of what these suitors are doing; see how they are wasting the estate, and doing dishonour to the wife, of one who is certain to return some day, and that, too, not long hence. Nay, he will be here soon; may heaven send you home quietly first that you may not meet with him in the day of his coming, for once he is here the suitors and he will not part bloodlessly."

With these words he made a drink-offering, and when he had drunk he put the gold cup again into the hands of Amphinomus, who walked away serious and bowing his head, for he foreboded evil. But even so he did not escape destruction, for Minerva had doomed him to fall by the hand of Telemachus. So he took his seat again at the place from which he had come.

Then Minerva put it into the mind of Penelope to show herself to the suitors, that she might make them still more enamoured of her, and win still further honour from her son and husband. So she feigned a mocking laugh and said, "Eurynome, I have changed my mind, and have a fancy to show myself to the suitors although I detest them. I should like also to give my son a hint that he had better not have anything more to do with them. They speak fairly enough but they mean mischief."

"My dear child," answered Eurynome, "all that you have said is true, go and tell your son about it, but first wash yourself and anoint your face. Do not go about with your cheeks all covered with tears; it is not right that you should grieve so incessantly; for Telemachus, whom you always prayed that you might live to see with a beard, is already grown up."

"I know, Eurynome," replied Penelope, "that you mean well, but do not try and persuade me to wash and to anoint myself, for heaven robbed me of all my beauty on the day my husband sailed; nevertheless, tell Autonoe and Hippodamia that I want them. They must be with me when I am in the cloister; I am not going among the men alone; it would not be proper for me to do so."

On this the old woman {150} went out of the room to bid the maids go to their mistress. In the meantime Minerva bethought her of another matter, and sent Penelope off into a sweet slumber; so she lay down on her couch and her limbs became heavy with sleep. Then the goddess shed grace and beauty over her that all the Achaeans might admire her. She washed her face with the ambrosial loveliness that Venus wears when she goes dancing with the Graces; she made her taller and of a more commanding figure, while as for her complexion it was whiter than sawn ivory. When Minerva had done all this she went away, whereon the maids came in from the women's room and woke Penelope with the sound of their talking.

"What an exquisitely delicious sleep I have been having," said she, as she passed her hands over her face, "in spite of all my misery. I wish Diana would let me die so sweetly now at this very moment, that I might no longer waste in despair for the loss of my dear husband, who possessed every kind of good quality and was the most distinguished man among the Achaeans."

With these words she came down from her upper room, not alone but attended by two of her maidens, and when she reached the suitors she stood by one of the bearing-posts supporting the roof of the cloister, holding a veil before her face, and with a staid maid servant on either side of her. As they beheld her the suitors were so overpowered and became so desperately enamoured of her, that each one prayed he might win her for his own bed fellow.

"Telemachus," said she, addressing her son, "I fear you are no longer so discreet and well conducted as you used to be. When you were younger you had a greater sense of propriety; now, however, that you are grown up, though a stranger to look at you would take you for the son of a well to do father as far as size and good looks go, your conduct is by no means what it should be. What is all this disturbance that has been going on, and how came you to allow a stranger to be so disgracefully ill-treated? What would have happened if he had suffered serious injury while a suppliant in our house? Surely this would have been very discreditable to you."

"I am not surprised, my dear mother, at your displeasure," replied Telemachus, "I understand all about it and know when things are not as they should be, which I could not do when I was younger; I cannot, however, behave with perfect propriety at all times. First one and then another of these wicked people here keeps driving me out of my mind, and I have no one to stand by me. After all, however, this fight between Irus and the stranger did not turn out as the suitors meant it to do, for the stranger got the best of it. I wish Father Jove, Minerva, and Apollo would break the neck of every one of these wooers of yours, some inside the house and some out; and I wish they might all be as limp as Irus is over yonder in the gate of the outer court. See how he nods his head like a drunken man; he has had such a thrashing that he cannot stand on his feet nor get back to his home, wherever that may be, for he has no strength left in him."

Thus did they converse. Eurymachus then came up and said, "Queen Penelope, daughter of Icarius, if all the Achaeans in Iasian Argos could see you at this moment, you would have still more suitors in your house by tomorrow morning, for you are the most admirable woman in the whole world both as regards personal beauty and strength of understanding."

To this Penelope replied, "Eurymachus, heaven robbed me of all my beauty whether of face or figure when the Argives set sail for Troy and my dear husband with them. If he were to return and look after my affairs, I should both be more respected and show a better presence to the world. As it is, I am oppressed with care, and with the afflictions which heaven has seen fit to heap upon me. My husband foresaw it all, and when he was leaving home he took my right wrist in his hand—'Wife,' he said, 'we shall not all of us come safe home from Troy, for the Trojans fight well both with bow and spear. They are excellent also at fighting from chariots, and nothing decides the issue of a fight sooner than this. I know not, therefore, whether heaven will send me back to you, or whether I may not fall over there at Troy. In the meantime do you look after things here. Take care of my father and mother as at present, and even more so during my absence, but when you see our son growing a beard, then marry whom you will, and leave this your present home.' This is what he said and now it is all coming true. A night will come when I shall have to yield myself to a marriage which I detest, for Jove has taken from me all hope of happiness. This further grief, moreover, cuts me to the very heart. You suitors are not wooing me after the custom of my country. When men are courting a woman who they think will be a good wife to them and who is of noble birth, and when they are each trying to win her for himself, they usually bring oxen and sheep to feast the friends of the lady, and they make her magnificent presents, instead of eating up other people's property without paying for it."

This was what she said, and Ulysses was glad when he heard her trying to get presents out of the suitors, and flattering them with fair words which he knew she did not mean.

Then Antinous said, "Queen Penelope, daughter of Icarius, take as many presents as you please from any one who will give them to you; it is not well to refuse a present; but we will not go about our business nor stir from where we are, till you have married the best man among us whoever he may be."

The others applauded what Antinous had said, and each one sent his servant to bring his present. Antinous's man returned with a large and lovely dress most exquisitely embroidered. It had twelve beautifully made brooch pins of pure gold with which to fasten it. Eurymachus immediately brought her a magnificent chain of gold and amber beads that gleamed like sunlight. Eurydamas's two men returned with some earrings fashioned into three brilliant pendants which glistened most beautifully; while king Pisander son of Polyctor gave her a necklace of the rarest workmanship, and every one else brought her a beautiful present of some kind.

Then the queen went back to her room upstairs, and her maids brought the presents after her. Meanwhile the suitors took to singing and dancing, and stayed till evening came. They danced and sang till it grew dark; they then brought in three braziers {151} to give light, and piled them up with chopped firewood very old and dry, and they lit torches from them, which the maids held up turn and turn about. Then Ulysses said:

"Maids, servants of Ulysses who has so long been absent, go to the queen inside the house; sit with her and amuse her, or spin, and pick wool. I will hold the light for all these people. They may stay till morning, but shall not beat me, for I can stand a great deal."

The maids looked at one another and laughed, while pretty Melantho began to gibe at him contemptuously. She was daughter to Dolius, but had been brought up by Penelope, who used to give her toys to play with, and looked after her when she was a child; but in spite of all this she showed no consideration for the sorrows of her mistress, and used to misconduct herself with Eurymachus, with whom she was in love.

"Poor wretch," said she, "are you gone clean out of your mind? Go and sleep in some smithy, or place of public gossips, instead of chattering here.

Are you not ashamed of opening your mouth before your betters—so many
of them too? Has the wine been getting into your head, or do you always
babble in this way? You seem to have lost your wits because you beat the
tramp Irus; take care that a better man than he does not come and cudgel
you about the head till he pack you bleeding out of the house."

"Vixen," replied Ulysses, scowling at her, "I will go and tell Telemachus
what you have been saying, and he will have you torn limb from limb."

With these words he scared the women, and they went off into the body
of the house. They trembled all over, for they thought he would do as he
said. But Ulysses took his stand near the burning braziers, holding up
torches and looking at the people—brooding the while on things that
should surely come to pass.

But Minerva would not let the suitors for one moment cease their
insolence, for she wanted Ulysses to become even more bitter against
them; she therefore set Eurymachus son of Polybus on to gibe at him,
which made the others laugh. "Listen to me," said he, "you suitors of
Queen Penelope, that I may speak even as I am minded. It is not for
nothing that this man has come to the house of Ulysses; I believe the light
has not been coming from the torches, but from his own head—for his hair
is all gone, every bit of it."

Then turning to Ulysses he said, "Stranger, will you work as a servant,
if I send you to the wolds and see that you are well paid? Can you build
a stone fence, or plant trees? I will have you fed all the year round, and
will find you in shoes and clothing. Will you go, then? Not you; for you
have got into bad ways, and do not want to work; you had rather fill your
belly by going round the country begging."

"Eurymachus," answered Ulysses, "if you and I were to work one
against the other in early summer when the days are at their
longest—give me a good scythe, and take another yourself, and let us see
which will last the longer or mow the stronger, from dawn till dark when
the mowing grass is about. Or if you will plough against me, let us each
take a yoke of tawny oxen, well-mated and of great strength and
endurance: turn me into a four acre field, and see whether you or I can
drive the straighter furrow. If, again, war were to break out this day, give
me a shield, a couple of spears and a helmet fitting well upon my
temples—you would find me foremost in the fray, and would cease your
gibes about my belly. You are insolent and cruel, and think yourself a
great man because you live in a little world, and that a bad one. If Ulysses
comes to his own again, the doors of his house are wide, but you will find
them narrow when you try to fly through them."

Eurymachus was furious at all this. He scowled at him and cried, "You
wretch, I will soon pay you out for daring to say such things to me, and in
public too. Has the wine been getting into your head or do you always
babble in this way? You seem to have lost your wits because you beat the
tramp Irus." With this he caught hold of a footstool, but Ulysses sought

protection at the knees of Amphinomus of Dulichium, for he was afraid. The stool hit the cupbearer on his right hand and knocked him down: the man fell with a cry flat on his back, and his wine-jug fell ringing to the ground. The suitors in the covered cloister were now in an uproar, and one would turn towards his neighbour, saying, "I wish the stranger had gone somewhere else, bad luck to him, for all the trouble he gives us. We cannot permit such disturbance about a beggar; if such ill counsels are to prevail we shall have no more pleasure at our banquet."

On this Telemachus came forward and said, "Sirs, are you mad? Can you not carry your meat and your liquor decently? Some evil spirit has possessed you. I do not wish to drive any of you away, but you have had your suppers, and the sooner you all go home to bed the better."

The suitors bit their lips and marvelled at the boldness of his speech; but Amphinomus the son of Nisus, who was son to Aretias, said, "Do not let us take offence; it is reasonable, so let us make no answer. Neither let us do violence to the stranger nor to any of Ulysses' servants. Let the cupbearer go round with the drink-offerings, that we may make them and go home to our rest. As for the stranger, let us leave Telemachus to deal with him, for it is to his house that he has come."

Thus did he speak, and his saying pleased them well, so Mulius of Dulichium, servant to Amphinomus, mixed them a bowl of wine and water and handed it round to each of them man by man, whereon they made their drink-offerings to the blessed gods: Then, when they had made their drink-offerings and had drunk each one as he was minded, they took their several ways each of them to his own abode.

BOOK XIX

Telemachus and Ulysses remove the armour—Ulysses interviews Penelope—Euryclea washes his feet and recognises the scar on his leg—Penelope tells her dream to Ulysses.

Ulysses was left in the cloister, pondering on the means whereby with Minerva's help he might be able to kill the suitors. Presently he said to Telemachus, "Telemachus, we must get the armour together and take it down inside. Make some excuse when the suitors ask you why you have removed it. Say that you have taken it to be out of the way of the smoke, inasmuch as it is no longer what it was when Ulysses went away, but has become soiled and begrimed with soot. Add to this more particularly that you are afraid Jove may set them on to quarrel over their wine, and that they may do each other some harm which may disgrace both banquet and wooing, for the sight of arms sometimes tempts people to use them."

Telemachus approved of what his father had said, so he called nurse Euryclea and said, "Nurse, shut the women up in their room, while I take the armour that my father left behind him down into the store room. No one looks after it now my father is gone, and it has got all smirched with soot during my own boyhood. I want to take it down where the smoke cannot reach it."

"I wish, child," answered Euryclea, "that you would take the management of the house into your own hands altogether, and look after all the property yourself. But who is to go with you and light you to the store-room? The maids would have done so, but you would not let them."

"The stranger," said Telemachus, "shall show me a light; when people eat my bread they must earn it, no matter where they come from."

Euryclea did as she was told, and bolted the women inside their room. Then Ulysses and his son made all haste to take the helmets, shields, and spears inside; and Minerva went before them with a gold lamp in her hand that shed a soft and brilliant radiance, whereon Telemachus said, "Father, my eyes behold a great marvel: the walls, with the rafters, crossbeams, and the supports on which they rest are all aglow as with a flaming fire. Surely there is some god here who has come down from heaven."

"Hush," answered Ulysses, "hold your peace and ask no questions, for this is the manner of the gods. Get you to your bed, and leave me here to talk with your mother and the maids. Your mother in her grief will ask me all sorts of questions."

On this Telemachus went by torch-light to the other side of the inner court, to the room in which he always slept. There he lay in his bed till morning, while Ulysses was left in the cloister pondering on the means whereby with Minerva's help he might be able to kill the suitors.

Then Penelope came down from her room looking like Venus or Diana, and they set her a seat inlaid with scrolls of silver and ivory near the fire in her accustomed place. It had been made by Icmalius and had a footstool all in one piece with the seat itself; and it was covered with a thick fleece: on this she now sat, and the maids came from the women's room to join her. They set about removing the tables at which the wicked suitors had been dining, and took away the bread that was left, with the cups from which they had drunk. They emptied the embers out of the braziers, and heaped much wood upon them to give both light and heat; but Melantho began to rail at Ulysses a second time and said, "Stranger, do you mean to plague us by hanging about the house all night and spying upon the women? Be off, you wretch, outside, and eat your supper there, or you shall be driven out with a firebrand."

Ulysses scowled at her and answered, "My good woman, why should you be so angry with me? Is it because I am not clean, and my clothes are all in rags, and because I am obliged to go begging about after the manner of tramps and beggars generally? I too was a rich man once, and had a fine house of my own; in those days I gave to many a tramp such as I now am, no matter who he might be nor what he wanted. I had any number of servants, and all the other things which people have who live well and are accounted wealthy, but it pleased Jove to take all away from me; therefore, woman, beware lest you too come to lose that pride and place in which you now wanton above your fellows; have a care lest you get out of favour with your mistress, and lest Ulysses should come home, for there is still a chance that he may do so. Moreover, though he be dead as you think he is, yet by Apollo's will he has left a son behind him, Telemachus, who will note anything done amiss by the maids in the house, for he is now no longer in his boyhood."

Penelope heard what he was saying and scolded the maid, "Impudent baggage," said she, "I see how abominably you are behaving, and you shall smart for it. You knew perfectly well, for I told you myself, that I was going to see the stranger and ask him about my husband, for whose sake I am in such continual sorrow."

Then she said to her head waiting woman Eurynome, "Bring a seat with a fleece upon it, for the stranger to sit upon while he tells his story, and listens to what I have to say. I wish to ask him some questions."

Eurynome brought the seat at once and set a fleece upon it, and as soon as Ulysses had sat down Penelope began by saying, "Stranger, I shall first ask you who and whence are you? Tell me of your town and parents."

"Madam," answered Ulysses, "who on the face of the whole earth can dare to chide with you? Your fame reaches the firmament of heaven itself; you are like some blameless king, who upholds righteousness, as the monarch over a great and valiant nation: the earth yields its wheat and barley, the trees are loaded with fruit, the ewes bring forth lambs, and the sea abounds with fish by reason of his virtues, and his people do good deeds under him. Nevertheless, as I sit here in your house, ask me some other question and do not seek to know my race and family, or you will recall memories that will yet more increase my sorrow. I am full of heaviness, but I ought not to sit weeping and wailing in another person's house, nor is it well to be thus grieving continually. I shall have one of the servants or even yourself complaining of me, and saying that my eyes swim with tears because I am heavy with wine."

Then Penelope answered, "Stranger, heaven robbed me of all beauty, whether of face or figure, when the Argives set sail for Troy and my dear husband with them. If he were to return and look after my affairs I should be both more respected and should show a better presence to the world. As it is, I am oppressed with care, and with the afflictions which heaven has seen fit to heap upon me. The chiefs from all our islands—Dulichium, Same, and Zacynthus, as also from Ithaca itself, are wooing me against my will and are wasting my estate. I can therefore show no attention to strangers, nor suppliants, nor to people who say that they are skilled artisans, but am all the time broken-hearted about Ulysses. They want me to marry again at once, and I have to invent stratagems in order to deceive them. In the first place heaven put it in my mind to set up a great tambour-frame in my room, and to begin working upon an enormous piece of fine needlework. Then I said to them, 'Sweethearts, Ulysses is indeed dead, still, do not press me to marry again immediately; wait—for I would not have my skill in needlework perish unrecorded—till I have finished making a pall for the hero Laertes, to be ready against the time when death shall take him. He is very rich, and the women of the place will talk if he is laid out without a pall.' This was what I said, and they assented; whereon I used to keep working at my great web all day long, but at night I would unpick the stitches again by torch light. I fooled them in this way for three years without their finding it out, but as time wore on and I was now in my fourth year, in the waning of moons, and many days had been accomplished, those good for nothing hussies my maids betrayed me to the suitors, who broke in upon me and caught me; they were very angry with me, so I was forced to finish my work whether I would or no. And now I do not see how I can find any further shift for getting out of this marriage. My parents are putting great pressure upon me, and my son chafes at the ravages the suitors are making upon his estate, for he is now old enough to understand all about it and is perfectly able to look after his own affairs, for heaven has blessed him with an excellent disposition. Still, notwithstanding all this, tell me who you are and where you come from—for you must have had father and mother of some sort; you cannot be the son of an oak or of a rock."

Then Ulysses answered, "Madam, wife of Ulysses, since you persist in asking me about my family, I will answer, no matter what it costs me: people must expect to be pained when they have been exiles as long as I have, and suffered as much among as many peoples. Nevertheless, as regards your question I will tell you all you ask. There is a fair and fruitful island in mid-ocean called Crete; it is thickly peopled and there are ninety cities in it: the people speak many different languages which overlap one another, for there are Achaeans, brave Eteocretans, Dorians of three-fold race, and noble Pelasgi. There is a great town there, Cnossus, where Minos reigned who every nine years had a conference with Jove himself. {152} Minos was father to Deucalion, whose son I am, for Deucalion had two sons Idomeneus and myself. Idomeneus sailed for Troy, and I, who am the younger, am called Aethon; my brother, however, was at once the older and the more valiant of the two; hence it was in Crete that I saw Ulysses and showed him hospitality, for the winds took him there as he was on his way to Troy, carrying him out of his course from cape Malea and leaving him in Amnisus off the cave of Ilithuia, where the harbours are difficult to enter and he could hardly find shelter from the winds that were then raging. As soon as he got there he went into the town and asked for Idomeneus, claiming to be his old and valued friend, but Idomeneus had already set sail for Troy some ten or twelve days earlier, so I took him to my own house and showed him every kind of hospitality, for I had abundance of everything. Moreover, I fed the men who were with him with barley meal from the public store, and got subscriptions of wine and oxen for them to sacrifice to their heart's content. They stayed with me twelve days, for there was a gale blowing from the North so strong that one could hardly keep one's feet on land. I suppose some unfriendly god had raised it for them, but on the thirteenth day the wind dropped, and they got away."

Many a plausible tale did Ulysses further tell her, and Penelope wept as she listened, for her heart was melted. As the snow wastes upon the mountain tops when the winds from South East and West have breathed upon it and thawed it till the rivers run bank full with water, even so did her cheeks overflow with tears for the husband who was all the time sitting by her side. Ulysses felt for her and was sorry for her, but he kept his eyes as hard as horn or iron without letting them so much as quiver, so cunningly did he restrain his tears. Then, when she had relieved herself by weeping, she turned to him again and said: "Now, stranger, I shall put you to the test and see whether or no you really did entertain my husband and his men, as you say you did. Tell me, then, how he was dressed, what kind of a man he was to look at, and so also with his companions."

"Madam," answered Ulysses, "it is such a long time ago that I can hardly say. Twenty years are come and gone since he left my home, and went elsewhither; but I will tell you as well as I can recollect. Ulysses wore a mantle of purple wool, double lined, and it was fastened by a gold brooch with two catches for the pin. On the face of this there was a device that shewed a dog holding a spotted fawn between his fore paws, and watching it as it lay panting upon the ground. Every one marvelled at the way in which these things had been done in gold, the dog looking at the fawn, and strangling it, while the fawn was struggling convulsively to escape. {153} As for the shirt that he wore next his skin, it was so soft that it fitted him like the skin of an onion, and glistened in the sunlight to the admiration of all the women who beheld it. Furthermore I say, and lay my saying to your heart, that I do not know whether Ulysses wore these clothes when he left home, or whether one of his companions had given them to him while he was on his voyage; or possibly some one at whose house he was staying made him a present of them, for he was a man of many friends and had few equals among the Achaeans. I myself gave him a sword of bronze and a beautiful purple mantle, double lined, with a shirt that went down to his feet, and I sent him on board his ship with every mark of honour. He had a servant with him, a little older than himself, and I can tell you what he was like; his shoulders were hunched, {154} he was dark, and he had thick curly hair. His name was Eurybates, and Ulysses treated him with greater familiarity than he did any of the others, as being the most like-minded with himself."

Penelope was moved still more deeply as she heard the indisputable proofs that Ulysses laid before her; and when she had again found relief in tears she said to him, "Stranger, I was already disposed to pity you, but henceforth you shall be honoured and made welcome in my house. It was I who gave Ulysses the clothes you speak of. I took them out of the store room and folded them up myself, and I gave him also the gold brooch to wear as an ornament. Alas! I shall never welcome him home again. It was by an ill fate that he ever set out for that detested city whose very name I cannot bring myself even to mention."

Then Ulysses answered, "Madam, wife of Ulysses, do not disfigure yourself further by grieving thus bitterly for your loss, though I can hardly blame you for doing so. A woman who has loved her husband and borne him children, would naturally be grieved at losing him, even though he were a worse man than Ulysses, who they say was like a god. Still, cease your tears and listen to what I can tell you. I will hide nothing from you, and can say with perfect truth that I have lately heard of Ulysses as being alive and on his way home; he is among the Thesprotians, and is bringing back much valuable treasure that he has begged from one and another of them; but his ship and all his crew were lost as they were leaving the Thrinacian island, for Jove and the sun-god were angry with him because his men had slaughtered the sun-god's cattle, and they were all drowned to a man. But Ulysses stuck to the keel of the ship and was drifted on to the land of the Phaeacians, who are near of kin to the immortals, and who treated him as though he had been a god, giving him many presents, and wishing to escort him home safe and sound. In fact Ulysses would have been here long ago, had he not thought better to go from land to land gathering wealth; for there is no man living who is so wily as he is; there is no one can compare with him. Pheidon king of the Thesprotians told me all this, and he swore to me—making drink-offerings in his house as he did so—that the ship was by the water side and the crew found who would take Ulysses to his own country. He sent me off first, for there happened to be a Thesprotian ship sailing for the wheat-growing island of Dulichium, but he showed me all the treasure Ulysses had got together, and he had enough lying in the house of king Pheidon to keep his family for ten generations; but the king said Ulysses had gone to Dodona that he might learn Jove's mind from the high oak tree, and know whether after so long an absence he should return to Ithaca openly or in secret. So you may know he is safe and will be here shortly; he is close at hand and cannot remain away from home much longer; nevertheless I will confirm my words with an oath, and call Jove who is the first and mightiest of all gods to witness, as also that hearth of Ulysses to which I have now come, that all I have spoken shall surely come to pass. Ulysses will return in this self same year; with the end of this moon and the beginning of the next he will be here."

"May it be even so," answered Penelope; "if your words come true you shall have such gifts and such good will from me that all who see you shall congratulate you; but I know very well how it will be. Ulysses will not return, neither will you get your escort hence, for so surely as that

Ulysses ever was, there are now no longer any such masters in the house as he was, to receive honourable strangers or to further them on their way home. And now, you maids, wash his feet for him, and make him a bed on a couch with rugs and blankets, that he may be warm and quiet till morning. Then, at day break wash him and anoint him again, that he may sit in the cloister and take his meals with Telemachus. It shall be the worse for any one of these hateful people who is uncivil to him; like it or not, he shall have no more to do in this house. For how, sir, shall you be able to learn whether or no I am superior to others of my sex both in goodness of heart and understanding, if I let you dine in my cloisters squalid and ill clad? Men live but for a little season; if they are hard, and deal hardly, people wish them ill so long as they are alive, and speak contemptuously of them when they are dead, but he that is righteous and deals righteously, the people tell of his praise among all lands, and many shall call him blessed."

Ulysses answered, "Madam, I have foresworn rugs and blankets from the day that I left the snowy ranges of Crete to go on shipboard. I will lie as I have lain on many a sleepless night hitherto. Night after night have I passed in any rough sleeping place, and waited for morning. Nor, again, do I like having my feet washed; I shall not let any of the young hussies about your house touch my feet; but, if you have any old and respectable woman who has gone through as much trouble as I have, I will allow her to wash them."

To this Penelope said, "My dear sir, of all the guests who ever yet came to my house there never was one who spoke in all things with such admirable propriety as you do. There happens to be in the house a most respectable old woman—the same who received my poor dear husband in her arms the night he was born, and nursed him in infancy. She is very feeble now, but she shall wash your feet." "Come here," said she, "Euryclea, and wash your master's age-mate; I suppose Ulysses' hands and feet are very much the same now as his are, for trouble ages all of us dreadfully fast."

On these words the old woman covered her face with her hands; she began to weep and made lamentation saying, "My dear child, I cannot think whatever I am to do with you. I am certain no one was ever more god-fearing than yourself, and yet Jove hates you. No one in the whole world ever burned him more thigh bones, nor gave him finer hecatombs when you prayed you might come to a green old age yourself and see your son grow up to take after you: yet see how he has prevented you alone from ever getting back to your own home. I have no doubt the women in some foreign palace which Ulysses has got to are gibing at him as all these sluts here have been gibing at you. I do not wonder at your not choosing to let them wash you after the manner in which they have insulted you; I will wash your feet myself gladly enough, as Penelope has said that I am to do so; I will wash them both for Penelope's sake and for your own, for you have raised the most lively feelings of compassion in my mind; and let me say this moreover, which pray attend to; we have had all kinds of strangers in distress come here before now, but I make bold to say that no one ever yet came who was so like Ulysses in figure, voice, and feet as you are."

"Those who have seen us both," answered Ulysses, "have always said we were wonderfully like each other, and now you have noticed it too."

Then the old woman took the cauldron in which she was going to wash his feet, and poured plenty of cold water into it, adding hot till the bath was warm enough. Ulysses sat by the fire, but ere long he turned away from the light, for it occurred to him that when the old woman had hold of his leg she would recognise a certain scar which it bore, whereon the whole truth would come out. And indeed as soon as she began washing her master, she at once knew the scar as one that had been given him by a wild boar when he was hunting on Mt. Parnassus with his excellent grandfather Autolycus—who was the most accomplished thief and perjurer in the whole world—and with the sons of Autolycus. Mercury himself had endowed him with this gift, for he used to burn the thigh bones of goats and kids to him, so he took pleasure in his companionship. It happened once that Autolycus had gone to Ithaca and had found the child of his daughter just born. As soon as he had done supper Euryclea set the infant upon his knees and said, "Autolycus, you must find a name for your grandson; you greatly wished that you might have one."

"Son-in-law and daughter," replied Autolycus, "call the child thus: I am highly displeased with a large number of people in one place and another, both men and women; so name the child 'Ulysses,' or the child of anger. When he grows up and comes to visit his mother's family on Mt. Parnassus, where my possessions lie, I will make him a present and will send him on his way rejoicing."

Ulysses, therefore, went to Parnassus to get the presents from Autolycus, who with his sons shook hands with him and gave him welcome. His grandmother Amphithea threw her arms about him, and kissed his head, and both his beautiful eyes, while Autolycus desired his sons to get dinner ready, and they did as he told them. They brought in a five year old bull, flayed it, made it ready and divided it into joints; these they then cut carefully up into smaller pieces and spitted them; they roasted them sufficiently and served the portions round. Thus through the livelong day to the going down of the sun they feasted, and every man had his full share so that all were satisfied; but when the sun set and it came on dark, they went to bed and enjoyed the boon of sleep.

When the child of morning, rosy-fingered Dawn, appeared, the sons of Autolycus went out with their hounds hunting, and Ulysses went too. They climbed the wooded slopes of Parnassus and soon reached its breezy upland valleys; but as the sun was beginning to beat upon the fields, fresh-risen from the slow still currents of Oceanus, they came to a mountain dell. The dogs were in front searching for the tracks of the beast they were chasing, and after them came the sons of Autolycus, among whom was Ulysses, close behind the dogs, and he had a long spear in his hand. Here was the lair of a huge boar among some thick brushwood, so dense that the wind and rain could not get through it, nor could the sun's rays pierce it, and the ground underneath lay thick with fallen leaves. The boar heard the noise of the men's feet, and the hounds baying on every side as the huntsmen came up to him, so he rushed from his lair, raised the bristles on his neck, and stood at bay with fire flashing from his eyes. Ulysses was the first to raise his spear and try to drive it into the brute, but the boar was too quick for him, and charged him sideways, ripping him above the knee with a gash that tore deep though it did not reach the bone. As for the boar, Ulysses hit him on the right shoulder, and the point of the spear went right through him, so that he fell groaning in the dust until the life went out of him. The sons of Autolycus busied themselves with the carcass of the boar, and bound Ulysses' wound; then, after saying a spell to stop the bleeding, they went home as fast as they could. But when Autolycus and his sons had thoroughly healed Ulysses, they made him some splendid presents, and sent him back to Ithaca with much mutual good will. When he got back, his father and mother were rejoiced to see him, and asked him all about it, and how he had hurt himself to get the scar; so he told them how the boar had ripped him when he was out hunting with Autolycus and his sons on Mt. Parnassus.

As soon as Euryclea had got the scarred limb in her hands and had well hold of it, she recognised it and dropped the foot at once. The leg fell into the bath, which rang out and was overturned, so that all the water was spilt on the ground; Euryclea's eyes between her joy and her grief filled with tears, and she could not speak, but she caught Ulysses by the beard and said, "My dear child, I am sure you must be Ulysses himself, only I did not know you till I had actually touched and handled you."

As she spoke she looked towards Penelope, as though wanting to tell her that her dear husband was in the house, but Penelope was unable to look in that direction and observe what was going on, for Minerva had diverted her attention; so Ulysses caught Euryclea by the throat with his right hand and with his left drew her close to him, and said, "Nurse, do you wish to be the ruin of me, you who nursed me at your own breast, now that after twenty years of wandering I am at last come to my own home again? Since it has been borne in upon you by heaven to recognise me, hold your tongue, and do not say a word about it to any one else in the house, for if you do I tell you—and it shall surely be—that if heaven grants me to take the lives of these suitors, I will not spare you, though you are my own nurse, when I am killing the other women."

"My child," answered Euryclea, "what are you talking about? You know very well that nothing can either bend or break me. I will hold my tongue like a stone or a piece of iron; furthermore let me say, and lay my saying to your heart, when heaven has delivered the suitors into your hand, I will give you a list of the women in the house who have been ill-behaved, and of those who are guiltless."

And Ulysses answered, "Nurse, you ought not to speak in that way; I am well able to form my own opinion about one and all of them; hold your tongue and leave everything to heaven."

As he said this Euryclea left the cloister to fetch some more water, for the first had been all spilt; and when she had washed him and anointed him with oil, Ulysses drew his seat nearer to the fire to warm himself, and hid the scar under his rags. Then Penelope began talking to him and said:

"Stranger, I should like to speak with you briefly about another matter. It is indeed nearly bed time—for those, at least, who can sleep in spite of sorrow. As for myself, heaven has given me a life of such unmeasurable woe, that even by day when I am attending to my duties and looking after the servants, I am still weeping and lamenting during the whole time; then, when night comes, and we all of us go to bed, I lie awake thinking, and my heart becomes a prey to the most incessant and cruel tortures. As the dun nightingale, daughter of Pandareus, sings in the early spring from her seat in shadiest covert hid, and with many a plaintive trill pours out the tale how by mishap she killed her own child Itylus, son of king Zethus, even so does my mind toss and turn in its uncertainty whether I ought to stay with my son here, and safeguard my substance, my bondsmen, and the greatness of my house, out of regard to public opinion and the memory of my late husband, or whether it is not now time for me to go with the best of these suitors who are wooing me and making me such magnificent presents. As long as my son was still young, and unable to understand, he would not hear of my leaving my husband's house, but now that he is full grown he begs and prays me to do so, being incensed at the way in which the suitors are eating up his property. Listen, then, to a dream that I have had and interpret it for me if you can. I have twenty geese about the house that eat mash out of a trough, {155} and of which I am exceedingly fond. I dreamed that a great eagle came swooping down from a mountain, and dug his curved beak into the neck of each of them till he had killed them all. Presently he soared off into the sky, and left them lying dead about the yard; whereon I wept in my dream till all my maids gathered round me, so piteously was I grieving because the eagle had killed my geese. Then he came back again, and perching on a projecting rafter spoke to me with human voice, and told me to leave off crying. 'Be of good courage,' he said, 'daughter of Icarius; this is no dream, but a vision of good omen that shall surely come to pass. The geese are the suitors, and I am no longer an eagle, but your own husband, who am come back to you, and who will bring these suitors to a disgraceful end.' On this I woke, and when I looked out I saw my geese at the trough eating their mash as usual."

"This dream, Madam," replied Ulysses, "can admit but of one interpretation, for had not Ulysses himself told you how it shall be fulfilled? The death of the suitors is portended, and not one single one of them will escape."

And Penelope answered, "Stranger, dreams are very curious and unaccountable things, and they do not by any means invariably come true. There are two gates through which these unsubstantial fancies proceed; the one is of horn, and the other ivory. Those that come through the gate of ivory are fatuous, but those from the gate of horn mean something to those that see them. I do not think, however, that my own dream came through the gate of horn, though I and my son should be most thankful if it proves to have done so. Furthermore I say—and lay my saying to your heart—the coming dawn will usher in the ill-omened day that is to sever me from the house of Ulysses, for I am about to hold a tournament of axes. My husband used to set up twelve axes in the court, one in front of the other, like the stays upon which a ship is built; he would then go back from them and shoot an arrow through the whole twelve. I shall make the suitors try to do the same thing, and whichever of them can string the bow most easily, and send his arrow through all the twelve axes, him will I follow, and quit this house of my lawful husband, so goodly and so abounding in wealth. But even so, I doubt not that I shall remember it in my dreams."

Then Ulysses answered, "Madam, wife of Ulysses, you need not defer your tournament, for Ulysses will return ere ever they can string the bow, handle it how they will, and send their arrows through the iron."

To this Penelope said, "As long, sir, as you will sit here and talk to me, I can have no desire to go to bed. Still, people cannot do permanently without sleep, and heaven has appointed us dwellers on earth a time for all things. I will therefore go upstairs and recline upon that couch which I have never ceased to flood with my tears from the day Ulysses set out for the city with a hateful name."

She then went upstairs to her own room, not alone, but attended by her maidens, and when there, she lamented her dear husband till Minerva shed sweet sleep over her eyelids.

BOOK XX

Ulysses cannot sleep—Penelope's prayer to Diana—the two signs from heaven—Eumaeus and Philoetius arrive—the suitors dine—Ctesippus throws an ox's foot at Ulysses—Theoclymenus foretells disaster and leaves the house.

Ulysses slept in the cloister upon an undressed bullock's hide, on the top of which he threw several skins of the sheep the suitors had eaten, and Eurynome {156} threw a cloak over him after he had laid himself down. There, then, Ulysses lay wakefully brooding upon the way in which he should kill the suitors; and by and by, the women who had been in the habit of misconducting themselves with them, left the house giggling and laughing with one another. This made Ulysses very angry, and he doubted whether to get up and kill every single one of them then and there, or to let them sleep one more and last time with the suitors. His heart growled within him, and as a bitch with puppies growls and shows her teeth when she sees a stranger, so did his heart growl with anger at the evil deeds that were being done: but he beat his breast and said, "Heart, be still, you had worse than this to bear on the day when the terrible Cyclops ate your brave companions; yet you bore it in silence till your cunning got you safe out of the cave, though you made sure of being killed."

Thus he chided with his heart, and checked it into endurance, but he tossed about as one who turns a paunch full of blood and fat in front of a hot fire, doing it first on one side and then on the other, that he may get it cooked as soon as possible, even so did he turn himself about from side to side, thinking all the time how, single handed as he was, he should contrive to kill so large a body of men as the wicked suitors. But by and by Minerva came down from heaven in the likeness of a woman, and hovered over his head saying, "My poor unhappy man, why do you lie awake in this way? This is your house: your wife is safe inside it, and so is your son who is just such a young man as any father may be proud of."

"Goddess," answered Ulysses, "all that you have said is true, but I am in some doubt as to how I shall be able to kill these wicked suitors single handed, seeing what a number of them there always are. And there is this further difficulty, which is still more considerable. Supposing that with Jove's and your assistance I succeed in killing them, I must ask you to consider where I am to escape to from their avengers when it is all over."

"For shame," replied Minerva, "why, any one else would trust a worse ally than myself, even though that ally were only a mortal and less wise than I am. Am I not a goddess, and have I not protected you throughout in all your troubles? I tell you plainly that even though there were fifty bands of men surrounding us and eager to kill us, you should take all their sheep and cattle, and drive them away with you. But go to sleep; it is a very bad thing to lie awake all night, and you shall be out of your troubles before long."

As she spoke she shed sleep over his eyes, and then went back to Olympus.

While Ulysses was thus yielding himself to a very deep slumber that eased the burden of his sorrows, his admirable wife awoke, and sitting up in her bed began to cry. When she had relieved herself by weeping she prayed to Diana saying, "Great Goddess Diana, daughter of Jove, drive an arrow into my heart and slay me; or let some whirlwind snatch me up and bear me through paths of darkness till it drop me into the mouths of over-flowing Oceanus, as it did the daughters of Pandareus. The daughters of Pandareus lost their father and mother, for the gods killed them, so they were left orphans. But Venus took care of them, and fed them on cheese, honey, and sweet wine. Juno taught them to excel all women in beauty of form and understanding; Diana gave them an imposing presence, and Minerva endowed them with every kind of accomplishment; but one day when Venus had gone up to Olympus to see Jove about getting them married (for well does he know both what shall happen and what not happen to every one) the storm winds came and spirited them away to become handmaids to the dread Erinyes. Even so I wish that the gods who live in heaven would hide me from mortal sight, or that fair Diana might strike me, for I would fain go even beneath the sad earth if I might do so still looking towards Ulysses only, and without having to yield myself to a worse man than he was. Besides, no matter how much people may grieve by day, they can put up with it so long as they can sleep at night, for when the eyes are closed in slumber people forget good and ill alike; whereas my misery haunts me even in my dreams. This very night methought there was one lying by my side who was like Ulysses as he was when he went away with his host, and I rejoiced, for I believed that it was no dream, but the very truth itself."

On this the day broke, but Ulysses heard the sound of her weeping, and it puzzled him, for it seemed as though she already knew him and was by his side. Then he gathered up the cloak and the fleeces on which he had lain, and set them on a seat in the cloister, but he took the bullock's hide out into the open. He lifted up his hands to heaven, and prayed, saying "Father Jove, since you have seen fit to bring me over land and sea to my own home after all the afflictions you have laid upon me, give me a sign out of the mouth of some one or other of those who are now waking within the house, and let me have another sign of some kind from outside."

Thus did he pray. Jove heard his prayer and forthwith thundered high up among the clouds from the splendour of Olympus, and Ulysses was glad when he heard it. At the same time within the house, a miller-woman from hard by in the mill room lifted up her voice and gave him another sign. There were twelve miller-women whose business it was to grind wheat and barley which are the staff of life. The others had ground their task and had gone to take their rest, but this one had not yet finished, for she was not so strong as they were, and when she heard the thunder she stopped grinding and gave the sign to her master. "Father Jove," said she, "you, who rule over heaven and earth, you have thundered from a clear sky without so much as a cloud in it, and this means something for somebody; grant the prayer, then, of me your poor servant who calls upon you, and let this be the very last day that the suitors dine in the house of Ulysses. They have worn me out with labour of grinding meal for them, and I hope they may never have another dinner anywhere at all."

Ulysses was glad when he heard the omens conveyed to him by the woman's speech, and by the thunder, for he knew they meant that he should avenge himself on the suitors.

Then the other maids in the house rose and lit the fire on the hearth; Telemachus also rose and put on his clothes. He girded his sword about his shoulder, bound his sandals on to his comely feet, and took a doughty spear with a point of sharpened bronze; then he went to the threshold of the cloister and said to Euryclea, "Nurse, did you make the stranger comfortable both as regards bed and board, or did you let him shift for himself?—for my mother, good woman though she is, has a way of paying great attention to second-rate people, and of neglecting others who are in reality much better men."

"Do not find fault child," said Euryclea, "when there is no one to find fault with. The stranger sat and drank his wine as long as he liked: your mother did ask him if he would take any more bread and he said he would not. When he wanted to go to bed she told the servants to make one for him, but he said he was such a wretched outcast that he would not sleep on a bed and under blankets; he insisted on having an undressed bullock's hide and some sheepskins put for him in the cloister and I threw a cloak over him myself." {157}

Then Telemachus went out of the court to the place where the Achaeans were meeting in assembly; he had his spear in his hand, and he was not alone, for his two dogs went with him. But Euryclea called the maids and said, "Come, wake up; set about sweeping the cloisters and sprinkling them with water to lay the dust; put the covers on the seats; wipe down the tables, some of you, with a wet sponge; clean out the mixing-jugs and the cups, and go for water from the fountain at once; the suitors will be here directly; they will be here early, for it is a feast day."

Thus did she speak, and they did even as she had said: twenty of them went to the fountain for water, and the others set themselves busily to work about the house. The men who were in attendance on the suitors also came up and began chopping firewood. By and by the women returned from the fountain, and the swineherd came after them with the three best pigs he could pick out. These he let feed about the premises, and then he said good-humouredly to Ulysses, "Stranger, are the suitors treating you any better now, or are they as insolent as ever?"

"May heaven," answered Ulysses, "requite to them the wickedness with which they deal high-handedly in another man's house without any sense of shame."

Thus did they converse; meanwhile Melanthius the goatherd came up, for he too was bringing in his best goats for the suitors' dinner; and he had two shepherds with him. They tied the goats up under the gatehouse, and then Melanthius began gibing at Ulysses. "Are you still here, stranger," said he, "to pester people by begging about the house? Why can you not go elsewhere? You and I shall not come to an understanding before we have given each other a taste of our fists. You beg without any sense of decency: are there not feasts elsewhere among the Achaeans, as well as here?"

Ulysses made no answer, but bowed his head and brooded. Then a third man, Philoetius, joined them, who was bringing in a barren heifer and some goats. These were brought over by the boatmen who are there to take people over when any one comes to them. So Philoetius made his heifer and his goats secure under the gatehouse, and then went up to the swineherd. "Who, Swineherd," said he, "is this stranger that is lately come here? Is he one of your men? What is his family? Where does he come from? Poor fellow, he looks as if he had been some great man, but the gods give sorrow to whom they will—even to kings if it so pleases them."

As he spoke he went up to Ulysses and saluted him with his right hand; "Good day to you, father stranger," said he, "you seem to be very poorly off now, but I hope you will have better times by and by. Father Jove, of all gods you are the most malicious. We are your own children, yet you show us no mercy in all our misery and afflictions. A sweat came over me when I saw this man, and my eyes filled with tears, for he reminds me of Ulysses, who I fear is going about in just such rags as this man's are, if indeed he is still among the living. If he is already dead and in the house of Hades, then, alas! for my good master, who made me his stockman when I was quite young among the Cephallenians, and now his cattle are countless; no one could have done better with them than I have, for they have bred like ears of corn; nevertheless I have to keep bringing them in for others to eat, who take no heed to his son though he is in the house, and fear not the wrath of heaven, but are already eager to divide Ulysses' property among them because he has been away so long. I have often thought—only it would not be right while his son is living—of going off with the cattle to some foreign country; bad as this would be, it is still harder to stay here and be ill-treated about other people's herds. My position is intolerable, and I should long since have run away and put myself under the protection of some other chief, only that I believe my poor master will yet return, and send all these suitors flying out of the house."

"Stockman," answered Ulysses, "you seem to be a very well-disposed person, and I can see that you are a man of sense. Therefore I will tell you, and will confirm my words with an oath. By Jove, the chief of all gods, and by that hearth of Ulysses to which I am now come, Ulysses shall return before you leave this place, and if you are so minded you shall see him killing the suitors who are now masters here."

"If Jove were to bring this to pass," replied the stockman, "you should see how I would do my very utmost to help him."

And in like manner Eumaeus prayed that Ulysses might return home.

Thus did they converse. Meanwhile the suitors were hatching a plot to murder Telemachus: but a bird flew near them on their left hand—an eagle with a dove in its talons. On this Amphinomus said, "My friends, this plot of ours to murder Telemachus will not succeed; let us go to dinner instead."

The others assented, so they went inside and laid their cloaks on the benches and seats. They sacrificed the sheep, goats, pigs, and the heifer, and when the inward meats were cooked they served them round. They mixed the wine in the mixing-bowls, and the swineherd gave every man his cup, while Philoetius handed round the bread in the bread baskets, and Melanthius poured them out their wine. Then they laid their hands upon the good things that were before them.

Telemachus purposely made Ulysses sit in the part of the cloister that was paved with stone; {158} he gave him a shabby looking seat at a little table to himself, and had his portion of the inward meats brought to him, with his wine in a gold cup. "Sit there," said he, "and drink your wine among the great people. I will put a stop to the gibes and blows of the suitors, for this is no public house, but belongs to Ulysses, and has passed from him to me. Therefore, suitors, keep your hands and your tongues to yourselves, or there will be mischief."

The suitors bit their lips, and marvelled at the boldness of his speech; then Antinous said, "We do not like such language but we will put up with it, for Telemachus is threatening us in good earnest. If Jove had let us we should have put a stop to his brave talk ere now."

Thus spoke Antinous, but Telemachus heeded him not. Meanwhile the heralds were bringing the holy hecatomb through the city, and the Achaeans gathered under the shady grove of Apollo.

Then they roasted the outer meat, drew it off the spits, gave every man his portion, and feasted to their heart's content; those who waited at table gave Ulysses exactly the same portion as the others had, for Telemachus had told them to do so.

But Minerva would not let the suitors for one moment drop their insolence, for she wanted Ulysses to become still more bitter against them. Now there happened to be among them a ribald fellow, whose name was Ctesippus, and who came from Same. This man, confident in his great wealth, was paying court to the wife of Ulysses, and said to the suitors, "Hear what I have to say. The stranger has already had as large a portion as any one else; this is well, for it is not right nor reasonable to ill-treat any guest of Telemachus who comes here. I will, however, make him a present on my own account, that he may have something to give to the bath-woman, or to some other of Ulysses' servants."

As he spoke he picked up a heifer's foot from the meat-basket in which it lay, and threw it at Ulysses, but Ulysses turned his head a little aside, and avoided it, smiling grimly Sardinian fashion {159} as he did so, and it hit the wall, not him. On this Telemachus spoke fiercely to Ctesippus, "It is a good thing for you," said he, "that the stranger turned his head so that you missed him. If you had hit him I should have run you through with my spear, and your father would have had to see about getting you buried rather than married in this house. So let me have no more unseemly behaviour from any of you, for I am grown up now to the knowledge of good and evil and understand what is going on, instead of being the child that I have been heretofore. I have long seen you killing my sheep and making free with my corn and wine: I have put up with this, for one man is no match for many, but do me no further violence. Still, if you wish to kill me, kill me; I would far rather die than see such disgraceful scenes day after day—guests insulted, and men dragging the women servants about the house in an unseemly way."

They all held their peace till at last Agelaus son of Damastor said, "No one should take offence at what has just been said, nor gainsay it, for it is quite reasonable. Leave off, therefore, ill-treating the stranger, or any one else of the servants who are about the house; I would say, however, a friendly word to Telemachus and his mother, which I trust may commend itself to both. 'As long,' I would say, 'as you had ground for hoping that Ulysses would one day come home, no one could complain of your waiting and suffering {160} the suitors to be in your house. It would have been better that he should have returned, but it is now sufficiently clear that he will never do so; therefore talk all this quietly over with your mother, and tell her to marry the best man, and the one who makes her the most advantageous offer. Thus you will yourself be able to manage your own inheritance, and to eat and drink in peace, while your mother will look after some other man's house, not yours.'"

To this Telemachus answered, "By Jove, Agelaus, and by the sorrows of my unhappy father, who has either perished far from Ithaca, or is wandering in some distant land, I throw no obstacles in the way of my mother's marriage; on the contrary I urge her to choose whomsoever she will, and I will give her numberless gifts into the bargain, but I dare not insist point blank that she shall leave the house against her own wishes. Heaven forbid that I should do this."

Minerva now made the suitors fall to laughing immoderately, and set their wits wandering; but they were laughing with a forced laughter. Their meat became smeared with blood; their eyes filled with tears, and their hearts were heavy with forebodings. Theoclymenus saw this and said, "Unhappy men, what is it that ails you? There is a shroud of darkness drawn over you from head to foot, your cheeks are wet with tears; the air is alive with wailing voices; the walls and roof-beams drip blood; the gate of the cloisters and the court beyond them are full of ghosts trooping down into the night of hell; the sun is blotted out of heaven, and a blighting gloom is over all the land."

Thus did he speak, and they all of them laughed heartily. Eurymachus then said, "This stranger who has lately come here has lost his senses. Servants, turn him out into the streets, since he finds it so dark here."

But Theoclymenus said, "Eurymachus, you need not send any one with me. I have eyes, ears, and a pair of feet of my own, to say nothing of an understanding mind. I will take these out of the house with me, for I see mischief overhanging you, from which not one of you men who are insulting people and plotting ill deeds in the house of Ulysses will be able to escape."

He left the house as he spoke, and went back to Piraeus who gave him welcome, but the suitors kept looking at one another and provoking Telemachus by laughing at the strangers. One insolent fellow said to him, "Telemachus, you are not happy in your guests; first you have this importunate tramp, who comes begging bread and wine and has no skill for work or for hard fighting, but is perfectly useless, and now here is another fellow who is setting himself up as a prophet. Let me persuade you, for it will be much better to put them on board ship and send them off to the Sicels to sell for what they will bring."

Telemachus gave him no heed, but sate silently watching his father, expecting every moment that he would begin his attack upon the suitors.

Meanwhile the daughter of Icarius, wise Penelope, had had a rich seat placed for her facing the court and cloisters, so that she could hear what every one was saying. The dinner indeed had been prepared amid much merriment; it had been both good and abundant, for they had sacrificed many victims; but the supper was yet to come, and nothing can be conceived more gruesome than the meal which a goddess and a brave man were soon to lay before them—for they had brought their doom upon themselves.

BOOK XXI

The trial of the axes, during which Ulysses reveals himself to Eumaeus and Philoetius

Minerva now put it in Penelope's mind to make the suitors try their skill with the bow and with the iron axes, in contest among themselves, as a means of bringing about their destruction. She went upstairs and got the store-room key, which was made of bronze and had a handle of ivory; she then went with her maidens into the store-room at the end of the house, where her husband's treasures of gold, bronze, and wrought iron were kept, and where was also his bow, and the quiver full of deadly arrows that had been given him by a friend whom he had met in Lacedaemon—Iphitus the son of Eurytus. The two fell in with one another in Messene at the house of Ortilochus, where Ulysses was staying in order to recover a debt that was owing from the whole people; for the Messenians had carried off three hundred sheep from Ithaca, and had sailed away with them and with their shepherds. In quest of these Ulysses took a long journey while still quite young, for his father and the other chieftains sent him on a mission to recover them. Iphitus had gone there also to try and get back twelve brood mares that he had lost, and the mule foals that were running with them. These mares were the death of him in the end, for when he went to the house of Jove's son, mighty Hercules, who performed such prodigies of valour, Hercules to his shame killed him, though he was his guest, for he feared not heaven's vengeance, nor yet respected his own table which he had set before Iphitus, but killed him in spite of everything, and kept the mares himself. It was when claiming these that Iphitus met Ulysses, and gave him the bow which mighty Eurytus had been used to carry, and which on his death had been left by him to his son. Ulysses gave him in return a sword and a spear, and this was the beginning of a fast friendship, although they never visited at one another's houses, for Jove's son Hercules killed Iphitus ere they could do so. This bow, then, given him by Iphitus, had not been taken with him by Ulysses when he sailed for Troy; he had used it so long as he had been at home, but had left it behind as having been a keepsake from a valued friend.

Penelope presently reached the oak threshold of the store-room; the carpenter had planed this duly, and had drawn a line on it so as to get it quite straight; he had then set the door posts into it and hung the doors. She loosed the strap from the handle of the door, put in the key, and drove it straight home to shoot back the bolts that held the doors; {161} these flew open with a noise like a bull bellowing in a meadow, and Penelope stepped upon the raised platform, where the chests stood in which the fair linen and clothes were laid by along with fragrant herbs: reaching thence, she took down the bow with its bow case from the peg on which it hung. She sat down with it on her knees, weeping bitterly as she took the bow out of its case, and when her tears had relieved her, she went to the cloister where the suitors were, carrying the bow and the quiver, with the many deadly arrows that were inside it. Along with her came her maidens, bearing a chest that contained much iron and bronze which her husband had won as prizes. When she reached the suitors, she stood by one of the bearing-posts supporting the roof of the cloister, holding a veil before her face, and with a maid on either side of her. Then she said:

"Listen to me you suitors, who persist in abusing the hospitality of this house because its owner has been long absent, and without other pretext than that you want to marry me; this, then, being the prize that you are contending for, I will bring out the mighty bow of Ulysses, and whomsoever of you shall string it most easily and send his arrow through each one of twelve axes, him will I follow and quit this house of my lawful husband, so goodly, and so abounding in wealth. But even so I doubt not that I shall remember it in my dreams."

As she spoke, she told Eumaeus to set the bow and the pieces of iron before the suitors, and Eumaeus wept as he took them to do as she had bidden him. Hard by, the stockman wept also when he saw his master's bow, but Antinous scolded them. "You country louts," said he, "silly simpletons; why should you add to the sorrows of your mistress by crying in this way? She has enough to grieve her in the loss of her husband; sit still, therefore, and eat your dinners in silence, or go outside if you want to cry, and leave the bow behind you. We suitors shall have to contend for it with might and main, for we shall find it no light matter to string such a bow as this is. There is not a man of us all who is such another as Ulysses; for I have seen him and remember him, though I was then only a child."

This was what he said, but all the time he was expecting to be able to string the bow and shoot through the iron, whereas in fact he was to be the first that should taste of the arrows from the hands of Ulysses, whom he was dishonouring in his own house—egging the others on to do so also.

Then Telemachus spoke. "Great heavens!" he exclaimed, "Jove must have robbed me of my senses. Here is my dear and excellent mother saying she will quit this house and marry again, yet I am laughing and enjoying myself as though there were nothing happening. But, suitors, as the contest has been agreed upon, let it go forward. It is for a woman whose peer is not to be found in Pylos, Argos, or Mycene, nor yet in Ithaca nor on the mainland. You know this as well as I do; what need have I to speak in praise of my mother? Come on, then, make no excuses for delay, but let us see whether you can string the bow or no. I too will make trial of it, for if I can string it and shoot through the iron, I shall not suffer my mother to quit this house with a stranger, not if I can win the prizes which my father won before me."

As he spoke he sprang from his seat, threw his crimson cloak from him, and took his sword from his shoulder. First he set the axes in a row, in a long groove which he had dug for them, and had made straight by line. {162} Then he stamped the earth tight round them, and everyone was surprised when they saw him set them up so orderly, though he had never seen anything of the kind before. This done, he went on to the pavement to make trial of the bow; thrice did he tug at it, trying with all his might to draw the string, and thrice he had to leave off, though he had hoped to string the bow and shoot through the iron. He was trying for the fourth time, and would have strung it had not Ulysses made a sign to check him in spite of all his eagerness. So he said:

"Alas! I shall either be always feeble and of no prowess, or I am too young, and have not yet reached my full strength so as to be able to hold my own if any one attacks me. You others, therefore, who are stronger than I, make trial of the bow and get this contest settled."

On this he put the bow down, letting it lean against the door [that led into the house] with the arrow standing against the top of the bow. Then he sat down on the seat from which he had risen, and Antinous said:

"Come on each of you in his turn, going towards the right from the place at which the cupbearer begins when he is handing round the wine."

The rest agreed, and Leiodes son of Oenops was the first to rise. He was sacrificial priest to the suitors, and sat in the corner near the mixing-bowl.

{163} He was the only man who hated their evil deeds and was indignant with the others. He was now the first to take the bow and arrow, so he went on to the pavement to make his trial, but he could not string the bow, for his hands were weak and unused to hard work, they therefore soon grew tired, and he said to the suitors, "My friends, I cannot string it; let another have it, this bow shall take the life and soul out of many a chief among us, for it is better to die than to live after having missed the prize that we have so long striven for, and which has brought us so long together. Some one of us is even now hoping and praying that he may marry Penelope, but when he has seen this bow and tried it, let him woo and make bridal offerings to some other woman, and let Penelope marry whoever makes the best offer and whose lot it is to win her."

On this he put the bow down, letting it lean against the door, {164} with the arrow standing against the tip of the bow. Then he took his seat again on the seat from which he had risen; and Antinous rebuked him saying:

"Leiodes, what are you talking about? Your words are monstrous and intolerable; it makes me angry to listen to you. Shall, then, this bow take the life of many a chief among us, merely because you cannot bend it yourself? True, you were not born to be an archer, but there are others who will soon string it."

Then he said to Melanthius the goatherd, "Look sharp, light a fire in the court, and set a seat hard by with a sheep skin on it; bring us also a large ball of lard, from what they have in the house. Let us warm the bow and grease it—we will then make trial of it again, and bring the contest to an end."

Melanthius lit the fire, and set a seat covered with sheep skins beside it. He also brought a great ball of lard from what they had in the house, and the suitors warmed the bow and again made trial of it, but they were none of them nearly strong enough to string it. Nevertheless there still remained Antinous and Eurymachus, who were the ringleaders among the suitors and much the foremost among them all.

Then the swineherd and the stockman left the cloisters together, and Ulysses followed them. When they had got outside the gates and the outer yard, Ulysses said to them quietly:

"Stockman, and you swineherd, I have something in my mind which I am in doubt whether to say or no; but I think I will say it. What manner of men would you be to stand by Ulysses, if some god should bring him back here all of a sudden? Say which you are disposed to do—to side with the suitors, or with Ulysses?"

"Father Jove," answered the stockman, "would indeed that you might so ordain it. If some god were but to bring Ulysses back, you should see with what might and main I would fight for him."

In like words Eumaeus prayed to all the gods that Ulysses might return; when, therefore, he saw for certain what mind they were of, Ulysses said, "It is I, Ulysses, who am here. I have suffered much, but at last, in the twentieth year, I am come back to my own country. I find that you two alone of all my servants are glad that I should do so, for I have not heard any of the others praying for my return. To you two, therefore, will I unfold the truth as it shall be. If heaven shall deliver the suitors into my hands, I will find wives for both of you, will give you house and holding close to my own, and you shall be to me as though you were brothers and friends of Telemachus. I will now give you convincing proofs that you may know me and be assured. See, here is the scar from the boar's tooth that ripped me when I was out hunting on Mt. Parnassus with the sons of Autolycus."

As he spoke he drew his rags aside from the great scar, and when they had examined it thoroughly, they both of them wept about Ulysses, threw their arms round him, and kissed his head and shoulders, while Ulysses kissed their hands and faces in return. The sun would have gone down upon their mourning if Ulysses had not checked them and said:

"Cease your weeping, lest some one should come outside and see us, and tell those who are within. When you go in, do so separately, not both together; I will go first, and do you follow afterwards; let this moreover be the token between us; the suitors will all of them try to prevent me from getting hold of the bow and quiver; do you, therefore, Eumaeus, place it in my hands when you are carrying it about, and tell the women to close the doors of their apartment. If they hear any groaning or uproar as of men fighting about the house, they must not come out; they must keep quiet, and stay where they are at their work. And I charge you, Philoetius, to make fast the doors of the outer court, and to bind them securely at once."

When he had thus spoken, he went back to the house and took the seat that he had left. Presently, his two servants followed him inside.

At this moment the bow was in the hands of Eurymachus, who was warming it by the fire, but even so he could not string it, and he was greatly grieved. He heaved a deep sigh and said, "I grieve for myself and for us all; I grieve that I shall have to forgo the marriage, but I do not care nearly so much about this, for there are plenty of other women in Ithaca and elsewhere; what I feel most is the fact of our being so inferior to Ulysses in strength that we cannot string his bow. This will disgrace us in the eyes of those who are yet unborn."

"It shall not be so, Eurymachus," said Antinous, "and you know it yourself. Today is the feast of Apollo throughout all the land; who can string a bow on such a day as this? Put it on one side—as for the axes they can stay where they are, for no one is likely to come to the house and take them away: let the cupbearer go round with his cups, that we may make our drink-offerings and drop this matter of the bow; we will tell Melanthius to bring us in some goats tomorrow—the best he has; we can then offer thigh bones to Apollo the mighty archer, and again make trial of the bow, so as to bring the contest to an end."

The rest approved his words, and thereon men servants poured water over the hands of the guests, while pages filled the mixing-bowls with wine and water and handed it round after giving every man his drink-offering. Then, when they had made their offerings and had drunk each as much as he desired, Ulysses craftily said:—

"Suitors of the illustrious queen, listen that I may speak even as I am minded. I appeal more especially to Eurymachus, and to Antinous who has just spoken with so much reason. Cease shooting for the present and leave the matter to the gods, but in the morning let heaven give victory to whom it will. For the moment, however, give me the bow that I may prove the power of my hands among you all, and see whether I still have as much strength as I used to have, or whether travel and neglect have made an end of it."

This made them all very angry, for they feared he might string the bow, Antinous therefore rebuked him fiercely saying, "Wretched creature, you have not so much as a grain of sense in your whole body; you ought to think yourself lucky in being allowed to dine unharmed among your betters, without having any smaller portion served you than we others have had, and in being allowed to hear our conversation. No other beggar or stranger has been allowed to hear what we say among ourselves; the wine must have been doing you a mischief, as it does with all those who drink immoderately. It was wine that inflamed the Centaur Eurytion when he was staying with Peirithous among the Lapithae. When the wine had got into his head, he went mad and did ill deeds about the house of Peirithous; this angered the heroes who were there assembled, so they rushed at him and cut off his ears and nostrils; then they dragged him through the doorway out of the house, so he went away crazed, and bore the burden of his crime, bereft of understanding. Henceforth, therefore, there was war between mankind and the centaurs, but he brought it upon himself through his own drunkenness. In like manner I can tell you that it will go hardly with you if you string the bow: you will find no mercy from any one here, for we shall at once ship you off to king Echetus, who kills every one that comes near him: you will never get away alive, so drink and keep quiet without getting into a quarrel with men younger than yourself."

Penelope then spoke to him. "Antinous," said she, "it is not right that you should ill-treat any guest of Telemachus who comes to this house. If the stranger should prove strong enough to string the mighty bow of Ulysses, can you suppose that he would take me home with him and make me his wife? Even the man himself can have no such idea in his mind: none of you need let that disturb his feasting; it would be out of all reason."

"Queen Penelope," answered Eurymachus, "we do not suppose that this man will take you away with him; it is impossible; but we are afraid lest some of the baser sort, men or women among the Achaeans, should go gossiping about and say, 'These suitors are a feeble folk; they are paying court to the wife of a brave man whose bow not one of them was able to string, and yet a beggarly tramp who came to the house strung it at once and sent an arrow through the iron.' This is what will be said, and it will be a scandal against us."

"Eurymachus," Penelope answered, "people who persist in eating up the estate of a great chieftain and dishonouring his house must not expect others to think well of them. Why then should you mind if men talk as you think they will? This stranger is strong and well-built, he says moreover that he is of noble birth. Give him the bow, and let us see whether he can string it or no. I say—and it shall surely be—that if Apollo vouchsafes him the glory of stringing it, I will give him a cloak and shirt of good wear, with a javelin to keep off dogs and robbers, and a sharp sword. I will also give him sandals, and will see him sent safely wherever he wants to go."

Then Telemachus said, "Mother, I am the only man either in Ithaca or in the islands that are over against Elis who has the right to let any one have the bow or to refuse it. No one shall force me one way or the other, not even though I choose to make the stranger a present of the bow outright, and let him take it away with him. Go, then, within the house and busy yourself with your daily duties, your loom, your distaff, and the ordering of your servants. This bow is a man's matter, and mine above all others, for it is I who am master here."

She went wondering back into the house, and laid her son's saying in her heart. Then going upstairs with her handmaids into her room, she mourned her dear husband till Minerva sent sweet sleep over her eyelids.

The swineherd now took up the bow and was for taking it to Ulysses, but the suitors clamoured at him from all parts of the cloisters, and one of them said, "You idiot, where are you taking the bow to? Are you out of your wits? If Apollo and the other gods will grant our prayer, your own boarhounds shall get you into some quiet little place, and worry you to death."

Eumaeus was frightened at the outcry they all raised, so he put the bow down then and there, but Telemachus shouted out at him from the other side of the cloisters, and threatened him saying, "Father Eumaeus, bring the bow on in spite of them, or young as I am I will pelt you with stones back to the country, for I am the better man of the two. I wish I was as much stronger than all the other suitors in the house as I am than you, I would soon send some of them off sick and sorry, for they mean mischief."

Thus did he speak, and they all of them laughed heartily, which put them in a better humour with Telemachus; so Eumaeus brought the bow on and placed it in the hands of Ulysses. When he had done this, he called Euryclea apart and said to her, "Euryclea, Telemachus says you are to close the doors of the women's apartments. If they hear any groaning or uproar as of men fighting about the house, they are not to come out, but are to keep quiet and stay where they are at their work."

Euryclea did as she was told and closed the doors of the women's apartments.

Meanwhile Philoetius slipped quietly out and made fast the gates of the outer court. There was a ship's cable of byblus fibre lying in the gatehouse, so he made the gates fast with it and then came in again, resuming the seat that he had left, and keeping an eye on Ulysses, who had now got the bow in his hands, and was turning it every way about, and proving it all over to see whether the worms had been eating into its two horns during his absence. Then would one turn towards his neighbour saying, "This is some tricky old bow-fancier; either he has got one like it at home, or he wants to make one, in such workmanlike style does the old vagabond handle it."

Another said, "I hope he may be no more successful in other things than he is likely to be in stringing this bow."

But Ulysses, when he had taken it up and examined it all over, strung it as easily as a skilled bard strings a new peg of his lyre and makes the twisted gut fast at both ends. Then he took it in his right hand to prove the string, and it sang sweetly under his touch like the twittering of a swallow. The suitors were dismayed, and turned colour as they heard it; at that moment, moreover, Jove thundered loudly as a sign, and the heart of Ulysses rejoiced as he heard the omen that the son of scheming Saturn had sent him.

He took an arrow that was lying upon the table {165}—for those which the Achaeans were so shortly about to taste were all inside the quiver—he laid it on the centre-piece of the bow, and drew the notch of the arrow and the string toward him, still seated on his seat. When he had taken aim he let fly, and his arrow pierced every one of the handle-holes of the axes from the first onwards till it had gone right through them, and into the outer courtyard. Then he said to Telemachus:

"Your guest has not disgraced you, Telemachus. I did not miss what I aimed at, and I was not long in stringing my bow. I am still strong, and not as the suitors twit me with being. Now, however, it is time for the Achaeans to prepare supper while there is still daylight, and then otherwise to disport themselves with song and dance which are the crowning ornaments of a banquet."

As he spoke he made a sign with his eyebrows, and Telemachus girded on his sword, grasped his spear, and stood armed beside his father's seat.

BOOK XXII

The killing of the suitors—the maids who have misconducted themselves are made to cleanse the cloisters and are then hanged.

Then Ulysses tore off his rags, and sprang on to the broad pavement with his bow and his quiver full of arrows. He shed the arrows on to the ground at his feet and said, "The mighty contest is at an end. I will now see whether Apollo will vouchsafe it to me to hit another mark which no man has yet hit."

On this he aimed a deadly arrow at Antinous, who was about to take up a two-handled gold cup to drink his wine and already had it in his hands. He had no thought of death—who amongst all the revellers would think that one man, however brave, would stand alone among so many and kill him? The arrow struck Antinous in the throat, and the point went clean through his neck, so that he fell over and the cup dropped from his hand, while a thick stream of blood gushed from his nostrils. He kicked the table from him and upset the things on it, so that the bread and roasted meats were all soiled as they fell over on to the ground. {166} The suitors were in an uproar when they saw that a man had been hit; they sprang in dismay one and all of them from their seats and looked everywhere towards the walls, but there was neither shield nor spear, and they rebuked Ulysses very angrily. "Stranger," said they, "you shall pay for shooting people in this way: you shall see no other contest; you are a doomed man; he whom you have slain was the foremost youth in Ithaca, and the vultures shall devour you for having killed him."

Thus they spoke, for they thought that he had killed Antinous by mistake, and did not perceive that death was hanging over the head of every one of them. But Ulysses glared at them and said:

"Dogs, did you think that I should not come back from Troy? You have wasted my substance, {167} have forced my women servants to lie with you, and have wooed my wife while I was still living. You have feared neither God nor man, and now you shall die."

They turned pale with fear as he spoke, and every man looked round about to see whither he might fly for safety, but Eurymachus alone spoke.

"If you are Ulysses," said he, "then what you have said is just. We have done much wrong on your lands and in your house. But Antinous who was the head and front of the offending lies low already. It was all his doing. It was not that he wanted to marry Penelope; he did not so much care about that; what he wanted was something quite different, and Jove has not vouchsafed it to him; he wanted to kill your son and to be chief man in Ithaca. Now, therefore, that he has met the death which was his due, spare the lives of your people. We will make everything good among ourselves, and pay you in full for all that we have eaten and drunk. Each one of us shall pay you a fine worth twenty oxen, and we will keep on giving you gold and bronze till your heart is softened. Until we have done this no one can complain of your being enraged against us."

Ulysses again glared at him and said, "Though you should give me all that you have in the world both now and all that you ever shall have, I will not stay my hand till I have paid all of you in full. You must fight, or fly for your lives; and fly, not a man of you shall."

Their hearts sank as they heard him, but Eurymachus again spoke saying:

"My friends, this man will give us no quarter. He will stand where he is and shoot us down till he has killed every man among us. Let us then show fight; draw your swords, and hold up the tables to shield you from his arrows. Let us have at him with a rush, to drive him from the pavement and doorway: we can then get through into the town, and raise such an alarm as shall soon stay his shooting."

As he spoke he drew his keen blade of bronze, sharpened on both sides, and with a loud cry sprang towards Ulysses, but Ulysses instantly shot an arrow into his breast that caught him by the nipple and fixed itself in his liver. He dropped his sword and fell doubled up over his table. The cup and all the meats went over on to the ground as he smote the earth with his forehead in the agonies of death, and he kicked the stool with his feet until his eyes were closed in darkness.

Then Amphinomus drew his sword and made straight at Ulysses to try and get him away from the door; but Telemachus was too quick for him, and struck him from behind; the spear caught him between the shoulders and went right through his chest, so that he fell heavily to the ground and struck the earth with his forehead. Then Telemachus sprang away from him, leaving his spear still in the body, for he feared that if he stayed to draw it out, some one of the Achaeans might come up and hack at him with his sword, or knock him down, so he set off at a run, and immediately was at his father's side. Then he said:

"Father, let me bring you a shield, two spears, and a brass helmet for your temples. I will arm myself as well, and will bring other armour for the swineherd and the stockman, for we had better be armed."

"Run and fetch them," answered Ulysses, "while my arrows hold out, or when I am alone they may get me away from the door."

Telemachus did as his father said, and went off to the store room where the armour was kept. He chose four shields, eight spears, and four brass helmets with horse-hair plumes. He brought them with all speed to his father, and armed himself first, while the stockman and the swineherd also put on their armour, and took their places near Ulysses. Meanwhile Ulysses, as long as his arrows lasted, had been shooting the suitors one by one, and they fell thick on one another: when his arrows gave out, he set the bow to stand against the end wall of the house by the door post, and hung a shield four hides thick about his shoulders; on his comely head he set his helmet, well wrought with a crest of horse-hair that nodded menacingly above it, {168} and he grasped two redoubtable bronze-shod spears.

Now there was a trap door {169} on the wall, while at one end of the pavement {170} there was an exit leading to a narrow passage, and this exit was closed by a well-made door. Ulysses told Philoetius to stand by this door and guard it, for only one person could attack it at a time. But

Agelaus shouted out, "Cannot some one go up to the trap door and tell the people what is going on? Help would come at once, and we should soon make an end of this man and his shooting."

"This may not be, Agelaus," answered Melanthius, "the mouth of the narrow passage is dangerously near the entrance to the outer court. One brave man could prevent any number from getting in. But I know what I will do, I will bring you arms from the store-room, for I am sure it is there that Ulysses and his son have put them."

On this the goatherd Melanthius went by back passages to the store-room of Ulysses' house. There he chose twelve shields, with as many helmets and spears, and brought them back as fast as he could to give them to the suitors. Ulysses' heart began to fail him when he saw the suitors {171} putting on their armour and brandishing their spears. He saw the greatness of the danger, and said to Telemachus, "Some one of the women inside is helping the suitors against us, or it may be Melanthius."

Telemachus answered, "The fault, father, is mine, and mine only; I left the store room door open, and they have kept a sharper look out than I have. Go, Eumaeus, put the door to, and see whether it is one of the women who is doing this, or whether, as I suspect, it is Melanthius the son of Dolius."

Thus did they converse. Meanwhile Melanthius was again going to the store room to fetch more armour, but the swineherd saw him and said to Ulysses who was beside him, "Ulysses, noble son of Laertes, it is that scoundrel Melanthius, just as we suspected, who is going to the store room. Say, shall I kill him, if I can get the better of him, or shall I bring him here that you may take your own revenge for all the many wrongs that he has done in your house?"

Ulysses answered, "Telemachus and I will hold these suitors in check, no matter what they do; go back both of you and bind Melanthius' hands and feet behind him. Throw him into the store room and make the door fast behind you; then fasten a noose about his body, and string him close up to the rafters from a high bearing-post, {172} that he may linger on in an agony."

Thus did he speak, and they did even as he had said; they went to the store room, which they entered before Melanthius saw them, for he was busy searching for arms in the innermost part of the room, so the two took their stand on either side of the door and waited. By and by Melanthius came out with a helmet in one hand, and an old dry-rotted shield in the other, which had been borne by Laertes when he was young, but which had been long since thrown aside, and the straps had become unsewn; on this the two seized him, dragged him back by the hair, and threw him struggling to the ground. They bent his hands and feet well behind his back, and bound them tight with a painful bond as Ulysses had told them; then they fastened a noose about his body and strung him up from a high pillar till he was close up to the rafters, and over him did you then vaunt,

O swineherd Eumaeus saying, "Melanthius, you will pass the night on a soft bed as you deserve. You will know very well when morning comes from the streams of Oceanus, and it is time for you to be driving in your goats for the suitors to feast on."

There, then, they left him in very cruel bondage, and having put on their armour they closed the door behind them and went back to take their places by the side of Ulysses; whereon the four men stood in the cloister, fierce and full of fury; nevertheless, those who were in the body of the court were still both brave and many. Then Jove's daughter Minerva came up to them, having assumed the voice and form of Mentor. Ulysses was glad when he saw her and said, "Mentor, lend me your help, and forget not your old comrade, nor the many good turns he has done you. Besides, you are my age-mate."

But all the time he felt sure it was Minerva, and the suitors from the other side raised an uproar when they saw her. Agelaus was the first to reproach her. "Mentor," he cried, "do not let Ulysses beguile you into siding with him and fighting the suitors. This is what we will do: when we have killed these people, father and son, we will kill you too. You shall pay for it with your head, and when we have killed you, we will take all you have, in doors or out, and bring it into hotch-pot with Ulysses' property; we will not let your sons live in your house, nor your daughters, nor shall your widow continue to live in the city of Ithaca."

This made Minerva still more furious, so she scolded Ulysses very angrily. {173} "Ulysses," said she, "your strength and prowess are no longer what they were when you fought for nine long years among the Trojans about the noble lady Helen. You killed many a man in those days, and it was through your stratagem that Priam's city was taken. How comes it that you are so lamentably less valiant now that you are on your own ground, face to face with the suitors in your own house? Come on, my good fellow, stand by my side and see how Mentor, son of Alcimus shall fight your foes and requite your kindnesses conferred upon him."

But she would not give him full victory as yet, for she wished still further to prove his own prowess and that of his brave son, so she flew up to one of the rafters in the roof of the cloister and sat upon it in the form of a swallow.

Meanwhile Agelaus son of Damastor, Eurynomus, Amphimedon, Demoptolemus, Pisander, and Polybus son of Polyctor bore the brunt of the fight upon the suitors' side; of all those who were still fighting for their lives they were by far the most valiant, for the others had already fallen under the arrows of Ulysses. Agelaus shouted to them and said, "My friends, he will soon have to leave off, for Mentor has gone away after having done nothing for him but brag. They are standing at the doors unsupported. Do not aim at him all at once, but six of you throw your spears first, and see if you cannot cover yourselves with glory by killing him. When he has fallen we need not be uneasy about the others."

They threw their spears as he bade them, but Minerva made them all of no effect. One hit the door post; another went against the door; the pointed shaft of another struck the wall; and as soon as they had avoided all the spears of the suitors Ulysses said to his own men, "My friends, I should say we too had better let drive into the middle of them, or they will crown all the harm they have done us by killing us outright."

They therefore aimed straight in front of them and threw their spears. Ulysses killed Demoptolemus, Telemachus Euryades, Eumaeus Elatus, while the stockman killed Pisander. These all bit the dust, and as the others drew back into a corner Ulysses and his men rushed forward and regained their spears by drawing them from the bodies of the dead.

The suitors now aimed a second time, but again Minerva made their weapons for the most part without effect. One hit a bearing-post of the cloister; another went against the door; while the pointed shaft of another struck the wall. Still, Amphimedon just took a piece of the top skin from off Telemachus's wrist, and Ctesippus managed to graze Eumaeus's shoulder above his shield; but the spear went on and fell to the ground. Then Ulysses and his men let drive into the crowd of suitors. Ulysses hit Eurydamas, Telemachus Amphimedon, and Eumaeus Polybus. After this the stockman hit Ctesippus in the breast, and taunted him saying, "Foul-mouthed son of Polytherses, do not be so foolish as to talk wickedly another time, but let heaven direct your speech, for the gods are far stronger than men. I make you a present of this advice to repay you for the foot which you gave Ulysses when he was begging about in his own house."

Thus spoke the stockman, and Ulysses struck the son of Damastor with a spear in close fight, while Telemachus hit Leocritus son of Evenor in the belly, and the dart went clean through him, so that he fell forward full on his face upon the ground. Then Minerva from her seat on the rafter held up her deadly aegis, and the hearts of the suitors quailed. They fled to the other end of the court like a herd of cattle maddened by the gadfly in early summer when the days are at their longest. As eagle-beaked, crook-taloned vultures from the mountains swoop down on the smaller birds that cower in flocks upon the ground, and kill them, for they cannot either fight or fly, and lookers on enjoy the sport—even so did Ulysses and his men fall upon the suitors and smite them on every side. They made a horrible groaning as their brains were being battered in, and the ground seethed with their blood.

Leiodes then caught the knees of Ulysses and said, "Ulysses I beseech you have mercy upon me and spare me. I never wronged any of the women in your house either in word or deed, and I tried to stop the others. I saw them, but they would not listen, and now they are paying for their folly. I was their sacrificing priest; if you kill me, I shall die without having done anything to deserve it, and shall have got no thanks for all the good that I did."

Ulysses looked sternly at him and answered, "If you were their sacrificing priest, you must have prayed many a time that it might be long before I got home again, and that you might marry my wife and have children by her. Therefore you shall die."

With these words he picked up the sword that Agelaus had dropped when he was being killed, and which was lying upon the ground. Then he struck Leiodes on the back of his neck, so that his head fell rolling in the dust while he was yet speaking.

The minstrel Phemius son of Terpes—he who had been forced by the suitors to sing to them—now tried to save his life. He was standing near towards the trap door, {174} and held his lyre in his hand. He did not know whether to fly out of the cloister and sit down by the altar of Jove that was in the outer court, and on which both Laertes and Ulysses had offered up the thigh bones of many an ox, or whether to go straight up to Ulysses and embrace his knees, but in the end he deemed it best to embrace Ulysses' knees. So he laid his lyre on the ground between the mixing bowl {175} and the silver-studded seat; then going up to Ulysses he caught hold of his knees and said, "Ulysses, I beseech you have mercy on me and spare me. You will be sorry for it afterwards if you kill a bard who can sing both for gods and men as I can. I make all my lays myself, and heaven visits me with every kind of inspiration. I would sing to you as though you were a god, do not therefore be in such a hurry to cut my head off. Your own son Telemachus will tell you that I did not want to frequent your house and sing to the suitors after their meals, but they were too many and too strong for me, so they made me."

Telemachus heard him, and at once went up to his father. "Hold!" he cried, "the man is guiltless, do him no hurt; and we will spare Medon too, who was always good to me when I was a boy, unless Philoetius or Eumaeus has already killed him, or he has fallen in your way when you were raging about the court."

Medon caught these words of Telemachus, for he was crouching under a seat beneath which he had hidden by covering himself up with a freshly flayed heifer's hide, so he threw off the hide, went up to Telemachus, and laid hold of his knees.

"Here I am, my dear sir," said he, "stay your hand therefore, and tell your father, or he will kill me in his rage against the suitors for having wasted his substance and been so foolishly disrespectful to yourself."

Ulysses smiled at him and answered, "Fear not; Telemachus has saved your life, that you may know in future, and tell other people, how greatly better good deeds prosper than evil ones. Go, therefore, outside the cloisters into the outer court, and be out of the way of the slaughter—you and the bard—while I finish my work here inside."

The pair went into the outer court as fast as they could, and sat down by Jove's great altar, looking fearfully round, and still expecting that they would be killed. Then Ulysses searched the whole court carefully over, to see if anyone had managed to hide himself and was still living, but he found them all lying in the dust and weltering in their blood. They were like fishes which fishermen have netted out of the sea, and thrown upon the beach to lie gasping for water till the heat of the sun makes an end of them. Even so were the suitors lying all huddled up one against the other.

Then Ulysses said to Telemachus, "Call nurse Euryclea; I have something to say to her."

Telemachus went and knocked at the door of the women's room. "Make haste," said he, "you old woman who have been set over all the other women in the house. Come outside; my father wishes to speak to you."

When Euryclea heard this she unfastened the door of the women's room and came out, following Telemachus. She found Ulysses among the corpses bespattered with blood and filth like a lion that has just been devouring an ox, and his breast and both his cheeks are all bloody, so that he is a fearful sight; even so was Ulysses besmirched from head to foot with gore. When she saw all the corpses and such a quantity of blood, she was beginning to cry out for joy, for she saw that a great deed had been done; but Ulysses checked her, "Old woman," said he, "rejoice in silence; restrain yourself, and do not make any noise about it; it is an unholy thing to vaunt over dead men. Heaven's doom and their own evil deeds have brought these men to destruction, for they respected no man in the whole world, neither rich nor poor, who came near them, and they have come to a bad end as a punishment for their wickedness and folly. Now, however, tell me which of the women in the house have misconducted themselves, and who are innocent." {176}

"I will tell you the truth, my son," answered Euryclea. "There are fifty women in the house whom we teach to do things, such as carding wool, and all kinds of household work. Of these, twelve in all {177} have misbehaved, and have been wanting in respect to me, and also to Penelope. They showed no disrespect to Telemachus, for he has only lately grown and his mother never permitted him to give orders to the female servants; but let me go upstairs and tell your wife all that has happened, for some god has been sending her to sleep."

"Do not wake her yet," answered Ulysses, "but tell the women who have misconducted themselves to come to me."

Euryclea left the cloister to tell the women, and make them come to Ulysses; in the meantime he called Telemachus, the stockman, and the swineherd. "Begin," said he, "to remove the dead, and make the women help you. Then, get sponges and clean water to swill down the tables and seats. When you have thoroughly cleansed the whole cloisters, take the women into the space between the domed room and the wall of the outer court, and run them through with your swords till they are quite dead, and have forgotten all about love and the way in which they used to lie in secret with the suitors."

On this the women came down in a body, weeping and wailing bitterly. First they carried the dead bodies out, and propped them up against one another in the gatehouse. Ulysses ordered them about and made them do their work quickly, so they had to carry the bodies out. When they had done this, they cleaned all the tables and seats with sponges and water, while Telemachus and the two others shovelled up the blood and dirt from the ground, and the women carried it all away and put it out of doors. Then when they had made the whole place quite clean and orderly, they took the women out and hemmed them in the narrow space between the wall of the domed room and that of the yard, so that they could not get away: and Telemachus said to the other two, "I shall not let these women die a clean death, for they were insolent to me and my mother, and used to sleep with the suitors."

So saying he made a ship's cable fast to one of the bearing-posts that supported the roof of the domed room, and secured it all around the building, at a good height, lest any of the women's feet should touch the ground; and as thrushes or doves beat against a net that has been set for them in a thicket just as they were getting to their nest, and a terrible fate awaits them, even so did the women have to put their heads in nooses one after the other and die most miserably. {178} Their feet moved convulsively for a while, but not for very long.

As for Melanthius, they took him through the cloister into the inner court. There they cut off his nose and his ears; they drew out his vitals and gave them to the dogs raw, and then in their fury they cut off his hands and his feet.

When they had done this they washed their hands and feet and went back into the house, for all was now over; and Ulysses said to the dear old nurse Euryclea, "Bring me sulphur, which cleanses all pollution, and fetch fire also that I may burn it, and purify the cloisters. Go, moreover, and tell Penelope to come here with her attendants, and also all the maidservants that are in the house."

"All that you have said is true," answered Euryclea, "but let me bring you some clean clothes—a shirt and cloak. Do not keep these rags on your back any longer. It is not right."

"First light me a fire," replied Ulysses.

She brought the fire and sulphur, as he had bidden her, and Ulysses thoroughly purified the cloisters and both the inner and outer courts. Then she went inside to call the women and tell them what had happened; whereon they came from their apartment with torches in their hands, and pressed round Ulysses to embrace him, kissing his head and shoulders and taking hold of his hands. It made him feel as if he should like to weep, for he remembered every one of them. {179}

Book XXIII

Penelope eventually recognises her husband—early in the morning
Ulysses, Telemachus, Eumaeus, and Philoetius leave the town.

Euryclea now went upstairs laughing to tell her mistress that her dear husband had come home. Her aged knees became young again and her feet were nimble for joy as she went up to her mistress and bent over her head to speak to her. "Wake up Penelope, my dear child," she exclaimed, "and see with your own eyes something that you have been wanting this long time past. Ulysses has at last indeed come home again, and has killed the suitors who were giving so much trouble in his house, eating up his estate and ill treating his son."

"My good nurse," answered Penelope, "you must be mad. The gods sometimes send some very sensible people out of their minds, and make foolish people become sensible. This is what they must have been doing to you; for you always used to be a reasonable person. Why should you thus mock me when I have trouble enough already—talking such nonsense, and waking me up out of a sweet sleep that had taken possession of my eyes and closed them? I have never slept so soundly from the day my poor husband went to that city with the ill-omened name. Go back again into the women's room; if it had been any one else who had woke me up to bring me such absurd news I should have sent her away with a severe scolding. As it is your age shall protect you."

"My dear child," answered Euryclea, "I am not mocking you. It is quite true as I tell you that Ulysses is come home again. He was the stranger whom they all kept on treating so badly in the cloister. Telemachus knew all the time that he was come back, but kept his father's secret that he might have his revenge on all these wicked people."

Then Penelope sprang up from her couch, threw her arms round Euryclea, and wept for joy. "But my dear nurse," said she, "explain this to me; if he has really come home as you say, how did he manage to overcome the wicked suitors single handed, seeing what a number of them there always were?"

"I was not there," answered Euryclea, "and do not know; I only heard them groaning while they were being killed. We sat crouching and huddled up in a corner of the women's room with the doors closed, till your son came to fetch me because his father sent him. Then I found Ulysses standing over the corpses that were lying on the ground all round him, one on top of the other. You would have enjoyed it if you could have seen him standing there all bespattered with blood and filth, and looking just like a lion. But the corpses are now all piled up in the gatehouse that is in the outer court, and Ulysses has lit a great fire to purify the house with sulphur. He has sent me to call you, so come with me that you may both be happy together after all; for now at last the desire of your heart has been fulfilled; your husband is come home to find both wife and son alive and well, and to take his revenge in his own house on the suitors who behaved so badly to him."

"My dear nurse," said Penelope, "do not exult too confidently over all this. You know how delighted every one would be to see Ulysses come home—more particularly myself, and the son who has been born to both of us; but what you tell me cannot be really true. It is some god who is angry with the suitors for their great wickedness, and has made an end of them; for they respected no man in the whole world, neither rich nor poor, who came near them, and they have come to a bad end in consequence of their iniquity; Ulysses is dead far away from the Achaean land; he will never return home again."

Then nurse Euryclea said, "My child, what are you talking about? but you were all hard of belief and have made up your mind that your husband is never coming, although he is in the house and by his own fire side at this very moment. Besides I can give you another proof; when I was washing him I perceived the scar which the wild boar gave him, and I wanted to tell you about it, but in his wisdom he would not let me, and clapped his hands over my mouth; so come with me and I will make this bargain with you—if I am deceiving you, you may have me killed by the most cruel death you can think of."

"My dear nurse," said Penelope, "however wise you may be you can hardly fathom the counsels of the gods. Nevertheless, we will go in search of my son, that I may see the corpses of the suitors, and the man who has killed them."

On this she came down from her upper room, and while doing so she considered whether she should keep at a distance from her husband and question him, or whether she should at once go up to him and embrace him. When, however, she had crossed the stone floor of the cloister, she sat down opposite Ulysses by the fire, against the wall at right angles {180} [to that by which she had entered], while Ulysses sat near one of the bearing-posts, looking upon the ground, and waiting to see what his brave wife would say to him when she saw him. For a long time she sat silent and as one lost in amazement. At one moment she looked him full in the face, but then again directly, she was misled by his shabby clothes and failed to recognise him, {181} till Telemachus began to reproach her and said:

"Mother—but you are so hard that I cannot call you by such a name—why do you keep away from my father in this way? Why do you not sit by his side and begin talking to him and asking him questions? No other woman could bear to keep away from her husband when he had come back to her after twenty years of absence, and after having gone through so much; but your heart always was as hard as a stone."

Penelope answered, "My son, I am so lost in astonishment that I can find no words in which either to ask questions or to answer them. I cannot even look him straight in the face. Still, if he really is Ulysses come back to his own home again, we shall get to understand one another better by and by, for there are tokens with which we two are alone acquainted, and which are hidden from all others."

Ulysses smiled at this, and said to Telemachus, "Let your mother put me to any proof she likes; she will make up her mind about it presently. She rejects me for the moment and believes me to be somebody else, because I am covered with dirt and have such bad clothes on; let us, however, consider what we had better do next. When one man has killed another—even though he was not one who would leave many friends to take up his quarrel—the man who has killed him must still say good bye to his friends and fly the country; whereas we have been killing the stay of a whole town, and all the picked youth of Ithaca. I would have you consider this matter."

"Look to it yourself, father," answered Telemachus, "for they say you are the wisest counsellor in the world, and that there is no other mortal man who can compare with you. We will follow you with right good will, nor shall you find us fail you in so far as our strength holds out."

"I will say what I think will be best," answered Ulysses. "First wash and put your shirts on; tell the maids also to go to their own room and dress; Phemius shall then strike up a dance tune on his lyre, so that if people outside hear, or any of the neighbours, or some one going along the street happens to notice it, they may think there is a wedding in the house, and no rumours about the death of the suitors will get about in the town, before we can escape to the woods upon my own land. Once there, we will settle which of the courses heaven vouchsafes us shall seem wisest."

Thus did he speak, and they did even as he had said. First they washed and put their shirts on, while the women got ready. Then Phemius took his lyre and set them all longing for sweet song and stately dance. The house re-echoed with the sound of men and women dancing, and the people outside said, "I suppose the queen has been getting married at last. She ought to be ashamed of herself for not continuing to protect her husband's property until he comes home." {182}

This was what they said, but they did not know what it was that had been happening. The upper servant Eurynome washed and anointed Ulysses in his own house and gave him a shirt and cloak, while Minerva made him look taller and stronger than before; she also made the hair grow thick on the top of his head, and flow down in curls like hyacinth blossoms; she glorified him about the head and shoulders just as a skilful workman who has studied art of all kinds under Vulcan or Minerva—and his work is full of beauty—enriches a piece of silver plate by gilding it. He came from the bath looking like one of the immortals, and sat down opposite his wife on the seat he had left. "My dear," said he, "heaven has endowed you with a heart more unyielding than woman ever yet had. No other woman could bear to keep away from her husband when he had come back to her after twenty years of absence, and after having gone through so much. But come, nurse, get a bed ready for me; I will sleep alone, for this woman has a heart as hard as iron."

"My dear," answered Penelope, "I have no wish to set myself up, nor to depreciate you; but I am not struck by your appearance, for I very well remember what kind of a man you were when you set sail from Ithaca. Nevertheless, Euryclea, take his bed outside the bed chamber that he himself built. Bring the bed outside this room, and put bedding upon it with fleeces, good coverlets, and blankets."

She said this to try him, but Ulysses was very angry and said, "Wife, I am much displeased at what you have just been saying. Who has been taking my bed from the place in which I left it? He must have found it a hard task, no matter how skilled a workman he was, unless some god came and helped him to shift it. There is no man living, however strong and in his prime, who could move it from its place, for it is a marvellous curiosity which I made with my very own hands. There was a young olive growing within the precincts of the house, in full vigour, and about as thick as a bearing-post. I built my room round this with strong walls of stone and a roof to cover them, and I made the doors strong and well-fitting. Then I cut off the top boughs of the olive tree and left the stump standing. This I dressed roughly from the root upwards and then worked with carpenter's tools well and skilfully, straightening my work by drawing a line on the wood, and making it into a bed-prop. I then bored a hole down the middle, and made it the centre-post of my bed, at which I worked till I had finished it, inlaying it with gold and silver; after this I stretched a hide of crimson leather from one side of it to the other. So you see I know all about it, and I desire to learn whether it is still there, or whether any one has been removing it by cutting down the olive tree at its roots."

When she heard the sure proofs Ulysses now gave her, she fairly broke down. She flew weeping to his side, flung her arms about his neck, and kissed him. "Do not be angry with me Ulysses," she cried, "you, who are the wisest of mankind. We have suffered, both of us. Heaven has denied us the happiness of spending our youth, and of growing old, together; do not then be aggrieved or take it amiss that I did not embrace you thus as soon as I saw you. I have been shuddering all the time through fear that someone might come here and deceive me with a lying story; for there are many very wicked people going about. Jove's daughter Helen would never have yielded herself to a man from a foreign country, if she had known that the sons of Achaeans would come after her and bring her back. Heaven put it in her heart to do wrong, and she gave no thought to that sin, which has been the source of all our sorrows. Now, however, that you have convinced me by showing that you know all about our bed (which no human being has ever seen but you and I and a single maidservant, the daughter of Actor, who was given me by my father on my marriage, and who keeps the doors of our room) hard of belief though I have been I can mistrust no longer."

Then Ulysses in his turn melted, and wept as he clasped his dear and faithful wife to his bosom. As the sight of land is welcome to men who are swimming towards the shore, when Neptune has wrecked their ship with the fury of his winds and waves; a few alone reach the land, and these, covered with brine, are thankful when they find themselves on firm ground and out of danger—even so was her husband welcome to her as she looked upon him, and she could not tear her two fair arms from about his neck. Indeed they would have gone on indulging their sorrow till rosy-fingered morn appeared, had not Minerva determined otherwise, and held night back in the far west, while she would not suffer Dawn to leave Oceanus, nor to yoke the two steeds Lampus and Phaethon that bear her onward to break the day upon mankind.

At last, however, Ulysses said, "Wife, we have not yet reached the end of our troubles. I have an unknown amount of toil still to undergo. It is long and difficult, but I must go through with it, for thus the shade of Teiresias prophesied concerning me, on the day when I went down into Hades to ask about my return and that of my companions. But now let us go to bed, that we may lie down and enjoy the blessed boon of sleep."

"You shall go to bed as soon as you please," replied Penelope, "now that the gods have sent you home to your own good house and to your country. But as heaven has put it in your mind to speak of it, tell me about the task that lies before you. I shall have to hear about it later, so it is better that I should be told at once."

"My dear," answered Ulysses, "why should you press me to tell you? Still, I will not conceal it from you, though you will not like it. I do not like it myself, for Teiresias bade me travel far and wide, carrying an oar, till I came to a country where the people have never heard of the sea, and do not even mix salt with their food. They know nothing about ships, nor oars that are as the wings of a ship. He gave me this certain token which I will not hide from you. He said that a wayfarer should meet me and ask me whether it was a winnowing shovel that I had on my shoulder. On this, I was to fix my oar in the ground and sacrifice a ram, a bull, and a boar to Neptune; after which I was to go home and offer hecatombs to all the gods in heaven, one after the other. As for myself, he said that death should come to me from the sea, and that my life should ebb away very gently when I was full of years and peace of mind, and my people should bless me. All this, he said, should surely come to pass."

And Penelope said, "If the gods are going to vouchsafe you a happier time in your old age, you may hope then to have some respite from misfortune."

Thus did they converse. Meanwhile Eurynome and the nurse took torches and made the bed ready with soft coverlets; as soon as they had laid them, the nurse went back into the house to go to her rest, leaving the bed chamber woman Eurynome {183} to show Ulysses and Penelope to bed by torch light. When she had conducted them to their room she went back, and they then came joyfully to the rites of their own old bed. Telemachus, Philoetius, and the swineherd now left off dancing, and made the women leave off also. They then laid themselves down to sleep in the cloisters.

When Ulysses and Penelope had had their fill of love they fell talking with one another. She told him how much she had had to bear in seeing the house filled with a crowd of wicked suitors who had killed so many sheep and oxen on her account, and had drunk so many casks of wine. Ulysses in his turn told her what he had suffered, and how much trouble he had himself given to other people. He told her everything, and she was so delighted to listen that she never went to sleep till he had ended his whole story.

He began with his victory over the Cicons, and how he thence reached the fertile land of the Lotus-eaters. He told her all about the Cyclops and how he had punished him for having so ruthlessly eaten his brave comrades; how he then went on to Aeolus, who received him hospitably and furthered him on his way, but even so he was not to reach home, for to his great grief a hurricane carried him out to sea again; how he went on to the Laestrygonian city Telepylos, where the people destroyed all his ships with their crews, save himself and his own ship only. Then he told of cunning Circe and her craft, and how he sailed to the chill house of Hades, to consult the ghost of the Theban prophet Teiresias, and how he saw his old comrades in arms, and his mother who bore him and brought him up when he was a child; how he then heard the wondrous singing of the Sirens, and went on to the wandering rocks and terrible Charybdis and to Scylla, whom no man had ever yet passed in safety; how his men then ate the cattle of the sun-god, and how Jove therefore struck the ship with his thunderbolts, so that all his men perished together, himself alone being left alive; how at last he reached the Ogygian island and the nymph Calypso, who kept him there in a cave, and fed him, and wanted him to marry her, in which case she intended making him immortal so that he should never grow old, but she could not persuade him to let her do so; and how after much suffering he had found his way to the Phaeacians, who had treated him as though he had been a god, and sent him back in a ship to his own country after having given him gold, bronze, and raiment in great abundance. This was the last thing about which he told her, for here a deep sleep took hold upon him and eased the burden of his sorrows.

Then Minerva bethought her of another matter. When she deemed that Ulysses had had both of his wife and of repose, she bade gold-enthroned Dawn rise out of Oceanus that she might shed light upon mankind. On this, Ulysses rose from his comfortable bed and said to Penelope, "Wife, we have both of us had our full share of troubles, you, here, in lamenting my absence, and I in being prevented from getting home though I was longing all the time to do so. Now, however, that we have at last come together, take care of the property that is in the house. As for the sheep and goats which the wicked suitors have eaten, I will take many myself by force from other people, and will compel the Achaeans to make good the rest till they shall have filled all my yards. I am now going to the wooded lands out in the country to see my father who has so long been grieved on my account, and to yourself I will give these instructions, though you have little need of them. At sunrise it will at once get abroad that I have been killing the suitors; go upstairs, therefore, {184} and stay there with your women. See nobody and ask no questions." {185}

As he spoke he girded on his armour. Then he roused Telemachus, Philoetius, and Eumaeus, and told them all to put on their armour also. This they did, and armed themselves. When they had done so, they opened the gates and sallied forth, Ulysses leading the way. It was now daylight, but Minerva nevertheless concealed them in darkness and led them quickly out of the town.

BOOK XXIV

The ghosts of the suitors in Hades—Ulysses and his men go to the house of Laertes—the people of Ithaca come out to attack Ulysses, but Minerva concludes a peace.

Then Mercury of Cyllene summoned the ghosts of the suitors, and in his hand he held the fair golden wand with which he seals men's eyes in sleep or wakes them just as he pleases; with this he roused the ghosts and led them, while they followed whining and gibbering behind him. As bats fly squealing in the hollow of some great cave, when one of them has fallen out of the cluster in which they hang, even so did the ghosts whine and squeal as Mercury the healer of sorrow led them down into the dark abode of death. When they had passed the waters of Oceanus and the rock Leucas, they came to the gates of the sun and the land of dreams, whereon they reached the meadow of asphodel where dwell the souls and shadows of them that can labour no more.

Here they found the ghost of Achilles son of Peleus, with those of Patroclus, Antilochus, and Ajax, who was the finest and handsomest man of all the Danaans after the son of Peleus himself.

They gathered round the ghost of the son of Peleus, and the ghost of Agamemnon joined them, sorrowing bitterly. Round him were gathered also the ghosts of those who had perished with him in the house of Aegisthus; and the ghost of Achilles spoke first.

"Son of Atreus," it said, "we used to say that Jove had loved you better from first to last than any other hero, for you were captain over many and brave men, when we were all fighting together before Troy; yet the hand of death, which no mortal can escape, was laid upon you all too early. Better for you had you fallen at Troy in the hey-day of your renown, for the Achaeans would have built a mound over your ashes, and your son would have been heir to your good name, whereas it has now been your lot to come to a most miserable end."

"Happy son of Peleus," answered the ghost of Agamemnon, "for having died at Troy far from Argos, while the bravest of the Trojans and the Achaeans fell round you fighting for your body. There you lay in the whirling clouds of dust, all huge and hugely, heedless now of your chivalry. We fought the whole of the livelong day, nor should we ever have left off if Jove had not sent a hurricane to stay us. Then, when we had borne you to the ships out of the fray, we laid you on your bed and cleansed your fair skin with warm water and with ointments. The Danaans tore their hair and wept bitterly round about you. Your mother, when she heard, came with her immortal nymphs from out of the sea, and the sound of a great wailing went forth over the waters so that the Achaeans quaked for fear. They would have fled panic-stricken to their ships had not wise old Nestor whose counsel was ever truest checked them saying, 'Hold, Argives, fly not sons of the Achaeans, this is his mother coming from the sea with her immortal nymphs to view the body of her son.'

"Thus he spoke, and the Achaeans feared no more. The daughters of the old man of the sea stood round you weeping bitterly, and clothed you in immortal raiment. The nine muses also came and lifted up their sweet voices in lament—calling and answering one another; there was not an Argive but wept for pity of the dirge they chaunted. Days and nights seven and ten we mourned you, mortals and immortals, but on the eighteenth day we gave you to the flames, and many a fat sheep with many an ox did we slay in sacrifice around you. You were burnt in raiment of the gods, with rich resins and with honey, while heroes, horse and foot, clashed their armour round the pile as you were burning, with the tramp as of a great multitude. But when the flames of heaven had done their work, we gathered your white bones at daybreak and laid them in ointments and in pure wine. Your mother brought us a golden vase to hold them—gift of Bacchus, and work of Vulcan himself; in this we mingled your bleached bones with those of Patroclus who had gone before you, and separate we enclosed also those of Antilochus, who had been closer to you than any other of your comrades now that Patroclus was no more.

"Over these the host of the Argives built a noble tomb, on a point jutting out over the open Hellespont, that it might be seen from far out upon the sea by those now living and by them that shall be born hereafter. Your mother begged prizes from the gods, and offered them to be contended for by the noblest of the Achaeans. You must have been present at the funeral of many a hero, when the young men gird themselves and make ready to contend for prizes on the death of some great chieftain, but you never saw such prizes as silver-footed Thetis offered in your honour; for the gods loved you well. Thus even in death your fame, Achilles, has not been lost, and your name lives evermore among all mankind. But as for me, what solace had I when the days of my fighting were done? For Jove willed my destruction on my return, by the hands of Aegisthus and those of my wicked wife."

Thus did they converse, and presently Mercury came up to them with the ghosts of the suitors who had been killed by Ulysses. The ghosts of Agamemnon and Achilles were astonished at seeing them, and went up to them at once. The ghost of Agamemnon recognised Amphimedon son of Melaneus, who lived in Ithaca and had been his host, so it began to talk to him.

"Amphimedon," it said, "what has happened to all you fine young men—all of an age too—that you are come down here under the ground? One could pick no finer body of men from any city. Did Neptune raise his winds and waves against you when you were at sea, or did your enemies make an end of you on the mainland when you were cattle-lifting or sheep-stealing, or while fighting in defence of their wives and city? Answer my question, for I have been your guest. Do you not remember how I came to your house with Menelaus, to persuade Ulysses to join us with his ships against Troy? It was a whole month ere we could resume our voyage, for we had hard work to persuade Ulysses to come with us."

And the ghost of Amphimedon answered, "Agamemnon, son of Atreus, king of men, I remember everything that you have said, and will tell you fully and accurately about the way in which our end was brought about. Ulysses had been long gone, and we were courting his wife, who did not say point blank that she would not marry, nor yet bring matters to an end, for she meant to compass our destruction: this, then, was the trick she played us. She set up a great tambour frame in her room and began to work on an enormous piece of fine needlework. 'Sweethearts,' said she, 'Ulysses is indeed dead, still, do not press me to marry again immediately; wait—for I would not have my skill in needlework perish unrecorded—till I have completed a pall for the hero Laertes, against the time when death shall take him. He is very rich, and the women of the place will talk if he is laid out without a pall.' This is what she said, and we assented; whereupon we could see her working upon her great web all day long, but at night she would unpick the stitches again by torchlight. She fooled us in this way for three years without our finding it out, but as time wore on and she was now in her fourth year, in the waning of moons and many days had been accomplished, one of her maids who knew what she was doing told us, and we caught her in the act of undoing her work, so she had to finish it whether she would or no; and when she showed us the robe she had made, after she had had it washed, {186} its splendour was as that of the sun or moon.

"Then some malicious god conveyed Ulysses to the upland farm where his swineherd lives. Thither presently came also his son, returning from a voyage to Pylos, and the two came to the town when they had hatched their plot for our destruction. Telemachus came first, and then after him, accompanied by the swineherd, came Ulysses, clad in rags and leaning on a staff as though he were some miserable old beggar. He came so unexpectedly that none of us knew him, not even the older ones among us, and we reviled him and threw things at him. He endured both being struck and insulted without a word, though he was in his own house; but when the will of Aegis-bearing Jove inspired him, he and Telemachus took the armour and hid it in an inner chamber, bolting the doors behind them. Then he cunningly made his wife offer his bow and a quantity of iron to be contended for by us ill-fated suitors; and this was the beginning of our end, for not one of us could string the bow—nor nearly do so. When it was about to reach the hands of Ulysses, we all of us shouted out that it should not be given him, no matter what he might say, but Telemachus insisted on his having it. When he had got it in his hands he strung it with ease and sent his arrow through the iron. Then he stood on the floor of the cloister and poured his arrows on the ground, glaring fiercely about him. First he killed Antinous, and then, aiming straight before him, he let fly his deadly darts and they fell thick on one another. It was plain that some one of the gods was helping them, for they fell upon us with might and main throughout the cloisters, and there was a hideous sound of groaning as our brains were being battered in, and the ground seethed with our blood. This, Agamemnon, is how we came by our end, and our bodies are lying still uncared for in the house of Ulysses, for our friends at home do not yet know what has happened, so that they cannot lay us out and wash the black blood from our wounds, making moan over us according to the offices due to the departed."

"Happy Ulysses, son of Laertes," replied the ghost of Agamemnon, "you are indeed blessed in the possession of a wife endowed with such rare excellence of understanding, and so faithful to her wedded lord as Penelope the daughter of Icarius. The fame, therefore, of her virtue shall never die, and the immortals shall compose a song that shall be welcome to all mankind in honour of the constancy of Penelope. How far otherwise was the wickedness of the daughter of Tyndareus who killed her lawful husband; her song shall be hateful among men, for she has brought disgrace on all womankind even on the good ones."

Thus did they converse in the house of Hades deep down within the bowels of the earth. Meanwhile Ulysses and the others passed out of the town and soon reached the fair and well-tilled farm of Laertes, which he had reclaimed with infinite labour. Here was his house, with a lean-to running all round it, where the slaves who worked for him slept and sat and ate, while inside the house there was an old Sicel woman, who looked after him in this his country-farm. When Ulysses got there, he said to his son and to the other two:

"Go to the house, and kill the best pig that you can find for dinner. Meanwhile I want to see whether my father will know me, or fail to recognise me after so long an absence."

He then took off his armour and gave it to Eumaeus and Philoetius, who went straight on to the house, while he turned off into the vineyard to make trial of his father. As he went down into the great orchard, he did not see Dolius, nor any of his sons nor of the other bondsmen, for they were all gathering thorns to make a fence for the vineyard, at the place where the old man had told them; he therefore found his father alone, hoeing a vine. He had on a dirty old shirt, patched and very shabby; his legs were bound round with thongs of oxhide to save him from the brambles, and he also wore sleeves of leather; he had a goat skin cap on his head, and was looking very woe-begone. When Ulysses saw him so worn, so old and full of sorrow, he stood still under a tall pear tree and began to weep. He doubted whether to embrace him, kiss him, and tell him all about his having come home, or whether he should first question him and see what he would say. In the end he deemed it best to be crafty with him, so in this mind he went up to his father, who was bending down and digging about a plant.

"I see, sir," said Ulysses, "that you are an excellent gardener—what pains you take with it, to be sure. There is not a single plant, not a fig tree, vine, olive, pear, nor flower bed, but bears the trace of your attention. I trust, however, that you will not be offended if I say that you take better care of your garden than of yourself. You are old, unsavoury, and very meanly clad. It cannot be because you are idle that your master takes such poor care of you, indeed your face and figure have nothing of the slave about them, and proclaim you of noble birth. I should have said that you were one of those who should wash well, eat well, and lie soft at night as old men have a right to do; but tell me, and tell me true, whose bondman are you, and in whose garden are you working? Tell me also about another matter. Is this place that I have come to really Ithaca? I met a man just now who said so, but he was a dull fellow, and had not the patience to hear my story out when I was asking him about an old friend of mine, whether he was still living, or was already dead and in the house of Hades. Believe me when I tell you that this man came to my house once when I was in my own country and never yet did any stranger come to me whom I liked better. He said that his family came from Ithaca and that his father was Laertes, son of Arceisius. I received him hospitably, making him welcome to all the abundance of my house, and when he went away I gave him all customary presents. I gave him seven talents of fine gold, and a cup of solid silver with flowers chased upon it. I gave him twelve light cloaks, and as many pieces of tapestry; I also gave him twelve cloaks of single fold, twelve rugs, twelve fair mantles, and an equal number of shirts. To all this I added four good looking women skilled in all useful arts, and I let him take his choice."

His father shed tears and answered, "Sir, you have indeed come to the country that you have named, but it is fallen into the hands of wicked people. All this wealth of presents has been given to no purpose. If you could have found your friend here alive in Ithaca, he would have entertained you hospitably and would have requited your presents amply when you left him—as would have been only right considering what you had already given him. But tell me, and tell me true, how many years is it since you entertained this guest—my unhappy son, as ever was? Alas! He has perished far from his own country; the fishes of the sea have eaten him, or he has fallen a prey to the birds and wild beasts of some continent. Neither his mother, nor I his father, who were his parents, could throw our arms about him and wrap him in his shroud, nor could his excellent and richly dowered wife Penelope bewail her husband as was natural upon his death bed, and close his eyes according to the offices due to the departed. But now, tell me truly for I want to know. Who and whence are you—tell me of your town and parents? Where is the ship lying that has brought you and your men to Ithaca? Or were you a passenger on some other man's ship, and those who brought you here have gone on their way and left you?"

"I will tell you everything," answered Ulysses, "quite truly. I come from Alybas, where I have a fine house. I am son of king Apheidas, who is the son of Polypemon. My own name is Eperitus; heaven drove me off my course as I was leaving Sicania, and I have been carried here against my will. As for my ship it is lying over yonder, off the open country outside the town, and this is the fifth year since Ulysses left my country. Poor fellow, yet the omens were good for him when he left me. The birds all flew on our right hands, and both he and I rejoiced to see them as we parted, for we had every hope that we should have another friendly meeting and exchange presents."

A dark cloud of sorrow fell upon Laertes as he listened. He filled both hands with the dust from off the ground and poured it over his grey head, groaning heavily as he did so. The heart of Ulysses was touched, and his nostrils quivered as he looked upon his father; then he sprang towards him, flung his arms about him and kissed him, saying, "I am he, father, about whom you are asking—I have returned after having been away for twenty years. But cease your sighing and lamentation—we have no time to lose, for I should tell you that I have been killing the suitors in my house, to punish them for their insolence and crimes."

"If you really are my son Ulysses," replied Laertes, "and have come back again, you must give me such manifest proof of your identity as shall convince me."

"First observe this scar," answered Ulysses, "which I got from a boar's tusk when I was hunting on Mt. Parnassus. You and my mother had sent me to Autolycus, my mother's father, to receive the presents which when he was over here he had promised to give me. Furthermore I will point out to you the trees in the vineyard which you gave me, and I asked you all about them as I followed you round the garden. We went over them all, and you told me their names and what they all were. You gave me thirteen pear trees, ten apple trees, and forty fig trees; you also said you would give me fifty rows of vines; there was corn planted between each row, and they yield grapes of every kind when the heat of heaven has been laid heavy upon them."

Laertes' strength failed him when he heard the convincing proofs which his son had given him. He threw his arms about him, and Ulysses had to support him, or he would have gone off into a swoon; but as soon as he came to, and was beginning to recover his senses, he said, "O father Jove, then you gods are still in Olympus after all, if the suitors have really been punished for their insolence and folly. Nevertheless, I am much afraid that I shall have all the townspeople of Ithaca up here directly, and they will be sending messengers everywhere throughout the cities of the Cephallenians."

Ulysses answered, "Take heart and do not trouble yourself about that, but let us go into the house hard by your garden. I have already told Telemachus, Philoetius, and Eumaeus to go on there and get dinner ready as soon as possible."

Thus conversing the two made their way towards the house. When they got there they found Telemachus with the stockman and the swineherd cutting up meat and mixing wine with water. Then the old Sicel woman took Laertes inside and washed him and anointed him with oil. She put him on a good cloak, and Minerva came up to him and gave him a more imposing presence, making him taller and stouter than before. When he came back his son was surprised to see him looking so like an immortal, and said to him, "My dear father, some one of the gods has been making you much taller and better-looking."

Laertes answered, "Would, by Father Jove, Minerva, and Apollo, that I were the man I was when I ruled among the Cephallenians, and took Nericum, that strong fortress on the foreland. If I were still what I then was and had been in our house yesterday with my armour on, I should have been able to stand by you and help you against the suitors. I should have killed a great many of them, and you would have rejoiced to see it."

Thus did they converse; but the others, when they had finished their work and the feast was ready, left off working, and took each his proper place on the benches and seats. Then they began eating; by and by old Dolius and his sons left their work and came up, for their mother, the Sicel woman who looked after Laertes now that he was growing old, had been to fetch them. When they saw Ulysses and were certain it was he, they stood there lost in astonishment; but Ulysses scolded them good naturedly and said, "Sit down to your dinner, old man, and never mind about your surprise; we have been wanting to begin for some time and have been waiting for you."

Then Dolius put out both his hands and went up to Ulysses. "Sir," said he, seizing his master's hand and kissing it at the wrist, "we have long been wishing you home: and now heaven has restored you to us after we had given up hoping. All hail, therefore, and may the gods prosper you. {187} But tell me, does Penelope already know of your return, or shall we send some one to tell her?"

"Old man," answered Ulysses, "she knows already, so you need not trouble about that." On this he took his seat, and the sons of Dolius gathered round Ulysses to give him greeting and embrace him one after the other; then they took their seats in due order near Dolius their father.

While they were thus busy getting their dinner ready, Rumour went round the town, and noised abroad the terrible fate that had befallen the suitors; as soon, therefore, as the people heard of it they gathered from every quarter, groaning and hooting before the house of Ulysses. They took the dead away, buried every man his own, and put the bodies of those who came from elsewhere on board the fishing vessels, for the fishermen to take each of them to his own place. They then met angrily in the place of assembly, and when they were got together Eupeithes rose to speak. He was overwhelmed with grief for the death of his son Antinous, who had been the first man killed by Ulysses, so he said, weeping bitterly, "My friends, this man has done the Achaeans great wrong. He took many of our best men away with him in his fleet, and he has lost both ships and men; now, moreover, on his return he has been killing all the foremost men among the Cephallenians. Let us be up and doing before he can get away to Pylos or to Elis where the Epeans rule, or we shall be ashamed of ourselves for ever afterwards. It will be an everlasting disgrace to us if we do not avenge the murder of our sons and brothers. For my own part I should have no more pleasure in life, but had rather die at once. Let us be up, then, and after them, before they can cross over to the main land."

He wept as he spoke and every one pitied him. But Medon and the bard Phemius had now woke up, and came to them from the house of Ulysses. Every one was astonished at seeing them, but they stood in the middle of the assembly, and Medon said, "Hear me, men of Ithaca. Ulysses did not do these things against the will of heaven. I myself saw an immortal god take the form of Mentor and stand beside him. This god appeared, now in front of him encouraging him, and now going furiously about the court and attacking the suitors whereon they fell thick on one another."

On this pale fear laid hold of them, and old Halitherses, son of Mastor, rose to speak, for he was the only man among them who knew both past and future; so he spoke to them plainly and in all honesty, saying,

"Men of Ithaca, it is all your own fault that things have turned out as they have; you would not listen to me, nor yet to Mentor, when we bade you check the folly of your sons who were doing much wrong in the wantonness of their hearts—wasting the substance and dishonouring the wife of a chieftain who they thought would not return. Now, however, let it be as I say, and do as I tell you. Do not go out against Ulysses, or you may find that you have been drawing down evil on your own heads."

This was what he said, and more than half raised a loud shout, and at once left the assembly. But the rest stayed where they were, for the speech of Halitherses displeased them, and they sided with Eupeithes; they therefore hurried off for their armour, and when they had armed themselves, they met together in front of the city, and Eupeithes led them on in their folly. He thought he was going to avenge the murder of his son, whereas in truth he was never to return, but was himself to perish in his attempt.

Then Minerva said to Jove, "Father, son of Saturn, king of kings, answer me this question—What do you propose to do? Will you set them fighting still further, or will you make peace between them?"

And Jove answered, "My child, why should you ask me? Was it not by your own arrangement that Ulysses came home and took his revenge upon the suitors? Do whatever you like, but I will tell you what I think will be most reasonable arrangement. Now that Ulysses is revenged, let them swear to a solemn covenant, in virtue of which he shall continue to rule, while we cause the others to forgive and forget the massacre of their sons and brothers. Let them then all become friends as heretofore, and let peace and plenty reign."

This was what Minerva was already eager to bring about, so down she darted from off the topmost summits of Olympus.

Now when Laertes and the others had done dinner, Ulysses began by saying, "Some of you go out and see if they are not getting close up to us." So one of Dolius's sons went as he was bid. Standing on the threshold he could see them all quite near, and said to Ulysses, "Here they are, let us put on our armour at once."

They put on their armour as fast as they could—that is to say Ulysses, his three men, and the six sons of Dolius. Laertes also and Dolius did the same—warriors by necessity in spite of their grey hair. When they had all put on their armour, they opened the gate and sallied forth, Ulysses leading the way.

Then Jove's daughter Minerva came up to them, having assumed the form and voice of Mentor. Ulysses was glad when he saw her, and said to his son Telemachus, "Telemachus, now that you are about to fight in an engagement, which will show every man's mettle, be sure not to disgrace your ancestors, who were eminent for their strength and courage all the world over."

"You say truly, my dear father," answered Telemachus, "and you shall see, if you will, that I am in no mind to disgrace your family."

Laertes was delighted when he heard this. "Good heavens," he exclaimed, "what a day I am enjoying: I do indeed rejoice at it. My son and grandson are vying with one another in the matter of valour."

On this Minerva came close up to him and said, "Son of Arceisius—-best friend I have in the world—pray to the blue-eyed damsel, and to Jove her father; then poise your spear and hurl it."

As she spoke she infused fresh vigour into him, and when he had prayed to her he poised his spear and hurled it. He hit Eupeithes' helmet, and the spear went right through it, for the helmet stayed it not, and his armour rang rattling round him as he fell heavily to the ground. Meantime Ulysses and his son fell upon the front line of the foe and smote them with their swords and spears; indeed, they would have killed every one of them, and prevented them from ever getting home again, only Minerva raised her voice aloud, and made every one pause. "Men of Ithaca," she cried, "cease this dreadful war, and settle the matter at once without further bloodshed."

On this pale fear seized every one; they were so frightened that their arms dropped from their hands and fell upon the ground at the sound of the goddess' voice, and they fled back to the city for their lives. But Ulysses gave a great cry, and gathering himself together swooped down like a soaring eagle. Then the son of Saturn sent a thunderbolt of fire that fell just in front of Minerva, so she said to Ulysses, "Ulysses, noble son of Laertes, stop this warful strife, or Jove will be angry with you."

Thus spoke Minerva, and Ulysses obeyed her gladly. Then Minerva assumed the form and voice of Mentor, and presently made a covenant of peace between the two contending parties.

FOOTNOTES

{1} Black races are evidently known to the writer as stretching all across Africa, one half looking West on to the Atlantic, and the other East on to the Indian Ocean.

{2} The original use of the footstool was probably less to rest the feet than to keep them (especially when bare) from a floor which was often wet and dirty.

{3} The [Greek] or seat, is occasionally called "high," as being higher than the [Greek] or low footstool. It was probably no higher than an ordinary chair is now, and seems to have had no back.

{4} Temesa was on the West Coast of the toe of Italy, in what is now the gulf of Sta Eufemia. It was famous in remote times for its copper mines, which, however, were worked out when Strabo wrote.

{5} i.e. "with a current in it"—see illustrations and map near the end of bks. v. and vi. respectively.

{6} Reading [Greek] for [Greek], cf. "Od." iii. 81 where the same mistake is made, and xiii. 351 where the mountain is called Neritum, the same place being intended both here and in book xiii.

{7} It is never plausibly explained why Penelope cannot do this, and from bk. ii. it is clear that she kept on deliberately encouraging the suitors, though we are asked to believe that she was only fooling them.

{8} See note on "Od." i. 365.

{9} Middle Argos means the Peleponnese which, however, is never so called in the "Iliad". I presume "middle" means "middle between the two Greek-speaking countries of Asia Minor and Sicily, with South Italy"; for that parts of Sicily and also large parts, though not the whole of South Italy, were inhabited by Greek-speaking races centuries before the Dorian colonisations can hardly be doubted. The Sicians, and also the Sicels, both of them probably spoke Greek.

{10} cf. "Il." vi. 490-495. In the "Iliad" it is "war," not "speech," that is a man's matter. It argues a certain hardness, or at any rate dislike of the "Iliad" on the part of the writer of the "Odyssey," that she should have adopted Hector's farewell to Andromache here, as elsewhere in the poem, for a scene of such inferior pathos.

{11} [Greek] The whole open court with the covered cloister running round it was called [Greek], or [Greek], but the covered part was distinguished by being called "shady" or "shadow-giving". It was in this part that the tables for the suitors were laid. The Fountain Court at Hampton Court may serve as an illustration (save as regards the use of arches instead of wooden supports and rafters) and the arrangement is still common in Sicily. The usual translation "shadowy" or "dusky" halls, gives a false idea of the scene.

{12} The reader will note the extreme care which the writer takes to make it clear that none of the suitors were allowed to sleep in Ulysses' house.

{13} See Appendix; g, in plan of Ulysses' house.

{14} I imagine this passage to be a rejoinder to "Il." xxiii. 702-705 in which a tripod is valued at twelve oxen, and a good useful maid of all work at only four. The scrupulous regard of Laertes for his wife's feelings is of a piece with the extreme jealousy for the honour of woman, which is manifest throughout the "Odyssey".

{15} [Greek] "The [Greek], or tunica, was a shirt or shift, and served as the chief under garment of the Greeks and Romans, whether men or women." Smith's Dictionary of Greek and Roman Antiquities, under "Tunica".

{16} Doors fastened to all intents and purposes as here described may be seen in the older houses at Trapani. There is a slot on the outer side of the door by means of which a person who has left the room can shoot the bolt. My bedroom at the Albergo Centrale was fastened in this way.

{17} [Greek] So we vulgarly say "had cooked his goose," or "had settled his hash." Aegyptus cannot of course know of the fate Antiphus had met with, for there had as yet been no news of or from Ulysses.

{18} "Il." xxii. 416. [Greek] The authoress has bungled by borrowing these words verbatim from the "Iliad", without prefixing the necessary "do not," which I have supplied.

{19} i.e. you have money, and could pay when I got judgment, whereas the suitors are men of straw.

{20} cf. "Il." ii. 76. [Greek]. The Odyssean passage runs [Greek]. Is it possible not to suspect that the name Mentor was coined upon that of Nestor?

{21} i.e. in the outer court, and in the uncovered part of the inner house.

{22} This would be fair from Sicily, which was doing duty for Ithaca in the mind of the writer, but a North wind would have been preferable for a voyage from the real Ithaca to Pylos.

{23} [Greek] The wind does not whistle over waves. It only whistles through rigging or some other obstacle that cuts it.

{24} cf. "Il." v.20. [Greek] The Odyssean line is [Greek]. There can be no doubt that the Odyssean line was suggested by the Iliadic, but nothing can explain why Idaeus jumping from his chariot should suggest to the writer of the "Odyssey" the sun jumping from the sea. The probability is that she never gave the matter a thought, but took the line in question as an effect of saturation with the "Iliad," and of unconscious cerebration. The "Odyssey" contains many such examples.

{25} The heart, liver, lights, kidneys, etc. were taken out from the inside and eaten first as being more readily cooked; the [Greek], or bone meat, was cooking while the [Greek] or inward parts were being eaten. I imagine that the thigh bones made a kind of gridiron, while at the same time the marrow inside them got cooked.

{26} i.e. skewers, either single, double, or even five pronged. The meat would be pierced with the skewer, and laid over the ashes to grill—the two ends of the skewer being supported in whatever way convenient. Meat so cooking may be seen in any eating house in Smyrna, or any Eastern town. When I rode across the Troad from the Dardanelles to Hissarlik and Mount Ida, I noticed that my dragoman and his men did all our outdoor cooking exactly in the Odyssean and Iliadic fashion.

{27} cf. "Il." xvii. 567. [Greek] The Odyssean lines are— [Greek]

{28} Reading [Greek] for [Greek], cf. "Od." i.186.

{29} The geography of the Aegean as above described is correct, but is probably taken from the lost poem, the Nosti, the existence of which is referred to "Od." i.326,327 and 350, etc. A glance at the map will show that heaven advised its suppliants quite correctly.

{30} The writer—ever jealous for the honour of women—extenuates Clytemnestra's guilt as far as possible, and explains it as due to her having been left unprotected, and fallen into the hands of a wicked man.

{31} The Greek is [Greek] cf. "Iliad" ii. 408 [Greek] Surely the [Greek] of the Odyssean passage was due to the [Greek] of the "Iliad." No other reason suggests itself for the making Menelaus return on the very day of the feast given by Orestes. The fact that in the "Iliad" Menelaus came to a banquet without waiting for an invitation, determines the writer of the "Odyssey" to make him come to a banquet, also uninvited, but as circumstances did not permit of his having been invited, his coming uninvited is shown to have been due to chance. I do not think the authoress thought all this out, but attribute the strangeness of the coincidence to unconscious cerebration and saturation.

{32} cf. "Il." i.458, ii. 421. The writer here interrupts an Iliadic passage (to which she returns immediately) for the double purpose of dwelling upon the slaughter of the heifer, and of letting Nestor's wife and daughter enjoy it also. A male writer, if he was borrowing from the "Iliad," would have stuck to his borrowing.

{33} cf. "Il." xxiv. 587,588 where the lines refer to the washing the dead body of Hector.

{34} See illustration on opposite page. The yard is typical of many that may be seen in Sicily. The existing ground-plan is probably unmodified from Odyssean, and indeed long pre-Odyssean times, but the earlier buildings would have no arches, and would, one would suppose, be mainly timber. The Odyssean [Greek] were the sheds that ran round the yard as the arches do now. The [Greek] was the one through which the main entrance passed, and which was hence "noisy," or reverberating. It had an upper story in which visitors were often lodged.

{35} This journey is an impossible one. Telemachus and Pisistratus would have been obliged to drive over the Taygetus range, over which there has never yet been a road for wheeled vehicles. It is plain therefore that the audience for whom the "Odyssey" was written was one that would be unlikely to know anything about the topography of the Peloponnese, so that the writer might take what liberties she chose.

{36} The lines which I have enclosed in brackets are evidently an afterthought—added probably by the writer herself—for they evince the same instinctively greater interest in anything that may concern a woman, which is so noticeable throughout the poem. There is no further sign of any special festivities nor of any other guests than Telemachus and Pisistratus, until lines 621-624 (ordinarily enclosed in brackets) are abruptly introduced, probably with a view of trying to carry off the introduction of the lines now in question.

The addition was, I imagine, suggested by a desire to excuse and explain the non-appearance of Hermione in bk. xv., as also of both Hermione and Megapenthes in the rest of bk. iv. Megapenthes in bk. xv. seems to be still a bachelor: the presumption therefore is that bk. xv. was written before the story of his marriage here given. I take it he is only married here because his sister is being married. She having been properly attended to, Megapenthes might as well be married at the same time. Hermione could not now be less than thirty.

I have dealt with this passage somewhat more fully in my "Authoress of the Odyssey", p.136-138. See also p. 256 of the same book.

{37} Sparta and Lacedaemon are here treated as two different places, though in other parts of the poem it is clear that the writer understands them as one. The catalogue in the "Iliad," which the writer is here presumably following, makes the same mistake ("Il." ii. 581,582)

{38} These last three lines are identical with "Il." vxiii. 604-606.

{39} From the Greek [Greek] it is plain that Menelaus took up the piece of meat with his fingers.

{40} Amber is never mentioned in the "Iliad." Sicily, where I suppose the "Odyssey" to have been written, has always been, and still is, one of the principal amber producing countries. It was probably the only one known in the Odyssean age. See "The Authoress of the Odyssey", p260.

{41} This no doubt refers to the story told in the last poem of the Cypria about Paris and Helen robbing Menelaus of the greater part of his treasures, when they sailed together for Troy.

{42} It is inconceivable that Helen should enter thus, in the middle of supper, intending to work with her distaff, if great festivities were going on. Telemachus and Pisistratus are evidently dining en famille.

{43} In the Italian insurrection of 1848, eight young men who were being hotly pursued by the Austrian police hid themselves inside Donatello's colossal wooden horse in the Salone at Padua, and remained there for a week being fed by their confederates. In 1898 the last survivor was carried round Padua in triumph.

{44} The Greek is [Greek]. Is it unfair to argue that the writer is a person of somewhat delicate sensibility, to whom a strong smell of fish is distasteful?

{45} The Greek is [Greek]. I believe this to be a hit at the writer's own countrymen who were of Phocaean descent, and the next following line to be a rejoinder to complaints made against her in bk. vi. 273-288, to the effect that she gave herself airs and would marry none of her own people. For that the writer of the "Odyssey" was the person who has been introduced into the poem under the name of Nausicaa, I cannot bring myself to question. I may remind English readers that [Greek] (i.e. phoca) means "seal." Seals almost always appear on Phocaean coins.

{46} Surely here again we are in the hands of a writer of delicate sensibility. It is not as though the seals were stale; they had only just been killed. The writer, however is obviously laughing at her own countrymen, and insulting them as openly as she dares.

{47} We were told above (lines 357,357) that it was only one day's sail.

{48} I give the usual translation, but I do not believe the Greek will warrant it. The Greek reads [Greek].

This is usually held to mean that Ithaca is an island fit for breeding goats, and on that account more delectable to the speaker than it would have been if it were fit for breeding horses. I find little authority for such a translation; the most equitable translation of the text as it stands is, "Ithaca is an island fit for breeding goats, and delectable rather than fit for breeding horses; for not one of the islands is good driving ground, nor well meadowed." Surely the writer does not mean that a pleasant or delectable island would not be fit for breeding horses? The most equitable translation, therefore, of the present text being thus halt and impotent, we may suspect corruption, and I hazard the following emendation, though I have not adopted it in my translation, as fearing that it would be deemed too fanciful. I would read:—[Greek].

As far as scanning goes the [Greek] is not necessary; [Greek] iv. 72, [Greek] iv. 233, to go no further afield than earlier lines of the same book, give sufficient authority for [Greek], but the [Greek] would not be redundant; it would emphasise the surprise of the contrast, and I should prefer to have it, though it is not very important either way. This reading of course should be translated "Ithaca is an island fit for breeding goats, and (by your leave) itself a horseman rather than fit for breeding horses—for not one of the islands is good and well meadowed ground."

This would be sure to baffle the Alexandrian editors. "How," they would ask themselves, "could an island be a horseman?" and they would cast about for an emendation. A visit to the top of Mt. Eryx might perhaps make the meaning intelligible, and suggest my proposed restoration of the text to the reader as readily as it did to myself.

I have elsewhere stated my conviction that the writer of the "Odyssey" was familiar with the old Sican city at the top of Mt. Eryx, and that the

Aegadean islands which are so striking when seen thence did duty with her for the Ionian islands—Marettimo, the highest and most westerly of the group, standing for Ithaca. When seen from the top of Mt. Eryx Marettimo shows as it should do according to "Od." ix. 25,26, "on the horizon, all highest up in the sea towards the West," while the other islands lie "some way off it to the East." As we descend to Trapani, Marettimo appears to sink on to the top of the island of Levanzo, behind which it disappears. My friend, the late Signor E. Biaggini, pointed to it once as it was just standing on the top of Levanzo, and said to me "Come cavalca bene" ("How well it rides"), and this immediately suggested my emendation to me. Later on I found in the hymn to the Pythian Apollo (which abounds with tags taken from the "Odyssey") a line ending [Greek] which strengthened my suspicion that this was the original ending of the second of the two lines above under consideration.

{49} See note on line 3 of this book. The reader will observe that the writer has been unable to keep the women out of an interpolation consisting only of four lines.

{50} Scheria means a piece of land jutting out into the sea. In my "Authoress of the Odyssey" I thought "Jutland" would be a suitable translation, but it has been pointed out to me that "Jutland" only means the land of the Jutes.

{51} Irrigation as here described is common in gardens near Trapani. The water that supplies the ducts is drawn from wells by a mule who turns a wheel with buckets on it.

{52} There is not a word here about the cattle of the sun-god.

{53} The writer evidently thought that green, growing wood might also be well seasoned.

{54} The reader will note that the river was flowing with salt water i.e. that it was tidal.

{55} Then the Ogygian island was not so far off, but that Nausicaa might be assumed to know where it was.

{56} Greek [Greek]

{57} I suspect a family joke, or sly allusion to some thing of which we know nothing, in this story of Eurymedusa's having been brought from Apeira. The Greek word "apeiros" means "inexperienced," "ignorant." Is it possible that Eurymedusa was notoriously incompetent?

{58} Polyphemus was also son to Neptune, see "Od." ix. 412,529. he was therefore half brother to Nausithous, half uncle to King Alcinous, and half great uncle to Nausicaa.

{59} It would seem as though the writer thought that Marathon was close to Athens.

{60} Here the writer, knowing that she is drawing (with embellishments) from things actually existing, becomes impatient of past tenses and slides into the present.

{61} This is hidden malice, implying that the Phaeacian magnates were no better than they should be. The final drink-offering should have been made to Jove or Neptune, not to the god of thievishness and rascality of all kinds. In line 164 we do indeed find Echeneus proposing that a drink-offering should be made to Jove, but Mercury is evidently, according to our authoress, the god who was most likely to be of use to them.

{62} The fact of Alcinous knowing anything about the Cyclopes suggests that in the writer's mind Scheria and the country of the Cyclopes were not very far from one another. I take the Cyclopes and the giants to be one and the same people.

{63} "My property, etc." The authoress is here adopting an Iliadic line (xix. 333), and this must account for the absence of all reference to Penelope. If she had happened to remember "Il." v.213, she would doubtless have appropriated it by preference, for that line reads "my country, my wife, and all the greatness of my house."

{64} The at first inexplicable sleep of Ulysses (bk. xiii. 79, etc.) is here, as also in viii. 445, being obviously prepared. The writer evidently attached the utmost importance to it. Those who know that the harbour which did duty with the writer of the "Odyssey" for the one in which Ulysses landed in Ithaca, was only about 2 miles from the place in which Ulysses is now talking with Alcinous, will understand why the sleep was so necessary.

{65} There were two classes—the lower who were found in provisions which they had to cook for themselves in the yards and outer precincts, where they would also eat—and the upper who would eat in the cloisters of the inner court, and have their cooking done for them.

{66} Translation very dubious. I suppose the [Greek] here to be the covered sheds that ran round the outer courtyard. See illustrations at the end of bk. iii.

{67} The writer apparently deems that the words "as compared with what oxen can plough in the same time" go without saying. Not so the writer of the "Iliad" from which the Odyssean passage is probably taken. He explains that mules can plough quicker than oxen ("Il." x.351-353)

{68} It was very fortunate that such a disc happened to be there, seeing that none like it were in common use.

{69} "Il." xiii. 37. Here, as so often elsewhere in the "Odyssey," the appropriation of an Iliadic line which is not quite appropriate puzzles the reader. The "they" is not the chains, nor yet Mars and Venus. It is an overflow from the Iliadic passage in which Neptune hobbles his horses in bonds "which none could either unloose or break so that they might stay there in that place." If the line would have scanned without the addition of the words "so that they might stay there in that place," they would have been omitted in the "Odyssey."

{70} The reader will note that Alcinous never goes beyond saying that he is going to give the goblet; he never gives it. Elsewhere in both "Iliad" and "Odyssey" the offer of a present is immediately followed by the statement that it was given and received gladly—Alcinous actually does give a chest and a cloak and shirt—probably also some of the corn and wine for the long two-mile voyage was provided by him—but it is quite plain that he gave no talent and no cup.

{71} "Il." xviii, 344-349. These lines in the "Iliad" tell of the preparation for washing the body of Patroclus, and I am not pleased that the writer of the "Odyssey" should have adopted them here.

{72} see note {64}

{73} see note {43}

{74} The reader will find this threat fulfilled in bk. xiii

{75} If the other islands lay some distance away from Ithaca (which the word [Greek] suggests), what becomes of the [Greek] or gut between Ithaca and Samos which we hear of in Bks. iv. and xv.? I suspect that the authoress in her mind makes Telemachus come back from Pylos to the Lilybaean promontory and thence to Trapani through the strait between the Isola Grande and the mainland—the island of Asteria being the one on which Motya afterwards stood.

{76} "Il." xviii. 533-534. The sudden lapse into the third person here for a couple of lines is due to the fact that the two Iliadic lines taken are in the third person.

{77} cf. "Il." ii. 776. The words in both "Iliad" and "Odyssey" are [Greek]. In the "Iliad" they are used of the horses of Achilles' followers as they stood idle, "champing lotus."

{78} I take all this passage about the Cyclopes having no ships to be sarcastic—meaning, "You people of Drepanum have no excuse for not colonising the island of Favognana, which you could easily do, for you have plenty of ships, and the island is a very good one." For that the island so fully described here is the Aegadean or "goat" island of Favognana, and that the Cyclopes are the old Sican inhabitants of Mt. Eryx should not be doubted.

{79} For the reasons why it was necessary that the night should be so exceptionally dark see "The Authoress of the Odyssey" pp. 188-189.

{80} None but such lambs as would suck if they were with their mothers would be left in the yard. The older lambs should have been out feeding. The authoress has got it all wrong, but it does not matter. See "The Authoress of the Odyssey" p.148.

{81} This line is enclosed in brackets in the received text, and is omitted (with note) by Messrs. Butcher & Lang. But lines enclosed in brackets are almost always genuine; all that brackets mean is that the bracketed passage puzzled some early editor, who nevertheless found it too well established in the text to venture on omitting it. In the present case the line bracketed is the very last which a full-grown male editor would be likely to interpolate. It is safer to infer that the writer, a young woman, not knowing or caring at which end of the ship the rudder should be, determined to make sure by placing it at both ends, which we shall find she presently does by repeating it (line 340) at the stern of the ship. As for the two rocks thrown, the first I take to be the Asinelli, see map facing p.80. The second I see as the two contiguous islands of the Formiche, which are treated as one, see map facing p.108. The Asinelli is an island shaped like a boat, and pointing to the island of Favognana. I think the authoress's compatriots, who probably did not like her much better that she did them, jeered at the absurdity of Ulysses' conduct, and saw the Asinelli or "donkeys," not as the rock thrown by Polyphemus, but as the boat itself containing Ulysses and his men.

{82} This line exists in the text here but not in the corresponding passage xii. 141. I am inclined to think it is interpolated (probably by the poetess herself) from the first of lines xi. 115-137, which I can hardly doubt were added by the writer when the scheme of the work was enlarged and altered. See "The Authoress of the Odyssey" pp. 254-255.

{83} "Floating" ([Greek]) is not to be taken literally. The island itself, as apart from its inhabitants, was quite normal. There is no indication of its moving during the month that Ulysses stayed with Aeolus, and on his return from his unfortunate voyage, he seems to have found it in the same place. The [Greek] in fact should no more be pressed than [Greek] as applied to islands, "Odyssey" xv. 299—where they are called "flying" because the ship would fly past them. So also the "Wanderers," as explained by Buttmann; see note on "Odyssey" xii. 57.

{84} Literally "for the ways of the night and of the day are near." I have seen what Mr. Andrew Lang says ("Homer and the Epic," p.236, and "Longman's Magazine" for January, 1898, p.277) about the "amber route" and the "Sacred Way" in this connection; but until he gives his grounds for holding that the Mediterranean peoples in the Odyssean age used to go far North for their amber instead of getting it in Sicily, where it is still found in considerable quantities, I do not know what weight I ought to attach to his opinion. I have been unable to find grounds for asserting that B.C. 1000 there was any commerce between the Mediterranean and the "Far North," but I shall be very ready to learn if Mr. Lang will enlighten me. See "The Authoress of the Odyssey" pp. 185-186.

{85} One would have thought that when the sun was driving the stag down to the water, Ulysses might have observed its whereabouts.

{86} See Hobbes of Malmesbury's translation.

{87} "Il." vxiii. 349. Again the writer draws from the washing the body of Patroclus—which offends.

{88} This visit is wholly without topographical significance.

{89} Brides presented themselves instinctively to the imagination of the writer, as the phase of humanity which she found most interesting.

{90} Ulysses was, in fact, to become a missionary and preach Neptune to people who knew not his name. I was fortunate enough to meet in Sicily a woman carrying one of these winnowing shovels; it was not much shorter than an oar, and I was able at once to see what the writer of the "Odyssey" intended.

{91} I suppose the lines I have enclosed in brackets to have been added by the author when she enlarged her original scheme by the addition of books i.-iv. and xiii. (from line 187)-xxiv. The reader will observe that in the corresponding passage (xii. 137-141) the prophecy ends with "after losing all your comrades," and that there is no allusion to the suitors. For fuller explanation see "The Authoress of the Odyssey" pp. 254-255.

{92} The reader will remember that we are in the first year of Ulysses' wanderings, Telemachus therefore was only eleven years old. The same anachronism is made later on in this book. See "The Authoress of the Odyssey" pp. 132-133.

{93} Tradition says that she had hanged herself. Cf. "Odyssey" xv. 355, etc.

{94} Not to be confounded with Aeolus king of the winds.

{95} Melampus, vide book xv. 223, etc.

{96} I have already said in a note on bk. xi. 186 that at this point of Ulysses' voyage Telemachus could only be between eleven and twelve years old.

{97} Is the writer a man or a woman?

{98} Cf. "Il." iv. 521, [Greek]. The Odyssean line reads, [Greek]. The famous dactylism, therefore, of the Odyssean line was probably suggested by that of the Ileadic rather than by a desire to accommodate sound to sense. At any rate the double coincidence of a dactylic line, and an ending [Greek], seems conclusive as to the familiarity of the writer of the "Odyssey" with the Iliadic line.

{99} Off the coast of Sicily and South Italy, in the month of May, I have seen men fastened half way up a boat's mast with their feet resting on a crosspiece, just large enough to support them. From this point of vantage they spear sword-fish. When I saw men thus employed I could hardly doubt that the writer of the "Odyssey" had seen others like them, and had them in her mind when describing the binding of Ulysses. I have therefore with some diffidence ventured to depart from the received translation of [Greek] (cf. Alcaeus frag. 18, where, however, it is very hard to say what [Greek] means). In Sophocles' Lexicon I find a reference to Chrysostom (1, 242, A. Ed. Benedictine Paris 1834-1839) for the word [Greek], which is probably the same as [Greek], but I have looked for the passage in vain.

{100} The writer is at fault here and tries to put it off on Circe. When Ulysses comes to take the route prescribed by Circe, he ought to pass either the Wanderers or some other difficulty of which we are not told, but he does not do so. The Planctae, or Wanderers, merge into Scylla and Charybdis, and the alternative between them and something untold merges into the alternative whether Ulysses had better choose Scylla or Charybdis. Yet from line 260, it seems we are to consider the Wanderers as having been passed by Ulysses; this appears even more plainly from

xxiii. 327, in which Ulysses expressly mentions the Wandering rocks as having been between the Sirens and Scylla and Charybdis. The writer, however, is evidently unaware that she does not quite understand her own story; her difficulty was perhaps due to the fact that though Trapanese sailors had given her a fair idea as to where all her other localities really were, no one in those days more than in our own could localise the Planctae, which in fact, as Buttmann has argued, were derived not from any particular spot, but from sailors' tales about the difficulties of navigating the group of the Aeolian islands as a whole (see note on "Od." x. 3). Still the matter of the poor doves caught her fancy, so she would not forgo them. The whirlwinds of fire and the smoke that hangs on Scylla suggests allusion to Stromboli and perhaps even Etna. Scylla is on the Italian side, and therefore may be said to look West. It is about 8 miles thence to the Sicilian coast, so Ulysses may be perfectly well told that after passing Scylla he will come to the Thrinacian island or Sicily. Charybdis is transposed to a site some few miles to the north of its actual position.

{101} I suppose this line to have been intercalated by the author when lines 426-446 were added.

{102} For the reasons which enable us to identify the island of the two Sirens with the Lipari island now Salinas—the ancient Didyme, or "twin" island—see The Authoress of the Odyssey, pp. 195, 196. The two Sirens doubtless were, as their name suggests, the whistling gusts, or avalanches of air that at times descend without a moment's warning from the two lofty mountains of Salinas—as also from all high points in the neighbourhood.

{103} See Admiral Smyth on the currents in the Straits of Messina, quoted in "The Authoress of the Odyssey," p. 197.

{104} In the islands of Favognana and Marettimo off Trapani I have seen men fish exactly as here described. They chew bread into a paste and throw it into the sea to attract the fish, which they then spear. No line is used.

{105} The writer evidently regards Ulysses as on a coast that looked East at no great distance south of the Straits of Messina somewhere, say, near Tauromenium, now Taormina.

{106} Surely there must be a line missing here to tell us that the keel and mast were carried down into Charybdis. Besides, the aorist [Greek] in its present surrounding is perplexing. I have translated it as though it were an imperfect; I see Messrs. Butcher and Lang translate it as a pluperfect, but surely Charybdis was in the act of sucking down the water when Ulysses arrived.

{107} I suppose the passage within brackets to have been an afterthought but to have been written by the same hand as the rest of the poem. I suppose xii. 103 to have been also added by the writer when she decided on sending Ulysses back to Charybdis. The simile suggests the hand of the wife or daughter of a magistrate who had often seen her father come in cross and tired.

{108} Gr. [Greek]. This puts coined money out of the question, but nevertheless implies that the gold had been worked into ornaments of some kind.

{109} I suppose Teiresias' prophecy of bk. xi. 114-120 had made no impression on Ulysses. More probably the prophecy was an afterthought, intercalated, as I have already said, by the authoress when she changed her scheme.

{110} A male writer would have made Ulysses say, not "may you give satisfaction to your wives," but "may your wives give satisfaction to you."

{111} See note {64}.

{112} The land was in reality the shallow inlet, now the salt works of S. Cusumano—the neighbourhood of Trapani and Mt. Eryx being made to do double duty, both as Scheria and Ithaca. Hence the necessity for making Ulysses set out after dark, fall instantly into a profound sleep, and wake up on a morning so foggy that he could not see anything till the interviews between Neptune and Jove and between Ulysses and Minerva should have given the audience time to accept the situation. See illustrations and map near the end of bks. v. and vi. respectively.

{113} This cave, which is identifiable with singular completeness, is now called the "grotta del toro," probably a corruption of "tesoro," for it is held to contain a treasure. See The Authoress of the Odyssey, pp. 167-170.

{114} Probably they would.

{115} Then it had a shallow shelving bottom.

{116} Doubtless the road would pass the harbour in Odyssean times as it passes the salt works now; indeed, if there is to be a road at all there is no other level ground which it could take. See map above referred to.

{117} The rock at the end of the Northern harbour of Trapani, to which I suppose the writer of the "Odyssey" to be here referring, still bears the name Malconsiglio—"the rock of evil counsel." There is a legend that it was a ship of Turkish pirates who were intending to attack Trapani, but the "Madonna di Trapani" crushed them under this rock just as they were coming into port. My friend Cavaliere Giannitrapani of Trapani told me that his father used to tell him when he was a boy that if he would drop exactly three drops of oil on to the water near the rock, he would see the ship still at the bottom. The legend is evidently a Christianised version of the Odyssean story, while the name supplies the additional detail that the disaster happened in consequence of an evil counsel.

{118} It would seem then that the ship had got all the way back from Ithaca in about a quarter of an hour.

{119} And may we not add "and also to prevent his recognising that he was only in the place where he had met Nausicaa two days earlier."

{120} All this is to excuse the entire absence of Minerva from books ix.-xii., which I suppose had been written already, before the authoress had determined on making Minerva so prominent a character.

{121} We have met with this somewhat lame attempt to cover the writer's change of scheme at the end of bk. vi.

{122} I take the following from The Authoress of the Odyssey, p. 167. "It is clear from the text that there were two [caves] not one, but some one has enclosed in brackets the two lines in which the second cave is mentioned, I presume because he found himself puzzled by having a second cave sprung upon him when up to this point he had only been told of one.

"I venture to think that if he had known the ground he would not have been puzzled, for there are two caves, distant about 80 or 100 yards from one another." The cave in which Ulysses hid his treasure is, as I have already said, identifiable with singular completeness. The other cave presents no special features, neither in the poem nor in nature.

{123} There is no attempt to disguise the fact that Penelope had long given encouragement to the suitors. The only defence set up is that she did not really mean to encourage them. Would it not have been wiser to have tried a little discouragement?

{124} See map near the end of bk. vi. Ruccazzu dei corvi of course means "the rock of the ravens." Both name and ravens still exist.

{125} See The Authoress of the Odyssey, pp. 140, 141. The real reason for sending Telemachus to Pylos and Lacedaemon was that the authoress might get Helen of Troy into her poem. He was sent at the only point in the story at which he could be sent, so he must have gone then or not at all.

{126} The site I assign to Eumaeus's hut, close to the Ruccazzu dei Corvi, is about 2,000 feet above the sea, and commands an extensive view.

{127} Sandals such as Eumaeus was making are still worn in the Abruzzi and elsewhere. An oblong piece of leather forms the sole: holes are cut at the four corners, and through these holes leathern straps are passed, which are bound round the foot and cross-gartered up the calf.

{128} See note {75}

{129} Telemachus like many another good young man seems to expect every one to fetch and carry for him.

{130} "Il." vi. 288. The store room was fragrant because it was made of cedar wood. See "Il." xxiv. 192.

{131} cf. "Il." vi. 289 and 293-296. The dress was kept at the bottom of the chest as one that would only be wanted on the greatest occasions; but surely the marriage of Hermione and of Megapenthes (bk. iv. ad init.) might have induced Helen to wear it on the preceding evening, in which case it could hardly have got back. We find no hint here of Megapenthes' recent marriage.

{132} See note {83}.

{133} cf. "Od." xi. 196, etc.

{134} The names Syra and Ortygia, on which island a great part of the Doric Syracuse was originally built, suggest that even in Odyssean times there was a prehistoric Syracuse, the existence of which was known to the writer of the poem.

{135} Literally "where are the turnings of the sun." Assuming, as we may safely do, that the Syra and Ortygia of the "Odyssey" refer to Syracuse, it is the fact that not far to the South of these places the land turns sharply round, so that mariners following the coast would find the sun upon the other side of their ship to that on which they'd had it hitherto.

Mr. A. S. Griffith has kindly called my attention to Herod iv. 42, where, speaking of the circumnavigation of Africa by Phoenician mariners under Necos, he writes:

"On their return they declared—I for my part do not believe them, but perhaps others may—that in sailing round Libya [i.e. Africa] they had the sun upon their right hand. In this way was the extent of Libya first discovered.

I take it that Eumaeus was made to have come from Syracuse because the writer thought she rather ought to have made something happen at Syracuse during her account of the voyages of Ulysses. She could not, however, break his long drift from Charybdis to the island of Pantellaria; she therefore resolved to make it up to Syracuse in another way.

{135} Modern excavations establish the existence of two and only two pre-Dorian communities at Syracuse; they were, so Dr. Orsi informed me, at Plemmirio and Cozzo Pantano. See The Authoress of the Odyssey, pp. 211-213.

{136} This harbour is again evidently the harbour in which Ulysses had landed, i.e. the harbour that is now the salt works of S. Cusumano.

{137} This never can have been anything but very niggardly pay for some eight or nine days' service. I suppose the crew were to consider the pleasure of having had a trip to Pylos as a set off. There is no trace of the dinner as having been actually given, either on the following or any other morning.

{138} No hawk can tear its prey while it is on the wing.

{139} The text is here apparently corrupt, and will not make sense as it stands. I follow Messrs. Butcher and Lang in omitting line 101.

{140} i.e. to be milked, as in South Italian and Sicilian towns at the present day.

{141} The butchering and making ready the carcases took place partly in the outer yard and partly in the open part of the inner court.

{142} These words cannot mean that it would be afternoon soon after they were spoken. Ulysses and Eumaeus reached the town which was "some way off" (xvii. 25) in time for the suitor's early meal (xvii. 170 and 176) say at ten or eleven o' clock. The context of the rest of the book shows this. Eumaeus and Ulysses, therefore, cannot have started later than eight or nine, and Eumaeus's words must be taken as an exaggeration for the purpose of making Ulysses bestir himself.

{143} I imagine the fountain to have been somewhere about where the church of the Madonna di Trapani now stands, and to have been fed with water from what is now called the Fontana Diffali on Mt. Eryx.

{144} From this and other passages in the "Odyssey" it appears that we are in an age anterior to the use of coined money—an age when cauldrons, tripods, swords, cattle, chattels of all kinds, measures of corn, wine, or oil, etc. etc., not to say pieces of gold, silver, bronze, or even iron, wrought more or less, but unstamped, were the nearest approach to a currency that had as yet been reached.

{145} Gr. is [Greek]

{146} I correct these proofs abroad and am not within reach of Hesiod, but surely this passage suggests acquaintance with the Works and Ways, though it by no means compels it.

{147} It would seem as though Eurynome and Euryclea were the same person. See note {156}

{148} It is plain, therefore, that Iris was commonly accepted as the messenger of the gods, though our authoress will never permit her to fetch or carry for any one.

{149} i.e. the doorway leading from the inner to the outer court.

{150} Surely in this scene, again, Eurynome is in reality Euryclea. See note {156}

{151} These, I imagine, must have been in the open part of the inner courtyard, where the maids also stood, and threw the light of their torches into the covered cloister that ran all round it. The smoke would otherwise have been intolerable.

{152} Translation very uncertain; vide Liddell and Scott, under [Greek]

{153} See photo on opposite page.

{154} cf. "Il." ii. 184, and 217, 218. An additional and well-marked feature being wanted to convince Penelope, the writer has taken the hunched shoulders of Thersites (who is mentioned immediately after Eurybates in the "Iliad") and put them on to Eurybates' back.

{155} This is how geese are now fed in Sicily, at any rate in summer, when the grass is all burnt up. I have never seen them grazing.

{156} Lower down (line 143) Euryclea says it was herself that had thrown the cloak over Ulysses—for the plural should not be taken as implying more than one person. The writer is evidently still fluctuating between Euryclea and Eurynome as the name for the old nurse. She probably originally meant to call her Euryclea, but finding it not immediately easy to make Euryclea scan in xvii. 495, she hastily called her Eurynome, intending either to alter this name later or to change the earlier Euryclea's into Eurynome. She then drifted in to Eurynome as convenience further directed, still nevertheless hankering after Euryclea, till at last she found that the path of least resistance would lie in the direction of making Eurynome and Euryclea two persons. Therefore in xxiii. 289-292 both Eurynome and "the nurse" (who can be none other than Euryclea) come on together. I do not say that this is feminine, but it is not unfeminine.

{157} See note {156}

{158} This, I take it, was immediately in front of the main entrance of the inner courtyard into the body of the house.

{159} This is the only allusion to Sardinia in either "Iliad" or "Odyssey."

{160} The normal translation of the Greek word would be "holding back," "curbing," "restraining," but I cannot think that the writer meant this—she must have been using the word in its other sense of "having," "holding," "keeping," "maintaining."

{161} I have vainly tried to realise the construction of the fastening here described.

{162} See plan of Ulysses' house in the appendix. It is evident that the open part of the court had no flooring but the natural soil.

{163} See plan of Ulysses' house, and note {175}.

{164} i.e. the door that led into the body of the house.

{165} This was, no doubt, the little table that was set for Ulysses, "Od." xx. 259.

Surely the difficulty of this passage has been overrated. I suppose the iron part of the axe to have been wedged into the handle, or bound securely to it—the handle being half buried in the ground. The axe would be placed edgeways towards the archer, and he would have to shoot his arrow through the hole into which the handle was fitted when the axe was in use. Twelve axes were placed in a row all at the same height, all exactly in front of one another, all edgeways to Ulysses whose arrow passed through all the holes from the first onward. I cannot see how the Greek can bear any other interpretation, the words being, [Greek]

"He did not miss a single hole from the first onwards." [Greek] according to Liddell and Scott being "the hole for the handle of an axe, etc.," while [Greek] ("Od." v. 236) is, according to the same authorities, the handle itself. The feat is absurdly impossible, but our authoress sometimes has a soul above impossibilities.

{166} The reader will note how the spoiling of good food distresses the writer even in such a supreme moment as this.

{167} Here we have it again. Waste of substance comes first.

{168} cf. "Il." iii. 337 and three other places. It is strange that the author of the "Iliad" should find a little horse-hair so alarming. Possibly enough she was merely borrowing a common form line from some earlier poet—or poetess—for this is a woman's line rather than a man's.

{169} Or perhaps simply "window." See plan in the appendix.

{170} i.e. the pavement on which Ulysses was standing.

{171} The interpretation of lines 126-143 is most dubious, and at best we are in a region of melodrama: cf., however, i.425, etc. from which it appears that there was a tower in the outer court, and that Telemachus used to sleep in it. The [Greek] I take to be a door, or trap door, leading on to the roof above Telemachus's bed room, which we are told was in a place that could be seen from all round—or it might be simply a window in Telemachus's room looking out into the street. From the top of the tower the outer world was to be told what was going on, but people could not get in by the [Greek]: they would have to come in by the main entrance, and Melanthius explains that the mouth of the narrow passage (which was in the lands of Ulysses and his friends) commanded the only entrance by which help could come, so that there would be nothing gained by raising an alarm. As for the [Greek] of line 143, no commentator ancient or modern has been able to say what was intended—but whatever they were, Melanthius could never carry twelve shields, twelve helmets, and twelve spears. Moreover, where he could go the others could go also. If a dozen suitors had followed Melanthius into the house they could have attacked Ulysses in the rear, in which case, unless Minerva had intervened promptly, the "Odyssey" would have had a different ending. But throughout the scene we are in a region of extravagance rather than of true fiction—it cannot be taken seriously by any but the very serious, until we come to the episode of Phemius and Medon, where the writer begins to be at home again.

{172} I presume it was intended that there should be a hook driven into the bearing-post.

{173} What for?

{174} Gr: [Greek]. This is not [Greek].

{175} From lines 333 and 341 of this book, and lines 145 and 146 of bk. xxi we can locate the approach to the [Greek] with some certainty.

{176} But in xix. 500-502 Ulysses scolded Euryclea for offering information on this very point, and declared himself quite able to settle it for himself.

{177} There were a hundred and eight Suitors.

{178} Lord Grimthorpe, whose understanding does not lend itself to easy imposition, has been good enough to write to me about my conviction that the "Odyssey" was written by a woman, and to send me remarks upon the gross absurdity of the incident here recorded. It is plain that all the authoress cared about was that the women should be hanged: as for attempting to realise, or to make her readers realise, how the hanging was done, this was of no consequence. The reader must take her word for it and ask no questions. Lord Grimthorpe wrote:

"I had better send you my ideas about Nausicaa's hanging of the maids (not 'maidens,' of whom Fronde wrote so well in his 'Science of History') before I forget it all. Luckily for me Liddell & Scott have specially translated most of the doubtful words, referring to this very place.

"A ship's cable. I don't know how big a ship she meant, but it must have been a very small one indeed if its 'cable' could be used to tie tightly round a woman's neck, and still more round a dozen of them 'in a row,' besides being strong enough to hold them and pull them all up.

"A dozen average women would need the weight and strength of more than a dozen strong heavy men even over the best pulley hung to the roof over them; and the idea of pulling them up by a rope hung anyhow round a pillar [Greek] is absurdly impossible; and how a dozen of them could be hung dangling round one post is a problem which a senior wrangler would be puzzled to answer... She had better have let Telemachus use his sword as he had intended till she changed his mind for him."

{179} Then they had all been in Ulysses' service over twenty years; perhaps the twelve guilty ones had been engaged more recently.

{180} Translation very doubtful—cf. "It." xxiv. 598.

{181} But why could she not at once ask to see the scar, of which Euryclea had told her, or why could not Ulysses have shown it to her?

{182} The people of Ithaca seem to have been as fond of carping as the Phaeacians were in vi. 273, etc.

{183} See note {156}. Ulysses's bed room does not appear to have been upstairs, nor yet quite within the house. Is it possible that it was "the domed room" round the outside of which the erring maids were, for aught we have heard to the contrary, still hanging?

{184} Ulysses bedroom in the mind of the writer is here too apparently down stairs.

{185} Penelope having been now sufficiently whitewashed, disappears from the poem.

{186} So practised a washerwoman as our authoress doubtless knew that by this time the web must have become such a wreck that it would have gone to pieces in the wash.

A lady points out to me, just as these sheets are leaving my hands, that no really good needlewoman—no one, indeed, whose work or character was worth consideration—could have endured, no matter for what reason, the unpicking of her day's work, day after day for between three and four years.

{187} We must suppose Dolius not yet to know that his son Melanthius had been tortured, mutilated, and left to die by Ulysses' orders on the preceding day, and that his daughter Melantho had been hanged. Dolius was probably exceptionally simple-minded, and his name was ironical. So on Mt. Eryx I was shown a man who was always called Sonza Malizia or "Guileless"—he being held exceptionally cunning.